THE NOVELS OF KENNETH ROBERTS
Storytelling in the Grand Tradition

Kenneth Roberts is the novelist who lifted American history out of the scholarly dust and gave it to the world in all its robust splendor. He has turned back the clock to our early beginnings and breathed lusty life into an era rich in romance, adventure and danger. His men and women . . . his heroes, traitors, soldiers, lovers and Redskins . . . come back, not as hollow echoes of a misty past, but as living, loving, fighting characters—worthy of the destiny they carved for themselves and for posterity. Here in the works of the "best historical novelist in America" is the thunder of battle, the whisper of intrigue, the marching of rebels, the war-whoop of savages . . . all the thrilling panorama of young America and the flames that fused it together in freedom and unity!

NOW AVAILABLE IN
FAWCETT EDITIONS

ARUNDEL
BOON ISLAND
CAPTAIN CAUTION
THE LIVELY LADY
LYDIA BAILEY
NORTHWEST PASSAGE
OLIVER WISWELL
RABBLE IN ARMS

"Those who fail after a glorious fashion, Raleigh, Cervantes, Chatterton, Camoens, Blake, Claverhouse, Lovelace, Alcibiades, Parnell and the last unknown deckhand who, diving overboard after a comrade, sinks without saving him: these interest us, at least they interest those who, armed with imagination, are thereby doomed themselves to the same failure as their heroes were."

—R. B. Cunninghame Graham; Cruz Alta.

KENNETH ROBERTS

NORTHWEST PASSAGE

A Fawcett Crest Book

FAWCETT PUBLICATIONS, INC., GREENWICH, CONN.
MEMBER OF AMERICAN BOOK PUBLISHERS COUNCIL, INC.

THIS BOOK CONTAINS THE COMPLETE TEXT OF THE
ORIGINAL HARDCOVER EDITION.

All characters in this book are fictional and any
resemblance to persons living or dead is purely coincidental.

A Fawcett Crest Book reprinted by arrangement with
Doubleday & Company, Inc.

Fourth Fawcett Crest printing, May 1969

Published by Fawcett World Library,
67 West 44th Street, New York, N. Y. 10036.
Printed in the United States of America.

To Booth Tarkington
Who Deserves the Credit for the Virtues
of This Novel
and Is in No Way to Blame
for Its Faults

For the assistance so generously and unfailingly given him in the accumulating of material for and the writing of Northwest Passage, the author is deeply grateful to

Anna Mosser Roberts
Major A. Hamilton Gibbs, Middleboro, Mass.
Stanley Pargellis, Department of History, Yale University
Dorothy M. Vaughan, Portsmouth, N.H., Public Library
Wallace H. White, Jr., United States Senator from Maine
S. H. P. Pell, Director, Fort Ticonderoga Museum
Dorothy C. Barck, New York Historical Society
R. W. G. Vail, Librarian, American Antiquarian Society
Chilson H. Leonard, Phillips Exeter Academy, Exeter, N.H.
Consul General and Mrs. Ernest L. Ives, Algiers, Algeria
Prof. Herbert Faulkner West, Dartmouth College
Gustav Lanctot, Public Archives of Canada
Richard Goddard, Shattuck Observatory, Hanover, N.H.
Milo King, General Manager, Fort Ticonderoga Museum
Paul Allen, Baker Memorial Library, Hanover, N.H.
Stephen Laurent, Odanak (St. Francis), P.Q.
Lucy Drucker, London
Harry deForest Smith, Director, Amherst College Library
Mary G. Nye, Vermont Historical Society
W. R. Gregg, Chief, U. S. Weather Bureau
Victor Hugo Paltsits, New York Public Library
Winold Reiss, New York City
Allan Nevins, Department of History, Columbia University
Nellie B. Pipes, Oregon Historical Society, Portland, Ore.
Zoltán Haraszty and Harriet Swift, Boston Public Library
Superintendent, Public Record Office, London
The Library of Congress

The hitherto unpublished courtmartials of Major Rogers and Lieut. Samuel Stephens, and other explanatory documents, as well as a complete bibliography, appeared in the Appendix of the special edition of this novel.

"I HAVE no special regard for Satan; but I can at least claim that I have no prejudice against him. It may even be that I lean a little his way, on account of his not having a fair show. All religions issue bibles against him, and say the most injurious things about him, but we never hear his side. We have none but the evidence for the prosecution, and yet we have rendered the verdict. To my mind, this is irregular. It is un-English; it is un-American; it is French. . . . Of course Satan has some kind of a case, it goes without saying. It may be a poor one, but that is nothing; that can be said about any of us."

MARK TWAIN
In Defense of Harriet Shelley
and Other Essays

The Northwest Passage, in the imagination of all free people, is a short cut to fame, fortune and romance—a hidden route to Golconda and the mystic East. On every side of us are men who hunt perpetually for their personal Northwest Passage, too often sacrificing health, strength and life itself to the search; and who shall say they are not happier in their vain but hopeful quest than wiser, duller folk who sit at home, venturing nothing and, with sour laughs, deriding the seekers for that fabled thoroughfare—that panacea for all the afflictions of a humdrum world.

BOOK I

CHAPTER I

THIS BOOK has not been written to prove a case. It is not an argument against what is called the crucible of war; nor is it an attempt to show that no man has ever been tempered in that crucible without bearing one of war's inevitable scars—without having become cruel, an ingrate, a wastrel; diseased, selfish, self-deluded, a drunkard; contemptuous of what is good, or without faith in God or mankind. It may, at times, seem to hint that patriots, steadfast defenders of their country against enemies in warpaint or scarlet, are still called patriots when, in times of peace, they sit traitorously irresolute or quiescent before those equally dangerous foes that lurk in the shadows of all wars—such foes as greed, short-sightedness, and the stupidity and cowardice of backyard statesmen.

My purpose has been more simple. It has been my lot to have some contact with a man who was remarkable and strange; and by chance I encountered him at periods important in the early history of my country. Given the proper guidance, he might have been a greater prince than Jenghiz Khan. To me, at times, he seemed almost a god: at other times possessed by demons. Yet I think that at his best he benefited his country more substantially than have warriors, statesmen and authors of greater renown; and at his worst, I suspect he fell no lower than any one of us might fall, provided we had possessed his vision and energy to begin with, and then had undergone the same exertions, the same temptations, the same ingratitudes and disappointments he endured. Therefore it has seemed to me worth while to write my recollections of the days when he fascinated me as no man has before or since.

In telling this story, I would like above all things to be truthful; yet at the very outset I find it difficult to remember accurately the beginning of the chain of circumstances that most affected my life.

I might, for example, blame my troubles on my habit of sketching scenes and faces in a commonplace book; I might ascribe them to my father's insistence that I go to Harvard College; or I might with equal accuracy say they were due to John Singleton Copley's words of encouragement. Some people, as I shall show, blamed Hunk Marriner and Cap Huff for visiting me in my college room in Cambridge and encouraging me to mock the Board of Overseers. I myself, for a long time, blamed Elizabeth Browne and my own youthful inability to keep my mouth shut. But it would be as reasonable to blame the terrible food in the Harvard Commons in the year 1759, or the French King for using St. Francis Indians to help him gain control of North America.

If any of those ingredients—my desire to sketch, Harvard College, its terrible food, John Singleton Copley, Cap Huff, Elizabeth Browne or the St. Francis Indians—had been lacking, my troubles, no doubt, would never have commenced, and I might have become a Portsmouth merchant, living comfortably and dully in a tall brick house and admiring the making of money, no matter how made.

Even though these subjects seem irrelevant, I must touch on all of them; for they have a bearing on what happened later.

Both my mother and my father had long lived in Kittery. My mother's home, before she married, was the square one at Pipestave Landing, the beautiful point which, near Salmon Falls, marks the limit of navigation on the Piscataqua River at low tide. Her great grandfather Richard Nason built that house in 1632.

My father, Humphrey Towne, owned a rope-walk at Kittery, opposite Badger's Island, where John Langdon of Portsmouth built his vessels. In his rope-walk my father made hawsers and cables for the King's ships—cables so large that when one was moved, eighty seamen took it on their shoulders and walked it through the streets, so that it had the appearance of a monstrous blue-legged centipede. Most of my father's work, however, was done for John Langdon's brigs, which helps to account for my name—Langdon Towne.

My father was a kind man, but inclined to be impatient with those whose opinions were at variance with his own. This trait, seemingly, was inherited. His own great grandfather William had removed from Ipswich to Kittery in a fit of impatience. Three of William's sisters, Rebecca, Sarah and Mary, all women of probity and good sense, had denounced the vicious children responsible for the beginning of the witchcraft delusion in Massachusetts, and as a result had themselves been put on trial for witchcraft. Rebecca was acquitted: then called back and convicted because of the pretended agonies of those same terrible children. Then Sarah was convicted for openly upholding Rebecca, and both were hanged. At that William, really losing his temper, loaded his wife, his belongings and his eight children on three cows and a horse and removed to the eastward. He refused to stop until he crossed the Piscataqua River and came to Kittery where, as he put it, he could breathe the air of Maine, uncontaminated by the choking flavor of Massachusetts imbeciles and murderers.

Our home was on Mendum's Point in Kittery, handy to Badger's Island and the main ferry to Portsmouth; and beginning with the days when I was knee-high to a grasshopper, I had gone up and down the Piscataqua between Kittery and Pipestave Landing, sometimes afoot and sometimes by canoe, to spend Thanksgiving or Christmas with my grandfather, or to fish in the spring of the year, or to shoot geese and deer in the autumn. That was how I had come to know Hunk Marriner and Cap Huff.

Hunk's mother, Anna Marriner, owned canoes which she operated from a wharf near our house, and was called the commodore of the Kittery canoe fleet that daily brought fish to Spring Wharf in Portsmouth.

She was a playful woman, addicted to jesting and practical jokes; and it was one of her whims to name her children after prominent residents of Portsmouth. She named them for Governor Benning Wentworth, his brother Hunking, Samuel Langdon who became president of Harvard, Archibald

Macpheadris who built the first ironworks in this country at
Dover, Judge Peter Livius and others, most of them proud
and wealthy Episcopalians. Thus she was anathema to Portsmouth society, which was composed exclusively of Episcopalians who had no relish for any sort of gaiety except their
own. Ordinary citizens of Portsmouth and Kittery thought
highly of her, however, because she worked hard, brought
plenty of fresh fish to Spring Wharf, and retained the affectionate regard of her children, which was more than most of
the Portsmouth Episcopalians were able to do.

Hunking Marriner had inherited some of his mother's
playfulness, as well as her love for hard work; and although
he worked at nothing but fishing and shooting, and was
therefore called lazy and a loafer, he worked three times
harder than any merchant ever worked at less exhausting
labors, and had six times as much fun.

He shot, as the saying goes, for the market; and I have
seen him come down the river, in the fall of the year, his
canoe loaded to the gunwales with Canada geese, brant,
black ducks and teal, all shot in one day. His skill was such
that he could successfully stalk Canada geese in an open field.

Knowing my partiality for gunning, he took me with him
for company, and we shot geese, deer and bear together as
far north as Dover and as far east as Arundel, where I had
relatives. Through him I met Cap Huff, another resident of
Kittery, who made a living carrying packages express from
Portsmouth to Falmouth. When business was slack, Cap
joined us, claiming he did it for a rest. He was a prodigious
eater, able to devour two dozen twelve-inch trout at one sitting; and it was his contention that a single goose was the
most embarrassing piece of game a gunner could bring home,
since it was more than one man could comfortably eat,
but not enough for two.

It is singular but true that Hunk and Cap took more interest
in my efforts to sketch than did any other person in Kittery
or Portsmouth. My father and my older brothers seemed
convinced that drawing was a waste of time, if not downright womanly, like painting on China, or embroidering. My
mother, I had reason to think, was secretly pleased at my
scratchings; but at the same time she saw no reason for depicting subjects she considered unpleasant. A sketch of our
kitchen, in which we lived, seemed to her to lack dignity.

She preferred a sketch of our best room, which we never sat in and seldom saw.

Hunk and Cap, on the other hand, breathed anxiously down my neck while I struggled to get things on paper. Some of their suggestions were worthless, but others showed their observation had been superior to mine.

"Wouldn't those birches look better," Hunk asked, "if you put black triangles, like brackets, where the branches sprout out of the trunk?"

It was Cap who showed me that to draw an impression of a thing is sometimes an improvement on drawing an exact likeness. "Listen," he said, "that aint the way a partridge looks when he's in a hurry! He's all pale, like a ghost, and twice as long as what he'd measure if you put a yardstick on him."

It was in 1757 that my father decided to send me to Harvard College. What led him to do so, I was never sure. My two older brothers were in the rope-walk, so there was no room for me. I had been sent to Major Samuel Hale's Grammar School in Portsmouth and had become friendly with all the young Episcopalians; and it may be my father figured a Hardvard education would provide me with a business opening that would be advantageous to the whole family.

If that was what he thought, he was probably right. Nearly all of those Episcopalian men of Portsmouth had gone to Harvard. We were Congregationalists, and it was almost a miracle when a Congregationalist was admitted by Episcopalians of Portsmouth as a social equal. Yet as soon as I was safely enrolled in Harvard, the Portsmouth Episcopalians seemed willing to accept me as one of themselves, whether I wished to be accepted or not.

It is barely possible I was sent to Harvard because my mother had hopes of seeing me a clergyman, just as every mother, seemingly, at some time dreams of her son in a pulpit, discoursing musically to weeping congregations. I mention this suspicion because there was rumor in Kittery and Portsmouth to the effect that I proposed to enter the ministry after leaving Harvard. This rumor may have been due to remarks which my mother let drop; or it may have been due to the erroneous belief that Harvard was a sort of religious institution, and that nearly every young man who went there from smaller towns in those days became a clergyman.

In my case there were three good reasons why the rumor had no foundation. For one thing, no system of Divinity or Ethics was taught in the College while I was there. For another, my aptitude for drawing inclined me toward the classes of the Hollis Professor of Mathematics and Natural Philosophy. Under him I studied Natural and Experimental Philosophy, which matters were of small worth to a clergyman, but of great value to me—Pneumatics, Hydrostatics, Mechanics, Statics, Optics; the doctrine of Proportions; the principles of Algebra, Conic Sections, Plane and Spherical Trigonometry; the general principles of Mensurations, Planes and Solids; the principles of Astronomy and Geography; the doctrine of the Spheres; the use of the Globes; the motions of the Heavenly Bodies according to the hypotheses of Ptolemy, Tycho Brahe and Copernicus; the division of the world into its various kingdoms; the use of the Maps; and so on. It was from him that I first heard mention of the Northwest Passage, which was to loom so large in my life.

The third and best reason why I never studied divinity was that I had no desire to do so.

Nevertheless, the rumor persisted in Portsmouth, and before long it got me into real trouble. That's one reason why I have always hated rumors.

CHAPTER II

In the summer of 1759, when Hunk Marriner and Cap Huff unexpectedly visited me in Cambridge, the College would have been something of an eyeopener to those who thought of it as a nest of budding clergymen.

It was not, as the reformer Whitefield had implied a few years before, a mere seminary of Paganism; but on warm nights in the spring of the year it was likely to be a tumultuous place because of the determination of the students to show their disapproval whenever they received a bad supper in the Commons. Since this was a nightly occurrence, there was almost a regular evening hullabaloo, followed by the ringing of bells and often a sprightly throwing of brickbats against the door of a Tutor.

Edicts and warnings were issued by the Board of Overseers of the College against these frequent disorders, complaining that there were combinations among the undergraduates for the perpetration of unlawful acts; that students were guilty of being absent from their chambers at unseasonable times of night; that the loose practice of going and staying out of town without leave must cease. The students must, the Overseers insisted, make an end of profane cursing and swearing. There could be no more frequenting of alehouses; no more fetching of liquors to the chambers of undergraduates; no further entering into extravagant and enormous expenses at taverns for wine, strong beer and distilled spirits.

Since it never seemed to occur to the Board of Overseers to see that our food was improved, the disorders naturally continued.

It even became the fashion to walk forth, on a warm evening, in search of disorders. The searchers were seldom disappointed; but when they were, they generously provided disorders of their own to keep late-comers from being disappointed too.

My rooms were on the top floor of a small house on Brattle Street; for since there were 134 students in Harvard at that time, and since only 90 could be accommodated in Massachusetts Hall, the rest of us were obliged to lodge where we could.

It was late on a June afternoon, a little before the Commons hour, that I heard my name hoarsely spoken in the street below. When I went to the open window and peered out, I saw one of my classmates pointing up at my room. Beside him Hunk Marriner and Cap Huff, all sweaty and dusty, stared upward with mouths agape.

At my shouted invitation they stumbled up the dark and narrow stairs and pushed their way into the room, seeming to fill it to overflowing, not only with their bodies and their muskets and the packages which each carried, but with a singular ripe odor compounded of rum and a musty smell unfamiliar to me.

"What's that smell?" I asked, when I had made them welcome.

"Smell?" Cap said. "Smell? I don't smell nothing, only these books here." He waved a huge hand at my desk.

"What you smell," Hunk said, "might prob'ly be either us or these skins—five sea-otter and twelve sables. Cap got 'em off to the eastward somewheres, and we're taking 'em to Boston to sell to Captain Callendar."

"Well," I said, "you're in luck! Who'd you get 'em from?"

"Oh," Cap said indifferently, "I just stumbled across 'em, and so I picked 'em up."

"Why didn't you sell 'em in Portsmouth?"

Cap's reply was impatient. "Listen: there's times I wisht I'd never bothered to pick up one of these skins. Every time anybody mentions 'em, there's as much talk about 'em as there'd be about a cart-load of gold horseshoes. Prob'ly it's those skins you smell, the way Hunk says, but don't give 'em another thought, because we're going into Boston as soon as we get something to eat. Then you wont smell 'em any more."

"If you're going to eat," I said, "I'll go out and eat with you."

Hunk shook his head. "One of the reasons we stopped here was so we could leave our muskets while we go to Boston. The other reason was we didn't have any money, and we wont have any till we sell the skins. We thought maybe you'd have some."

"I haven't," I said. "This is the end of the year, and nobody has any. You'll have to go over to Commons with me for supper. Maybe you wont like the food, but it can't be helped."

"We'll like it," Cap assured me. "Anybody that's hungry likes anything, and I'm hungry enough to eat a porcupine, quills and all."

They were not, Hunk protested, suitably dressed to appear in polite society; but this wasn't true, for they had on their city clothes—homespun breeches, gray woolen stockings and towcloth shirts—and carried brown coats tied to their belts in back. Thus a little brushing made them presentable, aside

from the wrinkles in their coats and the musty flavor of stale
sea-otter pelts that clung persistently to them.

Noticeable as was this faint perfume, it was wholly sub-
merged, when we entered Commons, by a noisome fragrance that struck against us in waves as we walked down the
aisle. These surges of ripeness seemed propelled against us
by an undercurrent of grumbling that rose from all the tables,
frequently increasing to a noisy angry clamor, only to subside again to discontented mutterings.

When we seated ourselves, it was evident that Cap and
Hunk might have worn buckskin hunting clothes and coonskin caps without exciting comment; for the attention of all
the students at my own table and those adjoining was riveted
on the pies which were being served. They had been baked in
deep dishes, about the size of a barber's bowl; and whenever
one of them was placed before a newcomer, all his neighbors
leaned forward to watch it opened. In every case the owner,
after piercing the protective covering, used forefinger, thumb
and nose in the supreme gesture of loathing, while all ad-
jacent colleagues groaned eloquently in unison. This, then,
accounted for the resurgent clamor; and when we in turn
received our own pies and opened them, we had little hope
of containing our own emotion.

On the instant that I punctured the crust of mine, a hot
and nauseous smell gushed upward—a smell so ripely evil
that it caught at the throat and at the stomach too.

At the sight of my face, all the others at our table joined
in the prevalent loud groan.

"For God's sake, what's in it?" I asked Wingate Marsh, a
classmate.

"Carrion!" Marsh said. "Carrion!"

"Look here," I said to him, "these friends of mine walked
all the way from Portsmouth today. Isn't there anything fit
to eat?"

"Not one damned thing!" Marsh said. "There's nothing but
this pie—carrion pie!" Then his eyes fixed themselves amazed-
ly on Cap Huff, who sat beside me.

Cap had neatly folded back the crust of his pie, and was
eating heartily. Hunk also delved into his with no sign of
repugnance.

"Hold on!" I protested. "Don't eat that! You'll be poisoned!
We can't leave the table till the tutors give the word, not

unless we want to be fined five shillings; but if you'll wait, I'll borrow some money and we'll go to the Tavern and get something to eat."

"What's wrong with this?" Cap asked. He scraped his bowl with his spoon; then looked amiably around the incredulously staring table. "Maybe mine was better'n what you had. Anyways, I aint more than took the edge off my appetite, and if there's anybody wants to get rid of this pie, I'll trade him for it."

He eyed my friends innocently. "I'll trade a drink of rum for every pie. Tomorrow night I'll be coming out of Boston with some rum, and you can come around to Langdon Towne's room and collect."

With one accord the eleven other men at the table pushed their pies toward Cap. He took them all, arranging them in a semi-circle in front of Hunk and himself.

"What would you figure was in these pies?" he asked, as he smiled blandly at my classmates.

Matthew Weaver of Watertown answered for all of us. "We don't know what was in yours, but ours must have been horse. Old horse, a long time dead."

Cap rolled up his eyes and swallowed hard. "No; it aint horse: it's rabbit; but a natural good eater easy gets used to rabbits that might have lost their lives some little time back. Besides, if a rabbit's tuckered when he gets killed, he tastes kind of lively. I don't say but these was both kind of over-kept and tuckered too; but on the other hand, look at all the flavor they gain by it."

Weaver stared at him incredulously. "Don't they taste *horrible* to you?"

Cap seemed to consult his inwards judicially. "No, not horrible exactly. I've had rabbit pies that you didn't have to lift the cover of, because it was already blew off. Maybe you wouldn't call it no furbelowed lady's feed, but I've seen cheeses that wasn't, either. The way to learn how to eat a pie like this is to turn your head to one side while you open it, and until it kind of dies down; but that's only for beginners. Eggs too old I don't claim I ever could master, even myself; but take a nice old kept-over rabbit and there's something mighty strong and wholesome about him. It builds up the stomach."

Samuel Wingate of Dorchester cleared his throat. "We live

and learn. Just let me have my pie back, will you?"

Cap stared at him. "Your pie? I already et yours. You aint got any! You traded it to me for a glass of rum tomorrow; and when you make a bargain, you got to keep it. Don't they learn you no morals at Harvard College?"

Sam was silent, and Cap conferred privily with Hunk, while I removed the crust from my pie and tried it. As Cap had intimated, it was not as bad as it smelled. Neither was it good.

Cap spoke benevolently to my friends. "This is how we figure it: all these pies belong to I and Hunk, but we wouldn't want to take advantage of a lot of nice young fellers—not if their education had been kind of neglected along some lines. If you fellers want to trade for what we got left, we'll trade. There's still enough of 'em so's each of you can have half a pie. You can have 'em back for a cigarro apiece, payable tomorrow night when you get your rum."

CHAPTER III

WORD SPREAD rapidly, seemingly, concerning my amiable and eccentric acquaintances; for when Hunk and Cap returned from Boston at dusk on the following day, there were as many as twenty undergraduates, a few of them unknown to me, lounging on the grass before the house in which I lived. As soon as Cap came in sight at the end of the street, we saw that he intended to keep his agreement. Over his shoulder was a canvas sling; and in the sling, resting above his left hip, was a five-gallon keg. Hunk was laden with a number of lesser bundles, among them a paper cylinder the size of a small cannon. Evidently their skins had sold well in Boston.

These two friends of mine, it was easy to see, had made a strong and favorable impression in a short time; for Marsh and Wingate and the others hailed them profanely, asking how much rabbit pie they'd eaten during the day, and saying they should have been at Commons for supper, as we'd had a poison ivy soup that they'd no doubt have found appetizing.

"We've got your cigarros," Sam Wingate told Cap. "Knowing your tastes, we had 'em made specially for you out of horse hair and hoof parings."

"That's good," Cap said. "That'll be a nice change from the chopped fish skins and oakum that us country fellers have to smoke." He looked apprehensively up and down the street. "Listen! We only got five gallons in this here keg, and I been lugging it five miles, so I got a good deal of a thirst. There aint more'n enough to give us a couple all round, so let's get out of sight somewheres and drink it pretty quick. If we don't, we'll have the whole college wanting a taste of it, and there wont be enough left for us to do more than spill on our chins."

There was some truth in what he said, for already our numbers had been augmented by other acquaintances of mine; so after Cap had dispatched Wingate and Marsh for jugs of hot water and an empty mixing-bucket, we trooped upstairs to my room and disposed ourselves as best we could —most of us on the floor.

Cap placed his keg upon a table; slapped it affectionately. "This here's the medicine for food-poisoning, like what you fellers prob'ly got from your insides not being built up strong and seasoned. It aint no ordinary rum, that's had all the good taken out of it by being strained and doctored and allowed to grow weak with age. This here's third-run rum, real powerful, more like food than drink. When you drink it, you can taste it. Rum's intended to take hold of you, and that's what this does. There aint no way of concealing what it is, the way you can with old, weak-kneed rum. Why, this rum, you could put onions in it, or the powerfulest dead fish, and couldn't taste a thing different about it! It's real honest rum!" His eye fell on my wash-bowl and pitcher in the corner. "Here, gimme that pitcher! First we'll try it raw; than we'll butter it, and you can see what I mean."

Worrying the bung from the keg, he decanted some of the contents into the pitcher. The room, on the instant, was permeated with an odor like that of a damp and dirty cellar in which quantities of molasses have become sour, mouldy and pungent.

Cap raised the pitcher to his lips. When he lowered it, his

eyes were watery, and he gasped spasmodically, like a dying haddock.

He handed it to the man beside him. "Now you try it, but don't spill none of it on you. You're a nice-dressed little gentleman, and you don't want holes et in your clothes." He turned to Hunk. "Don't waste time unwrapping that butter and the rest of the stuff we got in Boston. This rum's more penetrating than what I figured on."

When Marsh and Wingate returned with the required utensils, they found us garrulous and in a glow from our single swallow of Cap's remedy for food-poisoning.

Cap seized a bucket and went to work. In it he put two cups of maple sugar, added an inch of hot water and stirred until the sugar was dissolved. He poured in two quarts of rum, added a lump of butter the size of his fist, threw in a handful of powdered cinnamon; than filled the bucket to the brim with steaming hot water. So briskly did he stir the mixture that it splashed his shirt. And as we passed him our cups to be filled, he lectured us on the subject of hot buttered rum.

"This here," he said, "aint the proper way to make it. I put hot water in this here, but what you ought to have is hot cider. You take three or four drinks of this, made the right way, and you don't worry about what kind of food you're eating, or about anything else, either. You can't even remember what you et five minutes after you et it.

"And it aint a temporary drink, like most drinks. That's on account of the butter. No matter how much you drink of anything else, it'll wear off in a day or so; but you take enough hot buttered rum and it'll last you pretty near as long as a coonskin cap. Fellers up our way drink it when they're going out after catamounts, on account of catamount-hunting being hard work and requiring considerable persistence. After a man's had two-three drinks of hot buttered rum, he don't shoot a catamount: all he's got to do is walk up to him and kiss him just once; then put him in his bag, all limp."

The rum in the drinks which Cap passed us had been miraculously changed. The mixture seemed mild and sweet— as harmless-tasting as a soothing syrup. Murmurs of pleasure arose from my friends as they sampled it; and the glances turned toward Cap were almost affectionate.

At their gratified murmurs, Cap scooped up a cupful for himself and drained it; then stood with eyes upraised, meditating. "Yes," he admitted, "that aint bad! A few of those and you could play with me like a kitten." His mind seemed to slip off at a tangent.

"Hunk, give Langdon Towne that stuff we got in Boston and tell him what we thought up for him."

Hunk picked up the paper cylinder which had struck me with its resemblance to a small cannon. He cleared his throat in evident embarrassment. "That rabbit pie last night——"

"Don't beat about the bush!" Cap interrupted. "You Harvard fellers can't get good food out of the folks that run this college without you make it plain how rotten it is. That's what you thought, wasn't it, Hunk?"

"Yes," Hunk said. "It seemed to us that it doesn't do much good to go around *complaining* about bad food. That's why——"

Again Cap broke in on him. "What Hunk means is that you got to *show* 'em what you think about it—show 'em hard and quick, so's they can't make any mistake about the way you feel. S'pose a feller says a lot of things to you that you don't like: you can reason with him all day without getting anywheres; but if you crack him on the jaw, he understands the way you feel about him, and he's apt to be a little more careful. Wasn't that what you had in mind, Hunk?"

"Yes," Hunk said. "We kind of figured that if we got some good stout paper——"

Cap stopped him. "Wait a minute! You aint telling this right! You aint used to talking, like what I am. Here, bring up those cups and let's have just the merest taste of this rum before it cools off."

We crowded around him, my friends abusing him as freely as though they had known him all their lives. They called him an old Senior Sophister; an old Butter Whelk.

They hurled questions at him, demanding to be told whether a conscience invincibly erroneous may be blameless; whether private profit ought to be the chief end of moral actions; whether the dissolution of solids in corrosive liquors is performed by attraction.

They urged him to go ahead and explain himself in English instead of using Maine dialect as heretofore.

Cap drained his own cup and whacked it on the table.

With fumbling hands he set about mixing a second bucketful, and as he mixed, he discoursed. "I dunno nothing about them erroleous consciences or roguish liquors, because I aint never had dealings with no such things; but me and Hunk have given considerable thought to this moral action I'm talking about, and if you listen, you'll get some private profit out of it."

They cheered him lustily.

"We figured it all out while we was walking into Boston. I was kind of polite about those rabbit pies last night; but we're better acquainted now, so I don't mind saying they'd 'a' made a pole-cat think he hadn't never smelled nothing. What you fellers want to do is make this clear to the folks that run Harvard College, and we figured how to do it, didn't we, Hunk?"

Hunk just looked at him reproachfully.

"Yes," Cap went on, "Langdon Towne knows how to draw, because me and Hunk, we've watched him and helped him. We figured if Langdon Towne drew a nice big picture of Harvard College offering a supper to a pole-cat, and the pole-cat being kind of strangled by the smell——"

The rest of Cap's speech was lost in a tumult of cheers and laughter. The next thing I knew Cap and Hunk had peeled a sheet of heavy white cartridge paper from Hunk's cannon-like cylinder and were holding it flat against the wall, while somebody else thrust a black crayon into my hand.

I stood before the cartridge paper, a little unsteady on my feet, and marked off the points of the drawing as well as I could. To represent the Harvard Overseers, I blocked out a man in Pilgrim dress, holding a dish in his extended hand; and opposite him I lightly sketched a bushy-tailed pole-cat clutching his nose with a paw and shrinking disgustedly from the proffered plate.

To persons slightly in liquor, matters of little humor can seem irresistibly droll; and this was the case now. As the figures developed, my audience howled and slapped themselves, rolling on the floor with uncontrollable mirth; and I, too, felt I was producing a masterpiece of comicality.

When I stepped back to look at the sketch and incidentally wipe the tears from my eyes, I found, standing close behind me, a person I had not before seen. I took him for an undergraduate, for he seemed no older than others in the room. His thin face was pale and a little pock-marked and his eyebrows were so prominent and his eyes so small that there was a peering look to him, almost as though he stared inquisitively at life through quizzing glasses. His dress was elaborate for an undergraduate, being of rich dark brown broadcloth, with a waistcoat of orange watered silk.

"That's not bad, you know," he said to me. "Not bad at all." He fingered his lower lip. "What would you think if this gentleman"—he lightly tapped the figure of the Pilgrim—"were half concealed in the entrance of the dining hall? Then there'd be no opportunity for a misunderstanding."

He was right, of course. I went at it again, outlining the end of the Commons building, so that the Pilgrim's upper body seemed to be leaning from the open door.

While my audience whooped, the inquisitive-faced young man made another suggestion. "Try putting the dish in his other hand, and having him hold to the door-jamb with the hand nearer you. Wouldn't that give it more life?"

I did as he suggested, and was enraptured at the vitality which the sketch took on. With that I went to blacking it in, and in no time at all it seemed to me not only completed but perfect.

"Now," Cap said, "we'll all have another little drink, and then I and Hunk'll carry it out and nail it up where people can see it. Where you want it nailed? Against the President's front door?"

Disregarding the turmoil around us, the pale young man nodded and smiled at me. "That's really good. Let me take your crayon. I'll show you something—just a trick, but you might find it useful."

I gave him the crayon. Stepping close to my drawing, he made a single S-shaped line on the Pilgrim's cheek. The face as I had drawn it was merely stern and somewhat cadaverous. That one crayon stroke made it sly, narrow-minded, hypocritical, contemptuous, selfish, cruel.

I gazed from this surprisingly made-over face to the thin, inquisitive features of the stranger. "Where'd you learn to do that?"

"Oh," he said, "I've been at it since I was twelve years old. My stepfather——"

He stopped suddenly. So, too, did the laughter and shouting in the room, which had rung in my ears like the roaring of breakers on a beach. In the quiet that ensued, I heard a measured knocking at the door. This was what I had feared before Cap's buttered rum had robbed me of my prudence. I knew, now, that any such gathering as this must inevitably bring down the college authorities upon us; and I saw, too late, that I had been a fool.

Seeing all the eyes in the room turned toward me, I rubbed my hand over my face in an attempt to clear my mind of rum-fumes; then hoarsely called, "Come in."

The door swung open to reveal, in the light of the flickering candles, the spare, stooped form of Belcher Willard, my tutor. At sight of him those who were on the floor scrambled upright with a sound of thumping and rustling, to stand in respectful silence, as required by the college laws.

Cap and Hunk dropped the drawing which they had been holding against the wall. In the stillness I could hear it rolling itself up, as though to hide from this representative of our governing body.

Willard came in among us and walked straight to the table, on which were the keg, the pails of greasy liquid and a score of soiled tin cups. When he raised his eyes from that odorous and offensive chaos, he looked hard at the surrounding circle of faces; then fixed his attention on me.

"Langdon Towne," he said, "you are familiar with the laws of this college. No undergraduate shall keep by him brandy, rum or any other distilled spirituous liquors. Whosoever shall transgress against this law shall have the said liquor that is found with him taken from him, and disposed of by the President and Tutors; and he shall be further punished not exceeding five shillings."

Before I could reply, Cap Huff cleared his throat noisily. "That aint Langdon Towne's rum. That's *my* rum. I paid five shillings for that rum—a shilling a gallon—and three shillings for the keg. I'll give it to the President if he needs it; but he can't take it and dispose of it without my say-so."

Willard looked at him from under beetling brows. "You are not a member of this Society!"

"Well, no, I aint," Cap admitted. "I aint a member of any society. I just stopped in to let Langdon Towne know the salmon was biting in Kittery, and if I'd known there was any feeling against rum in these parts, I wouldn't have brought this keg here."

Willard set his lips tight together. "The laws of this Society further say, that if any scholar shall entertain at his chamber or familiarly associate with any person of loose or ill character, he shall be punished by the President and Tutors not exceeding five shillings; and if he persist in so doing he shall be publicly admonished, degraded or expelled, according to the aggravation of his offence."

Cap just stood there, scratching his head.

"Sir," I said, "Cap Huff isn't a loose or ill character—not according to my lights."

"The lights of your generation," Willard replied, "are false and audacious, and repugnant to the fundamental principles of wise and proper government."

I saw Cap stoop hastily and pick up my drawing. "I guess we'll be moving along," he said. "Hunk, you take all your stuff and I'll take the keg. We better be getting back to Kittery." To Willard he added mildly, "I kind of forced myself on Langdon Towne and these young fellers here. They aint done nothing but drink a little of my rum, and there aint no way to keep young fellers from drinking rum sometimes, no matter how many laws you make."

Willard looked disagreeable. "Your philosophical disputations have no interest for me." He stretched out a bony hand and with his forefinger tapped the drawing which Cap was attempting to stuff beneath his coat. "What is this?"

Cap put it behind his back. "That's mine."

"Indeed!" Willard said. "Indeed! Permit me to doubt it. Permit me also to remind you that the President or Tutors may require suitable assistance from any scholar for the preservation of the good order of the College; and if anyone so required shall refuse to give his assistance, it shall be looked upon as a high misdemeanor and a great contempt of the authority of the College, and be punished by degradation or expulsion."

Cap looked at him and breathed hard. "You mean if these boys don't help you to take my property away from me by attacking me, you'll up and raise all that hell with 'em?"

"Give it to him, Cap," I said.

Cap gave the roll of paper to Willard, who opened it. He slowly raised his eyes to mine. "Who did this?"

"That's mine," Cap repeated quickly. "I figured it out."

"I thought of it first," Hunk Marriner said.

The stranger who had altered the expression on the Pilgrim's face stepped close to Willard. "This is beside the point," he said mildly. "It's plain to be seen these gentlemen aren't artists, though they have other admirable qualitites. I think this will settle the matter." He leaned over and scratched a few lines on the margin of the drawing. Miraculously, the lines flowed together to form a likeness of Belcher Willard; a likeness so kindly and flattering that all of Willard's grim austerity was transformed into something almost beautiful.

Willard rolled up the drawing and set his fists on his hips. He looked from the stranger to me and back again. "Most opportune! Suspiciously opportune! This Society seems to have become a resort for characters who incite our members to luxury, intemperance or ruin. At whose invitation did you——"

"My name, sir," the young man said, "is Copley. John Singleton Copley of South Boston."

Willard laughed sourly. "I regret, sir, you are not a member of this Society, so that you could be dealt with as you deserve." He once more scanned the rest of us with a hard eye. "As for those of you who are students at Harvard College, you will report at my rooms at five tomorrow afternoon for discipline."

CHAPTER IV

I T WAS late in July when the college authorities notified my father that I had been placed on probation—not so much for my own sins, but as an object-lesson to the many undergraduates who were leaning more and more toward extravagances, irregularities and disorders. Probably, the authorities intimated, I would be allowed to return in the autumn, but possibly I might not.

To me this decision seemed so unjust that I hoped with all my heart I had seen the last of Harvard College; the more so as my father was in a great rage with me. He spoke his mind about the evils of drink and bad companions; but his bitterest remarks were directed against my seeming determination to waste my days and bring shame on my family by frittering away my time on an unmanly pursuit.

"We've got a position to maintain in this community," he said. "We've reached it by hard work, and by living in fear of the Lord. Your grandfather took his living off the land, and so did his father and his father's father. They labored from sunup to sundown; and by the sweat of their brows they fed their families, built snug houses, and laid aside a little from year to year. The money they made, and my own efforts, have given us our rope-walk and the house we live in. If it hadn't been for the toil of generations of hard-working men, Langdon, you'd never have had the chance to go to Harvard—the chance to excel all the rest of us in property and position. And now you've had the chance, you've been throwing it away by fiddling with pencils and crayons—by making hentracks on a piece of paper!

"Do you think that's any way to retain the respect of this community? Do you think you can support a family? How do you think the rest of us would feel if we had to see people's fingers pointed at you—if we had to hear 'em say: 'There goes Towne's boy: he draws pictures!'

"What do you think your great-great-grandfather would have said to you for it? He was the first settler in this region. He was Ensign of the town of Kittery! He'd have stood no such nonsense, and neither will I."

"Well, sir," I said, "I'm sorry for what's happened, and I'm willing to work as hard as anyone, but I'd do a lot better if I worked at something I liked."

"Pah!" my father cried. "Where'd we be if we did what we liked! I'd like to be a rich merchant in Boston, with a score of ships at sea! We don't work because we like it, but because we must!"

"Yes, sir," I agreed, "but Mother says my great-great-grandfather wouldn't go to church, and drank rum, and went off and fought the Indians every time there was a chance; so he must have done what he liked occasionally."

My father was only the angrier. "Wasn't it his duty to fight the Indians?"

"People don't seem to consider it their duty nowadays,"

I reminded him. "About the only ones who go to fight the French and Indians are those who enjoy going, or those who make more by going than they could by staying home."

"I wont argue the point, Langdon!" my father said. "I'd rather be dead in my grave than see you mincing around this town, drawing pictures and being supported like a female relative. Tomorrow you'll pack your duds and go to your grandfather's house, where you'll be out of reach of rowdies like Hunk Marriner and Cap Huff. You'll help your grandfather cultivate that farm, and you'll do it with a good grace, or he'll take a whip to you, old as you are! Yes, and I'll thank him for doing it!"

There wasn't any choice. I knew that my mother and my brothers thought my father too hard on me; but they didn't dare oppose him, any more than I did; so I went to Pipestave Landing.

I loathed the back-breaking slavery of farm life—the eternal brain-numbing monotony of crawling out of bed at dawn, half dead with sleep, to water the cattle, clean out their stalls, hoe the interminable rows of corn and beans, scythe the endless fields, pitch countless tons of hay from field to rick and from rick to barn, grub up alders, transport rocks from the fields to the long gray walls around them, split stove-wood, draw the water, milk the cows, currycomb the horses, oil the harness and do all the other chores that a farmer must, or be swallowed by his acres.

I hated to sit down to my meals, drenched with sweat, too tired to say anything except "Pass the butter." I hated the waves of weariness that swept over me each night, as soon as my supper was eaten, so that I, like everyone else in the house, was glad to stumble upstairs to bed.

I hated my hot room beneath the eaves; I even hated the leaden slumber that brought surcease from my labors, but no rest.

I had no time to sketch the scenes around me, although they kindled sparks within me all day long—the broad reaches of the Piscataqua, running down toward Portsmouth; the squat gundelos with lateen sails that came to the landing with their loads of goods for the back country; the small white houses on the Sligo shore across the river; the woods and skies and shadows of morning and noon and eventide. By and by, too, my hands were so calloused and my fingers so stiffened, I doubted they would hold a pencil.

What made my hatred of this drudgery almost unbearable was the impossibility of seeing Elizabeth Browne. I might, I think, have kicked over the traces and gone down to Portsmouth to see her if it hadn't been for my father's remark about the disgrace I had brought on my family.

What I had done at Cambridge had not, I knew, been disgraceful. I had been foolish, as most of my classmates had been at one time or another; and I had unjustly been made to suffer while others, equally guilty, had been allowed to go unpunished and even unrebuked. Yet my father's ratings had made a coward of me where Elizabeth was concerned— or perhaps it is fairer to say that my infatuation for her had made a coward of me. To put it bluntly, I dared not see her until I was sure I ran no risk of losing her.

My position was doubly insecure because her father was not only an Episcopalian, whereas my family were Congregationalists, but was also rector of Queen's Chapel—the church attended by all the big-wigs of Portsmouth, from Governor Benning Wentworth down. New England Episcopalians, as a rule, despised all other sects as being uncouth persons, devoid of social graces; and all other sects hated Episcopalians as being little better than Papists.

Worse, I was a resident of Kittery, a place held ignoble and clownish by every sprig of family in Portsmouth. I think it is safe to say I would never have met Elizabeth Browne if I hadn't been a student at Harvard; and I knew I was tolerated by her family because I was on good terms with the many Harvard graduates and undergraduates in Portsmouth—all of them Episcopalians and all of them propertied.

Consequently I was only too sure that if Elizabeth's family thought of me as being not only disgraced, but disgraced by Harvard, I would be forever barred from seeing her.

It was late in August when New England had the news that resulted in my release from Pipestave Landing. This was the capture, by General Amherst and his army of British and Provincial troops, of Fort Ticonderoga and Crown Point, strongholds of the French and Indians during our long wars with them. Even at Pipestave Landing we could hear the firing of cannon and the ringing of bells with which Portsmouth received the news—cannon firing and bell ringing that continued for twenty-four hours, so great was the rejoicing at this victory.

Two weeks later, early in September, I had a letter from my father. Because of the victory at Ticonderoga and Crown Point, he wrote, confidence had returned and trade had picked up wonderfully. Every merchant in Portsmouth was planning to build a ship, so there was more rope to be made than ever before in the town's history. My help, he said, was needed in the rope-walk, and he would be glad to have me come home at once.

Evidently he had forgiven me, and my difficulty at Harvard was henceforth to be treated not as complete disgrace but as something that could even be overlooked and at least not mentioned.

That afternoon I was on my way down river; and as would have been the case with any young man in my position, my own family came last in my thoughts. My first thought had been for Elizabeth Browne; and the first thing I meant to do in Portsmouth was to see her.

CHAPTER V

THE GUNDELO that carried me to Portsmouth found an anchorage beside the long wharf at the foot of Buck Street, where the brigs and ships were tied up as thick as bones in a shad. I left my bag of clothes at the Seaman's Tavern and set off up Buck Street, in high spirits at the thought of seeing Elizabeth again.

To those who think New England towns are drab and colorless, filled with sour-faced folk in stuffy raiment, Buck Street at eight o'clock on a warm evening would be an amazement. It is narrow and winding; crowded with warehouses, shops, taverns and residences. Odors of rum, coffee, lemons and spices lie thick along it, as clearly defined as the layers of cream and jam in a Boston pie; and due to one of the many singular customs of the town, it is as full of people as of odors. Every night the lively grandees of Portsmouth make a promenade of Buck Street, gabbling and laughing, their sticks and high-heeled shoes clicking on the pavement, their silks rustling, their powdered hair and shoe-buckles gleaming in the light from tavern doors and shop windows.

Merchants, shipbuilders, lawyers and bankers are there with their wives and daughters: naval officers from the King's ships: army officers from Fort William and Mary in scarlet and gold, their swords clutched tight beneath their arms: members of the King's Council, long crimson-lined capes swinging from their shoulders. All of Portsmouth, as the saying goes, whether Episcopalians, Congregationalists or dissenting Congregationalists, stroll up and down Buck Street in seeming amity on every pleasant evening.

At a distance, among the throng, I saw the Reverend Arthur Browne and his wife, but neither Elizabeth nor her sister Jane was with them. So, therefore, filled with eagerness and a lover's doubts, I hurried to the Brownes' house on Court Street; and as I had hoped, Elizabeth, being the youngest of the daughters, opened the door.

"Well, I declare!" she cried. "It's Langdon Towne, back from the dead!" She looked at me indignantly from the corners of her eyes—one of her ways that I found fascinating. "Never a word out of you for weeks! Are those the manners they teach you at Harvard?"

I had no mind for small talk. The sight of her seemed to have exploded something within me, so that my throat and brain were choked; and I stood there like a fool, gawking at her. Her hair was a glossy black, shot with gleams of shimmering purple when sunlight fell across it; and her eyes, which seemed enormous, were black as well, but a fathomless, velvety black in which swam flecks of gold. Her face was slender, like a narrow heart, and her eyes slanted upward a little at the outer corners; while her mouth, which was large, was a brilliant crimson against the clear pallor of her skin. Like her eyes, her mouth had a gay quirk at the corners; so that her expression, even when serious, was half amused.

She laughed a little at my silence, and pretended to turn away. Then I caught at her hand, but she snatched it from me and brushed a heavenly finger across my lips in silent warning. With that she moved quickly toward the door of the back parlor, where I heard the murmur of voices.

When I followed Elizabeth into that small, candle-lighted room, I saw why she had not been among the strollers on Buck Street; for three persons sat there chatting. One was her older sister Jane, and another was the man to whom Jane was betrothed—Sam Livermore, a Harvard graduate and a good friend of mine: the same Sam Livermore who later became King's Attorney for the Province of New Hampshire.

When my eyes fell on the third person, my first sensation was one of amazement and pleasure, for it was he who had stood beside me, two months before, and taken the responsibility for my drawing of the Pilgrim Father and the disgusted pole-cat: then politely given a name which I had never before heard, but was to hear countless times in the future—John Singleton Copley.

Before Elizabeth could speak, Copley jumped from his chair, seized my hand and shook it warmly. "Well, well!" he said, "this is delightful! I tried to see you the day after we had our little trouble, but they told me you were in difficulties. I hope they weren't serious!"

Of course I was instantly jealous, and Copley probably saw that I was; but when I said somewhat morosely that my difficulties had been of no consequence, he went out of his way to respond with kind and friendly speeches.

"Why," he said to Elizabeth and Jane and Sam, "I didn't know Towne was a friend of yours! Ever since I saw him in Cambridge, I've wanted to see him again and urge him to do something with his talent for drawing."

Elizabeth and her sister raised their eyebrows. They might almost have said aloud, "Oh, indeed! We thought you meant to speak of something worth hearing."

Then Copley gaily went on to give an account of Cap's and Hunk's visit to me, and what he'd heard of the results thereof.

Sam chuckled and slapped his knee at Copley's recital; but Elizabeth and her sister seemed to find nothing amusing in it.

"Horrible creatures!" Elizabeth exclaimed. "Who were they, Langdon?"

"Why," I said, "they weren't horrible! They were Hunk Marriner and Cap Huff."

Elizabeth made a gesture of distaste. "Oh, fie! Coarse and dreadful," she said. "Both profane swearers; and who in Portsmouth doesn't know Cap Huff has been in jail!"

"But Elizabeth," I protested. "It wasn't Cap's fault he was put in jail. He was put there for talking against Benning Wentworth."

Elizabeth made an outcry. "La, what spurious logic! If Cap Huff talked against Benning Wentworth, it was certainly Cap Huff's fault, wasn't it?"

"No, Elizabeth. It was Benning Wentworth's fault for deserving to be talked against."

"Langdon Towne!" she exclaimed. "What perversity! You know those vulgar creatures have done nothing for you except encourage you in idleness and folly. How can you speak for them after the trouble they made for you in Cambridge?"

I sat embarrassed and speechless; I'd hoped she didn't know anything about my Cambridge troubles. Copley spoke up for me. "I think you're a little hard on Mr. Towne's associates. I do indeed! They were kind young men, and most amusing. I found them so, and so did all the others there that night. Of course we'd none of us argue that they'd shine before the ladies; but if we restrict our acquaintances and friends to the highest circles, our knowledge of the world and of life is bound to suffer." He smiled at Elizabeth. "Don't you think so?"

Elizabeth made no answer.

"It seems to me," Copley continued, "that it's peculiarly essential for an artist to know all sorts of people, and to know them well. It's his business to portray life; and if he isn't familiar with all phases of life, he's bound to make a failure of portraying it. Don't you think that's a reasonable statement?"

"Langdon isn't an artist," Elizabeth said primly, and added with some dryness, I thought, "He lives in Kittery—but when he leaves Harvard he'll make his home in Portsmouth. Don't you hope to, Langdon?"

"But he *is* an artist," Copley protested. "He has a true eye for light and shadow, and a fine manner of composition. He has an unusual gift, and a man can't ignore a gift. He can't hide his light under a bushel."

I was so pleased with what this friendly young man said of me that for the moment I forgot Elizabeth. "Why," I said to him, "you must be already an artist yourself! That accounts for the line you put in the face I drew!"

Sam laughed. "Mr. Copley's a pupil of Joseph Blackburn. That's why he's here: to talk with Mr. Browne about arranging sittings for Mr. Blackburn."

That meant something to me; for Blackburn was the foremost portrait painter in North America. To have words of praise from one of Blackburn's pupils was more than I had ever expected. I could only stare humbly at Copley.

"All you need," he said pleasantly, "is study and practice. What have you been drawing this summer?"

"Nothing," I said. I turned up my hands and looked at the palms. In the light of the candles the heavy calluses on my fingers stood out in lumps and ridges.

Copley reached over and felt them. "See here; you ought to be careful of your hands! What have you been doing? Working at a forge?"

"I've been farming."

The room was so silent that even the motions of the moths as they swooped from candle to candle seemed to make a noise. We heard the front door open and close, and the voices of Mr. and Mrs. Browne in the entry-way.

"There's Father," Jane said quickly. "I'll take you to him, Mr. Copley."

"You're most kind," Copley said. "Ah—isn't your family in sympathy with your drawing, Mr. Towne?"

"No, they're not. My father doesn't like it. He thinks it's undignified. He thinks it's a waste of time." I glanced at Elizabeth. "Nobody likes it."

"I see. I see. Ah—did you have any definite ideas as to what you'd like to draw—what you'd like to paint?"

"Yes, but I never told my father. He wont even let me speak of it."

"What was it you had in mind?" Copley asked.

I looked apologetically at Elizabeth and hesitated.

"Oh, come!" Copley said. "I'm an artist. I've been trying to paint since I was fifteen years old. If you know what you want to do, say so! Not one person in ten thousand has any aim in life!"

"Well," I said, "you'll think I'm a fool, probably, but nobody in this country has ever painted Indians. I've hunted through every book in Harvard, and there isn't one that shows you how they look."

Elizabeth laughed. "Nobody cares! They all look alike!"

"No they don't," I said. "They all look different. All the nations wear clothes of their own, and paint themselves differently."

Copley rose and put his hand on my shoulder; but he spoke to Elizabeth and the other two, sitting silently on the couch. "I hope you'll agree with me that talent ought to be encouraged: not discouraged. I was so fortunate as to have Peter Pelham for a stepfather. He was an engraver and a painter. He died when I was fifteen years old, but he encouraged me and gave me all the training he could. Some day, I hope, I'll somehow repay that encouragement." He turned to me. "Don't let anybody discourage you if you have a talent and know how you want to use it. If you let yourself be driven out of it, you'll be unhappy all your life. Did you ever hear of Mark Catesby?"

I said I hadn't.

"Well," Copley said, "every naturalist in the world knows about Mark Catesby, and every painter in England and France. Mark Catesby wanted to draw the birds of South Carolina, and he did so in spite of opposition and discouragements. Probably Catesby never made much money, but he was happy, and I doubt he'd be willing to exchange his lot with that of any planter or merchant in South Carolina—and there are some mighty wealthy ones down there. Catesby'll be remembered when all the planters and merchants are forgotten."

He looked at Elizabeth again. She was sitting erect in her chair, her hands clenched tightly in her lap and her eyes downcast. "Well," he said. "Well——"

Then he turned to Jane. Without a word she rose from the couch and the two of them went from the room.

CHAPTER VI

THE REST of that evening seems dark and unreal, when I remember it.

Sam Livermore good naturedly tried to leave Elizabeth and me alone together, but she wouldn't have it so. Boylike, I had dreamed throughout the summer of the kind things she'd say to me when I should see her again; the reality was bitter. Stumblingly I tried to argue that painting was a respectable profession, but somehow she contrived to twist every timid word I said upon the subject, and made it appear very like an insult to herself.

For the first time I knew the sharp adroitness of an angered girl, and learned the dismal lesson that almost every man eventually learns when his hopes are contrary to his lady's. Try as I would to hold her to the argument, she seemed determined to fly off at tangents, so that we were perpetually losing our way and getting nowhere.

By clever tricks of her tongue she made it appear that because I upheld Cap Huff and Hunk Marriner, it was entirely due to them that I wished to be an artist: that I preferred their approval to her own: that because I valued their friendship, it was of more importance to me than that of any great man in Portsmouth: that I was by nature, therefore, inclined toward vulgarity and the dregs of society.

She referred to my "terrible friends." Rascals, she called them; riffraff; and she made it clear to me that unless I renounced such companions, I too was a rascal and riffraff, unfit to associate with decent people.

The reason for her steadily increasing sharpness with me I didn't understand at all; my belabored mind fell into a dull and hopeless confusion, permeated naturally by a rising resentment. I sat before her and Sam, sore, and rubbing stupidly at the calluses of my palms: furious, I wanted to rise in cold dignity and leave the house; but at the same time, after being so long lonely for the sight of her, I couldn't bear to go away from her.

Rather abruptly, her sister Jane came back into the room and said: "Elizabeth, Father wants to see you and Langdon."

Elizabeth jumped up, went out decisively; and as I was morosely following, Sam caught me warningly by the elbow. "Don't talk back," he whispered. "Don't argue. Everything'll be all right . . . If you don't argue, I'll wait for you . . ."

That made me feel very like a convicted evil doer in whom his lawyer tries to instil a little courage just before sentence is passed by a hanging judge. I crossed the hall, entered the parlor and saw Mrs. Browne and the Reverend Arthur Browne sitting rigidly in their chairs, staring darkly at me.

Two candles on the center table threw wavering shadows on their deeply-lined faces, giving both of them a cadaverous appearance. Hitherto I had thought of Mr. and Mrs. Browne only as pompous, perhaps because of pride at their position in Portsmouth society; but the lines now etched by the candle-light showed more than that. Unless I was mistaken, they were disappointed people—disappointed and frightened—and I vaguely wondered why. Elizabeth seated herself stiffly in a corner, leaving me to stand alone before her father and mother—a prisoner at the bar.

The Reverend Mr. Browne cleared his throat. "Langdon, we could hardly credit what we've just been hearing from young Mr. Copley." He threw back his head and looked at me along his nose. "He'd have us believe you seriously contemplate becoming a painter—an artist! We'd like you to tell us that he is misinformed."

When I was silent, he leaned forward persuasively, resting his elbows on the table and placing his fingertips together. "Come, come, Langdon: surely you'll never throw away all the advantages you've had—the advantages you've acquired through sacrifices made by your father and your mother! Surely you'll never toss them aside for a mere whim—a mere wayward caprice. A foolish son is a grief to his father and a bitterness to her that bare him."

"It's not a whim, sir," I said. "Mr. Copley said I had a knack for drawing. I've been at it for years."

Then Mr. Browne became gentle with me. "Now, my boy!

You don't understand! Years ago, before I came to this country, I was secretary to Dean Swift in Dublin. It was while he was writing *Gulliver's Travels*. I daresay you've heard of it—a fanciful tale for children, and better known than works of higher merit. As secretary to the Dean, I made the acquaintance of all sorts of folk: actors, even: authors: artists. Almost the worst of the lot were the artists: a rude and clownish crew, unsavory and irreligious! They had no standing whatever! Painters, actors, mountebanks—they were all in the same boat: a wicked and adulterous generation! Even the family solicitor was preferable to an artist. I've seen artists left kicking their heels for hours in gentlemen's antechambers. They were poor men, too. All their lives they lived miserably, in dire poverty." He coughed behind his hand and I saw him glance at Elizabeth. "For the most part they were drunkards."

"Not all artists were like that, sir," I reminded him. "Velasquez and Rubens were great gentlemen. Lely and Kneller were knighted."

Behind me I heard Elizabeth stir quickly, as if in sudden unbearable impatience. Mrs. Browne tossed her head. Her husband spoke impressively. "I had rather be a doorkeeper in the house of my God, than to dwell in the tents of wickedness. And for every Lely and Kneller, there were thousands of unsuccessful paint-daubers who thought they were artists. They rolled in gutters: starved and froze in garrets: filled their bellies with the husks that the swine did eat. I mean no offense, my boy, when I say you're not a Velasquez or a Kneller."

I stood before him like a fool, my head filled with things I might have said, but certain that nothing I could say would stir his sympathies.

He coughed again, delicately. "I fear you haven't given this matter proper thought. We have made you welcome in this house, and my daughter has made you welcome. It has been our understanding that you proposed to enter the ministry. I had hoped that your education, coupled with your connections in this town, might incline you toward the Church of England. That would have given us great satisfaction. But even if you had chosen to remain a Congregationalist, Langdon, we should not altogether have thought the worse of you. This family is a liberal family—a very,

very liberal family. *Very* liberal! Congregationalist ministers from this town have become presidents of Harvard College, and although I cannot agree with their doctrinal views, I respect their position. That is one thing on which I have always insisted, where this family is concerned: a respect for position. As you well know, sir, three of my sons are in the British army; one is a clergyman in Newport; my oldest daughter is married to a colonel in the British army; another to a captain in the British navy; another is engaged to Mr. Livermore, an attorney of great ability and promise. Surely, Langdon, you can understand how repugnant a loose-living, poverty-stricken artist would seem to each and every one of them."

"But Mr. Copley isn't repugnant to you," I protested.

"Indeed," Mr. Browne said politely. "Isn't it just possible that you aren't fully aware of my feelings concerning Mr. Copley? He is a student of Mr. Blackburn, who wishes to paint portraits in this town. Consequently Mr. Blackburn sends Mr. Copley to me to beg for my influence in obtaining commissions for him. Joseph Blackburn is the foremost artist in this country, sir, but he must beg for commissions. Mr. Copley himself is an artist of ability, I'm told: yet he must beg for his master—must humble himself like Ahab! And do you know what this great artist Blackburn asks to be paid for such portraits as he may paint? Five pounds apiece! He has risen to the head of his profession, sir; but his reward for painting a person of wealth and position is a beggarly five pounds! How many portraits must he paint, Langdon, before he is able to support himself and a family in decency?"

There was nothing to be said. I shifted from one foot to the other and numbly watched the sputtering of one of the candlewicks. My poor brain, I thought, sputtered as feebly and impotently in my own defense.

Behind me I heard Elizabeth's voice. "Langdon doesn't want to paint portraits," she said. "He wants to paint Indians." Her voice, I thought, sounded almost kind; but when I turned to look at her, she stared at me defiantly.

"Yes," Mr. Browne said softly. "Yes. Indians. So Mr. Copley intimated. May I ask why you wish to paint Indians?"

"Because nobody knows how they look, for one thing," I

said. "For another thing, they're a peculiar warm color, and they'd lend themselves to harmonious, bold, striking designs. I think I could use them against the foliage, against the sky and the water, in a way that's never been done before."

Mrs. Browne gasped. My words, I saw, filled her with immeasurable disgust. Browne threw himself back in his chair and eyed me sardonically. "There is the proof of your lack of foresight. Without knowing how to paint, you have decided to be a painter, even though you alienate your own family, to say nothing of all persons of position in this town. As subjects for your paintings you have selected creatures without property, distinction, religion, humanity, morals, art or literature. Not only will you beggar yourself to paint them, but in doing so you will violate all the rules of painting. You are young, Langdon. You have seen nothing: read nothing. Why don't you read Richardson, a great critic, on painting? Then you'll know that common nature is no more fit for a picture than plain narrative is for a poem. A painter must raise his ideas beyond what he sees. In his own mind he must form a model of perfection which is not to be found in reality. In painting, as in poetry, a beautiful, genteel woman must have her defects overlooked. A brave man must be imagined more brave, more wise, more exactly and inflexibly honest than any we know or can hope to see. A gentleman must be more so: a peasant must have more of the gentleman. An artist must use the same methods that an historian uses: that a poet adopts. Do you suppose an historian or a poet can set down the crude and ugly details of his subject?"

"I don't see why not," I said.

Seemingly Mr. Browne's question had been rhetorical; for he stared at me with surprise that changed quickly to contempt. "Exactly! You don't see why not! Richardson knows, as does every artist of importance, that life would be an insipid thing indeed if we never saw or had ideas of anything but what we commonly see. Perhaps you find something of interest in a company of people performing petty acts of no consequence to anyone but themselves! You think that persons of gentility and refined taste could possibly take pleasure in paintings of horrid savages?"

"It would depend on who painted them," I told him.

Mr. Browne raised his hands from the table and let them

drop upon it, as if calling heaven to witness that strength failed him to combat my stupidity. "My boy, I wont debate with you. I'll only say that if you persist in this course, nothing can save you."

He rose majestically, moved past me to the door and held it open. I looked at Elizabeth. She just sat there in the corner, staring at the wavering candle-flames as though unconscious of my presence. As for her mother, there was no mistaking Mrs. Browne's expression. She hated me. I knew I couldn't say anything that would have any sense to it, and I knew too that my under lip was trembling. I made a sort of bow and walked out into the hallway.

Then Mr. Browne, making small grumbling noises in his throat, followed me and closed the parlor door. I felt him press my hat into my hand: saw him throw open the outer door. The tall elms across the street were a dark cliff against the star-sprinkled sky. It seemed to me that the stars would go out and only the black cliff remain, once the house door closed, shutting me away from Elizabeth.

Sam Livermore came through the doorway, grasped my arm. "Langdon'll feel differently in the morning, Mr. Browne," he said. "A good night's rest and second thoughts . . . Much brighter in the morning! Depend on me, sir." The door closed emphatically.

I went down the street with Sam, stupidly repeating "Brighter in the morning: brighter in the morning."

I couldn't have felt worse, not even if I'd known that when morning came, I'd be miles to the northward, fleeing a worse enemy to my freedom than the Reverend Arthur Browne.

CHAPTER VII

"DON'T TALK about it," Sam told me kindly. "You'll only say things you'll regret. Mr. Browne is a fine, good man, but he's a clergyman. Clergymen can't endure contradiction, and they're pretty apt to be scared to death of anything that might damage their high standing in the community. Always remember *that* when you talk to a clergyman. I know how you feel. You've got knots in your brain because of the things he said to you. I get them myself whenever he talks to me. We'll go to Stoodley's and have some rum to loosen the knots."

I may have felt a little better by the time we stood beneath the twin whale-oil lamps that flank the front door of Stoodley's Tavern; but my mind was numb, and though I was conscious that someone nearby was talking, the words spoken meant nothing to me.

Sam shook me a little. "He's talking to you."

When I looked up, I saw the bulky figure and the moist round face of Cap Huff. He was in working garb of leather shirt and leather small clothes; and I could only think, as I stared at this clumsy ox of a man, how Elizabeth and her father would hate the sight of him.

"What do you want?" I asked.

He came closer, exuding a powerful odor of sweat and rum. "Where you been? I aint seen you for months. You aint drunk, are you?"

I shook my head, but he continued to scrutinize me closely.

"If you'd like a drink," I said, "come into Stoodley's. That's what we're going in for: to get a drink. Sam tells me if I have a drink, it'll take the knots out of my brain."

"Knots?" Cap said. "You are *too* drunk! You better go down to the Deer Tavern. They got rum down there that'll burn knots out of a pine plank and that'll sober you up good." He lowered his voice. "I got to find Hunk. You seen Hunk?"

When I said I hadn't, he asked when I expected to cross the river to Kittery.

I seemed unable to make up my mind.

"I *knew* it," he said. "You better wait right here, and not try to cross alone in this condition. I'll be back pretty quick, so's to see you get over all right."

Sam Livermore coughed politely and said, "I'll keep him here till you come back."

Cap nodded approvingly and went lumbering down the street, while I wondered vaguely what was in the wind.

Stoodley's, when we entered, was doing a roaring business. It was the most fashionable of all the Portsmouth inns —so fashionable in fact, that from the profits of its nightly sales of lobsters and liquor, Stoodley, only two years later, built his Earl of Halifax Tavern, which for the comfort of its beds, the cosiness of its tap-room and the quality of its food and drink, has no superior in Pennsylvania, Maryland or even Virginia.

The tap-room at Stoodley's was long, wainscoted and ceiled with first-growth pine the color of maple syrup; and at its far end was a bar with a sort of Dutch oven behind it. A bed of coals burned nightly in this open oven, even in hot weather, for broiling the small lobsters, fresh from the Piscataqua, for which Stoodley's is famous. In summer, the hinged roof above the oven was drawn up, allowing the heat to escape and the room to remain cool. In winter, with the roof closed, the oven radiated a rosy glow; and no matter how wildly the wind howled from the Isles of Shoals, or how high the drifts were piled in the streets without, Stoodley's tap-room was a delight. Young bloods, and old ones too, dropped in after an evening of business or pleasure for a glass of buttered rum while waiting for their lobsters to broil: then washed down the lobsters with a quart or two of Stoodley's ale.

Because of the number of King's Councillors who frequented Stoodley's, the rich merchants who entertained their ship captains and supercargoes, and the members of St. John's Lodge of Masons who trooped down for refreshment from their lodge-room on the third floor, Stoodley had built connecting private rooms along one side of his tap-room; and it was toward one of these rooms that Sam turned me.

He patted my shoulder. "Everything'll be all right," he assured me. "In a day or two you'll forget this ever happened." He called cheerfully for a pitcher of buttered rum, and gave instructions for four small lobsters to be broiled six minutes if the fire was a hot one. In spite of his cheerfulness, I knew he was wrong. I'd never get over what Elizabeth had done to me.

"Here," Sam said, when the rum was put before us, "here's the one sure cure for what ails you." He watched me critically while I drank; then spoke earnestly. "Langdon, you're making a mistake! The Brownes are gentlefolk. They're afraid of anything that's different from what they're accustomed to. Never tell people what you really think, if it's at all different from what *they* think, because it sets 'em against you on general principles. You handled 'em badly. You started wrong-end to. You ought to have told 'em you wouldn't be an artist for a duke's income, and then fixed so they'd have begun begging you to be an artist."

"It's possible," I admitted.

"It's certain!" Sam exclaimed. "There's plenty of rich men in Portsmouth. Let me go around and talk to 'em a while, and in a few years they'd contribute the money to make you an artist. You could even make money yourself while you're waiting. Why, this town's a-crawl with opportunities! If I weren't aiming to get into the government, I'd give up the law tomorrow, so to take advantage of some of 'em. Look: all you need is a schooner! Load her with anything—beaver hats, barrel staves, salt fish, warming pans, ice—and sail her to the Sugar Islands. Sell your cargo there, buy rum and coffee with the proceeds: then sail her to England and dispose of vessel as well as cargo. You could make five hundred percent profit on a venture like that!"

"That may be," I said, "but I don't believe that would help me with Elizabeth."

"Certainly it would," Sam protested. "She wouldn't care what you did as long as you had money."

At the look on my face he coughed. "I don't mean it just that way," he added hastily. "She couldn't marry without her father's consent, of course, and she'd know that if you were able to accumulate property, you'd eventually reach a position of importance in the community." He poured himself another glass of rum and drank it.

"I'm afraid you're right," I said. "I'm afraid the best people in this town don't care what you do as long as you have money. And I'm afraid that if anyone was able to make money, and wilfully stopped making it in order to be something undignified, like an artist or an author, he'd just be cast out and stoned."

"Nonsense!" Sam said.

"As for letting rich men help me study painting," I continued, "I couldn't do it. If they help me, they'll expect me to paint the way they like instead of the way *I* like."

"Oh, my God!" Sam protested.

"What's more," I said, "if I went to making money, as you

suggest, I might not be able to stop. It might do to me what it's done to the best people in this town."

Sam's voice was suddenly brittle. "Well, well! We're a little above ourselves this evening, aren't we? Just who do you mean when you speak of the best people?"

"You know who I mean. I mean the chosen of God: the Episcopalians! They sing *God Save the King* and think Benning Wentworth a great and good man."

"Huzza! Huzza!" Sam cried satirically. "Here are the lobsters."

The door opened. One of Stoodley's slaves—all of whom were named Duke, Prince, King, Earl, Baron or something similar—bustled in with four lobsters on a platter, and two mugs of ale. When he saw me sitting glumly, making no move to regale myself, he cried, in a shrill voice, "Heah! Ah grabbed those lobsters right offa coals! Whyn't you git at 'em, Mist' Towne? 'Ey's sweeter'n hot lobster-milk, yarsuh!"

At that I joined Sam in attacking the lobsters, forking the tender bodies from their shells and dipping them in melted butter. They were, as Duke had said, not unlike hot curds, juicy and tender, and sweet as scorched honey from ocean depths. Sam, his mouth full, speared half a lobster tail and waved it appreciatively at Duke, who shuffled from the room, appeased.

Neither Sam nor I spoke again until we had demolished even the claws, and washed them down with Stoodley's creamy ale.

"There!" Sam said, passing me a Cuban cigarro and lighting one himself, "I guess the world looks brighter to you, doesn't it? Come to think of it, not all honest men are dead yet, are they?"

"Certainly not," I admitted. "There's a lot of honest men in Portsmouth—men who don't approve of the way the province is being milked. My father's an honest man. So are the Langdons and the Pickerings and the Penhallows and others I could name. But they're Congregationalists. They haven't any power. The power's in the hands of those who distribute the positions—those who chuckle and slap themselves every time Benning Wentworth makes a joke."

"Not so loud, cully," Sam said. "Better lower your voice! There's too many tale-bearers in this town." He glanced over his shoulder at the door separating us from the adjoining private room.

"So," I said, "I mustn't speak the truth then! I mustn't be a painter and I mustn't speak the truth, or else I'll be in trouble!" I waggled a forefinger at him. "Especially I mustn't speak the truth about the best people! Did you ever hear what the best people of Ipswich did to some ladies of my family? They were good women; but they were called witches and hanged! Haven't you heard what happened to Richard Shortridge for marrying Molly Pitman when Benning Wentworth wanted her?"

Sam shrugged his shoulders. "You can't prove it!"

"Can't I? Go talk to seamen who know what's happening in the British navy! Two weeks after the wedding, Benning Wentworth arranged for a press gang to steal Shortridge out of his own home, press him into a British ship and keep him there for life. He's on a British frigate today; and for all I know, Wentworth's still trying to coax Molly down to Little Harbor."

"Who told you this claptrap?" Sam demanded. "It sounds like Anna Marriner's tarradiddle, or something out of your flannel-mouthed friend Cap Huff."

"Well," I said, "what about the grants of land being made by Benning Wentworth in this province? He's granting big tracts to outsiders at enormous fees, isn't he—or is that claptrap and tarradiddle, too?"

Sam eyed me warily.

"Isn't Benning Wentworth," I persisted, "reserving a five-hundred-acre piece for himself out of every grant, with the understanding that each piece must be improved by the settlers on the grant?"

"I know nothing about it," Sam said.

"That's strange! I thought everybody knew about it! I thought everybody knew he'd stolen a hundred thousand acres from this province! Why, it's common talk that thanks to Benning Wentworth and his brother Mark, the whole province has been stripped of its forests, and half the money for the lumber's in Benning's pocket. Where've you been that you don't know about it? How does it happen a lawyer doesn't know it's impossible to get justice in this province unless you go on your knees to the Wentworths? My, my! Think of a lawyer not knowing that they own Wyseman Clagett, the new

King's Attorney, right here in this town! Maybe you never heard Wyseman Clagett knows a hundred and seven different ways to have you put in jail if he doesn't like your looks! Maybe you never heard you'd be Clagetted if you try to run contrary to Benning Wentworth's schemes! Maybe you never heard how Clagett and High Sheriff Packer take pennies off dead men's eyes and divide 'em with Wentworth!"

Sam buried his nose in his mug of ale and said nothing.

"I had to listen to the Reverend Arthur Browne," I said, "because he's Elizabeth's father; but I don't have to keep silent when you want me to think you admire the leaders of this town. Do you admire Lettice Mitchel's father and mother for making her marry Wyseman Clagett—for having a higher regard for any rogue in a King's uniform than for an honest man in ordinary dress? Do you admire Wyseman Clagett for beating Lettice twice a week? Do you admire Clagett and Packer for sending constables to incite seamen to resist arrest; then fining 'em ten shillings apiece so the King's Attorney and the High Sheriff can be kept in food and wines? I suppose if Wyseman Clagett and Thomas Packer came in here and took my clothes by force, you'd admire them!"

Upon that, as by some disastrous coincidence, the door behind Sam—not the door into the big tap-room, but one leading into the private room adjoining ours—swung open, revealing a face and figure that sent a chill down my spine. Wyseman Clagett, King's Attorney for the Province of New Hampshire, stood there looking at me horribly.

He was a large man with heavy eyebrows, black eyes and a dismaying nervous affliction. Every moment or so his mouth, convulsively contorted, was drawn so far to one side that he seemed to be trying to eat his ear, and at the moment of this distortion his bushy eyebrows jerked together like two black caterpillars wrestling. Temper made Wyseman's facial disturbance worse; children screamed and mules ran away at the sight of it.

He was worse now as he looked at me through the open door; while I, speechless, looked back at him.

Sam jumped to his feet and turned toward the door; then Clagett walked in, and close behind him came Thomas Packer, the High Sheriff—the same Thomas Packer who later hanged the school teacher Ruth Blay. Packer was a gloomy-looking man, as indeed he should have been.

In a room from which they emerged I saw a table littered with lobster shells and ale mugs, so I was sure they had been there as long as we, and probably longer—long enough, certainly, to have heard easily, through the thin partition, every word I'd said.

Sam was the first to find his voice. "To what are we indebted for the pleasure?" he asked politely.

Clagett, grotesque but imposing in his long, scarlet-lined councillor's cloak, spoke in his surprisingly high-pitched voice. "Mr. Livermore, I've nothing against you, but I find you in dangerous company. I think you and I can understand each other without unnecessary formalities, so I'll bid you good evening."

"Mr. Attorney," Sam said, "Langdon Towne's my guest. If you're here to say something to him, say it to me as well."

Clagett's reply was ironic. "Ah! The gander asks the same sauce as the goose! Sir, you'd like me to think, would you, that you're in sympathy with all Mr. Towne's opinions?"

"I'm not familiar with all Mr. Towne's opinions," Sam said. "As for my sympathies, they're nobody's business but my own —until they're expressed. But that's not the question, sir. The question is why you've joined us without an invitation—without doing us the courtesy of knocking, even."

"Oh," Clagett said, "that's easily answered. I'm here to prevent repetitions of libels upon His Majesty's government and officers. Perhaps, sir, you wish to defend libels upon His Majesty's representatives?"

"Certainly not!" Sam protested. "Certainly I don't wish to defend libels, no matter who it is that's libelled."

Clagett's high voice was stern. "Then, sir, you've no business here, and I must again wish you a very good evening. Sheriff, open that door and give Mr. Livermore any necessary assistance!"

For all Packer's heavy appearance, he could move rapidly when he wished; and he moved rapidly now. Reaching for the door into the tap-room, he drew it open, placed a huge hand against Sam's back and ejected him as easily as a man lifts an ale-mug. With equal rapidity he closed the door behind Sam and shot the bolt. I saw the latch rise and fall, and knew Sam was vainly trying to force his way back in.

I realized that my goose, as they say in Kittery, was cooked, and that Sam could do nothing for me without ruining himself. Clagett looked at me, his eyebrows wrestling and his mouth trying to eat his ear.

"Do you wish to make a statement?" he asked me.

I tried to keep my voice from shaking. "Why should I make any statement?"

"Because you've made yourself liable to serious charges."

"What charges?"

"Slander and libel!" Clagett struck the table with his open palm. "You slandered me; you slandered my wife. You libelled that great and good man, our Governor, Benning Wentworth. You repeated shameful rumors concerning the whereabouts of Richard Shortridge—lies, all lies! Now I want to know the source of them. Who spread these poisons to you? Who told you?"

I breathed hard and shook my head; that was all I could do.

"You stand in some peril," Clagett warned me. "I want the source of these calumnies."

"Calumnies?" I tried to speak up. "I'd be the last to repeat calumnies about innocent men."

"What!" Clagett shouted. "What do you say?"

I was a frightened boy, but at his shout I somehow contrived to hold my head up. "I don't believe they're calumnies."

"Ah," said Clagett and turned to the sheriff. "Dangerously intoxicated and a threat to the safety of a peaceable community. No communication permitted with such a prisoner, Sheriff! No communication whatever with anyone!"

"You don't dare!" I told him. "You don't dare to bring me into a court and have me repeat what I said to my friend in this room."

Clagett made no answer; he just pulled his cloak around him and grinned. Then I understood that of course I'd never see the inside of a court; that I'd never have recourse to the processes of justice; that I'd never even know the mercy of a judge owned by Benning Wentworth. Clagett planned to treat me, I realized, as Richard Shortridge had been treated. He planned to have me pressed aboard a British man-of-war—a prison from which there would be no appeal and almost no escape.

"Wait!" I cried out like a fool. "I demand to have word taken to my family! I demand the right to see a lawyer: to see Sam Livermore."

Clagett spoke almost smilingly to Packer. "Raving from the effects of drink! Not to be spoken to or even approached by anybody! I hold you responsible!" He waved Packer toward the door.

In the next room—the private room from which Clagett and Packer had descended upon us—there was a clatter, followed by the crash of an overturned table and breaking chinaware. A hoarse voice cursed loudly, bellowing, "Who's raving from drink? I want to hear him doing it! Ain't there enough for other people to get raving from?"

The half-closed door swung open, and in the doorway stood Cap Huff, breezy, enormous, bright-eyed, almost sober.

CHAPTER VIII

CAP STOOD looking at us earnestly: then hitched up his breeches and came in ponderously, closing the door behind him. "Which one's raving from drink?" he asked. "Clagett, maybe? Hunk Marriner tells me his mother, old Anner Marriner, had a good bit of money twisted out of her by Clagett only today, so of course I don't say it wouldn't be right and natural if he's drunk and raving this evening. How you feeling, Mr. Clagett? Good?"

Clagett turned to Packer. "Take them both, Sheriff. No communication with anyone for either of them."

"Take who both, Sheriff?" Cap asked heartily. "I just stepped in to see that no communications from Royal representatives of the Crown didn't get young Langdon Towne here into evil associations, and ruin him with their liquor. You three gentlemen been having a nice supper together? I don't like to interfere in friendship's jolly hours, but it's time this here boy went home, or his family'll be fretted." He went to the window and ripped down the curtain that covered it. "Why," he said inconsequentially, "this room's on an alley, just like the jail that everybody gets out of. The tide's fall-

ing, and it's a hell of a paddle across the river. Aint you
about ready to go home, Langdon?"

"I can't," I said. "I've been arrested."

"You'd ought to be," Cap said solemnly, with a gesture toward Clagett and Packer. "Consorting with evil companions!
You'd ought to be!"

"Sheriff!" Clagett spoke harshly to Packer. "You have your
orders. These men are under arrest. Are you going to take
them to——"

"I will," Packer said; but he didn't. Instead he tried to imi-
tate the King's Attorney's manner. "You," he said to Cap
Huff, "are a hissing and a by-word in this town. You've attempted to interfere with the King's justice, and you're a
hissing and a by-word."

"I'm a by-word," Cap said, "but I aint no hissing. I been a
by-word in this town since I was seven years old and stole the
minister's breeches. I can prove I been the best by-word this
town ever had, and still am, but the man that calls me a hissing, he's got to take and set down and eat it!" He took Packer
by the shoulders, rammed him down into a chair. "Packer, set
down!"

Clagett strode toward the door that opened into the tap-
room. "You fool," he said to Cap Huff. "Do you suppose
there was ever a night when there were no constables in Stoodley's tap-room?"

"Call 'em in," Cap Huff told him. "Open the door and call
'em in!"

Clagett jerked the door open, and the opening was almost
filled with the broad-shouldered figure of Hunking Marriner.
Hunk pushed Clagett back into the room, came in himself,
closed the door behind him, and bolted it.

Hunk's mouth was drawn down at the corners. His face was
white and his clothes were torn and muddy. He stood with
his back to the door and, not speaking, looked hard at Clagett.

Cap put heavy hands on Clagett's shoulders and sat him
down beside Packer. "Don't make much of a noise, gentlemen," he said, "because if you try, I'll load up your mouth
with lobster shells till you wont be able to make even no
hissing. It's a word I don't like, and wont allow to be applied
to me, and if you make the sound it means, I'll think you're
calling it at me again, and when my feelings get hurt, I aint
responsible! Hunk Marriner don't like you neither, Mr. Clag-

ett." Cap, standing before the two seated men, with one hand on Packer's shoulder and the other on Clagett's, turned his head to speak to me. "Hunk's going with you, Langdon."

"Going where with me?" I asked.

"Where you aint neither of you arrested," Cap said. "Where you wont neither of you get pressed on a King's ship, and maybe never get back. Hunk's feelings got hurt with Clagett this afternoon, Langdon. Hunk's mother got Clagetted over a load of fish, just around sundown. Clagett wanted fish for supper, but he didn't want to pay for it, so he played the old trick him and Packer have played so often; Packer had a couple of constables arrest her for profanity, and fined her five dollars. She paid her fine with the fish, and Clagett and Packer divided 'em."

Cap gave Clagett an admonitory slap on the top of the head. "How'd you come to forget about Hunk, Mr. Clagett? You'd oughta remembered Hunk wouldn't like such goings on! I'm surprised you got any constables left, seeing that two of 'em wont be out of the hospital for a month, and that it took four more to throw Hunk in that damned old jail of yours. And you'd oughta known you couldn't keep Hunk in that jail, Mr. Clagett!"

He spoke to Hunk. "Wasn't there something you wanted to say to Mr. Clagett before you and Langdon set off on your travels?"

"Yes," Hunk said, "there was. I wanted to tell him that if he didn't keep away from my mother——"

"Wait a minute," Cap said. "You aint used to talking, like what I am. In case Mr. Clagett don't understand what you mean about your mother, I'll explain it to him later." His tone became querulous. "Why don't you fellers get started so I can stop talking?"

Hunk swung himself over the ledge of the open window and dropped lightly to the ground. I scrambled after him, and then, standing on tiptoe, looked back into the lighted room. "Hurry, Cap," I said. "You know you've got to come too, don't you?"

"I certainly do," he answered, laughed boorishly and, for so huge a man, became a marvel of agility. With his ponderous hands still upon the two shoulders, he kicked the chairs of the King's Attorney and the High Sheriff from under them, left them rolling and grunting upon the floor: then sprang across the room, squeezed himself through the window and dropped at my side.

"Good-bye, bully boys," he said. "There's three of us better leave town a spell. It just happens I got a dear old grandma I oughta visit—keeps the Seaman's Tavern in Newburyport; so I'm off to the south'ard while you two go north. I hope you'll——"

He checked himself as an outrageous uproar was heard from within Stoodley's. "Well, suppose we all commence a-running," Cap said, and these words, and a hoarse laugh from the darkness, and a heavy padding of his feet down the alley, were the last Hunk Marriner and I heard from Cap Huff as we turned and ran for the river.

CHAPTER IX

HUNK AND I crouched in the canoe under Spring Wharf and kindled a lantern. The tide was half in, and the wharf piles, perhaps because of the glimmering of the slimy green weed with which they were coated and the pressure of the rapid current against their lower ends, seemed about to engulf us, like a dripping dark forest. They had a dank, oppressive odor—a singular combination, seemingly, of mud, sulphur, saltpeter and decay; and as I crouched among them in that wet canoe, I laughed feebly, thinking that as dusk had fallen that same night, I'd sat with Elizabeth Browne in her mother's parlor, a respectable young man who'd been a student at Harvard and hoped to be a painter.

Hunk had with him a letter to me from Sam Livermore, hastily scrawled in the tap-room of Stoodley's.

"Hurry up and read it!" Hunk urged me. "Sam said not to waste any time getting away. He said I hit one of those constables kind of hard."

I broke the seal on Sam's letter and unfolded two sheets.

While Hunk held the lantern close, I spelled out the first one.

"Cap and Hunk will help you get away [it read]. Go to Crown Point and give the enclosed letter to Col. Zaccheus Lovewell or Maj. Rogers. Either of them can get you in the army. All the fighting is over, and you'll have a good time, probably nothing to do but catch trout and hunt raccoons. You can come back before too long. Nobody will try to make trouble for you, as you will then be a hero. Trust me to look out for your interests with Elizabeth and Mr. Browne. Tell your father you couldn't help what happened. Providence was against you today."

"Be careful of that other letter," Hunk said. "Sam's a Mason, and he's put Masonic signs in it. Lovewell and Rogers belong to St. John's Lodge, here in Portsmouth; and when one Mason makes a sign at another Mason to do something, he's supposed to do it. My mother says that's why people join the Masons—so to get other Masons to do favors for 'em."

I examined the letter for secret symbols, but could find none. I read it to Hunk:

"To Colonel Zaccheus Lovewell or Major Rogers at Crown Point: The bearers of this letter, Langdon Towne and Hunking Marriner, both of Kittery, are friends of mine and good woodsmen. Mr. Towne has been educated at Harvard. Owing to a slight difference of opinion with the civil authorities of this locality, I have suggested to them the advisability of temporarily exercising their talents in your vicinity. If you can find places for them in your detachments, I will consider it a personal favor and will also guarantee they will make good soldiers. Accept, gentlemen, the assurance of my deepest consideration and high personal regard. Yr. obedient humble servant, Sam'l Livermore."

We dowsed the lantern, pushed out from under the wharf, and set off across the swirling black water of the Piscataqua. Half an hour later Hunk left me at our front door, promising to return as soon as he had rolled his blanket.

I entered the house reluctantly, dreading the ordeal before

me. The downstairs rooms were heavy with the feel of sleep. As I mounted the stairs, I heard my mother's drowsy voice: "Is that you, Langdon?"

When I said it was, she murmured something about "all hours of the night" and told me to bolt the front door. I went on up the stairs and into the back room overlooking the river, which I shared with my younger brother, Odiorne. When I struck a light, Odiorne blinked, muttered inarticulately, and turned his face to the wall.

Pulling off my jacket and shirt, I dragged my horse-hide trunk from beneath the eaves. Crown Point, I suspected, would be cold, so I took my leather shirt and breeches, woolen undershirts, a towcloth shirt for hot days, three pairs of stockings, and both tanned and untanned moccasins. Mindful of Sam's hint that I might have spare time on my hands, I also added a sketching book and a small box of paints and pencils.

My mother pattered into the room, a shawl thrown over her nightdress. "Why, Langdon! What's this mean? Did you know you didn't bolt the front door?"

"Mother," I said, "I had a little trouble. I got to go away for a while."

Odiorne muttered complainingly in his sleep. My mother sat down suddenly on the bed, looking weak and tired.

"What kind of trouble, son?"

"Trouble with Wyseman Clagett. He heard me talk against him and the Governor and pretty near the whole Episcopal Church. He almost put me in jail, Mother."

I gave her Sam Livermore's letters. She felt at her breast for her spectacles, and I saw that her eyes were full of tears.

"Here," I said, "I'll read 'em to you." When I had finished reading the letters, Odiorne sat up in bed.

"There wont be a window left in Clagett's house tomorrow night," he said. "I know just who to get."

My mother turned on him. "Odiorne Towne! Don't let me hear another word from you! You march yourself downstairs this instant and lay out that cold beef and a loaf of bread."

Odiorne crawled out of bed and padded downstairs.

My father came slowly in, rumpled and gray in his nightgown, and behind him I saw Eben, Richard and Enoch, my older brothers. My father's face was rigid, and I felt that now I was in for it and no mistake. I took my brown blanket from the trunk and arranged my effects on it, so to roll it. When I picked up my sketch book, my ears burned in anticipation of what he would say.

"Son," my father asked, "how'd you happen to be talking against Wyseman Clagett and the Governor? Haven't I warned you repeatedly to keep your eyes open and your mouth shut?"

"It was because of the Brownes," I said. "They're bound I shan't be an artist. John Singleton Copley says if I don't use my talent, I'll regret it all my life, but Mr. Browne says an artist isn't a gentleman. He said his door was closed to me."

"Oh, he did, did he?"

"Yes, sir. I felt pretty bad about it, so Sam Livermore took me to Stoodley's. I felt so bad that I said anything that came into my head. Clagett and Sheriff Packer were in the next room."

My father looked stern. "You should have gone to the Bell Tavern. Didn't you have sense enough to know Stoodley's would be full of royalists?"

My mother sniffed. "I'm glad he spoke out! It's high time somebody spoke out!"

My father nodded. "Yes, there's lots of others in Portsmouth who'll be glad you spoke out, but still they wont speak out themselves. It looks as if us common people would have to stand the Clagetts and the Packers and the Wentworths for some years to come!" Ruminatively he added, "All things considered, you might be worse off, my son. As your friend Livermore says, Clagett'll have to be careful about touching you, once you've been in the army; and by the time you get to Crown Point, the summer campaign'll be over."

He spoke more cheerfully. "It ought to be an interesting experience. You can't tell what it'll lead to; you might even get a grant of land out of it. Anyway, there's got to be one of the Townes fight the French every generation, so maybe this trouble of yours will leave our family in peace for the rest of our lives."

He eyed me thoughtfully. "I've said some pretty sharp things about this painting idea of yours; but if Copley says you can paint, and you've got so much faith in yourself that you'll hold out against Arthur Browne, I guess I'll have to admit I was wrong."

He cleared his throat. My mother coughed and my brothers stared up at the ceiling, as if trying to remember something —a sign they were greatly impressed by my father's sudden change of heart.

"It's too bad about the Brownes," my father said. "Too bad; but you did well to take a stand. A man's got to make it understood in the beginning that his wife's folks can't plan his life or regulate his conduct. You got to stand up to 'em, son, or your life wont be worth living!"

My brother Enoch rubbed one bare foot against the other. "I got two half-Joes and twelve shillings in hard money. If it'll do you any good, Langdon, you're welcome to it."

My brother Richard coughed. "You can have that light musket of mine, Langdon. She's new, and you can drive nails with her at fifteen paces."

I said I'd take it and Enoch's hard money as well.

"If there's anything of mine you want," my oldest brother Eben said, "you can have it." After some thought I settled on his new braided fishing line, a box of salmon hooks, two silk handkerchiefs and the big powder-horn scraped thin on shipboard by my great-uncle James during the expedition to Cartagena in 1741.

New Englanders, I have heard it claimed, are tight-lipped and tight-fisted: as close as the bark on a tree, and cold as a brass doorknob. Some of them probably are, but I have never noticed any particular closeness among New Englanders in my section—though they are often close-mouthed about their benefactions; and I'm not sure, indeed, they're not inclined to be close-mouthed in moments of emotion.

At all events, when my father and brothers came to the kitchen with me and sat silently while my mother brought food for all of us, I knew their silence was due neither to coldness nor tightness.

Hunk Marriner whistled outside. My mother kissed me, and my father and brothers helped me shoulder my blanket and pack, then went with me to the door.

There I shook hands with them, none of us saying anything except "Good-bye"; but as I stepped forth into the darkness, my mother's voice called quaveringly from behind the nightgowned figures in the doorway: "Hunk Marriner, you take good care of Langdon. He's always been a good boy."

I'm afraid I gulped a little at that, and again when I turned and looked back from the landing-stage at the river's edge and saw that in the candle-lighted doorway two figures still stood looking toward what they could not see.

CHAPTER X

THE WAR in which we found ourselves so unexpectedly embarked seems vague and far-off now; but to us, at the time, it seemed as important as it did endless.

Almost since I could remember it had been going on. We called it, simply enough, The War, because it was the only one of which we knew or expected to hear. In reality it was a war against the French and their Indian allies. With the passage of the years we called it the Old French War; and to those of us engaged in it it seemed older, even, than Robert Matlin, the Portsmouth baker, who walked to Boston and back every week to buy his flour, and lived to be 115 years old.

Since the beginning of 1755 the colonists had fought under British generals who were blunderers and incompetents, and under far too many British officers who considered themselves insulted if forced to meet colonial officers on a basis of equality. Year after year the colonists, led by British, had fought to drive the French from their line of forts and trading posts, which extended from Quebec and Montreal, through Crown Point and Ticonderoga and out into the Indian country of the West; and year after year the French, with subterfuges, surprise attacks and Indian cunning, had fought to hold the English back.

The prize for which they struggled was one that aroused the cupidity of every king in Europe; and the King of France and the King of England would gladly have sacrificed the life of every general in their employ if by so

doing they could win. That prize was the ultimate owner-
ship of the Ohio Valley, with its endless forests, fertile
plains, tremendous rivers and wealth of furs—the richest
empire for which two nations ever contended.

Each year, since the war began, the stupidity of one British
general or another had brought overwhelming catastrophe
upon us, so that every home and tavern in Portsmouth, and
doubtless in hundreds of other towns as well, had buzzed
with anger against the bunglers who were directing our
destinies and doing it unbelievably badly.

In 1755 Braddock, a brutal and foolish man, had fallen
into a French ambush near Fort Duquesne with horrible results. In the same year Sir William Johnson, by his pig-
headed refusal to follow up his victory over Dieskau and
wipe out the fleeing French army, had prolonged the
war for years. In 1756 the Earl of Loudoun, an experienced
soldier, had come from England to lead our men, and had
labored tirelessly to surmount the difficulties that confronted
him. He soon became cordially detested, however, when, in
1757—due partly to his own mistakes and partly to the
cowardice of his subordinate, General Webb—Fort William
Henry on Lake George was captured and demolished by Montcalm, and its unarmed, captive garrison of English and Provincials horribly massacred or maltreated by Montcalm's
Indians. In 1758 Abercrombie, master blockhead of them all,
had led the finest army ever seen in America against Ticonderoga, ordered a general assault from the worst possible
position, and sacrificed the victory and the army to his own
stupidity. Seven men from Portsmouth had been caught in
that French spider's web of fallen tree-tops, at Ticonderoga,
shot to shreds by French bullets, and left hanging there to
rot.

And now, in 1759, the French had retreated from Ticonderoga and Crown Point before General Amherst's superior
forces, and there was talk on all sides that the French were
at last certain to be beaten. If only the English would
avoid further blunders, everybody agreed, Montreal and
Quebec would be captured, and Canada would at last fall
into the hands of England.

There was one good feature of this British mismanagement,
and only one. It had shown that Provincial troops could fight,
if properly led, as well as any of the King's regiments that

had been brought to America; but we remained as distrustful of British leadership as ever.

This, then, was the war toward which Hunk Marriner and I were bound—not because we had any fondness for war, but because war seemed a lesser evil than Wyseman Clagett. Anything, I eventually learned, is preferable to war; but that knowledge is something every man must learn for himself— usually at considerable expense.

Our first objective was the fort on the Connecticut River known as Number Four, that being the crossing place of all roads, paths and Indian trails between the Atlantic Coast, Canada and the West. Once past Number Four, we knew, we were safe from Wyseman Clagett; so we drove our canoe upstream from Kittery at top speed, around Boiling Rock and through Long Reach, and swung to the westward with the rising tide, past Hilton's Point and into the channel that leads to beautiful Great Bay.

At sun-up we left our canoe with a farmer near Durham, giving him the use of it until we should return, which we hoped might be reasonably soon. Then, strapping on our blankets and packs and shouldering our muskets, we set off due west on the beaten path to Dunbarton and Number Four.

We fully intended, on reaching Number Four, to follow the old road to Lake Champlain, which goes by way of Lake George; and if we had done so, the course of our lives would have been altered. Whether the alteration would have been for the better or for the worse, I cannot say; but I am certain that if we hadn't stopped at the Flintlock Tavern in Dunbarton, and there met Sergeant McNott, we would have taken the Lake George road and been another two days reaching Crown Point. That delay of two days would have made all the difference.

Dunbarton is half way between Portsmouth and Number Four. It lies in fertile, rolling country, sprinkled with handsome fenced farms on hilltop meadows; but the town itself is nothing to brag about, since it consists of a church, a smithy, a school and the Flintlock Tavern, all grouped at the crossroads and all built of squared logs.

In the center of the crossroads stood a signpost reading "No. 4: 54 mls," and on the front of the tavern hung a board

lettered "Last chance: No more rum for 54 mls. S. Flint,
Prop."

The tavern appeared to be as quiet as two fugitives like
ourselves could wish. There was no sign of life to be seen
near it, except for a wolfish-looking dog that reclined in the
dust beside the front steps, slumbering heavily, and dreaming
of something that caused him to emit muted, falsetto barks.
Since our canteens needed filling, we went in. We at once
discovered the seeming quietness of the tavern to be con-
find to its outside. Indoors, there rose from a dark corner
of the tap-room a dreary rendition, in male voices, of the
hymn,

> "Awake, my soul, and with the sun
> The daily stage of duty run;
> Shake off dull sloth and joyful rise
> To pay thy morning sacrifice;
> Redeem thy mis-spent life that's past
> And live this day as if thy last;
> Improve thy talent with due care;
> For the great day thyself prepare."

Being still too close to Portsmouth to run risks, we attempted to withdraw quietly; but as we turned to go, we were
hailed so brusquely and explosively that I thought for a moment the speaker must be one of Wyseman Clagett's agents.
"Here you!" the voice shouted from the group of hymn-
singers in the corner, "where you think you're going! Come
back here!"

We stopped and looked back. The man who had spoken
had risen from the table in the corner and was glaring fiercely
at us. It seemed to me he was the most violent-looking man I
had ever seen. He was a little over medium height. His hair,
what we could see of it, was a sort of carroty scarlet, and
his face was not only brick red, as though he were on the
verge of exploding with rage, but was pitted with smallpox.
His eyes were a pale, frosty blue, and one of them was half
concealed by a drooping eyelid, so that he seemed to be
squinting with cold calculation. A scar ran from the drooping eyelid across his cheek-bone to his ear, which had been
slashed through in the middle, so that it was divided into
an upper and a lower ear, and the two halves were held neat-

ly together by a flattened gold ring. His arms were so long that they reached nearly to his knees, and he held himself tilted forward, with his elbows flexed, as though he intended to leap at and strangle anyone who disagreed with him.

"What's the matter?" Hunk said. "We aint broken any laws, have we?"

The angry man left his corner and came close to us. He wore a hunting smock of greenish buckskin, circled at the waist with a broad belt from which depended small leather loops, evidently for the carrying of light baggage. His leggins were buckskin, with a flap below the knee. The flap was tied tight around the ankle and calf, which gave him a trig look. The strangest part of his garb was his headgear. It was a stiff little cap of green wool, brimless, with two short ribbons dangling from its back; and it was pushed over to one side, so that its front edge rested almost on the angry man's eyebrow. Nevertheless, it clung to him like a limpet, giving him an indescribably rakish and reckless appearance. I had seen such caps in Portsmouth, but there they were worn by girls and were called Scotch bonnets.

"Listen," he said. "You can sing, can't you?"

As politely as possible, I told him we were in a hurry and had no time for singing.

"In too big a hurry to sing?" he demanded. "Then wha'd you come in here for? Where you going to?"

I told him Crown Point.

"Listen," he said again, and his anger seemed to rise and boil within him, "why don't you talk sense? An hour more or less aint going to make any difference to you if you're going to Crown Point. You don't know the way to Crown Point, anyhow! You come on over here to this table and do some singing, like I say! I tell you I got to find somebody that knows how to sing! It's important!"

When I mistakenly laughed at this, I thought he might rupture a blood vessel. His right hand clenched convulsively, and he seemed about to fly at my throat.

"All right," I said hastily. "We don't want any trouble with anyone. We'll sit down and sing if you want us to, but what in God's name is important about it?"

The red-headed man pulled off his green cap and wiped his forehead on his sleeve. "By God," he said passionately, "if you'd ever had anything to do with drunk Indians, maybe you'd understand; but if you haven't, there's no use talking about it. I got John Konkapot over here. He's a Stockbridge Indian, and he's drunk. Stockbridge Indians are psalm-singing Indians; and this here John Konkapot, he wants to sing. There aint none of us can sing well enough to suit John, and he's showing his dissatisfaction. When he's dissatisfied, he wont drink nothing but rum. If I can get him to drinking beer, it'll make him sick, and unless he drinks beer and gets sick, he wont be fit to travel. That's what's important about it!"

"Why don't you leave this Konkapot here to sober up by himself and go on without him?" Hunk asked.

The red-headed man clapped his green cap on his head, and with the palm of his hand gave it a quick push that anchored it securely, tilted though it was. He glared at Hunk. "Because he was sent here to get me!" he said bitterly. "Because I got to get back to Crown Point and take him with me! Because we need him! That's why! Now, by God, you come over to that table without any more talk, or you'll get some of that trouble you aint looking for."

Hunk and I glanced at each other and decided we'd better comply. We stood our muskets against the wall, hung our blankets and packs over them and went to the table in the corner.

Three men sat at it. One was Flint, the tavern-keeper, as we soon discovered. The others were Flint's hired man and the Stockbridge Indian, John Konkapot. Flint and his hired man were evidently ill at ease.

Konkapot was a strange-looking Indian. His leggins were of greenish buckskin, like those of our red-headed acquaintance; but his upper body was covered by a black-and-white checked shirt of almost unbelievable foulness. The shirt hung down outside his leggins, and was daubed across the shoulders with red paint. His head was shaved, except for a scalp-lock in the center of his skull, and the scalp-lock was confined at the base by a brass shoe-buckle. Although his face was buried in his hands, I could see he was crying.

Our friend tapped Flint on the shoulder. "Beer!" he said peremptorily. "Bring beer for everybody, and keep bringing it to Konkapot whenever his mug gets low."

"He won't drink it, Sergeant," the inn-keeper protested. "He'll only pour it on me, the way he did the last mugful."

Our friend turned on him furiously. "You do as you're told! If he wants to pour it on you, let him pour it! I'm paying for it, and he can use it the way he wants to! Hurry up with that beer! We got to do some more singing!"

The inn-keeper hurried away.

"Just go ahead and sing," our friend told us. "Don't pay no attention to Konkapot. He's crying about his grandfather."

"What happened to his grandfather?"

"Oh, the regular thing! Prob'ly they buried him without his bracelets, or maybe he had the misfortune to die in bed. Everybody knows why Indians cry when they get drunk. Anyway, all you got to do is sing."

Hunk hummed the first line of "There is a land of pure delight where saints immortal reign."

"That's a good one," our friend said. "Let out on it, so's to get Konkapot interested."

"I'll carry the air," I told Hunk, "and you take the tenor. If anyone else has a voice, I'll take the second bass."

We went to work on it. Hunk's voice, which was high and sweet, soared powerfully on the next-to-last line—"Death, like a narrow sea divides——" Our new friend, whose voice was execrable, joined us deafeningly, and beat time with a forefinger. The hired man, too, chimed in, but feebly. When Hunk hit the high notes, the Indian Konkapot raised his head from his hands and stared at us from red, drunken, tear-filled eyes.

He was the dirtiest-looking Indian I had ever seen. His face had been painted white not long before, but much of the white had rubbed off, so that he made me think of a pig-sty in need of white-washing.

Flint, the inn-keeper, came back to the table with three mugs of beer in each hand, stood behind us and joined disconcertingly in the last lines; but when we'd finished, he set the mugs on the table and slid into his seat.

Our red-headed friend showed signs of exasperation. "What's the matter with you?" he asked Konkapot belligerently. "Here I got you some real singers, and you never open that big mouth of yours. If you want to sing, sing!"

Konkapot wiped his face clumsily with the palm of his hand. "Moe," he said. "Moe." He gulped down half his mug of beer, blinked stupidly at us, and again said, "Moe!"

"Give it to him," the red-headed man exclaimed. "Keep right at it!"

When we had moistened our throats, we went at the second verse. To my surprise, Konkapot had a good baritone, and thus I could insert a bass. The second verse was pleasing to all of us—so pleasing that, at the end, we applauded ourselves freely and drained our beer-mugs to ourselves, after the manner of tap-room singers since time immemorial.

When Flint left to fill our empty mugs, Konkapot swayed in his chair and examined us owlishly. "You know Dusty Fiddles?"

"We know 'em all," Hunk said. "We're just as civilized as you are."

Konkapot threw back his head and gave tongue like the Bull of Bashan.

> *"O come, all ye faithful,*
>   *Joyful and triumphant——"*

We let him negotiate the first "O come, let us adore him" by himself; then swung in with him on the second with such overwhelming success that the wolfish-looking dog came in from outside and lay by the door, moaning mildly. No sooner had we finished than Konkapot started the song anew. He couldn't seem to get enough of it. He started it again and again, as tireless as a machine, and the more we sang, the oftener Flint hurried back and forth between our table and the beer keg.

Just as I had decided Konkapot would never stop, he laid his dirty arm across my shoulders and said thickly, "You my sweet bludda!"

"Who?" I asked. "I'm your sweet what?"

"His sweet brother," the inn-keeper explained. "He likes you, but don't be scared. He wont kiss you. Them heathen aint learned how."

Konkapot hiccuped, rose unsteadily to his feet, stumbled over a chair, and went toward the door, stepping high, as though laboriously ascending a steep hill.

"Climbing a mountain now," Flint explained admiringly. "When he thinks he's got to the top, he'll fall down and roll like hell if somebody doesn't stop him. But come on, Joe." He and his hired man rose, charitably placed themselves one on each side of Konkapot, and conducted him out to the open air.

The man with the split ear sighed gustily. "There! That finishes *him*. When he comes to, he'll be practically sober."

CHAPTER XI

THE NAME of our red-headed acquaintance was McNott. He was a sergeant in the army; and like most sergeants, he was set on having his own way. A more intolerant and bossy man I had never encountered. One of the most singular things about him was that he was not cowardly at heart, as are most bossy men, but would have flown at anyone twice his size if he thought the occasion demanded it. Since he couldn't bear to be contradicted, and since he was unable to see any point of view except his own, he seemed perpetually on the verge of fighting someone. To give him his due, he was more often right than not; and no doubt his contentious attitude was due to his knowledge of the errors under which the great majority of mankind perpetually labor.

Alone with Hunk and me, he abruptly seemed wholly sober, looked us over with a quick, keen eye: then spoke up briskly, "Who am I?" and answered himself. "Me, I'm McNott. What's my business? Being a sergeant. What's yours? Who are you, and what takes you to Crown Point?"

It was Hunk who replied. "Thought maybe we'd go see what it kind of looks like," he said. "Thought maybe after we got there we might take a notion to join the army—that is, if we feel like it after we get there."

"You don't say!" McNott returned. "Was you intending to join the Royal Regiment, or the Highlanders, or General Amherst's staff, or one of them lousy Provincial regiments?"

"To tell you the truth, I don't know," I admitted. "We have letters to Colonel Lovewell and Major Rogers, but we haven't decided which one to see first."

"Well, well," McNott said. "When you going to make up your mind? It's kind of a shame, aint it, to keep two good officers like Colonel Lovewell and Major Rogers all excited and nervous, on account of not knowing which one of 'em might get you?" He looked severe and called to Flint, who had left Konkapot to the hired man, and, returning, was just entering the doorway. "Three mugs more, Flint."

"Maybe," I ventured, "you could tell us which officer we ought to see first?"

"Oh," McNott said carelessly, "it depends what you want to do. Colonel Lovewell's a nice feller: a fine old feller. He keeps his regiment pretty busy, digging latrines and working on the fort. If you like to dig latrines, I'd see Lovewell. If you like to chop down trees, maybe he'll fix it so you can chop some down and raft 'em across the lake; but if you'd rather use a pick-axe and shovel, maybe that can be arranged, too. He's a real accommodating feller, Lovewell is."

"We don't want to do any of those things."

"Then you better keep away from armies," McNott said. "Once you're in the army, you do anything you're told to do. Most always you're told to do something you wouldn't choose to do if you had the say-so."

"You don't do things like that if you're under Major Rogers, do you?" I asked.

Sergeant McNott eyed me suspiciously. "Listen! Don't you know about Rogers' Rangers?"

I said everybody knew about Rogers' Rangers. "They kill Indians, mostly, don't they?"

McNott spoke sharply. "Mostly they get along without sleeping, and a good part of the time they get along without eating. Sometimes they lay in one spot for twelve hours without moving, while the mosquitoes and the black flies chew 'em to pieces. Other times they run seventy-eighty miles in a day and kill a few Indians when they get where they're going. If they can go afoot, they do so; but if they can't go afoot, they go in canoes, or on rafts, or on skates or on snowshoes; and if none of those ways work, they walk on stilts or swim. Sometimes one or two of 'em gets hurted. They eat their food raw, a good deal of the time. They're up prowling around when everybody else is a-bed; and long before anybody else is up in the morning, Rogers' men have most generally been up a couple hours, cleaned their muskets, shaved, got their breakfasts, rolled their blankets, sewed up the rips in their buckskins and maybe shot a few Indians out of a tree. Then they do a little drilling and camp-cleaning, and later in the day they're pretty apt to lay out a road to somewhere; and if they have an hour or two to spare, they build the road in addition to laying it out. Then they parade, and maybe teach the English Regulars a little something about fighting. If any Regulars or Provincials desert to the French, Rogers' men wait till after sundown, and then they go into the French camp and get the feller that deserted, and bring him back and cook his goose for him. That's what they do mostly!"

"They don't do things like that this late in the year, do they?" I asked.

"Late!" McNott exclaimed. "Late! This aint late! This aint the middle of September yet! Why, the year's just started! Damn it, we aint killed our average yet! We've got to slaughter five Indians a day, and so far we're abut fifty-eight behind. Hell! It aint till the leaves get off the trees, so we can see 'em through the undergrowth, that we really get 'em nice! The best battle we ever fought was the Battle on Snowshoes."

"We?" I asked. "We? Are you in Rogers' Rangers?"

"For God's sake!" McNott cried, "couldn't you tell? Of *course* I'm in the Rangers! There aint nobody wears green buckskins, only Rogers' Rangers! There aint nobody wears Scotch caps, only Rogers' Rangers! Do you think I'd wear one of those damned caps if I wasn't in the Rangers? Hell, I'd be afraid of being mistook for a shemale; but if you're in the Rangers, you can do any damned thing you please, and nobody dares to say 'Boo!' "

Suddenly, as he spoke, I began to have an unexpected powerful yearning; I wanted one of those green caps to wear. In my mind's eye I saw myself returning to Portsmouth and Kittery, swaggering in green buckskins and with a green Scotch cap tilted becomingly on the side of my head—yes, laughing hoarsely and giving Elizabeth Browne and the Reverend Arthur the mere tail of a jeering eye as I passed by across the street.

I looked at Hunk and saw that he, too, was staring, fascinated, at the green cap so securely perched above Sergeant McNott's ear.

McNott, I suddenly realized, was looking at both of us

hungrily; then all at once he seemed satisfied, nodded, and grunted in short laughter. "Good enough," he said. "Soon as Konkapot's got over what ails him, us soldiers'll start for Crown Point and Major Rogers."

"You know Major Rogers well, Sergeant?" Hunk asked deferentially.

"Do I know him well!" McNott stared at Hunk intolerantly. "Ever had fleas on you? How well do you reckon they knowed you? Him and me's been that thick ever since our very first Indian massacre, when we was little more than red-cheeked children. If you've made up your mind you want to be in the Rangers, and I tell the Major to take you, it's all settled."

"Major Rogers always does what you tell him?" Hunk asked.

"Always," McNott said firmly; then added, with a reasonable air, "except sometimes when I do what he tells *me*. Right now, for instance, I'm doing something to oblige him, on account of him having sent me to collect his rents at Dunbarton. I'd been laying out a road for him between Number Four and Crown Point, but he had to have these rents from the Dunbarton farmers that owed 'em to him; so I been down here collecting 'em."

"Isn't that unusual?" I asked. "Unusual, I mean, for an officer to detach one of his men to go and collect money for him?"

"Unusual!" McNott shouted. "Unusual! Hell, this aint no usual army! Last year the Major raised five companies of Rangers out of his own pocket! He never got a cent back from the British: not a damned cent; and if it wasn't for the Rangers, the British wouldn't know where they was or how they got there! Why in God's name shouldn't he use one of his own men to get money for him? Massachusetts wont give it to him! New Hampshire wont give it to him! The British wont give it to him, and there aint nobody but his own men he can trust, and no money he can get except his own! Unusual, for God's sake! That's a hell of an idea about unusualness!"

I thought best to change the subject. "This Konkapot that's with you," I said. "He isn't in the Rangers, is he?"

McNott looked fierce. "Why aint he?"

"Nothing, only I thought he didn't look——"

"That's because he's wearing his shirt," McNott said. "It aint because he's drunk: it's because he's wearing a shirt. Shirts aint regulation for Stockbridge Indians. There's a whole company of 'em in the Rangers, and when they're on ranging service, they aint allowed to wear shirts. General Amherst says it don't look soldierly, and I dunno but what I agree with him. A feller that's got a dirty shirt hanging down around his knees, he don't look as if he was good for much. Indians don't see it that way, though. They all carry their shirts, and the minute they get free of regular duty, they put 'em on. They put 'em on to be stylish. Outside of that, shirts help to keep off the rain and the mosquitoes, if they're greasy enough—and they are! I aint got much use for Indians, taking 'em by and large. You can't count on 'em for nothing except getting drunk when it aint convenient and running away when you need 'em most. But these Stockbridge Indians, they fight like civilized people. They'd just as soon get killed as anybody."

Despite the variety of topics on which Sergeant McNott discoursed, he returned again and again to Major Rogers.

To the Sergeant's way of thinking, the Major was the greatest man and the greatest soldier the world had ever seen.

McNott, it appeared, had lived most of his life in Dunbarton, and so, too, had Rogers, except during those periods when the French-led St. Francis Indians, coming down from the north, had burned the farmhouses, destroyed the crops, slaughtered the cattle, chopped down the fruit trees, scalped settlers and stolen women and children, and so forced farmers to seek sanctuary in block-houses in the larger settlements.

"Why," McNott said, "seems like Rogers begun to chase Indians before he was weaned! Fifteen years old, he was, when he started fighting 'em; and in a year's time the smartest Indian ever made couldn't think half as much like an Indian as Rogers could. He knew what they aimed to do before they knew themselves; and from that day to this, he aint changed one damned bit. No, sir! He hates a St. Francis Indian worse'n poison—he hates 'em worse'n I do, pretty near; but much as he hates 'em, he aint never got mad at 'em. No, sir: I and him just sit down and figure what they're going to do, and then I and him go out and stop 'em from doing it. Before he was seventeen years old, them St. Francis Indians was as careful of I and him as they'd have been of a thousand rattlesnakes! They was awful dainty how they showed themselves around here, just on account of how I and Rogers bothered 'em."

"What was he doing when he wasn't fighting Indians?" I asked. "Farming?"

McNott shook his head contemptuously. "Hell, no! Rogers couldn't never settle down. He had to find out about things. Damnedest feller you ever saw for asking questions. He aint never satisfied with what he learns. He asks and he asks; and if he can't find out what he wants to know by asking, he'll run a thousand miles to look at something. Why, by God! when he was eighteen-nineteen years old, after that first Indian war, he'd go off alone, where there hadn't never been any white settlers, and he'd travel day and night, just looking —all alone, mind you! He traveled up through the Cohase Intervales, and up beyond Lake Memphremagog, where there hadn't no white men ever been, only those that the Indians had captured. He went back and forth between here and Canada, just looking and figuring out the best trails and the best passes. He knows this country better'n any book. Yes sir! He knows it better'n any man alive, red or white!"

"How'd it happen the Indians never caught him?" Hunk asked.

McNott put his elbows on the table and glanced quickly over his shoulder. "By God," he said, "I dunno! I dunno how he does it! He's the size of a moose, but he goes drifting through the woods like a owl. He'll stand right in plain sight, in the middle of some trees, and if you take your eyes off him for a second, he aint there. No sir: you can look for him all day, and you can't find him! The Indians, they call him a devil. White Devil. That's their name for him: Wobi madaondo: White Devil. They say he disappears into rocks, and pops out of 'em, like Pamola, the Evil One. That's what the braves say; but what the squaws say, I dunno. He's learned to talk their language, Rogers has, and you can't talk that language and spend your time popping in and out of rocks. No sir! You got to spend a good deal of it with Indians—mostly young, good-looking ones."

We drank our beer contemplatively.

"Well," McNott continued, "when this French war broke out in 1755, I and him went to it. Right away we picked up some of the young fellers around here that had a knack for slaughtering Indians, and we went right to work doing it. That was the start of Rogers' Rangers. One company of us, there was, under that old yeller-bellied windbag Sir William Johnson."

McNott became excited and shook his fist at us. "We watched the French day and night. They never made a move but what we knew about it and told Johnson. We killed their Indians and sunk their boats and burned their crops and took prisoners; and after we'd been at it a month, the French would 'a' paid five thousand pounds, hard money, for Rogers' scalp. The next year Rogers had two companies of Rangers, and the next year he had four, and now he's got eight, not counting his Stockbridge Indians; and if the English win this war, it'll be because of what Rogers and his Rangers have done for 'em, by God! Why, this feller Rogers, he'll march fifty-sixty miles in a day, with three feet of snow on the ground and the glass down to thirty below, or he'll march the same distance when it's up to hundred and twenty, like a furnace, and he'll take the britches and the hides off any Frenchmen and Indians that get in his way! He's a hell-roarer and a caution, that's what he is! There aint a soldier anywhere, French or English, colonel or general, that can hold a candle to him! The English know it, too! The best man they had, young Lord Howe, he went to school to Rogers, so to learn how to fight a battle the way it ought to be fought in this country; but before he learned his lesson, he got killed fighting the English way, and there never was a damneder shame!"

So moved and excited had McNott become as he spoke that he slid from his chair and went to prowling up and down the tap-room. His moccasins made no sound, and in his greenish buckskins and his green Scotch cap he was like a shadow against the dark pine walls.

Abruptly he stopped and thrust his face close to ours. "Listen," he said, "if they'd let Rogers alone, he'd do things the English never dreamed of! They don't know nothing about this country! Not nothing! Compared with Rogers, they're little boys playing toy soldier. They're——"

The tap-room door swung open and Konkapot came in. He stood staring mournfully at us, a dark and unhappy figure. "Rum," he said hoarsely. "Feel bad."

Sergeant McNott walked over to him and examined him

earnestly. "No," he said, "you're well! You feel bad, but you're well! Get your musket and blanket. We'll sleep in the brush."

"Rum!" Konkapot said. "Konkapot sick Indian! Oh, oh, oh! Konkapot so sick!"

"You aint!" McNott told him sternly. "You already been sick! Didn't I hear you? I did! Konkapot all well again! Get your musket and blanket, but I'll let you wear your shirt a while yet, now you're so well again. Get 'em!" Konkapot looked at him dumbly, wept feebly, then with meekness went to the corner of the tap-room where he had left his musket and blanket.

McNott looked at Hunk and me. "This here Konkapot," he said, "Major Rogers sent him from Crown Point to where I was collecting rents to tell me to get back to Crown Point in kind of a hurry. That means Rogers and Rogers' Rangers are going somewhere pretty soon. I expect you two was aiming to go to Crown Point by way of Lake George after you'd passed Number Four. We wont go that way. We'll go by this new road I was laying out, and that'll save two days."

He stepped closer to us; stood stiffly. "You've heard me talking. Still think you'd like to join in with Major Robert Rogers and Rogers' Rangers?"

Hunk and I began to gather up our belongings. "That's what we think, Sergeant," Hunk said.

In the deep dusk, ten minutes later, as we moved off to the westward into the black forest with those two strange soldiers, I could hear Konkapot snuffling and hiccuping, like a child who has been severely spanked.

CHAPTER XII

A̲t noon the next day we came down from the hills to the broad meadows along the Connecticut River and stopped at the log fort that gives the place its name of Number Four. All my life long I had heard tales of Number Four; for it was at this very spot, always, that the St. Francis Indians, coming down from the north, crossed the Connecticut and headed eastward to raid the settlements. On their homeward journey, too, they made straight for Number Four with captives and booty: then turned north, up the Connecticut, on the long trail to the Cohase Intervales and far-off St. Francis.

I stared hard at this tranquil meadow with its stockaded fort called Number Four at the river's edge. Across it had pelted the red devils who, eighty years before, travelled all the way to the Piscataqua, stole up to the door of the very house in which I had spent the summer just past, and drove a tomahawk into the brain of my mother's great-granduncle, Richard Nason. Back over this level clearing had raced those same red men, dragging with them to St. Francis another Richard Nason, eight years old. It was over the spot where I stood, perhaps, that red men had carried my great-great-aunt Sarah, a child of six, to St. Francis and held her there five years, until Thomas Hutchins ransomed her and brought her back to Kittery. For my mother's sake I made a drawing of of the place in my sketch book—of the fort and stockade, the settlers' cabins, and the swelling hills beyond—thinking I might never see the place again.

I have smiled often, looking at that rough drawing of a sunny intervale—not so much because of its defects, but because it proves conclusively that although premonitions of approaching disaster may be common occurrences in romances, they are rare in real life. If I'd had a premonition of the circumstances under which I should next see Number Four, my sketch of the place would have shown it as forbidding as the pit of Acheron.

On the new road staked out by Rogers' Rangers between Number Four and Crown Point, we passed rapidly over hills that grew ever higher and steeper; through streams that grew constantly more turbulent; and on the morning of September 13th, a day and a half after leaving Number Four, we came to the edge of the plateau overlooking the narrows of Lake Champlain.

Spread before us, as on a map, was that gateway between Canada and the American Colonies—that narrow, watery highway for which the English and the French had so long contended, and over which such a vast deal of blood had been spilled.

If there is a pleasanter sight, on a golden autumn morning, I have never seen it. Directly before us, on the far side of the narrows, Crown Point lay flat on the water like a blunt hook. At the bend in the hook were the low parapets of a square stone fort, surmounted by a tall stone watch-tower. It looked wholly useless, being so close to the shelving bank that it could never have brought a gun to bear on a rowboat that knew enough to keep close to its walls. Behind the square fort, on the high land which formed the thick shank of this enormous hook, men were crawling like ants, constructing the ramparts of a new and greater fort. The strip of water guarded by these two forts, the old and the new, was so narrow that no vessel, small or large, could traverse it without the consent of those behind the guns, provided the guns were effectively placed; and for the first time I saw why Crown Point, properly fortified and garrisoned, was a sure barrier to any hostile army that sought to pass. Only in boats could the supplies necessary to an army be carried between Canada and the American Colonies; and so long as Crown Point forbade the passage of supplies, an army dependent on those supplies could not exist.

To the left of Crown Point the narrows wound southward like a tranquil river to the distant heights of Ticonderoga. To the right the broad and placid surface of Champlain stretched to the north—and somewhere beyond its far blue reaches, I knew, the French and their Indian allies lay waiting.

On our side of that narrow inland sea rose the sharp peaks of the Green Mountains: on the other the rolling, tree-clad ramparts of the New York shore. In the morning sun the crowded spruces that clothed those hills stood out sharp and clear; so that, instead of seeing merely hills, I saw an infinity of trees, close-packed. I had a dim vision of countless other hills stretching off to the north and west, mile upon mile—hundreds of miles: thousands, perhaps—all clothed with billions upon billions of close-packed trees.

It seemed irrational to me that the human ants crawling slowly over the surface of Crown Point should have come a wearisome journey from their native ant hills to wrangle and strive eternally with other similar ants, and perhaps be killed doing it. Did all these ants consider themselves important, and ordained by heaven to have a hand in regulating the world's affairs?

When Konkapot had guiltily removed his dirty checked shirt and hidden it in his rolled blanket, we went down to the shore and crossed the narrows toward the new fort.

The Provincial soldiers in charge of the raft stared respectfully at McNott. "Where's this Suagothel the Rangers are going to?" one of them asked.

McNott eyed him noncommittally. "Who told you we were going?"

"Enoch Simms," the Provincial said. "He's the barber in our company, and he gets to know everything. Five hundred Rangers, Enoch said, was going to Suagothel tonight."

"If he knows so much," McNott said, "go back and make him tell you where Suagothel is."

The Provincial withdrew, offended, whereupon McNott glanced at me impassively. "Wha'd I tell you?" he said calmly. "The Major's just waiting for I and Konkapot."

"Where's that place?" I whispered. "Where's Suagothel?"

"Never heard of it," McNott said, "but we'll all damned soon find out!"

The rocky point we approached was alive with men. Squads were breaking up the lumber raft that had come in ahead of us, and carrying off the logs on their shoulders. Along the shore stood Provincials in homespun and British Regulars in canvas overalls, fishing with alder poles and handlines. As we jumped ashore, one of the Provincials fell off a rock, scrambled yelling up the bank, and dragged onto the shingle a pickerel the length of a man's leg. It must have weighed fifteen pounds. Two other Provincials fell on it, knocked it on the head with a rock and carried it away in triumph.

"Stink-fish!" McNott said contemptuously. "Provincials don't balk at eathing nothing—not even bad, diseased cats!"

He set off at top speed along the shore, skirted the star-shaped earthworks, and passed the half-finished ramparts of the new fort. Within the enclosure of the walls I could see the beginnings of two enormous stone barracks. The place was alive with men. There must have been nearly two thousand of them at work—digging, shovelling, hewing timbers, carrying rock. Behind the fort scarlet-clad companies drilled

against a background of acres of tents. I could hear the
rattle of wheezy drums, thumping out orders to the drilling
men.

The ceaseless and all-pervading activity filled me with
anxiety, for I longed to be a part of that activity, and I was
afraid there might not be room for me.

On the northern side of the new fort, the ground sloped to
a small bay, formed by the tip of Crown Point's hook. The
bank fell away abruptly to a shingly beach; and on the beach,
concealed by the bank from the forts and the parade
ground, was a miniature camp—a camp of perhaps eighty
tents, neatly following the line of the beach, and facing the
long blue expanse of lake that stretched northward between
misty mountain ranges.

We stood at the edge of the bank, looking down at this
little colony of tents, and saw that they were divided in sections, and that at their extreme right, in the angle of the hook
of land that formed the bay, stood an officer's markee.

As if to emphasize the divisions, twenty overturned whaleboats lay on the beach, the bow of each boat pointing at one
of the tent-clusters. The appearance of the boats would have
pained a seaman, for they were rudely daubed with brown and
green paint. They were, however, uniform in their slovenli-
ness.

The whaleboats seemed to awaken fond memories in Mc-
Nott's mind. "There they are!" he said delightedly. "There
aint a drop of water in this whole damned lake that I aint
rubbed against in one of those boats!"

Most of the men at work around the tents and boats wore
Scotch caps similar to McNott's, and barring a few who were
tossing pine cones in the air and shooting at them with
muskets, they were a busy lot. They were mending and greas-
ing moccasins, washing shirts, stitching buckskins, cleaning accouterments, fastening protecting-cloths around the
breeches of muskets, cutting bullet patches, filling powder-
horns, calking the whaleboats, and piling supplies close beside
those unwieldy craft.

At the left of the encampment I saw a group of Indians.
They had their own tents and whaleboats, apparently. Like
Konkapot, they were naked from their waists up and were

squatted at the water's edge or on rocks, gazing at themselves in mirrors and daubing themselves with paint.

McNott gestured largely at Konkapot. "Go ahead down and join your company! I've never seen a man need a coat of paint worse'n what you do, Konkapot! I'll report to the Major for you." Konkapot, solemn, looked down at himself thoughtfully—planning design, color and composition, I suppose—then left us without a word.

McNott wagged his head. "Yes, sir!" he told us. "Yes, sir! They're going out! When the Indians paint themselves, there aint no doubt about it! Somebody's going to be stirred up! Yes, sir: there's certainly trouble boiling for someone!"

On a log outside the markee sat five or six Rangers. From time to time a head appeared at the tent-opening and called one of them. He jumped from the log, received instructions and went pelting up over the bank and away toward the main camp behind us.

There was a constant movement of officers and men toward and away from the markee—of British officers in scarlet coats: of Provincial officers in blue jackets and breeches, undecorated save for brass gorgets at their throats: of Rangers carrying written messages, heavy barrels, oddly-shaped bundles.

McNott took me by the arm and pointed out men to me, men whose names meant nothing then, but were to mean much to me later.

"You see those two Ranger officers waiting to go in the markee?" McNott asked—"that sour-faced feller and the sanctimonious one? The sour-faced one's John Stark. He was in command of us when we laid out the road to Number Four—the road you just came over. The other one's Jonathan Carver. He's an engineer, and he worked on the road, too. They're captains, both of 'em. If you scratched either of 'em anywhere, you'd probably split your finger on an Indian bullet or maybe a busted piece of tomahawk."

I hoped fate would throw me with neither of them; for Stark was gray-faced and tight-lipped, and frowned constantly; whereas Carver had a sly and soapy look—a sort of false humbleness. Both of them, I suspected, would be hard to get along with.

"That feller checking over the pile of supplies," McNott went on, "the one in the green uniform: he's a Britisher—

cap'n in the Royal Regiment. Cap'n Williams. He's studied with Rogers for a couple years. He can fight as good as a Ranger, and if he keeps on the way he's going, he'll be a general. He's better'n any British officer ever *I* see. He knows enough to take orders from a Ranger officer, and that's more than most of 'em know. Last winter we marched fifty miles through the snow—twenty below it was—and fought three battles. If it hadn't been for Williams, we'd all froze to death on the way back. Williams can build a fire out of snow and just a little mud."

I tried to remember the things McNott told me, and the men he indicated, but as I couldn't, I got out my sketch book and made quick sketches of the hurrying officers and men, writing their names beneath the sketches. I caught hurried outlines of Captain Ogden, Captain Butterfield, Captain Brewer, Lieutenant Dunbar, Lieutenant Turner, Ensign Avery.

Hunk and McNott came and peered over my shoulder. "Look at that!" McNott exclaimed. "Aint that Ogden to the life, peeking out of the sides of his eyes! Yes, sir! That's the way he always looks: as if he didn't believe something!" He was diverted. "And that's Dunbar! Yes, sir! Hanging his mouth open so a bluebird could nest in it! Aint he an Englishman, though?"

A thought seemed to strike McNott. "Look," he said. "You stand right here. Don't move an inch. I'll go down and wait till I get hold of the Major, and then I'll tell him. Yes, sir! I'll tell him he's got to take you; and by God, he better!"

He jumped down from the bank, ran to the markee, and a moment later there came to us from there the sound of his irascible voice: then that of a heavy, deep one—the thickest sounding voice I had ever heard. It had a clabbery quality, too, as though it came bubbling up from under water.

Hunk and I studied the sketches I had made, and memorized the names—Captain Stark, Captain Carver, Captain Williams, Captain Butterfield, Captain Ogden, Captain Brewer, Lieutenant Dunbar, Lieutenant Turner, Ensign Avery—and not a face in the lot but bore a scar of one kind or another; some of the faces seemed to be mostly scars. Some were pitted with smallpox, too. I'd never seen so much autobiography written on faces.

From the markee-opening McNott's scarlet hair suddenly emerged, and he jerked his head at us violently. We scrambled down the bank, pulled off our hats and went in.

CHAPTER XIII

IN ONE corner of the markee was a rough bunk, spread with the tips of fir-branches, and beside it stood a small hair-trunk. In the center of the tent was a table, and behind it sat a man who eyed us expressionlessly. This blank scrutiny had a peculiar effect on me; I became short of breath; and my hands and knees began to tremble unmanageably. He was perhaps twenty-eight years old; and it was he, I instantly knew, who had spoken with the thick voice; for the man himself was thick. That was my first impression, one of solid thickness: not mental thickness, but physical—a kind of physical unkillableness, it might be called.

His lips were thick, and so was his long, straight nose. His hands, clasped before him on the table, were enormous and muscular; and their fingers, pallid by comparison with the brown of his face and hands, looked parboiled, as though left overlong in water. Beneath his large eyes the flesh was puffy; and his shoulders, sloping down from a bull-like neck, filled his buckskin hunting shirt so solidly that the leather might have been shrunk to fit them. The breadth of his chest and upper arms gave him the look of holding a deep breath.

He wore a tight little infantryman's hat which had a sort of semicircular black plate or visor cocked straight up in front, as if to protect the wearer's forehead from bullets or blows; and a curved ornament which I thought was leather rose from the back and swept over the cap's top like a squirrel's tail. The eyes that stared at me from beneath that upstanding black visor were the color of the round gray pebbles that lie along our Maine beaches, scoured by the surf. Yet when he spoke, his manner was genial, as though he addressed an equal—which was contrary to the attitude of important military men, according to my understanding. When he smiled, it was hard to tell the meaning of his smile. It might have been considered admonitory, or kindly, or even as sheepish, depending on the state of mind of the person to whom he spoke; but to me it seemed to indicate that he was, at heart, a good-natured man.

"Sergeant McNott tells me you've got a letter for me." It almost seemed that the thickness of his lips made it hard for him to form words as rapidly as he wished.

"Yes, sir." I gave him Sam Livermore's letter. He studied the address upon it; then flipped it open and read, moving his heavy lips as he did so.

"Yes," he said, putting the letter on the table, and slapping it with his huge hand, "I know Livermore. Ordinarily I'd be glad to do him a favor, but Livermore knows nothing about Ranging service. Nobody knows anything about it till he's been through it. I don't believe I'd be doing him a favor if I took you in the Rangers."

McNott spoke to him almost ferociously, and I marveled that a sergeant could speak in such a tone to a major. "I tell you he can draw pictures! Why don't you look at his pictures?" To me he said angrily, "Show him that book."

Rogers took the book and turned the pages with his thick fingers. At one point he said, as if surprised, "That's Number Four." A little further along he made a singular explosive noise, held up the book to McNott and pointed at a page.

"Aint it the spit of him?" McNott asked complacently.

Rogers closed the book, gave it back to me and stood up. He was tall—taller than Hunk or myself; and we then saw that his hips and legs were as slender as his upper body was thick. He picked up Livermore's letter and read it again, moving his lips as he had on the first reading. "Harvard!" he said doubtfully. "I don't know how some of these boys of mine would make out with an educated man. They're a pretty rugged lot! Pretty rugged!"

"I'm not very educated," I told him. "You don't get much education in two years—not out of books."

McNott, behind me, spoke contemptuously. "He aint educated at all! He don't even know why Indians cry when they're drunk!" He pointed at Hunk. "Look at him, Major. Does he look like he's been at Harvard?"

"No," the Major said, and smiled at me. "I suppose at Harvard they don't teach you about country like this."

"No, sir," I said. "What I learned about the woods, I learned from Hunk Marriner."

"I don't mean that," Rogers said. "I mean I suppose they don't teach you about the undeveloped sections—sections like the Ouisconsin and the Northwest."

"No, sir," I said. "They don't know much about it. Anyway, they don't bother themselves about what's going on nowadays. They teach you about Greece and Rome and Egypt and places in the Bible. Last year Professor Winthrop lectured about Captain Middleton's voyage and all the argument over the Northwest Passage, but he was illustrating a point in philosophy."

"Argument over the Northwest Passage?" Rogers asked. "What argument's that, and who's Captain Middleton?"

"Well, sir," I said, "Captain Middleton, as near as I can recall, got permission from the British government to sail into Hudson's Bay in search of the Northwest Passage to Japan, but he went back to England saying he couldn't find it. Then a gentleman published a book saying the Hudson's Bay Company had offered Middleton five thousand pounds not to make the voyage and——"

"Why?" Rogers interrupted. From his half-grin I suspected he disbelieved me. "Why did they offer him money for not going?"

"Because they had a monopoly, sir. They were afraid Middleton might discover the Passage. Then everyone in the world would rush to it, and the Hudson's Bay Company would lose its monopoly. England would have benefited, and the world; but the twelve stockholders in the Hudson's Bay Company would have been out of pocket, so they tried to stop Middleton."

"But they didn't stop him?"

"No, sir! Leastways, he sailed his voyage; but the gentleman who wrote the book says he must have taken a bribe, because it can be proved from Middleton's Journal that he was in the Northwest Passage, although Middleton claims he wasn't. He says Middleton was a liar, and the Hudson's Bay Company are charlatans, forgers, bribers, suppressors of the truth, and no better than traitors to their country."

"How'd it happen you remembered all this so pat?"

"Because the book told about the Indian nations to the westward. I got it and read it, so to find out how the Indians look."

"Find out how they look? Find out how they look? Why would you want to find out how they look?"

I fumbled for words. "Well," I said, "I'd like to draw people from the different Indian nations—draw 'em and paint 'em. Nobody ever did it. If you try to find out how they look, you can't. Nobody knows how they look. Mark Catesby made a great name for himself drawing the birds of South Carolina, and I don't see why Indians aren't as important as birds. I thought the book about Middleton might tell me how the Indians looked; but it was like all the others: it didn't tell you anything you really wanted to know."

"Who wrote the book?"

"An English gentleman named Arthur Dobbs."

"Arthur Dobbs? Arthur Dobbs? What happened to him after he wrote the book? Where is he now?"

"I don't know, sir."

Rogers eyed me intently, his lips moving almost imperceptibly, as though he sought to memorize each word. When I stopped speaking, he stood there, his heavy hands hanging slack, his thick lips parted, as if he expected me to continue. I thought he intended to ask other questions; but he went back to his stool behind the table, read Sam Livermore's letter once more, then placed it beneath a pile of papers.

"All right," he said. "You two say you want to join the Rangers. If McNott says you're qualified, I'll take his word. Just make up your mind you've got your work cut out for you. Understand? I don't care what you do when you're not under my command; but when you're on Ranging service, you'll obey all orders promptly and willingly, and they wont be easy ones." He once more made that singular explosive noise, which I now recognized as a laugh. "Some of the orders you'll get would make an ordinary man drop dead. We have to have discipline in the Rangers—and that's pretty hard to teach a Provincial. If you're willing to join the Rangers on that understanding, I wont stop you."

In the boundless ignorance of youth, I answered confidently for Hunk and myself: we wanted to be Rangers.

"All right," Rogers said. He turned to McNott, "Take 'em out, get 'em their equipment, and begin teaching 'em what they ought to know. Be sure they have bayonets. You'll be in charge of Number Two whaleboat, with Sergeant Rice next in command." He picked up a paper from the table. "Here's your list of men and supplies: Gillis is crossed off. He's got hay fever and can't go. Can't have any sneezing this trip! Use Marriner in place of Gillis."

He eyed me reflectively. "You're pretty handy with a pen, I s'pose. I s'pose in Harvard you had to write examinations on Greece and Egypt and those places in the Bible."

I nodded.

"I'll put you in Number One whaleboat under Captain Ogden," Rogers continued. "I'll be in Number One myself. If I need letters written and don't have time to tend to 'em, you can write 'em, can't you?"

"Yes, sir."

"All right," Rogers concluded, waving us from the tent. "We'll try to teach you some of the things Harvard College overlooked."

CHAPTER XIV

W E SAT on the bank where McNott stationed us, while he and some others puttered around Number Two whaleboat. From our post we looked down on the camp as at a stage. The scene at which we stared, as well as those who acted in it, seemed remote: a part of a drama, in which we were not equipped to act.

This theatricality was heightened by the milky blue lake, which stretched into the north between diminishing headlands and mountains that looked like flat profiles of mountains painted for a theater's scenery.

Seventeen boats, we saw, were going on this venture of which we had so unexpectedly become a part. That meant, probably, twelve men to a boat.

"Hunk," I said, "maybe we made a mistake not to go over

and join Lovewell's regiment. Maybe we don't know enough to be Rangers."

"I dunno why we don't," Hunk said. "We can keep going through the woods all day. We can stop a deer at two hundred paces. That's good enough shooting to kill anyone we need to kill. If you can hit a deer's shoulder-blade at two hundred paces, you can hit a man's head at the same distance; and a man aint good for nothing if he's hit in the head, is he? You know he aint, Langdon! We can look out for ourselves in the woods, and what more can any of these Rangers do? I bet I could do as good shooting as any of those fellers over there if I had me a little practice, and so could you."

He indicated a group of Rangers on the beach. One of them threw pine cones in the air. The others, in rotation, shot at the cones. When one of the cones failed to burst into fragments, a derisive howl arose. It was first-class shooting; for from the manner in which the cones exploded, the muskets must have been loaded with a single ball.

In spite of Hunk's seeming confidence, I suspected from the carelessness of the question he now asked me, that he was really as nervous as I was. "Where's this Suagothel we're going to, d'you s'pose?"

"God knows," I said. "It's got to be north, if we're going in boats. Twelve men is about as many as one whaleboat ought to carry, so there wont be enough of us to make much of a fight. Maybe we're just going to look at something and bring back word about it."

"You don't need seventeen whaleboats full of men to look at something, do you?" Hunk asked. "With that many you could look at the whole of North America!"

I gave it up and watched McNott and his men. They overturned Number Two whaleboat and slid it into the lake with a thunderous grating of pebbles: then climbed in and rocked it, peering intently at the floorboards. Seemingly they found no leaks. McNott hopped out, made his way between the tents and came up the bank to us.

"Let's get at it," he said. "There's papers to sign, caps and buckskins to get, and rations to draw. You got to be ready to start by roll-call tonight."

"Start where?" Hunk asked.

McNott might have been deaf. "All you need to know," he

continued, "I can tell you in ten minutes. I aint going to tell you twice, so listen to what I say, and remember it! Don't forget *nothing!* If you do, you'll pay high. It might cost you your scalp, and maybe you aint particular, but that's something most people don't like. Got that straight?"

We said we had.

"In camp," he explained, "you're paraded and inspected every sundown. Have your musket clean as a whistle, hatchet scoured, sixty rounds powder and ball, and be ready to march at a minute's warning.

"When you're on the march, act the way you would if you was sneaking up on a deer. Just remember the deer you're hunting now aint going to run away if you do anything wrong, or if he sees you first. These deer got two legs: they carry knives and muskets, and what they enjoy best is putting bullets where it hurts the worst and using your hair to make the girls look up to 'em at home. You're looking for them and they're looking for you; you'll feel better afterwards if you see them first. If you don't, you most generally lay where they left you. It aint convenient for Rangers to get detained by what's useless—funerals and all such."

He became more cheerful. "That aint going to happen, but you got to be careful about everything. You got to tell the truth about what you see and what you do. You can lie all you please when you tell other folks about the Rangers, but don't never lie to a Ranger or an officer. There's an army depending on us for correct information. Don't never lie, and always be careful! Don't never take a chance you don't have to. That's the way the French and Indians fight, and it's the way *we* got to fight. That's what the Major's always telling us: don't take chances."

He snorted, as if he found the Major's insistence irresistibly amusing.

"Now then," he went on, "when we're on the march we march single file, far enough apart so one shot can't go through two men—sensible, aint it? If we strike swamps, or soft ground, we spread out abreast, so it's hard to track us. When we march, we keep moving till dark, so to give the enemy the least possible chance at us. When we camp, half the party stays awake while the other half sleeps. If we take prisoners, we keep 'em separate till we've had time to examine 'em, so they can't cook up a story between 'em. Is that all clear?"

We said it was.

"Now then," McNott continued, "we have to make allowance for all sorts of trouble. That's why we carry skates on marches. S'pose you've marched somewhere. Don't never march home the same way. Take a different route, so you wont be ambushed.

"No matter whether we travel in big parties or little ones, each party has to keep a scout twenty yards ahead, twenty yards on each flank and twenty yards in the rear, so the main body can't be surprised and wiped out. That's something you don't want to forget. You never know when you may have to lead a party yourself.

"Another thing you never know is when you're going to run into an enemy force too big to handle. If you do, there aint no sense standing still and letting yourself be wiped out, the way the British do. So every night, when you're on the march, you'll be told where to meet in case we're surrounded. If we're surrounded, we just scatter and go it alone. Don't make any mistake about where we're going to meet in case we have to scatter. Be sure to find out where the place is, and don't never forget it—never!

"Don't sit down to eat without posting sentries. Don't sleep beyond dawn. Dawn's when French and Indians attack. Don't cross a river by a regular ford, because if anybody's laying for you, that's where he'll lay. If you find out somebody's trailing you, make a circle, come back onto your own tracks, and ambush the folks that aim to ambush you. Don't stand up when the enemy's coming against you. Kneel down. Lie down. Hide behind a tree. Let him come till he's almost close enough to touch. Then let him have it, and jump out and finish him up with your hatchet. That's simple enough, aint it?"

"That's just plain common sense," Hunk said.

"Of course it is," McNott agreed, "but you'd be surprised how often it never occurs to those fellers"—he jerked his head toward the flat land behind us, whence still came the hoarse thumping of the drums of the drilling British Regulars—"how often it never occurs to those fellers to do anything sensible. British generals, they march a regiment right up to the muzzles of a battery of guns, and feel real bad when the whole regiment has to be buried. Then they start think-ing what ought to be done next, so they bring up another regiment just the same way, and get it buried too. If they didn't have Rogers and his Rangers to scout for 'em, there'd be a fresh army of British Regulars wiped out by the French every year. And if Rogers could 'a' been put in command of everybody, British and Colonials too, about four years ago, there wouldn't be any French left in North America by now. No, sir! He'd have pushed 'em clear way back to Quebec, and then he'd have thrown scouts all 'round Quebec and starved 'em to death!"

The mention of starving put him in mind of food. "Now we'll go eat." He seemed to marvel at our astounding luck. "My, my! First day in camp, and you get to eat Ranger food! When we're in camp, there aint no soldiers anywhere eat like Rangers. Wine and rum and the best of everything, the Major gets for us." Somewhat ruefully he added, "We don't eat so well on the march."

"Look here," I said, "where's this Suagothel we're bound for? Uncertainty's a curse to newcomers like us."

"Nobody's supposed to know till we've started. Somebody might blab."

"You know us by now," I protested. "We wont blab. We didn't blab much to you coming over the road, did we?"

McNott cast a cautious glance over his shoulder at the Rangers at work around the tents and whaleboats: then came closer to us. "All right; I'll tell you. Don't forget it when you're writing the Major's letters and have a chance to do me a good turn. Did you ever hear of St. Francis?"

We both nodded. All New England, to its sorrow, had heard of St. Francis.

"That's it," McNott said.

"That's it? How do you mean, that's it? What's Suagothel got to do with St. Francis?"

"There aint any such place as Suagothel!" McNott said. "Rogers said Suagothel so to fool the French if they should get to hear about it. It's St. Francis we're for!"

"St. Francis!" I exclaimed. "St. Francis!"

"That's right!" McNott said comfortably. "Those red hel-lions have hacked us and murdered us and burned our houses and stolen women and killed scouts and brained babies and scalped stragglers and roasted officers over slow fires for five

whole years, but they've done it once too often! They took
Captain Kennedy out from under a flag of truce, a week ago;
and they captured James Tute, the best Ranger officer we
got. Well, they've had their fun, and now they got to learn
that war's a serious business; so *that,* my boy, is going to be
the end of St. Francis!"

CHAPTER XV

ALL THE rest of that day,
the camp remained as we had first seen it. Not a tent was
struck. Not a boat was launched, except temporarily, to hunt
for leaks. The sun swung into the southwest and slid down
behind the mountains of the New York shore, leaving them
masses of purple against an orange sky. A chill September
wind swept across the flat surface of Crown Point, ruffling the
waters to the north and darkening them to a steely drab; but
still the Rangers dawdled about their tents, laboring at tasks
that might have occupied them on any ordinary day. One
who spied upon them from the heights on either side would
have seen nothing but the commonplaces of approaching night.

Before each row of tents, as the twilight grew, a generous
fire brightened the dingy canvas, so that the tent-fronts
gleamed whitely in the glow, like beacons of their owners'
innocent pursuits and peaceful intent.

The orange sky softened to a rosy yellow: dimmed slowly
to a pallid green. The mountains bulked black against the
fading light, and as the stars began to appear above them the
lake darkened until there was no telling where water ended
and shore began.

Then, between the tents and the beach, there was unseen
movement, and faint noises were heard—the sound of wood
rubbing against wood: of low-pitched voices: of splashings.
More than ever the row of tents seemed erected upon a stage;
for before each fire, throwing its light against the canvas, a
movable palisade of brush had been set in place, screening

the flames from the lake. Thus, although the tents were il-
luminated as by a row of giant footlights, the boats and those
around them were left in blackness.

When, with the placing of the screens, Hunk and I, following McNott's instructions, left the shelter of a tent and entered the darkness near the water, we found that narrow
space thronged with men—men who multiplied and grew
thick about us as though they rose noiselessly from out of the
ground. We could hear sergeants monotonously muttering
the numbers of their boats—"Seven, seven, seven, seven"—
"three, three, three!"

Hunk left me. I worked to the eastward along the shingle,
through milling men who growled and murmured, until I
heard, hoarsely reiterated, the words "One, one, one, one."
Number One was the whaleboat to which Rogers had assigned me.

Three officers stood close by the beached stern of Number One. I recognized the tight-fitting cap of Major Rogers.
"Get in," he told me.

A sergeant, clutching the stern, asked my name. When I
told him, he said, "Take the third thwart."

Two men, vague figures in the darkness, already occupied the outer ends of the third thwart. Each held an upended oar.

Others climbed in and stumbled between us, walking on our
feet and rapping musket butts against us, and the boat seemed
to float in an aroma of greasy buckskin, sweat, gun-oil and
damp wool. From where I sat, shivering, I looked back at
the shining tents and at black shadows passing swiftly between us and the fire-screens. I heard one of the shadows report, "Number Fifteen filled and ready." Close on the words
another muttered, "Number Twelve filled and ready."

Rogers asked amiably about Number Seventeen. "Anybody
dead in Number Seventeen? Maybe they aren't going."

A whisper went down the beach like a shadow dying in a
thicket. A breathless voice said, "Number Seventeen filled and
ready."

"Send 'em off!" Rogers ordered.

Up the beach I heard gratings, thumpings, and the sound
of water slapping and slapping. An officer came in over the
stern of Number One, and in the faint light I recognized
Captain Ogden. Dimly I saw the boat beside us slide slowly

away from land. Its oars creaked and dipped softly as it moved beyond my line of vision.

"Push out!" Rogers said. The boat stirred beneath us, rumbling on the pebbly bottom: then floated clear. Rogers and two others—one of them the sergeant—climbed in over the stern. The sergeant picked up a steering oar and pushed, while the men beside me set their oars softly in the gunwales and pulled. We moved out to find the other whaleboats drifting as silently as dark shadows and as we passed them one by one, a voice from each identified it.

"Number Seventeen," the first boat said; and in reply Rogers' thick voice called "Buttonmould Bay." They lay there in a long line, sixteen of them, seeming to wait avidly for this word that Rogers flung at them. When we had passed the sixteenth, we kept on into the north, the oars creaking. Behind us, against the dim radiance of the tents we had left, I could see the oars of the other whaleboats moving rhythmically in our wake, like the legs of a gigantic centipede.

Faintly I could see the bulky figure of Major Rogers leaning over the stern of the boat, unshipping the rudder from its slings, hanging it in place on the stern-post; and I thought I could feel an emanation from him—a sort of warmth, as from a hidden flame. It seems to me now that if I could make others feel that warmth, which forced us on and on, and ever on, when all hope of going onward had long died within us, it is possible that they might in the end have a clearer understanding of that singular indomitable figure, in whose brain was stored a fund of knowledge possessed by no other living man. If I could convey to others his astounding fortitude, which held us up and held us up, long after we had lost the power to stand, it is possible that even his harshest contemners might be more lenient in their judgment of him.

The boat moved slowly, with a small, uneasy rocking. From the waters of the lake rose a cold dampness and a brackish smell, unlike the clean salt freshness of the Piscataqua. This reflection turned my mind to Elizabeth. Wait, I thought: wait till she sees me with my green Rangers' blanket fastened at my shoulder with a silver brooch; my Scotch cap cocked rakishly toward my right eyebrow, as Rangers wore them!

Would she weep because once she had been hard to me: had scorned me? She hadn't understood me when I wished to be a painter; but when I came home a hero—ah, she'd understand that! She had despised me for associating with improper persons—"Vulgar creatures"—and, wondering what she'd think if she could see some of the persons I was associating with now, I laughed bitterly—and unfortunately I laughed aloud.

The sergeant at the steering oar made a clucking noise. "For laughers that got to laugh out loud," he whispered hoarsely, "they're hereby granted leave to swim under water till they get to shore, where they can laugh like hell while getting unbowelled with a hatchet."

I sat rigid, and thanked my stars for the darkness. Behind me the boat was silent, save for the cautious slight splash of oars. Before me, on the stern thwarts, Rogers, Ogden and the third officer huddled together, whispering. The darkness of this brackish lake was the close, clammy darkness of a warehouse in winter. The slow, monotonous beat of oars became, in my sleepy mind, a sort of threnody to whose tune we moved inexorably, a dark procession, toward a distant open grave.

Hours, it seemed to me, elapsed before the sergeant at the tiller hoarsely whispered "Oars!" The man at my left pulled at my arm and slid toward me. It was my turn, I saw, to row. I crawled over him and got my hands on the handle of the clumsy sweep. Even the steersman was relieved, and by Rogers himself. Every half hour there was a similar shifting of oarsmen on every thwart.

To me the strangest thing about this stealthy parade of boats was the silence of the rowers. Never before had I been for hours in the company of men who were entirely silent. I thought I understood why Rogers' Rangers had the reputation of doing wild and outlandish things when not on military service. If they were thus bottled up for nights and days on end, it seemed to me, they must indeed be on the verge of bursting when restraint was at length removed. Rumor, no doubt, was right when it credited them with drinking powerful liquors in prodigious quantities and seeking the society of women who were wild and gay.

Toward morning we moved more slowly. We were close in shore—so close that we could see pointed spruces against the faintly luminous sky; hear the lap of wavelets on the rocky banks.

Rogers stood in the stern, sniffing the air; he really seemed to smell his way. Without lights or landmarks to guide him, he called back to Number Two boat, "Turn in here: pass the word." We headed for the loom of the land. Beneath our bows there was the scrunching of a sandy beach, and we heard the other boats slide ashore, one by one.

In a thick whisper Rogers gave his orders for posting sentries—six men to the north beyond the headland: six over the ridge in front of the boats: six to the flat land to the south. He spoke as though the shore were distinct before him in the rays of an afternoon sun, instead of a black mass from which emerged the soft scent of pines and dying grasses. He spoke, too, as though an unseen enemy might be lurking close at hand, waiting to hatchet the lot of us in case so much as one precaution should be overlooked.

CHAPTER XVI

WHEN DAWN came, the seventeen boats lay close together under the bank, screened beneath bushes. Their crews were camped on the high land above, far enough back among the spruces to be invisible from the lake.

I say they were camped, but it was a poor apology for a camp. There were no tents: no fires: no kettles: no hot food.

We had been told to build no fires till we knew ourselves to be free from French and Indians; and this was a warning that needed no repetition.

The boat-crews had orders to stay together, so in reality there were seventeen small camps grouped about the knoll. The men could go only to the latrines, or to a spring for water; so they sat quietly, blankets around them, waiting for rations to be distributed. Thus they were not only under the surveillance of the sergeants who camped with them, but of their lieutenants, who occupied posts on higher ground, and of Rogers himself, who had arranged his captains and his belongings on the summit of the knoll.

It seemed to me, when the pale dawn light had brightened into day, and the crew of Number One whaleboat were flesh and blood instead of dim shadows that growled and muttered, that I had never seen men who looked less companionable. They ignored me; and I, unwilling to thrust myself upon them, thought gloomily that if it ever came to fighting, I would be unfortunate indeed with such comrades.

There were twelve of us, aside from Rogers, Ogden, Williams and the sergeant, and I studied them when the opportunity offered. Our sergeant's name was Bradley. His face was pale and a little bitter, and he was given to standing stock-still and staring accusingly from one to the other of us, as if he expected to catch us in something underhanded.

One of our crew was a jet-black Negro, about whom there was something vaguely familiar, though I had seen so few Negroes that they all looked alike to me. He carried his head a little forward, so that he seemed always to be looking slyly upward. When speaking, he half-laughed, as if he found the world and everyone in it irresistibly amusing. He was called Pomp by some and Whip by others.

The Ranger beside me, Jesse Beacham, was old and stooped. His hair was almost white; and the calm detachment of his face put me in mind of a setter dog sitting sleepily in the sun with upraised head, enduring the attentions of obstreperous children.

Half our boat's company were Irish, though I wouldn't have known it except by the names they bandied back and forth—Killian, Foyle, Healy, McLock—for in their manner of speaking they were New Englanders. They used insulting language to each other at one moment, and immediately afterward were almost sickeningly affectionate and conciliatory.

There were two corporals, Webster and Crofton.

Webster, thin and lugubrious, had charge of the rum rations. Crofton, a small man, quick in his movements and of a suspicious and contentious nature, had charge of the boat rations. In each boat was a breaker of rum, from which a gill was supposed to be issued to each man twice a day while we were on the lake: also every boat carried cold rations of biscuit, chocolate, ginger and bologna sausage, and in addition each man carried a bladder filled with corn meal, which was to be the only ration when we had left the boats and were on the march.

Feeling heavy-hearted and homesick, I got to my feet and stared around, hopeful of seeing Hunk or McNott, but I could find no familiar face among the scores of green-clad figures who sat or lay among the fallen logs and mossy rocks that were thick on the knoll. In the early morning light that filtered down through the tall trees around us, those dim figures seemed unreal; and I felt cold, lonely and miserable. Mosquitoes by the thousand whined around my face and ears. Infinitesimal insects—no-see-'em—pierced my hands and neck, as with red-hot needles.

I sat down again. Jesse Beacham, motionless beside me, stared into space like a benevolent white hound.

"Don't they bite you?" I asked.

He said, simply, that they didn't, and the tone in which he said it was courteous, but seemingly final.

"You got something on you so they don't bite?" I asked.

He said "Yes," in the same courteous tone.

Soon afterward I discovered that Jesse seldom said more than "Yes" or "No" until he had, in his own mind, satisfactorily phrased a more extended reply. He liked to be exact in what he said—an excellent trait, but one that can be carried to excess. Not knowing Jesse's peculiarities, I was thoroughly discouraged and wished I'd never been such a fool as to become a part of an army.

Although none of the men about me had appeared to be aware of me, I found that most of them had heard what I'd just said. Crofton, on his knees sorting out rations, looked up at Jesse. "Tell him about your woolen strings, Grampa," he said. "Tell him how the mosquitoes can't bite while you got on your woolen strings."

Jesse stared mournfully into space. "The woolen strings aint for insects."

One of the Irishmen rose on his elbow. "Of course they aint for insects! The woolen strings keep off toothache. The thing that keeps off the insects is two acorns a day, eaten raw, aint it, Grampa?"

"No," Jesse said. "No. The woolen strings don't have no virtue for toothache."

Sergeant Bradley came quickly among us, stared bitterly around him; then began to distribute biscuit and a bologna sausage apiece. Webster followed him sadly, pouring rum from a wooden canteen into our horn cups. As each man received his ration, he glanced up at Webster with a sort of furtive curiosity.

When Bradley reached me, he spoke defiantly. "In dry weather Jesse rubs soap on himself. He hates to talk about it, because that's the only use he has for soap. In wet weather he greases like an Indian." In a milder voice he spoke to Jesse. "Aint that what you do, Grampa?"

"Yes," Jesse said, caressing his knuckles.

Bradley snorted and walked away, and Webster, having filled our cups, went on in silence, his face contemplative. I was surprised when Jesse looked solicitously after him; then the old man's eyes met mine, and he cleared his throat. "Webster got a letter yesterday. His wife just died, and he don't feel good."

"That's too bad."

Jesse nodded. "Yes, I s'pose a man gets interested in a woman after living with her a few years."

The jet-black Negro, Whip, got up, came and stood beside me, and without a word held out an old brass snuff box.

"What's this?" I asked.

The box, he explained, contained bear's grease, and if I rubbed it on myself, the mosquitoes and no-see-'ems would be less troublesome, since they disliked getting their feet greasy.

I thanked Whip and rubbed some of it on my face and neck. While I did so, Whip said: "Aint you remember me? I'm one of the Braveboat Harbor Whipples. I'm Pomp Whipple." Braveboat Harbor was a section of Kittery to the eastward of my home.

"Then you must be one of Captain Whipple's boys," I said—"one of the boys he brought from Africa!" Captain William Whipple was a highly respected resident of our section, who had made a fortune out of sailing a slave-ship before he was thirty years old.

Pomp nodded. He'd often seen me around Kittery, he told

me, when he was younger—before he ran away and joined the Indians.

Crofton leaned forward to wag the uneaten portion of his sausage at me. "Kittery? You don't talk like you come from Kittery. I come from Epping my own self. Where'd you get to talk like an Englishman, the way you do?"

I said I wasn't conscious of talking like an Englishman.

Sergeant Bradley came over to stare, with what seemed his customary bitterness, at Crofton. "You fellers up in Epping," he complained, "think anybody talks foreign if he don't sound as if he had a mouse up his nose!"

He turned his attention to me. "Funny I never see you before. I was born and brought up in Portsmouth."

I confessed that Portsmouth had seen little of me in recent years, because I had been away at college.

"College!" the sergeant said incredulously. "What college?"

When I said Harvard, he uttered an exclamation of comprehension. "Harvard! No wonder you don't sound right to Crofton! The most educated person Crofton ever heard talk was somebody up in Epping that was thinking about studying common fractions." He eyed me speculatively. "What would you want to join the Rangers for, if you got a good home and book-learning to boot?"

"Well," I said, "I joined on account of a man you probably know—seeing you're a native of Portsmouth."

The sergeant looked interested. "Is that so? Who would that be?"

"Wyseman Clagett."

The sergeant's face was blank. Elderly, white-haired Jesse Beacham turned mournful eyes on me, and Pomp Whipple laughed nervously. "Well, well!" Bradley said. "I never expected to see a friend of Wyseman Clagett in the Rangers."

"I'm not exactly his friend," I said. I told him how, in a private room in Stoodley's Tavern, I had unwittingly insulted Clagett and Sheriff Packer, and been helped to escape by the intervention of Cap Huff and Hunk Marriner. My boatmates gathered around and listened, and Pomp Whipple, rolling his eyes, chuckled delightedly at inopportune moments.

Bradley ruminatively sucked a pine splinter; and when I had finished, he said carelessly, "When you go home, some of us better go along, so if Clagett says anything to you, we can take his house to pieces, just to give him the idea."

From the others arose a muttering of assent. All at once it seemed to me I had never seen a kindlier or pleasanter-looking set of men. It struck me as incredible that I could have thought them churlish; and I was glad my lot had been cast with such intelligent and sympathetic companions.

A distant, hoarse voice shouted for Sergeant Bradley. My new-found friend left me, running. When he came back, he addressed me brusquely. "Towne, Major wants you."

CHAPTER XVII

Rogers, when I had first seen him on the preceding day, had impressed me, because of his thick lips, his long, fleshy nose and the puffy circles beneath his eyes, as one of the ugliest of men. Now I found nothing ugly about him, and was chiefly concerned with his intense and violent energy of mind and body.

He was forever on the move—prowling among his men and staring at them, as if weighing the state of their health or equipment: eyeing a tall pine speculatively: squinting at distant landmarks: kicking at the soil underfoot as if to judge its quality: walking in circles and moving his heavy lips with the air of studying some bothersome problem: casting quick and rather furtive glances at the faces of those near him.

When I came up the knoll, he was walking in circles around a lofty spruce, at the base of which sat Captain Ogden and handsome, yellow-haired Captain Williams of the Royal Regiment; and scattered here and there were other officers, rolled in their blankets, their heads on knapsacks.

The sun had just topped the rise behind us. From the knoll the lake, half shrouded in early morning mist, looked milky. Rogers peered into that pale expanse: then stared upward and whistled sharply. "See anything?"

A guttural "No!" emerged from the tree top. I looked up and saw Konkapot wedged against the trunk.

Rogers went to his knapsack and fumbled in it. He drew out a note book and handed it to me. "Here, I want you to write down the names of men I send out, and where I send 'em, and when they get back—if they *do* get back. Put down the places we stop and what the weather's like. I want to keep a map of this trip. This place is Buttonmould Bay. Tonight I figure on getting beyond Otter River—maybe as far as Split Rock."

"Split Rock?" Captain Williams asked. His voice was polite.

Rogers grinned. "Probably you think we ought to go farther, Captain. Maybe you think we ought to be able to reach the Winooski."

"Well, Major," Captain Williams said apologetically, "we've got quite a way to go. Split Rock's only about ten miles, isn't it?"

"That's all," Rogers agreed, "but it's better to take your time going ten miles and get there than trying to go thirty miles in so much of a hurry that you don't."

Williams said nothing.

"These Frenchmen," Rogers continued patiently, "pop right up out of the water when I'm around. You'd think they were frogs! Yes, Indians do it, too." He laughed. "Seems to be something about me that kind of attracts 'em. Yet, on the other hand, they don't much like me. Anyway, we'll take it slow and dodge 'em. You'll see what I mean when this fog burns off."

A pine cone landed with a thump near Rogers, and he looked up inquiringly. Konkapot's mournful voice said, "Six men in canoe!" We stared between the tree trunks at the New York shore, dimly seen through the lifting fog, but saw nothing.

A sentry ran through the heavy underbrush and up the knoll to Rogers. "Two canoes and a bateau," he said. "There's a canoe scouting each shore; and the bateau's keeping out in the middle. It's full of Frenchmen. Fifteen Frenchmen. Six Indians in each canoe."

"How close are the canoes?" Rogers asked.

"About pistol-shot off shore at the headlands."

"All right," Rogers said. "Tell Captain Jacobs I want him. I'll use his Indians and the Mohawks too."

Captain Jacobs was captain of the Stockbridge Indians, and he was a nightmare. His upper body was painted black;

the lower part of his face white. On his chest was neatly depicted, in yellow paint, a representation of an officer's gorget. His head was shaved; the base of his scalp-lock was wrapped tightly, to the height of five inches, with a rattle-snake skin. Thus the top of his scalp-lock sprayed out above the snakeskin like a ragged shaving brush. Among the hairs of the scalp-lock were bound the rattles of several rattle-snakes.

Rogers was more military with this Indian officer than with any of his white officers. They saluted each other punc-tiliously, and Rogers not only addressed Jacobs as "Captain," but also as "Brother Nawnawampeteoonk," which was his real name, Jacobs being his Christian or civilized name.

All the Stockbridge Indians, Rogers told him, were to fol-low the canoes and bateau and report their movements. The Mohawks were to scout north toward Otter River in an attempt to find out where the party of French and Indians had been camped the night before.

These orders given, Rogers pulled at his lower lip, rolling his protuberant eyes from his concealed whaleboats to the open lake, still innocently empty of enemies. He beckoned to Captain Ogden.

"Take twenty men," he told him, "and post 'em in the brush above our boats. If that scout canoe gets sight of any of our boats, and comes in to investigate, let it get close up and then destroy every man in it. Don't let any of 'em get away. Finish 'em all. If they don't see our boats, let 'em go by."

Ogden summoned Sergeant Bradley, and Bradley walked around the knoll, calling off names: Beacham, Foyle, Orford, Bennett, Rice, McRae, Murphy, Thacher. I saw them moving cautiously toward the boats: saw Ogden pointing out the posi-tions they should take.

Rogers turned to his other officers, who had folded their blankets and picked up their packs and muskets. "Join your detachments. Stay with 'em till we find out where these scout boats are bound. Tell your men to get what sleep they can. They're not to talk or move till everything's clear."

Instantly they hurried away, leaving the knoll deserted, except for Rogers and me. The Stockbridge Indians, stripped to leggins and breech-clouts, came over the shoulder of the knoll and stood looking out over the calm blue lake. It seemed to me that the black and white paint on their upper bodies had the effect of making them look more like shadows than men. A man's body, sometimes, seemed to terminate at the white paint, so that one needed to hunt carefully in order to find his complete outline.

Fascinated, I began sketching them as they stood there, but stopped when one of the Indians pointed at something on the water and another made a grunting noise. Turning my head, I saw a canoe had slid into sight from behind the headland.

"There they are," Rogers said. It wasn't one of the big canoes, called *canot du maître* but the next smaller size, known as a half canoe. In it were six Indians: a steersman, a bow-man, and four who were doing the paddling. All six shone in the early morning sun as if lacquered. Their faces were painted green and yellow: their bodies black and red.

When the canoe swung into the bay on a long curve, about fifty yards from shore, we could see the shaved heads of the bow-man and steersman moving slowly from side to side: see them lift their eyes, white in their painted faces to the treetops—hunting, no doubt, for signs of smoke. I looked for the Stockbridge Indians, to see what they thought of these strangers, but they had vanished, and the knoll where they had stood seemed to lack all human life. There was no movement on it: no sound.

Even the groups below me had melted away. Wrapped in their green blankets, the Rangers looked like moss-covered logs or boulders.

The canoe slid around the bay. Far out in mid-lake a bateau slowly held a straight course toward Crown Point. The oarsmen wore buckskins; but in the bow and stern were men in white uniforms—French officers. These were the first French soldiers I had ever seen, and in the distance, on the bosom of the placid lake, they looked like painted little toy soldiers for children to play with.

I couldn't feel that they were dangerous, or deadly enemies, or that they, and others like them, had fought our colonists for five long years: had sent Indians by thousands aginst our settlements: had allowed Indians to butcher women and children and unarmed colonists two years ago at Fort William Henry: had slaughtered thousands of our men a year ago at Ticonderoga.

When the bateau and canoes had vanished beyond the

southern headland of Buttonmould Bay, the knoll was suddenly busy again. They hadn't seen our whaleboats, and the camp was at ease once more. Men puttered with knapsacks and muskets; entered into involved and endless arguments; spread blankets on the ground and played at five-card loo with a deal of finger-wetting and slapping down of cards; slept, rolled up like cocoons in green strouds.

It was noon before I could sleep myself; for Rogers kept me with him, even though he must have seen I found trouble in staying awake; and in that time I came to have, from Rogers' remarks to me, a clearer understanding of the Rangers and of the men who made up that body. Most of them, both officers and men, had enlisted as Rangers, and were nothing but Rangers at any time. A fair number, however, were temporarily attached to the Rangers because they were officers or men from other parts of General Amherst's army who seemed well equipped to become skilled in the type of marching and fighting for which Rogers was famous.

General Amherst, Rogers said, regarded the Rangers as a school in which his most promising officers and men could learn the only type of warfare that could ever be successful in forest fighting, and having learned it, they would be able, in future campaigns, to impart their knowledge to others. Thus Captain Williams was normally a captain in the Royal Regiment; Captain Dunbar from Gage's Light Infantry; Captain Butterworth a Provincial Captain; Ensign Avery from Fitch's Provincial regiment; and a full quarter of the men were selected from Provincial regiments, from the Royal Highlanders, from Gage's Light Infantry and from other British regiments whose fighting experience, up to now, had been limited to meeting the enemy in close formation in open fields—a suicidal method when employed against French and Indians accustomed to forest warfare.

The Stockbridge Indians, too, were Rangers; but the Mohawks were not. The Mohawks had been sent to General Amherst by Sir William Johnson, who lived in the Mohawk Valley and was the Superintendent of Northern Indians for the British Government; and the General, having no other use for them, had ordered them to accompany Major Rogers as scouts. From the Major's tone when he spoke of them, I gathered he was not enthusiastic about Mohawks.

Every moment Rogers was more of a marvel to me. He

seemed unable to feel fatigue. Almost continually he prowled around the camp, examining boats, talking with sentries, scrutinizing the lake; even stopping to watch the progress of card games.

I was always surprised to see the small distinction he made between officers and men. He stood over a group rolling dice on a blanket, and took part in it by throwing down a shilling. The shilling became two: then four. The men were familiar with him, daring him to let it stay. He took up his shillings, however, and prowled away, abusing them good-naturedly; telling them they knew nothing about the game, at which they guffawed.

Even though I was new to the army, I had lived near a British garrison and knew that a British officer would rather be dead than to put himself on an equality with his men like this.

Twice when we were alone, he returned abruptly to the fragmentary conversation we'd held in his tent at Crown Point on the preceding day. Had I, he asked, read the book about Captain Middleton's voyage in search of the Northwest Passage? I said I had; that it was a short book; and then he cross-examined me upon it as though he had no other interest in life.

He could think of more things to ask in a minute than I could have thought of in a week. What, he wanted to know, had interested Dobbs in the Northwest Passage? What made Dobbs so sure of its existence? What reasons did Captain Middleton have for thinking there wasn't a Northwest Passage? Did the book mention other attempts to find it? Who were the Spaniards who had tried it? What Indian nations were mentioned in Dobbs's book? Did the English seem greatly interested in the Northwest Passage? Did Dobbs's book have a large sale? How large? Did Dobbs have anything to say concerning the expenses connected with finding the Northwest Passage?

Some of his questions I could answer and some I couldn't, but I knew the answer to the last one. Dobbs, I told him, had said the expenses were large, and he had persuaded the Lords of the Admiralty to offer a standing reward of £20,000 to the person who should discover the Northwest Passage.

Rogers whistled. "Twenty thousand pounds!" he murmured meditatively. "Twenty thousand pounds!"

What he thought, there was no way of knowing. Whatever he was doing or saying or hearing, he wore always a semi-deferential, semi-apologetic, semi-amiable smile, just as some men perpetually wear a preoccupied frown.

He let me go, finally. Only twenty-four hours had passed since, leg-weary from my long march with Hunk, I had looked for the first time on Crown Point and the army; and it began to seem to me I had been in the army all my life, and had never rested.

CHAPTER XVIII

THE NIGHT we left Buttonmould Bay we rowed a bare ten miles to Otter River; but short as the journey was, it was long enough to rob me of my only friends, and to come within an inch of putting an end to the expedition. It was long enough, too, to give me a respect for Rogers that endured.

Toward sundown the Mohawks had returned from the northward with the news that they had found no signs of a place where the bateauload of Frenchmen might have camped. Rogers listened without comment to the report of their spokesman, but he was far from satisfied. "Damn it," he complained to Williams, "those Frenchmen camped *somewhere!* If I'd been in their place, I'd have camped at Otter River. They came past us early in the morning—just the proper time for 'em to get here if they'd started from Otter River at daybreak. I know damned well they didn't row all night! By God, I wonder if those Mohawks just went far enough from camp to lie down and take a good comfortable sleep themselves! I never liked anything Sir William Johnson had a hand in, and it was he who sent those Mohawks to General Amherst!"

When Captain Ogden opined that the Mohawks were, probably, no different from any other Indians—as good scouts, doubtless, as Stockbridge Indians, Rogers stared at him owlishly. "Maybe they are," he said, "but whatever white man's discipline they got, they got from Johnson, and Johnson doesn't know any more about discipline than he does about war. I've had these Stockbridge Indians with me for three years, and they do what they're told. If the General had left it to me, I wouldn't have taken Johnson's Mohawks, any more than I'd have taken those men from the regular army."

Captain Jacobs and his Stockbridge Indians came back at dusk and reported that the French in the bateau and the Indians in the two canoes had gone to a headland from which they had an unobstructed view south to Crown Point, and camped there. Rogers looked thoughtful and shook his head, but gave orders for the whaleboats to be uncovered and launched, and for the oars to be wrapped with strips of blanketing. When the men were aboard, he went from boat to boat, warning the crews to be silent. Under no condition, he told them, were they to talk. The cry of a loon, given twice, would be the signal to stop rowing: given once, the signal to go ahead.

The night was cold—so cold that my neck ached and my muscles seemed made of wood. A heavy mist hung low over the water, thrusting clammy fingers against our flesh and through our garments. Rogers, a towering figure in the stern of our boat, explored the air currents with his beak of a nose, seeming to feel them as an animal might. From time to time, startlingly, the vacant, hysterical laugh of a loon burst from his lips, and we lay drifting silently, rocking a little on the black water; then in the profound stillness of that cold night we could hear him sniffing and whuffling like a suspicious bear.

Four miles of rowing brought us to the shallows that lie off the mouth of Otter River; and it was here that his snuffling was rewarded. He had stopped us with that singularly vacant burst of laughter, and so long did he hold us motionless that it seemed to me our boat itself vibrated with our shivering. Not a sound could we hear save the faint chirping of small birds, far overhead, moving south; yet Rogers, apparently, was aware of something. We could feel him lean from side to side: hear him sniff as a questing dog sniffs, blowing outward as if to freshen his organs of scent: then drawing the air jerkily into his nostrils.

Of course it couldn't actually have been altogether smell; he had some sort of sixth sense that the rest of us lacked. Just when I thought our waiting would never end, a faint but unmistakable sound came out of the mist dead ahead—a sound that I had heard a thousand times on the Portsmouth docks, when brigs and schooners stirred uneasily at the push of a rising tide. It was the muted screaking of the jaws of a boom, working against a mast.

Rogers sank down in the stern of the boat. "Frenchman anchored off the mouth of the river," I heard him whisper to Captain Williams.

"We can row around it," Williams breathed.

"No telling how many vessels there are," Rogers said softly. "We got to get past 'em, and there's only one sure way. We'll have to go where they can't go."

Obeying his whispered orders, the seventeen whaleboats silently floated backward, like the ghost of some strange lake monster: then nosed off to the eastward, into a bay so shallow that our oarblades scraped bottom—so shallow that long before the boats had reached the shore, we had climbed overboard to drag them through the mud and the clustered water plants. It seemed more like a dream than a reality that two hundred men and all those boats should move across that mud-puddle of a bay without a shout, without a curse, without the splashing of water, or the thump of a dropped oar against a thwart, or the rumble of one boat colliding with another. That was how they moved, however, so that we came safely to a dark, low-lying bank from which mosquitoes rose by the million to devour us.

We covered ourselves as well as we could from the bloodthirsty insects, and when the dawn came we went to work carrying the boats.

Otter River has a peculiar mouth. In the centuries during which it has poured its brown flood down from the sharp hills to the eastward of Champlain, it has brought with it so much soil that it has built for itself a narrow spit of land, projecting a mile into the lake. This spit of land has made two bays out of the one into which it extends, and along the spit runs the river. A sketch of the bay and the river-mouth, therefore, would resemble the distended jaws of a gigantic animal thrusting out an eager tongue as if wishful of gulping down the succulent little island that lies a mere three-quarters of a mile away.

Above the tongue is North Otter Bay, which is deep; below it is South Otter Bay, so shoal as to be dangerous, in spots, to anything but a canoe. It was through the shallows of South Otter Bay that we dragged our boats ashore on the tongue of land along which the river pours itself into the lake; and it was across this tongue of land that we were obliged to carry the boats in order to get to the northward of the French.

After an hour of back-breaking labor, steaming with sweat, up to our middles in water, almost eaten alive by mosquitoes, we finally brought the boats to the edge of North Otter Bay and covered them with brush at the foot of the wooded hill that lies to the north of the river mouth. There we lay, simmering and fuming, while Rogers set off for the top of the hill with Lieutenant Turner and Ensign Avery to obtain additional information about the French.

I say that we simmered and fumed, but those words are inadequate to express the current of rage against the Mohawks that ran through the camp as flame runs through dry grass. The heat, perhaps, had set our nerves on edge: perhaps our long and silent labors had made our anger keener. Whatever the reason, the whole camp was furious at the Mohawks: and when Rogers came back, bringing word that there had been and still were three French sloops ranged between the river mouth and Diamond Island, the language used to describe Sir William Johnson's Indians became Biblical.

Every man in the detachment knew that the Mohawks had been sent on a scout toward Otter River on the preceding day. These French sloops, almost necessarily, had been anchored in this same spot during the entire time the Mohawks were on their scout; for the occupants of the bateau and two canoes that had passed us must have been sent out from these very vessels. The failure of the Mohawks to bring back word of the three French craft had endangered the whole expedition.

Lacking a leader as astute as Rogers, we would probably have been discovered if there had been only one French sloop. With three of them lying across the channel, our escape was miraculous.

All around us the men cursed the Mohawks openly and bitterly, calling them murdering red hellions, dirty red skunks, and names unfit to repeat; and only the Mohawks themselves seemed unconscious of the temper of the detachment.

They sat at the water's edge, looking like thirteen skinned foxes, and complacently daubed vermilion bands across countenances previously blackened with soot; and those who had business in their vicinity sheered away from them as though they were vipers.

Rogers prowled restlessly at the foot of the hill, making sure that the boats were properly concealed, and issuing orders for the picketing of the camp. My brief experience of the day before had taught me how to stick close to his left elbow, ready to note down his orders, and at the same time keep out from under foot. He paraded Turner's and Avery's detachments and the Stockbridge Indians, fully equipped: then sent them off to join Avery and Turner on the slope of the hill overlooking the river mouth, where they had been left to watch the sloops. He kept Captain Jacobs with him, and sent word to Turner by Captain Jacobs' Indian lieutenant, Lieutenant Solomon, that he and Jacobs would also come to watch the sloops as soon as the camp was in order. Then, followed by Jacobs and me, he went to the northern slope of the hill, where the whaleboat crews had settled themselves, and there, beside a tall spruce, he halted.

"Now," Rogers said to Jacobs, "tell those Mohawks I want to see 'em. Their hash is all loose in 'em: we'll have to settle it."

CHAPTER XIX

THERE WERE thirteen of the Mohawks, and when they stood before Rogers, staring at him out of eyes as dull and black as the soot on their faces, it seemed to me they looked more like snakes than like humans. Their heads were flatter than those of the Stockbridge

Indians, and that flatness was accentuated by the scalp-locks which lay against their shaved and blackened skulls. From ear to ear, across their eyes and the bridges of their noses, they had painted vermilion bands that seemed to me unpleasantly like the stripes upon serpents. All of them wore their blankets fastened around their waists and hanging down in folds, and above those folds their thin, soot-daubed upper bodies rose lithe and tense. Unquestionably the thirteen were contemptuous, defiant and dangerous.

Rogers stared at them: then glanced around the knoll—at the officers on either side of him; at the groups of Rangers chewing busily at their morning rations, their faces turned toward the little knot of painted Mohawks. It was a smolderingly silent audience that the commander had when he began to speak.

"Our brothers the Mohawks," he said, and his thick voice was almost kindly, "are known to all the world as great warriors. They have come a long journey from their homes in the Mohawk Valley, and we, their friends, understood they had come to raise their hatchets in behalf of the great King their father. Because they are known to be terrible in war, the great King, speaking from the mouth of his most trusted leader, General Amherst, gave orders that they should go with me to act as my eyes and ears against our enemies, the French. Now it may be that we have not understood correctly why our friends the Mohawks came to Crown Point to join the army of General Amherst, so we will ask them to tell us why they came."

He nodded to Captain Jacobs, who interpreted his words to the Mohawks in a language that was pleasant to hear, even though the listener understood none of it. When Captain Jacobs had finished, one of the Mohawks replied, and the gist of his speech, again translated by Captain Jacobs, was that their father was Sir William Johnson, and that Sir William Johnson had asked them to come to Crown Point in order to show the great King across the water that his children the Mohawks were still his children, obedient to his wishes and to the wishes of their friend and benefactor, Sir William Johnson.

"Our father, Sir William Johnson," the Mohawk said, "understands that there is a time to fight and a time not to fight, but there are some who do not understand this. We left our homes before the corn was harvested, and we have no way of knowing whether our crops were large or small. If they were small, we must start at once to kill game for our families unless we wish them to starve. Any wise man knows this. Yet instead of thanking us for coming to Crown Point to show our friendship for the great King and giving us presents to carry back to our families, your general without consulting us sent us off on a long journey to kill someone we have never seen. If we had known we would be sent on such a journey, we would never have come to Crown Point."

The officers behind Rogers moved impatiently and muttered, but Rogers again spoke amiably. "I see that we did not understand why Sir William Johnson sent our brothers the Mohawks to join us. He sent them to eat our food and drink our rum and do nothing, and we have not been accustomed to expect such behavior from warriors. We expect such actions from old women, but not from brave men. We did not understand, probably, because Sir William Johnson did not tell us that he had instructed his children the Mohawks to behave like old women. He should have told us. Since he did not, we cannot blame our brothers the Mohawks for not wishing to go on this journey.

"There is another thing, too, that we do not understand, and we will be pleased if our brothers the Mohawks will explain it to us. Yesterday, knowing that the Mohawks were skilled in tracking enemies, we sent them to Otter River to discover the camping ground of the French. Since they made no complaints, we supposed that they went willingly, and would faithfully carry out their orders. There were three vessels at Otter River: yet our brothers the Mohawks failed to see those vessels. They returned, saying they found nothing. We trusted them; and because we trusted them, all of us have this morning been in danger of losing our boats and our lives. How do our brothers the Mohawks explain their blindness?"

The spokesman of the Mohawks replied as gravely and with as noble a bearing as though he gave utterance to the most rational and sagacious sentiments. "Sir William Johnson," he said, "allows his children the Mohawks to do what they will. If he wishes his children to go somewhere, he asks them whether it would give them pleasure to go; and unless the Mohawks are agreed that it would give them pleasure, they do not go. At Crown Point it is different, and here it is also different. We are told to do the thing that one man wishes us to do, regardless of our own desires. We do not like to be ruled as any man may choose to order us. When we were told yesterday to go on a scout to Otter River, we went a short distance and then held a council to decide whether we wished to go further. Some were willing, but others were not. Each man made an oration, and when all had spoken, more were in favor of returning than of going forward. Therefore we returned."

I know now that Indians are peculiar people, and cannot be judged as white men are judged. I have learned that some of them are so direct and honest in their manner of thinking that they are as wise, in many ways, as the wisest white men; but most of them are simple to absurdity—so simple that they can only be depended on to do the wrong thing: to waste food when it should be saved: to rely on dreams when reason is essential: to be reckless when caution is advisable and cautious when recklessness is imperative: to lie when truthfulness is required, and tell the truth when tactful evasion is preferable: to run home when they are most needed, and get under foot when they are least wanted: to punish harmless transgressions with death and ignore the most heinous crimes. In those days, however, I knew nothing about Indians, and the Mohawks seemed to me to be treacherous, and as dangerous to us as mad dogs: shooting, I thought, was far too good a death for them.

Rogers had different ideas, and his reply was as gentle in its manner as though he were praising the Mohawks for faithful service. "We are grateful to our brothers the Mohawks for explaining to us the things which we did not understand, and we are greatful to them, also, for coming such a long journey to show their friendship. We need their help, and we hope they will always be our friends. We also hope that some day they will learn our method of making war, as have our brothers from Stockbridge. Our brothers say that Sir William Johnson allows them to do what they will; but if our brothers should only do what they wanted to do in this section of the country—if, when they were put on guard over a camp, they should prefer to wrap themselves in their blankets and sleep—they would soon lose their scalps. What is worse, those whom they were supposed to guard would also lose their scalps.

"We have discovered that this is not a good way to make war. It is impossible to make war if you are dead, and the only way to stay alive when fighting the French is for wise men to give orders beforehand as to what must be done; then for everybody to obey those orders without arguing, whether he wants to or not. That is why, in our army, soldiers are shot when they do not obey orders—when they decide to do as they will.

"Since our brothers the Mohawks are accustomed to do as they will—accustomed to disobey orders if they find those orders displeasing—they should be careful to serve only under Sir William Johnson. If they serve under anyone else, they will probably be shot. Since the Mohawks are our friends, I do not wish to hurt their feelings or the feelings of Sir William Johnson by shooting any of them. Neither am I willing to keep them with us any longer; for they will only eat our provisions and drink our rum and refuse to obey orders. Therefore they must go back to Crown Point. But if they should tell the truth as to why they went back, General Amherst might have them shot, so they must say they became sick. They can say they became sick from something they ate. It may seem remarkable that all the Mohawks on this expedition should become sick together, all at one time, and probably they will be called old women for doing so; but it is better to be called old women than to be shot."

He leaned casually upon a musket and waited for Captain Jacobs to translate. The Mohawks, seemingly indifferent to Jacobs' words, stared straight ahead out of lacklustre eyes.

"They're to go at once," Rogers said, when Jacobs had finished. "We need their boat, so they're to go by land. Have 'em get their belongings from their boat and set off immediately." He turned to Captain Williams. "You're in command, Captain, until I come back. I'll have to find out what those sloops are doing."

CHAPTER XX

ONE OF the fundamental differences, it seems to me, between Indians and white men who are known as civilized is that the white man has been more or less disciplined, whereas Indians, as a rule, are free of disciplinary measures from their earliest days. Indian children are never whipped for wrong-doing; drunken Indians are held guiltless of crimes committed while intoxicated; no Indian is forced by his tribe or nation to do anything he doesn't want to do; lazy Indians are supported by more industrious ones. Because of that lack of discipline, Indians are supposed to be more savage, cruel, treacherous, cowardly, shortsighted than any other race. Yet I doubt that an Indian at his worst can outdo white men who, because of panic, mob excitement or lack of leadership, have temporarily broken away from the discipline that is supposed to be the white man's birthright.

The Mohawks went quietly enough to their boat when Rogers and Jacobs were out of sight, and all over the knoll Rangers rose to their feet to see them go, and never before had I heard profanity to equal that which accompanied them. On rejoining the crew of Number One whaleboat to devour my delayed breakfast, I found even Jesse Beacham gazing mournfully after the red men and mildly repeating the words "drammed red bustards." The Irishmen among Number One's boat-crew were in such a temper that they were wrangling passionately with one another, while in the adjoining crew Sergeant McNott, purple-faced with rage, stared belligerently about him, as if for someone to attack.

Hunk Marriner crawled over to sit beside me. "Aint it a shame," he said, "that Indians don't have pelts half as good as a weasel, so they'd be worth shooting!"

McNott violently urged me to write down in my book, where Rogers would see it, that it would pay the British government not to make presents to Mohawks except those who had kept farthest away during three consecutive campaigns.

Indeed I was conscious myself of a sort of suffocating resentment at those dreadful Indians, who would have sacrificed all of us to their own senseless stupidity, and so hot was this resentment that it seemed to me I would have had as little hesitation in killing a Mohawk as in shooting a porcupine that had filled my dog's mouth and tongue with quills.

Someone shouted near the river bank, where the boats were hidden in the brush, but so engrossing was my anger that the sound made no impression on me: I forgot noise had been forbidden: forgot, that is, until McNott leaped to his feet and violently hurled a stick in the direction of the shout. Captain Williams ran down from the knoll, and there was sudden and unaccustomed movement in all the groups. Hunk scrambled back to his detachment, seized his musket and snapped up the pan. All around me, I saw, men were picking up their muskets and getting to their knees, peering toward the boats.

Out from the brush in which the boats had been hidden stumbled one of the Mohawks, and close behind was Captain Butterfield, a Provincial officer from New Hampshire. Butterfield, burly and red-faced at all times, looked even redder now. He was clutching at the Indian's greasy shoulder; and the Indian, encumbered by a musket, his pack and a bulky powder bag, staggered but was not stopped.

Captain Williams went past the Mohawk on the run, caught Butterfield's outstretched arm and swung him abruptly to a halt. The whole knoll boiled with men in green buckskins. A phalanx of them seemed to spring from the ground behind Williams, and without knowing how I got there, I found myself in the front row of this formation, with Hunk and McNott crowded close against me. The Indian, halted by the wall of men, turned and would have gone back past Williams and Butterfield toward the boats, but Butterfield thrust out his foot and tripped him.

"For God's sake!" Williams cried. "You can't do that, Captain!"

The Indian had bounced to his feet like an enormous red squirrel, his eyes darting here and there as if seeking a hole through which he might scramble; but Rangers had run between him and the boats: he was penned in a ring of men with Williams and Butterfield.

"Can't!" Butterfield cried. "Can't! Why can't I? Those red skunks stole the powder and the rum out of the boat! It aint theirs: it's ours! They can't wreck us and rob us too—not without learning a lesson! I caught this one, by God, and I'll make an example of him!"

From the circle of men came angry words: "Blow his head off! Stick a knife in him!"

"Where'd the rest of 'em go?" Williams asked.

"They went up river," Butterfield said angrily. "They got away, but this one wont!"

"Lieutenant Dunbar!" Williams called. "Lieutenant Grant! Take your men to the river bank and see there's no trouble. I want all the other officers to take their men out of this crowd. Get 'em back to their camps where they belong." He never took his eyes off Butterfield.

Behind me I heard the voices of officers calling their men by name.

"Now, Captain," Williams said to Butterfield, "just step to one side and let this Indian join his company. We want 'em out of camp, all of 'em."

"I don't care what you want!" Butterfield said. "That red hellion aint going to get out of here with that bag of powder! I wont back down for those dirty rats."

"You've got your orders, Captain Butterfield," Williams said coldly. "Let this man through."

"You go to hell!" Butterfield shouted furiously. "You damned Britishers think you can throw us any kind of an order, no matter whether there's sense to it or not. Well, by God, you can't! We've got brains: just as many as you have—and better ones, too, most of the time!"

From somewhere in the circle of silent Rangers came a hoarse whisper, clearly heard by everyone. "You lousy Provincial!"

The ring of men wavered and shifted. I saw three or four Provincials move around behind Butterfield, and realized that nearly all the men close to him were Provincials. Butterfield's face, which had so recently been scarlet with excitement, had grown pale.

"Lousy Provincials!" he said in a shaking low voice. "Lousy

Provincials! That's what *you* think, but where would you pig-headed Englishmen be if it wasn't for us—you and your damned murdering Highlanders and your drunken black Irishmen. You'd be two feet underground, where you damned well belong! You aint Rangers! You're brass-button soldiers filled with pizened skunkwater and sawdust!"

On the edge of the circle a man from a Highland regiment suddenly hit one of the Provincials on the jaw. Two Provincials jumped at him and the three went down in a tangle of fists. McNott leaped for the struggling men, dragged them apart, sent the Highlander flying with a tremendous kick, jerked one of the Provincials to his feet, and slapped his face resoundingly. Then, as if he'd completed one slight task and was ready to take up another, he looked about him invitingly, waiting for further infractions of discipline.

"Captain Butterfield," Williams said, "if Provincials have a bad reputation among regular troops, it's because of actions like yours. That Mohawk is going safely out of this camp. If you interfere, I'll have you courtmartialled."

Instead of answering, Butterfield snatched at the bag of powder beneath the Mohawk's arm. The Mohawk threw himself on the ground, and in a moment the circle of men had turned into a sort of human whirlpool—a maelstrom of struggling, kicking, shouting, cursing maniacs, all filled, seemingly, with the desire to tear each other to shreds.

I saw the Mohawk, still clutching his musket and powder bag, creeping among the feet of these grunting, fist-swinging madmen; saw Butterfield kick him brutally in the side.

The Mohawk writhed like a snake, grasped the knife that hung by a thong on his breast, and plunged it into the powder bag. I heard McNott shouting violently in my ear. Hunk's contorted face appeared close to mine: his flailing arm struck my cheek and swept me out of the circle and flat on my back.

Then I heard a musket shot, followed instantly by a gigantic thump—more of a stupendous concussion than an explosion. It seemed almost to pluck the moccasins from my feet, the clothes from my body, the hair from my head: it pressed me down as though an invisible feather bed had fallen on me.

When I got to my knees, dazed, the cluster of men who a

moment before had been the incarnation of violent energy
were stretched on the ground, a smoldering, feebly-moving
tangle of human wreckage from which came groans and in-
coherences. The air was filled with the thick and salty smell
of gunpowder, the musty odor of burning leather; and high
in the trees hung a slowly-drifting cloud of bluish smoke.

I was conscious of men running from all sides toward this
writhing, smoking heap. I crawled among them myself, looking for Hunk Marriner. I recognized him by his fair hair. He
was on his knees, pawing with one hand at the shoulder of
his Ranger's smock, from which came wisps of gray smoke,
and his face and hands were black.

"Wait," I said. "Let it alone. I'll cut it away." With my
knife I sawed the sleeve from his shirt and peeled it down
his arm. Powder had somehow blown inside his shirt and
burned there, leaving his whole shoulder black and streaked
with blood.

"Can you put it out?" Hunk asked. "It's still burning."

"No," I said. "It's out. It's all out. Put your arm around me
and I'll get you away from here."

Hunk lifted his hands. Both palms were blown full of
powder grains. "I damned near got that powder bag from
him," he said. "I almost had my hands on it when he fired
his musket into it. What happened to the Mohawk?"

I heard McNott's voice behind me, husky and sour. "He
got away." I looked around. McNott sat with his legs
stretched straight in front of him. His face was as black as
Hunk's. The left leg of his breeches had been slit open, and
burning powder had so seared his knee that the tendons
showed white through the blackened, bloody flesh.

Ogden came behind us and looked closely at the sergeant.
"Here's McNott," he told the Rangers with him. "Move him
up on the ridge." Two men stooped down and got him under
the arms. "Careful of that leg," McNott said, "or I'll wring
your damned necks! Half my leggins got blown into that
hole."

"I'll take Marriner," I told Ogden. "They'll hurt his shoulder if they try to carry him." I got him around the waist and
hoisted him to his feet. When I turned him toward the knoll,
Captain Williams came up to us and looked hard at Hunk's
shoulder. The captain was almost unrecognizable. The whole
side of his face was blown full of powder, his left eye was

completely closed, and the tow-colored hair on half of his head had been singed off, leaving a charred stubble.

Captain Ogden, at his elbow, spoke to him imploringly. "That eye ought to be looked at, Captain. You ought to have it tended to."

"It's nothing, Captain," Williams said cheerfully. "I'm quite all right. Just take care of the others and don't worry about me." To Hunk he said, "You behaved well. You very nearly saved us all."

"I thought I had it," Hunk said. "I ought to known what he figured on doing when he stuck his knife in the bag."

"Not at all," Williams said. "Not at all. You acted as quickly as anyone could have. You'll make a good Ranger. I'd be pleased to have you in my company." He peered at Hunk's wound out of his one good eye. "Yes," he added with simulated cheerfulness. "You'll be all right—all right."

Swaying like a drunken man, he turned to leave us, but Ogden took him by the arm and steered him between the trees. From his closed, puffed eye a stream of moisture had washed a white furrow on his blackened cheek. The sickening thought struck me that in all probability he would never lead another company; that Hunk might not only never serve in any company, but never even hold a musket to his shoulder again.

I had made my friend as comfortable on the knoll as I could and was picking powder from his wound when I saw Rogers coming back to the camp from his excursion to look at the sloops. I had expected him to show violent anger at what had happened, or pehaps grief; but what I seemed to read in his face was a sort of grim amusement and a kind of regretful relief. Then Sergeant Bradley came to look after Hunk and I left them and went to Rogers with the orderly book. Officers crowded close around him, and before him stood Captain Butterfield, making a halting explanation. He seemed entirely unhurt.

"We needed that powder," Butterfield said. "If Captain Williams hadn't interfered, I'd 'a' taken it away from him without any trouble, and none of this would have happened."

Rogers laughed. "You don't know *what* would have happened. You were dealing with an Indian, and you ought to have known you can't take liberties with an Indian. No matter how these Indians behave, we need to keep 'em friendly.

We've got enough unfriendly ones yowling around us without adding to the number!"

He pulled his hat down on his head, glared at his officers; then fixed his eyes upon Butterfield again. "That's all beside the point. The point is that you didn't maintain discipline, and the moment discipline's gone, everything's gone. You lost your head, and maybe it's a good thing for the rest of us that you did! An officer who loses his head once will usually do it again, so it's better to have it happen now than later, when we might not have got out of it so easy."

"Major," Butterfield said earnestly, "I didn't lose my head. I knew what I was doing every minute. It was the others lost their heads."

"I wont argue the point," Rogers said, "but when somebody loses his head, you can usually count on one thing: the only one who isn't hurt is the one who lose his head. Everybody else suffers in one way or another. I notice *you* didn't get hurt.

"Anyway, Captain Butterfield, you're going back! You've done enough damage to my men; and if I have you courtmartialled, you'll probably do more. I guess it'll be enough punishment if you go back and report to General Amherst that sickness prevented you from going farther than Otter River. You're sick, and so are the Provincials who'll return with you, and the Rangers and the Regulars who'll have to go back because of this. These men are either sick or burned with gunpowder: that's all you're ever to tell anybody about what happened."

He moved a few steps toward the boats, then turned and called, "Captain Williams."

Williams moved forward, supported by Captain Ogden.

"Captain Williams," Rogers said, "I'm putting you in charge of all these sick men—Indians, Rangers, Regulars and Provincials. Move 'em back, away from this camp, and start home at once. The rest of us'll stay right here."

Captain Williams was a pitiful spectacle; for although Captain Ogden had made an effort to wash off the powder stains, the flesh around his damaged eye was raw and bloody, and his other eye was almost closed in sympathy, so that he was obliged to throw his head far back in order to see. Blisters had formed where the hair had been burned from his scalp. "Major," he said, moving his lips with difficulty, "I'll be all right in a day or two. This isn't anything. I can see out of my right eye. I could sight a musket right now if I had to. I can march as well as——"

"You're going back, Captain," Rogers said. "Those are your orders. You'll have to go back by land. I'm taking all the boats with me. You'll take every Ranger and every Regular who was burned or who has powder marks on his uniform."

"Major," Captain Williams mumbled, "I'd like to say one more word."

"All right," Rogers said. "Say it."

"Major," Williams continued, "that'll mean sending back pretty near thirty men, not counting the Mohawks. Counting the Mohawks, you'll lose over forty men. That's twenty percent —a higher percentage than you'd lose in two battles if you had bad luck. I don't believe you can afford that many, Major. Couldn't you reconsider those orders, Major? I figure practically all of us could make the trip, Major—Captain Butterfield and all the rest of us."

"Look here, Captain," Rogers said. "You can't bandage that eye properly. You don't even know what's happened to it. You can't keep the flies out of it. What'll happen if you go blind in the woods? I'll have to send another man home with you! I won't take the chance! Captain Williams, you're going back because you're incapacitated and so are some others, but the most are going because they haven't shown themselves subject to discipline. If there'd been a hundred in it, I'd send a hundred back. I don't give a damn how big a percentage of 'em I lose if they aren't subject to discipline. By God, I'd make this expedition with fifty men—yes, with *ten* men—and do more with those ten than I could do with two hundred that didn't obey orders."

He lowered his head and stared at his officers out of stony eyes. "All the men in this detachment are Rangers, understand? Rangers! They aren't Scotchmen or Englishmen or Irishmen or Provincials or Regulars or anything else: they're Rangers! If I find two Irishmen leagued together as Irishmen and not as Rangers, by God, I'll send 'em home if we're within twenty feet of where we're going."

CHAPTER XXI

I WONDERED, that night, as we pulled silently out of North Otter Bay into the teeth of a northeast storm, why I felt no sense of loss at leaving Hunk and Sergeant McNott behind. I thought, at the time, it was because I was numb from bodily misery and lack of sleep—because of the drenching rain that trickled coldly down my neck to form a puddle in my soggy buckskins. I know now that when we lose a friend in war, he never quite seems gone. We think of him as being somewhere near, in another company, where we can find him readily enough—if the everlasting work is ever done, and the everlasting discipline permits.

The worst part of our water journey lay behind us; for although we still had twice as far to row as we had already come, we had passed the narrowest part of the lake and would henceforth be in more open waters, less likely to be seen and attacked by French vessels.

Because of this I thought, for a time, our progress might be easier, but instead it became more difficult. For five successive days after we left Otter River the storm howled out of the northeast, drenching us with rain, numbing us with cold, and making travel an agony. As we approached the eastern arm of Lake Champlain, which ends blindly in Missisquoi Bay, the eastern shore along which we coasted each night became flatter and flatter; and on this flat land we were obliged to find complete concealment before dawn each day for a hundred and sixty men and seventeen whaleboats. A mile or two away we could see Grand Isle and Isle la Motte, rich in rocky coves and wooded country; but Rogers grinned like a satyr at the suggestion of camping there.

"Yes, sir," he said, when he saw Ogden studying the heavy timber of Grand Isle, "that's might pretty country. When the French come looking for us, they'll look there first of all. If

122

they found us there, we'd be in a box. We'd have no place to retreat to, and that would be the end of us."

"I suppose so," Ogden admitted.

Rogers laughed abruptly. "You bet it's so! The place to hide is in the last place the French would think of looking— a place we can escape from if they find us. We'll camp right out on the flat land, and nowhere else!"

It takes time to conceal a hundred and sixty men and seventeen whaleboats in open country, but we did it—did it in the darkness, without lights or fires, and so thoroughly that when daylight came, we had apparently vanished from the face of the earth.

Through the 20th of September we lay opposite Grand Isle in a pelting rainstorm and saw nothing.

On the 21st, hiding abreast of a passageway between the islands, we saw four scout canoes prowling from cove to cove along the western shore. At mid-afternoon they went back to the southward again, passing half a mile from where we lay, but paying no attention to the low expanse of brush that screened us—brush so insignificant that a deer, standing in it, would have stuck out like a blue heron in a frog pond.

On the 22nd, our long row almost over, we made our camp on the peninsula separating Missisquoi Bay from the main body of Lake Champlain. At our left was the narrow strait between the Bay and the Lake; and ahead of us, beyond Missisquoi's blue surface, lay the endless flat expanse of Canada.

What we would find when we set out to cross that flat expanse, I didn't know. Rogers himself didn't know. Not even Captain Jacobs and his Stockbridge Indians knew. We were certain of just two things: the town of St. Francis was ninety miles due north, and in all that ninety miles there was no house, no road, not even a path.

When the men speculated as to what lay before them, Sergeant Bradley shut them up. "What do you care what it's like?" he growled. "You fellers been grumbling about not liking to row whaleboats, and about the blisters on your tails, and about having to shiver all day and work all night. Well, after tomorrow there wont be none of that! You wont have no boats to row; and you wont have no time to sit down, so you wont be bothered by blisters where you got 'em now. You'll march by day and sleep by night, like regular civilized human beings; so you'll have everything just the way you want it!"

I was so sick of whaleboats that what he said sounded, to me, encouraging. As long as I lived, I thought, I wouldn't care if I never saw another whaleboat; I wouldn't care if I never saw another boat of any kind again.

CHAPTER XXII

THE NEXT night we rowed cautiously into Missisquoi Bay, curved sharply to the right, and at dawn landed at its southernmost tip.

"This is the best we can do," Rogers told us. "There's firm land to hide the boats on, and the French may not find them there. Firm land's pretty scarce in this section." He laughed in a way I didn't like.

When we hauled the boats ashore, we found the bank almost flush with the water. It was land and yet not land. The trees grew from a spongy soil that oozed water at the smallest pressure; and as the lot of us went back and forth between the boats and the places where we deposited our belongings, our sloshings put me in mind of thousands of frightened fish caught in the shallows of a tide river.

The activity of Rogers was unremittently furious. He stationed men in trees to watch for the French: then drove the rest of us at cleaning, calking and storing the whaleboats; and when it came to hiding them, he laid hold of Number One with Ogden and the rest of us, and helped us drag it halfway to where we were to put it: then ran back to Number Two and did the same. The weight of our boat, as we dragged it, forced our legs deep into the marshy soil. Sergeant Bradley, helping to heave it across a deadfall, had his breeches pulled from him by the muck. One of my moccasins was sucked off, and both of Corporal Webster's, and when we went back to dig them out, we could scarcely find them, so completely were they engulfed. The mud seemed animate, pulled at us and squeezed us like some huge, half-slothful python that hoped to hold us and in time digest us.

When we had carried the boats a hundred yards to dry earth and packed their lockers with provisions we'd use after our return, we hid them beneath screens of pine. I had expected Canada to be cold, but the marshy forest steamed with a breathless, sultry heat. Clouds of mosquitoes rose from the swamp, whining and singing about our heads. With every breath, we drew them into our throats, and coughed and spat mosquitoes.

We all fared alike: every man carried a whole bologna sausage, a bag of meal, two cakes of chocolate and a canteen of rum, and I heard Rogers warning the officers: "Be sure each man fills his meal bag as full as he can. God knows when we'll get more! Make 'em carry enough for two weeks."

No sooner were the boats hidden than he paraded us. Possessed of a demon of impatience, he was up and down our lines and everywhere, urging us to move faster, and at the same time strapping on his knapsack and blanket, hanging his belt with hatchet and corn-meal bag. He hovered around us like a persistent bee, buzzing at us to be quick—to hurry. He went from man to man, tweaking knapsack straps, shaking powder-horns, looking at moccasins.

To me he said, to be noted in my orderly book, "I'm leaving two Indians on the high land to watch the boats—Lieutenant Solomon and Konkapot. They'll stay here till we come back, unless the French find the boats. In that case Solomon and Konkapot'll come after us to bring the report."

As the men jostled into position, fastening the last of their equipment to their belts, Sergeant Bradley hustled me into place behind Ogden and beside Jesse Beacham. Captain Jacobs and eight of his Stockbridge Indians, stripped to the waist and covered with grease and paint, ran ahead to act as advance scouts and stopped at the end of the high land to look back at us.

"Follow the lake shore to the northeastern tip of Missisquoi Bay," Rogers called up and down the lines. "That's our meeting place in case we have to scatter. We'll strike inland there. Until we're out of the swamps, we'll march abreast."

He looked from one end of his tiny army to the other, and I saw a hint of a dubious smile appear upon his heavy lips, as if we were only partly to his liking. From neck to thigh we were hung with clumsy equipment. Our labors in the heat and dampness had given us a sweaty and raffish look, and splashed us with mud and water; and some had even rubbed themselves with mud to protect themselves from mosquitoes. No wonder Rogers wore that dubious smile.

The advance guard of Indians ranged forward, vanished, and then the long advance of the rest of us began. We struck wet ground at once, of course, and plodded into it. I hoped that we might pass it soon, and that my breeches, unlike poor Bradley's, might remain upon me. Through the dense trees, to our left, we caught glimpses of blue Missisquoi Bay, as cool and tranquil as we were hot and uncomfortable.

Rogers led us silently, moving apparently with miraculous ease, while we followed him as noiselessly as men could who were half the time sloshing through marsh, and the other half forcing themselves through heavy undergrowth, fending branches from eyes and freeing knees of shrubs. Except for side glances to gauge our distances, we kept our eyes on the ground, so to be sure where to put our feet.

We stopped every hour at Rogers' orders. "Saves straggling," he said. "Can't afford straggling on *this* trip." Every time we thus stopped, he walked the length of the line, examining each man: then went behind us to stare toward the rear.

When, at dusk, we reached a dry ridge, he gave the word to camp for the night. The straps of my blanket and knapsack had cut me like iron bands, and to sit down was torture, but to get up was worse.

I stood there watching Rogers; wondering how he did it. He had called Bradley and Lieutenant Farrington, and with their help had hoisted himself to the lower branches of a tall spruce.

He went up it like a big squirrel, almost to the top, and clung there, peering back along our route. There was nothing, no exertion or hardship, he couldn't bear and be fresh at the end of it.

Through the dull fatigue that numbed me, his thick voice, mumbling to Ogden, was the last thing I heard at night, and it was that same thick voice that, in the morning, awakened me to a wet blanket and aching joints.

I can hear him now, shouting to the officers: "Get 'em up! They got ten minutes to get started! Get 'em up! Get 'em up!"

We were two days reaching the northern end of Missisquoi Bay; and it was at the end of the second day that I understood one of the reasons why Rogers so often studied the country we'd left behind us.

We had just made camp. From the penetrating feel of the windless air, which cut into us the moment we stopped moving, I knew we were in for a frost. We needed fires badly, not only to dry our blankets, but to warm our aching feet: to make hot food and hot rum; but since our orders forbade fire, we were doing what we could to make ourselves comfortable; and it was at this cheerless moment that we saw Bradley running into camp, and with him came Solomon and Konkapot.

"They found our boats!" Bradley called. "The damned French found our boats!"

I heard a hundred men repeating the words incredulously. "They found the boats: the damned French found our boats!"

The Rangers around me did simple and foolish things. One dusted the corn meal from his sausage and replaced it in his knapsack. Another pulled off his Scotch cap and peered within it. A third took his blanket from the ground and shook it like a tidy housewife. Perhaps they, like myself, were trying not to remember that our means of transportation were gone, our reserves of food lost: that we were deep in enemy country, with an enemy force behind us and entire enemy armies ahead of us and on our flank.

Perhaps they were merely trying not to wonder how many days of life were left to us.

CHAPTER XXIII

R_OGERS_ AND the two Indian runners were hemmed in by silent clusters of Rangers whose eyes seemed to glitter whitely in the semi-dark.

Lieutenant Dunbar made a move to push the men back, but Rogers stopped him. "All right, Lieutenant," he said. "We're all concerned in this."

He looked up at Solomon. "When was it? When did they find the boats?"

It was at sundown the day before, the Indian lieutenant told him. He and Konkapot must, therefore, have travelled in twenty-four hours as great a distance as we had covered in two full days. Consequently those who had found the boats must be at least one day behind us.

"How many?" Rogers asked.

Solomon ran a knotted string through his fingers to refresh his memory. Four canoes filled with Indians, he said, had entered the bay just at sunset. Behind them were twenty bateaux, each one loaded with twenty Frenchmen.

Almost immediately one of the canoes had discovered where we'd disembarked; then they followed our trail to the concealed boats, and whooped and fired muskets in great joy. When the bateaux had landed, Solomon and Konkapot, hidden, had seen the Indians cast about for further traces of us: then give it up because of darkness.

When the Frenchmen lit campfires, Solomon squirmed nearer them, saw the French commander divide his force into two parts, and to something more than half of the men distribute the supplies taken from our boats. From this, Solomon argued that in the morning half of the four hundred Frenchmen and probably all of the forty to fifty Indians would be sent in pursuit of us. Solomon and Konkapot had travelled all night, necessarily making slow progress, but as soon as light came, they'd come at top speed, not stopping all day for food or the slightest rest.

Rogers reached behind him, picked up his shot pouch, and fumbled in it. He brought out two six-inch carrots of tobacco, which he handed to Solomon and Konkapot, who went silently away. They were tired Indians. The circle of men opened to let them through: then crowded together once more with furtive movements and whisperings. As they stood there, staring at Rogers, their eyes gleamed whitely in the dusk.

Rogers again fumbled in his shot pouch, and this time he brought forth a phosphorus bottle and a piece of paper. He gave the bottle to Captain Ogden, unfolded the paper, and looked at the circle of faces. "We'll make up our minds right here and now," he said rather quietly, in a steady voice. "You men have all guessed where we're supposed to be going, but you haven't yet heard the orders. I'll read 'em to you."

Ogden pulled the spunk from the phosphorus bottle and held it, glowing, over the paper.

Rogers' eyes, in the bluish glare of the phosphorus, looked cavernous; and his heavy nose, enlarged by shadows, gave him the look of a grotesque, carved from stone.

"General Amherst signed these orders," he said, "and here's what they say:

"You will proceed to Missisquoi Bay, from whence you will march and attack the enemy's settlements on the south side of the River St. Lawrence, in such a manner as you shall judge most effectual to disgrace the enemy, and for the success and honor of His Majesty's arms. Remember the barbarities that have been committed by the enemy's Indian scoundrels on every occasion where they had an opportunity of showing their infamous cruelties on the King's subjects which they have done without mercy. Take your revenge, but don't forget that though those villains have dastardly and promiscuously murdered the women and children of all ages, it is my orders that no women or children are killed or hurt. When you have executed your intended service, you will return with your detachment to camp, or join me wherever the army may be."

Rogers wagged the paper at us. "Those are the orders!" I could see his head turning, like that of a gigantic owl, as he scanned our dim faces. "The French think they've trapped us. They've caught us where we can't get reinforcements, and they think this is the end of Rogers' Rangers. They've been trying to wipe us out for five years. Probably they're telling each other, right this minute, that they'll have our scalps inside three days. They're counting the money they'll get! They'll get a thousand pounds just for my head alone. Probably they've already arranged how to divide the money."

The circle of men swayed and muttered.

"They want us pretty bad, the French do," he continued, "but if you want to know how I feel, I'll tell you. I've worked too damned long and too damned hard over this corps, and so have you, to see it destroyed by two hundred lousy Frenchmen and a little parcel of Indians. We've always done things they thought couldn't be done, and I don't propose to stop now."

Almost irrelevantly he added, "Some of you fought in the Battle on Snowshoes last year. Lieutenant Phillips and Lieutenant Crofton, with twenty Rangers, were surrounded in that battle. The French offered 'em good terms, so they surrendered—they and their party. None of 'em ever came back. Maybe you remember what happened to 'em. Lieutenant Crofton's brother can tell you, in case you've forgotten. He's in Number One Company right now. Maybe he'd care to speak up and say."

Crofton spoke up. His voice was shrill. "They tore my brother's arms out of him. They chopped the ends of his ribs away from his backbone and pried 'em out through his skin, one by one. I don't care how many French and Indians there are! I don't care if there's a million of 'em! If there's only two hundred, I can pretty near kill 'em all myself!"

Nobody said a word.

Rogers nodded. "That's what happened to Lieutenant Crofton. Lieutenant Phillips had a strip of skin ripped upward from his stomach. They hung him in a tree by it while he was still alive. They chopped up his men with hatchets and threw the pieces up into the pines, so there wasn't any way of putting 'em together again."

The frosty air around us was so still that I could hear sentries, a hundred yards away, moving with sucking sounds in the wet soil.

"I've heard tell," Rogers continued, "that Rogers' Rangers are as well known in France and England as they are in America. I can't say as to that; but I know this: if there ever was a body of men that could march better or shoot better or fight better than Rangers, nobody's ever known about 'em."

He cleared his throat. The men around him were dark and quiet, like shadows, and seemingly as devoid of opinions.

"They think they've got us," Rogers said. "They think we're as good as dead. Well, they haven't got me, by God! They haven't got you: not yet they haven't! And I don't believe they ever will—not if we use our knowledge and fight the way we have in the past."

From the shadowy circle rose a babel of cries. I found myself repeating, over and over, "No, no! No, no!" I felt as though I had been one of these men all my life: as though the Indians had torn Crofton's ribs from his still-living body before my own eyes: as though I myself had seen Phillips hanged to a tree by a strip of his own flesh. Like all the green-clad men around me, I was confident that all the Frenchmen in the world couldn't harm us while Rogers led us.

I sat half the night with Rogers and Ogden in a sort of cave made of fallen logs. In it we had a fire, screened above and on three sides with blankets. Captains, lieutenants and sergeants crawled in on hands and knees to report the health of their detachments. None of the officers was sick, and only six of the men were unfit for duty. While I copied their reports in the orderly book, Rogers worked on a birch-bark map and conferred with Ogden over the location of rivers and valleys. Between the two of them they seemed to know every brook and hill south of Canada; but it was midnight before the map was finished to their satisfaction.

"Here," Rogers said to me,. "copy this map in the book. It's important." To Ogden he said, "Well, there's got to be an officer work his way back with those half-dozen sick men." He pulled at his heavy lower lip. "I can't spare any of 'em. I can't even spare any of the sergeants."

"McMullen's been limping," Ogden said.

"I know he has," Rogers said, "but I can't send McMullen. I had trouble with him last spring when Captain Burbank was captured. McMullen thought he ought to be made captain of the company in Burbank's place, and instead of that, I took over the company myself. McMullen was wild. He complained to Amherst, and tried to quit the Rangers. If I send him back, he'll be sure I'm doing it to get even with him."

Ogden said nothing. Rogers rubbed his huge hands together and breathed heavily. "All right," he told Ogden, "get McMullen in here."

Ogden thrust his head from the opening of our smoky den and told the sentry to call Lieutenant McMullen, and the night was so still we could hear McMullen groan when his sergeant waked him. He crawled in to us soon after, his eyes puffed half-shut with sleep and mosquito bites.

Rogers grinned at him. "What's the matter with your leg?"

"Leg?" McMullen asked. "What leg?"

"You know what leg."

McMullen shook his head. "Major, there isn't anything wrong with my leg, any more'n there is with the folks' tails that still got whaleboat blisters on 'em."

"Well," Rogers said, "there's six sick men out of this detachment, and somebody's got to lead 'em home and carry a message to Amherst at the same time. You're the one I've picked."

They stared at each other. Twice McMullen opened his lips to speak, and twice closed them again. A vein stood out in his forehead, and his puffed face seemed about to sizzle and explode.

"Now, Lieutenant," Rogers said, "I know what you're thinking. You're thinking I'm doing this out of cussedness, the way I kept you from getting command of your company."

"Yes," McMullen said, "I *am* thinking that."

"Look here," Rogers said, "I kept you from being captain of Burbank's company because you haven't had enough experience, and you're too impulsive besides. You're better as a lieutenant, right now, than as a captain; and I haven't got a better officer at getting through the woods. This message to Amherst has got to go through. If it doesn't get through, there'll be a lot of us, probably, that'll never be seen again. If you get through safely with it, I'll mention you in despatches, and it'll mean twice as much to you as just being one of twenty officers on this expedition."

"I'd rather be one of the twenty," McMullen said. "If you want to be sure the message goes through, why don't you send somebody who hasn't hurt his knee?"

"There's nothing the matter with your knee," Rogers said. "You just told me so yourself."

McMullen, fumbling at his swollen neck, stared helplessly at Ogden: at me. "Well," he said, "well—where's the message?"

Rogers unrolled the piece of birch-bark and held it before McMullen. "Now look here. You can remember this map as being a big inverted V. The base of the western leg rests on Crown Point, runs up Lake Champlain and ends at St. Francis, nearly on the St. Lawrence. The eastern leg runs from St. Francis down past Lake Memphremagog to the Connecticut River and rests on Number Four." He tapped the map with a thick forefinger. "Take a good look at this eastern leg—the one from St. Francis to Number Four. See those two big curves in the Upper Connecticut River? Those are the Cohase Intervales. I built a fort in the Cohase Intervales for Benning Wentworth four years ago, so I know 'em pretty well; but I don't believe anybody else knows anything about 'em. If we can reach those Intervales, we ought to be all right. I doubt anybody'd run the risk of following us farther than that. Is that clear?"

McMullen, running his finger along the eastern leg of that inverted V, nodded.

Again Rogers tapped the map. "Look: at the lower end of the Cohase Intervales, the Ammonoosuc River and Wells River run into the Connecticut right opposite each other. It was at the mouth of the Ammonoosuc that I built the fort. That's sixty miles above Number Four. It's easy to find. Lieutenant Stephens was stationed at Number Four last winter. He can tell Amherst just where I want the provisions left."

"I can tell him myself," McMullen said.

"All right," Rogers said. "Start for Crown Point first thing in the morning. No matter what happens, get there. Get there as fast as you can, but don't take chances. The French and Indians that found our whaleboats will keep on following the main body of us, of course, so you make a circuit to the eastward and get around 'em—a fifty-mile detour if you have to. If you're discovered, abandon your sick men and let 'em look out for themselves. You've got to get through! You've *got* to!"

McMullen nodded.

"Don't tell any of those six men what I tell you, unless you're dying. If you're sure you're done for, and the others have a chance to get away, tell the likeliest one. Otherwise keep it to yourself. No matter what happens to you, no matter what they do to you, don't let any Frenchman get these plans out of you." McMullen eyed him bleakly and again nodded.

"When you reach Crown Point," Rogers continued, "go straight to General Amherst. Tell him we lost the boats. Tell him I didn't give you a written message for fear you'd be captured. Tell him that when we leave St. Francis, we'll go by way of Memphremagog and the Connecticut. Tell him I want provisions sent to my old fort at the mouth of the Ammonoosuc and left there under guard—provisions for a

hundred and fifty men—a hundred and fifty hungry men.
Just repeat those orders, Lieutenant."

In a wooden voice McMullen said, "Provisions for a hundred and fifty men to the mouth of the Ammonoosuc, opposite the mouth of Wells River, at the end of the Cohase
Intervales. You're coming back by way of the other leg of
the triangle whose base rests on Number Four."

Rogers grinned. "That's right. That's how we'll come back
—if we come back."

CHAPTER XXIV

Two HUNDRED Frenchmen
and nearly fifty Indians were hard on our heels, Jacobs had
said; and when McMullen and the six sick men had drifted
off to the eastward in the misty dawn of September 26th,
there were a hundred and fifty-three of us left to outdistance
those two hundred and fifty Frenchmen and Indians, do
what had to be done at St. Francis; then get away—if we
could.

No sooner had we left the northern end of Missisquoi Bay
that morning than we entered a spruce bog. The water was
a foot deep, and in places even deeper, where the current
had hollowed out channels like running brooks, into which
we sometimes stumbled and sometimes fell full length. When
Indians went out on either side to scout for ridges along
which we might make greater speed, they returned with the
word that there was no dry land: that it was all bog. Although they climbed trees to look for solid footing, they saw
none, came down and reported the whole land to be a vast
wet sponge.

Water stood everywhere between the trees, concealing irregularities in the ground. Young growth, choked to death
by its own profusion, lay ankle deep, knee high, belt high,
breast high, head high. Blown-down trunks rotted in the
water with small spruces sprouting densely along their

length. Dead branches were heaped in windrows; and one who stepped upon them plunged through the tangle, raking his leg from ankle to thigh on jagged points. Living branches clutched the garments, scratched at the eyes, plucked the caps from our heads, tore holes in our clothes, and gored us through the holes.

Through this terrible country we marched in triple file, and the men on either side of me seemed crackling and splashing shadows in the undergrowth. Sometimes I heard the voice of Rogers, huskily calling the course to Konkapot, who moved between him and the Stockbridge Indians to relay messages.

It was part of my duty to write down these changes of directions in the little book. "There's never been a map of this country," Rogers had told me, "and we'll make one now. If we get out of this, we'll probably have to do it all over again some day!"

There was little imagination to his description of our travels, but he worked hard to make it accurate.

It read simply enough—"September 26th. North-north-east a mile and a half, northeast one mile, crossed two small brooks running southwest, went a northeast course half a mile, north a mile, northwest half a mile, crossed a brook running west by north, travelled north a mile, north-north-east half a mile, went three miles due north, and came to a brook about two yards wide, running due west, crossed it, and encamped about thirty yards from it. This day saw no game."

To attain this simple record, he kept his compass perpetually in his hand: he counted the number of steps he took, and had others do the same: he went back and forth along the detachment, stopped and watched them pass him, sweating and cursing, wrestling their way through the dead growth, crashing through windfalls of branches. He climbed trees: went circling off by himself: came splashing back to shout to Captain Jacobs to slant off to the north-north-east.

All day we saw no really dry land, and we ate standing in water. Sundown found us still laboring through the swamp. I felt parboiled, burned out, and at the same time sopping wet, soaked and chilled. It seemed to me that every muscle of mine had been beaten with hammers, and I knew from the look of Bradley and Crofton and the other men near me that they felt no better than I did. Their faces were liver-colored with fatigue: their eyes sunk in their heads: the outline of their teeth revealed, as is a mummy's. Their lips were slack; their mouths half-open.

Jesse Beacham, who was sixty years old if he was a day, seemed to stand it better than any of us, barring Rogers himself.

When we were finally halted, it was almost dark and we had made nine miles. The water was halfway to our knees, so that the only way we could be free of it was to cut trees and climb into the branches. Working in pairs, we chopped young spruces with our hatchets, and by placing three close together and lopping the limbs from their upper sides, we made something like platforms, held above the water by the limbs underneath; and the tips of boughs, properly placed on these platforms, made passable sleeping places.

Jesse Beacham, working with me, seemed able to see in the dark, and he could make a bed of spruce boughs more rapidly than an inn-keeper could make one from two blankets and a feather-mattress.

As soon as we could, we settled ourselves, soaked from head to foot with perspiration and brown swamp-water, although the branches, beneath our wet buckskins, felt like the ridges of washboards. We put our knapsacks beneath our heads, placed our muskets between us where we could get at them quickly, and ate our supper of sausage, corn meal and rum.

"Jesse," I said, "don't you get sick of sausage and corn meal?"

"No," Jesse said. "No. If there aint nothing to eat but sausage and corn meal, you like it. If you had to choose between sausage and corn meal and sausage and beans, you'd hate both of 'em." That helped me to eat, and I began to realize that old Jesse was more of a comfort than a younger man could have been.

We chewed our sausages and listened to curious noises— the sound of articles falling in the water: breaking trees: the blundering splashes made by men whose platforms were insecure: the snuffling and coughing of those who had caught colds. I could hear Rogers' heavy voice, locating his officers —calling Jacobs, Dunbar, Turner, Avery, Grant, Farrington; fixing their positions in his mind. I heard him ordering out sentries, rear, front and both flanks, and thanked God I could lie on knobby branches, uncomfortable as they were, and wrap myself in a blanket, sopping wet though it was.

"Jesse," I said, "I wish I had his energy, don't you?"

"Hell, no," Jesse said. "I'd ruther be like me."

CHAPTER XXV

WE ENTERED the bog on the 26th of September, and were in it nine days.

On the 27th Rogers routed us from our spruce hammocks with the first graying of the sky, and in ten minutes we were wallowing forward—north, north-north-east, north-east by east, north by east, and then north again—sweating, straining, stumbling through a boggy tangle of spruce in no way different from that of the day before.

On the 28th, on the 30th, on the first of October, the 2nd of October, the 4th of October, it was all the same—the same water, the same trees, the same tangled hoorahs' nests of dried branches, the same snags under water, the same knobby platforms at night, the same incessant hurry to keep ahead of the Frenchmen and Indians in our rear.

Only the men changed. Jacobs and his Indians looked little different, since they were thin to begin with, and naturally malignant in their appearance, in addition to being free of the curse of whiskers; but the others grew more and more hairy every day and, for the most part, more evil looking.

A few were improved by their changed appearance. Sergeant Bradley, that pale and soured man, sprouted red whiskers that gave him an air of raffish gaiety. Jesse Beacham's beard was white as snow, and as it lengthened, the younger Rangers took notice of it, calling him Grandad, old Kriss Kringle, the Snow King, or the Spirit of Niagara. To all such epithets Jesse only looked benevolent, as an ancient angel might look, peering through the interstices of a fleecy cloud.

Our buckskins, too, from the constant whipping of the spruce branches and the everlasting wetness, gave way here and there, developing rips which we had no chance to mend.

Worst of all, our moccasins became pulpy, so that we either had to take them off and tie them around our necks, or have no footgear left by the time we reached dry land—if that time ever came.

I asked Jesse Beacham whether, in his opinion, it was better to go barefoot, or to trust to luck that we might soon be out of the bog. "I don't know," Jesse said. "I got to give it some thought; but I guess I better take off my moccasins while I do my thinking, so's I'll have 'em when I decide what to do about 'em." I followed Jesse's example and went barefoot. The chill of the water seemed to have driven blood and feeling from my feet, so that stumbling or stepping on sharp branches was only painful at first.

It was when the moccasins began to wear out that now and then we became aware that one and another of us had simply disappeared. We had started from Missisquoi Bay with one hundred and fifty-three. On the 29th of September a man was missing from Lieutenant Grant's detachment. On the 30th another vanished from Lieutenant Dunbar's.

When the first man's absence was reported to Rogers, he sent Jacobs and Konkapot back along our trail to search. They couldn't find him, and we never knew whether he had fallen so far behind that the French had caught him, or whether he had stumbled into a hole and drowned.

Rogers seemed to think the first explanation was the right one. He went back among the men and told them to move faster. "If some of those Frenchmen get ahead of us, so we're caught front and rear," he said, "you wouldn't like it! You'd understand you'd better have kept moving—so keep moving!"

So we did. We splashed doggedly onward, and as for me, I was going as fast as I could all the time.

On the 2nd of October two more men disappeared—one from Lieutenant Farrington's detachment and one from ours. The one from our own was Webster, the lugubrious corporal who had learned of his wife's death the day before our expedition started.

I had come to like Webster. He never grumbled, and twice he had carried my musket while I made notes for Rogers. It was toward sundown when I missed him from his regular place in the line. I looked back, thinking he might have changed his position. When I couldn't find him, I shouted his name, but heard nothing except the splashing of the nearby men.

"When'd you see him last?" Jesse Beacham asked me.

I couldn't remember.

"I'd better go back and look for him," I told Jesse.

"I wouldn't if I was you," Jesse said. "I'd keep travelling."

"My God, Jesse," I said, "we can't leave Webster like this, feeling the way he does about his wife."

"Maybe," Jesse said, "it'll be kind of a relief to him to be left alone."

Rogers heard us arguing and came back to walk with us. "Who's gone?" he wanted to know.

When we told him, he said it was too bad. "Maybe," he added, "he was discouraged. They go quick when they're discouraged."

He looked hard at me. "There's no use hunting for Webster. If you found him, you couldn't carry him. It would only mean the French would get both of you."

Then, seeing that I was silent, he said abruptly, "Webster knew what would happen if he couldn't keep up. He understands you'd like to help him—that we all would. He understands, the same as I would myself."

With that he splashed ahead to overtake Ogden, and I tried to keep my mind off Webster. I thought probably he'd made himself one of those soggy spruce platforms and lain down upon it. Maybe the French and the Indians wouldn't find him. . . .

On the 4th of October, early in the afternoon, we crossed a mound on which white Indian Pipes grew from a smooth bed of pine needles—the first dry patch we had seen since the 26th of September. It wasn't much of a mound, being about a hundred yards long and thirty yards wide; but it put heart into us. We had come to think there was no dry land left in the world.

When some of the men stopped upon it, staring as if in surprise at their pallid, parboiled feet, Rogers drove them on, into the bog beyond.

"Keep going!" he urged. "Get off this mound and don't

leave traces! We're damned near there. Keep going! It's not much farther. Keep going!"

We stumbled on into the bog; it seemed to me the water was shallower, and by mid-afternoon I was sure of it. I sank in only to my ankle-bones. Again and again we crossed patches of dry land—patches the size of a kitchen table: of a whaleboat: of a barn door.

In place of the muck and tangled roots through which we had wallowed for nine long days, we began to feel firm ground beneath our feet; and then, toward sundown, there was solid earth everywhere, except for puddles in scattered hollows. We were out of the bog at last.

Like new men we hurried on over dry ground until stopped by thick darkness. To sleep on dry land once more, without the labor of chopping a platform of boughs, seemed a heaven-sent luxury, even though my clothes and blankets were as wet as ever, the camp as devoid of fire, and my supper only a handful of corn meal.

We were close to our goal, and watching Rogers, I knew it. He climbed a tree and made Lieutenant Turner and Jacobs do the same. Then, when he was down, he made a circuit of the camp, warning every sentry as he came to him. "Use your eyes and your nose!" I heard him say. "If they catch us, it'll be tonight. Keep watching and keep sniffing!"

God knows when he slept—if he did. Again and again I heard his voice, dimly, in my sleep. When Sergeant Bradley rolled me from my blanket in the morning, it was still dark, and the first thing I heard was Rogers, warning Captain Jacobs not to let the Indians get out of hand if we stumbled unexpectedly on St. Francis. "You tell 'em to spend their time killing," he said. "No torture! Kill fast!"

We were on the march with the first faint light of dawn. The ground continued to rise and to harden, and our breeches and what was left of our moccasins began to be almost dry. The worst of our journey, I felt, must be behind us, since nothing could be worse than that endless spruce bog.

War, however, is one of the things that never improve with age. We had no more than started when Konkapot and Solomon came running back to Rogers. "River!" Solomon said exultantly. "Big river!"

"That's it, by God!" Rogers cried. "It's the St. Francis!"

CHAPTER XXVI

W<small>HEN WE</small> had drawn the charges from our muskets and reloaded, we lay concealed in the brush on the river bank, looking for enemy Indians and for the town we had come so far to attack. We saw only a brown flood that I took to be thirty to forty yards wide. It surged between gravelly banks so high that in places they were cliffs. So turbulent and swollen was the stream that all the water in the bogs we had just crossed might have been trying to force its way to freedom between its banks. Its brown current swirled in whirlpools; in midstream the sharpness of its riffles gave it the look, I thought, of brown ice.

"Let's see that book," Rogers said to me. He took it and pored over the records of our journey, his thick lips moving as he read. He got out Stark's rough map and scrutinized it. Finally he went up a tree. When he came down, his mind was made up. "I can't see any low land to the north of us," he said. "The town's only two miles from the flats of Lake St. Peter, so we're nowhere near it. We ought to be as much as fifteen miles upstream, so we'll cross right here. Then we'll be on the same side as the town."

"How many rafts shall we make?" Ogden asked.

"Rafts be damned!" Rogers cried. "There's no time for rafts! Tell 'em to plug their muskets! Have 'em lash their packs and blankets on their shoulders! We'll wade it!"

The banks of the St. Francis were covered with hardwood growth—maples, beech and oak. Their leaves, bitten by recent frosts, had turned fiery scarlet, smoldering red, blazing yellow; and my companions, against this flaming foliage, put me in mind of demons crawling blunderingly out of hell. We had stripped off our leggins and tied them to our packs; and our packs, in turn, were lashed high on our shoulders, so that our heads protruded turtle-like from bulging humps. These misshapen upper bodies were supported by lean legs, bleached pallid by days of soaking in the bog. We must have made a strange and ludicrous spectacle, crowded close together to watch Rogers, who knelt half-naked at the water's edge and thrust with a long spruce pole to test the depth.

Behind us, sprawled at the top of the bank, lay the Stockbridge Indians, peering back into the forest on the lookout for the French. Before us the river brawled and roared, a disconcerting sight.

Captain Ogden, at a word from Rogers, stepped off the bank and into the stream. His arms waved frantically; his legs flew from under him, and his body plunged beneath the surface in a welter of yellow foam. Rogers caught him, swung him back to shore, and the half-drowned officer crawled out on hands and knees, coughing and choking.

Then using the pole as a prop, Rogers himself stepped in. The current boiled around his knees: the pole vibrated. He looked back at us and grinned, and it seemed to me that instead of our commander, I saw, in this exultant grin, the look of a reckless boy who laughs at his fellows because he outdoes them.

I could make out that he was bawling something to Ogden, but I could hear nothing above the roar of the river. A tall Ranger put down his musket on the bank, edged into the stream and caught Rogers by the belt. Another Ranger followed, seizing the belt of the man who had preceded him. Headed by Rogers, a line of Rangers moved into the rushing water with painful slowness.

The water rose around their waists; caught at their clumsy packs. They leaned against the roaring current, a human chain, slowly fighting their way across.

In midstream, the riffles splashed over Rogers' head. He stared owlishly back at us, gasping, his eyes pouchy, his long hair dangling like seaweed in his eyes and along his thick nose.

Inch by inch he passed through the riffles. The water was shallower. He moved more rapidly, pulling his line of Rangers after him. He was waist deep: then thigh deep. Like a draggled merman he reached the bank and hooked his arm around a tree.

Between him and us stretched a causeway of Rangers, the

brown water of the St. Francis piling against them and boiling downstream in yellowish foam.

One by one we made our way along this causeway, fumbling from human link to human link like mountain climbers on a cliff, moving from one precarious toe-hold to another.

Many of us carried an extra musket, since those who formed the chain had carried none; and where to carry those two muskets seemed to me the greatest problem that life could hold. I buttoned them inside my shirt and strapped my belt around them, so that their muzzles stood three feet above my head. At each step their locks tore at my stomach.

The stones at the bottom of the river-bed moved beneath my feet; the icy current dragged at thighs and hips. There was a singular dizzying fascination to the swirling torrent that wrenched at me with a continuous sucking roar.

When halfway across I heard a chorus of yells. The French, I thought, had caught us; but the Ranger to whom I clung urged me onward. "It's Foyle," he said. "Lost his footing. Dropped his muskets."

It was Rogers himself who pulled me to the bank. "Get the men out of the river," he was calling to his officers. "Get 'em out dead or alive! If any of 'em float down to St. Francis, we're done for!"

I ran downstream, and found Ogden running with me. We could see someone rolling like a log in the sharp waves. We got him by cutting across a bend. It was Foyle. His arms were tangled in the straps of his knapsack, and he was dead; but we put him on the bank, head downward, in the vague hope that the water might drain from him and let him come to life. There was nothing else we could do.

When we returned, the human chain still held, and the Stockbridge Indians, who were like dogs in the water, were diving and groping for lost muskets. Another Ranger besides Foyle had been drowned; and six more, wrenched from the living chain at the beginning of the crossing, had been spewed out on the far bank by the boiling current. Two lay at the edge of the stream, unable to crawl from the shallows. Four had dragged themselves to higher land and sprawled there, naked, looking over at us. When Rogers signalled to them to cross, they sat motionless, too exhausted to move.

"One of 'em's mine," Lieutenant Avery said. "He's got the flux. I'll go over and get him."

Rogers shook his head. "You'll stay where you are! You'd get drowned yourself if you tried to carry him over. We'll have to leave those men. They're better off back there than they'd be over here, and that chain of men can't stand where they are, waiting for sick men to get better!"

He gave sharp orders to the nearest man of the living chain. "Tell those sick men to move to the eastward and try to keep out of the way of the French who'll follow us. Pass the word, and tell the last man to let go when he's delivered the message."

Those who had crossed, officers and men alike, stood silent, staring over at the six men, and in the silence Rogers seemed to feel disapproval. "Too bad," he said. "Too bad, but if they can get far enough to the eastward, they've got a chance. We've got to keep moving, gentlemen."

Captain Jacobs crawled out on the bank, dragging three muskets with him. Several, he said, were still at the bottom of the river, and he thought if he had time, he could get them.

"Time!" Rogers echoed. "We're moving on!"

One by one the human links of the chain emerged shivering from the rapids and came stiffly among us, seeking their muskets.

Rogers herded us rapidly from the water's edge. "Get away from this river bank," he ordered. "Get onto high land and get dressed. Draw your loads and reload with buckshot!"

Ogden asked whether men should be sent to bury Foyle. Rogers shook his head. "We've got fifteen miles to go! Maybe it's more! Get forward!"

When the officers made their returns, there were one hundred and forty-two of us left. Five were without muskets.

Rogers hitched up his leggins and settled his black infantryman's hat more firmly on his head. "Why," he said, "that's not bad! Things might be worse—lots worse! I could take Quebec with a hundred and forty-two men as good as this! We'll keep the same order. Stockbridge Indians in advance: Lieutenant Turner's detachment in the rear."

After what we had been through, the Indian trail along the high bank of the river was as easy to travel as a postroad. The trees were enormous: the undergrowth long since killed down. Beneath our feet was packed earth and brown pine needles, springy to the touch. If I could have had a de-

cent dinner in me, in place of the few scrapings of corn meal
that my pouch had yielded, and if there had been no Frenchmen following on our heels, I think I might really have enjoyed that hurrying march down the St. Francis.

The long line of men in ragged buckskins and green
Scotch caps slipped through the darkening forest as noiselessly as owls on the hunt.

It was nearly night when Rogers, finding a tall pine from
which to make an observation, gave the order to halt. He
was on his way up the tree before the file-closers had come
in.

We stared up the tree after him. The detachment gathered
around it, their upturned faces blobs of pallor in the dusk.
He came sliding and scratching down and dropped among
us like a big cat. He straightened his clothes and dug pine
needles from his neck. "Well," he said, "we're there! I can
see the fires, not three miles away. It's the town!"

It was the fifth day of October—the twenty-second day of
our journey from Crown Point. We had been twenty-two
days without fires; without cooked food; without dry blankets; without shelters over our heads; without clean clothes.
And this was the campaign my father, over a month ago,
had characterized as being almost over.

CHAPTER XXVII

ROGERS, IT seemed to me,
could go beyond the limits of human endurance; and then,
without rest, buoyantly hurl himself against the fiercest opposition of Nature or man, or both. There was something
elemental about him—something that made it possible for
men who were dead with fatigue to gain renewed energy
from him, just as a drooping wheat-field is stirred to life by
the wall of wind that runs before a thunder-storm.

We'd no sooner made camp that night than he called for
Lieutenant Turner and Ensign Avery; and the three of them

moved silently off into the darkness, Rogers leading at a gait so sharp it was a sort of inaudible run.

He left one order behind him. "Make 'em sleep," he told Ogden. "They're going to need it!"

Sleep, for me, I thought, was out of the question, for I was in a turmoil over the thought that in a few hours we would be fighting. There was no possible way to escape it; and I suspected that I was already as good as dead. I saw with dreadful clarity what a fool I had been about everything, and wished to God I had stayed at home, content with an orderly existence. Of what use to me was my foolish, youthful desire to paint, and how would my knack for drawing and for color benefit me when I lay scalped and mangled in a Canadian forest? If I had stayed at home, where I could see Elizabeth's eyes darting amused and sidelong glances at me: where I could have sat comfortably in our warm kitchen on a frosty morning and watched my mother pouring flapjack batter . . .

Sergeant Bradley shook me to consciousness. "Come on," he was saying. "Come on! The Major's back. Everything's all right! Come on: we're going to attack!"

The moon, almost full, touched the tall trees with silver and gave us a faint light, even in the blackest shadows. All around me I could see men moving: hear straps being tightened; ramrods being drawn and rapped home again. "What time is it?" I asked Bradley.

"Time to get up! Come on, for God's sake. The Major's going to talk to us."

I collected my equipment and felt myself all over to be sure I had everything—orderly book, bayonet, hatchet, flints, bullets, powder, blanket, knife, cup, fork, salt, razor, soap. The soap was little smaller than when I had left Crown Point, but when I sniffed at it, wondering whether I'd ever have another opportunity to clean myself, Bradley pulled at me impatiently, pressing me toward a tight-packed throng of men. They had a steamy, animal smell—a smell of wet buckskins, musky bodies, oily hair. Over their shoulders I could see the blue-green glow of a sulphur spunk shining on Rogers' big nose and thick lips. He was comparing his compass with Ogden's and Dunbar's. When he looked up, the spunk threw shadows over his eyes and the hollows of his face, giving it the look of a grinning death's head.

"Everybody accounted for?" he asked.

There was a muttering of "all present" from the sergeants.

"All right," Rogers said. "Now pay attention! Lieutenant Turner and Ensign Avery went with me to look at the town. It stretched along the high bank, just the right size and position for an attack, and the trail leads straight to it. Everything's in our favor—even the wind. It's in the west, and the dogs can't get our smell."

"Good thing for the dogs," somebody muttered. The men tittered with the sound of wind stirring dry leaves.

Rogers seemed not to hear. "We went up trees and watched 'em. They haven't got a sentry out—not one! They've been dancing nearly all night. They were dancing when we got there, and dancing when we came away at midnight—howling and whooping and having a hell of a time. Maybe they're drunk, but don't count on it."

From the mass of Rangers before him there rose a pleased murmuring.

"Now bear this in mind," Rogers went on. "We can't waste time! We got to work fast and get away, because they'll be after us like hornets. We're under orders to wipe out this town, so see you do it! There's only one way to do it and that's to kill every Indian capable of bearing arms. Kill 'em quick and kill 'em dead! Don't let a damned Indian get away, provided he's big enough to fight. But for God's sake don't kill any of our own Indians, and don't kill any white captives. Our own Indians have white stripes painted around their bodies, and the tops of their heads are painted white. As for captives, there'll be some around; so keep your eyes open and don't make mistakes."

He paused. There was something so peculiarly exciting about those thick accents of his that I found myself shaking. His voice grew harsher. "Our food's gone. So's our clothes. We'll need food and clothes if we expect to be alive this time next week."

His sulphur spunk flickered and went out, and his face disappeared as though it had been that of a grinning demon who, having warned us, had vanished into the realm of disembodied spirits, but his voice went on. "Don't forget how they treated Phillips and Crofton. If we don't wipe 'em out now, they'll go down into New England and skin our people alive, the way they always have."

There was a moment of silence, as heavy as the forest gloom around us.

"Here's the way we'll do it," that thick voice continued. "We'll move up to the edge of the woods and wait for daylight. Captain Ogden's detachment and Captain Jacobs' Indians will attack the right of the town. That's the downstream end, and downstream's the way they'll run if they get the chance."

Everything was planned, as neat as a pin. We were to move out of the woods in a long line, Captain Ogden, Captain Jacobs, Lieutenant Farrington and Lieutenant Grant leading; in the center, Lieutenant Dunbar, Lieutenant Turner and Ensign Avery; in the rear, Lieutenant Jenkins, Lieutenant Campbell and Lieutenant Curgill. When Rogers whistled, the officers and their sergeants were to break down the doors of the houses; and the rest of us, ten paces back, were to wait for the Indians to come out. One man from each detachment was to hunt out a kettle, find food to fill it, take the kettle to a common center, and get the food to cooking as soon as possible.

Rogers himself would be at the downstream end of the town—in case anyone wanted him, he said. Prisoners were to be brought to Lieutenant Dunbar, who would halt his detachment at the drum.

I asked Jesse Beacham what he meant by the drum. Jesse said patiently that when I got where we were going, I'd probably see something that looked like a drum, because if Rogers spoke of anything, you could usually depend on seeing it when you got there.

"Ready," Rogers said. "As they've got no sentries out, we'll travel single file. We'll use no flankers and no advance scouts. Keep in touch with the man in front. That's all. Come on."

I heard Ogden call for Sergeant Bradley, who took me by the knapsack and pulled me forward. Someone caught the slack of my buckskin shirt and shuffled me, and hands fumbled at me as we moved off past men who whispered irascibly and breathed hard.

The hurrying of the men along that dark and narrow lane between the trees caused a rubbing, whispering, hissing sound that might have been made by a gargantuan serpent. They seemed to flicker through the patches of moonlight like specters.

I felt a stirring in the still, cold air—the stirring of approaching dawn; and at last, on that faint and frosty breeze, I caught the scent of wood-smoke.

Ogden, standing in the path, stopped us. "Dump your packs."

We put our blankets, our knapsacks and everything we could spare in compact piles beside the path: then squatted in the trail, working our bayonets over our musket-sights.

The moonlight on the treetops had dimmed, now, and the shadows around us were pallid in a ghostly light—the light of false dawn. In that ghostly light Captain Jacobs and his Indians, crowded close behind us, had the look of dismembered phantoms. Because of the white paint upon them, they seemed like human lobster-buoys, bobbing silently in the murk. I could faintly see the other detachments; hear them dump their packs and adjust their bayonets.

Somewhere in front of us I heard the strident crowing of a rooster.

The false dawn had passed and the shadows were blacker than before. Not far from us a dog barked mournfully, perfunctorily. The men whispered and muttered, fearful that the barking might arouse the sleeping town. I wanted to speak to Jesse Beacham about that dog, but I knew that if I did, my teeth would chatter. I was cold and hungry; worse of all, I was afraid: afraid of the dog: afraid of what lay before us: afraid of being afraid. The dog, as if dissatisfied with his first attempt, barked again—a bark lugubrious beyond belief —and Jesse Beacham sighed shiveringly. It came to me that Jesse was as hungry and cold and afraid as I.

Then I realized that real dawn was coming upon us, and I saw Rogers and Ogden, gray figures against dark tree trunks, staring out at a clearing that began to be revealed before us.

Rogers looked up at the sky: then came back to us, and Sergeant Bradley rose to meet him. "You'll take the down-stream end," Rogers said. "Don't make a noise, and don't let 'em get away." He moved along the recumbent line, which was still strung out in single file along the trail, and I saw Lieutenant Farrington, Lieutenant Dunbar, Lieutenant Grant, rising one by one to take his orders: then lying down again.

The mist in the clearing was thin. It rolled up like smoke from the bed of the river, billowing slowly; and through it, as through a veil, we saw the houses of St. Francis. They were strewn along the river bank, on each side of a church with a skeleton steeple, in which hung a bell. Some of the cabins were made of logs and some of planks, like the homes of white men; but they stood at odd angles, as if each one had been pushed a little out of position, so that they had the unreality of houses seen in a dream. It was hard to realize that out of this miserable line of hovels had come the painted demons who had terrorized all New England for a century: that it was in this very town that young Richard Nason and little Sarah Nason, ancestors of mine, had lived for years as captives.

The place looked deserted—dead. Nothing moved in the clearing or near the houses, and that look of deadness was heightened by the frost that lay whitely on every roof as well as on cultivated patches in the clearing. The patches were little farms—corn fields: melon and pumpkin patches. In some were piles of pumpkins.

Rogers came back, loosened his hatchet in his belt, picked up his musket; then swung his arm, scythe-like. The white-smeared Indians, the whole long line of green-clad, bearded men, rose to their feet and began to run into the clearing.

CHAPTER XXVIII

At every step I took, I expected the doors and windows of that misty village to fly open: to spout fire against the long thin line of Rangers running toward it.

The noise we made seemed loud enough to wake the dead. Our feet crunched the frosty ground: our powder-horns and shot pouches thumped and rattled at our hips.

What I was doing seemed familiar, as if I had often done this very thing; and it came to me, as I ran, that it was like the final stealthy race to reach a river bank before hidden ducks leaped out of range.

There was a pink streak in the eastern sky, and by its pale light, as we ran panting on, I could see poles before the black cabins—poles with hairy discs hanging from their tips; and I could smell the place. It had a rank but pleasant odor, as of herbs mixed with grease, sweet-grass and wood-smoke. The strip of ground before the houses was as hard and level as the roadway in a city: as smooth as a dance floor; and I understood that it was indeed a dance floor, where the Indians danced. In its center stood a drum, made of a tree trunk as big around as a washtub and almost shoulder-tall.

The windows of the houses were unglazed: some were black holes: others were covered with paper on which were painted fish, birds, animals. Skins lashed to frames leaned against the walls. The hairy discs on the poles, I now saw, were scalps, and there were hundreds of them, moving gently in the dawn breeze. I wondered if the scalp of Crofton's brother was among them.

We ran on and on across the clearing, our eyes fixed upon that line of dark houses on the river bank, expecting each moment that Indians would burst out of the doors and that fire would leap at us from the windows. I was near the head of our people, and with those who were to attack the far end of the village. We passed the flimsy little church with its skeleton steeple: we passed the cabins beyond the church, and came abreast of the last buildings at the lower end of the town. A skinny black dog with a yellow face ran out at us. His hackles rose and his lips drew back over his teeth, but before he could even snarl, a thrown hatchet struck his head and he fell on his side, his legs jerking.

The whole line had stopped, crouching, their muskets ready. Rogers, ahead of us, whistled through his fingers—a whistle that cut our straining ears like a knife. And then, toward the silent houses, raced the lieutenants and sergeants, while Jacobs and his Stockbridge Indians dodged among the cabins like shadows. Directly before me I saw a low log house with the river running dimly behind it. Sergeant Bradley and Lieutenant Farrington threw themselves against the rough door of that house; the door broke from its hinges with a splitting crash.

Then, almost in the same instant, the whole village seemed

to erupt with yells, crashes and screams. From the doorway smashed by Bradley and Farrington there came stumbling an old Indian with a blanket tied around his waist; he tripped on the blanket and fell. Bradley sank a hatchet into the small of the brown back, then jumped to one side.

Out through the doorway burst three squaws, their faces contorted. Bradley thrust his foot before them and they fell in a heap. A well-sized Indian boy, trying to leap over them, fell too, and Farrington was on his back like a cat. I saw white eyes roll upward in the twisted, copper-colored face: then Farrington's hatchet cut down through them.

The squaws, covered with blood, scrambled to their feet. Bradley caught two by the arms, rammed his bayonet through their upper garments and rushed them, whimpering, behind our waiting line. The other ran like a frightened duck, toeing in.

Two faces showed in the doorway, and Jesse Beacham's musket roared in my ear. One of the faces vanished: the other, half shot away, came slowly into full view: the body beneath it sank forward across the threshold.

A girl and two boys squirmed around it as it fell and ran toward us, dodging from side to side, as if hunting a hole. One of the boys was almost the size of my brother Odiorne. When Crofton's musket swung toward him, I pushed it away and caught the boy.

He was greasy and like an eel in my hands, writhing and twisting to break my hold, but I dropped my musket and got him between my knees, where he squirmed and bucked so hard that it seemed impossible one boy could move in so many directions at one time. Crofton stood before me, looking for an opportunity to sink his bayonet in the writhing red body.

"Too young," I said. "Prisoner."

Crofton stared wildly at me; then turned back to watch the doorway. I rapped the base of the boy's skull with my fist; and when he lay still, I picked up my musket, took him by the arm and dragged him to Dunbar's detachment.

Dunbar's men were in a ring around the drum, and Dunbar himself stood upon the drum, giving orders. Pressed close to the drum were squaws, covered with dirt, their clothes half torn off: a few young girls, one wholly naked: another boy.

They were huddled on the ground, not moving or making a sound, and not one looked toward the bedlam beyond.

I threw the boy at the feet of one of Dunbar's Rangers: then ran back to my own detachment.

The strip of pink in the eastern sky had turned to a brilliant red, and in its rosy light the darting movements of the Rangers seemed purposeless, like the erratic scuttling of water-beetles on a placid pond. The rattling of their muskets was as rapid as the crackling of twigs in a newly-lit fire, and overhead everywhere drifted layers of gunpowder smoke turning pink in the sunrise.

Two more Indians lay on the ground before the end house when I got back, one a woman—a squaw. Crofton, his face crimson, was shouting like a madman: "There's more of 'em! I saw 'em! I tell you I saw 'em!"

Captain Ogden took him by the arm and shook him; then ran forward and into the house. From within came the sound of two shots, almost together. Ogden backed out again, stepped to one side for shelter, drew the ramrod from his musket, reached for his powder-horn: then leaned against the wall, looking down at his side. The hand that held the powder-horn was covered with blood, and when Bradley and Crofton ran to him, he coughed and sat down heavily. Upon that, both Bradley and Crofton swung away from him, but only to spring into the doorway from which he had emerged.

From the dark interior came a sound of agonized choking: then a sickening pounding and a muffled musket shot.

Then Lieutenant Grant came running from behind the house, shouting, "They're getting away! They're going down river in canoes!"

Jesse Beacham and I ran around the house and down the bank of the river, and although we went as fast as our legs could take us, Rogers was ahead of us, and his voice rang out, not thick, but high and keen. It brought Captain Jacobs and a dozen white-barred Stockbridge Indians tearing after him like a pack of wolves; and behind us I could hear others running and shouting.

The St. Francis at this point was deeper than where we had crossed, and the water ran smooth and brown, with a glassy look. Sunrise was full upon us, and on the shining river was mirrored the blazing colors of the trees on the opposite bank. Black heads moved slowly on this gaudy stream, making for the further shore; and lower down were five canoes, driving swiftly toward the shadowy north. In one were six Indians, paddling raggedly: in another four. The canoes lurched and wobbled from the over-hasty paddle strokes of the naked red men. The three hindmost canoes were small ones, and the savages in them, having no paddles, were paddling with their hands and singing a wild, defiant song.

Rogers dropped to his knee and fired. In the leading canoe an Indian stood upright, stumbled backward and fell sideways against the paddlers in the stern. The little craft made an abrupt curve and overturned, and its six passengers disappeared in a flurry of yellow foam.

Along the bank Rangers began to follow the canoes, and around me others were kneeling and firing. I heard them calling their shots. "I'll take the one coming out on the bank," Jesse said. His musket jetted smoke, and an Indian who had reached the shallows of the farther shore stopped where he was. His head fell forward, and his legs, floating, slowly swung downstream.

I heard myself saying, "Good shot!"

"That's three I got," Jesse said mildly. "I got a nice one while you was hauling that boy away—pretty a shot as ever I made. Just caught a flash of him between the houses—snap shot, from the hip."

From between the middle fingers of his left hand he dropped a ball in his musket and smoothly pressed it with his ramrod, staring eagerly downstream at a head that moved at the apex of a wedge of riffles—riffles that were flame-colored from the reflection of the young maples. I raised my musket and drew a bead on the head. It was easy, like dropping a slow-flying partridge. The head plunged under water: the tip of the wedge of ripples became a swirl: the man's whole back came to the surface, rolling sluggishly, and I was aware, with a dully horrified astonishment at myself, that I felt the same satisfaction I'd often felt in seeing a partridge fold up in midflight.

The banging of muskets was continuous. Abreast of us, where heads had moved across the gaily colored stream, there were dark bodies floating, face downward. The singing had stopped, and of the five canoes, four were empty, half-full of water, broadside to the current. In the fifth, one man, kneeling, paddled desperately with both hands, while spouts of water shot upward from the surface beyond him.

Jesse shook his white head. "Those fellers must be excited! I wisht we was down there. I'd like to get just one more."

The paddler half-rose to his feet and seized the gunnels with both hands. One of the gunnels went under water, and as the canoe overturned I saw that it threw out a squaw with a baby upon her breast. She'd been lying full length in the canoe, and perhaps she was already dead, for she made no effort to swim, but disappeared at once. The male Indian rolled twice, like a porpoise, and it seemed to me he was vainly trying to dive for the woman, or to swim under water; he came up once, but not again.

Then I heard Rogers shout, recalling the men who'd gone along the bank; and turning, I saw the lifting disc of the sun clearing itself above the line of shattered cabins. Jesse Beacham blinked, as if awakened by the golden light. The shadows of the Rangers near us stretched out across the trampled, frosty grass, gigantic though cast by human mites. Everything except the wide sun and the long shadows seemed to have shrunk and become small.

Lieutenant Turner and Lieutenant Farrington were standing with Rogers, who swung his arm at us and shouted angrily, "Get those men back here! Call 'em back to the drum! I want this detachment paraded!"

We started back toward the houses, running.

"Towne!" the Major called. "I want you! You'll be needed when we examine the prisoners."

CHAPTER XXIX

THE SMOOTH dance-ground before the houses was littered with the bodies of Indians, and the houses themselves seemed to have aged immeasurably in the half hour since we had started across the clearing— unbelievably it was only half an hour since then. Their doors

stood open or were broken down: the paper at the windows
hung in strips: fragments of cloth and buckskins trailed across
the thresholds: blankets and household goods were strewn
around them. The poles erected before each cabin stood at
drunken angles or lay flat, and in the brilliant light of the
newly risen sun, St. Francis was squalid beyond belief.

Clumps of Rangers stood before the dwellings, eating from
Indian bowls and staring watchfully at the roofs and upper
parts of the cabins; for we knew that a few Indians were still
hidden in the shallow cellars and shallower lofts. Among the
dead moved other Rangers, prodding at bodies with bayonets,
looking for silver bracelets, and peering intently at dusky
faces to be sure that they were dead. Still others were busy
wrapping strips of cloth around their lower legs, fitting themselves with moccasins, drawing Indian leggins over tattered
buckskins. Behind us burned a circle of fires, each one tended
by a Ranger; and over each fire hung a steaming kettle—a
sight which made my stomach squeak for food.

Around the drum, herded like sheep by Dunbar's men,
were twenty-five women and children. For the most part the
women wore short skirts of blue cloth, and blue cloth upper
garments that came to their thighs. A few carried brats with
dirty noses. The naked girl had somehow clothed herself, and
the boy I had cracked on the head and dragged away from
Crofton was hunkered down against the drum with another
smaller boy, both staring slack-mouthed at Ogden, who sat,
stripped to the waist, on the ground nearby.

On Ogden's ribs were the double purple bruises of a bullet-
hole and beside him sat Bradley, sopping a piece of white
strouding in a kettle and pressing it to the two wounds.

Rogers hurried across the dance-ground, followed by Farrington and Lieutenant Turner, and when Lieutenant Dunbar
saw the commander, he jumped down from the drum and
went to meet him. "They're looting already," he told Rogers.
"Some of 'em wont have any place to put food if they're not
stopped."

"God almighty couldn't stop 'em from looting," Rogers said
bitterly, "but I'll make it as hard for 'em as I can." To Farrington and Turner he said, "You'll have to work fast. Round
up all the sergeants and start the detachments going for their
packs. Have Numbers One and Two go first: when they're on
their way back, send Three and Four; then Five and Six.

Have the packs dumped in a line in front of the drum, where I can see 'em. When all the packs are brought in, parade the full detachment. Lieutenant Turner, you tend to that. We're moving out of here quick because we'd better."

He looked down at his tattered leggins. "I want some food and I want those houses burned—all but the three storehouses. Lieutenant Farrington, take charge of that. Leave the storehouses so we can stock up, and before you burn the rest, get me some leggins and moccasins. If you can't find any big enough, get me a good blue blanket, so I can wrap my legs; but don't get me a lousy one. If we get lousy, we'll never get clean. If you come across anything good—blankets, leggins, moccasins—pile it in front of the storehouses. Try to get some of those white summer strouds. We may need 'em for bandages."

He fingered his lower lip. "Who went through the church?"

When nobody answered, he tapped a finger against his palm. "The ornaments in that church were silver; and according to what I hear, they're heavy. Anybody who carries silver instead of food is going to be sorry—mighty sorry!" He shrugged his heavy shoulders, as if he knew his warning went unheeded.

"Get Captain Jacobs," he said to Farrington. "Tell him I'm going to examine the prisoners. And those scalps on the poles ought to be counted. Tell Avery to do it. Use the last three detachments to set the fires, and have the center detachments stand guard, front and rear, to pick off those in the lofts. There's always a few hide there or down cellar." Farrington nodded comprehendingly.

"All right," Rogers said. He flirted his huge hand. Turner and Farrington ran toward the irregular line of dead bodies, among which Rangers still prowled, poking with their bayonets like workers in a new-cut meadow, forking hay.

Rogers went to Ogden and knelt beside him, peering closely at his wound. "How's it feel?"

Ogden laughed gruntingly. "Like I spilled some hot soup on myself."

"Think you can walk?"

"I can if it doesn't get worse."

"Don't let it get worse," Rogers told him and, rising, took the white strouding from Bradley. "Sergeant Bradley, get your detachment together, and have 'em get their packs.

Bring mine: Captain Ogden's and Towne's too, and others that need to be brought."

With that, Rogers lifted Ogden to his feet as if he had been a child. "Ogden, you know we've got to be moving out of here. Walk around a little and see if you bleed much. If you do, maybe we can carry you in a blanket till it stops."

"You don't have to worry about me, Major," Ogden said. "I'll look out for myself somehow."

Rogers went quickly back to the drum, upon which Lieutenant Dunbar still stood and now was staring at the cabin farthest upstream. A lazy wisp of smoke was drifting up from it, and a dozen Rangers stood around it, their muskets ready.

"Send half your men for the packs of this detachment, Lieutenant," Rogers said. "We can't waste a minute. Move those prisoners out into the open, where they can't hear what we say. I'll use the drum. Bring 'em up to me one by one. Bring 'em up yourself. You know how to handle 'em."

Dunbar jumped down and Rogers leaped upon the drumhead. His tight hat with its upturned crest, his pouchy eyes, his ragged beard and his tattered buckskins gave him the look of a ruffled, angry bird of prey. And he looked more so when one of Farrington's men held up to him a bowl of the mixture of corn and beans that the Indians call succotash; for he pulled out his spoon, hunched himself over it and fairly shovelled it into his mouth. Then, while he was ravenously eating, he caught sight of me and beckoned me to join him. I did; and, still eating but not speaking, he proffered me a share of his bowl. I got out my own spoon and shovelled as rapidly as he did. When the last bean and the last grain of corn were gone, he ran his fingers around the inside of the bowl, licked them, and wiped them on his leggins.

"Where's your book?" he asked. He took it from me, opened it and laughed that abrupt laugh of his. "For anybody that wants to draw Indians, you haven't taken advantage of your opportunities. Look at 'em!" He waved his big hand toward the sprawled red bodies that lay between us and the houses. The end house was a mass of flames, dull by comparison with the scarlets and yellows of the trees on the far bank of the river, against which the village loomed dark, as against a glowing curtain. Out of the flames burst two figures—one an Indian, naked: the other a squaw, with little arrowheads of flame darting among her clothes. At a musket shot, the man tripped, recovered himself: then sprawled headlong: the woman seemed to become all one flame and ran screaming in a circle.

"You couldn't draw that, could you?" Rogers asked. "Not and keep your stomach in you, hardly?"

The screaming woman ran down to the river and was heard no more. Half a dozen cabins were burning lustily now; and others were beginning to smoke. Detachments of Rangers came toward us across the clearing, bringing the packs we had left in the woods before attacking; they seemed very slow, walking wearily under their loads.

"Stop that dawdling!" Rogers cried from the drum-head. "Haven't you got any sense of time?" He thrust two fingers between his lips and whistled piercingly, waved his right arm with violence, and the tired burden-bearers broke into a run.

CHAPTER XXX

So MANY houses were ablaze that we could feel the heat oppressively, and along with the heat came, worse, an irregular banging of muskets, stricken howlings and wails of passionate despair.

Rogers stamped upon the drum-head. "Bring 'em on!" he told Dunbar. Drawing his chronometer from inside his leggins, he thrust it before my face. "Look at this! We attacked at 5.17 and here it is 6.10, twenty minutes after sunrise, and look at us! Just sitting here doing nothing!"

I wrote down the time.

Dunbar came to us, dragging by the wrist an old woman with stringy gray hair who was dressed like an Indian in blue skirt, blouse and trousers, but whose face was lighter than an Indian's. "This woman's a captive," Dunbar said. "She's no Indian."

Captain Jacobs ran up, breathing heavily. His scalp-lock was singed; on his shoulder was a knife scratch; the greasy white paint on his face and middle body was smeared with ashes and cinders; his arms and leggins were clotted with blood, and tied to his belt were six new scalps.

"Ask her what's her name and where she's from," Rogers told Jacobs.

When Jacobs spoke to her, she burst into such a flux of talk that Rogers and Captain Jacobs looked at each other blankly.

"She's German," I told Rogers. "She's talking half German and half English. She was taken from near Albany about twenty years ago, and she wants to stay here."

"She can't do it!" Rogers said. "She'll damned well go home where she belongs! Ask her this: ask her if she expected the Rangers to come here? Whether anybody knew St. Francis was going to be attacked?"

The woman rattled on and on, as though words, dammed within her during all her twenty years with the Indians were now loosed for the first time. Rogers kept interrupting. "What's she say? What's she talking about?" but the woman talked on and on, telling why she wanted to stay with the Indians.

"To hell with her!" Rogers said. "Tie her up till we're ready to start." To Captain Jacobs, he added, "If they can't answer simple questions intelligently, tell 'em they'll get a bayonet in the rump! Where's the next?"

"There's four more captives," Dunbar said. "You want 'em brought up together?"

"Good God, no! Most of these captives are more Indian than the Indians! We'll take 'em separately! Hurry 'em up!"

All the cabins in the long line now were crackling loudly— all except the three windowless provision houses. Above the flames towered a rolling, eddying cloud of smoke that must have been visible for miles, and I saw Rogers glancing up at it anxiously. The irregular firing of muskets had stopped save for a desultory shot or two, and along the great dancing-floor before the burning cabins the officers were beginning to form the men into something like marching order. Not far from me I saw Jesse Beacham, spreading blankets in the warm sunlight and puttering with packs—one of them mine, I knew; and it seemed impossible that Jesse, looking like a dilapidated but benevolent Kriss Kringle, could be the same person who had shot off the side of one Indian's head and neatly slain two others not many minutes ago.

Dunbar pushed another woman close to the drum. She was about thirty-five, and white, but dressed in every respect like the Indian squaws. Her hair was gray and stringy: her back bent: her face dirty and streaked with tears. Her dress, too, was dirty—covered from breast to knees with old grease spots and stains. Her name, she said, was Sarah Hadden: she had been captured seven years before in the vicinity of Lake Winnepesaukee. She had seen her husband killed at the same time, and although she had carried her baby with her, it was sick, and her captors had knocked its head against a tree before they reached Lake Memphremagog.

"You married an Indian after that?" Rogers asked.

She said she had.

"Still married to him?"

She shook her head.

Rogers scrutinized her closely. "They make you work for the old men, don't they?"

She rubbed her mouth with the back of a hand knotted like birch-roots. "I chop their wood and carry it; cook their food and scramble for bones with the dogs."

"Look here," Rogers said. "Did you hear any talk about my force being on its way to this town?"

"Not this town," she said, "but French officers came up here five days ago and made an oration. Fifteen young men went with them to Wigwam Martinic. They said that's where Rogers was going. You're Rogers, aren't you?"

"Look," Rogers said, "did they say how many French were going to Wigwam Martinic?"

She nodded. "They said four hundred. They said they had the whole country roused up to get you. They said they'd found all your boats—all seventeen of 'em—and got you cornered in here somewheres. They didn't know where, but they said you couldn't get away."

"Wait a minute," Rogers said. He motioned to Lieutenant Farrington, who was waiting uneasily behind Dunbar. "Find Lieutenant Turner. Start those men filling their knapsacks with corn. Keep 'em moving. Did you make a count of the killed?"

"There's two hundred dead, counting the ones we shot in the river," Farrington said, "but we don't know how many were burned. A lot of 'em's in the cellars, and can't get out; you can smell 'em roasting."

The woman laughed and twisted her hands in her dress.

"How many scalps?" Rogers asked.

"About five hundred and twenty."

The woman put her hand on Rogers' knee and spoke earnestly. "There was seven hundred scalps on those poles! Seven hundred! I used to look up at 'em and count, when I hauled the wood! Seven hundred scalps: nearly every scalp from a white man. My own husband's was there among 'em."

"Some of the poles had fallen in the fire," Farrington said defensively.

"You get Turner," Rogers told him. "Send word to all officers that I want the whole command paraded. Then I want every officer here for a council. Find Captain Ogden. I'll have an Indian to carry his pack. Have his stuff and mine and Towne's filled with corn and brought right here—packs and blankets—so we can get away in a hurry."

Then he spoke again to the woman.

"They think they've got us, do they? If they sent all their men to Wigwam Martinic, what did they think would stop us from finding another way out?"

"They know the paths. And they know you'll have to go up this river, or the Beçancour or the Chaudière. Well, they've got forces at every river. There's three hundred at the mouth of this one, so to stop you in case you tried to come up it— three hundred French and some Indians."

"That many?" Rogers said carelessly. "You don't expect me to believe you, do you?"

"I tell you it's true!" the woman cried. "There's three hundred Frenchmen and another band of braves from this town, camped where the St. Francis runs into the St. Lawrence! It's only four miles from here. If you go downstream, they'll kill you; if you go upstream, they'll catch you! For the love of Heaven, don't let 'em corner you in this hell-hole!"

Rogers took out his chronometer again. "Put her with the German woman," he told Dunbar. "Captain Jacobs, bring up the rest of those captives, all three of 'em! We'll get through with this."

The woman went down on her knees and clawed at Rogers' leg. "Every word's true!" she snuffled. "I can't stay here! It's like living with pigs. I can keep up with you. Don't go off without me! I'll do your work: I'll do your cooking: I can use a musket: I'll——"

"I'll look out for you," Rogers said. "Where are those others?"

Captain Jacobs brought up three white women. One looked feeble and decrepit. Another was middle-aged. The third was young, perhaps eighteen years old. Her hair was yellow, her eyes dark brown, and she had the boldest, most brazen look I had ever seen on a woman.

Rogers wasted no time. "I'm Rogers," he said. "You're captives here, and if I get the truth out of you, you'll be treated well."

The yellow-haired girl looked up at him from under her brows, coquettishly adjusting her hair with a pretty hand. Her fingernails, I saw, were bitten close off. She had no trouble catching Rogers' eye.

He leaned forward from the drum. "You understand me, don't you? You understand English, don't you?"

"Oh, I understand much," she said. "Much." Her voice was harsh and hoarse, like that of the Portsmouth fish women who are obliged to make themselves heard above the noise of the sea and the rolling of wheels on wharves.

The decrepit old woman at her side eyed her venomously. "Keep a civil tongue in your head for once," she said. To Rogers she added, "She wasn't much more than a baby when she came here, and she's worse than any of these dirty red rips."

"Rip yourself, you old broomstick," the yellow-haired girl said calmly.

Rogers stamped upon the drum-head again. "Look here: how many fighting men were there in this town?"

The two older women looked puzzled: then began to mutter and count on their fingers. But the yellow-haired girl spoke up confidently.

"Hundred and fifty," she said.

The decrepit old woman turned on her fiercely. "You've been in the bushes with more than that!" she cried.

The yellow-haired girl shouted, "You're a liar. You're a——"

Rogers stamped again. "We *killed* over two hundred!" His

slate-gray eyes narrowed till they were half-shut. "How many fighting men were there in this town?"

"Maybe two hundred," the girl said.

Rogers made a careless gesture. "That's near enough. Why didn't they all go down river with the French when the French asked 'em?"

"The French only asked for thirty," she answered.

"Why didn't they want more?"

"They said they had enough without more! Said they'd destroyed your boats and you couldn't get away."

Rogers laughed. "Boats! What do they know about boats! If they'd found any boats of mine, they'd have followed me."

"Yes," the girl said, "some of 'em *did* follow you, too. Still following you, aren't they? Now they've got you front and rear, haven't they?" The girl looked sullenly at the column of smoke; then abruptly she laughed.

Rogers took her by the ear and she looked up at him provocatively, whereupon he shook her: then slapped her upon the cheek.

"You know who I am, don't you?" he asked.

She spat. "Wobi madaondo."

He nodded. "Major Rogers to you! If you understand such a hell of a lot, where's Lake Memphremagog?"

She looked at him open-mouthed: then pointed up river.

"All right," he said. "Don't forget what you know when you talk to me. You're going with us, and if we don't get safe to Memphremagog, you don't either!" He turned to Dunbar. "Put these women with the other two. Bring up the Indian prisoners—all of 'em."

He looked down at my book. "I guess we've got what we wanted. Those stories tally." He took off his black cap and scratched his tousled head. "Funny about these white Indians! You have to look out for 'em! If they get started young enough, they're worse than the red ones, sometimes. I'll bet that yellow-head would give you something to remember her by!"

"Why don't you leave 'em here, those that want to stay?"

"Can't do it," he said. " 'Tisn't good policy to admit white people prefer Indians to their own people. Besides, the Indians would kill 'em as soon as we left, probably. Anyway, they're white, and they got to *be* white if they get a chance."

Dunbar, assisted by four men from his detachment, moved

the captured Indians close to the drum, and beyond them I could see a stream of Rangers moving back and forth between the three unburned storehouses and the long row of heaped blankets, knapsacks and muskets.

The captured Indians seemed a pitiable spectacle, grouped against the background of their smoldering homes, the windrows of dead bodies and the plodding Rangers with their burdens of corn from the storehouses. Most of the women held half-naked children in their arms, and those who didn't were old. To me, in my ignorance, these old ones seemed venerable; but afterward I recalled that they were fat and pigeon-toed; so probably they weren't really as elderly as I thought they were. Others were indeed bent with age, their faces like frost-rotted apples.

In response to the questions which Captain Jacobs, prompted by Rogers, put to them, they said that the braves who had gone down river with the French officers had gone in canoes; that the French officers themselves had arrived in canoes; that all the land between St. Francis and the St. Lawrence was marshland, cut with false channels of the St. Francis.

When Rogers looked at his chronometer again, I saw what he was driving at. For the French and Indians down river to attack us, they would have to come upstream in canoes, slowly. Since no smoke had risen from the burning houses till after sunrise, the French and Indians could hardly reach us until the sun was an hour high, and half of that hour was still left to us.

Rogers studied the Indian women. They seemed to have no curiosity about what might happen to them: no feeling about what had already happened. Never once did they look around at the blackening embers of their homes. All of them must have lost husbands, fathers or children at our hands, but their faces were stolid.

"Turn 'em loose," Rogers said suddenly. "They wouldn't add to our speed, and they wouldn't be much use to us anyhow."

He laughed, jumped down from the drum and settled his hat more firmly on his head. Then, raising his arm in a theatrically commanding gesture, he spoke to Jacobs in a deep voice, like that of an actor, "Tell these prisoners I'm letting 'em go, so that they can take a message to their people. They're to tell their people that it was I, Wobi Madaondo, who burned their town and killed their young men. Rogers did it, but he never would have done it if they'd behaved honorably toward the Great Father across the water and toward the children of the Great Father. Go ahead and tell 'em!"

While Captain Jacobs translated, Rogers stood before the drum, staring across at the remains of the village. His heavy body was still, but his eyes were restless and seemed to see everything—every pack and every man in the long line of Rangers now completely formed: every corner of the clearing in which the town had stood: every cloud in the sky: every movement of the officers who had gathered for the council of war to which he had summoned them.

Captain Jacobs stopped.

"Tell 'em," Rogers continued, "that what has been done was done because they trampled on the white flag sent to them by the Great Father. If the white flags of the Great Father are not honored, those who dishonor them will be destroyed. On the poles before their houses were the scalps of six hundred children of our white brothers, but so far I have slain only two hundred of their people in return. But if this town again rises from the ashes, and sends other young men to take the scalps of our people, Rogers will have no mercy on St. Francis or on anybody he finds the next time he comes."

When Jacobs had translated, Rogers stepped close to the knot of Indian women. His big nose gave him the look of an eagle, puffed up with anger, ready to strike and keep on striking as long as there was life in him. "Five women were held captive in this town. Tell these people to carry word that anything taken from us shall be paid for. This is the payment for the five captives." He reached forward and caught the arms of the two Indian boys—the one I had made prisoner and the smaller one who stood beside him. He held them with one enormous hand, and with the other drew out from among the women the Indian girl who, when I first saw her, had been naked. Two smaller girls beside her, shrank back among the women.

"Bring out those two girls," Rogers told Jacobs.

Jacobs went in among the women, pushing them out of his way. The girls dodged and fell on the ground to crawl among the women's legs, but Jacobs caught them by the hair and dragged them, squirming and kicking, to Rogers, who pawed the two boys and the three girls together and got his long arms around the five of them. They stood quietly enough, pressed against his stained and tattered buckskins, petrified with fear.

"Tell 'em just one more thing," Rogers said. "Tell 'em to say that if we're followed, it will be bad for those who follow. Bad! Tell 'em Wobi madaondo himself said it. And tell 'em this shows how much he fears being caught: he will go home by way of Lake Memphremagog!" He motioned to Dunbar to scatter the Indian women.

They went away like stolid hens, across the dance-ground, separating as they went and waddling off in different directions, while the Rangers bawled pleasantries after them.

The officers who crowded around Rogers to stare at the five Indian children looked more like soldiers than when they had attacked; for they had either drawn seatless buckskin leggins over their tattered breeches, or had cut blue strouding into strips and bound their legs, as Indians often do. Lieutenant Farrington carried extra leggins and moccasins, which he gave to Rogers.

"My God!" Rogers said, "haven't any of these red hellions got man's sized feet?" Seated on the ground, he took off his own broken moccasins and struggled with the new ones.

"Where's Ogden?" he asked.

Ogden came out from behind the group, walking lopsidedly.

Rogers looked up at him. "Can you travel?"

"I'm all right," Ogden said, trying to speak heartily. "I'm first rate." He licked his lips and darted a quick glance at his brother officers.

Rogers dropped his eyes to his new moccasins, and the other officers stared at the sky or at the ground; for Ogden wasn't all right. He'd had a bullet through his body, and he looked it. His cheeks, above his matted beard, were a greenish straw color.

"Here's two boys for you, Captain," Rogers said. He jerked his head toward the two little Indians. "Let the big one carry your pack and your musket. Use the little one to lean on."

"Major," Lieutenant Farrington said, "I aint feeling too

good myself. Maybe I better have one of those girls to help me—the biggest one."

The circle of officers guffawed, and Rogers laughed too. Even the three girls, watching Rogers' face, smiled faintly, pretending to understand.

Rogers beckoned to Captain Jacobs, who seemed to me a ludicrous spectacle. Not only had his singed scalp-lock drooped forlornly over his chalk-white forehead, but the yellow of his painted gorget had run into the white of his body stripe, and the two colors, mixed with perspiration, had trickled down into his exposed navel. "Captain," Rogers said to the Indian, "you'll have charge of the captives at night. These three girls belong with 'em, always. See they help the old woman. Tie 'em up at sundown, so they can't run away."

He got up, stamped his feet in his new moccasins; then dragged on the leggins. As he fastened them to his belt, he spoke to his officers: "According to what the prisoners tell me, there's two forces after us—three hundred downstream, and about two hundred trailing us from Missisquoi Bay. That's five hundred. There's a hundred and forty-two of us."

"I lose one man," Captain Jacobs said.

"Dead?" Rogers asked.

Jacobs nodded. "We put him in house to burn, so nobody get."

"Any other losses?" Rogers asked.

Four officers spoke together. Six of their men, it appeared, had been cut with knives or gashed a little with hatchets, but not seriously.

"All right," Rogers said. "There's a hundred and forty-one of us, then, and five hundred against us. Two hundred of those haven't any more food than we had when we got here, and the other three hundred probably haven't as much as we have right now. They can't chase us unless they have supplies, and when they get here they wont find much to eat: not unless they want to eat roasted Indians." His laugh was like the neighing of a horse.

"Now," he went on, "I told the prisoners I was leaving here by way of the St. Francis River, and then I turned 'em loose to spread the word. There's just a chance that nobody'll believe it—just a chance the French may not bother us if we go up the St. Francis. They don't tell the truth themselves, and they don't expect others to. Anyway, we've got to make up our minds how we're going to get away: make yours up quick!"

"How many ways are there?" Dunbar asked.

"Damned few!" Rogers said. "There's the way we came. We can go back on our track and try to ambush the two hundred that followed us from Missisquoi. They're pretty near here, and they must be tired; so we might be able to wipe 'em out; but those from down river might catch us in the rear before we did it. Even if we were lucky, we'd still have that damned spruce bog to wade through; and when we got to Missisquoi Bay, we'd find no boats. That means we'd have to go all the way to Crown Point along the lake on foot."

Farrington spoke sharply. "I say to hell with that, Major! I'd rather try anything than that lousy spruce bog." The other officers murmured, assenting.

"There's only one other route, then," Rogers said. "It's about as far from here to Lake Memphremagog as to Missisquoi Bay, and Memphremagog is on the way to the Cohase Intervales. There'll be food at the Cohase Intervales —at the mouth of the Ammonoosuc, sixty miles north from Number Four. Ever since we started I figured that would be how we'd have to go back. To get to Memphremagog we follow this river to its forks: then take the west branch." It sounded easy the way he said it.

"How far to the forks?" Farrington asked.

"Maybe eighty miles," Rogers said carelessly.

"How far from the forks to the mouth of the Ammonoosuc?" Lieutenant Grant asked.

Rogers stared at him unwinkingly. "I don't know. If we get past Memphremagog we'll be all right."

"Is it three hundred miles?" Lieutenant Grant persisted.

I heard one of the officers mutter "Jesus! Three hundred miles!"

Rogers reached for his pack, swung it to his shoulders and spoke reassuringly. "That's something we don't have to worry about. If we get past Memphremagog, you wont mind how much farther you've got to go. If you *don't* get there, it wont matter a damn."

Guffawing, the officers slapped their knees and made game of Grant.

"Well," Rogers said brusquely, "what's the sense of the council? Do we go by way of Memphremagog?"

In a hasty chorus they agreed: "Yes, yes! Memphremagog; Memphremagog!"

To my mind that name, Memphremagog, had a sinister and forbidding sound, as of storms and bogs and threatening shadows, and I wondered how many of us would live to see that dark and distant lake.

Well, anyhow, that's where we were going. "Set fire to those storehouses," Rogers called, and the crackling was loud; embers dropped through the smoky air as we lined up to leave that dreadful place.

CHAPTER XXXI

WE HAD the poverty-stricken uniformity of a long line of mendicants from an institution when we moved out of the clearing where St. Francis had stood. We were clothed partly in our own poor rags and partly in the odds and ends salvaged from the cabins which now were smoldering embers. We wore our battered green caps still, jammed hard down over our matted hair; and our packs bulged fatly; but the buckskins and the leg-wrappings that covered our lower limbs might have come from the rag-bag of the poorest fisherman.

The October sun was hazy through the smoke, and in that light the bodies of a dozen slain savages that lay in a kind of horrid cluster not far from me had the look of being about to move and disentangle themselves.

Some of the brown faces were toward me; and the eyes, wide open, seemed to be watching me as the order came for us to march; to save my life I couldn't help staring back at those staring eyes. And as we moved on, I had to step around another tangle of bodies—there seemed to be thousands of bodies of Indians, dead men I had helped to kill

My insides crawled at the sight—and I wasn't the only one. Two of these brown corpses were lying athwart upon another, and an arm of this lower stuck up rigid in the air, the fist clenched. Crofton ran out from our line and seized this arm at the wrist, tried to twist it back as if to make it rest more decently; but the arm resisted him and wouldn't bend. Crofton ran back again, eyeing the rest of us half slily and half defiantly.

I began to yawn and yawn. It seemed to me that given the opportunity, I could sleep for a year: that it had been years since I had rested: that this one day had already been longer than any week I had ever known: that I was dreaming, and it must be a dream that I had taken part in the destruction of St. Francis and in the death of all those strangely twisted dark men.

How long, how long ago had it been since McNott had shouted angrily at Hunk and me that the St. Francis Indians had played their tricks once too often. I remembered how he had said "And that's going to be the end of St. Francis!"

For the first time I realized that those words of his had meant nothing to me. I had heard them; but, like a witless child, I had given them no thought. They hadn't meant to me—as they must have if I had used my brain—hunger, cold, interminable labor, destruction, torture, death, and possibly the end of what was known as Langdon Towne. Harvard, I saw, hadn't taught me to think properly—and I remembered, now, that Rogers had said "We'll teach you something you never learned at Harvard College."

When we came to the end of the clearing, where the yellow and red leaves of the hardwood growth arched above the hard-packed Indian trail on which we travelled, I looked back at what had been St. Francis. Our narrow column of swiftly-moving men seemed like a brown and green snake, slipping into the shelter of the forest. From end to end and from side to side of that long clearing, there was no other living thing in sight—not a crow; not a bluejay, even. There was nothing but the smoking embers; the windrows of dead bodies.

The trail along the high bank of the river was a good one, trodden hard by the feet of generations of Indians; and as we hurried along it in the brilliant golden light of that Oc-

tober morning, I felt a singular and unexpected affection
for the ragged men with whom I travelled—for Rogers, setting the pace at the head of the column, moving with a
peculiar lurching stride above which his thick neck and his
heavy sloping shoulders seemed to glide smoothly along: for
Ogden, following just behind him, listing heavily to favor
his wound, and supported on either side by a half-naked
Indian boy: for Sergeant Bradley, close in front of me, turning sour glances upon the rest of us: for white-bearded Jesse
Beacham, swinging placidly along behind me: for black Pomp
Whipple, grinning at nothing: for little Corporal Crofton,
furtively eyeing his companions—for all the other men strung
out behind me: men who had been half-seen shadows on our
journey to St. Francis. Now, it seemed to me, I knew them
all: not only Farrington, Dunbar and Jacobs, the Indian Captain; not only Curgill, Grant, Turner, Avery and the other
detachment leaders, but all the men under them. Never, I
thought, would I forget one of them with whom I had
crossed the clearing at St. Francis.

Because of their quickness and determination, no harm
had come to us; and I was grateful to them for their dis-
regard of danger, the deadly accuracy of their shooting. No
other men, it seemed to me, could have done what they did:
no other leaders could so well have led us. Except for them,
I thought, I might not be alive; and so I loved them all,
and among them felt secure. If there was any possible way of
getting home, I was confident these men would find it.

To travel this smooth trail, even though it rose steadily,
was child's play after our terrible nine-day journey through
the bogs. Rogers came back at intervals to walk alongside
the women, and though they seemed to need no urging, he
urged them just the same.

"If you fall behind," he warned them, "we'll have to leave
you, and if we leave you, you're goners! You'll be caught,
and when they catch you, they'll pry up your scalps and
put red-hot hatchets against your skulls. They'll show no mercy
to anybody who's been a part of this detachment. The whole
line will stop for five minutes every hour. When it stops,
do what you have to do, and do it without straying. Don't
try to be modest—not yet!" His laugh was explosive, like
snow falling from a roof.

The women kept up. The Indian girls trotted like dogs.

The white women, during their captivity, had learned to walk like Indians. They swung their hips as if they were potato sacks, and toed in so that there was no understanding why their big toes didn't interfere and trip them. Sometimes one of their Stockbridge guardians, finding a woman underfoot, would scowl and silently raise his hatchet. At once all five would scuttle close up behind our detachment, like a covey of frightened partridges, and there they would cling—the German woman; dirty Sarah Hadden who had eaten bones with the dogs: feeble and decrepit old Mrs. Coit; her yellow-haired daughter Jennie; and the middle-aged woman who seemed to hate Jennie Coit more than anything in the world. The three Indian girls stuck to Mrs. Hadden, Mrs. Coit and the German woman like shadows.

The name of the middle-aged woman was Mrs. Wick. She had forgotten where she lived before the Indians captured her, and she was foggy, even, about her first name, telling some of us that it was Deborah and others that it was Abigail.

As for yellow-haired Jennie Coit, she thought of nothing but men, so far as I could see. She wanted a man, and she didn't care who he was or how he looked: whether he was white, Indian or Negro. Unless I was mistaken, she would have taken white-haired Jesse Beacham as quickly as Rogers; and when I saw Jesse looking at her with benevolent interest, I was uncomfortable until he told me she reminded him of a pointer bitch to which he had been attached. She was white, he said, with yellow eyes, and so determined to escape from the house that she somehow scrambled up the chimney while fire was burning in the fireplace. Her judgment, he said sadly, didn't equal her resourcefulness; for she made advances to a bear, and that was the end of her.

Rogers, in his determination to get us safely away, led us on and on, forever on and on, until it seemed to me my feet and legs were seared and tortured stumps.

We made seventeen miles that first day of our retreat from St. Francis. Plodding, plodding on, we made fifteen miles when we passed the ford we'd tragically crossed on our way to the hated village; but we didn't cross now—or linger. Our way now was to continue on the north side of the river; the French who'd followed us from Missisquoi were somewhere to the south, coming up; and though we were dead on our feet, Rogers led us on two miles beyond the ford before he let us stop. When we camped, I thought I'd reached the extreme limit of my endurance. How Captain Ogden kept going with a bullet-hole through him was beyond me. How the women had done it was a mystery. How I had kept going myself, I couldn't understand. Like most young men, I didn't know much about endurance or about anything else. I know now there is almost no limit to man's endurance, provided the determination is there, either within him or close to him.

We rolled ourselves in our blankets where Rogers halted us, and I was too tired to lean forward and untie my moccasins. Down the line behind me I could hear the gritting and crunching of the men's teeth on dry corn. I couldn't eat: I didn't want to, and yet I couldn't sleep. My arms twitched: my knees and thighs quivered and jerked. My eyelids ached and my brain felt hot. Behind my throbbing eyelids I saw quick pictures: a canoe capsizing to spill a dead woman and her baby into a cold river: the distorted faces of children leaping over blood-stained bodies: a red man's face in a doorway, turning abruptly to a bloody pulp: windrows of sprawling corpses with white eyes that never ceased their staring. In the end all the pictures gave way to those staring eyes—eyes that faded to pin-points and swelled to glaring saucer-like discs: that multiplied until my whole head seemed filled with images of straining irises; then diminished to long and wavering lines of distant watching eyeballs.

It seemed to me I would never sleep again. I felt myself strangling when all those whirling, sightless eyes turned into one enormous white orb that hung above me, shooting out piercing rays that stabbed me like arrows. I must have shouted, for I found Jesse shaking me and saying "Now, now! Now, now!" Through the overhanging branches the glaring disc of the full moon shone straight into my face.

"Come on," Jesse said. "Rogers says it's bright enough to see the path."

He helped me to my feet, and when I stumbled and fell to my knees, he hoisted me up again. "It'll wear off," he assured me. "It'll be easy, too, because we got to go kind of slow on account of Ogden."

He folded my blanket and slung it over my shoulder with my pack.

"My God, Jesse," I said. "Aren't your feet sore?"

He said "Yes" in a mild voice. As a sort of afterthought he added that he hadn't slept well, and had already limbered himself by moving around a little. Remembering that Jesse was three times my age, I tried to forget my aches.

In the moonlit path ahead I could see Ogden holding to Rogers' shoulders, while Bradley and the two Indian boys stood beside him, watching.

"We could cut poles," Bradley said, "and fasten a blanket between 'em like a hammock."

"I wont do it," Ogden protested. "I tell you I can keep up with you if I can stay on my feet!"

"He's right," Rogers told Bradley. "If he lets us carry him, he'll be like a baby for weeks, and we'd never get him over the mountains." He stepped backward, forcing Ogden to hobble forward; then added cheerfully, "By the time we reach the mountains, Captain, you'll be as good as ever."

The sight of Ogden made my feet feel better.

"Here," Rogers said to Bradley, "help the boys hold him up till he gets going. I don't want him to fall."

"No," Ogden whispered, "don't let me fall. I wouldn't want to fall. As long as I don't fall I'll be all right."

"Come ahead," Rogers called down the line. As we moved forward he came back to make sure we were all on our feet.

We saw him peering at us hard in the moonlight as we passed him. "Step along," he kept saying, "step along! It'll be daylight in a couple of hours. We'll stop to eat when it's daylight."

As his voice faded behind us, I could hear Pomp Whipple's oily chuckle: Lieutenant Dunbar's reedy voice; the querulous tones of Mrs. Wick; the rustling scuffling of many moccasined feet on the path; the rattling thumps of men tripping and falling, and scrambling up again. We moved slowly, but when Rogers returned and took his place at our head, we went more rapidly.

"If we keep going this way," I said to Jesse, "starting two hours before dawn, we'll reach Memphremagog in no time."

"I guess so," Jesse said. His voice was not enthusiastic— a fact which I hoped was due to his great age.

The trail was still hard and smooth, and easy to follow in the moonlight; and when dawn came, and we had our short rest for food, as promised, we saw the river was narrower and the land flatter. The country had a bleak and miserable look: a look of gray sterility—of deadness; and as the day wore on, this dreariness was more pronounced. The trail seemed less travelled, and was no longer packed and smooth. Wet patches were more frequent, and we found ourselves climbing over or crawling under trees that had fallen across the path: scrambling aside, sometimes, where earthslides had blocked the way. What path there was began to lead now and then through watercourses with boggy sides. I didn't see how Ogden could keep going, but somehow the two Indian boys contrived to pull and hoist him forward.

Around mid-afternoon, Rogers halted us where a small stream ran into the St. Francis and then he sent word down the line that we could eat again. While we got our handfuls of corn from our knapsacks, he called Konkapot and Captain Jacobs, and the three of them crossed the stream and vanished.

"Jesse," I said, "this trail's pinching out." I hoped he'd deny it, but I knew he couldn't.

He tossed half a handful of grains of dried corn into his mouth; then passed his hand caressingly over his white whiskers as though he had eaten a full meal. "Yes," he said, "I shouldn't wonder if it was."

The whole line was restless. Two of the Stockbridge Indians, clownish-looking because of their streaks of white paint, left the women and studiously examined the banks of the little stream that crossed our path. Bradley, unwinding Ogden's bandage, shouted after them, asking if they'd found anything; but they shook their heads and continued to nose around like dogs hunting a scent.

Ogden, stripped to the waist, stood with his eyes closed, leaning on the two Indian boys. His bandage, a long piece of white strouding, was badly yellowed, though not bloody. Bradley took it to the stream, washed it and wrung it out.

The bullet had gone in low down on Ogden's ribs and come out near his backbone. The two holes were white and puckered: the flesh between them green and purple, as though he had been beaten half to death.

"Jesse," I said, "I'm mighty glad that hole isn't in me."

"Yes," Jesse said, "but that's as nice a place for a hole as I could think up if I thought all day—if you got to have one."

Ogden opened his eyes and looked at us, and to me the uncomplaining patience of that look was heartrending. "How far have we come?" he asked.

"You mean today?"

"Yes, today," he whispered.

"About fifteen miles, as near as I can figure," I said.

He closed his eyes and hung on the two Indian boys as a drunken man hangs to a fence-rail. You could see he'd just dragged on and on, half-conscious; but tragic as was the man's plight, heroic as was his struggle, I think, except for a moment of pity now and then, most of us weren't really moved by his suffering and indomitable pluck. No, at the time it seems to me we took what he was doing as a commonplace. Yet I think that later no-one forgot; and now-adays, when I hear able-bodied people complain at having to do something unpleasant or tiresome, or when I see someone abandon a task half completed, I see Ogden with his naked side and its sinister discolorations—I see Ogden wavering and sagging between his two Indians but not falling.

When Rogers returned with Konkapot and Captain Jacobs, he took Ogden's bandage from Bradley, and sent the sergeant down the trail to order all detachment leaders to the head of the line. "I want the women and the Indian girls too," he told Bradley. After he had stooped to look at Ogden's wounds, and had even sniffed at them, he adjusted the bandage himself. "That's doing fine," he said briskly. "If you got through yesterday and today all right, you ought to get through anything."

Ogden didn't even open his eyes. "How far to Memphremagog?" he whispered.

Rogers' reply was hearty. "Oh, it's quite a piece yet: quite a piece. Better sit down, Captain."

"No," Ogden said. "I better not. If I sat down it might be pretty hard to get up. I better not."

"Prop yourself against a tree, then," Rogers said. "I want to ask these boys some questions."

Farrington, Dunbar, Turner, Grant and the rest of the lieutenants had crowded up close. Jennie Coit and her mother, with Mrs. Wick and the German woman, were in the midst of them. Jennie was leaning against Ensign Avery, who looked down on her with slack lips. When Rogers beckoned to her, she left Avery quickly enough.

"Grind some corn for Captain Ogden," he said. "I told you to keep busy."

"There's nothing to grind it with," Jennie said, and gave him a languorous look.

Rogers grinned unpleasantly, and his protuberant eyes were fierce. He looked like Wobi Madaondo—a White Devil, and a threatening one. He must have looked the same to Jennie, for she went immediately to Ogden, and I saw her sulkily fumbling for corn in his knapsack.

Rogers turned to his silent officers. "The trail's pinching out. It splits here, and the trail up the St. Francis is pretty old. I'd say nobody'd travelled it for a year or two. If anybody knows anything about it, speak up."

Nobody said a word.

"Maybe there isn't a trail," Rogers said. "Captain Stark thought there was, and the map he drew shows one. He said he was brought down the east side of the river when he was captured ten years ago." To Captain Jacobs he said, "What's the names of these Indian boys? I've been too busy to ask."

"Big one Abissanehraw," Captain Jacobs said. "Little one Tatabekamateosis."

"Nonsense!" the Major cried. "We're in a hurry! They're Billy Rogers and Bub Rogers!" He tapped the larger one impressively on the shoulder, saying "You Billy." Billy looked pleased. He pinched the ear of the smaller boy. "You Bub."

Bub turned an agonized glance toward the rest of us, but finding us stony, he stared up at Rogers, pop-eyed.

"Now," Rogers told Captain Jacobs, "ask Billy and Bub whether they ever went to Memphremagog and down on the other side to the Connecticut and Number Four."

Captain Jacobs spoke rapidly to the boys. Billy replied first, at considerable length, while Bub's answer was dignified.

Jacobs turned to Rogers. "They say Yes. Bub says Mrs. Cheney at Number Four old friend. Gave him molasses on bread once."

"How'd they get there? Did they use this trail?"

Jacobs shook his head. "They go other side river."

"Does the trail follow the river on the other side?"

"Too wet," Jacobs said after conferring with the boys. "Goes away away. Goes straight. River goes like snake."

Rogers' officers stared at him. What Jacobs had just told us was bad news—the worst kind of news; but the officers seemed undisturbed by it.

"Is that a good trail on the other side of the river?" Rogers asked.

The boys agreed that it was.

Mrs. Wick cackled. "Good! What do you think Indians know about what's good? I went over that trail once, after a two months' drought, and pretty near drowned. These red buggers wrap a piece of deer's belly around a stick and think it's good! They sleep in a houseful of smoke and think it's good!"

"Can you remember the trail?" Rogers asked.

"Remember it?" Mrs. Wick cried. "No! I couldn't remember it to save my life."

"Ask those Indian girls," Rogers said. "Ask that big one there. If she had to go from here to Memphremagog, would she use the trail we're on or cross the river to the other."

Jacobs questioned her; then grunted. "She knows nothing. She say she do neither: she say she go back to St. Francis."

Rogers laughed. "She's not such a fool!" He spoke almost confidentially to his officers. "I guess we're all right! If Stark came down this side of the river, we can go up it. I figure we'd be better off on this side, anyway. If the French take the other trail, and cross the river to look for us, they'll have a hell of a time locating us. If they stay on this side, they can't go faster than we can." He looked around at Ogden. Jennie Coit was working his shirt around his shoulders and down over his bandage. "They can't go faster than we can," Rogers repeated, "not if you keep up with me. See you keep up with me; that's all. Get your men started. We'll keep going till it's too dark to see!"

CHAPTER XXXII

THE NEXT day, the third of our retreat, the trail vanished in a bog, not as bad as the one in which we had spent nine days after leaving Missisquoi, but bad enough. There were deadfalls all through it, and masses of young growth that whipped at us whenever we moved.

Through this bog the river curved in enormous loops, and somehow Rogers felt where they were without seeing them. It is true that he kept four Stockbridge Indians ahead of our line with orders to report any alteration in the river's course, and it is also true that he had Captain Stark's rough map, drawn from the vague memories of his captive days. The loops were indicated on that map, but Stark hadn't remembered just where they were. Rogers anticipated them.

There was something animal-like about the manner in which he always took the proper turning: always knew when he had gone the proper distance. I shall always think he possessed an instinct the rest of us didn't have—the same instinct that infallibly brings a dog home, no matter how winding the trackless course he follows.

When Rogers turned us at right angles to the river and sent us splashing and stumbling to the westward, I had complete faith in him. When, at the end of three hours of struggling, we found ourselves once more looking out over the brown and turbulent St. Francis, it seemed an everyday occurrence instead of the miracle that it really was.

To put down those words, "three hours of struggling," is easy; but I could write forever without learning how to describe the endlessness of those three hours: the aching legs; the twig-whipped face and hands; the trickling sweat that stung my eyes; the recurring anger at the tree trunks which lay with hellish ingenuity in the path, the under-water holes and trenches that tortured our blistered feet; the little sticks that crawled beneath belt and collar to rub the sweaty skin; the perversity with which knapsack and musket snagged themselves on stumps and branches; the dodging and bending to escape the clutching undergrowth; the eternal necessity of hurrying on and on and on; the never-absent knowledge that close on our heels were men whose sole object in life was to put bullets through us—to sink hatchets in our brains.

No one can know these things who has never fought his way through a pathless forest, with enemies behind him, immensity before him, and a sackful of corn between him and starvation.

So at the end of three hours of struggling we came to the river again, and slept that night on dry land, which we couldn't have done unless Rogers had led us across the bend.

Some of the nights of our retreat aren't clear to me. They lose themselves in each other, as sequential nightmares blend indistinguishably into one horrible dream. The third night I remember clearly because it was the night Jennie Coit attached herself to Ogden, and the night Rogers figured out for us how much corn we could allow ourselves to eat a day.

We had no sooner stopped, settled our packs and muskets, got out our handfuls of corn and gone to crunching them, than I heard Jennie's voice, harsh and hoarse, say something in the Abenaki language, and I thought, from her tone, she was saying something unpleasant. A moment later she ran in among us, with Konkapot after her.

In the bright light of the moon, her face looked pale blue; her yellow hair green. She was furious.

Rogers had gone down the line as soon as we stopped, to make sure everything was all right; so Sergeant Bradley stepped forward as acting commander of the detachment. "What the hell you doing?" he asked Jennie. "Get back where you belong!"

"I'm going to see Captain Ogden," she said, "going to fix his bandage."

"We got two Indian boys looking out for Captain Ogden," Bradley told her. "If the Major finds you up here, you'll lose your hair."

With her lips Jennie made an unladylike noise; stepped quickly past Bradley and started for Ogden. Bradley caught her by the arm and jerked her back. As she turned, she

swung her fist, catching Bradley on the ear with the sound
of a rock hitting a bag of walnuts. He let her go and staggered back, pawing at the side of his head. She darted to
Ogden, and I saw her kneeling beside him, holding him
up and fumbling with his shirt.

"Well," Jesse Beacham said mildly, "she's getting rough,
aint she?"

Bradley walked after her, stood looking down at Jennie
and Ogden, then turned to Konkapot. "All right, Konkapot,"
Bradley said, "don't worry about this mink. We'll let the
Major tend to her. You go on back and tell Captain Jacobs
the Major'll look after her."

Jennie had Ogden's shirt off by then, and crouching over
him she unwrapped his bandage, making mothering sounds.
When she'd got it off, she began to knead the flesh about
his wounds gently, and she was doing this when Rogers returned. Moving without a sound, he came close behind her
and just stood there, watching her.

Then she rose to her feet, with the bandage in her hand,
and bumped against him and recoiled, as from a stone wall.

"Who sent you up here?" Rogers growled.

"Who do you think sent me?" she snarled. "Not those foul
old strumpets I have to march with!"

"Nobody else, either!" Rogers said. "When I want women
around me, I send for 'em! Don't start raising hell with these
men of mine or I'll turn you loose in the woods."

"Go ahead!" she cried. "Go ahead and turn me loose! I
didn't ask to be brought, did I? I'd rather take a chance with
Mohawks or looservees than with you and your men! Turn
me loose and turn Captain Ogden loose, too, why don't you,
so I can take care of him! Maybe I could find him a cow
moose to lick his bullet-holes. If he stays with you, there
wont be nobody or nothing bother with 'em—only maggots.
Look at this!" She thrust Ogden's bandage almost against
Rogers' face and shook it at him. "Look at it! Why don't you
have him tended to? Who changed that bandage last? I did,
last night! It ought to be changed three times a day, so it
don't dry on him. He ought to be washed!"

"These Indian boys can wash him," Rogers said.

"You're a liar! No wonder they call you Wobi madaondo!
Those boys never washed themselves or anything else in their
lives! They wouldn't know how to! They're lousy, both of

'em, and so's Captain Ogden, probably, from leaning on 'em.
Look at 'em in the morning and see if they aren't. He's got to
be stripped and cleaned, and he's got to have his bandage
washed. Get out of my way, you big spider, so I can tend
to him!"

She pushed past Rogers and stamped off toward the river
through the moonlit brush. Rogers thrust a thick finger under
his black hat and scratched his head: then went closer to
Ogden. "We'll have to look out for that girl, Captain," he
said. "I don't believe she's much good."

"She's pretty handy," Ogden said faintly. "I guess I *would*
feel better if she fixed that bandage three times a day, like
she said."

"Well," Rogers said reluctantly, "I'll let her move up and
fix it, but when she's fixed it, send her back to her mother.
I don't want her around the other men. Somebody'll get into
a fight over her."

Ogden just whispered, "How far is it to Memphremagog?"

"Ask the girl," Rogers said. "She's going to take care of
you." He laughed indulgently. "Memphremagog! Doesn't anybody think about anything except Memphremagog?"

Jennie came back, went down on her knees beside Ogden
and lifted him so that he leaned against her shoulder.

She looked up at Rogers. "Why don't you tell him how far
it is?" As she spoke she was binding the white strouding
around Ogden's two bullet-holes. Still holding him against her
shoulder, as a mother holds a sick child, she slipped his
buckskin shirt over his head and put his arms in the sleeves
for him. Then she picked up his knapsack, unstrapped it,
peered within and shook her head. "You've been overeating!
How much of that corn did you eat today?"

Ogden looked a little ashamed. "I had two handfuls. I got
pretty hungry. I guess it was maybe losing blood that made
me want so much."

"It doesn't make any difference what makes you want it,"
she cried. "You can't have it! You can have one handful of
corn a day. One handful: understand?"

"You talk like a fool!" Rogers said.

Jennie leaped to her feet and shook her fist at him. "Tell
him how far it is to Memphremagog! It's not knowing what
to expect that drives anyone crazy—Frenchmen behind us,
nobody knows where; Memphremagog ahead of us, nobody

knows how far! I'd tell him if I knew! I'd be telling him all the time, if I stayed with him—yes, and that's where I'm going to stay!"

Rogers stared at her with protuberant eyes. "Lord, but you're noisy!" he said, and sat down a few feet away, took a handful of corn from his knapsack and began to eat, making smacking noises with his thick lips.

"Bring me the book," he called to me; and by the light of the moon he began to study the map I had copied long, long ago—on the night before we struck into the spruce bog from the shores of Missisquoi Bay. Afterward, he lay on his back, staring up at the shafts of moonlight that pierced the trees above us, and I could see that he was moving his lips as if he were reading. Ogden had fallen asleep; and Jennie, sitting beside him, looked down at his face intently. She no longer seemed bold and hard, but helpless and gentle, though I knew she was neither; yet I knew, too, that the rest of us had ceased to exist for her. Yesterday we had been potential prey: today we were potential nuisances who were like to interfere blunderingly with her care for the sick man.

Rogers gave the book back to me. "Here, write down what I tell the sergeant, so there wont be any misunderstanding about it."

He whistled to Bradley, who came to him, covertly eyeing Jennie.

"How much corn you used, Sergeant?" Rogers asked.

"About half," Bradley said. "I guess my knapsack's half full still."

"That wont do," Rogers said. "You're using too much. So's everybody else. We only made eight miles today."

"Well," Bradley said, "that only leaves us forty miles to go, doesn't it?"

Rogers' face looked wooden. "I've been going over Stark's map. Sometime tomorrow, probably, we'll strike pretty bad going. I don't believe this command can make a great many miles a day from now on. The going'll mostly be up hill."

"We could split up and hunt for food," Bradley said.

"Not here we couldn't," Rogers told him quickly. "There's only one way to go, and that's along the banks of this river. Anybody that leaves the river any distance wont get back, and would likely get scalped before long. We've got to stick together till we're past Memphremagog."

Bradley looked doubtful. "I'll tell 'em to eat less." And somewhat unnecessarily, I thought, he added, "They're right hungry."

"Can't help it! They're to do as I say, or they'll be a hell of a lot hungrier! Tell 'em to divide their corn into six parts—six, say, or seven or eight—and not to eat more than one of the parts every day, no matter how hungry they get! If they can eat less than that, they'd better."

"I'll tell 'em, Major. There's another thing, though. They're all arguing about how far it is from here to the Ammonoosuc, where you said there'd be food. They keep talking about it all the time. Not knowing nothing about how far it is, they're making some pretty wild guesses."

"Make 'em stop it!" Rogers ordered. "I'll tell 'em how far it is. It isn't much over a hundred miles, as the crow flies, from the northern end of Memphremagog to the Ammonoosuc. Call it a hundred and ten. That's all it is. I've been over it myself."

"As the crow flies!" Bradley's mouth dropped open. "My God, we aint crows, Major!"

Rogers shrugged his shoulders. "Well, that's how far it is. Only a hundred and ten miles."

His use of the word "only" struck me as characteristic. So far as I could see, he drew no distinctions between small events and large—between great hazards and minor ones. All obstacles, apparently, looked the same to him—perhaps because he meant to surmount them all.

But my knapsack, like Bradley's, was only half full of corn. There may have been about three quarts in it; about twelve cups. Twelve cups of corn to get us to Memphremagog, mysteriously distant, and from there a hundred and ten miles to the Ammonoosuc. I felt myself go suddenly hot all over, like a man with a bad tooth just before the blacksmith pulls it out for him with pincers. For I saw that the distance we'd marched on the way to St. Francis must be less than half as far as we had now to go before we could reach the Ammonoosuc and the store of food waiting for us there.

Bradley walked away with his head down. Jennie Coit had lain down beside Ogden and was asleep, one arm across his blanketed figure.

"Damned mink!" Rogers growled. "Sergeant, get her blanket and pack and send it back here. It kind of looks to me as if she wouldn't bother anybody but Ogden for the next few days."

I can't even imagine how Rogers knew we'd strike bad going on the following day; but we did, and by midmorning —it was the fourth day—we began to see hills ahead: miniatures of those abrupt hills peculiar to the northern portion of the section now called Vermont. The river grew narrow, racing over a rock-filled bed between steep banks cut with brooks. By noon we were among them, laboring up steep slopes through tangles of undergrowth; slipping down their far sides: clambering up and stumbling down all through the rest of the day.

Rogers gave orders to Lieutenant Solomon and Konkapot, scouting ahead, to shoot a deer, bear or moose if they saw one, but nothing smaller. Our crashing through the undergrowth and our rustling in the dead leaves must have frightened the game away, for there seemed to be none. At night we had heard, high up, the squawking of ducks going south, or the shrill and mournful comments of geese; and nearer at hand the unending exchange of complaints between owls; but during the day we saw nothing; heard nothing save an occasional crow or the far-off, thrice-repeated call of a hungry hawk.

Ogden did well. He walked with his hand hooked in Jennie's blanket strap; and behind him went the Indian boy Billy, pushing at his rump to help him up hills, and holding to his belt to keep him from falling down them. Behind Billy went Bub, carrying Ogden's blanket, knapsack and musket. The group of them, scrambling up hill and down, put me in mind of Sisyphus, forever rolling his boulder up a slope, only to have it slip to the bottom so that he must start all over.

Ogden had the look of a man doomed to everlasting labor. He never glanced to either side: never raised his eyes from the ground before him: just stumbled on, pulled and pushed onward by his tireless shadows. Not only did Jennie help him on: she fed him, washed his bandage and changed it, clipped his hair, sewed up the rents in his clothes—all within the five-minute halts that we still made hourly, to make sure no one straggled. He seemed to have become her one interest in life, and it was plain that she would have given him her clothes if he'd have taken them: her few remaining kernels of corn; would have done anything to get him on and endlessly on.

That day we made fourteen miles; but the fifth day was bad. The hills were higher: the logans between steeper; the brooks more torrential: the boulders in them larger and more slippery. That was the day Ogden, for the first time since he was wounded, looked around to see how the rest of us were doing. It was difficult, a little later, to tell the days apart; but in the early days of our retreat there were distinguishable features that made them easily remembered.

The fifth day—the day Ogden first looked around—was the tenth day of October.

The sixth I recall because to the southward we saw real mountains in our path—sharp, jagged peaks; and because on that day a few men ran out of corn. They were the ones who had looted; and they began trading their loot for food—a wampum collar for a handful of corn: a silver brooch for a cupful.

The seventh, too, I remember, because when, at night, I returned from filling canteens with water, I saw Crofton kneeling in a singular dog-like posture. When I came quietly up behind him, I saw he had drawn something large and round from his knapsack, and was gnawing at it—gnawing and pulling, as a dog wrenches at the gristle on a bone.

"For God's sake, what's that?" I asked.

Crofton gave the thing a quick push into his knapsack and rubbed his mouth with the back of his hand. His push had been too hurried, and the thing rolled out again, like something alive, creeping out to look around. It was a head—an Indian's head.

I can't recall what I said, but Crofton came close to me —so close that I backed away and wanted to run. "It's mine," he whispered. "No harm taking what's mine, seeing what they did to my brother!" He laughed with the bubbling sound that a horned owl makes when it holds a rabbit in its claws.

Yet it struck me at the time that his argument was reasonable. Perhaps my mind was strange because of a month of insufficient, uncooked food—of daily forced marches and wet clothes—of never knowing when the French and Indians might come up with us. At all events, it seemed to me that if Crofton's brother had been horribly killed by Indians, he

too had every right to kill Indians horribly and do what he
pleased with those he killed. Not until later did I realize
that war robs us of our reasoning powers, so that we think
and believe strange things.

It was on the day after this, the eighth since St. Francis,
that we sighted Memphremagog—a beautiful, narrow lake
set among hills and mountains the shape of sharks' teeth:
hills so steep they seemed to have been made by a giant beneath the earth's crust, thrusting upward with a stick before
the crust was cold.

That day, I then thought, was the darkest we would know.
It was the thirteenth of October. But it was only the beginning of a nightmare that even still comes back to set me ex-
claiming and groaning in my sleep, until strangers wake in
other rooms and pound upon the wall.

CHAPTER XXXIII

IT WAS during the forenoon
that we stumbled over the shoulder of a hill and sighted
Memphremagog through the brown leaves. The day was a
weather-breeder if ever I saw one: a brilliant, glittering day,
so clear that we could see, in seemingly unending ranks to
the southward, a host of sharp toy mountains, bright blue
against the pallid, cloudless sky. Across the lake rose even
higher mountains, crammed together helter skelter, so that
the land was overcrowded with them. We were coming to a
terrible country: no doubt of that.

From the murmuring that arose from the scarecrow men
behind me, I knew the sight of Memphremagog, to which we
had so long looked forward, meant safety, rest, food—chiefly food. There must be fish in it: deer would come to it to
feed: its coves, no doubt, were full of ducks in the early
morning.

Food had become an obsession with all of us, for now all
our knapsacks were as empty as we were. I was lucky; in

the bottom of mine there remained a single cupful of corn, and if I dropped a grain, men hunted for it on hands and knees. For days we had lived in hope that when we reached Memphremagog, we would be free of the fear of pursuit: could build ourselves roaring fires, broil trout by the thousands beside them, sleep warm and undisturbed once more.

Marvelously, though Jennie Coit still marched beside Ogden, he needed her support no longer. The Indian boy Billy carried his pack, but he had taken to carrying his own musket, and he held his head up and looked about him as he walked.

To those who marched near him, Jennie had come to seem almost a part of him—so much a part we scarcely noticed her. She seemed content to keep an eye on him, as a dog keeps an eye on his master. When we sighted the lake, she skipped a little, gaily, clapped her hands and said in that harsh voice of hers: "We'll have trout for supper!"

The words were scarcely out of her mouth when Rogers turned on her. He looked pretty wild. The curved decoration had long since disappeared from the rear of his little hat; the upright black visor was broken, and had the appearance of an enormous misplaced eye-patch. His brown beard was fiercely bushy, and the pouches beneath his slate-colored eyes had grown more pronounced.

"Trout!" he cried. "How'll you get trout! Maybe you think you'll find someone up here who'll lend you a boat and some bait!" He snorted and went swinging on through the trees, obliquing away from the lake instead of going toward it.

Jennie shot a quick glance at Ogden and was silent. Now that he was better, she was more careful how she answered Rogers. I was sure that she had never before been afraid of anything in her life, but that now she was afraid—afraid of losing Ogden.

Around mid-afternoon Lieutenant Dunbar came up to the head of the line to speak to Rogers. Officers and men alike, during the last few days, had altered so startlingly that sometimes I had to look at them hard to remember who they were. Dunbar was a different man from the stooped, reedy-looking, thin-haired Britisher I had first seen at Crown Point; for from under his dilapidated green Ranger's cap, his blond hair hung down over his ears, and a fluffy blond beard broadened the lower part of his face. For warmth he had wrapped his upper body with strips of green strouding from St. Francis and over it pulled his ragged buckskin shirt, so that he seemed almost corpulent by comparison with what he had been. Even his voice had become hoarser and less reedy.

"Major," he said to Rogers, "is there any possibility of stopping to hunt food?"

"Not just yet, Lieutenant," Rogers said kindly. "We've still got a little food left, and the chances are the French have, too."

"When do you think we might stop, Major?" Dunbar asked. "All the men expected to stop when we reached Memphremagog; and now we're swinging away from it, they're worried."

"Don't they have any corn left?"

"Most of 'em haven't. They think they're going to starve to death. They say if they could stop at the lake for just one day, they'd shoot enough and catch enough to get anywhere."

Rogers went swinging on, almost as if he hadn't heard him. Then he said, "Well, Lieutenant, they can't stop. Encourage 'em all you can. Tell 'em we're liable to stumble on a deer almost anywhere along here."

"What's a deer for a hundred and forty men?" Dunbar asked.

Rogers marched straight ahead. Lieutenant Turner and Ensign Avery came up while Dunbar still walked beside Rogers, evidently loath to take No for an answer.

Rogers glanced at Turner out of eyes that looked as though he hadn't slept for a month—and I think he scarcely had. "Well, Lieutenant, what's troubling you?"

"Major," Lieutenant Turner said, "I don't believe some of my men are going to last much longer."

"So you want to stop and hunt, do you?" He gave an explosive whoop that passed for laughter.

"No, sir," Turner said. "The men seem to think they'd be all right if they could split into small detachments and take different routes. They say we'll never find game, travelling in such a big party as this—never."

"That's what my detachment thinks," Avery said. Avery, when I first saw him in Crown Point, had been a round-faced boy with a clear, tanned skin. He didn't look like that now. Two deep grooves like sabre-cuts extended from his nostrils to his chin, and between those grooves the flesh was a bluish white. His eyes were half-closed, as if he were almost asleep on his feet.

It was Turner and Avery that Rogers had taken with him to reconnoiter St. Francis the night before we attacked, so I knew he had a good opinion of them.

"You say that's what your detachments think," Rogers said. "Is that what you think too, gentlemen?"

With one voice Dunbar, Turner and Avery replied "Yes, sir."

Lieutenant Farrington and Lieutenant Grant came up behind Avery, looking draggled and worried. All of them together put me in mind of a picture I had once seen of Robinson Crusoe, a hairy, strangely-clothed man in a wilderness of trees; and it came to me with something of a shock that I looked like that myself.

Rogers seemed to see Farrington and Grant out of the back of his head. "Your men grumbling too?"

"Not grumbling, Major," Farrington said. "They just want a little food."

"Oh," Rogers said, "if they *all* feel that way about it, I suppose we'll have to hold a council of war, but we'll have it tonight: not before. Tell your men to keep going hard, and when we camp, we'll decide what to do."

He looked up at the sky; lifted his big beak of a nose and sniffed the air. "Just bear this in mind, though. My wounds hurt. We're going to get weather, and I don't believe the hunting'll be much good for a day or two."

No one replied, and Rogers had nothing more to say. The officers waited for their detachments to catch up. It was the first time I had ever seen one of Rogers' officers do that. Hitherto they had always hurried back down the line to join their men.

We stopped for the night on a flat-topped knoll above a brook that flowed toward Memphremagog. The entire command, barring sentries, had gathered at Rogers' orders into a tight circle around the knoll. There was no way of telling whether he'd thus pulled the men close together because he expected an attack, or to give it more warmth and confidence.

He held his council of war on the crest of the knoll, which was black as a smoke-house. It was the dark of the moon, and the stars had dwindled to faint points, instead of being made brighter by the darkness. The men around me were vague shadows: I felt the loom of their bodies rather than saw them.

"Let's get this decided," Rogers said. "There's been talk of splitting up into hunting parties. I'll listen to the opinion of every officer. Ensign Avery, are you still of the same opinion?" Avery was the youngest, and so entitled to express himself first in the council of war.

"Yes, sir," he said. "My men can't go much farther unless they have something to eat. They're beginning to get stomach cramps."

The officers murmured in agreement. I could see opinion was strong in favor of splitting up.

"Captain Ogden," Rogers said, "what's your idea? You've had more to contend with than most of us."

Ogden was silent so long that in the darkness I thought he might have slipped away somewhere, with Jennie. Rogers had to call his name again.

"Well," Ogden said, "it's pretty hard to drive men when they're as hungry as these. If they all felt like me, I'd say keep on the way we are for another day or two. I believe we'd be better off in the end."

Lieutenant Dunbar spoke up. "Major, when we started this retreat, you said we'd be all right if we could reach Memphremagog. We've reached it, and there's no signs of any French behind us. Maybe they *aren't* behind us. Perhaps they couldn't locate enough supplies to carry 'em this far. Maybe they figured we went another way. Has anything led you to alter the opinion you gave us at St. Francis?"

"You misunderstood me, Lieutenant," Rogers said. "I told you we'd be all right when we *passed* Memphremagog. We haven't passed it yet. We're still abreast of it."

The others were silent.

"Now," the commander said, "we'll put it to a vote; but before we do, there's a few things I'd like to mention. A hungry man can keep going lots longer than he thinks he can, if only he keeps his courage. Look at Captain Jacobs and his Stockbridge men. They're as well off, almost, as when they started, and they've had no more than any of us.

I've seen Indian boys go ten days without any food at all, just so they could dream better dreams about what to carry in their medicine bags. Another thing, this country in here is tricky country. It's full of ravines, bad corners, bogs you'll have to skirt—a mighty easy place to stumble into an ambush. I know a little about it, because I've been through here once myself. But those behind us—if they *are* behind us—know *all* about it."

A voice on the edge of the circle quietly said, "Vote."

"All right," Rogers said. "I'll hear from those in favor of continuing in a body."

The only one to speak was Ogden, who loudly said "Aye!"

If Rogers was disappointed, he failed to show it. "That's enough! We'll divide into parties around noon tomorrow. I want to march 'em to the eastward a little, to get 'em clear of the bogs at this northern end of the lake; and I'll have to rearrange the detachments, so each one can have as good guides and leaders as possible. I'll make maps tonight, so each party'll have one.

"There's just two things I want you to remember. The place we'll head for is the mouth of the Ammonoosuc, where it runs into the Connecticut at the Cohase Intervales, opposite Wells River. The Ammonoosuc: don't forget it. That's where food'll be. All you've got to do is hold out till you reach the Ammonoosuc. I can show you exactly where it is on the map. There's probably food there right now, waiting for us.

"The second thing you want to remember is to keep moving southeast. The Connecticut is southeast of us. The more you bear to the south, the easier the going is, and the farther it is to the river. Once you reach the river, you're all right. It runs through intervales all the way—the Cohase Intervales: prettiest country you ever saw. It's all cleared land—cleared and cultivated by the Indians. At the lower end of the Intervales is the Ammonoosuc. Get that far and you've got nothing more to worry about. Is that all clear?"

They mumbled that it was. Then in silence I could hear Rogers getting to his feet, and could imagine him pressing his dilapidated little hat down over his untidy growth of hair with enormous hands. "All right, gentlemen: we march at dawn as usual. Just warn your men I'm building a small fire on the southern slope of the knoll, so to draw the maps."

He called to me and Ogden. I heard Jennie murmuring to

Ogden and helping him to his feet. When we got a fire going and carefully screened, she sat behind Ogden in the fire pit, her back to his, to let him prop himself against her as against a chair.

Rogers and Ogden went over and over the map. Rogers traced the route he had followed when he had explored the Cohase Intervales with Captain Powers in 1754, and built the fort at the mouth of the Ammonoosuc in 1755. He had a mind that held more things than my grandfather's attic. "If you leave the Connecticut here," he said, tapping the map with a huge forefinger, "and strike across to the upper waters of the Ammonoosuc, you can save ten miles." I wrote down the landmarks to be followed: a sugar-loaf mountain: the scar of a snowslide on a hill: a giant boulder shaped like a frog: a solitary elm blasted by lightning.

He remembered where dead trees had jammed in the stream: where there were falls: the height and length of the falls: where there were eagle nests, woodchuck colonies, cliff-swallows' holes. He had forgotten nothing he had seen. It seemed impossible for any head to retain such a mass of information without bursting.

I made ten copies of the map. When I had finished, Rogers took the book from me, tore out the ten pages; then pushed both book and maps into the front of his buckskin shirt.

"Don't you want me to keep the book?" I asked.

He shook his head. "No: you've got a chronometer and know how to take a sight. Ensign Avery doesn't. I'm going to lend you to Avery in case he gets lost."

I tried to look unconcerned. "You've got education," Rogers went on, "and Avery hasn't. If a man has education, he isn't as apt to get discouraged as quick as one who hasn't. . . . Avery's a good officer. I want him to get out safe. I guess the two of you together'll be all right, but if anything *should* happen to him, you'll be able to take care of his detachment."

I wanted to tell him that I wasn't nearly so educated as he thought I was, but my mind spun from one irrelevant subject to another: to McNott, who had said I wasn't educated at all; to Hunk Marriner, who hadn't been in my thoughts for days; to Elizabeth, and our own kitchen, and Odiorne, who had wanted a tame Indian brought home to him.

Rogers, I found, was watching me closely. He grinned

heepishly. "Don't worry," he said. "You've got one advantage
over all the others. The others just want to stay alive, but
you want to stay alive and paint pictures. It's pretty hard to
destroy a man who's got a real incentive for wanting to live."

CHAPTER XXXIV

THE MAJOR'S aching wounds
were right, and the blue skies and far horizons of the day
before had been weather-breeders; for at dawn a northeast
blow set in, wrapping streamers of dirty gray mist around
the tops of the cone-shaped hills; sending brown leaves
whirling every which-way through the ravines between them.

I was filled with foreboding by the broken, irregular country; by the gloom of the wet fog and the mournful wind that
would surely bring rain; by the topsy-turvy manner in which
the watercourses flowed, so that no dependability could be
put upon them; by the knowledge that I must leave Jesse
Beacham and Ogden and Bradley and Rogers and those with
whom I had marched during all the long, long days, and
throw in my lot with men I knew far less well.

My breakfast of a dozen kernels of corn made me no more
cheerful as I pushed on behind Ogden and Jennie, up hill
and down, across brooks and through bogs. When noon came,
we might have been where we started at dawn. The hills
looked the same; the trees looked the same; the ravines were
as rocky and precipitous: only the storm was different. The
mist had turned to cold rain, which hissed maliciously upon
the few dead leaves that still clung to the dripping trees, and
drifted down-wind in sheets that thinned and thickened.

Rogers halted us on the southern side of an overhanging
cliff, first sending Captain Jacobs and Konkapot to the cliff-
top above us. At such a time as this, it struck me, he was
carrying things too far. I knew we wouldn't be here long;
and to station sentries against attack during a driving northeaster seemed ludicrous. Still, I had watched him long enough

to know he would persist in his methods, no matter what any of us thought.

The place where we halted might have been the center of a maze; for opposite us were four sharp hills, and at the end of the ravines between them we could see other hills, equally abrupt, and the mouths of more ravines that staggered off in half a dozen directions.

When Rogers signalled the detachments, they assembled before him—a draggled and miserable horde, their buckskins black from the downpour: their battered Scotch bonnets pressed down as far as they'd go. Water trickled from their beards and musket barrels: their moccasins and leggins, stuffed with leaves, made their feet and legs seem grotesquely distorted; the rents in their garments were mended with strips of blanket or strange odds and ends picked up at St. Francis. Nothing they wore seemed to fit, and their faces had the gaunt look of hairy, fleshless saints painted by Byzantine artists. The whites stood packed together, staring contemplatively at the Stockbridge Indians, who had squatted at the foot of the cliff, got out their mirrors and paint, and gone to daubing themselves with vermilion.

The officers gathered close to Rogers, but there was nothing in their dress or appearance to mark them as officers, for they were as tattered and bearded and harried-looking as any Ranger in the ranks—barring Crofton. Crofton had taken to crouching in his walk, as though he might, at any moment, help his movements by putting his hand to the ground like a monkey. He had a way of looking up frequently at those near him as does an ape, out of defiant eyes. His knapsack bulged. Some of the men in the detachment had complained of the smell that came from it, though I doubt they knew what caused it. Crofton looked worse than anybody else, which is the same as saying he looked like something out of a very strange and painful hell.

Mrs. Coit, Sarah Hadden and the German woman were just tired old hags, their hair straggling over their faces in dripping rattails. Mrs. Wick, who was shoeless, reminded me of a worn-out cat. She moved her bare feet up and down, as a cat does, and, like a cat, glared fixedly at Jennie Coit.

With the back of his hand, Rogers sloshed rainwater from his nose and cheeks, but drops remained upon the pouches beneath his eyes. "Still of the same mind?" he asked of nobody in particular.

There wasn't any answer; everybody's mind seemed made up to the change.

"All right," Rogers said. "What we'll do is split into twelve parties. It'll be best if some of those parties stay fairly close to each other, in case one party finds game and another doesn't. We'll find mighty little, anyway, till this storm lets up. I'm going to put five Rangers and five Indians with the women and start 'em straight for Crown Point. It's a long trip, but hunting's best in that direction, and as small a party as that, taking that route, isn't likely to be followed."

The women just looked helplessly at each other. Jennie Coit, standing close beside Ogden, moved behind him and put her cheek against his back.

"Lieutenant Solomon and Sergeant Clark," Rogers said, "you're in charge of the women. Choose five men, each of you, and get going. Don't waste time till you get around the southern end of Memphremagog: then you can march southwest. Take that middle ravine over yonder; the rest of us are starting in a few minutes."

Clark and Lieutenant Solomon called out the names of their followers, picked up their belongings and pressed through the throng of Rangers. The German woman shooed the three Indian girls ahead of her, and Mrs. Coit picked up her kettle—the kettle that had not yet been used. Only Mrs. Wick waited, moving her bare feet in the wet leaves. "She's got to come too, aint she?" she asked spitefully, pointing at Jennie.

Rogers, peering around Ogden, spoke sharply to the yellow-haired girl. "What you waiting for?"

She looked up at Ogden and pulled at his arm, but he stared straight ahead. Jennie pulled at his arm again; then she hoisted her pack heavily to her shoulder and turned away, stooping as if scarcely able to move. Mrs. Wick burst into a scream of laughter, slapping her hands on her knees to laugh the louder. Jennie, walking slowly, reached her; then suddenly took her by the hair, jerked her forward so that she sprawled grunting among the leaves. Jennie kicked her.

Rogers ran to them, pulled Jennie away, jerked Mrs. Wick to her feet, turned their backs to him, set a big hand upon each of those backs and pushed them forward. "If I were you I wouldn't fight," he said. "Not each other! You'll need considerable gimp to get to Crown Point! Better not waste it on somebody you don't like. Keep it for yourselves! Get on!" Neither Jennie nor Mrs. Wick answered or looked back. They went on, stumbling, following that miserable little column of women, ragged Rangers and painted Indians who were already dim to our sight in the drifting rain squalls.

A minute or two later four of the remaining eleven parties into which we were now divided moved away, more or less keeping one line, so that the four groups, though somewhat separated, were really a tiny army on its own. This body was headed by Lieutenant Farrington, Lieutenant Campbell, Lieutenant Curgill and a sergeant, each commanding his own group of ten men. Rogers had told them to head southeastward for the Ammonoosuc; and the rain hid the last man of them from us before they'd floundered two hundred yards from the cliff.

I was of the next party to move; we were to keep to the eastward of the first; and after us, and to the east of us, Rogers with the last of the command—thirty-eight men— was to follow. The party to which I belonged consisted of four groups, commanded by Dunbar, Turner, Jenkins and Avery. I went to stand with Ensign Avery, while the others were deciding with which of our four groups the five Stockbridge Indians assigned to us should travel.

Avery was so young that his beard lay on his cheeks like wet silk. "Look," he told me confidentially, "you don't know these men of mine. If they wasn't so hungry, they'd be the nine best in the whole command! We'll be put in the rear, on account of me being the youngest, but if we can find some way to get up front, these men of mine'll hit anything that shows its head." He spoke proudly. "They can hit flying squirrels at night—on the wing."

I hardly heard him, because of my impatience to be off and my uneasiness at leaving Rogers. He, too, was impatient. Twice he spoke sharply to Dunbar for his slowness in starting, which was unusual; for Dunbar was a British officer, and Rogers liked to be formal and polite to the British.

"Off with you," Rogers shouted harshly. "Get on!" And at that we began to move. Walking with Avery at the rear of our own party of ten, I looked around at Rogers, thinking he might give us a word of farewell, but he seemed already to have forgotten our existence, and was looking up at the cliff behind him and whistling through his fingers for Captain Jacobs and Konkapot.

The rain was trickling down the back of my neck. "You'll be glad you're with us instead of *them*," Avery assured me, plodding heavily, "as soon as these men of mine get something to eat. They're pretty hungry right now, but as soon as you get to know 'em, we'll have some good times."

I never got to know them.

CHAPTER XXXV

IF THERE is worse country— for men in a hurry—than that to the east of Memphremagog, I have yet to see it. Ordinarily, during storms in a forest, there are signs to indicate the points of the compass; and if a brook or river can be found, one needs only to go up it—or down it, as the case may be—in order to go farther on his way.

Memphremagog isn't like that. Its hills and mountains are packed together like fish-balls on a platter; and wind, blowing between two hills and striking another, is twisted about so that it blows in circles. Thus rainstorms, instead of hitting trees properly and causing moss to grow on the northerly side, strike from all directions at once. As for the water-courses, there are brooks within half a mile of each other, flowing in four directions at the same time. Streams turn at right angles for no apparent reason, or make almost complete loops; and the valleys through which some of them flow are so deep and so involved that they seem to have been planned and dug by an insane god.

Our course was a snake's all the rest of that day, winding along ravines and around the shoulders of hills. The men strayed out on side excursions looking for something to shoot, so that they had to be watched and urged back into line. It seemed to me we were getting nowhere; and because of that slowness, and the howling rain-laden wind and the constant aching discomfort within me, I was irritable and apprehensive. I had the feeling someone would tread on my heels if I couldn't get forward.

The afternoon seemed no more than started before the sheets of rain and the low-lying clouds brought a dismal twilight upon us. When we came up with some of Jenkins' Rangers cutting spruce boughs, I looked at my chronometer. It was only a little past three. When I showed it to Avery, he cursed under his breath.

"What's this?" Avery asked the men. "What you stopping for?"

"Going to camp here," one of them said.

Avery spoke sharply to his own followers, who had halted. "Keep your packs on! We'll see about this!"

We pressed on to where Dunbar and Turner were helping their groups of men to settle themselves. Just beyond them the ground fell away into a ravine so broad that the far side was blurred in rain and dusk.

"Lieutenant," Avery said to Dunbar, "can't we get on a little farther? It aint half past three yet."

Dunbar's voice was thin and tired. "It's nearly dark, Mr. Avery, no matter what the hour is. Have you seen what's ahead of us?"

He led us closer to the ravine. It was a bad one, perhaps two hundred feet deep and while the bank on our side was steep and thinly wooded, the far side was rocky and even steeper. The distance from the level spot on which we stood to the top of the opposite bank was a good six hundred yards, and the stream at the bottom, even in the murk, was a silvery ribbon of quick water.

"If we try to cross that stream tonight," Dunbar said, "we stand to have men drowned, or lose muskets and wet what little powder we've got left. In the morning, when it's light, they'll be rested and ought to be able to cross without trouble."

Avery turned and looked behind him: raised his eyes to scan the sky: then once more stared into the ravine. Lieutenant Turner came up to us and stood staring down too. Avery eyed Turner questioningly. "What you want to camp here for? This is a hell of a place!"

"Maybe so," Turner said. "Some of these men aint feeling

too good. That's an awful easy place to break a couple legs."

"What you think?" Avery asked me.

I said I thought we ought to cross while the light held: that the water might rise much higher if the rain kept falling; I urged that we could make better time the next day if we crossed now.

Avery looked apologetically at Dunbar. "That's what I think, Lieutenant."

Dunbar nodded. "I wont try to stop you, Mr. Avery. We're each of us responsible for his party. You're subject to no one's orders but your own," and I took this to be a hint that Dunbar could get along without suggestions from Avery or me.

"Well," Avery said, "well——" He hesitated; then added: "We'll hunt on the far bank till you come up with us in the morning."

"That's not necessary," Dunbar said. "We might take a few fish from the stream for breakfast, or hunt a little on this side, so don't have us on your mind. You'll find us close behind you before night."

Avery called sharply to his men; we moved forward; and when the others saw the ravine, they pulled at their caps and fastened their powder-horns and pouches more securely.

"We got to get across this tonight," Avery said. "Watch where you put your feet."

He went down the bank, slipping, saving himself by grasping at trees. I slid after him, put my foot through a tangle of dead branches, pitched headlong and rolled against a tree with a thump that made me grunt. When Avery helped me up, I saw Dunbar's and Turner's heads thrust out over the lip, watching us. Probably, I thought, Avery and I were fools to pit our judgment against theirs; but there was nothing to do now but go on.

The men stumbled and fell repeatedly on the slippery steep slope, deep with wet leaves and soft mold. The lower we went in the ravine, the less the wind howled above us and the louder became the rushing of the stream. When we reached the bottom at last, we found a white torrent surging over boulders, and the tops of the boulders looked disgustingly slippery.

I suspected, when I felt this roaring stream pull my feet out from under me and hurl me gasping against an icy rock, that Dunbar had known best. Yet, when I reached the far bank, I was little wetter than I had been at any time during the day.

I looked back up the steep slope down which we had floundered, but I could see nobody. The top was a blur of gray treetops dimly traced against a wet obscurity.

-Some of the men overturned boulders at the edge of the stream, in the vain hope of finding something living that might be eaten, and one muttered about camping here, so to fish in the morning.

"Listen," Avery said, "we'd be all day catching a mess in this stream. They wont bite in a northeaster, anyway. The place to get 'em is a pond. Maybe we'll find one tomorrow."

"You don't mean to say there's *ponds* around here!" one of the men exclaimed.

Another laughed weakly—probably because we had found ponds wherever we turned—and continued to laugh and laugh, like a girl overcome with mirth at her own brainlessness. We all laughed with him out of sympathy.

"Well," Avery said, "there aint none of us dead yet, so we might be worse off."

We worked our way slowly up the farther declivity, holding by sodden shrubs and pulling ourselves over ledges and blown-down trees wedged precariously among them. We could just see to do it; and even so, when we worked hard to surmount bad spots, we had.to rest a little until our legs stopped shaking and our muscles quivering.

When we reached the top and looked back, we saw a red glow on the bank we had left. "Look at that!" Avery cried. "That's something I aint seen in some little time! Wouldn't Rogers give 'em hell if he saw it? Guess they must be cooking their moccasins and shirt fringes!"

He went crawling off to look for shelter and found it in a little grove of spruces pressed close against a rock. Nobody so much as mentioned a fire, probably because we would have been so long in finding dry wood. We packed ourselves into the shelter, one against the other, with our wet blankets tight around us. This is not as cold as it sounds when the weather isn't frosty, for a steam seems to lie next to the body after a time.

I had perhaps half a cup of corn left, and Avery had fifteen or twenty grains. The others had a few, so we put them all together and doled them out, one at a time, till the last kernel was gone. Everybody had eight apiece, and three had nine. I felt myself a scoundrel for being one of the three who had nine, but ate them.

The wind howled all night, and the rain slatted and hissed through the trees and on the dead leaves. Long before dawn we had slept ourselves out, and the men, in soggy misery, spoke of what sort of food would be waiting for us at Ammonoosuc. They referred longingly to John Askin, the Rangers' sutler, wishing he might be the one to bring supplies; and the Rangers' fare of which they spoke was tantalizing. They mentioned a red wine which Askin alone was able to procure: large, tender sausages; a special ham so cured that it was almost black; chocolate cakes, round red cheeses, cigars from the Sugar Islands, and a pale brown rum that could be drunk by the bottle without causing anything but a delightful exhilaration and quickening of all the senses.

When we could finally see our hands before our faces, we had been rolled in our blankets for nearly thirteen hours.

Avery crawled out from among us, wrung the water from the remnants of his Scotch cap and made his tattered blanket into a sodden roll. "The first pond we strike," he said, "we can try the fish, but prob'ly we wont have any luck to speak of till the wind changes—nothing but little stink-pans."

A thought seemed to strike him, and he counted rapidly on his fingers. "By God!" he said. "What is this? The fifteenth?"

I said it was.

"New moon's about due," he said. "If this storm don't break pretty damned quick, we'll have weather all the way to the Ammonoosuc!" The men, busy on hands and knees with their blankets, groaned and spat.

Avery walked off toward the lip of the ravine. The sound of his footsteps in the soggy leaves ceased suddenly—so suddenly that I rose to my feet and looked after him.

He stood there, fifteen paces away, frozen, one hand before him to ward off branches, one half-raised to his cap, as a hunter freezes when he unexpectedly sees a distant deer. Thinking he *had* seen a deer, I picked up my musket and scrambled toward him. He whipped behind a tree, dropped to his knees, and looked back at me. His face, above his beard, was ghastly.

Beyond him, from the ravine, I heard an awful sound—a thin, high squeal made by a man. I heard yells, half-howl and half-caterwaul, that made the skin move behind the ears, as at the shriek of a lynx.

When I reached Avery, he snapped up the lock of my musket and knocked the powder from the pan so it couldn't be fired.

The whole bottom of the ravine, at first glimpse, appeared alive with moving figures. I could distinguish men plunging downward through the trees of the opposite slope: others scurrying confusedly at the edge of the stream.

"Christ!" Avery whispered. "They'll get 'em all! Every damned one! It's an ambush!"

The confusion in the ravine became clearer to me. Upstream and downstream, in two scattered groups, were Indians crouched behind boulders: lying behind fallen tree-trunks. They were painted black and vermilion. Those rushing down the bank, and stumbling jerkily at the edge of the stream, were Dunbar's, Turner's and Jenkins' men. Rushing with them and darting among them were other black-painted Indians and a horde of small men—Frenchmen—in a brighter green than the greenish buckskins of the Rangers. There must have been two hundred Frenchmen and Indians.

If one of the stumblers broke loose from those around him and started upstream or downstream, a hidden Indian rose from behind a boulder and sank a hatchet in him.

I made out Dunbar, standing at the edge of the water, defending himself with his bayoneted musket against three Frenchmen. Seemingly the powder was wet; for not a musket was fired. An Indian came out of the foaming water behind Dunbar, split his head with a hatchet, and leaped forward on him as he fell. He knelt on Dunbar with one knee and chopped off his head.

From the struggling, confused throng came agonized cries that made me sweat and shake. I saw two Indians, upstream, holding down a Ranger, head and foot, while a third Indian dismembered him with a hatchet, although he was still alive and screaming.

"Don't let any of our men come up here!" Avery said to me. "Get 'em moving! There aint a damned thing we can do but get out quick! If we don't——" He didn't finish: he didn't need to.

So suddenly had this horrible thing happened that our men were where I had left them, crouched over their muskets to keep off the rain while they re-primed them.

They stood up and came toward me. "Get on your packs and blankets," I said.

"Aint we going to help 'em?" one of the men asked.

"There's two hundred to our eleven," I said. "They're out of range, and there's nothing we could do but get ourselves wiped out if a hair of us is seen. Avery says to get going."

"What about the ones that get away?" a Ranger asked.

Avery came up behind me, reached down and got his musket. He looked sick. "None of 'em got away. They killed 'em all. They're playing ball with their heads!"

I think we might have got clear away if we hadn't shot the moose; though there's no telling about such things. If we hadn't shot the moose, we might have caught up with Rogers and then Rogers would have been the one to suffer, which would have been a terrible thing for everyone. It's worse than fruitless, I find, to speculate on what might have happened under different circumstances; for too much of such speculation sometimes makes a man afraid to do anything.

It seemed best to Avery and me to bear sharply to the eastward. That direction, we knew, would bring us across the trail of Rogers' party; and by hurrying we could give him intelligence of the French and Indians and put him on his guard.

All that day the northeaster blew and the rain drove in our faces while we plodded miserably to the east. It seemed to me I had never had enough to eat, and never again could have; but in spite of our emptiness, we went on and on without a halt, clambering along watercourses, scrambling over the shoulders of hills, pulling ourselves out of ravines, dragging ourselves across bogs—and forever looking fearfully behind. We spoke no more of fishing. We would have needed bait to catch fish, and time to catch them, and a fire for cooking. It was the fire that bothered us. Its odor would have carried miles down-wind; and headed as we were, that scent would have been as good as a sign-post to the French and Indians who killed Dunbar and his parties.

On the next day, the sixteenth of October, the rain stopped, but the wind held on from the northeast, howling and screaming through the treetops. That afternoon we struck tracks, bearing to the southeast. The tracks seemed to be made by between thirty and forty men; and since we knew Rogers' detachment consisted of thirty-eight in all, we were sure they were his. We made certain when, in muddy spots, we found the prints of bare feet protruding from broken moccasins. We turned along them, feeling greatly cheered and almost safe once more; and to add to our satisfaction, the northeast wind faded toward sundown. Then, when we huddled together to get what sleep we could, we saw an occasional star through the breaking clouds—a Godsend, since we dared not wrap ourselves in our blankets after seeing Dunbar's finish. We could only pull them over us, so to leave our arms and legs free.

Unfortunately the clearer weather brought a heavy frost. Our blankets froze, and to better our condition we covered ourselves a foot deep in wet leaves.

When we crawled out in the morning, we were so stiff with cold that we were like drunken men. The wind, however, had gone into the south, so we hurried cheerfully onward, hopeful of soon coming up with Rogers, of striking good hunting in warm October weather, and of an easy journey to the Ammonoosuc.

It occurred to none of us to regard the moose as an omen. We thought of her as just a cow moose, brought out of hiding by the south wind and impelled to move about in search of food. She came over a hardwood ridge in front of Avery, looking as big as a Kittery barn, and Avery let her have it in the brain for good luck; and the eleven of us jumped on her.

Moose meat has less fat than any other, so there is little nourishment to it; but it is meat, nonetheless; and not one of us had eaten meat since we ate our last fragments of bologna sausage the day before we attacked St. Francis. For eleven days we had eaten nothing but corn, and mighty little of that; so Avery had his knife into the moose's throat before she stopped kicking, and the men were on her hindquarters with knives and hatchets.

Avery stopped them. "You know better'n that! If you eat that meat fresh killed and raw, you'll be sick! You wont be able to move!"

"I've eaten worse'n this!" one of the men said. They went

right on cutting. They intended to eat: no doubt of that.

"Look," Avery said, "take off the skin first. We need it for moccasins. The rest of you open her up and take out the liver, and we'll cook it. Then we'll divide the meat and catch up with the Major and eat the rest tonight. That way it wont make anyone sick."

One of the men sat back on his heels, a chunk of bloody meat in his hand. "Cook hell! This wood here is all hard-wood! It wont never burn!"

"Put that meat down, Higgins," Avery shouted. The man obeyed him reluctantly.

"Now for God's sake," Avery said, "don't eat it raw! We passed some spruce growth a ways back. I'll take Higgins and Peters, and the four of us'll go back and get a couple dead trees that'll burn. The rest of you skin her and cut her up, and by the time that's done the food'll be cooked and it'll do us some good."

They slowly went to work slitting the skin on the legs and belly.

"Come on," Avery said to me. Peters and Higgins followed us reluctantly. They were the recalcitrant ones, who had been most determined to eat. "Prime your muskets," Avery warned us. "There might be a full moose hanging around waiting for that cow, and the waiting might have upset him."

When the four of us worked back along our trail, we found the stand of spruces that Avery had noted, two hundred yards to the rear; and wherever there are spruces, there are blow-downs of dead trees. We picked out two small ones, trimmed off the upper branches so they were easy to carry, and went to work dragging them into the clear. It was hard work freeing them. The starvation rations of the past few days seemed to have made my knees limber, but we had them almost out when Avery looked up at me. "What's that?"

I had said nothing.

"I thought you'd hurt yourself," he explained. He glanced at Peters and Higgins, struggling with their spruces: then went to them.

"Anything the matter? Didn't one of you let out a yelp?"

They stared at him in surprise.

Avery turned his head slowly toward me, a look of in-credulity in his eyes. Then, leaving us, he ran out of the spruce thicket, and a little way along our tracks; crouched where the ground rose a few feet. I saw that he was peering toward where we had left our seven men and the dead moose. On the instant when he crouched, I realized sickeningly what had happened. Like Dunbar, Turner and Jenkins, we too had been caught.

Avery sank flat on his stomach and squirmed back into the shelter of the spruces.

"Have they killed 'em?" I asked.

He shook his head. "Not with all that moose meat to be carried! They're prisoners and'll be made to carry the meat till it's eaten. Then they'll finish 'em."

He began to move off to our left, stooping. "Now we've *got* to get to Rogers."

Rogers! The thought of Rogers then was like the thought of home and safety.

CHAPTER XXXVI

Like four shadows we crept across our tracks, careful to leave no traces. By taking cover in depressions and behind boulders, we reached the shelter of a rocky knoll; and hidden among its ledges we watched thirty swarthy, stunted Frenchmen and a dozen painted Indians hustle our seven comrades off to the northeast. They had become beasts of burden: on their shoulders they bore gory fore- and hind-quarters; bundles of moose meat; the neck and hide. Frenchmen, carrying two muskets apiece, prodded the captive Rangers with their own bayonets, amid thin bursts of distant laughter.

We were helpless. If we made a move to rescue the luckless seven, they would be instantly hatcheted and we most certainly would lose our own lives as well.

"That's where that moose came from!" Avery said bitterly. "It was moving ahead of 'em!" He looked at me despairingly. "Who'd have expected to find 'em in *front* of us?"

"You don't suppose it was their tracks we'd been following?" I asked.

"Oh, God, no!" Avery said. "That moose came on us at an angle—diagonally across our trail; and that's the way those damned French rats were moving. They must have been sent out by those that caught Dunbar. They must have known a short way to get here. If they hadn't struck us, they'd prob'ly have turned after Rogers."

"Well," I said, "they'd have caught us either way, it seems to me. I don't see how you're to blame for killing the moose. Anybody'd have killed it, under the circumstances."

The lines of trouble on Avery's young face deepened. He was hardly more than a child, and was more concerned over making a mistake than over a catastrophe to someone else.

When there was no further sight or sound of the Frenchmen and Indians, we crept back to where we had shot the moose, to see whether anything had been left. A pack of wolves couldn't have stripped the carcass more thoroughly. They had taken the nose, the tongue, the brain; even the eyes, the ears and the intestines. Only the skull was left. "I guess they're as hungry as we are," Avery said. "I was hoping the French and Indians that were after us would starve to death; but it kind of looks as if these wouldn't be the ones."

He picked up the skull and a few scraps that lay among the blood-stained leaves. "I wish they'd left the hoofs. You can get a pretty good soup out of four hoofs and a moosehead—kind of gluey; sticks to your insides."

"If we'd et it raw, the way we wanted to," Higgins said bitterly, "we'd have *something* in us, anyway."

Avery turned on him. "By God, you aint got as much sense as a squirrel! Even a squirrel knows enough to look out for tomorrow! You'd have something in you—yes; but you'd be sick, and you'd be a prisoner, and tomorrow you wouldn't have anything in you but hatchet-holes! It beats hell how full the world is of people that don't know enough to thank God they're alive!"

The outburst seemed to make him feel better. He led us down that dim trail to the southeast as though he had food in him. Speed, I knew, was urgent; for the wind had turned back into the northeast again, and the sky was covered with a dingy pall of swiftly-moving clouds that foretold more rain.

We caught up with Rogers about an hour before dark. We knew we had reached him when, out of a seemingly empty forest, a bullet rattled through the branches above us, and the report of a musket whanged among the trees, echoing against far-off hills. We stood where we were, our muskets raised above our heads. I looked everywhere for the afterguard who had fired, but saw no sign of anyone until John Konkapot came out from behind a tree and made motions to someone to the rear of him. On that Sergeant Bradley and Jesse Beacham ran to him and stood waiting for us, and I own that the sight of them affected me. I had never expected to see their familiar faces again. As we came up, the three of them stared hard at the bloody moose-skull under Avery's arm.

Bradley looked beyond us. "Where's the rest of your detachment, Mr. Avery?"

"Tooken," Avery said. "How far's the Major?"

Bradley turned to Konkapot. "Go on ahead and tell the Major it's Mr. Avery and Langdon Towne and two Rangers." He took the moose-head from Avery and sniffed at it. "Fresh!" he exclaimed. "Where's the rest of it?"

"The French got it."

Bradley cursed feelingly and motioned Avery to go ahead. Jesse and I fell in behind them.

"Haven't you had anything to eat yet?" I asked Jesse.

"No," he said contemplatively. He plodded on silently; then thoughtfully added, "No, the weather aint been very good for hunting." He shot a quick glance at me from under bushy white eyebrows. "How'd you get away from 'em?"

"Just luck," I said. "We got away twice—the first time when they finished Dunbar, Turner and Jenkins."

Jesse made commiserative humming sounds. "Dunbar and Jenkins and all them men? Too bad. I'm glad you four got away. Better come and tell the Major now, I guess."

We found Rogers' detachment re-forming. At the sound of Konkapot's warning shot, the Major had thrown them out in a crescent-shaped line, and he stood in the center with Ogden and Lieutenant Grant, waiting for us. I think our misfortunes of the past few days may have had a weakening effect on me, for a wave of fondness swept over me when

I stood before them—such a wave as I had only felt, as a boy, when I saw my father after a long separation.

Rogers took us in at a glance. His eyes were more staring than they had been three days before, his black hat had lost the remaining half of its cockade, and his moccasins were reinforced with strips of strouding. Ogden, however, looked better. His face no longer resembled a greenish skull, but was merely emaciated.

"How'd they happen to get you, Mr. Avery?" Rogers asked.

"We killed a moose," Avery said. "When four of us went back to hunt firewood, the French jumped the others."

"You went *back!* Then they were in front of you!"

Avery nodded.

"How many? How far off were you when it happened? Which way'd they go?"

When Avery told him, Rogers spoke sharply to Bradley, telling him to send four sentries to the rear.

"Could we catch 'em?" he asked Avery.

Avery shook his head. "I doubt it. They'll have that moose meat to eat, and there's no telling when you'd strike the main body—the one that massacred Dunbar and Turner and all the men with 'em."

"What? What did you say?" The Major started and grunted with pain, as if he'd been kicked. "When was that? Did they kill 'em all? How do you know they did?"

"We saw it," Avery said. "It was the morning after we left you. We crossed a ravine, but Dunbar and the others stayed back on the other side. At dawn they were pushed into the ravine and ambushed. None of 'em got away."

Rogers stared at Avery. "And you were near enough to see it! How many were there?"

Avery looked sick. In a shaking voice he said: "About two hundred that we could see. There was eleven of us."

I felt called on to put in my oar. "They were out of range, Major. We couldn't have helped. If we'd been seen, they'd have got us, too."

Rogers nodded and cleared his throat. "Did they treat 'em pretty bad?"

"Yes, sir; they did. They treated 'em bad."

I heard a peculiar snuffling titter. Near us I saw Crofton crouched on the ground like a young bear. His hands were tied, he was on a rope, like a bear, and, like a bear, he swung himself from side to side and clawed at the ground.

"I told you to keep him in the rear," Rogers said angrily. "Hitch him to a tree and let him dig if he wants to!"

"Is he crazy?" I asked Jesse.

"Yes," Jesse said. "The Major found that head of his and took it away from him. Crofton's possessed to dig it up. That's all he thinks of: digging! If he aint on a rope, so he can be pulled along, he just stays wherever he is and digs."

Rogers looked up at the sky: then down at the moose-head that Bradley held. "Well," he said, "here's what we'll do. Just ahead of us there's two hills with a little valley between. It's only an hour to dark. We'll build a fire at the far end of that valley, and we'll make camp beyond the fire. That'll give us an hour to hunt for something to put with this soup-bone of moose-head; and if any of Avery's seven men have the luck to get away, they might hear the guns or see the fire and come in. We got to give 'em a chance. If the French should make up their minds to come this far, we'll make trouble for 'em before they ever get a look at us."

We hunted in a circle around those two hills until darkness came down on us, accompanied by more rain from the northeast. There were forty-two of us to be fed; and when we assembled around the fire we had a moose-skull, six black spruce partridges, five owls, a duck-hawk, a porcupine, three red squirrels and a crow, most of them badly damaged by musket balls. We boiled the mess in three of the kettles brought from St. Francis, dividing it as evenly as possible. I gave three cups of soup apiece. The soup wasn't rich enough to hurt an invalid, and I have no doubt it would have disgusted my Harvard classmates who cavilled at a rabbit pie; but it was hot, and it went a long way toward helping us endure the rain without discouragement. We were almost contented as we sat around the fire, crunching the little bones that were left in the bottom of the kettles.

Rogers wandered restlessly among us. "Don't swallow those bones," he kept saying. "With your stomachs empty, they'll cut holes in you. Don't swallow the bones. We'll be at the Ammonoosuc before long."

Jesse Beacham, gnawing fruitlessly at a chunk of moose-skull, said mildly that he'd come to think the Prodigal Son hadn't made such a bad trade when he sold his birthright for a mess of pottage. For his own part, he'd be glad to sell his birthright, or anything else, for half a mess of pottage, and would consider he was getting the best of the bargain.

There were beech trees near where we camped; so before we marched in the morning, we went to them and pawed among the sodden leaves for beech-nuts—nuts so small that one must hunt an hour under the best of circumstances to find a cupful, and then from them obtain scarcely enough meat to feed a wren. In wet weather a beech-nut becomes perverse and disappears entirely, leaving behind it nothing but the tantalizing burr from which it emerged.

While we thus hunted, we heard the sentries shouting, and when they came up with us, they were leading Andrew McNeal and Andrew Wansant, two of the seven who had been captured on the preceding day. Neither of the two had muskets, blankets, pouches or powder-horns. Their Scotch caps were gone. Both were naked above the waist, and they were scratched and clawed, as if by wildcats.

We crowded around them to hear their story. The first thing Rogers wanted to know was whether the Frenchmen had seemed to be still in search of us. McNeal said No: that they were going back to the north. They were hungry, he said: worse off than we when seen at close range; and like us, they had eaten nothing for days. Their uniforms, McNeal said, were as tattered as our own; all of Wansant's and McNeal's clothes had been taken from them at once to patch garments.

The other five, McNeal said, had not yet been killed or tortured. Neither he nor Wansant had been able to understand the lingo of the French or the Indians, but from their gestures he had understood that the prisoners would be made to carry game and kettles until they returned to Canada, when they would be turned over to squaws to be tortured.

They had been given split moose-bones to gnaw, and had been tied back to back, in pairs. McNeal had saved a sharp-pointed sliver of moose-bone. By driving the point into one of the cords that bound him, and patiently turning it round and round for two hours, he had frayed the rope and broken it. Another hour's work had freed him and Wansant; and the two of them, moving inch by inch, had crept beyond their sleeping captors.

"If it hadn't been for the noise of the rain and the wind," McNeal said, "we couldn't 'a' done it."

Wansant said simply, "I don't know yet how we done it."

"Thank God the Major lit a fire," McNeal said. "Wansant climbed a tree around midnight and thought he saw just a little glimmery spark, way away off. That's what kept us going."

We looked at them as at men who had been buried before our eyes, only to rise from the grave unhurt.

"Got anything to eat?" McNeal asked.

We gave them a few beech-nuts. The palms of McNeal's hands were raw; and the flesh was worn from the thumb and forefinger of his right hand so that the bones and tendons showed. He tossed the nuts in his mouth and chewed them, shell and all.

On that day, which was the eighteenth of October, the country seemed to grow even worse. The streams still ran in all directions, and while we thought the rain was coming from the northeast, we couldn't be certain of it because of yesterday's unexpected double change of wind. At length even Rogers began to suspect that our compasses had gone wrong: that we might be lost. I know there are some who can find their way in the forest by the manner in which moss grows on the trees, the greater number of limbs on the south sides, and the direction of the watercourses; but if we had lacked compasses, we couldn't have done it.

Rogers shook his head at the continued downpour. "I'm going to build a camp," I heard him tell Ogden, "and get something into these men. Half of us'll fish: the rest can build fires and stand guard. We'll try to dry out the blankets, too. If this storm comes off cold, we might have a little trouble."

I called Jesse Beacham's attention to this. "A little trouble!" I said ironically. "We might have a little trouble!"

"Well," Jesse said thoughtfully, "I dunno but what he's right."

Rogers spotted a squirrel and shot him for bait and we got our lines in the first stream we reached. If there was a trout in it longer than five inches, we couldn't find it. Five-inch trout make good enough eating, but they find difficulty in getting their mouths around hooks designed for fish considerably larger. After persistent work and endless cursing we collected a few hundred minnows, and since there is no more nourishment to a trout cooked without pork than to a handful of snow, Rogers set us to work scraping rock tripe to boil with them. Rock tripe is a greenish-gray crust that grows on boulders and ledges. When boiled it has a sickish and offensive smell, like stale paste, but supposedly it is nourishing.

We were all afternoon getting the trout and the tripe. We had become awkward and fumbling in our movements, and seemed to do everything slowly. Time after time we hooked midget fish, only to have them wriggle magically from our hands and squirm between our clutching fingers to safety. Ordinarily I would have found it amusing to see a score of hairy, hollow-eyed men on hands and knees among the boulders, pawing for escaped minnows and falling clumsily on their faces; but there wasn't anything funny about it now. We needed the minnows.

When we boiled the trout and the rock tripe, the mixture was like slush from a fish-pier. It wasn't for enjoyment we ate it, however, but for the strength to get us to the mouth of the Ammonoosuc. No matter how it tasted; it was food.

That was all we could talk about—food: the food we'd find at the Ammonoosuc—what sort of food it would be: whether John Askin, the Rangers' sutler, would be there with delicacies for us. Some thought he would: others were sure we would find nothing but regular army rations—salt pork, biscuit, coffee, chocolate, sugar and rum. We didn't care what it was, so long as it was food.

Next day we came to a stream that struck a familiar chord in the breast of the Indian boy Billy; but like all Indians, he was unwilling to commit himself until he was sure. He was a good boy, as was Bub. They still carried Ogden's blanket and pack, and had taken Rogers' blanket as well. They were friendly, like dogs, thin as little skeletons from lack of food, and pot-bellied from eating grass, buds, snails and small snakes. They seemed to have forgotten their previous existence, and to be genuinely attached to us.

The stream, a brawling, shallow one, differed from those

we had encountered since we first saw Lake Memphremagog by being crystal-clear and holding steadily to one direction. It ran northwest, however; and what puzzled all of us, including Rogers, was how it could still be running to the north, toward Lake Memphremagog, when we must already be far south of the headwaters of the Connecticut, which runs almost due south.

At length Billy freely admitted to recognizing the stream. He had, he said, travelled beside it, going from the Connecticut to Memphremagog with his mother at the end of a summer of raising corn and beans in the Intervales. By following it to its source, he told the Major, we would come to a beautiful pond with an island in the middle. Only a mile from that pond, he said, was the Nulhegan River, and the Nulhegan flowed downhill into the Connecticut. Once we had come to the Nulhegan, he insisted, the Connecticut was only a short march. He put his hands on his pot belly and added apologetically, "No meat, take longer."

There are spells, as every hunter knows, when game vanishes from where it ought to be. At such times a hunter, no matter how skillful, is helpless. The forest seems stripped of birds and animals. There is no great mystery about it. Usually it results from unusual weather conditions—heavy and long-continued rains, or excessive drought—and the game has merely changed its feeding grounds, and gone to eating things no hunter expects it to eat. Partridges, for example, abandoning their usual diet of birch buds, thorn apples and checkerberry leaves, might go into the high oaks and eat acorns, which no hunter in his right mind would think them capable of doing. That is why hunting parties of Indians so frequently starve to death in forests full of game which can't be found.

This was such a time. There were plenty of owls—little ones, with voices like the rasp of files on iron, and big ones with wild yellow eyes—but we didn't shoot them for fear of frightening something more worth having. Of all living creatures, an owl makes the worst eating, being three-fifths head and one-fifth bone, and the rest mostly voice. To make even a ghost of a meal for the forty-four of us, we would have needed eighty owls; and the entire eighty would have held no more nourishment than an equal number of trout, since they, too, are without fat.

We spread out on both sides of that brawling, clear stream, going slowly and carefully in the hope of jumping a deer; but never a deer did we see: only a damnable owl now and then, and occasionally an eagle, flapping laboriously toward some distant destination.

The sky remained overcast, and the trackless forest through which we marched was dark and somber; and that somberness was reflected in our own spirits. Only Rogers and Ogden and the Indian boys seemed cheerful; but their cheerfulness had no effect on me. I had suddenly realized that I didn't believe anything. I didn't believe we would ever find game: ever emerge from this endless forest: ever see the Connecticut: ever feel the sun's warmth or dry clothes or happiness. I didn't believe I would ever again set eyes on my home or on Elizabeth. When we rested I could only sit and brood, heavily, vacantly, sullenly resentful against all the world.

It was the same with Jesse Beacham: with Avery: with Bradley. If we were spoken to, we made no answer. When Rogers walked among us, grinning his piratical grin, and telling us in his thick voice that we'd be out of the woods soon, and at the Ammonoosuc before we knew it, we just sat and stared at the ground.

Billy had been right. We found the pond with the island in it, and nearby the Nulhegan, running to the southeast. Dejectedly and silently we made our way down it like scarecrows half-alive, watching and hoping for the deer or moose that no one ever saw.

On the 20th hope sprang up in us again, and our lowness of spirit left us, for we cut across the shoulder of a mountain and looked up a broad valley that stretched far to the north—the Connecticut Valley. Through the trees that filled the cut between the mountains we could see a broad ribbon of river, riffled and streaked with quick water. To us the Connecticut meant that the Ammonoosuc wasn't far away—the Ammonoosuc and food. We tittered weakly and made childish jokes as we stumbled toward that distant gleam.

The Cohase Intervales of the Connecticut are unlike other river intervales. The valley, at the Intervales, goes down to the river in two giant steps. It looks as though the river was once infinitely larger and deeper, held back by some vast dam, and had deposited a rich, flat river bottom at a high level. If such a dam had burst, lowering the level of the river by fifty feet, the river at that lower level would have laid down a new rich valley bottom; and that, seemingly, is what happened at the Cohase Intervales. The upper shelf of flat land is wide in some places and narrow in others: cut by incoming brooks that have made the edges of the upper shelf irregular, and occasionally left islands of earth rising from the flat surface of the lower shelf.

At the point where the Nulhegan flows into the Connecticut, the intervales are small and infrequent: farther to the southward they increase and flow together until they embrace the whole broad valley. Some of these intervales are clear by nature: others have been cleared in times past by northeren Indians, who found the Cohase Intervales the richest and most beautiful of all the farming-land within their reach.

When we came out of the forest onto the small intervale where the Nulhegan runs in, we could look down the valley for miles, and see on the far side a range of mountains that put me in mind of the sharp peaks along the shores of Memphremagog. The sky was a leaden gray still, but to us it seemed blindingly brilliant; for not since we had paraded on the dance-ground at St. Francis had we been clear of the forest.

While we stood looking to the southward and wondering where, among those sharp mountains, the Ammonoosuc flowed in, there was a commotion at the rear of the party. When I looked around, Crofton was hurrying back across the intervale toward the forest we had just left, but scrambling on his hands and knees, like an animal. He had gnawed the rope that tied him and broken it. When we shouted at him in chorus, he whirled and stared at us over the top of a bush, as a disobedient dog stares; then ambled more slowly to the edge of the forest, looked here and there, like a dog, and began to dig.

"Shall I go after him, Major?" Lieutenant Grant asked. Grant, a bluff, good-natured officer with small, squinting eyes, had been portly, even at St. Francis; but now he was cadaverous, and his once-rounded cheeks we're creased and crumpled.

Rogers shook his head. "You couldn't catch him. Nobody could catch him. He's crazy. He can run forever."

Crofton, at the edge of the forest, stood up straight and peered at us. He looked like a bear standing on his hind legs. When he saw we weren't following, he dropped on all fours again, dug a little, and then, after a final apprehensive glance over his shoulder at us, he passed slowly from our sight, back into the forest.

Something about that strange departure into hell made us take furtive stock of each other in the bright light of the open intervale. What we saw wasn't reassuring. I realized for the first time that Rogers was stooped. I had noticed Ogden's stoop some days before, and knew it was due to his wound; but he had recovered from his wound now, and he still stooped. So did Lieutenant Grant. So, I realized, did Jesse, Sergeant Bradley, Whip and most of the others. And so, it dawned on me, did I. I knew, too, why I did it. My stomach had a peculiar rubbed-together feeling—a sort of knotted tightness that could only be relieved by stooping. I wondered how long I had been doing it. I hadn't been conscious of it before. When I straightened up, I had a stomach cramp, so I stooped over again and felt better.

Next to that stoop, the thing that struck me most forcibly about my companions was their eyes. I had become accustomed to their beards and their grotesque garments—their bare feet, and the odds and ends with which their lower legs were protected from the brush—but I had been almost unconscious of their eyes until this perturbed moment. Their eyes seemed to have been pressed into their skulls with hot irons that had seared the surrounding flesh to the color of fresh liver. In those dark rings the eyes were flat and staring above noses so fleshless they resembled beaks. Between the eyebrows were deep grooves, as if from insupportable worry. Because of these eyes, and the thin beaks of noses, every man at whom I glanced—even gentle Jesse Beacham—seemed fierce and predatory. I wondered then if people I'd seen elsewhere whose look was fierce and rapacious weren't really, at heart, harassed.

CHAPTER XXXVII

WE WENT as far down the Connecticut as we could, that afternoon. It was bad going, because of the rain-swollen tributaries that crossed our path. Never once did we see a deer. To try for fish in the swollen streams or the muddy river would have spoiled the best part of a day, so we went on and on, thinking always of the divine food waiting for us at the Ammonoosuc.

"Not far now," Rogers said cheerfully, when somebody asked him; and we, taking him at his word, stumbled on and on.

On the 20th we found ourselves in the true Cohase Intervales. In our weariness and stooped emptiness, the labor of climbing up and down those treeless shelves—of going far from the river to skirt gullies and returning only to encounter more—was harder on us, more exhausting, than our travels through the mazes of Lake Memphremagog. It was disheartening, too, to look far ahead, and see the slowness of our progress. In the forest, necessity had kept our eyes upon each succeeding step we took, and trees and thickets blocked the view; but here we could see the endlessly stretching miles, and felt ourselves snails upon them.

That was the day we lost Bradley. He came to Rogers to say his men were almost dead, and he thought he'd better hunt a little in the hills beyond the Intervales. He looked singularly defiant, but I thought nothing of it. In the condition we were in, a man's face was apt to assume all sorts of unexpected expressions without his intending it.

"Better stay with me, Sergeant," Rogers said. "We've been together a long time now. I believe you'd do well to keep on the way you are. This doesn't look like good hunting grounds to me."

"I guess we'll hunt here just the same, Major," Bradley said.

He moved off to one side with his detachment; and we expected they'd catch up with us by nightfall, or at the worst by next day; but they didn't. At night we reached the fording-place, marked, as Rogers had told us weeks before, by a saddle-shaped mountain. The weather had come off cold, and the dark peaks into which we must venture on the morrow had the look of threatening blue waves. To my aching eyes they seemed to surge and roll: the sharp line of their ridges to undulate.

We built a heap of stones in the morning, so Bradley and his men might know where we had crossed: then we floundered through the quick shoal water and clambered up the sandy bank on the far side. From here, looking back, we saw, on the bank we'd left, a scant line of men making their way toward the cairn we'd set up for their guidance.

"Here comes Bradley," Rogers said. "We'll wait for him."

It was difficult to realize, watching their devious, fumbling progress, that we had moved equally slowly and gropingly across that same intervale.

"There's only eight of 'em," Grant remarked.

"Yes," Ogden said, "and Bradley's not one of 'em."

Since Bradley had ten men under him, that meant three were missing.

They made bad going of it crossing the river. Those who slipped and fell took a long time to regain their feet: then stood, stooped over, to cough up water. Occasionally they fell again.

They crawled up our bank weakly, like half-drowned dogs.

"Where's Bradley?" Rogers asked.

"Major," said Kelly, a red-headed Irishman from Suncook, "he went home."

"Home!" Rogers cried. "What you talking about?"

"Major, he said the Cohase Intervales was just two days from his home in Concord, and the quickest way to get back was head straight for Concord. He said all of us could have supper at his father's house day after tomorrow if we went that way."

"Concord!" Rogers said. "Where in God's name does he think Concord is?"

"Major, the sergeant said the Cohase Intervales are north west a half north from his father's house in Concord; so he took a sight—south east a half south."

Rogers' mouth twisted. "How'd it happen you didn't go with him?" he asked in a husky voice.

"We didn't like the looks of the mountains," Kelly said. "We told him we'd go our own way. We'd rather follow the Major."

Rogers stared off to the northeastward and we stared with him. Through a gap in the hills we could see, low on the horizon, a dim silvery bulk of snow-covered mountains, like a far-off cloud.

"Who did go with him?" Rogers asked.

"Pomp Whipple and Lew Pote."

Rogers looked at the far, far, faint snow on the mountains. "Well," he said, "let's get moving again toward the Ammonoosuc."

Kelly spoke timidly. "Where does the Major think Bradley and them two will be landing up?"

"In the middle of the White Hills," Rogers said. "I noticed that Bradley was wearing a leather hair ribbon and some Indian jewelry. Maybe next summer somebody'll find a strip of leather and a few beads, and be Christian enough to bury what he finds with 'em. Let's get on."

Now we followed, as Rogers had promised, a blazed trail: the first we'd seen since the day the path beside the St. Francis vanished in a bog.

It took us high up over the shoulder of the mountain—a crest from which we looked back at a world devoid of life, and forward to a wilderness equally empty. Behind us the Connecticut, like a toy stream, wound back between its intervales; and on all those small drab shelves above the river nothing moved. I wondered where, in the expanse of forest and mountains beyond the river, Farrington and Campbell and Curgill still stumbled with their men—or where they might be lying, unable to move. To my vague surprise, I hardly remembered those officers. It was with difficulty, even, that I recalled their names.

Ahead of us was a rugged, wooded valley, almost inviting by comparison with those along which we had so recently struggled, and we could look straight down it, as along a gun-sight, into the misty distance where our food was waiting.

"There it is," Rogers said. "There's the Ammonoosuc!" He

hitched doggedly at the belt of his torn and soggy buckskins, as a man does when at last he's conquered a difficult task.

Konkapot and Captain Jacobs went ahead to the stream, hoping to surprise a deer; for they had stood the scarcity of food better than the rest of us. They could still move lightly, whereas the rest of us went blundering and staggering, kicking up noises wherever we walked.

The Ammonoosuc at last—and we were almost there. The whole valley, it seemed to me, must be a land flowing with milk and honey: a place in which we would be free at last from misery and painful endeavor. When we heard the reverberation of a musket shot, we went slipping and sliding eagerly down the rough trail, as to a banquet. In my mind was a picture of a two-hundred-pound buck—a fat, ten-point animal that might dress out to give each of the thirty-eight of us two full pounds of clear meat, a happy prelude to the great store of food awaiting us not far beyond.

What Captain Jacobs had shot was a fish eagle—a wretched bird, smelling of carrion. We made it into soup, cooking all of it, even the feet, head and intestines. After it had been boiled half an hour, each of us had a cupful of broth, and then Rogers divided the meat. I can see him now, straddling a flat rock, with the fishy-smelling body before him, marking the carcass into thirty-eight sections. He would hold a portion behind him, in a big hand that shook: Ogden would call a name; and the man he called would go up and take the portion. An eagle is not unlike many humans of great repute: dressed up in his feathers and wings, he looks important; but divested of those trappings, he is sadly wanting in impressiveness and substance, being mostly beak, wing-bone and leg muscle. The little portion that each of us received was a mere phantom of unsatisfactory food: a bad breath, so to speak; but it was tough, and lasted longer than five times the amount of something more savory; so our imaginations, no doubt, were strengthened by it, even though our stomachs weren't.

The valley, when we got into it, wasn't flowing with milk and honey. It was barren and miserable. We forded the rocky bed of the river, returning toward the Connecticut again. The trail, washed out by rains and long disused, dragged at our feet. The best we could do, even downhill, was twelve miles. When men tripped and fell they got to their knees like babies, and pulled themselves up by clinging to saplings or low branches.

That was the 21st of October, and all that day and all the 22nd we saw no more eagles nor even a chipmunk; yet, eating nothing at all, we made fifteen miles on the 22nd. And when we tripped and fell, we fell forward, not minding what happened to our faces so that we fell toward the fabulous meals we'd eat at the mouth of the Ammonoosuc. Spurred on by Rogers and by the food that awaited us, we made fifteen miles through a forest stripped of wild life.

Rogers shambled back and forth along that tottering, wavering, hastening line. His voice was hoarse and rasping. "Keep your feet, Kelly!" he shouted. "Pull that man up, you, next to him, there! You, there, Wansant! Get up and move along! We're almost there! We'll be there tomorrow, sure! McNeal! Wake up, McNeal! We're almost there!"

We were forced to make camp, that afternoon, while it was still light; for the men were so troubled with hunger cramps that their sense of balance seemed to have gone awry. All through the day, whenever the trail had come close to the Ammonoosuc, I had found myself leaning away from the bank to avoid pitching over the edge. My hands were numb; and when I stretched myself upon the ground, the earth seemed made of prickly mist, on which I floated undulatingly. I had the impulse to ask Jesse Beacham whether he felt the same. Out of the corner of my eyes I could see him lying like a dead man, his tangled white beard pointed straight upward, but I couldn't ask him. I couldn't get the words from my brain to my tongue.

I heard Rogers' voice far away; far, far away. I had heard voices like that during a boyhood illness, coming to me from behind a screen at my bedside, faintly, as if they spoke from outside the house.

He was talking about smoke. I heard the word again and again. It woke me.

I rose and crawled forward to where Rogers talked with Ogden, Grant and Avery.

"I tell you it's smoke!" Rogers insisted. "Open your mouth when you breathe, and breathe easy. Isn't that smoke?"

I sniffed and sniffed, and then I caught it—a faint, elusive fragrance of wood-smoke.

"By James!" Ogden whispered. "I *can* smell it, Major. Sure as you're born, it *is* smoke!"

I felt rather than heard Grant laughing convulsively, breathlessly, gasping and gasping for the strength to unleash another convulsion.

Rogers' voice was exultant. "There's only one place that smoke could come from! We're there! We're all right! The food's here! We'll have it by noon tomorrow. I knew we'd make it, by God, and we have!"

CHAPTER XXXVIII

W E CRAWLED and stumbled down the last three miles of the trail that next morning—the 23rd of October—beneath cold gray skies and against a raw wind that smelled of snow; but we cared nothing for cold or snow when we heard, faint and far ahead of us, a sharp report, followed by two others in quick succession.

There was no mistaking them. They were musket shots, and we had come back again to civilization—back to a land where there were friends and food: warmth and decent homes.

Rogers raised his arms triumphantly. Holding his musket like a pistol, he fired an answering shot.

Even Jesse Beacham seemed excited. "Here we come!" he said; and he, too, sent a bullet straight upward.

"Put on the kettle!" Avery croaked. His musket spat fire at a solitary crow, high above us. It swerved and increased its speed.

Up and down the line men called jubilantly in quavering voices, their guns banging in a happy fusillade. McNeal, whose musket had been taken from him by the French, begged the loan of Avery's so to celebrate our safe arrival. He was badly off, and entitled to celebrate. Having no upper garments, he wore Avery's blanket during the day, just as Wansant wore mine. Already the damp blankets had rubbed sores on their shoulders and backs, for the skin was tight over their bones, and therefore tender.

Hungry men can smell smoke enormous distances; and the scent of it now was powerful in our nostrils. We could see, before us, the end of the Ammonoosuc Valley, blocked by the hills on the far side of a greater valley. We had come back to the Connecticut once more, and not only could we glimpse the river itself, swift and turbulent, through the naked trees, but we could see smoke lying against crowded spruces like a veil upon a bride's dark hair.

Rogers, in advance, was shouting hoarsely, thickly—shouting, I supposed, to the men who awaited us with provisions. He must have reached the juncture of the rivers. "Rogers!" I heard him shout. "Major Rogers' detachment, back from St. Francis!" It fantastically occurred to me that we might be taken for a herd of animals from the forest and shot.

Again he shouted, and now there was something in the sound of his voice that vaguely worried me—a queer uncertainty. I broke into a leaden-footed run and came out of the forest beside Ogden, Grant, Captain Jacobs and Konkapot on a high clearing overlooking a pointed intervale, through which the Ammonoosuc ran to join the broad Connecticut. In the clearing stood a tumble-down deserted fort made of logs from which bark hung in strips. Half the logs in the palisade had rotted off, and there were holes in the roof of the log house within the palisade. In this we had no interest at all. All our eyes were upon the smoke across the river.

Rogers, fifty yards ahead of the foremost of the rest of us, slipped down the bank with a sound of rattling stones, sprawled to his knees and rose painfully to his feet. The two Indian boys slid down behind him like little brown skeletons.

On our side of the Connecticut, just below us, was the mouth of the Ammonoosuc, but there was nothing there except water and earth; the intervale was empty of any visible human life. But across the Connecticut from us we saw the foamy mouth of Wells River, entering the greater stream between high banks; and it was from the top of the southern bank of the lesser that the smoke rose and in thinning layers drifted over the Connecticut to us.

There was nothing near the fire—nothing at the water's edge: no canoe, no bateau, no food: nobody. What was a fire doing, then, burning away with no man near it, where there should have been many men and piled full sacks and boxes and great store of food. Was something wrong with our starved eyes, that they seemed to see only an abandoned fire, a nightmare ghost of a fire?

But the smell of the smoke came to us sharply on a cold and damp wind, and we knew that there are no odors in dreams, not even in nightmares. Behind me I heard men stumbling from the forest, making grunting, panting sounds.

Rogers looked quickly upstream: then down. "Rangers!" he called huskily. "Rangers!" His voice cracked. Snatching his musket from Billy, he primed and fired it.

There was desperation in the glance he threw us, and his voice was hoarse.

"They've gone and they've taken our food with 'em! They brought it and then took it away! God knows why!"

He dumped powder in his musket, rapped the butt on the ground and fired it again.

"Come back!" he shouted downstream. "Come back here!"

My knees and thighs seemed to have turned to jelly: my upper arms to pipe-stems. I got down the bank somehow. I think I fell head over heels down it with a dozen others, and crawled feebly from the heap like an unweaned puppy.

"Fire your guns and shout!" Rogers cried. "Look at the fire! They can't be more than a mile down river! We got to make 'em hear us! We got to get that food back! Oh God! If only I had a canoe!" He went to the river's edge and waded in, up to his knees, so to see farther downstream.

We fired and fired; shouted and shouted.

"Listen!" Rogers cried at intervals. Then we'd stand with sagging legs and open mouths, listening; but never a sound did we hear save the rollicking, chuckling murmur of the flowing river.

The smoke from the fire across the Connecticut wavered and swung downstream. Cold raindrops spattered on the dry grass of the intervale with the sound of stifled tittering. Captain Jacobs and Konkapot settled back on their heels at the river's edge, their heads and hands hanging. One by one the men sank down, seeming to collapse into wasted heaps of rags and bones.

Rogers came out of the water and contemplated them. His eyes were puffy and red, like those of a weasel caught in a trap. His Rangers just lay there, looking at nothing. Some of them made groaning sounds, and some muttered; the rest were sprawled angularly, as though dead. To me they looked finished, might already have been corpses.

The rain grew more earnest: came thick, pelting and icy. Captain Ogden cast a quick look at the gray clouds that had shut down over the valley, obscuring the hills beyond Wells River; then he went close to Rogers. "You mean to say some pack of damned dirty rats brought food all the way up here, and haven't waited for us?"

"They *did* wait for us," Rogers answered haggardly. "They waited clear up to almost right now. They waited for us until we heard those shots of theirs a little while ago. They waited until they heard our answering shots, and maybe that's why they left—they thought our firing was from a hostile party. I don't know. Maybe they didn't hear it: the wind was from them. Maybe they were just shooting as they started down river."

"Down river," Ogden repeated. "Gone down river and left us to die here—after what we've been through?"

Abruptly Rogers' face showed an anger that I thought forced. I was watching him wanly, and it seemed to me that although a final bitter anguish had entered into him, he controlled it suddenly, seeming that if he allowed us to despair utterly we should indeed all of us, as Ogden had just said, die.

"No, damn it, no!" Rogers shouted roughly. "Don't be a fool. They're only a mile or so down river! They heard our guns, just the way we heard theirs! They'll be back!"

"Why don't they answer, then?" Ogden cried. "That's the rule—always answer when a man's lost and you hear a musket!"

Rogers caught Ogden's arm and shook it. "I tell you that food'll be back! It'll be back!" He raised his voice. "I guarantee it! It'll be back! Now, Captain Ogden, we'll get all the men up to the fort and build a fire! Get the men on their feet and start 'em toward the fort."

Ogden just stared at him, and I knew what he meant: to have lived days and days in hell, but always with this spot where we now stood held out to us as bright Heaven if we could reach it—and then to attain it, perishing, only to find

it empty: a cul-de-sac of despair and death. We too stared as
Ogden did. The ghastly sarcasm of his look was upon all our
faces.

Not until I saw Rogers dragging and kicking them upright
did I realize that his optimistic words had been solely for
their benefit: had been spoken in one last effort to save them
from giving up.

"Get up!" Rogers was shouting at everybody. "Get back up
the bank! Get up to that fort and start your fires crackling!
Don't you even want to be warm? Get up! Get up!" He was
jerking the arms of prostrate men and pulling them upon
their feet. "Get up! Get up! Shelter and warm fires! That's
something, isn't it? Get up! Get up!"

Somehow, driving us, shouting at us, pulling and pushing
us, he got us up the bank and into the ruined palisade. Then
this grinning, bearded, tatterdemalion of a leader turned on
his pack of crawling skeletons, storming at them in hoarse
and breathless whispers. "By God," he panted, "I'll do my
part, but you'll have to do yours! You've had as much to
eat as I have, and you'll stand up on your feet like men and
do what's to be done, or I'll read out your names in every
town in New England! You're Rangers, and you're going to
act like Rangers! I'll get food for you! I'll have food for you
damned soon! I never yet promised you anything you didn't
get! I promised there'd be food at this place, and there *will*
be, but while I get it, you've got to make this place fit to live
in. To live in, why? Because you're not fit to go any further,
and when that happens, you've got to stop and live where you
are, don't you? So now get to work and begin living here!"

He stopped, visibly ready to drop himself. He swept a
gleaming look around the palisade and at the log house.
"Clean up that house! The logs on the south side are rotten,
so break 'em out! Build a fire in front of the south side. Make
it a long one, and use rotten logs. Save all the sound logs.
I'm going to use 'em! Get up, those of you that can work!
Let's see who's still fit to be called a Ranger! The rest of you
can lie and be damned for all I care!"

He walked to the door of the log house and stood there,
holding to the casing and looking inside.

Jesse Beacham, his face a tangle of white hair and his back
so bent that it was almost a hump, followed him groaningly.

"Look at that litter!" Rogers said. "Rake it against the south wall. Then pull down the wall, pull the litter into the open and start your fire!"

He turned and stared at the rest of us out of sunken eyes. Every last man—even Andrew McNeal, from whose hands the flesh had been torn—was crawling or shambling toward the log house.

"That's better," Rogers said. "Captain Ogden, take charge of the house. Lieutenant Avery and Lieutenant Grant, put part of those men to work on the palisade. Take down the rotten logs for firewood. Save the sound logs and roll 'em over the bank, where they can't be burned. I want 'em."

He rubbed his eyes. They were so deep in his head that the rain lay in the pouches beneath them. "Here!" he said, "here! I want help. I'll take Captain Jacobs—Towne—Billy —Bud—Konkapot!" He lurched away. Stumbling and slipping, the five of us followed him down the bank and to the edge of the intervale, where the Ammonoosuc, flowing into the Connecticut, formed a shallow backwater. He seemed to me to avoid looking down river, or across to the intervale where the fire now had been quenched by the rain.

Rogers lowered himself heavily to his knees and pawed in the shallows at the water's edge, among dried-up plants whose dead leaves were shaped like arrow-heads. With his hands he dug among them, pulling up a cluster of roots that looked like miniature sweet potatoes. He showed them to us. "You know those?" he asked Captain Jacobs.

Jacobs shook his head, as did Konkapot, Billy and Bub.

"Well," Rogers said, "I don't recommend 'em, but you can eat 'em if you have to. They're katniss."

We repeated the word after him.

Konkapot pulled one of the roots from the cluster and raised it to his lips. Rogers took it from him.

"That's why I don't recommend 'em to hungry men," he said. "Nobody eats 'em unless he's hungry, and if he's hungry, he's apt to be in too much of a hurry. Don't eat 'em the way they are now, or they'll burn your gizzard out."

We stared at him numbly.

"Go ahead and dig 'em," Rogers said, "but don't eat 'em: not yet."

We fumbled and splashed in the shallows like draggled, hairy, feeble raccoons, until we could find no more of the roots, but Rogers, eyeing the pile we had accumulated, shook

his head. "Not enough, we'll have to have more." To Captain
Jacobs and Konkapot he said, "You know tawho?"

They said they didn't.

"Damn it," Rogers cried, exasperated, "your *women* do!
Why don't you listen to your women once in a while!"

We carried the katniss roots to higher land, and there
Rogers began to crawl through the wet, frost-bitten grass like
a hound dog snuffing after a rabbit. We straggled along behind
him, our heads bent before the pelting rain.

Rogers came to a halt, crouched on all fours and staring intently at a clump of withered leaves from which a dried stalk
protruded. He put me in mind of a mud-stained, half-dead
setter, forced by instinct to point game, even though it was
the last thing he did. The leaves at which he stared had once
been long and narrow.

"That's tawho," he said. "Tiger lily." He dragged out his
knife. Resting on his elbows, he hacked painfully at the
turf beneath the leaves and brought up a bulb the size of a
crab-apple. "Tawho," he repeated. "Don't eat 'em raw or
they'll kill you. Bury 'em under a foot of earth with the
katniss, and build a fire over 'em. Let 'em stay there all night.
That draws out the poison. Then in the morning dig 'em up
and eat 'em, and they'll keep you alive."

With that we began to crawl over the intervale, hunting
dead tiger lily plants, like sick cattle dejectedly foraging for
a bare subsistence. My own case, as I look back on it, was
no better than that of an animal. I had no memories of the
past: no thoughts for the future. I wanted nothing except to
stay alive.

When we returned to the fort with our load of katniss and
tawho, we found the entire southern end of the log house removed, and a long fire burning before the opening. Ogden,
poking at the blaze, licked his lips when he saw our wretched
load of roots.

"Where's Grant and Avery?" Rogers asked.

"Asleep," Ogden said. "Everyone's asleep. You'd think they
were dead. Are those things good to eat?" He swallowed
hard.

Rogers shook his head. "Not yet. How many sound logs
did you find?"

"Twelve."

Rogers looked pleased. "Help us dig a trench for these Cohase potatoes, Captain. I guess that's all we can do today." To Captain Jacobs and Konkapot he added: "If you're too proud to go on digging, you might go back into the woods and look for game." They left us immediately, as dignified as two red skeletons could be.

While Rogers, Ogden and I hacked out a trench with our knives, close to the fire, Billy and Bub, like two skinny squirrels, scratched away the dirt as we loosened it, and when we had buried the bulbs in the trench, we raked hot embers above them.

Rogers sat back on his haunches. "There," he said. "Those ought to keep us going till we get the raft built."

"Raft?" Ogden echoed blankly. "Raft?"

"How else can I get to Number Four, Captain?" Rogers asked. "That's where our food's gone: back to Number Four! I've got to get that food; and if it's the last thing I do, I'm going to get even with the rats that never even came where I told 'em to come—the mouth of the Ammonoosuc, not across the Connecticut where they left their damned fire! I've got to reach Number Four somehow, Captain."

"It's sixty miles, Major," Ogden protested. "You'll never make it alone!"

"I thought I'd take Billy," Rogers said mildly, "and maybe a couple of men in case I get hurt—if I can find a couple who'd risk it."

"Well," Ogden said slowly, "I guess I could make it."

"I believe I can too," I said.

I thought Rogers hadn't heard me, for he just stood there, rubbing the back of one of his huge hands with the other. The dirty skin peeled off in little rolls, revealing a star-shaped red mark—an old bullet wound. Then he looked up and grinned at me wearily. "That's good. We'll make a Ranger out of you yet."

CHAPTER XXXIX

THE REST of that day and all the next was a dim bad dream. Gray sheets of rain slanted across gray trees and gray mountains: the dirty gray river wound along a brownish-gray trough, through sodden intervales of smutty gray.

We lay in a feeble stupor through the 23rd. Early on the morning of the 24th Rogers raked away the fire, unearthed the smoking brown bulbs, and divided them equally among us. We had four apiece, and I could easily have eaten a bushel. Epicures, I suspect, would have scorned them; but none of the epicures I know have ever been almost dead from starvation. If they had, they would know that foods commonly regarded as repulsive by those who have always been well-fed—such foods as dog, horse, snake, sea gull, wildcat, skunk, raw fish—are sweeter than ambrosia to men who are truly hungry.

All through the 24th, Rogers devoted his strength to cheering up his men, and when they had swallowed their miserable portions of tawho and katniss, he did a grotesque thing: he made them shave.

"If I'm going to get food for you," he told them, "you've got to make yourselves recognizable! I can't tell you apart now; and if you keep on getting hairier while I'm away, why, when I get back here with men carrying food for you, we might take you for catamounts and shoot hell out of you instead of feeding you!"

It was a task to get some of the men to the river bank, and an even greater task to make them soap their faces—if the soap hadn't a most horrible taste, I think we'd have eaten it long before. The disappointment of the preceding day seemed to have robbed most of them of all their remaining strength. Their razors, unused since the 13th of September, had rusted in spite of the oily rags in which they were wrapped; and their greasy beards, full of pitch, ashes and dirt, resisted blades painfully.

When that sorry company had washed the blood from their mangled faces and used their pocket scissors on one another's matted hair, they were startling to see. The cropped heads seemed skull-like; their ravaged faces were so emaciated it seemed shameful to reveal them thus naked. And yet these barbering processes put a little new life into the men. I suppose they were reminded that, after all, they were still human beings. They were even able, when spurred on by Rogers, to hunt for lily bulbs, and to unearth many times the amount we had dug the day before.

He let them go back to the log house, then; and there they lay, half-asleep and half-awake, all through the afternoon, while the downpour still thundered on the roof and Rogers made loud and hearty conversation.

"Why," he said, talking ostensibly to Ogden, Avery and Grant, but in reality speaking to the hearing of everybody, "I'll be back here with food in ten days. You can count on it! In the meantime, you can dig lily bulbs; and even if you shouldn't shoot a deer or a moose, you'll have no trouble—no trouble worth mentioning."

He spoke to me. "Towne, you told me, back in Crown Point, that you'd made a study of the Bible. Wasn't there somebody in the Bible who went forty days without any food at all?"

It was an effort to remember. Everything I had learned in the past seemed to have retreated into the folds of my brain, like frightened sea-anemones retiring into nothing; but under Rogers' insistent prodding, my memories partly revived.

"Forty days?" I said heavily. "Forty days? Yes, I think somebody in the Bible fasted forty days. Maybe it was our Lord—maybe Moses—maybe Elijah—I think maybe they all did."

"There!" Rogers cried triumphantly. "Do you hear what Towne says, all of you? Towne says even in the Bible there were men that went forty days without the slightest taste of food. Didn't have any good cooked roots—didn't have any nice hot katniss—didn't have any warm fresh tawho—— No sir, not a damned thing! Not a single bite, did they, Towne?"

My brain was stirred into being a little bit more useful, and I was able to quote what Moses himself had said in Deuteronomy: that he had gone forty days and nights without eating bread or drinking water.

"Bread?" Rogers asked, and for a moment he looked blank. "Didn't have any bread? That doesn't mean that he *did* have potatoes and maybe turnips and lettuce and parsnips and . . ."

"No, no; indeed not!" I explained that when Moses said "bread," he meant edible matter of all sorts: that the word "bread" was a synonym for all food; and upon this Rogers looked relieved.

"You hear that?" he said loudly. "Moses was forty days and nights without a bite of food or a drink of water. Of course he couldn't have gone entirely without water that long, because a man can't do it, and I wouldn't ask any of you to believe that Moses went forty days without water. When Moses said he went forty days without a drink of water, he was careful to use the word 'drink.' He didn't say he didn't have a drop of water now and then—at least, according to Towne he didn't. Probably that's reasonable, because Moses was a holy man and wouldn't have said what he knew nobody could believe; so what he meant by the word 'drink' was that he never once had a real good drink of water the whole of the forty days. But when he said he didn't have any food at all, he meant just exactly what he said. It's in the Bible anyhow, so that settles it! He didn't have a single bite of food for forty days. You believe that, don't you, Ogden?"

"Me?" Ogden said. "Do I believe . . ."

"Why of course!" Rogers shouted. "Ogden believes it. Grant believes it. Avery believes it! Everybody believes it! We all know it was exactly the way Towne says Moses says it was! Well, look at the difference! Look at the water *we've* got! Never a day during the whole expedition that every last man of us couldn't have all the water he wanted. Look at the water we've got now! Good, fresh, cold rain water! What do you suppose Moses would have given for a nice mug of it, let alone buckets full? Look at sailors going crazy, hanging to spars out on the ocean after a wreck! What wouldn't they give for a millionth part of the water we got here, all around us! Look at Moses and wrecked sailors—and Elijah—without a single drink of decent water, and no food at all, let alone bushels of roasted tawho and katniss and . . ."

He was interrupted. Grant, with knobby thin hands pressed tight over his mouth, began to sputter through bony fingers, a haggard sort of tittering was heard from here and there, and then throughout the ruined fort there came the wholesome and saving sound of laughter on the air. The sound increased, grew louder and more voluminous until it finally had body and life to it.

Hell, with such laughter in it, wouldn't be altogether hell, I thought. And after all, the country through which Rogers had led us must have been worse than that through which Moses led the Children of Israel. Moses had led the Children of Israel to safety, and Rogers would do the same for us.

CHAPTER XL

O<small>N THE</small> 25th the rain stopped and we began to build the raft. The task of rolling the twelve sound logs across the intervale and into the Connecticut seemed, in the beginning, beyond our powers; for at the smallest exertions our muscles quivered and relaxed, so that we could neither grip with our hands nor set our feet firmly against the ground.

Each log resisted us, as might a giant boulder. In the end we learned to kneel before a log and roll it toward us, a few inches at a time—five men to a log that one man, ordinarily, could easily have handled alone.

Those who were weaker cut alder and willow shoots, and dug roots of the red spruce. The spruce roots, knotted together, made lashings as tough as ropes; and the alder and willow shoots, laced from log to log and bound with spruce roots, held the logs firmly.

As a support for ourselves we lashed a spruce sapling across the middle of the raft, leaving a row of branches standing straight up like the teeth of a comb; and to these branches we tied our muskets, powder-horns, haversacks and blankets, to keep them from the water. For paddles we cut young swamp maples, lacing their end-crotches with spruce roots.

All the time we groaned and whimpered as we worked; for so bungling and futile seemed our labor that we feared it would never be done. Yet it *was* done on the morning of the 26th, and the raft wasn't a bad one. The dry logs made it float well. When we tried it, with Billy at one end as a lookout, Ogden and me at either side with paddles, and Rogers in the stern with a pole for pushing, she rode high, without dipping as small rafts often do.

We made a final effort, through the 26th, to find a deer, a porcupine, even a rabbit for food, but never a thing did we see—possibly because all our senses were dulled: perhaps because of our blundering movements; but more likely, it seemed to us, because of the frightening odor of anxiety and despair that must have emanated from our sorry company.

When at night Captain Jacobs and Konkapot came back last of all, empty-handed, Rogers refused to wait longer. At dawn on the 27th Grant and Avery went with us to the raft, while the others hobbled and wavered along behind, straggling like lost sheep. At the water's edge Rogers turned suddenly on Grant. "Repeat your orders."

Grant made an effort to stand straight. "I'm in charge. I'm to keep the men alive till food gets here. I'm to make the men dig bulbs every afternoon. I'm to send out hunting parties every morning." He paused and looked numbly at his feet.

"Whether they want to go or not," Rogers said sharply.

"Yes," Grant said, "whether—whether they want to go or not."

"And whatever they shoot," Rogers said, "you're to save some of it for Farrington, Curgill, Campbell, Evans and their parties. There's forty of 'em, and they'll have to eat when they get here. Something's got to be saved for those men. Bear 'em in mind all the time! Understand?"

Grant and Avery nodded.

"What else?" Rogers asked patiently.

"If I bring all of 'em in safe, you'll make me a Captain," Grant said.

"Just your orders, Lieutenant," Rogers said. "Don't try to think of anything but your orders. What are the rest of your orders?"

The other men, tattered, stooped, haggard specters in the gray dawn, had come to the edge of the bank. They stared down at Rogers, slack-lipped, dull-eyed.

Grant rubbed a claw-like hand over his face. "I'm to stay here ten days. I'm to tell Farrington, Curgill, Campbell and Evans that you'll be back in ten days."

"Ten days from today," Rogers said.

"Yes," Grant said. "You'll be back ten days from today."

"I'll be back ten days from today," Rogers repeated. "Ten days from today you'll have all you can eat."

"What'll we do if you don't get back?" Avery asked.

"You heard me," Rogers said. "I'll be back. All you've got to do is wait! Just wait!"

He motioned Ogden, the little Indian boy and me to get aboard the raft, edged it into deeper water, and crawled aboard himself. "Push us off," he told Grant.

We moved out into the current. Without a word, without any sound at all, the horde of tatterdemalions, crouching on the bank, watched us go. Their gaunt eyes followed us with a weary, dumb anxiety; and I thought perhaps they were wondering, as I was, whether our wabbly craft, when she reached midstream, would hold together.

We thrust and thrust with our porous paddles, but they took no grip on the water, and I had to go down on one knee to keep from slipping overboard.

"She's all right now," Rogers said. "Let her go!"

We stopped paddling. The raft, slowly turning and sidling, began to move downstream swiftly; and all at once there was mist and distance between us and the men we were leaving. To us it was as though we left them helpless behind bars, listless animals in cages. Some of them, at the brown river's edge, fumbled in the shallows as bears do. They looked enlarged, grotesque, not human.

When we passed through riffles, the raft undulated and water spurted between the logs. If we stood, we were dizzy; if we lay down, we were drenched and nearly frozen. We relieved each other at the steering pole, and on relinquishing it hooked our arms around the uprights of the center sapling and clung there like draggled, crucified scarecrows. When the current threw the raft toward either shore, we crawled to the edges and plied our flimsy paddles furiously until it was back in midstream once more.

It turned and twisted, facing now up river and now down;

coasted around sharp bends: through valleys whose sides rose steeply: past intervales miles in width.

The sky was the color of skimmed milk, and the sun no brighter or warmer than a pewter button. There was a peculiar penetrating bitterness to the air; and every breath I took seemed to lodge behind my eyeballs and make them ache. From the chill that lay above that dark stream, we might have been passing through a valley of invisible ice.

"There's cold weather coming," Rogers said. "We'll have to lay up at night; and when we do, we'll tie her in quick water, where she wont get ice-bound."

We went ashore on a sandy spit where a brook ran in, and anchored by pushing stakes around the raft; but no sort of anchorage we could devise was satisfactory. Neither Rogers nor Ogden said anything about what would happen if the raft froze in the shallows, or got away from us. None of us had much to say about anything; but in my own mind there was no doubt what would happen.

"What we better do," Rogers said, "is cut wood for a fire and fence. Then we can make some sort of rope, and I'll tie it to me."

A fire and fence is only used when there's danger of freezing. The fence is of brush, two feet high: the fire burns before it, and those who lie between the fire and the fence are warm—provided they have enough firewood.

While we built fire and fence, Billy cut flexible twigs, and later we braided them together until they were long enough to reach the raft; then made one end fast to the center sapling: the other end to Rogers' waist.

As Rogers had predicted, that night was a bad one—so bad that when we had finished cutting brush for the fence, we had trouble chopping firewood. Our wet clothes were frozen stiff, and we would have been glad for the warmth that comes with hard work, but to swing a hatchet was difficult. By slow hacking—waiting a little and then hacking a little—we felled one tree, a dead one; and when it was down, I knew how women feel when they burst into tears after a long trying day's back-breaking over a washtub.

That one tree was gone before daylight. To rise and stamp our feet for warmth seemed beyond our powers. We could only roll ourselves closer and closer to the ashes of the fire, until at last, when morning came, we were lying in them.

I had dreamt all night, over and over, that the raft was gone: that it was floating far downstream, piled high with dead Indians with staring white eyes crawling all over them; and when I woke, I'd just seen John Singleton Copley pointing at those eye-spangled corpses after promising to teach me how to paint the riffles of a river with a paddle dipped in blood.

The biting cold had held, and next morning, to save ourselves from slipping overboard, we had almost constantly to chip ice from the logs; but we made progress and came disastrously to White River Falls in the Connecticut River before noon.

Rogers had told us dully we had to look out for the falls: he wasn't sure the raft could get through them. He had droned the words "Watch out for the falls; watch out for the falls!" until they buzzed unendingly in my head. Even the waves of the Connecticut, slapping against the raft, seemed to mutter "Look out for the falls; look out for the falls!"

Just how we saved ourselves from going over the falls with the raft, I'll never know. One moment the river was clear and open ahead: the next moment Billy was piping something in a feeble voice, while Rogers shouted "Push! Push! Left! Push to the left!" Before us hung a cloud of white mist, boiling upward, and below the rolling vapor there were glimpses of broken and foamy water—downhill stretches of horribly speeding silver.

I splashed with my makeshift paddle until I thought my eyes would burst from my head. I heard straining grunts from Ogden; saw Rogers on his knees, poling like a madman.

The raft trembled, surged and heaved, spun round in a sinister hurry; and all too close we heard the dismaying great solid sound of a whole river plunging to a lower level. The shore was close, but not close enough. The raft wouldn't go to it.

"Get your guns and jump!" Rogers cried. "Take everything! Take mine! Jump!" He tried to wedge the pole against the bottom. I heard it split.

Ogden and I wrenched muskets, blankets and powder-horns from the fence of branches in the center of the raft. I saw Billy, a brown streak, leaping into the brown icy torrent, and then I was conscious myself of the shock of that same cold and speeding brownness all over me, and of uneven rocks beneath my feet; then of being swept under, and of clinging, even so, to a monstrous load of muskets and blankets that I was expected to save, whether I drowned or not.

A hand grasped my shirt and pulled me upright. Rogers had me, and he had Ogden too. Billy, in the shallows, helped us with the blankets and muskets, and then we were all in the chill mud of the river bank, with the noise of the falls in our ears, and complete anguish in our souls.

"Look!" Rogers shouted, and we saw the raft, midway of the sloping water, rise on edge and turn completely over. It appeared again, broken in the middle, V-shaped, like a cabin roof. A log burst from it and stood upright. What had been a raft became loose logs which rolled and tossed in a creamy smother; hung for a moment on the lip of the falls; then vanished.

"We're lucky," Rogers said. "It looks to me like a good sign, our not staying on that raft any longer."

CHAPTER XLI

SOMEWHERE I have heard that after the first three days of fasting a man has no further desire for food, and that after thirty days he feels no discomfort whatever: that his brain is clear, his body pure, and his endurance almost unlimited. I suspect that statement in toto. I don't believe in the benefits of fasting, and ever since I tried it in the company of Major Robert Rogers on the St. Francis Expedition, I have been strongly opposed to it.

After we had seen the logs of our raft plunge over the edge of the falls, we dragged ourselves higher up the bank, dropped to the ground and lay there. Even Rogers was supine for a time—though not for long. He got to his knees. "This is no place to stay," he said. "We can't stay anywhere without a fire. We'd freeze. There'll be wood on the bank below the falls." He stood up, swaying. "That's where we go next," he said. "Come on."

We crawled after him; and it was as he said. There was wood in plenty along the shore beyond the falls, though not such wood as would build a raft. There were whole trees, hardwood for the most part, and waterlogged; windrows of twigs and branches; untold quantities of splintered pines of varying sizes, shattered by the ice-jams of previous springs.

Rogers shook his head when he had crawled over the largest of those wood-heaps. "The only thing we can do today," he told us, "is try to get warm. Maybe tomorrow we can figure out something better."

We built ourselves another fence and a roaring fire of drift-wood: then stripped ourselves and dried our shredded blankets and our sorry remnants of garments. So tattered and so rotted were those wretched rags that they were next to worthless as covering, and worse than worthless as protection against cold.

Our persons, in a way, were as bad as our clothes. I was ashamed, almost, to look at Rogers and Ogden. Their scrawny bodies seemed caricatures of what they ought to be —like bodies formed by a sculptor with no knowledge of anatomy. Their muscles were stringy as those of a skun wildcat: their knees and elbows strangely knobby: their stomachs hollowed and their ribs protuberant like those of a hake that has lain for days upon a beach.

Rogers was covered with scars—red scars, blue scars, white scars. Some were bullet wounds, while others looked as though made by the claws or teeth of animals. Ogden's two bullet-holes, so recently healed, were a flaming purple, rimmed with crimson.

When the strips we called our clothes were dry, we huddled close to the fire, listening to the everlasting roar of White River Falls. The fire warmed me, and drugged by that warmth and the thunder in my ears, I neither knew how we could move from where we were, nor did I care.

It was a good thing for us, in a way, that we were wrecked at White River Falls. If the falls had not been there to provide us with windrows of firewood: if we had spent the night in a spot where we would have had only the fuel that we cut, we would probably have died of exhaustion and cold.

Our exertions on the raft had drained us of our last reserves of strength, and it was beyond our power to drive a hatchet into a tree. As for the cold, it was so bitter that in the morning the mist from the falls had cased every branch and rock and dead leaf in a glittering envelope of ice.

We lay beside the fire until the sun had come up to take off the knife-like bite of the air.

"We'll have to eat," Rogers said. "If we don't get something in us we can't stick on the raft."

"What raft?" Ogden asked.

"We'll get a raft," Rogers said.

"I don't know how," Ogden said. "If I try to swing a hatchet, I'll cut off my legs."

"Don't worry about that," Rogers said. "I'll get the raft if you'll find the food. Listen!"

Behind us, on the dark slope of the valley, a red squirrel chirred. Far away another answered. We could hear them chipping and chapping at each other: I knew just how they looked, jerking their tails and sliding spasmodically around tree trunks with outspread legs.

"There's the food," Rogers said. "There's only one good mouthful to a roasted red squirrel, even if he's hit in the head, but all we need is a few good mouthfuls."

"I guess we can knock down a few," Ogden said. "I don't know about getting 'em back here, if I shoot more than one. One's about all I can carry." He reached for his musket. "We better draw our loads and reload," he told me. "We can't afford to miss."

"Before you go," Rogers told us, "help me with the wood. There's only one way to get trees for a raft, and that's to burn 'em down."

We stacked piles of firewood at the base of six spruces near the water's edge: then dragged ourselves up the bank, leaving Rogers and Billy crawling from pile to pile, kindling the fires that were to fell the trees we no longer had the strength to hack down ourselves.

Ogden and I shot five squirrels during the morning, and found it difficult—not only because we couldn't hurry to a squirrel when we heard one, but because we had to wait for the squirrels to sit still: then shoot from a rest because of being unable to hold the sights steady unless we did so. Hunger cramps caught us with increasing frequency, and if a hunger cramp took hold while we were drawing a bead on a squirrel, there was nothing to do but double up and wait until it went away.

We came back, late in the morning, to find Rogers and Billy still nursing the fires at the bases of the six dry trees.

We skinned and roasted the squirrels, dividing the fifth one equally; and while we picked the meat from their mouse-like bodies, one of the trees came down with a crash.

Rogers drove us out again as soon as we had eaten. "Keep on hunting," he told us. "Shoot anything you find. I'll have these trees burned into lengths by the time you get back."

It seemed to me I couldn't drag my legs up the slope of that valley again, but somehow we did it, using our muskets as walking sticks and leaning frequently against trees. So far as I could feel, my roast squirrel had done me no good: I needed a side of mutton or a cow's hind-quarter to quiet the aching void within me. I thought bitterly of Cap Huff's idle remark about a goose being a little more than one man could eat alone, but not quite enough for two. How little Cap had known of hunger! A whole goose would no more than take the edge off my appetite.

Not far from us a partridge went out of a thicket with a thunderous roar. From the blundering sound he made among the branches, I was sure he had lit at no great distance.

"He's in a tree," I whispered to Ogden. Ordinarily, the breast of a partridge makes a toothsome preliminary to a simple meal; but as a meal itself it's not worth considering. Just now, however, this partridge seemed more desirable than anything on earth.

"Can you see him?" Ogden asked faintly.

I said I couldn't, but knew about where he was.

"Go ahead and get him," Ogden said. "I'll move off to the left and make a noise doing it, so he'll watch me. You sneak around and take him in the rear."

He lowered himself among the dead leaves and threw his arms and legs about, making feeble moaning sounds. I hoped the partridge would find such a noise impressive as I crept around the thicket and stood watching breathlessly. The trees were naked: leafless. In none of them could I see anything that looked like a bird, and I was about to call to Ogden when I saw a movement at one end of a swelling on the branch of an oak. It was the partridge, cocking an eye at Ogden's strange behavior.

I found a good rest, took careful aim and let him have it. When he scaled away from the limb on a long slant, Ogden and I stumbled as fast as we could to where he came down. It was rocky ground, clear of heavy undergrowth, and dotted with an occasional juniper bush and a thin covering of leaves; but the partridge was nowhere in sight.

"You sure he came down here?" Ogden asked.

I said I was; that he was hit hard.

"Yes, I saw him. I guess he was hit all right," Ogden agreed, "but I don't believe he came down here. We'd see him if he had. He must have gone beyond those rocks."

We went there and searched; we walked in circles, sought beneath every juniper: almost looked under every fallen leaf; but we found nothing.

"You're sure he came down at all?" Ogden asked finally.

I just nodded. The thought of losing that partridge shut off my voice completely; I was afraid that if I tried to speak, I'd sob instead.

Ogden, hollow-eyed, stared at the ground. "Guess you— guess you missed him," he said in a whisper. And then his wretched staring eyes seemed to enlarge. "Well, if that don't beat all!"

He was staring at a flat juniper that had a few brown oak leaves on it. Before my eyes the oak leaves magically altered and became a partridge—an enormous cock partridge, with ruff-feathers four inches long and a tail the size of a fan. We must have walked across him and around him twenty times.

I went down on my knees and picked him up. He was still warm—the fattest, most beautiful, angelic partridge I had ever seen. The musket ball had broken his back and left his breast untouched.

I looked up at Ogden. "I'm mighty glad you found him, Captain. Mighty glad."

"I *knew* you hit him," Ogden said. "That was a mighty pretty shot, Langdon—the best shot I ever hope to see."

When we returned to the falls, all six trees were down, and under each burned two fires, so to separate them into proper lengths for a raft. Rogers sat at the edge of the stream, his forehead resting on his drawn-up knees, and beside him lay Billy, asleep.

The Major looked up. He was a sight. His face and hands were black with soot: as black as Pomp Whipple's; and his eyes glared at us whitely, looking to see whether we had shot anything. I slipped the partridge's head from under my belt in back and held it up for him to see.

"Oh, by God!" he whispered. "Let's eat it before our luck changes!"

We ate the intestines first, washed and placed on a hot stone to roast. Then we had half a squirrel apiece, cut along the backbone. The partridge was more difficult to divide evenly. Having agreed that a newly-shot partridge is better raw than cooked, we seared him no more than enough to hold the meat together. Then we took off the breasts and, after considerable discussion and measuring, split them in what we agreed were equal parts. The carcass, mattering less, was quartered without argument.

Before we slept that night the twelve fires had done their work, and twelve logs lay on the bank, with nothing more to be done to them except get them into the water and fasten them together into a raft. To me, that night, the task appeared about as easy as pushing a porcupine through a musket barrel.

CHAPTER XLII

Nowadays whenever I dream of the building of that second raft, I wake myself up by whimpering aloud, because I've been straining to move a vast log that will not budge, yet must, or death awaits me.

We drove stakes in shallow water where the bottom was soft. Then we inched a log to the bank, tumbled it to the shingle, and worried it into the stream. We couldn't roll it, because we had to leave protruding branches for binding the raft together.

In moving a log, we worked however we could: levering it with stakes: sliding it over driftwood: lying on our backs to ease our hunger cramps, and pushing with heels or shoulders, so that from head to foot we were black with soot.

When we had a log in the water, we drew it to the fixed stakes, which held it in place while we went for another log. To each one we fastened a hazel switch, so there might be something by which to seize and guide it if it broke loose; and Billy stood guard at the stakes to do what he could in case they gave way.

It was noon before we had finished our labors, lashed our muskets and other wretched belongings to the uprights, cut new paddles and woven a long rope of hazel shoots.

Rogers insisted on the rope. "We don't want this one to get away from us," he muttered over and over. "We really got to keep hold of *this* one." We thought he was right about that. We couldn't have made a third raft.

Whether it was because of the steadily increasing cold—a cold that threatened snow—or the long struggle with the logs, I cannot say; but whatever advantage we had gained from our mouthful of partridge and two mouthfuls of squirrel had now been lost. We were finished; if our lives depended on our marching a mile, we couldn't have done it.

By the time we started, poor young Billy had bad cramps and couldn't even sit upright, so we laid him on some spruce tips in the middle of the raft. With his sharp nose, his closed eyes, his mouth stretched tight over his teeth, and his dusky color, he looked tragically like a mummy without its wrappings.

We worked free of the stakes, poled ourselves slowly into midstream and sank breathless on the raft, regardless of the icy water that welled up between the logs to soak our trembling bodies. Some day, I thought, I must paint a picture of this and call it Purgatory; and then I realized such a picture would have little meaning: it couldn't show the endlessness of these journeyings—the eternal wetness and shiverings, the aching bruises to soul and body, the everlasting hunger, everlasting toil, and everlasting exhaustion.

Rogers got to his knees, and I heard him say something about falls. The word shocked me into full consciousness. "Falls?" I asked. "More falls?"

"Not bad ones," he said thickly. "Just little falls. Wattoquitchey Falls, seven miles from here. Fifty yards long. Maybe we can ride 'em."

Ogden and I struggled painfully to our feet.

"For God's sake," Ogden said, "why didn't we go there to build the raft?"

"I said 'seven miles,' " Rogers reminded him. "You couldn't march seven miles. And what about him?" He pointed at Billy. "Why, maybe I couldn't even hardly do it myself."

"Can we see these falls before we're on top of 'em?" I asked.

"See 'em?" Rogers said. "We've *got* to see 'em, haven't we?"

We strained our eyes downstream. A few snowflakes drifted out of the heavy sky, and from the surface of the eddying brown water rose a vapor like a faint ghost of the mist that had billowed up from White River Falls. The thought of more falls was sheerly nauseating, and I knew that if the snow came down too thickly, we might not see them until too late. . . .

Rogers broke the silence at the end of three miles. "Maybe we can ride 'em," he said again. He repeated the words in another quarter-hour. Those falls, I realized, hadn't been out of his mind all day. That was why he had insisted on making the rope of hazel switches. I wondered what would happen if we couldn't ride them; but I didn't dare ask.

We sighted the falls through thickening snowflakes at three o'clock, and paddled the raft over toward the left bank, so we might have opportunity to see how they looked.

At first I thought we might indeed possibly ride them, for their total drop was only about ten feet; and the quick water wasn't over fifty yards long. The closer we came, however, the more apparent it was that the raft would never get down safely unless every possible ounce of weight was removed from it. Gouts of foam shot up from the middle of the rapids, proving that the ledges beneath were sharp and dangerous; we could hardly hope to live if the raft broke up or spilled us in that turmoil.

We let the raft drop down to within a few yards of the quick water, laid one end of it against the bank and held it there with our paddles. We could see the pool at the bottom —a brown, deep pool, streaked with streamers of foam.

"I don't believe we'd better try it," Rogers said.

"Somebody's got to," Ogden said wearily. "It's the only chance we've got."

"No it isn't," Rogers said. "The best chance is for me to go down to that pool and try to catch her when she comes down."

Ogden, seized with a cramp, clutched his middle. "You can't!"

Rogers seemed not to hear him. "That's what we'll do. Take Billy ashore. Take the muskets and the rest of the stuff. I'll hold her while you do it."

Ogden hesitated.

"Captain Ogden!" Rogers said sharply. "You heard me!"

Ogden moved quickly to obey. We hurriedly collected our rusty muskets, our soaked and tattered rags of blankets, and all our other accouterments that now were rubbish; then, taking Billy by his pipestem arms, we dragged him to the bank, where he lay all asprawl, no better than a shrivelled little red corpse. At Rogers' orders we made fast the rope of hazel shoots to the stoutest of the uprights; and Ogden tested the rope while I fastened our paddles to the raft's protruding branches. The rope was firm as a cable.

"Now for God's sake!" Rogers said, "don't let go that rope till I give the signal. It'll take me some time to reach the pool, and I got to undress. When I hold up my arm, turn her loose. Let the rope trail. If I miss the raft, maybe I can catch the rope." He fastened his own paddle beside ours and went ashore.

I joined Ogden, and together we clung to the rope. The raft plucked insistently at it, as if eager to be gone from us.

Picking up his musket, powder-horn and other belongings, Rogers went slowly from our sight into the dark woods, walking crouched over. The snowflakes had thickened, helping to hide him from us; and I thought it likely that I'd heard his voice for the last time.

The raft seemed more and more determined to swing out into the stream and go down the falls. For fear it might pull us off our feet and drag us into the rapids, we sat in the shallows, water up to our waists, our feet wedged against rocks.

"I'll bet my way was best," Ogden muttered. "One of us ought to *tried* to ride down on it. If the Major gets a stomach cramp when he's swimming to it——" He was silent. There wasn't much more to say.

At the edge of the pool the bushes moved apart, and Rogers, a dim figure through the steadily-falling snow, could be seen peering along the shore to left and right, seeking, evidently, for a suitable position. Then he went back into the bushes, and reappeared nearer us, crawling out on a flat rock. With agonizing slowness he put down his musket, blanket, knapsack and powder-horn, and painfully undressed.

He crouched at the edge of the rock, staring up at the falls—a lonely, naked, helpless atom in that immensity of roaring white water, drifting snowflakes, screaking forest and towering dark hills. Then he held up his arm and waved.

We let go the rope and floundered to our feet. The raft swung slowly broadside to the current and moved downstream. When it reached the quick water, it bobbed on the white riffles; flung itself forward.

It rolled and rocked. Halfway down it nosed completely under: a surge of white foam swept it from end to end. It rose again, reeling and sliding in the surges, and seemed to fling itself breathlessly to the bottom of the long slope. It plunged heavily into the swirling pool, and hung there, tilted forward, half under water. We looked to see it fall apart; but with labored slowness it came to the surface, turning gently among the clots and streaks of froth.

Rogers lowered himself from the rock. He swam arduously, with awkward jerks, as if his rump strove to rise and force his head under. He stopped once, freed his face from gouts of foam, and rolled on his side to look for the raft, which, again in the grip of the current, moved more rapidly.

He altered his course and swam spasmodically on. He found himself so close to it that he clutched for a log— clutched and missed. He kicked again; got a hand on the raft: another hand. He hung there for a time, his chin on the edge, his legs and body carried beneath the logs by the current; and I, watching him, felt my muscles quake; for I knew that no mere human, with an icy torrent plucking at his starved and weakened limbs, could cling for long to those charred tree trunks. As if in answer to my fears, he struggled sluggishly, hitched himself along with fumbling hands, gripped one of the branches we had left as uprights on the logs, and drew himself partly from the water, so that his upper body lay upon the raft—lay so long motionless, that I thought he was sped. Then we saw that he was making futile upward movements with his knee. It caught the edge eventually, and he squirmed aboard to lie flat.

"I never thought he'd make it!" Ogden whispered; and I, shaking all over, found that my tongue and throat were dry as chips.

Now Rogers had got to his knees, and we saw him unlash a paddle from the uprights, and begin to work slowly toward shore.

CHAPTER XLIII

DRIFTWOOD FROM Wattoquitchey Falls warmed us and kept us alive that night; and with the first faint grayness of that miserable last day of October—miserable and yet ever-memorable—we put Billy in the middle of the raft, with our blankets under and over him, and pushed out into midstream. The snow had ceased, and had been followed by a wind so bitter that it cut and slashed us like frigid knife-blades.

There were no more falls between Wattoquitchey and Number Four: no more quick water, Rogers said—no, there was nothing but the malignant cold, which seemed determined to finish what the French and the Indians and the evil spirits of the forests and streams had tried so hard to do to us.

But on both sides the intervales grew broader: the hills retreated; and though the glacial wind could thus howl at us unrestrained, we thought it had the voice of a raging demon of the wilderness, frantic to see us at last slipping from his grasp.

Out of his streaming eyes, Rogers stared at the widening intervales. "We're going to make it," he said. "By God, I believe we're going to make it!"

It was mid-afternoon when he seized Ogden by the arm. "Look!" he cried. "Look!" He doubled over with a cramp;

but thus bent he pointed awkwardly, like an actor playing the part of a hunchback. On the river bank, a hundred yards ahead, two men with axes suddenly stood.

"Why," Ogden said incredulously, "it's people again!" But I don't think Rogers could speak at all, and I know I couldn't.

The two strange, strange figures, men that weren't skeletons, men that were clothed, men that swung axes easily in ruddy strength and health—those two unbelievable men saw us, and came back along the bank, hurrying toward us.

"Don't tell 'em anything," Rogers warned us huskily as we swung the raft toward the shore. "I'll do the talking. Don't tell anyone a damned thing till we find out all about the dirty skunk that ran off with our food!"

One of the men splashed toward us, caught our rope of hazel switches and drew us to land.

"Where's Number Four?" Rogers asked.

They just stared.

"I'm Rogers," Rogers said. "Where's Number Four?"

"Rogers!" one of the men said, and a kind of horror was in his face. "You say you're Rogers?"

"I do!"

"I've often seen you," the man said, swallowing. "It's hard to believe!" He shook his head. "We heard you was dead, Major; and I guess it's true! You was! But anyhow, you're at Number Four, Major. It's right here, and we'll help you to the fort!"

With that, slipping and splashing in excitement, they gave us the unfamiliar help of muscular arms and got us off the raft, lifted Billy to the bank, put our belongings in a heap, and made the raft fast to a stake. They gawked at the burned ends of the logs and at the alder and hazel witches that held them together, and kept staring at Rogers as if he'd been a hippogriff.

We sat down just beyond the water's edge and watched them as they made the raft fast.

"Happen to have anything to eat?" Rogers asked them, whereupon, after another look at him, they sprang up the bank and departed, running. They were back in five minutes, bringing with them a bottle a third full of rum and a piece of bread the size of my fist. "That's all we got, Major," one said. "We're out chopping wood and et the rest, but there's plenty supplies at the fort. There's turnips and fresh pork."

Rogers broke the bread in four pieces. "Why, it's bread!" he said. He gave us our portions, took a mouthful of rum, then went over and looked at Billy. He poured a little rum between his lips. When Billy opened his eyes and coughed, he gave him the bread and passed us the bottle.

That mouthful of bread moistened by rum had incredible sweetness and savor. I could feel it moving warmly inside me, as though hastening to assure my cramped and aching stomach, my thumping heart, my laboring lungs and my shivering body that their long agony was over.

"Now we'll go up to the fort," Rogers told the staring woodcutters. "Guess maybe you'd better help us a little. Leave our stuff here: then come back for it. One of you carry this Indian boy. Then we'll just lean on the two of you."

One of the men picked up Billy and carried him. The other gave Ogden and me each a shoulder, and Rogers staggered along, now and then bumping into the man who carried the Indian boy; and thus we set off for the fort, which we could see, low and square, in the middle of its dismal, snow-covered clearing—that same peaceful clearing I had idly sketched on a warm September evening less than two months ago.

There was no sentry at the gate of the fort; no one on the small parade ground on which the snow had been trodden to dirty, frozen slush. Our helpers took us across the parade to the log barrack in the center. A squat tower of hewn plank rose from its northern end. The man on whom Ogden and I leaned pulled the latch-string of the door and kicked it open. In a broad stone fireplace opposite the door a fire burned, and at either end of the room were rows of bunks. In front of the fire a blanket was spread on the floor, and around it were a dozen Provincials, rolling dice.

They looked up. One said angrily, "Keep that door shut!"

"This here's Major Rogers," one of the woodcutters said in a voice that choked with excitement.

The Provincials got slowly to their feet and faced us, stared at us and frowned with unbelief, then seemed to see something terrifying.

"Who's in command of this fort?" Rogers asked.

"We don't know his name, Major," a soldier said huskily. "We're strangers here."

"Go get him," Rogers ordered.

Three Provincials jumped together for the door at the end of the room, jostling and tripping in their haste.

Rogers walked drunkenly to a bench, and the staring soldiers fell away before him.

"Put Billy on the blanket and go back and get our muskets," Rogers told the woodcutters.

Ogden and I got to the bench with difficulty. The feel of a roof over my head and of a closed room, warmed by a fire, almost suffocated me.

The door at the end of the room burst open. A stolid-looking man in a wrinkled blue uniform peered at us, blinking. "Which?" he asked. "Which one?" He came to us. "They said Major Rogers! None of *you* are Major Rogers!"

"I'm Rogers," the Major said. "Now here: write down what I say. I can't repeat. What's your name?"

"Bellows," the officer said, "in charge of the King's stores." He clapped his hands to his pockets, looked confused, then hurried from the room. When he returned he had pencil and paper. "We didn't know——" he stammered. "We heard —where did you——"

"Get canoes," Rogers said. "Load 'em with food. Send 'em up river. Mouth of the Ammonoosuc."

"These men are Provincials," Bellows said apologetically. "They're bound home. There's only——"

"Get settlers," Rogers said. "Good canoemen. Hire 'em!"

"It's pretty bad weather," Bellows said doubtfully. "Maybe when it clears off——"

Rogers rose wavering to his feet, then straightened himself to his full height and seemed to fill the room. In a strained, hoarse voice he said: "Today! Today! Now! Can't you realize there's a hundred Rangers at the mouth of the Ammonoosuc, starving! Get men and pay 'em! Get all the settlers into the fort! Call 'em in! Drum 'em up! I'll talk to 'em! For Christ's sake, get started!"

Bellows stared at him wildly: rushed back to the door and shouted a name, adding, at the top of his lungs, "Assembly! Assembly!"

Three private soldiers tumbled into the room, one a drummer. At a gesture from Bellows he ran out on the parade ground, fumbling with his drum braces. His drum rolled and rumbled, sending chills down my spine.

To one of the other soldiers Bellows shouted, "Run to Mrs. Bellows. Get a pail of milk and a bottle of my rum."

"And some bread," Ogden said.

"All the bread she's got!" Bellows shouted.

Rogers sank down on the bench, rubbed his gaunt face with huge skeleton hands, ran his fingers through his hair. "Write an order for the food to go up river. What you got in this place?"

"Pork," Bellows said. "Fresh beef. Turnips."

"How much bread you got?"

"Not much," Bellows said. "These Provincials——"

"Provincials be damned! Let 'em go without! Put all the food you can find in those canoes, and send out for more. Send out for everything there is! Those men of mine are going to be fed, or by God I'll raid every house in the settlement!"

The drum rattled and rolled, rumbled and banged.

Bellows scribbled hastily on a sheet of paper and sent the third soldier flying from the barrack with it. There were people crowding in at the door, goggling at us.

Rogers raised his voice to be heard over the continuous rolling of the drum. "Tell me something," he said to Bellows. "Supplies of food were to meet us at the mouth of the Ammonoosuc. They were sent, weren't they?"

"Oh yes," Bellows replied, and he looked frightened. "They were in charge of Lieutenant Stephens."

"So? What did he do with 'em?"

"He brought 'em back," Bellows said. "He waited several days; then he thought you and your command must have been wiped out—and he heard firing one morning and thought it might be French and Indians, so he decided he'd better start for home."

"Listen," Rogers said, and he spoke as much to the settlers and Provincials who had crowded in through the doorway as he did to Bellows. "We finished St. Francis for you. There isn't any more St. Francis, and you can begin to move up that way and clear the land and live in peace whenever you're a mind to. But this Lieutenant Stephens who got frightened and took our food away when we were firing muskets to show him we were coming—we'll have to have a settlement with him. He isn't here, is he?"

"No," Bellows said tremulously. "He's gone back to Crown Point. You'll be going that way, too, Major, I take it?"

"No, not till afterwards," Rogers answered in a choking voice.

The crowding people stared stupidly at him as he stood before them in the firelight, unbelievably gaunt, barefooted, covered with bruises, tattered strips of strouding sagging around his legs. The shredded buckskin leggins hung loosely on his emaciated flanks; singular torn bits of garments concealed little of his ribs and bony chest: his hands were scarred, burned, sooty and pitch-stained from his labors with the raft.

"No, we'll see Lieutenant Stephens at Crown Point afterwards," Rogers said. "Now get me some beef—fat beef. I'm going back to the Ammonoosuc myself."

CHAPTER XLIV

I T SEEMED impossible that the man who routed me from sleep at sun-up on the following morning had been at death's door from starvation and exhaustion only twenty-four hours earlier. Already, before waking us, he had been to the river to make sure the canoe-loads of supplies had set off for the Ammonoosuc. I had the feeling that the man was indestructible—this Rogers of Rogers' Rangers—this paladin who had destroyed St. Francis, had led us into hell and through it and out of it: that this colossus couldn't be killed or beaten. As I saw him then, it seemed to me his determined soul was such that even had his body perished, his ghost would have continued to lead us: would have threshed and fought the way through to bring us into safety.

I knew that now I was to part from him, which for me meant to walk tamely into a tamer world: when I thought of it, it seemed like a parting from glory; for the plain truth is that the Rogers I'd known until now was glorious, nor could

I have believed then that under other circumstances he could ever be less, or anything different. Thus, when we're young, or under great stress, do we see the heroes who lead and save us.

"Come on," he said that morning, when he'd wakened me, "I still need you a while." He wore borrowed buckskins, made for a smaller man—which was only natural, since he was bigger than most: bigger, even, than Cap Huff. He and Ogden and Billy and I ate a whole side of bacon, mopping up the grease with our loaves of bread, and washing it down with a kettleful of tea the color of the water in a spruce bog, and it made me feel as though I had swallowed a bag of bullets.

"I'm going to leave Billy here to fatten up," he told me. "When you come back from Crown Point, stop and get him. Take him home and keep him for me. I'm in Portsmouth every few months. When I need him, I'll ask for him. Meanwhile, if you're going to paint Indians, you can start on him. They're all about the same color."

Then, after breakfast, he set to work framing his report to General Amherst. I have heard it said, often, that everything Rogers wrote was written for him: that he was ignorant and illiterate. That isn't so. He was a bad speller—as bad a speller as I ever saw, barring Peter Pond the trader and John Stark's brother William, the two worst spellers in the world. Aside from that, he expressed himself not only fluently and well, but in simple language, which is a gift denied to many writers who are called great. What was more, his thoughts were clear and logical; and considering that he was working in a hurry, and that a meal or two and dry clothes don't make a man whole when horrid day on day and night on night have shattered him, I say that this report was as accurate and comprehensive as could have been made by either of his two great enemies, General Thomas Gage and Sir William Johnson, at their best.

He dictated eight pages, telling briefly what he had done and what he proposed to do; and what with consulting the notebook of our travels, and correcting here and inserting sentences elsewhere, it was almost noon before he reached the concluding paragraph—"I shall set off to go up the river myself at once, to seek and bring in as many of our men as I can find, and expect to be back in about eight days, when I shall, with all expedition, return to Crown Point. As to other particulars relative to this scout, which your Excellency may think proper to inquire after, I refer you to Captain Ogden, who bears this, and has accompanied me all the time I have been out, behaving very well. I am, Sir, with the greatest respect, Your Excellency's most obedient servant, R. Rogers. No. 4, Nov. 1st, 1759."

When it was finished, he took it from me and immediately went to work copying it. I never knew a man like him for keeping perpetually busy.

All the time he was writing, settlers were crowding in to stand near him and stare. They looked at him as we look at great men: that was plain in their eyes; and I think Rogers had a not unpleasant consciousness of their admiration. He kept at his work till he finished it: nevertheless I could see he was fully aware of the increasing throng of visitors and of their staring. When he finally signed the report, he folded it neatly; then stood up and looked about him with a bright and complacent glance.

"Well, friends," he said, "I suppose you know now that all danger from the Indians is over. Do any of you propose to take advantage of that improved condition?"

Several of them responded deferentially, yet eagerly. They said they thought of moving up river: as far up, perhaps, as the Upper Cohase, which was reputed to be fertile and beautiful.

"Cohase! That's nothing!" Rogers exclaimed, and launched out into a description of Lake George and the country north of the Mohawk River. His voice strengthened, became resonant with enthusiasm as he spoke; and his kindling eye roved over the room. He made us almost see eagles wheeling above majestic mountains; vast stretches of hardwood groves, devoid of undergrowth; the heavenly, unearthly blue of the fairest of all lakes; glass-clear streams packed with pink-fleshed trout; soil sufficiently fertile to cause apple trees to bear the year after planting; meadows carpeted with grass so rich that the cows that fed upon it could yield only cream; corn-stalks as tall as elms; a land of laughter and golden sunlight; of cool summers and mild winters—a terrestrial paradise.

Rogers paced the floor, gesturing, confident and prophetic. There in that wonderland, he told us, he would himself build a State—a little principality—a little Eden. Twenty-five thousand acres he and his officers would ask from the Crown, to begin with; and to that tract, when the war was over, would go his officers and their families: his best Rangers and their families. Thus within his principality would be built up an army more perfect and more dangerous than had ever before been seen. Those who accompanied him would have not only their own army, but their own governor, their own legislative body, their own laws. All would work together; help one another; and there in the wilderness would flourish a community of contented, rich and united people, wholly self-supporting and independent of foreign interference. No enemy would dare approach them: they would be safe forever from aggressors and from tyrants. Traders would come from Montreal, from Philadelphia, from all of North America for security, sending goods to the far West and receiving furs in return. It would supplant Albany, Boston, New York as the great clearing house; the great cross-roads of America.

Already this was a Rogers I hadn't known: an orator: a projector of dreams: a schemer: a man of business, blowing vast and brilliant bubbles—a Rogers strange and new to me—but when he stopped, the listening settlers were staring at him with glistening eyes, entranced.

"Jest Rangers goin' to settle it?" a bearded man asked.

"No," Rogers said. "There'd be room for you—room for every honest man who'd be willing to throw in his lot with me. I'd see you got your land on easy terms."

He put his hands on his hips and grinned that half-bashful grin of his. "How many here would go with me?"

I wasn't surprised when all those who hung upon his words—men and women and even the half-grown boys in the back of the room, staring slack-lipped and pop-eyed over the shoulders of their elders—said they'd go. Indeed, I wanted to go myself.

When I woke at dawn the next day, I heard someone already stirring in the bare room where Rogers, Ogden and I had spent the night. It was Rogers. He was on his feet, rolling his blanket and getting it fast to his shoulders; but as I watched him, he paused to set a brown bottle to his lips and drink long and unctuously. He finished his pack, drank again, looked down at us thoughtfully—then went toward the door, and I thought he lurched a little as he walked. His hand was on the latch when Ogden sat up and spoke.

"Not saying good-bye, Major?" Ogden asked. "No further orders?"

Rogers laughed a little more thickly than usual. "You two go to sleep again," he said. "Sleep a couple of days. It's no weather for you to be going overland to Crown Point. I'll just be sitting comfortable in a canoe myself—good place to drink a little, a canoe. You lay up till the weather clears. When you get there, just tell the General I'll be back here in about eight days." Then, as casually as though he were only going around the corner, he left us, and we heard him calling to Bellows to fill the empty flask. After that there came to us the sound of his footsteps outside, tramping across the frozen slush of the parade, and finally there was the distant sound of his voice, thick and loud, as he went down to the river. So, for that time, he passed from our ken.

He was right, as usual, about the weather; and we should have waited till it cleared before we set off for Crown Point. But Ogden—with Jennie Coit in his mind, I knew—insisted on starting that morning. We made miserable work of the comparatively safe and short journey through snow and rain and slush and mud. The truth is we were sick men, and by nightfall of the first day's march my legs had swelled horrifyingly. Ogden's legs swelled too, and one of his wounds was giving him trouble again.

Five days and nights it took us to cover those fourscore miles; the frigid lemon-colored glare of a November sunset shone in our faces when, on the 7th, I stood again on the bank where Hunk Marriner, McNott, Konkapot and I had stood, seven weeks before, looking across to the broad hook of Crown Point.

It was a desolate-looking place now. The ramparts of the new fort were dusted with snow, like lemon frosting on a giant cake, the tents gleamed coldly yellow in the declining sun, and the countless pointed spruces on the heavy hills beyond were powdered with an icy coating.

While we waited for the bateau to ferry us across, Ogden was consumed by a fever of impatience. He couldn't stand still, but limped up and down, fumbling with his accouterments, feeling his bristly chin; and when at last we were in the bateau, he was as fidgety as a caged fox: jumping up to stare toward the shore; shifting his powder-horn and cartridge box, only to shift them back at once, scratching himself; clearing his throat; staring about as if the place were strange to him; ignoring the bateau-man's questions; talking to me at random.

When the bateau touched shore, he blundered up the bank like a blind man. Officers stopped to stare open-mouthed at us; but he walked past them as if they didn't exist. If they had stood in his path, I have no doubt he would have tried to walk straight through them. His trembling eagerness to reach the fort and the general's markee was like that of a man half-dead with thirst hurrying toward water.

Amherst's markee was at the near end of the parade ground within the towering earthern ramparts. It was a double one—two big square tents placed close together, with a connecting corridor—and flanked on either side by two others, one for aides and one for the adjutant. In front of all three stood sentries so magnificent in their uniforms that I, part emaciated, part swelled, and clothed in a kind of ragged patchwork given me by charitable kind settlers at Number Four, wished myself elsewhere.

They wore scarlet coats with white belts whose buckles shone like gold, brilliant canary-yellow waistcoats, breeches so white that they were dazzling, and black gaiters that came above their knees. On their powdered heads were high, pointed hats with glittering regimental badges, and around their necks were stocks made of shining black leather. I had never dreamed that anything could look so beautiful and at the same time so coldly repellent.

Ogden hobbled to the closed flap of the middle tent, said "Message for General Amherst," and started in. Both sentries dropped their bayoneted muskets across the entrance. One of them snorted. The other said "Go over to the adjutant's tent first."

Then out of the tail of my eye I saw the sentries in front of the other two tents looking at us with an air of amused contempt; and my shame at my disreputable appearance vanished.

Ogden stepped back a pace from the crossed muskets and looked the two men up and down. They stopped smiling.

"You're lucky today," Ogden said. "I'll only ask you to announce me. Captain Ogden of His Majesty's Rangers, returning from St. Francis with despatches for General Amherst from Major Rogers. Go ahead! Read it out!"

The two sentries rattled their muskets and brought their hands up in a smart salute. Their faces were as red as their scarlet jackets: their backs so straight that their noses seemed to point to the sky. The sentries at the other tents stared haughtily into infinity. The man who had directed us to the adjutant's tent opened his mouth and bellowed "Captain Ogden of His Majesty's Rangers, returning from St. Francis——"

The flap of the markee was pulled aside to reveal the face of a handsome young officer. "Great Guns!" he shouted. "Stop that racket!" With his eye on Ogden he weakly exclaimed, "Great Heavens!" He held up the tent flap. "Come in here, Captain! That is to say—just a moment! By any chance are you lousy?"

Ogden looked at him distastefully. "Not yet," he said. "Thanks for warning us, but we've got to come in to see the General, even if we *do* get that way."

"What!" The young man stared. "No, no! You misunderstand me! I'll tell the General at once! A most remarkable sight! Fortunate the General's dined! Enough to take away a man's appetite! No offense, Captain! Splendid work! Splendid work!"

He turned toward the inner door of the markee, only to encounter a lean man with beetling brown eyebrows and grooves in his cheeks as deep as though gashed by a chisel. He wore a little tight wig, and over his uniform a loose green coat lined with brown fur. The Aide said "Captain Ogden, General. He——"

The General stopped him and came up close to us. Ogden was standing as rigid as a fence-post. "We're happy to have you back, Captain." He put out his hand.

Ogden relaxed and shook it. "Thank you, General! Thank you, sir." He fumbled in his haversack for Rogers' letter.

Amherst took it and sniffed at it without taking his eyes from Ogden. "Turn around, Captain," he said. "I'd like to have a picture of you, the way you are."

Ogden obediently turned around.

The General whistled softly; then looked at me. "Who's this?"

"Langdon Towne of Kittery, sir," Ogden said. "Acted as secretary to the Major."

"Private soldier or volunteer?" the General asked.

"Volunteer, sir," I said.

"Volunteer," the General repeated. "Ah yes—expedition finished—get your discharge now. Good." Then he sat down on his aide's bench and broke the wax wafer on Rogers' despatch.

"Hm, hm," he grumbled, running his eye over it. "Discovered the town from a tree—hm, hm—first found Indians in a high frolic or dance—hm—surprised the town when all fast asleep—hm, good!—chiefly destroyed—good, good!—destroyed both them and their boats—ha! yes!—set fire to all their houses—by Jove!—killed at least two hundred Indians and took twenty of their women and children prisoners—yes, yes, yes!—retook five English captives——"

He looked up at Ogden. "Interesting thing, Captain. Stockbridge Indian fellow came in last night. Those five captives the Major mentions have arrived at the mouth of Otter River with five Indians. I sent three whaleboats for them at once. They'll be in tomorrow morning."

Ogden made a strangled sound like a loud gasp, and the General looked at him sharply. Outside the sentries rattled their muskets, and through the tent-opening came a gaudily dressed officer, all scarlet, gold and white. As he entered, I caught sight of a throng of soldiers standing nearby, and in the distance others hurrying toward the General's markee.

"Oh, there you are, D'Arcy," Amherst said. "You've been out with the Rangers, so this'll interest you. Here's Captain Ogden, back from St. Francis all dressed up in the latest ranging costume, mostly holes. Thought you might like to have it copied to wear when we march on Montreal."

D'Arcy shook hands with Ogden: then stepped back, as had Amherst, to have a comprehensive view of us. The General's servant came in with a pair of candles. "By Jove!" D'Arcy exclaimed. "By Jove!"

"Quite!" Amherst said dryly. He resumed his reading of Rogers' letter. "Hm. Ah, yes. Found Captain Ogden badly wounded in his body——" He looked up at Ogden. "How'd that happen, Captain?"

"Well, sir, there was some question as to whether one of

the houses was empty. I went in to find out, and it wasn't."

"I see," Amherst said. "I see."

He went back to the letter. "Badly wounded in the body—yes, yes—examined prisoners and captives—hm—party of three hundred French and Indians down the river, boats waylaid, second party of two hundred French and Indians—hm, yes, yes!—return by Number Four—assemble at the mouth of the Ammonoosuc River—ah, yes: a great march: a great march!"

He frowned at Captain Ogden. "Badly wounded in the body, eh? How did you get through the woods? Did they carry you?"

"No, sir," Ogden said.

"Well," Amherst said impatiently, "didn't you bleed? How'd you keep up?"

"I don't know, sir. I *had* to keep up."

"No doubt," Amherst said blankly. "No doubt." He sighed. "Let's see: ah, yes: came to Cohase Intervales—yes—put down the river on a small raft to this place—dispatched provisions up river in canoes—why, what's this?" He rose to his feet, fumbling with the letter to find the last page. "Dated Number Four, November 1st. What's he mean by saying he dispatched provisions up river after reaching Number Four? I sent Lieutenant Stephens up river with provisions—provisions enough for all of you! Didn't you find them?"

"No, sir," Captain Ogden said. "Lieutenant Stephens went up, but he came back and brought the provisions away with him. His men heard our guns and—and didn't bother to wait. We found their fire burning. We could hear them firing guns, down river. We fired ours, but they didn't seem to notice." Under his breath he added, "We were pretty near gone."

Amherst's face turned dark red, a blue vein stood out on his forehead. "D'Arcy," he said, "have Lieutenant Stephens put under arrest and confined to his quarters. Have it done immediately." He turned a cold blue eye on Ogden; then added, "No: not confined to quarters. Better put him in the guard house in the fort, where he'll be safe from visitors."

D'Arcy clicked his heels together. "Yes, General."

Amherst spoke fretfully to his aide. "John, make a note about Stephens. Life is full of Stephenses. No matter what we do, we're surrounded by Stephenses who can't obey orders. All the Stephenses of this world ought to be shot, and the

Rogerses ought to have statues. Write something to that effect, only put properly, John.

The handsome young aide, his lips moving spasmodically, scribbled furiously in a note book.

The General looked from Ogden to me. "It's customary," he said, "to confer some small reward for a scout of this nature —for one that proves both arduous and successful. Captain Ogden will receive recognition in due course. But at present I'd suggest complete Ranger uniforms—D'Arcy, I'd be obliged if you'd see to that. Complete. All accouterments, D'Arcy. Scotch caps, green strouds, shoulder brooches—all. Gift of His Majesty, so to speak, what?" He glanced at the end of Rogers' letter. "Yes. Behaved very well. Yes, yes. Let's see, Captain Ogden; you reached Number Four the last day of October. You haven't had much to eat, I take it."

"No, sir. We could crawl, but we couldn't lift a hatchet."

"Mm. So you've come eighty miles since then, in these clothes and through the storm."

"Yes, sir."

"Mm. Legs trouble you?"

"Yes, sir."

"Very well," Amherst said testily. "Come back here tomorrow afternoon when you're clothed and in your right mind. I'll write Major Rogers. Oh, and D'Arcy: have this gentleman"—he pointed to me—"entered on the rolls as an ensign. When he's discharged, let him draw pay as an ensign from September 13th. Now take these gentlemen to your tent and give orders for what they need. They probably need a drink as much as anything."

D'Arcy smiled. "May I have the honor, gentlemen?" He stood aside to let us precede him from the markee. We came out, and there were hundreds of soldiers—Rangers, Provincials, British Regulars in work overalls and in the uniforms of half a dozen regiments—standing at a respectful distance and staring at us. But staring wasn't all they did. They began to cheer and kept on cheering.

CHAPTER XLV

I HAD BEEN under the impression that the young men of Harvard College knew how to drink, and I had often marvelled at Cap Huff's capacity; but they were the merest novices by comparison with Captain James Tute and Captain Jonathan Carver, the two Ranger officers to whom Captain D'Arcy turned us over and who entertained us in their tent that night.

After we'd had the hardihood to scrub ourselves in the lake, and our hair had been trimmed by the sutler's assistant, Ogden and I dressed ourselves in our new green buckskins, fastened our green strouds at the shoulder with silver brooches, cocked our new Scotch caps at the proper angle over our right eyebrows, and Captain Tute and Captain Carver took charge of us.

They made flip from rum and beer, flavored with cinnamon and blended with a hot poker, so to take out the poison, according to Captain Carver, who had a serious and ponderous air. They drank it absent-mindedly at first; then almost unconsciously, as a man knocks ashes from a cigar. We had some before supper, and even more with supper, and so much after supper that although Tute and Carver drank three for my one, I could hardly hear what was being said.

I took no particular fancy to these two officers, and never expected to run across either of them again, which shows that I was not one of those who have premonitions of the future.

Captain Tute was a careless, swaggering young man, tall and fair-haired. He had the pear-shaped head with bulging temples so often seen on precocious youths who know more in their boyhood than they ever do later. He had been captured by the French just before our departure to St. Francis, had recently been exchanged, and was now full of large talk as to how he would have escaped capture if conditions had been different. I thought him light-minded and something of a braggart, and yet I'd heard that Rogers held him in the highest esteem of all his Ranger captains.

Captain Carver reminded me of a tailor in Cambridge who had been able to persuade students that any ill-fitting coat made them look like Adonises. He had the same ingratiating, deferential manner. There was something feline about his caressing voice; and his habit of closing his eyes while talking put me in mind of our cat soliciting a chin-scratching.

From Tute and Carver we learned that Captain Williams had gone to New York with a terribly burned face. Sergeant McNott, they said, had lost a leg and had recovered; but of Hunk Marriner they could tell us nothing at all.

Ogden, looking self-conscious, tried to ask carelessly about the whaleboats that had been sent to Otter Creek to bring in to Crown Point the captives we'd rescued at St. Francis.

"The female captives?" Captain Tute asked innocently; and as Ogden immediately turned red, both Tute and Carver slapped each other's shoulders and laughed aloud. Then uproariously they asked what the St. Francis squaws were like and how they had been divided among us. I told them we'd driven the squaws away, whereupon Tute and Carver, wholly incredulous, laughed all the louder. After that they had a long, drunken discussion of Indian women of different nations—a discussion that proved Tute and Carver knew what they were talking about, and that the different nations had special peculiarities.

These two officers also found the question of plunder vastly interesting. Had either of us, they wanted to know, brought back anything pretty good; and when we said we hadn't, they wanted to know why. We ought to have taken a few fur robes, they said—preferably black squirrel robes; and there were Indian brooches and bracelets that were worth having.

Then, over fresh bottles, they got into an endlessly-involved argument about whether Indians are ever jealous of their wives; and long before it was over, Ogden was heard snoring in his chair. For my part, I thought courtesy could ask no more of either Ogden or me than what we'd already been through; so I shook him half-awake, and he stumbled after me to drop upon a pile of blankets at the side of the tent. We slept like dead men, and dawn was coming when I drowsily opened my eyes for a moment and saw Tute and Carver mix-

ing more flip by the light of the two candles. Tute was telling
Carver about a superb squaw; this Juno, it appeared, had so
loved Tute that she followed him about like a dog. Carver,
at the same time, was telling Tute about two superb squaws;
impassioned for Carver, they followed him about like two
dogs. I closed my ears again and slept till the sun was high.

It was mid-afternoon when Ogden and I, standing on the
high bank, sighted the three whaleboats heading in for Crown
Point.

Poor Ogden was trembling. All day his answers had been
slow in coming, his preoccupied eyes restless and his smile
forced.

As the whaleboats came slowly toward the sickle-shaped
beach on which the Rangers' tents were pitched, I made out
Mrs. Coit's white hair; the tight knot at the back of Sarah
Hadden's head; the fat face of the German woman; the dishevelled locks of Mrs. Wick; the yellow braids and flat back
of Jennie Coit; the shining black heads of the three Indian
girls. They were all there. They had all come safely through.

The beach was a-swarm with Rangers and Regulars
who had gathered to see the women come in. Strangely, when
the boats grated on the pebbles and the rowers shipped their
oars, Ogden hung back. The occupants of the boats began to
disembark. I saw Jennie rise from her seat, swing a bundle
to her shoulder and pick up a kettle. Then she sprang ashore,
and began to push through a crowd of laughing and shouting
soldiers and make her way up the beach.

"Well——" Ogden said in a voice that shook, even upon
that monosyllable, and went down to meet her, walking stiffly
and almost uncertainly. She looked him straight in the face
with bold brown eyes, but would have gone on if he hadn't
caught her arm; and I realized that she didn't recognize
him, shaven and trim in his new uniform.

"Jennie!" he said. "Jennie!"

She dropped her bundle and kettle. "My land!" she cried.
"How'd you ever get here? How's your side?"

"It's all right. All right, Jennie. How've you been? I didn't
know—I hope—by James, Jennie, I thought we weren't going
to get through. I wondered how you were making it. I was
afraid—afraid——"

"We did all right," she said carelessly. "We took it easy.

When it rained, we denned up. We killed five deer and a bear and half a dozen raccoons."

Ogden kept hold of her arm as though he never intended to let go. He had to release her, though, when she stooped to pick up her bundle and kettle. "Here, let's get up on the bank," she said, and looked angrily at the dozen Rangers and handful of Regulars who seemed disposed to crowd around her, staring and chaffing.

"What's in that pack?" Ogden asked. "You oughtn't to be carrying anything as heavy as that, Jennie! Give it here: I'll take it."

"No," Jennie told him. "I'll keep it. It's mine. It's some things from St. Francis—wampum—furs."

She scrambled up the bank, near to where I stood, and I noticed that she glanced back over her shoulder at one of the Stockbridge Indians who had all the time kept close to her.

Ogden followed her. "I didn't remember you had any such mess of truck when we left St. Francis, Jennie," he said. "I'll get a soldier to carry it when we start home."

"Home!" Jennie cried. She glanced again at the Stockbridge Indian; then looked up into Ogden's face and laughed impudently.

"Jennie," Ogden said, "I've got my discharge. We can start for Jersey today if you want to."

"Jersey?" Jennie said. "Jersey? I can't go to Jersey! I'm going with my mother."

"Your mother can come to Jersey too," Ogden said. "There's room for her. I figured you might want to bring her."

"No," Jennie said, "I can't."

"You can't!" Ogden cried. "Why can't you? Look, Jennie——"

But Jennie rolled her eyes upward, as she had rolled them at Rogers when I first saw her on the dance-ground at St. Francis, only now she was rolling them at the Stockbridge Indian—smiling at him.

Ogden's gaze followed hers. He turned helplessly to me: then back to Jennie. He seemed confused and slow-witted. "No, Jennie," he said. "No. Now wait. Now wait, Jennie. You can't do that. You—your——"

She turned on him. "Can't do what! I can do any damned thing I please! I don't owe anybody anything! I didn't ask

anyone to take me away from St. Francis! I'm going to Stockbridge to live!"

"Stockbridge!" Ogden whispered. "Stockbridge!"

Jennie looked at him defiantly. When he said nothing more,
she spoke to the Indian. He set off at once toward the fort.
Jennie huddled her bundle of plunder under her left arm,
picked up her kettle and ran after him, sagging a little from
the weight of her baggage.

Ogden felt his belt, his hatchet, his cap, as if uncertain
whether he had them on. Then all at once he laughed loudly
and emptily. "What do you think of that! She's white outside; but inside she's an Indian! Damned wanton little slut!"
Then he looked at me furtively and seemed to be ashamed of
what he'd just called Jennie. "She was—she was very kind to
me, though," he said in a low voice. "Guess I wouldn't be
alive——"

There swept over me the feeling that has, at one time or another, almost suffocated most men who have ever been a part
of any army. Such homesickness came upon me that my spirit
was ill of it. I wanted no more of imbecile war. I wanted
nothing but my own home, my own endeavors, my own
friends, my own people—the only things on earth in which
I could put faith. To my dying day, I knew, I would refuse to
be a part of any other war, even though I should be drawn
and quartered for my refusal.

CHAPTER XLVI

W HEN, FOLLOWING Rogers'
instructions, I picked up Billy at Number Four, he seemed
in no way put out at having to leave his new-found friends at
the fort, but followed me cheerfully. All the young Indians
we had taken had been the same, seeming to accept the
fact that since they were prisoners, they must belong to any
master who claimed them, and accompany him uncom-
plainingly.

Billy and I made rapid progress eastward, through the leafless forests of Hillsboro and Dunbarton. I stopped at the Flintlock Tavern at Dunbarton crossroads to see whether Sergeant McNott had returned to his home; but he hadn't, and neither Flint nor his hired man could tell me anything definite about him. They'd heard that he'd been taken to a hospital in Albany, and that was all.

Flint seemed to regard Albany and its Dutch inhabitants as a danger almost as grave as the French and Indians. When I said I had heard poor McNott had lost his leg, he nodded gloomily. "I don't doubt it! Them Albany Dutchmen, they'd take *anything* off a New Englander! If McNott only lost one leg there, it's because it was the only one the Dutchmen could get off."

Proudly he added, "There's *one* New Englander the Dutchmen better not try to get around, by God, and that's Major Rogers! He'd skin their eye-teeth for 'em! If they tried to outtrade *him,* they'd find their pockets full of bad bills of credit."

I studied Flint. There was nothing but admiration in his voice or face.

"Why should they get bad bills of credit from the Major?"

"Because he'd print 'em!" Flint said, and guffawed.

"Look here," I said. "The Major's a friend of mine. He saved my life. It's counterfeiting to print bad bills of credit —but perhaps you don't understand that you're stating the Major would do such a thing."

Flint made an apologetic sound. "Pshaw! I didn't mean nothing! Why, there's any quantity of folks in this section who've printed bills of credit! The fact is, the Major was up before the Superior Court in Portsmouth for it, four-five years ago."

"Major Rogers?" I cried. "Major Rogers was up for counterfeiting?"

"It didn't amount to nothing!" Flint assured me. "Why, he got a commission from old Benning Wentworth hisself before the case ever came to trial; and when he started fighting Indians, nobody ever gave it another thought! My land, the Major's too smart to be caught *that* way!"

"You must be mistaken!" I said angrily. "You've got the Major mixed up with someone else!"

At that Flint gave me a peculiar look, whereupon I

walked out of his tavern, indignant, and went on my way with Billy.

My anger grew cooler as we tramped on through the bleak settlements toward Epping and Newmarket, but I felt a strong contempt for Flint and all those like him who love to repeat little giggling sly stories of a hero. And yet—and yet, underneath this contempt for slanderers I felt a sneaking uneasiness. After all, I'd known only the magnificent side of the hero, and heroes are men; and there's only been one perfect man.

Hunk Marriner and I had left our canoe with a farmer on Oyster River in Durham—a part of Great Bay; so it was for Great Bay that Billy and I headed, hoping that Hunk had long since reached the canoe and gone back to Portsmouth in it. If he hadn't, and if the farmer had no word of him, I thought sadly that Hunk would never have any use for the canoe or for anything else, so there'd be no need to leave it for him, and Billy and I might as well take it for ourselves.

I'd liked Hunk: I'd liked Hunk well, and it was heavy news to me when we found the farmer and the canoe too in the barn, and the man shook his head when I asked for news of my friend. "No, not a word," he said. "Never expected to see either of you again for that matter." Then he showed interest in Billy.

"Where's *he* from?" he asked.

"St. Francis."

"Well, I vum! Where'd *you* pick him up?"

"I was there," I said. "Major Rogers loaned him to me."

"By Gosh!" he said. "By Gosh! You was at St. Francis with Rogers! There's been considdable talk about that!" He seemed to labor for words, but only brought forth an inquiry about the weather on our trip.

I said it was terrible, which led him to say, almost gaily, "We been getting a awful lot of rain down here."

After some contemplation he asked, "What about that other one you was inquiring for: that was with you when you left the canoe?"

"He was burned. Burned with gunpowder. Badly burned."

The man shook his head. I could see this really meant something to him, but he only asked bleakly whether Billy would like an apple pie.

When we had carried the canoe from the barn, we ate the pie while the farmer and his wife stood nearby, pretending to take no notice of us. Not only did they refuse to accept pay for storing the canoe, but they seemed almost pained when I tried to thank them. When I set the canoe in the river, the woman said, "If you're up this way again, you can make yourself to home." Her husband said, "If you ever see the other one again, tell him we're mighty sorry he got burned." As we set off, the two of them stood there unmoving, watching us go. There was something comforting about them, and I was glad to be back among such folk; for while our native New Englanders are not as garrulous as some, they are pretty good people at heart: pretty good people.

With Billy in the stern, doing most of the work, we slid rapidly down the bay and swung around the point into the Piscataqua. I could almost see, up river, my grandfather Nason's house at Pipestave Landing, and it seemed strange and unreal that I should be bringing Billy from St. Francis, just as Billy's grandfather may have been the one to take my own forebears from their home at Pipestave Landing and carry them to that far-off clearing beyond the ravines of Memphremagog.

We had always regarded the capture of whites by Indians as dreadful; yet I saw nothing dreadful in taking Billy home with me. In fact, I had even thought of Billy as fortunate to be thus captured; and certainly he seemed to be enjoying himself. It came to me that the Indians who stole my people may not have felt they were doing anything particularly terrible; indeed, may have thought, as I did of Billy, that their captives were fortunate. Could it, I wondered, have been possible that my ancestors even took a certain amount of pleasure in the experience? Was there a possibility, even, that the behavior of those savages from St. Francis was no worse than that of white men?

These ideas, I suspected, were unorthodox and not to be publicly mentioned unless I wished to get into more trouble in Portsmouth.

In spite of the November bleakness of the meadows that bordered the broad Piscataqua, the sight of the river stirred me; for it is different from other rivers, and has an influence upon those who live beside it. It is so deep and so swift that the two harbors of Portsmouth never freeze, and along its shores are peculiarly spacious bays and coves, bordered by fertile meadow-lands. Its waters surge down to the sea and back from it in swirling eddies, so that they seem to boil perpetually. Its color, too, is unusual—a steely grayish-purple, like the color of midocean seen from a small boat; and there is something of the sea about it—not the sea's restlessness and coldness, but its fresh fragrance. Women born within sight of it are black haired, as was Elizabeth, and fair-haired girls are as rare in Portsmouth as in Havana.

Two months before, when I returned from my grand-father's farm, I had gone straight to Elizabeth; and perhaps I'd have done so now if I dared. I found, however, that I was somehow altered—changed, perhaps, by two months of doing what I was told to do, whether or not I wanted to do it: by two months of obeying orders: by two months of Rangers' discipline.

Discipline, I have heard, is a good thing for our characters, but I'm not convinced of it. I've seen too many disciplined soldiers turn worthless away from their discipline. At all events I wanted to see my mother and my father and to find out whether Hunk Marriner's mother had heard anything from him.

When the canoe passed the mouth of Great Cove, the small gray houses were thick along both banks, the spire of Elizabeth's father's church rose above the swelling top of Heron Island, and before me lay all that familiar flotilla of islets that protects Portsmouth from the open ocean.

It was a sight I had often longed to see during the past two months: yet now that I actually saw it, it seemed to me that everything looked smaller and drearier than I had re-membered it.

I swung the canoe to the eastward, into Mendum's Cove, where Hunk's house stood. It wasn't much of a house; and it looked forlorn and lonely. Billy laid the canoe along the ramshackle wharf and remained in it to keep guard. There was no one in sight, so I walked to the house and pounded on the door, and Hunk's sister, Lady, named for Lady Pepperell, wife of Sir William Pepperell, opened it. She didn't say anything: just opened the door for me to come in.

"Is Mrs. Marriner here?" I asked.

"No," she said, jerking her head toward the little room off the kitchen. "Hunk's in yonder, though."

I went into the little room which was more a closet than a room, and in a sort of bunk against the wall Hunk lay looking up at the ceiling. The bed-clothes were raised above him by a contraption of slats, like a lobster pot. "Hey," he said in a thin, flat voice, "when'd you get back?" His eyes never moved from the ceiling.

"I just got back," I said. "I got the canoe with me. I thought you might want it."

"No," he said. "I don't want it." He closed his eyes. "You keep it."

"Does it hurt you to talk?"

"Not so long as I don't move." His lips scarcely stirred. "They shipped me home," he said, "mainly lying in wagons. It seemed a long ways. Guess it was."

His apathy gripped at my heart like an icy hand. "Hunk," I said, "hurry up and get well, so we can go gunning. There's more game around here in a minute than there is in Canada in a year." I tried to speak cheerfully.

"Yes," Hunk said wearily, "I'd certainly like to. I certainly would. I've been hanging on till you got back. I kind of thought you'd be back. Cap Huff thought you'd be back any day, now."

"How is Cap?" I asked. "Same old bumbler?"

"Yes," Hunk said.

It was something of a shock to realize that both of us had spoken of Cap as though I'd been away from Kittery for years.

"Hunk," I said, "have you had a good doctor?"

"There aren't any good ones," Hunk said. "None of 'em know anything. One'll say the way to cure a burn is to put oil on it: the next one says oil's terrible, and the only cure is spiders' webs. Army doctors are worst. I guess I'd be better off if I'd never seen one."

"It's still the burn, is it?"

"Yes. It wont heal. No matter what you do to it, it wont heal."

I couldn't think of anything to say.

"It don't hurt much, though," Hunk went on. "Anyway, it don't hurt as much as it did the night it happened—only when I cough. What happened to Captain Williams and Sergeant McNott?"

I thought I might as well lie as tell the truth. "They're getting along all right—doing fine."

"That's good," Hunk said. "I thought the Sergeant might lose a leg. And I'd certainly hate to be Williams. I guess there wasn't much left of his face. How'd you get along after we left you?"

"Very well," I said heartily. "Very well!"

"What? We heard you lost your boats, and that's the last we heard of you."

"Oh, yes. We lost our boats. Come to think of it, we didn't get along so very well."

"No," Hunk murmured. "That's what Cap heard. If you got time, I'd kind of like to hear about it."

"I got a St. Francis Indian boy with me," I said. "Billy, his name is. That's the name Rogers gave him. His real name's something like 'Absence-makes-the-heart-grow-fonder.'"

Hunk smiled faintly. "I'd like to see him. I certainly would."

"I'll get him. He's in the canoe."

"No," Hunk said. "Bring him over some other time. Let's hear about the trip. I'd rather hear about that than anything—that is, if you got time."

I brought a chair from the kitchen and told him the whole story. He lay there under his lobster pot, his eyes closed, and to me he seemed to be scarcely breathing.

The rest of the Marriners came home from their day's fishing and fish-selling and stood by the doorway listening silently; but one of them went to the wharf and tried to lure Billy ashore. Billy paid no attention to him, he told me later: just pushed the canoe out from the wharf and watched him distrustfully.

It was night when I finished. "Probably I've forgotten a lot of things," I said, "but I'll remember 'em later."

"Yes," Hunk agreed, "I'll learn about 'em later. You had a tough time—a tough time. I'm glad you got back all right. I was getting to be kind of afraid I wouldn't—well, I'm glad you're back."

I went out of the house without saying anything to any of the Marriners, though they called after me that word had been sent to my mother and that she was waiting supper for me. When I shouted to Billy, he ran the canoe inshore, out of the gloom. We paddled around the point to our own landing, where there was a fire burning; and when we slid toward it, I saw my father and brothers between the fire and the shore.

"It's a tame Indian!" I heard Odiorne shouting. "He's got me a tame Indian!"

My father caught the bow of the canoe and held her from rubbing. "Welcome home, son," he said. "It aint Thanksgiving till next Thursday, but we killed the turkey when we heard you'd been sighted."

CHAPTER XLVII

HUNK MARRINER died just before dawn the next morning, and I was glad of it. Nobody who loves the woods ought to be cooped up in a little room, doing nothing but suffer and just barely keep alive.

Billy went with my family and me to the funeral, because he couldn't be kept from going wherever I did; and as we walked out of the graveyard, I heard one of the neighbors muttering to another something about "Dirty murdering savage!" and "Hatchet 'em all if I had my way!" The man who said this had never been injured by the Indians, and he regarded himself as a good Christian—which was puzzling, because Billy, whose family and people I'd helped to massacre, looked upon me with an affection that was sometimes almost embarrassing.

He was a little embarrassing in other ways, too. With Odiorne teaching him, he learned many things quickly; but it took him some time to understand that he mustn't freely use the bad words he had picked up with the Rangers; and it was especially difficult for him to grasp why a snowstorm could be called goddam snowstorm when only men were present, but must not be called anything except a snowstorm when there were women within hearing.

He followed me up and down the streets of Portsmouth,

where I fear I strutted somewhat swaggeringly in my new and dashing uniform, and wasn't loath to be stared at, or to be stopped and congratulated and called deferentially "Ensign Towne." As for King's Attorney Clagett and Sheriff Packer, I met the pair of them full front one day on Water Street and laughed in their faces. Their wattles reddened like a turkey cock's, but that was all: who were they to interfere with one of Rogers' young heroes, come home from the taking of St. Francis with the insignia of an Ensign of Rangers on his uniform—a pet companion of the glorious Major and a friend of General Amherst's too!

I wondered how long before I'd encounter Elizabeth on the street, and she'd see the change in me, and be heartsick to think how she and her family had once treated this warrior home from the wars with his red captive behind him, running tame at his heels. Had she already seen me—from a window, perhaps—and did she weep on her pillow at night and hope that my heart would be softened toward her?

I thought perhaps she'd write me a humbled note, asking me to come to her; but she didn't, and after I'd been home a week, I decided that it was my part to be magnanimous. Of course the truth is I couldn't keep away from her.

When I slammed down the Reverend Arthur Browne's brass knocker in a military manner, it was Elizabeth's mother who opened the door and greeted me with dignified surprise that bordered on warmth. Then she took me straight out to the kitchen, where she and Elizabeth and Jane were making mince meat, baking pies and preparing—as was, I suppose, every woman in the New England provinces—for Thanksgiving.

Elizabeth was flushed and beautiful from the heat of the oven, and the sight of her overwhelmed me, she was so much lovelier than all my yearning dreams of her in absence had been.

I could say not a word, but didn't need to; for instantly the two girls began to chatter like bluejays, telling me how they had known I would soon be home, because of Sam Livermore going to see my poor friend in Kittery, and learning that I must surely return before long; how excited their whole world was when the news of the destruction of St. Francis had been printed in the Portsmouth newspaper; how their friends had asked and asked for news, thinking they might have heard everything from me.

"Now," Mrs. Browne said weightily, "we can provide them with a fund of information."

"What was it like, Langdon?" Elizabeth asked. She shot me a sidelong glance that made my heart leap.

"What was *what* like?" I asked.

"Oh," Elizabeth said, "everything. What was it like to go all that way and do such a wonderful thing?"

"Well," I said, "it wasn't so wonderful. It was a good deal like going hunting."

The three women were silent. I must, I realized, be guarded in my answers, or before I knew it I might find some of their aversions buzzing around my ears like bees. "Of course," I said quickly and meaninglessly, "the Indians made it different. I brought one home with me."

Mrs. Browne exclaimed "My land!" Elizabeth clasped her hands and stared at me from eyes as black as midnight. "An Indian! You brought home an Indian? Where is he?"

"I left him in the canoe at Spring Wharf." At the look on their faces I hastened to add: "He's only a boy, but as I was coming here, I thought I might as well leave him in the canoe."

"Why, Langdon Towne!" Elizabeth cried. "He'll freeze! Do you mean to say you brought him all the way from——"

Mrs. Browne spoke severely. "Elizabeth, your father will be vastly annoyed if he isn't here when Mr. Towne relates his adventures in our wilds."

To me she said, "We expect Mr. Livermore to join us for supper. Your presence would add to his pleasure and to Mr. Browne's. I suggest that Elizabeth accompany you to the wharf, and that you bring back this—ah—Indian. He can be permitted to remain in the kitchen during the supper hour."

I could see that she disliked referring to an Indian by any term so simple as "Indian." I wondered, too, whether she addressed her husband, in the privacy of their bedchamber, as Mr. Browne; and I decided she unquestionably did.

What I said, however, was that I would be delighted to stay for supper, and that we could go for Billy whenever Elizabeth was ready.

To be alone with her, even on the street, filled me with pride and happiness. "You'll never know," I told her, "how real you seemed when we were almost starved, and I saw you in my dreams."

"La!" she said. "Did you really dream of me?"

"Dream of you!" I cried. "There were times, toward the last, when our dreams were like life! I could touch you: hear you speak! You said beautiful things!"

She looked apprehensively over her shoulder.

"When we were at the end of our rope," I told her; "when there was no food to be had, and I thought we'd never get through, I tried to send messages to you. I tried to think myself into your mind, so you'd know how I felt. I thought perhaps, if I died, I might be allowed to see you before I—well, before I was sent anywhere."

"Don't say such things," she murmured.

"Couldn't you feel me near you, Elizabeth?" I asked; but she wouldn't answer.

I wasn't sure that she wholly understood what I'd been saying, and yet I was happy enough in realizing that, at all events, we were back where we had been before that unhappy night when all of us had said things we didn't mean.

When, on the wharf, I called to Billy, he came up out of the darkness like a silent brown ghost in a green stroud. Elizabeth would have patted him on the head, but he ducked like a dog with sore ears and ran from us to the edge of the wharf.

"See that!" I said. "That shows you how senseless an Indian can be!"

As we returned to the Brownes' in the dusk, with Billy at our heels, wrapped in his green blanket, everybody we passed turned to look at us. Elizabeth was pleased and excited. "The whole town'll talk about nothing else tomorrow, Langdon," she said, and I felt her shoulder against my arm. I had never seen her happier, and certainly I had never been so happy myself.

Mr. Browne was as affable to me as his wife and daughters had been. "Home from the wars!" he exclaimed dramatically. "You have earned the gratitude of this community! Our frontiers at last are safe from the encroachments of the red horde. You have stood at Armageddon and battled for the Lord." Nothing that he said was true, and I was heartily glad when he turned his attention to Billy. "Ah," he said cheerfully. "A young Scythian! A heathen, having the understanding darkened, being alienated from the life of God through the ignorance that is in him, because of the blindness of his heart!"

"Well," I said, "he's been a pleasant surprise to me. He carried Captain Ogden's musket and blanket for two hundred miles, and never let out a whimper. Billy hasn't had many advantages, but he's as good a boy as you'd find anywhere."

"Billy?" he asked. "Is it possible that savages take the names of Christians? He was named William?"

"No, sir," I said. "There's no pronouncing his name, so Major Rogers called him Billy."

Mr. Browne spoke unctuously. "Major Rogers! A true soldier in the Lord, who beareth not the sword in vain. Ah—ask the boy his true name."

"Sir," I said, "they don't tell their own names. It's bad luck."

Mr. Browne gave me a look deploring the placidity with which I spoke of heathen customs, and I was thankful that just then Sam Livermore came in, slapped me on the shoulder and began to exclaim over Billy.

The boy kept beside me, standing straight as a ramrod and woodenly dignified while he was being stared at and talked about. Mrs. Browne pronounced him vastly diverting. Elizabeth and Jane called him monstrous sweet and a perfect love, and Elizabeth asked whether I wouldn't give him to her for a slave boy. I thought she was joking; but from the quick scrutiny which Mr. Browne and his wife turned upon me, I realized that the request was meant to be taken seriously. Moreover, "He would be as a gift of God," Mr. Browne said. "The Word would be taught him and he would gain eternal life."

"The trouble is he isn't mine. He belongs to Major Rogers." I explained. "The Major told me to keep the boy until he came for him. An order's an order. I'm responsible, so I'm afraid I'll have to keep him."

Elizabeth pouted a little—a habit of hers that I found irresistibly fetching—and she slanted a reproachful glance at me. Mr. Browne, however, continued to stare at Billy as if he longed to exorcise the demons from this young savage with a horsewhip. I wondered why I was always so uncomfortable in the presence of one so righteous and godly as the Reverend Arthur Browne; but I consoled myself, as have so many young men, by remembering it wasn't Mr. Browne I hoped to marry.

When Mrs. Browne said that Billy was to sit in the corner of the kitchen while we were at supper, Mr. Browne protested that his cook, a bent and wrinkled Negress, would resent the presence of this heathen boy, but yielded when I said I would screen him from the cook's eye with a big chair. The chair proved to be unnecessary, however; for when I took Billy out to the kitchen, the old black woman shouted with fond laughter at sight of him. Before I had closed the door on them, they were both chattering, neither understanding a word of the other's, but thick as thieves.

In the dining room we'd no sooner sat down than Mr. and Mrs. Browne began to volley questions. They were almost like ghouls in their eagerness to be told the cruellest details of the attack on St. Francis, and it was a relief to me that their daughters and Sam Livermore were curious to hear everything I would tell them about Major Rogers.

Upon that subject, even I could be eloquent; I told them of the Major, and I spoke with an emotion that had its effect, as I could see. As I talked on, I knew I was holding an almost entranced attention from all of the little party at the table; and Elizabeth's brilliant soft gaze and her quickened breathing were lovely to see. She sat with parted lips, not missing a syllable; so that I, poor foolish orator, felt elate and inspired to speak so well in my lady's presence, and was happy so to kindle her with my own worship of the hero.

"They think as highly of Rogers around here," Sam said when I came to a stop, "as they do of Amherst."

"Yes, yes," Mr. Browne agreed. "Though Rogers is only a Provincial, he's risen to the heights—to the heights!"

"The regular army officers," Sam went on, "have never been able to see any good in any Provincial; but Rogers has shown 'em. He's a great man! Everybody knows there isn't an officer in the British army who could have made such a march."

"No, nor in *any* army," I said. "There isn't another man alive who could have done what he did."

Elizabeth's eyes were on me ardently. "What does he look like?" she asked. "Describe him, Langdon."

"It isn't easy," I said. "I'd have to make you see a man standing in fire and not burning: a man buried in a block of ice and not freezing: a man chained under water and not drowning: a man who comes out of the ice and the water and the fire and keeps all his friends alive and kills all his enemies. I don't know what he'd be like walking the streets of Portsmouth in a tie wig and brown velvet clothes and buckled shoes; but in a Canadian morass, up to his neck in mud, he looks like a shaggy god."

She clapped her hands. "You're doing pretty well," she said.

"Perhaps I could make a pastel sketch of him for you," I told her. "You know what pastels are, don't you, Elizabeth? Pigments ground to a paste with white lead and water; then bound together with honey and worked up into sticks? I've been doing a little with pastels, lately. Perhaps I could persuade them into some sort of likeness of the Major for you."

"Oh do!" she cried. "When will you bring it to me?"

"Elizabeth!" Reverend Arthur Browne said with some severity, a warning note in his voice; and I perceived that my mention of pastels had the effect upon him and his wife of an impropriety. Here was dangerous ground.

"You shouldn't be coaxing Langdon to waste his time in frivolities, Elizabeth," Mrs. Browne said, pretending to speak with some lightness. "Now that his career has opened so splendidly, and the whole community expects so much from him——"

"With your permission, Mrs. Browne," I interrupted, "what career is that?"

"My dear boy!" It was her husband who responded, and he bowed to me benevolently. "You've won your spurs, and it's the hope of all your friends that you'll continue to wear them—with glory! Always, my dear Langdon! We're all delighted to see how the way's opened before you to a commission in His Majesty's army."

I didn't want to open that old quarrel again: I hadn't the heart for it. I meant to be a painter—I was all the more determined on that now—but I meant to marry Elizabeth too. And so, just then, I kept the peace. "Sir, I thank you for your good wishes," I said. "I think it wont interfere with my career if I bring Elizabeth the sketch I've mentioned."

Elizabeth took my part. "He must!" she said to her father.

"I've set my heart on it, and it wont hurt Langdon to use his colors to delight a lady. Will it, sir?"

"No, no," Mr. Browne said indulgently. "So long as it's done only to oblige the ladies, or as a man might do anything for a day's pastime, of course there's no harm in it. By all means bring my daughter the sketch when you've finished it, my dear boy."

"I shall," I said, and I kept my word.

I think I must have made a hundred attempted sketches of Rogers in pastel before finally I got something that partly satisfied me. Elizabeth was always asking me when I'd be done; and I was as continually putting her off; for now I was delightfully in and out of the Reverend Arthur Browne's house perhaps a dozen times a week, and the light of that family's countenance was not denied me. Working from memory on the sketch that pleased me, I think I contrived to catch something of Rogers' character in the posture, and, too, in the vaguely-seen features revealed by the campfire into which I depicted him gazing. The suggestion was of a huge man, seated upon a rock and brooding over this fire in the night; and Elizabeth seemed to understand—perhaps because I told her—that I meant to show him as I'd so often seen him: awake, while all the detachment slept, calculating within himself the chances of success and failure, of life and death, and making sure that the outcome was to be neither death nor failure, but success and life.

Elizabeth was pleased. She took the little picture from me, gazed at it glowingly and gave me a touch on the cheek with two ineffable fingers.

"It's splendid," she said. "It shows real talent, Langdon, because it tells what the very spirit of him must be. Now make me a larger one, so that I can see what he *really* looks like."

This praise from her seemed to me almost like an admission that she wouldn't mind my ambition to be a painter after all. It was like a tacit consent; I laughed in sheer happiness, promised her the portrait, and went away itching to begin it.

CHAPTER XLVIII

WAR HAS an ennobling effect on a few, perhaps, a ruinous effect on others, and no effect at all on many. The same thing, doubtless, can be said for politics, as well as for business and professions. Even my short experience with war, however, did something for me that no business or profession could have done: it somehow made me willing to work indefinitely in order to reach a given goal; willing, too, to forego the little pleasures and relaxations that had once seemed so important. By comparison with the hated labors of those endless marches through the swamps of Canada, any work seemed pleasant: any hours, no matter how long, seemed short.

Billy and I built a shack on the high land of our farm, looking north toward Mount Agamenticus and the Dover hills. We built it out of boards with battens nailed over the cracks, and racked salt hay around the bottom in an attempt to parry the knife-thrusts of New England winter; but when a keen northwest wind was blowing, the shack was sometimes so cold, even with an iron stove roaring, that newly-applied paints would freeze if left more than ten feet from the fire. Only pastels, being dry, were safe.

Thus I was not disturbed by visitors, which is always something for an artist to be thankful for; and in the quiet of this rude haven I did my first finished portrait in red chalk and pastel. It was a half length, and about half life size, done partly from the pencilled sketches I'd made and partly from memory too. Sometimes my fingers, stiffly gripping the pencil, were so cold that I might not have gone on, except that I kept reminding myself how Rogers crawled from tree to tree at White River Falls to refresh the fires that saved our lives: how Ogden wavered and sagged between the two Indian boys, but still came on: how Andrew McNeal hacked at his bonds with a sliver of moose-bone until the tendons of his fingers were laid bare.

I was a novice, finding out everything for myself as I went ahead; yet I believe today that this portrait of Rogers in his green coat and his black infantryman's hat with the curved ornament, a knapsack-strap of Indian-work across his chest and a musket held in the crook of his arm, might have been worse. I confess that the thing took me months to do, and that I sometimes put it aside in despair for other months. Before it was finished we'd had the news of the taking of Montreal; and of course my hero-worshiping thought of that was that the surrender must have been made entirely to Major Rogers, with General Amherst figuring insignificantly in the background.

Another portrait I made simultaneously—it was an unfinished sketch rather than a portrait—was of Elizabeth in her dress of orange wool, as I had seen her before Thanksgiving in the kitchen, glancing obliquely at me from brilliant soft eyes. I did it for relaxation when my muscles ached from working over-long on Rogers; but in spite of that, the likeness distracted me from other work, so that I turned it to the wall before it was completed and thereafter got my relaxation from sketching Billy in a score of poses.

Elizabeth was always asking me when her portrait of Rogers would be done, and she pouted sometimes at the length of time I was spending on it; but when I brought it to her finished, I had my reward. She gazed and gazed at it, and any artist knows what it means when a lady of his heart is thus enchanted with his handiwork.

"Why, Langdon!" she cried. "I didn't *dream* you could do such things as this! I do believe it's as good as a real painting by a real artist."

"It *is* a real painting," I said, smiling.

"I mean an *oil* painting," she explained. "Probably if you took some lessons, you could make oil paintings, too."

"Pastels have their advantages, Elizabeth. They keep their brilliancy forever, unless they're smudged; but almost all oil paintings are sure to darken and crack in time."

"This one wont get smudged," she said in a voice that made me tingle. Then she added, "You've made him a pretty large nose and mouth, Langdon."

"Have I? While I was doing it, Elizabeth, it seemed to me

that perhaps I was softening and refining the features too much. I'll admit that when I first saw him, I thought he was one of the ugliest men I ever——"

"What!" Elizabeth interrupted. "No! No! Not ugly at all! There's a grandeur about his face! The large mouth shows generosity, and the large nose is aristocratic. All true aristocrats have large noses; and so have all great men. I wont hear him called ugly! You sha'n't talk so about my picture! I'll hide it away where you can't see it!" Then, laughing gaily, she tapped me on the shoulder, ran upstairs; and when she came back, charmingly flushed and still laughing, she fairly enraptured me.

"Langdon," she said, "have you made other pictures in your studio?"

"Well," I said, "I've sketched Billy a lot, and made studies of Indians. That's what I hope to do, you know: paint Indians."

She looked a little petulant. "Indians," she exclaimed. "I thought you were going to do portraits?"

"Well," I admitted, "I've done one other—from memory."

"Of anyone I know?"

Then, as I looked steadily at her, she dropped her eyes and asked softly, "Is it good, Langdon?"

"It's beautiful," I said. "Beautiful! You're looking at me over your shoulder. Every time I see it, my heart comes into my throat."

"Oh, Langdon!" she murmured in a gentle protest: then asked, "And what am I wearing?"

"Your orange cashmere."

At that she frowned quickly. "Oh, no! Not that orange cashmere! It's woolen!"

"I know, Elizabeth, but it makes a nice harmony. You're in the kitchen, and there's the most beautiful blue bowl on the table."

"In the kitchen!" she breathed. "Kitchen! Oh, Langdon! How could you do such a thing! I have a new gown—it's canary satin—a divine color! Mr. Blackburn's going to paint me in it. You could have painted me in that!"

"But Elizabeth!" I protested, "I've never seen you in it! It means nothing to me. I've seen your orange dress a score of times. It means warmth and home—there's nothing artificial about it."

To my complete astonishment and acute distress she burst into tears.

I took her hand. It lay in mine, clenched and unresponsive. "Elizabeth," I begged, "wait till you've seen what I've done. You'll feel differently when you see it, I'm sure! I'm proud of it. Whenever I go in the room, it's the first thing I look at. When I go away, it's the last thing I see. I'll bring it to you."

She turned her face from me. "I don't want to look at it! Don't bring it here! What if anyone should see it! That awful dress! And in the kitchen! The *kitchen!*"

"But you're in and out of the kitchen all day long, and so it's the room I love best in this house."

My words had no effect on her.

"I'd die of shame," she said. "I'd die of shame if people had to see a picture of me in the kitchen."

"What people?"

"The Wentworths or the Atkinsons or the Warners or the Masons or the Meserves! Think if Major Rogers should see it!"

"Oh, for God's sake!" I said; but before I could go on, her clenched hand opened within mine pleadingly. "Oh, promise me you'll tear it up! Promise me you'll burn it!"

"You don't understand. It's beautiful!"

"Please, Langdon! Please promise!"

So, of course, I promised. The next day I tore the picture in four pieces and threw it in a corner of my shack, where it lay among the fragments of other pictures of mine, most of them unfinished, that I'd condemned and tossed away.

It was my portrait of Rogers that brought Copley to Kittery on a Sunday in March. He went to my father's house first, found where I was, came on to the shack and knocked upon the door.

"Dear me," he said, when he'd come in. "How long has this been going on?" The place was littered with my sketches; many of them I'd tacked upon the walls—Konkapot, drunk, a shoebuckle caught rakishly in his scalp-lock; a line of Rangers, streaming water, locked together to resist the rush of the river; a canoe overturning in a flurry of yellow foam to spill out a dead woman and her brown baby; a windrow of red bodies strewn before the ruins of St. Francis; fleeing canoes driving at top speed down a placid river that reflected the scarlet, oranges, yellows and crimsons of a Canadian autumn; an Indian, at the bottom of a ravine, dismembering an enemy; a laughing, crouching red man, threatening with his knife an unarmed Ranger who cowered behind the body of a half-skinned moose; two tattered, hairy, animal-like Rangers, digging for lily bulbs in the shallows of the Connecticut.

"Dear me," Copley said again as he looked about him. "You've been busy! Ah—I saw that portrait you did of Major Rogers. Miss Browne was kind enough to show it to me. Where'd you learn pastel?"

"I got it out of books," I said. "What did you think of that portrait?"

"You got it out of books!" He exclaimed. "You can't get things out of books! You can only get them out of yourself! What else have you done beside these sketches and the Rogers portrait? Any other portraits?"

"Nothing of any consequence," I said. "Nothing fit to show you, anyhow."

"So?" Then he went to my workbench, sniffed at the stone on which I ground my colors; picked up one of my crayons and rubbed it on the back of his hand. "What's this mixed with?" he asked.

"That's a special one. It's mixed with clay precipitate as a white color, and bayberry wax emulsion for binding."

"Who told you how to do that?"

"Nobody," I said. "I've always made my own crayons, because I couldn't get brilliant, rich colors unless I mixed them myself. That one you're holding is just an experiment —one of several I made, using materials I'll find in the Indian country when I go there to paint Indians."

He eyed me thoughtfully. "Oh, it is, is it? How does it work?"

"Not bad," I said. "This was done with it." I fished out of a drawer a pastel memory sketch I'd made of the naked Indian girl kneeling before the St. Francis drum, and I set it upon the crude easel I'd patched up for myself. Copley scratched his jaw, looked at it and frowned, glanced at the crayon in his hand, put it down on the bench; then went to the easel and stared so hard, and at such close range, that I told him apologetically I didn't believe in fixatives and hadn't applied one.

He stepped back, shook his head and said sourly, "Let's see some others."

I felt a little sick. He didn't like it, and I had considered it one of my best. I got out some others that I'd thought well of, and placed them on the easel, one after the other.

But presently Copley stopped me. "Are these the first you did?"

"No," I said. "I made a good many tries at most of 'em before I got 'em the way I wanted 'em."

"What did you do with your first ones?"

When I pointed to the corner behind the stove, he walked over and picked up a handful. He was so long silent that I went to him and looked over his shoulder. He had found the picture of Elizabeth and had pieced it together.

"Who tore this?" he asked.

"Oh," I said, "that's nothing. Just forget you saw it, will you?"

He made a contemptuous sound, threw the drawings back in the corner, and went once more to the easel to place his nose almost against a sketch I'd left there—five canoes filled with Indians.

"Look here," he said irritably, "you can't do things like this!"

"I'm mighty sorry to hear it," I said. "I thought some of those were pretty good. What's wrong with 'em?"

"Wrong with 'em? *Wrong* with 'em? They're terrible! What are you thinking of? Who do you think would ever pay for things like this? Good heavens, man! Good heavens!"

"Are they good or bad?" I asked.

"Langdon," he said, "you'll have to get out of here! You'll have to go to London!"

I laughed, thinking he was joking. "When do you want me to leave?"

"The sooner the better."

I saw he was in earnest. "How would I ever get to London?" I asked. "It takes money to go to London." The thought of Elizabeth flashed into my mind, and I added, "Besides, I don't want to go there."

"It doesn't matter whether you do or not, Langdon. You've *got* to go. Let's see the rest of those sketches."

With a rather tremulous hand, I placed one on the

easel: then another. "But you don't think there's any good in them?" I said.

"Oh, for God's sake!" Copley exclaimed impatiently. "Of *course* there is! I don't know how you did it, but you've already learned more about pastel than anybody in this country could teach you. Yes, Langdon, you've got to go to London!"

"It's out of the question," I said, "so you might as well stop talking about it."

He paid no attention. "Who's seen these drawings besides me?"

"Billy," I said. "Billy's an Indian boy. They don't interest him very much. I haven't shown 'em to anyone else."

Copley tapped me upon the breast. "Don't! Don't show 'em to a soul! They'll say you're non compos! We're not supposed to paint things the way they occur. Things aren't allowed to happen on canvas the way they do in life. Men can't die the way they really die. Soldiers can't die as they must and always have died."

He picked up my drawing of the windrows of dead bodies before St. Francis. "See that! See the way that arm sticks up in the air?"

"That's the way it was!" I protested.

"Of course!" he cried. "Of course! But you're not allowed to do it! You know how an officer really dies in battle, usually —on his hands and knees, spitting blood, or under a bush where somebody dragged him, all crumpled and dirty. But in paintings, things mustn't happen so! Those who die must do it beautifully, in a fitting pose. If it's a general, he must be wearing Roman armor or a toga, and be held up by two colonels in Greek helmets; and in the background there should be a great deal of smoke, flying banners, a lop-sided cannon, and about seven soldiers addressing heaven and doing other things with lifted, cross-hilted short swords. A large figure of Mars floating against a yellow satin curtain held up by ropes and long tassels would also get you a great deal of praise from the critics. You have much to learn, my friend!"

"In London?" I asked him with some sarcasm.

"Tush," he exclaimed. "I'm only telling you a little of what you'd learn in London, and you could easily unlearn that part of it afterward."

When I shook my head, Copley stubbornly refused to believe me. "Langdon," he said, "I wonder whether you realize where paintings are used in this country—where they're hung —what sort of rooms they're placed in?"

"I think so," I said. "In the best homes—in the best and largest rooms."

Copley spoke slowly and impressively. "They are confined to sitting rooms. No American has yet been able to visualize a portrait hung anywhere except in a sitting room. And the quality of a portrait is calculated on just one thing: the resemblance it bears to the original. If you achieve fame as a painter under such circumstances, do you think the fame can be durable?"

When I hesitated, he asked me what I thought of Greenwood's paintings. Greenwood, one of the most highly regarded American artists, had at an earlier day painted Portsmouth's wealthiest citizens—John Langdon, for one, and the Cutts's and Moffatts.

I said I thought they were stiff.

"Stiff!" Copley cried. "Those bodies are hacked out of ice with a tomahawk! Their hair is made of cast-iron; their eyes carved from ebony." He raised clenched fists in exasperation. "But look at what they're wearing! Real silk! There's no mistaking the coverings of those ivory breasts! The richest satin, at 42 shillings a yard! If any lady who sat to Greenwood went to the trouble of buying silk stockings, he let the fact be known. If they wore lace, Greenwood made it clear that it was the best lace: the best and most expensive! Every gentleman he painted was satisfied. There was no need of a price-tag on the broadcloth of their coats! Greenwood's paintings showed the quality, so almost everybody in America vowed he was a great artist!" He grumbled and growled, muttering something about tin pleatings and hatchet-faces.

Then we were silent, cogitating. He went to the sketch of Konkapot which I had pinned upon the wall, scrutinized it with half-shut eyes and made humming noises. "I can smell the rum," he murmured.

Suddenly a thought seemed to strike him, "Here!" he said, "let me have some paper." He snatched up a sheet, put it down on the rough table I had made, and with a bit of chalk lightly outlined a graceful staircase mounting to a landing, whence rose a high arched window. On each side of the window was a rectangular panel.

He gave me the chalk. "There: fill each of those spaces with an Indian—a formal Indian—a pretty Indian, nicely dressed."

I did as he told me, incidentally touching up the staircase with a little color, so that the effect was lively and even brilliant.

Copley took the sketch from the table, rolled it and put it beside his hat. "Now," he said, "suppose you had a free hand to paint one of the distinguished early residents of this section. He ought to be a military man, of course. Who would you pick?"

"Sir William Phips, or Sir William Pepperell," I said promptly.

"I said *this* section. Why take a Governor of Massachusetts? Why go so far from home?"

"Phips was born at the mouth of the Kennebec," I said. "He was a shepherd and a shipbuilder on the Sheepscot River in Maine. He was a native of these parts."

Copley seemed surprised. "He was, was he? I thought he was just a damned fool Bostonian who didn't know enough to stop the sittings of the witchcraft court until hundreds of innocent people had been murdered."

"No," I said. "He was more than that. He was the luckiest man in the world till his luck turned. First he married a rich woman. Then he found a sunken galleon and took three hundred thousand pounds in gold from it. He took Port Royal from the French, too."

Copley meditated. "Well, let's see. If you had the chance, how would you paint him?"

"On the deck of a brig—thin, thirsty, black from the sun, coatless, stewing in the heat, watching half-naked sailors bring golden bars from under water."

Copley shook his head. "There you go again! Why, nobody'd be able to tell Phips from one of the sailors! Can't you understand the first principles of painting? He was a general, wasn't he?"

"Yes, but——"

"No 'buts' about it!" Copley cried. "A dead general must be held in somebody's arms; a live general has to be on a horse."

"But Phips was a seaman!" I protested. "He attacked Port Royal by sea. He——"

"You can't do it!" Copley reiterated. "You *cannot* do it! People wont have it! You'd like to paint Phips tending sheep or getting a drink from the water-butt; but if you did, you'd only have to tear up your work, the way you tore up that sketch of Elizabeth Browne in her orange dress." He spoke more emphatically. "Generals and women are *not* painted the way you know 'em! A woman wears her latest gown—the one that shows the most flesh. A general wears his newest horse. Surely you understand that there are times when it's useless to fly in the face of public opinion."

"Yes," I admitted. "I understand that."

"What I'm getting at is this," Copley said. "If somebody wanted to commission you to paint Pepperell on a sway-backed horse, would you feel obliged to argue that you ought to paint Phips? Or would you be willing to paint what you were asked to paint?"

"Why," I said, "I'd be glad for the opportunity to paint anything."

"Good!" Copley said. "Good! Artists complain because most rich people have bad taste and insist on showing it; but a rich man with bad taste is no worse than a stubborn artist with bad manners and a determination to starve to death rather than paint something that might give pleasure to someone else. As I see it, an artist who's trying to get somewhere ought to be willing to turn his hand to anything—to do what people want. When he's established himself, he can give people what he thinks they ought to have. It's only the little man who refuses to do anything that isn't perfect art; but little men, singularly enough, never produce anything perfect."

"What is it you want me to do?" I asked. "It must be pretty bad!"

Copley laughed. "Well," he said, "it's a means to an end. Mr. Blackburn has just started to paint Jonathan Warner, and Warner's wife and mother-in-law, and I'm helping him. Warner, you know, married the Macpheadris girl a short time ago."

I nodded. "Well," Copley said, "all three of 'em are a little excited by having the Macpheadris fortune fall in their laps, and young Mrs. Warner is the most excited of 'em all. She's only a child anyway, and she's drawn some pictures that she's possessed to have painted on the walls of her front hall. She wants 'em painted just the way she's drawn 'em."

"She can't draw, can she?" I asked.

"No," Copley admitted, "she can't but she's a nice girl and she's going to have a baby. If she doesn't get someone to paint her walls pretty quick, I'm afraid she'll go crazy, so I'm going to show her your sketches of Indians and talk her into letting you paint her drawings all over the front hall—and then, Langdon, you're going to London!"

CHAPTER XLIX

Mrs. WARNER'S drawings were worse than anything I could have imagined; but mindful of Copley's remarks about artists, I followed her childish designs to the letter; and to my surprise I found that I enjoyed the work and that the days flew past on flashing wings.

Never, it seemed to me, had I been so content. Day after day, from early morning to dusk, I spread my colors on the Warners' walls, painting in oils on the plaster, a scant square foot at a time, and in a month the two Indians stood completed at the head of the stairs, gazing darkly at the hall below, as they might have gazed at Mrs. Warner's father when he cannily paid them a forty-shilling barrel of watered rum for a ninety-pound bale of sea-otter skins. At the end of two months Sir William Pepperell, overdressed, sat stuffily on an elongated horse which pawed the air at the head of the stairs in what young Mrs. Warner called a monstrous exciting manner.

In another two months rolling fields, wooded hilltops, romantic castles bloomed on the walls below the caracoling Sir William. Last of all to be done was a woman alone in an open meadow, spinning, a dog that seemed part pig, and an atrocious scene showing Abraham offering up Isaac as a sacrifice.

"What in God's name," I asked Copley, "does it all mean, and why, Oh, *why* did young Mrs. Warner, just before the baby was born, conceive the idea of perpetuating that treacherous, lecherous old rip of an Abraham at the foot of her stairway?"

Copley looked at me gravely. "What have you got against Abraham? You're getting paid for him, aren't you?"

"I'd forgotten that," I said. "I take back what I called him. I see that he must have been a noble gentleman after all."

"Why of course, Langdon, and you'll paint many a worse before you're through."

I was willing; and I was grateful to Mrs. Warner and Abraham and Sir William Pepperell and his horse because they were helping me to get enough money to marry Elizabeth.

Early in May Copley came in to see me slap the last brushfuls of paint on the pig-dog—the last and most offensive figment of Mrs. Warner's imaginaton to be transferred to the wall. When I stood up, with back half-broken, and contemplated that dreadful animal, Copley took me by the arm and led me to the front lawn, from which we could see the furled white sails and yellow masts of Warner's new brig, the *Governor John Wentworth*, taking in cargo for England. It was she, and not Abraham and Isaac, that I would have liked to put upon the plaster of Mrs. Warner's hall.

"I shouldn't have done it!" I said. "I can't look at that dog without gagging!"

"Now, now!" he said. "That's Mrs. Warner's dog. I don't deny he's been a trial to you, and I think you've earned a rest. Why don't you go fishing?"

I said I'd like nothing better, if he'd come with me.

"I can't," he said. "I ought to be in Boston right now. You go ahead, and don't come back for a week. And *don't* let the dog or Abraham or the kind of horse Mrs. Warner thinks Sir William Pepperell ought to ride get working on your conscience. It isn't everybody whose first commissioned work is not only horrible, but gets 'em enough money, as this does, to take him to London."

Elizabeth seemed to look at me over his shoulder. "I'll never go," I said.

"No?" he smiled. "Well, go fishing first, and when you come back, we'll talk of it again."

That was how it happened that Odiorne and I took rods, guns, fish baskets and blankets, loaded Billy with salt, sugar, pork, corn meal, coffee-pail and fry pan, and set off in Hunk's canoe for the upper reaches of the Salmon Falls River.

A thousand things put me in mind of Hunk that week: the red buds on the steel-blue maples; the haze of green around the willow branches; the tremulous symphony of the baby frogs, that might have been written by a master musician to accompany the twilight scents of Maine meadows in the spring; the small white clouds, their bases flattened; the dazzling brilliance of our Maine atmosphere; the clucking of blackbirds in the bayberries; the squeals of porcupines at night; the sizzling and curling of trout in the bright brown fat. . . . I thought how much Hunk would have loved all this, and wondered whether friends aren't sometimes more alive to us when dead than when living.

It wasn't only my lost friend that I saw in the new color of the springtime and in the flicker of the evening campfire. The face of the girl I was going to marry was here and there and everywhere, and the breeze never stirred but I seemed to hear her whispering, "Langdon, dear!"

At the end of the week, when we came back down the Piscataqua with sunburned faces, tangled hair and stomachs full of fish, our canoe was loaded with a doe's hind-quarters, a young raccoon, five pounds of spruce gum and a bark box filled to the brim with fourteen-inch trout. As we neared Mendum's Point, my mother came down to the wharf and waved to us to hurry.

"My land!" she cried, when we shot alongside, "I thought you'd never be home in time! You can't dream who's been here!" Then, as if fearful I'd guess before she told me, she hurriedly added, "Major Rogers!"

Of course I was excited. "Here? He came to see you? What did he do and what did he say?"

"He came to see you," my mother said. "It was five days ago. I told him you'd be back Saturday, probably, and he said to tell you that he'd be at Stoodley's Saturday, expecting you to supper. On Sunday he's going to Concord."

I sprang shore. "I'll get dressed, and hurry over. Think if I'd missed him!"

"Ma!" Odiorne shouted, "kin I go see Major Rogers, Ma? Hey, Langdon: kin I see Major Rogers!"

"You'll see him," I promised. "But not today."

My mother clicked her tongue. "I should say he wouldn't! My land, it's like trying to see the King! Whenever he goes out, a crowd follows him around! They say people stand in front of the Brownes' house half the night."

I stared at her. "The *Brownes'* house! Is he staying at the Brownes'?"

My mother spoke soothingly. "Why shouldn't he, Langdon? The Major's a Mason, and so's the Reverend Arthur Browne. You'd naturally expect a minister to be the first to show hospitality to a soldier who fought on the Lord's side! If they're both Masons, that makes it even more natural."

That, I insisted to myself, was true, and there was no reason for the depression that began to weigh upon me.

"Did he see any of my sketches?" I asked. "It would have been all right for *him* to see 'em."

"Why, Langdon!" my mother said. "You know we agreed nobody was to go into that barn unless you took him. Anyway, the Major wouldn't have stopped. He had Elizabeth with him, and she was in a hurry to get back because that was the night the banquet was given to the Major, and she wanted to have her hair dressed in the new French fashion."

"Elizabeth was with him?" I asked blankly. "Only Elizabeth? Just the two of them came?"

My mother placed her hand upon my arm. "Now, Langdon! There's no reason why a gentleman like the Major shouldn't take a lady out on that great broad river. There'd be a thousand eyes on 'em every inch of the way!"

I made myself presentable with all possible speed, and paddled across the river in the twilight. My mouth and throat felt dry and uncomfortable. I couldn't force the canoe through the water fast enough. I stood up, tilted her so she'd have less water-resistance, and drove her. When I tied up at Spring Wharf, my fingers were all thumbs; and when I reached Stoodley's, I could hardly get my breath.

The moment I went in, I heard that heavy, thick voice I had learned to know so well in the swamps of Canada and on our terrible raft. I pushed open the door of the tap-room. There he sat at the center table, a score of men about him, some seated and some standing, but all staring at him with slack lips and dilated eyes, as were the black waiters. Wyseman Clagett was among his audience, and Sheriff Packer, and a number of Portsmouth merchants only known to me by sight.

"Another little jaunt you'll probably never hear about," he was saying, speaking in a loud and husky voice, "was my taking of St. d'Estrese last spring. There wasn't so much as a twig in the plain around that fort, and we'd heard there wasn't any way for us to get into the stockade. I knew there *had* to be a way in. Amherst wanted it taken, and it *had* to be taken; so we waited and we waited, in the forest, till they started to cart hay through the big gate. When the horses were halfway in, we came out of the forest, running as if all hell was after us. When they tried to back the horses out of the gate, we shot one of 'em; and before they could do anything about it, we were through the gate and into the stoackade, and the place was mine."

He cast a quick glance at the intent faces around him, laughed abruptly and drained a glass. Then, seeming to see me out of the back of his head, he jumped up, took both my hands and shook them violently. "Langdon, my boy!" he cried, "I thought I might miss you!" He circled my shoulders with a massive arm and turned to those who stared so admiringly at him. "I guess you know this gentleman. He helped me get the raft to Number Four! Yes sir! If it hadn't been for Langdon Towne, I don't believe I'd be here today. When we were so starved we couldn't even get on our feet, Langdon Towne shot a partridge and kept us alive just long enough—just long enough!"

He squeezed my shoulder in a bear's grip and put me in a chair beside him. "What'll you have to drink?"

"Flip," I said, and those strange vague fears of mine all fell away from me as I looked at him worshipingly and basked in reflected glory.

"Bring a bowl of flip," Rogers called to Stoodley. "There's no flip in the world to equal New England flip! I could drink a gallon of it—I mean, another gallon!" He exploded his sudden laugh, and the others laughed with him.

It was plain that all of the company looked upon him as the greatest man they'd ever seen.

There was something about him brilliant and bulky, as there is about an eagle, and the clothes he wore were such as had never been seen in Portsmouth. His green coat was made of flowered cloth; and his long weskit of yellowish brocade

had an edging of gold lace that must have weighed five
pounds. His neatly clubbed hair was glossy, and he smelled
powerfully of a pleasant perfume which emanated from his
head as well as from his garments.

He beamed upon me, toasted me sonorously, tossed down
a full glass of flip to my health; then instantly filled again.
"How's your painting coming along?" he asked. Before I
could answer, he explained to the deferential audience that
I was one of the greatest artists in the world. "You don't
know what painting is," he told them, "not until you've seen
Langdon Towne's."

They favored me with quick, expressionless glances: then
turned back to Rogers with obsequious smiles. Clagett was
polite as pie to me; whenever I looked at him, his eyes slid
aside, embarrassed.

I sat exalted by the great man's friendship; and he addressed me principally, as if I were the most important person present. "Langdon, you didn't know that now, since
we've got Quebec, Montreal and all Canada, I've become
quite a figure of state, did you?" He laughed. "Oh yes,
quite a figure!"

I laughed too. "That isn't precisely news to us, Major."

"Ah, my boy," he cried, "you should have been with me.
General Amherst sent me West, out to the Great Lakes, to
take over our magnificent new territory and accept the surrender of the French posts. Fifteen whaleboats flying the
English colors—two hundred Rangers—Toronto, Niagara
Falls, Presque Isle, Pittsburgh, Detroit—Indians by the hundreds: Indians by the thousands! Hurons, Ottawas, Missis-
saugas, Mingos, Chippeways—deer in droves, and lakes full
of the finest fish in the world: whitefish. They look like
mackerel, a little; but you never ate anything like 'em." He
licked his thick lips, looked toward Stoodley's grill, whence
came the incense of broiling lobsters; then added: "And Indians! Indians everywhere, spearing whitefish; Indians net-
ting whitefish—why, you don't know anything about Indians!"

He poured himself more flip and leaned on the table, rapping it for emphasis with an enormous forefinger. "Detroit!
A fort on a knoll, with the French flag waving over it: a
field of grass sloping down to a lake as blue as a velvet
coat: in front of it seven hundred Indians, all dressed in their

best—all painted vermilion, blue, yellow, black, white—all their heads shaved—all decked out in wampum! There's a picture for you! The lilies of France coming down, and the British flag going up, and then the French marching out, all in white uniforms; Indians leaping and shouting, howling and dancing! It was like seeing flames turned into men."

"Flames turned into men!" I shut my eyes and imagined that assembly. I could see the color—a brilliant pageant, blazing like autumn foliage. How I wished I had indeed been with him to see those flames turning into men. Rogers had seen that—while I'd been painting Abraham, Isaac, a pig-dog, and Sir William Pepperell on a sway-backed horse.

"No, sir!" Rogers went on, and we all hung on his words. "No, sir: you don't know what this country is till you go to the westward. You live here on a little strip of seacoast that's like—that's like"—he looked around for a simile—"that's like the braid on my weskit. You don't know what's beyond the braid! Why, you see lakes like oceans: tremendous mountains rolling off for a thousand miles into a golden haze. There's cliffs of solid copper along the lakes"—he took from his pocket a water-worn chunk of copper the size of a horse chestnut and tossed it on the table—"there's springs that gush three rods in the air: oil lying on top of the ground, so you can touch a coal to it and put your meat to broil: rivers so long you can travel for months on 'em! There's bones out there—bones of animals so big they couldn't be put in this tavern! You can't even dream what it's like! Why, I've seen——"

He broke off and reached for his glass. It was empty. So was the flip bowl. He rubbed his lips with a huge hand, grinned sheepishly at me and rose to his feet.

"Well, gentlemen," he said, "Mr. Towne's having supper with me and it's time for our lobsters. We've got things to talk over. Old campaigners, together." He rapped out his abrupt laugh.

The others pressed around him, shaking his hand, proud of the privilege and telling him so. If he loved flattery—and he was human—he had his fill of it that night, and of course had been having his fill of it many other nights and all day too.

"Come back later," he told them. "I'll have plenty of rum for more flip after supper. Come back and we'll make a night of it, gentlemen. I see you like it as well as I do," and at that they all laughed loud and long, as if at some sidesplitting witticism.

"Come, Langdon," he said, taking my envied arm; and thus, flushed and jocose, the center of all eyes, he led me into that very room from the window of which I'd dropped, a fugitive, the night Elizabeth's father put me from his door. How different—and how happy—were all things now!

The waiters scrambled around us, grinned and breathed hard, and bumped into each other in their anxiety to serve the Major.

"We want a dozen lobsters," the Major told Duke, the blackest of the waiters, "big fat lazy lobsters—not tough, skinny army ones. And two quarts of ale."

Stoodley himself rushed to the grill to fill this order.

"And a bowl of flip, quick!" Rogers added. "Mix it yourself, Duke, and don't be too careful with the rum."

Duke made mirthful, watery sounds, drawing his breath through his mouth in admiration, and departed, galloping.

Rogers took up the conversation where he had dropped it. "If you told the truth when you said you wanted to paint Indians, you'll have to see that Western country, Langdon! This is nothing, here in the East! It's what a child might use to build a doll's house on. Most New Englanders are like ants crawling on the stem of a fruit basket, and thinking the stem is the whole world. The thing for you to do is to figure on going out there with me."

"When are you going, Major?"

"God knows! All I know is, I'm going. I'm on call right now, in case the General wants me; but I'm going back. Don't fret about that! Did you ever hear of Michilimackinac?"

I said I hadn't.

"You will," he said. "That's the greatest *you* ever saw. It's north of Detroit. It's the bottle-neck of the Great Lakes. There isn't a mosquito anywhere near, and it's lousy with whitefish and game! Every pelt that comes from the northwest, and every package of goods that goes there, has to pass through Michilimackinac. What do you think of *that!*"

I said it ought to be a busy place.

"Busy!" Rogers cried. "It's a gold mine!" He wagged his head knowingly. "You'd never believe the things you see out there. I ran into a chief named Pontiac. I'll bet ten dollars you never heard of him?"

I shook my head.

"Well, that'll help to show you what you're missing! That red Indian is as able a man as ever I hope to see! If Indians' brains weren't lop-sided to begin with, that Pontiac would be as great a man as Julius Caesar or Alexander the Great. Yes, sir: this whole continent would be his. I don't know: maybe he can teach 'em, even now. Maybe he can; but I doubt it."

Duke set down a bowl of flip and filled our glasses. Rogers tossed off a half glass, smacked his lips and looked at me owlishly. "The trouble with Indians is, you can't control 'em. They're like children. They'll play as long as they can have their way; but if you tell 'em they can't do something, they'll pick up their playthings and go home—probably picking up a few scalps as they go. If Pontiac can knock that out of 'em, he'll own the whole of North America. He'll never let France and England treat it as if it was theirs, and trade it around among themselves as if the whole world belonged to them by Divine Grant. He'll chase 'em out so fast they wont know what hit 'em."

He glowered at me. "You and your tuppenny Eastern Indians!" he said contemptuously.

"Did they all look and dress differently?"

Rogers laughed. "Listen: Pontiac can call 'em in from two thousand miles away! He could produce an army of ten thousand Indians if he wanted to. Some of 'em are big and handsome, and some are little runts that can't hardly walk if they get off a horse. Some of 'em are pretty near white, and let their hair grow so long they trip on it if they don't carry it in a hammock. It would take me an hour to tell you the names of half the Indian nations! Make you die laughing, some of their names do! Names like the Stinkers and the Big Bellies and the Pierced Noses." He shot a quick glance over his shoulder as if to make sure no one was near. "Why, some come from as far west as the Shining Mountains!" He lowered his voice to a whisper. "Some of 'em have seen the Western Ocean!"

"They've seen the Western Ocean," I exclaimed. "Why that means they've——"

"Doesn't mean a thing," Rogers interrupted carelessly. "That's just between us. Don't mention it to anyone. I tell you because you say you want to paint Indians; and because, to tell you the honest truth, I might need some of 'em painted sometime." He gave me a warning look from protuberant eyes. Stoodley, Duke, King and Prince bustled to us, as busy as four hound dogs on a scent. They put down platters of lobsters, quart mugs of ale, loaves of bread and a dish of fresh butter.

"Keep that flip warm for about half an hour," Rogers told Stoodley.

We fell on the lobsters like wolves.

When each of us had demolished one, I asked Rogers what he was doing in Portsmouth.

He looked disgusted. "I'll tell you what I'm *trying* to do, Langdon—and it's more of a chore than leading an expedition against St. Francis! I'm trying to get the pay I ought to have had five years ago! If you want to get into trouble, do something useful for your country. The better you do, the worse they treat you!"

"Why can't you get it?" I asked. "Is somebody complaining of something you did?"

"No," Rogers said, "it's just that legislative bodies always act the same way. They squander money on things that don't amount to a hill of beans, but never pay their obligations. Massachusetts says I wasn't fighting for her but for the Crown; New Hampshire says the same; but His Majesty's Government says I was fighting for Massachusetts and New Hampshire. All I know is, I was fighting, while all these legislators were sucking sugar-tits. There's no doubt about that!" He thrust his huge hand under my nose. There upon it was the same star-shaped bullet wound I had first seen when the rain was pelting us at the mouth of the Ammonoosuc.

"They weren't there when I got this," he said. "They were glad enough to have me do their fighting for 'em; but now the danger's over, they leave me with a debt of over eight hundred pounds, and thirty-six lawsuits on my hands from officers, men and the families of dead men—suits for back pay. Being their commanding officer, I'm responsible. Over eight hundred pounds, and I'll never get it! Never! It's an honest debt, but there's something about these lousy legislators that makes 'em vote against paying honest debts. I guess soldiers have always been treated so, and always will be; and I know I'm a fool to think they might make an exception in my case."

"When'll you find out?" I asked, aghast at the sum he mentioned.

"June," he said carelessly. "I'm to appear in person before the New Hampshire Assembly in June: late in June. I've got my muster rolls, and a strong letter of recommendation from General Amherst; but I wont get the money. Starting around the end of June, I'll be mixed up in so many lawsuits that I can light fires with the processes all the rest of my life. Anyway, I wont find out till June."

The word "June" seemed to remind him of something. "You've got Billy all safe and sound, haven't you?"

I said yes: that he was a fine boy, and had been a great help; that we had taught him to read and write, and hoped to make a useful citizen out of him.

"Well," Rogers said, "I'm ready to take him off your hands. Let's see: I've got to go to Concord tomorrow, but I'll be back in a week. Suppose you send him over to me then."

This was a blow. Billy had come to be a member of my family, and I'd really put out of my mind the possibility of parting with him. He and Odiorne were inseparable, and each boy was learning from the other something he could otherwise never have known. I gave considerable thought to my answer.

"Yes," I said slowly. "I'll do as you say. I don't know how I'll get along without him. I use him a lot for posing and color-work. My young brother'll feel terribly if we have to give him up. He's teaching Billy to think like a white boy. If Billy could go on the way he's started, I think he might do great things." I looked at Rogers hopefully, but he was busy cracking lobster claws and forking out the meat.

I kept on trying. "I'm to receive quite a sum for my paintings in the Warner house. If you'd set a price on Billy, I'd like mighty well to buy him from you. If you wanted more than the Warners pay me, maybe you'd be willing to take out the balance in a painting. I believe I could do something you'd like."

Rogers shook his head. "That's too bad," he said regretfully. "It never occurred to me you'd get attached to him. The truth is, I've promised him to Miss Elizabeth Browne. She wants him."

The blood went out of my heart. "You—you've given him to Elizabeth?" I said.

My voice rang loud in my ears. The room seemed to have become an echoing vacuum in which the two of us hung suspended, with that broad face of Rogers, chewing vastly upon lobster meat, revolving slowly about me. I was physically dizzy with apprehension.

"Why, yes; to Elizabeth," Rogers said. "I'll tell you a secret," he went on, and laughed, drank hugely, so that the laughter ran into a gurgling chuckle, "Billy's my wedding present to her."

"Your wedding present—to Elizabeth?"

For a moment, then, I thought Elizabeth must have told him she and I were going to be married, though it's true that had never been definitely settled between us in spoken words—I thought she must have told him, and this was his kind way of announcing he was giving Billy to me as well as to her. I learned better quickly.

"I call it a secret," Rogers said, "but all the Browne family's neighbors and relatives know it, and God knows how many they've told!" He laughed uproariously. "We'll have in that bowl of flip we didn't finish, Langdon; and you can drink my sweet Betsy's health and mine. You know she's sweet, almost as well as I do, my boy! She tells me that of all the young fellows about here, you're the best friend she's got. Yes sir; she talks a lot about you, Langdon!" He slapped my shoulder. "She says that picture of me you gave her is really what made her fall in love with me."

"In love—with you," I somehow found voice to say. "Then you—and Elizabeth——"

"Yes, sir," he shouted jovially. "I'm a gone man, Langdon! I took just one look into those stars of eyes of hers, and it was all over! We're to be married on the last day of June." He pounded the table. "Here, Stoodley! Fill up this bowl of flip and don't spare the rum! You'll stand up with me at my wedding, wont you, Langdon?"

I filled a glass, rose, and drank to him and Elizabeth.

"No, I can't do that, Major," I said. "I can't stand up at your wedding. I can only say God bless you—and her—now. Before the end of June I'm crossing the seas to learn my trade."

"In the multitude of middle-aged men who go about their vocations in a daily course determined for them in much the same way as the tie of their cravats, there is always a good number who once meant to shape their own deeds and alter the world a little. The story of their coming to be shapen after the average and fit to be packed by the gross, is hardly ever told in their consciousness; for perhaps their ardour in generous unpaid toil cooled as imperceptibly as the ardour of other youthful loves, till one day their earlier self walked like a ghost in its old home and made the new furniture ghastly. Nothing in the world more subtle than the process of their gradual change! In the beginning they inhaled it unknowingly: you and I may have sent some of our breaths toward infecting them, when we uttered our conforming falsities or drew our silly conclusions: or perhaps it came from the vibrations from a woman's glance."

—MIDDLEMARCH.

BOOK II

CHAPTER L

Wʜᴇɴ ɪ ᴛʜɪɴᴋ of London I think of a study in black and gray—black and gray buildings, columns, domes, statues, dark with the soot of years, but shining white where the rain has washed the stone in streaks, as if the city's everlasting bones showed through.

I think of black trees in a gray fog, outlined against a pale sky; of gray pavements; of floods of gray-garbed people pouring along them through the fog; of white faces; of the triangles of white kerchiefs over the shoulders of the women.

I think of a gray river, swarming with those gargantuan waterbugs of the Thames—the many-oared ferries and barges on which the passenger-cabins gleam whitely: a river alive with merchant vessels and men-of-war whose sails stand out like new-washed linen aganst the gray houses of Lambeth.

Even now I can smell London—its acrid fragrance of sea-coal smoke pressed to earth by the soft and heavy London air. I can hear it, too—hear the unending grinding and thumping of coach wheels and cart wheels on the round boulders of the streets; the bellowing of chariot drivers, chair boys, draymen, street hawkers, with which the roads are filled; the clacking of women's pattens on the sidewalks; the screaking of the heavy signs that overhang every street.

I can see it, hear it, smell it; but I can't describe it satisfactorily; for nowhere in the world is there such a city of opposites. In no other hive of humanity are there so many kind and generous people or so many thieves and rascals; so many beautiful homes and so many hovels; so many wise

statesmen and so many political dolts; so much honesty and
so much knavery; so much education and so much pitiable
ignorance; so much cleanliness and so much filth; so much
patriotism and so much treachery; so much sobriety and so
much drunkenness; so much virtue and so much vice; so
many frigid natures and so many warm hearts.

I think of London now with affection; but on the morning
when I walked ashore from the *Governor John Wentworth*
and wandered along crowded, noisy, dirty streets, my heart
sank deeper with every step I took, and I thought of London
as the coldest, gloomiest, and most unfriendly city I would
ever find if I lived to be a thousand years old.

The truth was that I was homesick, and I strongly suspected
I was on the verge of falling ill and dying, with nobody to
care whether I did or not.

I stumbled into the Strand unexpectedly, and in watching
the passersby scuttling up and down the steps from one sidewalk level to another—for each abuttor built his sidewalk
at the level that pleased him—and dodging the jets of muck
that spurted from mire-holes whenever cart wheels jolted
into them, I forgot to be homesick.

The shop windows, filled with such brocaded waistcoats,
boots, ladies' dresses, hats, silverware and saddlery as I never
knew existed, were as good as a stage show. They led me on
and on until I was confronted by the surprising spectacle
of St. Paul's Church, which seemed to loom up magically from
a locality where a moment before there had been nothing
but narrow streets and mean houses. When I went to see it,
I found the enormous structure surrounded by a churchyard, and the churchyard in turn bordered by shops that entirely distracted me from St. Paul's—for many of them were
print-shops with windows full of prints.

I moved from one print-shop window to another, thinking to myself that I could draw as well as the designers of
most of the prints.

And then I came across another sort of print.

It hung in the center of a window. What first caught my
eye was a uniform in the foreground—one like those worn by
the sentries who had challenged Ogden and me when we
attempted to enter Amherst's markee on our return from St.
Francis. What held my attention, however, was the picture
itself—a turbulent, riotous, colorful depiction of a regiment

of Guards departing for Scotland. Soldiers, sutlers, camp-followers, spies and spectators roistered, kissed, brawled and generally played the devil amid a hopeless confusion. Every face, every figure of the hundreds in the print was perfect. The whole thing was human nature, fatuous, childish, incurably impenitent. A Representation of the March of the Guards Toward Scotland, it was called.

Feeling someone's eyes on me, I looked up to see a hatless man standing in the doorway of the print-shop and staring coldly at me. "To the devil with him," I thought, and resumed my study of the print. The original had been painted, I saw, by William Hogarth. I had vaguely heard of Hogarth as being a painter of grotesques: of exaggerated illustrations for books; but I had known nothing of him or of his work. Henceforth he would rank, in my thoughts, as one of the world's greatest artists.

The man in the doorway spoke to me in a supercilious voice. "Just published last week. Nice little piece of work."

"Nice!" I said. "My God, it's astounding!"

"Ah!" the man said, looking at me closely. "You're familiar with Hogarth?"

"No," I said. "No, I'm not."

"Gin Lane?" he asked incredulously. "The Harlot's Progress?"

I shook my head.

He stared me up and down, but not offensively. "Might I ask your nationality?"

"American."

"Indeed! Yes, yes! Have you ever, by any chance, encountered an acquaintance of mine, Harmon? A resident of North Virginia, I believe, or some nearby portion of New England."

I said I hadn't.

"Well," he said, as if a distasteful task had been successfully disposed of, "just step in a moment. I have Gin Lane, The Harlot's Progress, The Rake's Progress—all of Hogarth's most famous."

"I'm sorry," I said. "I'm not in a position to buy anything just now."

The print seller glared at me, said "Bah!" in a contemptuous voice, and stamped inside his shop. When I hesitated, he called to me testily, "Come in! Come in! Good God!

How much longer do you want to go without knowing Hogarth?"

When I followed him into the dark of his shop, I found him taking portfolio after portfolio from racks.

He selected a print, slid it behind a fixed frame on each side of which a candle burned, then stepped back from it. "Gin Lane," was all he said.

It was a study of drunkenness: of reeling, staggering houses, debauched children, of poverty all a-reek with alcohol; of a neighborhood steeped in gin, corruption, despair, death.

I examined it carefully. The work was beautiful and at the same time horrible.

"What medium does Hogarth work in?" I asked.

"Ah!" he said. "What medium! Ah, hah! Well, Gin Lane was done in red chalk."

"Red chalk!" I cried. "Red chalk!" If Hogarth could do such work as this in red chalk, I could, as I had suspected, learn to do whatever I needed to do with pastels.

"You're a painter?" the print seller asked.

"I've done a few things in pastel," I admitted. "A few."

He made puffing sounds of doubt and suspicion, opened another portfolio and took out a series of six prints. "Something a trifle less—ah—gruesome," he remarked. "Marriage à la Mode." He stepped back and looked at me.

The six prints were magnificent: even more horrible than Gin Lane in their truth, their richness, their exposure of the futility of greed and vice; their march to inevitable catastrophe.

"Now then," the print seller said defiantly. "What about those? Bad drawing, people say—especially that of the husband in the bagnio, run through by the paramour."

"What's wrong about it?"

"Impossible for a dying man to fall that way," he explained.

"Nonsense! People who say so never saw men die. Sometimes they dissolve, the way this man is dissolving, with everything running out of 'em—life, hope, soul, consciousness. There's no doubt about this man. He's dying. He'll be dead when he hits the floor. What damned fool called it bad drawing? I thought Hogarth painted comic things; but the man who did these is a great man; a great artist."

The print seller shook his head. "Bosh! Hogarth has no

ranking as an artist in England. No! His designs are bad: his colors are worse: he's vulgar—common. Critics put him below third-rate copyists of third-rate foreigners. The originals of this series were painted in oils, and when those originals were sold, they brought one hundred and twenty-six guineas: twenty-one guineas for each painting. Mm! What have you got to say to that!"

"Say to it!" I cried. "Say to it! All I can say is that I came to London because I was told a painter's encouraged to do better work here than in America, but I've got the wrong place! The art critics of this country must be the damnedest fools alive!" I turned away, sick with discouragement. If Hogarth wasn't recognized in England, what chance had I?

The print seller went with me to the door. "My name is Hight," he said. "Jonas Hight. Where do you lodge?"

"I lodge aboard the brig I came here on," I said, "and if she hadn't come to London to be sold, I'd go home on her."

"No you wouldn't," Hight said. "Not if you're an artist. An artist doesn't let a little thing like lack of recognition or lack of money discourage him. That's why artists receive the treatment they do. That's why noblemen give them commissions; then break their words. That's why publishers buy their books and treat them like dogs. That's why rival print sellers make cheap prints of their paintings and cheat them out of the proceeds—as Hogarth was cheated for so many years. That's why they live in garrets, producing beauty for lords and ladies who live in jeweled sties. That's why they fill themselves with gin and roll in kennels—to forget the dolts who see nothing in artists but a race of idiots. You can't go home—not unless you're just an ordinary tradesman —a cheese-parer; a print seller, say! Now, then, where'll you lodge when your brig changes hands?"

When I said I didn't know, he went to the rear of his shop and returned with a map of London so extraordinarily well executed and engraved that after a glance or two I saw where the brig lay, where I now was, and how all of London was situated.

"You want a map," Hight said, "and this one of Roque's is the best map ever made of a city."

"How much is it?"

He peered at it. "Well, this one's a little torn. None of my customers ever buy anything but the best—unless they're buying paintings, when they usually buy the worst—so this map's no good to me. I'll make you a present of it."

"Mr. Hight," I said, "I'll take it, but I've seen folks like you before. We have some where I live in America. Occasionally they get to be shipowners, and sometimes they're supported by the neighbors, who send 'em flour and pork and such-like in their old age. You tore that map yourself, not two minutes ago."

He stared at me coldly. "I don't know what you're talking about! You're like all these artists, forever saying some stupid thing or other. Now look here: here's the Fleet Prison, right near us, and Fleet Street running into the Strand. At the far end of the Strand, between there and Piccadilly, there's all sorts of publishers and picture dealers and print-shops —none of the print-shops as good as mine, of course! Most of the other print sellers are a terrible lot of thieves —terrible! A few honest men among 'em, of course—a few. Hm! Yes! At all events, that's not a bad section. Not bad. It's new, mostly, and there's more air than down here. Your pastels wont get dirty so quick.

"Now if I had a relative hunting a place to live—a relative who wanted to work hard, keep down expenses, keep up his self-respect and press his nose to the grindstone, I'd tell him to look for lodgings in two neighborhoods—Cavendish Square or Leicester Fields. Quite the rage, Cavendish Square is. You'll find John Wootton there—animal painter: splendid man to become acquainted with: great influence! You'll need influence in this town! Yes, yes! And Francis Cotes: best painter we have—extremely influential—knows everybody."

"I want to learn all there is to learn about pastels," I said. "What good is influence if I don't learn?"

"An artist!" Hight exclaimed disgustedly. "I knew it! You can't make 'em listen to reason!" He shrugged his shoulders, as if resigned to my folly. "Have a look about Leicester Fields, then. It's near the beginning of Piccadilly." With a pencil he drew a circle around that small, near square. "It's an airy little neighborhood, and not fashionable. Lots of lodgings around Leicester Fields: good ones. Street floor, one guinea a week; next floor ten shillings; top floor five shillings. Hogarth lives in Leicester Fields—Hogarth and young Joshua Reynolds. Ever hear of Reynolds?"

"No," I said, "but that's where I want to be—Leicester Fields."

Hight seemed almost disgusted. "Remember, Hogarth has no influence—none! He's a dreadful man! He makes fun of noblemen and uses a whip on society! It's too terrible to talk about, almost."

I looked carefully at Hight; then laughed. It was easy to see he held Hogarth in tremendous esteem.

"Oh, yes!" Hight said disdainfully, "laugh all you want; but I'm telling you the turth. Take that, for example." He jerked this thumb toward the print of The March of the Guards Toward Scotland. "Hogarth thought of dedicating that picture to George II, God bless him; but the King wouldn't have it. No, no! He said Hogarth deserved to be picketed for satirizing the gentlemen of the army."

"I don't see any satire to it," I said. "Wasn't the King familiar with his own army?"

Hight shrugged his shoulders. "Anyhow, that's what made Hogarth inscribe the print to the King of Prussia, as an encourager of Arts and Sciences. Oh, that man Hogarth doesn't care what he does! He'll die in debtors' prison, that's what he'll do!"

I thought a few unprintable thoughts about King George II, thanked Mr. Hight and started away.

"Here!" Hight cried. "What have you decided about Leicester Fields?"

"I'm going there at once to hunt a lodging."

"Well," Hight said, "don't say I didn't warn you! When you've settled down to being an artist, come back occasionally and I'll give you some hints on keeping body and soul together."

What I most needed in London for the first few months was what every young man needs in a strange city—something to stave off the curse of homesickness and loneliness. Of all the world's cities, it seems to me, London possesses more free spectacles, more galleries, more theaters, more great men and women, more of life's peculiar facets than any other; so that a stranger in it ought to be able to occupy himself from dawn till midnight.

None the less, as every young man knows, one takes little pleasure in viewing the finest of spectacles alone; and I was homesick with a homesickness from which I thought I would never recover—so homesick that I spent my first months in my small third-floor room off Leicester Fields, working and working at a portrait in pastels of Elizabeth—a portrait that depicted her in the gown, the canary satin gown, she had described to me: the one with rosettes of blue velvet, and white lace frills.

It was an experiment, I told myself repeatedly—merely an experiment, so that the time I spent on it was justified. It was an experiment in color; for only the high lights of the dress were yellow: the deepest shadows were red, changing to orange in the transitions, yet the whole effect was yellow. The background, instead of being dark, as were the backgrounds of all portraits I had ever seen, was light, so that Elizabeth's figure appeared rounded and breathing in an envelope of brightness.

Of what went on around me I was only half-conscious— or so thought at the time. After that terrible first month I made acquaintances in the coffee houses to which I went each morning for coffee, and to read the daily paper and the *Gentleman's Magazine;* but when these acquaintances thought me a fool for spending my days in painting and my nights in sketching, they remained acquaintances only. I had to work, for only by producing sketches for prints at the direction of Hight was I able to pay for my food and my third-floor room.

Occasionally I stood outside Hogarth's home, vaguely hoping he might come out and speak to me; but I never so much as saw him.

There seemed to be no way at all in which to make headway in my ambition to paint Indians. Nobody wanted pictures of Indians, and Hight discouraged me; told me to forget them. London's interest was centered on the coronation of King George III: on the angry rioting of the people over the resignation of the popular favorite William Pitt, England's wisest statesman, and his replacement by the new King's favorite, the Earl of Bute, one of England's many crack-brained statesmen. So violent were these riots that Bute, wherever he went, was accompanied by two prize-fighters for protection against the anger of the mob.

England talked of these things and of the recent return of Clive from India with a personal fortune of £300,000;

of French preparations to invade England in 6000 flat-bottomed boats; of Pitt's desire to fight Spain before Spain could—as she inevitably would—attack England, and of Bute's determination to delay until too late; of the 50,000 women of the streets who wielded so much influence in London; of the eight kept women with whom a noble lord invariably travelled. Would any of these chattering people pay two shillings—or one—for a print depicting Indians? No: for two shillings they could sit on a bench in the pit of Drury Lane and see the great Garrick in *The Beaux' Stratagem, Richard III, Hamlet, Cymbeline,* or any of a dozen others, or hear scores of fat-legged Italians sing atrociously and dance heavily at the Haymarket.

As for artists, the whole town seemed a-swarm with them, mostly bad ones—artists painting the ceilings of Lord Billington's home, or the walls of Lady Dripster's town house; artists painting coach panels, fans, tavern signs, miniatures, coffee-house decorations, government offices, royal palaces; artists studying at Thornhill's Academy, at the Duke of Richmond's school, at the Free School of Artists; artists exhibiting at the Royal Academy in the Strand.

Each of these artists, seemingly, had or hoped to have a patron to help him in his work. I made the rounds of all the picture-dealers with my crayon sketches of Indians, but most of them laughed drearily at me. Some of them were kind enough: some even retained a picture or two for a few weeks; but nothing ever came of it. The fact of the matter, they let me know, was that my pictures were vulgar: common. If I had depended on them for my livelihood, I would have starved within a year.

I think it was the realization that every artist had to have a patron that finally gave me the courage to approach the representative of Pennsylvania in England. I should, perhaps, explain that next to nothing could be done in England except by preferment. If a man wanted to hold an important post in the army or the navy—except under Pitt, who was supposed to have recognized and rewarded true ability—he had to know somebody who knew somebody who stood high in the King's favor. A clergyman couldn't exist unless he could persuade a wealthy family to supply him with what the English call a "living"—a ready-made, rent-free parsonage and church on a rich man's estate, together with an annual income ranging from a hundred to a thousand pounds. One who wished anything from the government— a remunerative position in one of England's colonies, a grant of land, authority to explore unknown territory—had to be able to present his case to an influential member of the Lords of Trade or the Privy Council.

Once let a soldier, sailor, architect, poet, artist, be given the opportunity to achieve something noteworthy for England, and England rewards him as does no other country in the world. Victorious generals are given fortunes, titles and great estates; artists are knighted; sailors are enriched in one engagement—as when, early in my London stay, the British ship *Active* captured the Spanish *Hermione,* and the officers and crew of the *Active* divided £250,000 in prize money. The difficulty lies in obtaining an opportunity; and it often happens that able men year after year plod the weary round of London government offices, all to no avail, while nincompoops rise to high estate and shame the nation—as was the case during the disgraceful administratons of Bute and Lord North.

The agent for Pennsylvania in England at this time was Benjamin Franklin, and it might almost be said that he was in England to obtain preferment for Pennsylvania. At all events, he wished to get something done that was right and reasonable; but he couldn't get what he wanted unless he was able to enlist the assistance of influential Englishmen. Since I couldn't either, I went to call on him; and I called and called until at length he saw me.

He was a stout, amiable-looking gentleman, with the benevolent appearance of a cat that has just made way with a platter of finnan haddie. He sat behind a flat desk; and while I told my story, he kept his eyelids lowered and his lips prim. If it hadn't been for this primness about the mouth, I'd have thought perhaps he was asleep, but he wasn't.

When I had said my say, he raised his eyes and examined me with a stare that was a singular blend of benevolence and penetration.

"I quite understand you wish to paint Indians," he said,

"but I am still at a loss to know who, in your opinion, would consider such paintings as an investment. Would it be the government?"

"I don't know why not," I said. "The government ought to have a record of the different tribes in its colonies. If the government didn't want such a record, perhaps the British Museum might. I don't know how the English feel about such things, but I read in the *Gentleman's Magazine* that you're friendly with David Hume and William Robertson and Adam Smith. If there's anything about England those three men don't know, I can't imagine what it is."

Franklin's eyebrows elevated themselves slightly. "I should suppose the way to paint Indians," he said, "is to paint Indians. Is it your theory that strangers should be asked to help you do it?"

I felt hot and uncomfortable. "I've painted the Indians I know about," I said, "but nobody'll have anything to do with 'em. Somebody's got to recognize what I do before I can go to the westward and paint Western Indians. That can't be done without support; for I'd have to take two or three years to it, and carry a canoe-load of presents. I haven't the money to do it."

"Mm!" Mr. Franklin said. "What sort of presents?"

"Cheap quizzing glasses, mostly, with a few bales of colored prints showing an Indian chief with his foot on the neck of the biggest bear in the world."

Mr. Franklin looked surprised and rubbed his chin. "An excellent assortment! Excellent! Any Indian would gladly murder his mother for a quizzing glass. When you speak of painting the Indians you know, what Indians do you mean?"

"St. Francis," I said. I brought out from my portfolio the last thing I had done—a pastel of a tranquil lake on which floated a big *canot du maître,* loaded with fourteen painted Indians and two French officers, all of them peering malignantly in the direction of the beholder. I'd shown them hunting an enemy—an enemy very sure to fare badly.

Mr. Franklin examined it closely. "Yes," he said, "they look natural—almost too natural for comfort. I had a little experience with some—ah—gentlemen like that five years ago, when I had my dealings with unfortunate General Braddock. How did you happen to encounter these—ah—virtuosos?"

"I went to St. Francis with Major Rogers."

"Did you indeed!" Mr. Franklin cried. "Did you indeed! An astounding feat! Let me hear about it."

While I told him the story, he continued to look from time to time at the drawing of the Indians in the canoe. When I had finished, he asked politely, "Would you care to have me buy this?"

"No, sir," I said. "It's part of a series, and the series shouldn't be broken. All the sketches together are a record of an interesting exploit; and some day I may need them to prove I'm able to do what I want to do."

Mr. Franklin laughed. "What you say is quite true; but how does an artist expect to live if he wont sell his pictures when he has a chance?"

I laughed too. "I daresay I seem unreasonable, sir."

At that Mr. Franklin began to hum to himself, looked up at the ceiling with a bland smile, folded his hands and tapped his fingers against his knuckles. He sat so long in this position that I thought his busy mind had turned to other matters, and I coughed deferentially to let him know I was still there. Then, as he paid no attention to that, I rose in considerable embarrassment to go.

"Ah," he said suddenly. "You've seen Amherst, and you've seen Crown Point; and after all Amherst has done for England, there must certainly be painted a panel in Vauxhall showing him at Crown Point. It's an inevitability, like thunder after lightning." The kind old gentleman beamed on me.

I spoke huskily. "But only great artists, like Hayman and Hogarth, are asked to paint panels for Vauxhall."

"Ah, yes!" Mr. Franklin admitted, "but not even Hayman and Hogarth know what Indians look like, or Crown Point looks like, and I doubt if they know what Amherst looks like. As it happens, I'm not acquainted with the management at Vauxhall, but in all modesty I believe I can assume that they've heard of me."

He drew a sheet of paper from a drawer in the table, reached for a quill, and beamed comfortably at me. "All I shall do," he assured me, "is to lay the matter before a dear friend of mine—an artist—Mr. William Hogarth: then let Nature take its course."

CHAPTER LI

A LETTER from Benjamin Franklin, in every country in Europe, was a key that unlocked any door; and Hogarth's door was no exception to the rule.

After working a day and two nights on a cartoon of Amherst at Crown Point, I presented myself at Hogarth's home with Franklin's letter. Ten minutes later I was conducted to the top floor and admitted to a studio, where I found a strange-looking little man crouched over a metal plate with an engraving tool. His head, which I later found to be bald as a potato, and about the same color, was swathed in a bright red turban. His whole appearance was bulbous. His nose was bulbous in a button-like way; his cheeks were round; so was his stomach, his hands, his knees, the calves of his legs. He seemed almost to be made of a great number of various-sized spheres cleverly joined together. Even his speech burst from him roundly, as soap-bubbles emerge from a pipe.

He bounced upright and gave me a button-bright look from his satiric eyes. "Friend of Benjamin Franklin—friend of mine! Glad to be of service!" He seized my hand and shook it, but glanced dubiously at the portfolio under my arm. "Artist," he said.

He perched himself abruptly on a high stool and eyed me contemptuously. "I suppose you've read Athenian Stuart's book and love to chatter about it with the rest. What? A book called *The Antiquities of Athens Measured Architectonically and Delineated!* Bah! Cant—hypocrisy—tittupy! Hocus pocus and tarradiddle! When I hear the numbskulls prating about Art, I wonder I can contain myself, by God, I swear I do! Critics damned near stunned, like ducks in thunder—barely able to twaddle—spellbound, sir, over the prodigious, inexpressible genius of this Athenian Stuart!"

When I shook my head and said I hadn't read the book, he rocked himself backward and forward on his stool, slapping his knees irritably. "You can't be much of an artist!" he cried. "Why, the whole Art world's agog! Genius! Stuart measured a couple of temples, so he's a genius! He's so burdened with honors he walks hump-backed!" As suddenly as he'd mounted the stool, he jumped down from it and tapped me upon the chest with his bulbous forefinger. "Since you're an artist, I suppose you've been measuring something architectonically."

He snatched the portfolio from me. "Here! Let's see!" With that he went to the window and let the light fall on my sketch of Amherst. For background I had shown the hook of Crown Point, the ramparts of the new fort and the misty blue headlands of Lake Champlain. The middle distance showed soldiers busy about whaleboats and canoes, and the uniforms I'd flecked in with faint scarlets, greens and blues. In the foreground Amherst stood, a commanding figure, about to step into a war canoe manned by Stockbridge Indians daubed with their fighting colors. I had tried to put into the sketch an air of suspense—a feeling as though all that strange assemblage of British, Provincials, Indians and Rangers, brought together in a wilderness by Amherst's efforts, would in another moment be off to the northward behind their leader to complete the conquest of Canada.

Hogarth examined it so long that I felt called on to make an explanation. "Maybe I haven't made it quite plain. Most of the large paintings I've seen are all foreground with a slurred conventional background. I want to develop my middle distance and background so they have as much character and life and truth as the rest of the picture."

Hogarth shook his head wonderingly. "That Franklin! You think he's just a smug-faced old putterer that stumbles into things by accident, and then he does something he has no business doing! Invents stoves! Stops fire-places from smoking! Ends sooty chimneys on street lamps! Finds out what causes earthquakes, lightning and thunder! Invents lightning rods, water-tight compartments, floating anchors, unspillable dishes! And now, by God, he invents someone to paint Indians!" He glared at me. "You're one of Franklin's inventions, aren't you?"

"I wish I were," I said. "Perhaps somebody'd look at my work."

"Somebody!" Hogarth cried. "Who? Nobody in England looks at a picture that isn't by an Italian!"

Then he picked up Franklin's letter from a table and glanced over it, evidently reviewing the contents. "Hm! Oh yes!" he murmured. "Panel of Amherst for Vauxhall. Hm! Very good sketch, very good pencillings, but I'll have to see what you can do with a palette on your thumb, young man! Where's your studio?"

I told him, and he scratched the back of his neck. "I'll bid you good morning," he said. "I'll be there in two hours," and he was as good as his word.

After he'd climbed my stairs, he went peering at everything upon the walls, much as Copley had done; and what detained him longest, strangely enough, was the portrait of Elizabeth Rogers I'd made in my folly of homesickness when I first came to London.

"Excellent!" he said. "Excellent! Must be like the sitter." And then, to my dumbfounded amazement, he chuckled and went on, "Character there! Ambitious to dazzle the rabble —somewhat sly—wouldn't trust her—pretty face, going to be shrewish when she's older, shrewish and——" He caught himself and turned to me apologetically. "Dear me; no offense! Not your sister, is she?"

"No, Mr. Hogarth."

"Good," he said, and chuckled. "When they're like that, paint 'em but keep away from 'em. Now where's the rest of it? I'll see all you've done."

I showed him everything I had, and his patient interest amazed and flattered me. He gave me a hundred hints and suggestions beyond price for improving my work, but he did far more than that; and when he left me, I thought that I was a made man; for he'd promised his influence on my behalf for the Amherst panel at Vauxhall, and I knew that was as good as the commission in my pocket—and it was.

Moreover when, in the spring, the fashionable world of London flocked to those magnificent gardens, I found myself no longer fearful of lacking the money to pay my landlord; for the Amherst panel brought me other commissions.

I remember little about them now, though I recall that one was from a print seller to do a series of Indian prints for children (the stipulation being that the Indians should be too pleasant to frighten the children); and another was to illustrate a novel in which the hero, a British officer, fell in love with an Indian princess whom he addressed in moments of passion as "esteemed female."

Those illustrations were a dreary task; I had forever to be altering them to suit the publisher, and they weren't finished till the end of my second year in London. After that I contrived to turn to mural painting; and if the plaster hasn't fallen, I suppose there are still Indians and trappers of mine slinking around the walls of perhaps a dozen gunrooms in certain English country houses to this day.

I'd been so long away from home I'd begun to think of myself, half-consciously, as almost a Londoner; so much so, indeed, that at Lord Bute's resignation in '63 I felt it my formal duty, as a true blue English heart, to get myself songfully tipsy in celebration. Young Benjamin West, who'd come over from Philadelphia to paint, took me to task the next day for profane ballads I'd been called upon to sing—called upon principally by myself—on a table in Tom's Coffee House.

Letters from home came, in time, to seem missives from a place I'd known not in reality but in my boyhood dreams. And yet, of course, in years I was still little more than a boy, being but in my middle twenties. Then one day a thing happened that made home—home and other poignant places—realities indeed to me.

On a misty summer morning I had gone to the Turk's Head Coffee House in Gerrard Street to gossip, mostly about commissions, with fellow painters who patronized that hotbed of the Arts. I found not an acquaintance in the place when I arrived, so sat down at a table by myself and began to peruse a copy of the *Morning Advertiser*.

Suddenly I sat up straight and stared unbelievingly at a paragraph that I'd begun to read with but little attention:

UNEXPECTED ENCOUNTER ON HOUNSLOW HEATH

While returning across Hounslow Heath from a visit to the home of a member of the Privy Council, Major Rogers, the famous American commander of His Majesty's Rangers in North America, was halted by one of the highwaymen who have so long and audaciously intimidated travellers in that locality. Doubtless thinking that he saw evidences of trepidation in the Major's behavior, the highwayman advanced close to the coach window, upon which Major Rogers thrust forth an arm, plucked the highwayman from his horse with one hand and dragged him through the window into the coach. Accompanied by his captive, the Major continued his journey to his destination, The White Bear Tavern, Piccadilly, where he had the culprit bound hand and foot by the tavern's people and confined in the cellars until the watch could be summoned. The highwayman will be arraigned before Mr. Justice Fielding. Major Rogers is said to have offered to wager a member of the Ministry that with a small detachment of his Rangers he could, within three months, wholly suppress the plague of highwaymen and footpads not only in London but in all of England.

I dropped the paper and took up my chocolate with a hand so unsteady that the cup rattled against my teeth. Rogers in London! Rogers among Privy Councillors and Cabinet Ministers! Unbelievable! Elizabeth would be with him, of course —and at that what Hogarth had said of my poor portrait of her rushed shockingly into my mind. . . . "Ambitious to dazzle the rabble . . . wouldn't trust her . . . shrewish." Ah, no! Elizabeth could never be like that!

CHAPTER LII

THE WHITE Bear Tavern was as comfortable a hostelry, provided one liked the noise and bustle of such a place, as there was in London. Its front was small and unprepossessing; but it extended back in two long wings which flanked a courtyard, and inside the wings were galleries with carved balustrades. The galleries in bad weather could be closed with sliding windows. Thus each room had a commodious balcony that could be used as a

sitting room. Like all good London taverns, it was as clean
as a whistle; and what was more noteworthy, it had a high
reputation for food, its soups—especially its turtle soup—
being the best in town. Its mutton chops were so large that
the sheep from which they were cut might well have come
from Brobdingnag; and its egg flip was delicious. It was a
popular tavern with Americans. Benjamin West lived there,
using his glassed balcony as a studio; and I would have done
the same if I hadn't felt obliged to save for the travels I
hoped to undertake in the Western Indian country—if I ever
could.

I found the landlord and his wife superintending the cleaning of the lower rooms. When I asked to be announced to
Major Rogers, they seemed to feel injured. "Sir!" the landlord's wife protested. "It's not yet eight! Sometimes the
Major doesn't ring his bell for breakfast till four." As an
afterthought she added, "In the afternoon."

"Ah—but Mrs. Rogers—the Major's wife," I faltered. "Is
she——"

The landlord's wife made a peculiar gasping sound. The
landlord looked blank. "Wife? Wife!" Then, as if recollecting
himself, he hastily said, "No indeed, sir: no indeed! No wife!"
He seemed to think I'd been strangely misinformed. "No
wife," he repeated. "Dear me, sir, no! None at all!"

Then, as a waiter came down the stairs, swinging an empty
tray, he spoke to him. "Andrew, you haven't been serving the
Major this early, have you?"

"None other," the man said. "Rang his bell 'arf an hour ago,
and I took him up the usual. Hard at it the Major is, too,
putting it right down into him, the Major is. I made bold to
ask him would he invite his friends to see 'Andsome Ned do
his dance on Tyburn Hill when that joyous event comes off.
Larfed like artillery saluting, the Major did, and went right on
eating."

"Off with you, Andrew!" the landlord said. He turned to
me. "You're in luck, sir. I'll show you in to the Major at
once," and he added, not flatteringly, "the Major's always
willing to see anybody—anybody at all."

On the stairway, as I followed the landlord, everything
half-forgotten seemed to come back upon me, reality indeed;
and when we stood outside Rogers' door, and I heard the

familiar thick voice shout "Come in! Come in!" in response to the knock, my heart was shaking within me.

I opened the door and stepped into a big corner room: as disordered a room as I ever saw in my life—and at that I'd been living among artists, musicians and actors! All around were trunks and boxes, most of them open; garments lay on chairs and on the floor; in a corner were a tray, pitchers, a couple of punch bowls, dirty glasses, and a dozen empty bottles. Between the two windows was a table littered with papers and the remains of breakfast. Sitting at the table, turning his head to stare at me, was the Major himself in a brilliantly-brocaded, much-soiled dressing gown, and with his hair—he wore his own—showing the half-ruinous remains of curls put into it by a Jermyn Street hairdresser. I had advanced a few steps into the room when he jumped up, oversetting his chair, and began to shout at me.

"Langdon Towne, by God!" he cried. "I was thinking of you yesterday: this morning too; and whenever my thoughts run on a person, he turns up! Langdon, my boy, I'm glad to see you! I'll bet I thought of you a thousand times when I ran across Dobbs in North Carolina! Dobbs and the Northwest Passage, remember? If it hadn't been for what you told me about Dobbs, I don't know as I'd have—— Here, sit down!"

He spilled a modish green coat and half a dozen neck-cloths from a chair, banged it down beside his writing-table, picked up his own chair, shouted "Natty!" in peremptory tones, and snatched up a rum bottle from where it stood among the remains of his breakfast.

"Here, have a taste! This is St. James's. Look!" He pointed at the label, which read "Forty years old."

"Rum that old's a medicine—not a drink! It wont hurt you! My God, Langdon! What a city this is! The best of rum, the best of food, the best of company, the handsomest women ——" He broke off to bellow "Natty!" again; then added contemplatively, "No, Langdon; there wouldn't be one damned thing wrong with London, hardly, if they'd only scrape about two inches of pigeon-droppings off the fronts of their buildings."

The door to the next room opened, and a thin, stoop-shouldered, youngish man came in. He looked distinctly resentful. "Scream and shout and yell!" he said venomously. "Never a damned hell's trifle of refinement! What is it?"

"Listen, Natty," the Major said. "This is Langdon Towne, one of my Rangers. He's a great painter." He turned to me in sudden contrition. "Should have asked before, my boy! How's your painting coming along? Tell me everything! No, never mind! I'll talk to you about that later. For God's sake, Natty, bring us a couple of clean glasses, will you, and take these sheets to Millan."

He grinned at me sheepishly. "I'm writing a book—two books. That's why I was thinking of you yesterday. I was just touching up the St. Francis raid. Look: here it is: right here. Look: here's my report to Amherst. Following the report I've added a lot more, telling how Stephens deserted us at the Ammonoosuc; how we built the rafts. Didn't know I was an author, did you? Hell, yes! Learned to spell some and everything!"

I glanced at the sheets of paper on his desk. "Why," I said, "that report to Amherst—you've got it dated November 5th here. You wrote it on November 1st: don't you remember?"

"Oh, dates!" Rogers cried contemptuously. "I'm writing history, and dates have got damned little to do with it, if you write it right! November 5th is Portsmouth's big day—Guy Fawkes' Day—but I want to get it celebrated hereafter as the day Rogers got back from St. Francis."

Natty put three glasses on the corner of the table, coughing with the sound a hatchet makes when driven into a tree. Rogers poured each tumbler a third full. To me he said, "This is Natty Potter, my secretary. I couldn't get along without Natty. He came over from Portsmouth with me. I found him there. You wouldn't know him; he drifted in long after you left. Who'd ever expect to find a nephew of the Archbishop of Canterbury in Portsmouth, New Hampshire! That's what Natty is, though: nephew of the Archbishop of Canterbury. Looks like it, doesn't he? He does not."

Potter winked at me, downed his rum, coughed that strange cough again. "Archbishop's nephew!" he exclaimed. "I'm sick of being the Archbishop's nephew. What's the matter with telling 'em I'm the Archbishop himself? Change my wig a little, wear bands, change my complexion from rum to port, and who'd know? Most people never see a clergyman after they're baptized—until they get in Newgate! Where's the manuscript for Millan?"

Rogers gave him the papers he had just shuffled together.

"Tell Millan he can have the rest of this the end of the week, Natty, and tell him anything you want about *Concise Account*. Find out the last possible date he'll give us on *Concise Account*. And for God's sake, Natty, write out a list of questions for me to ask Campbell when I go there to dinner. Write 'em out before you get too drunk, will you, Natty? And send out some paragraphs to the papers. There hasn't been a line in the *Advertiser* yet."

"Yes there has," I said. "That's how I knew you were here. It was about the highwayman on Hounslow Heath and your wager with a Cabinet Minister."

"Splendid," Rogers cried, and banged the table with his fist. "I'm glad I grabbed that rascal. In the *Advertiser*, is it? Ha! The journals make talk, and talk's what we want. Talk about Rogers: that's what we want! Tell the landlord to buy a dozen *Advertisers* for us, Natty, and see they reach the right people." He turned to me.

"You'd never think Natty's a Cambridge graduate and a man of letters, would you, not to listen to him and not to look at him. He is though, Langdon, and I'll have him up with the best of 'em yet! Why, there never *was* a town with so many opportunities in it as this town! Look at what they go to see—Italian opera, with singers that screech like an Indian squaw: that damned dull Four woman, scraping music out of wine glasses with her finger! Look at some of the plays Garrick puts on! *The Careless Husband, The Intriguing Chambermaid, Polly Honeycomb!* Damned if I don't think *I* could write better plays myself! Anyway, Natty can; and if we stay here long enough, he *will*, or I'll know the reason why!"

Potter snorted. "Blow, winds, and crack your cheeks! rage! blow!" He looked pleased, none the less, and went out more amiably than he had come in.

Rogers threw himself down in his chair, poured out an inch of rum, offered me the bottle: then looked me up and down with an almost paternal interest. "Quite the Londoner!" he said. "Quite the young man of fashion! Cinnamon coat, gray weskit—quite the quiet young blade! Married to some rich old woman, I suppose! No? no? Where do you live and how? By painting?"

I gave him my address, and told him that I'd contrived to live somehow by my art, but was no nearer my ambition to paint Indians on their own ground and from the living model than I had been five years ago.

Rogers slapped my knee. "The trouble with you is you're too damned quiet. This isn't a quiet man's town. Go out and break windows! Beat up the watch! Tear a bagnio to pieces! Get known! It's a good thing I'm here to help you! I'll take care of your Indians for you. Wait a bit and I'll put you to painting Indians! I thought of you at Vauxhall the other night. Saw a painting there of Amherst at Crown Point. Looked just like the place. I was with Ellis—Governor of Georgia, you know. I said, 'Ellis, I know a man who can do every bit as good as that—one of my Rangers—man by the name of Langdon Towne.'"

"That was mine," I said.

"What! That painting of Amherst? That was yours? Why, it's the best painting in the place! What else have you been doing?"

"I've done nothing but work," I said. "I'd rather hear about Portsmouth." I'm afraid my voice got a little husky then, but he didn't observe it. "How's—how's Mrs. Rogers?"

"Her health was good when I left," Rogers said. "Lovely girl! Too bad that old ass of a father of hers can't fall down and break his neck! Do you know what he did to me a couple of years ago? Naturally Elizabeth and I had always stayed in his house when we were in Portsmouth—he begged us to do so—great talk of hospitality. Then he made out a bill for board, lodging, washing and other odds and ends—a bill for £2600! Twenty-six hundred pounds, by God; and he set a sheriff on my heels!"

"Surely that's not possible!" I exclaimed. "Twenty-six hundred pounds for board and lodging? You could board and lodge the whole corps of Rangers for a year on that!"

"Don't I know it?" Rogers cried. "Anyway, that's what happened. His own daughter, too! I've got a copy of the charges if you don't believe it! He seized all my property in part payment, and I'm under bond for the rest! A man's got a hell of a chance to lead a pleasant life if he's got to be son-in-law to that old haddock!"

"Yes," I said. "He's a strange, uncomfortable man."

"Strange!" Rogers echoed. "Uncomfortable! About as strange and uncomfortable as so much mud! Enough of him! I've got irons in the fire here, and I'll tell you about 'em, now that Potter's not in the room. Potter talks a lot when he's drunk—and it seems you can't move around much in this town without getting drunk."

"Is Mr. Potter really the Archbishop of Canterbury's nephew?" I asked curiously.

Rogers looked hurt. "Certainly he is, but the Archbishop's not boasting. Family threw him out. He told me what for—some peculiar naughtiness—I forget. You can't tell when he's speaking the truth; so when he talks about himself I don't pay much attention. He wrote for the public journals, then was a strolling player, and I don't know how he got to America—likely doesn't know himself." Rogers laughed explosively. "Anyway, he's a big help with these books I've been writing. You see, I never wrote a book before, and you'd be surprised how much work it is if you never tried it. All the harder when you write two at once, the way I'm doing."

"What are they?" I asked. "I've illustrated some books."

"These wont be illustrated," Rogers said. "This publisher I've got—he wouldn't spend a farthing unless he was sure of getting a shilling for it. By God, these publishers beat anything ever I saw! If you'd written the Bible and offered it to 'em, they'd talk about hard times and high taxes, and try to buy it for five guineas! There isn't one of 'em that wouldn't cut your throat for half a crown! Anyway, Campbell says these books aren't intended to be read so much as they are to prove what I can do. Campbell got my publisher for me—made me publish in Whitehall, with the man who publishes the books on tactics. One's my *Journals;* the other's a *Concise Account of North America.* It was Campbell made me write *Concise Account.* Why, Campbell says if we can get the King interested, it'll be one of the greatest things that ever happened for England—and for us, too."

I was bewildered. Rogers in London, Rogers as an author—he was too much for me. "Who's Campbell?" I asked him feebly.

"Campbell? Thought everybody knew of Dr. Campbell, the great and learned Scottish author who knows everything about everything! You're responsible for my knowing him, Langdon."

"I am? But Major——"

"Yes you are!" Rogers cried emphatically. "You're respon-

sible for Campbell and Dobbs and Ellis and this whole Northwest Passage business. Listen: don't you remember telling me
about Arthur Dobbs, the day you joined the Rangers: the day
we started for St. Francis—Arthur Dobbs, who wrote the
book about the Northwest Passage?"

I said I remembered.

"Well, hark to this," Rogers said. "Six days after I married
Betsy, Amherst sent for me to go to South Carolina and help
fight the Cherokees. On my way down I stopped to pay my
respects to the Governor of North Carolina, and I'll be
damned if his name wasn't Arthur Dobbs! Well, sir, I remembered what you'd told me, and I said to Dobbs, 'No relation,
I suppose, to the gentleman who wrote the book on the
Northwest Passage?'

"You know, it was the very same Arthur Dobbs? He almost jumped down my throat. I believe he'd have given me
half the province if I'd asked for it. Nice country, too, but
too damned many mosquitoes!"

"Did you talk about the Northwest Passage to Governor
Dobbs, Major?"

"Did I! Dobbs told me that after he wrote that book, he
persuaded some gentlemen here in London to contribute
fifteen thousand pounds toward finding the Northwest Passage. With that money he bought two ships—the *Dobbs
Galley* and the *California*.

"They went to Hudson's Bay to hunt the Passage, and with
'em went one of the gentlemen who had contributed the
money—a gentleman named Henry Ellis. They didn't find
what they were after; but when Ellis came back, he wrote a
book too and insisted there *is* a Northwest Passage. And do
you know what Ellis is doing now? He's Governor of
Georgia, and he's right here in London!"

Rogers held the rum bottle to the light. Finding it empty,
he tossed it on the bed.

"Do you remember," he asked, "I told you about meeting
Pontiac, and how some of the Indian nations with him had
come all the way from the Western Ocean?"

"Yes, Major."

"All right," he said. "As soon as I found out Dobbs was
your Arthur Dobbs, I said this to him. I said, 'Governor,
you're looking in the wrong place for the Northwest Passage.
You're wasting your time sailing around Hudson's Bay. I

can show you Indians who've come all the way to Lake Michigan from the Pacific Ocean, and I know how to go there myself. I can take a brigade of canoes and go from the Hudson River to the Pacific, and I think I can go all the way by water. If I can't go all the way, I can go all but a few miles of the way. Anyway, I can go there, and that's more than all these explorers have been able to do with all the years of labor, and all the ships, and all the hundreds of thousands of pounds they've spent to find a Northwest Passage.' "

He rose to his feet and strode up and down the room, a fantastically powerful figure to be wearing a brocaded dressing gown. "Where an Indian can go, by God, I can go! I can put an end to this Northwest Passage talk for good and all! I can show England how to get all the trade of Japan and the Indies!"

He was excited, and so was I; for I now saw what he had meant when he had said he would show me all the Indians I wanted.

"What did Dobbs say?" I asked.

"Say?" Rogers cried. "He wanted to kiss me! He talked all night! That man's a drinker! He can drink almost half as much as I can! Lord, Langdon, how drunk we got! He said I'd got to go to London and tell Ellis what I'd told him. If I knew where the Northwest Passage had to be, he said, it was my duty to my country to go through it and prove it. Ellis would show me how to get funds, he said—Ellis and Dr. Campbell."

"I don't understand how Dr. Campbell enters into this," I said.

"Simplest thing in the world! He's written books about South America and the Indies and California and every other place in the world—especially about the Northwest Passage. Whenever anyone wants to write anything about the Northwest Passage, he goes to see Dr. Campbell. Campbell knows more than Dr. Samuel Johnson, and he can eat almost as much. I dined with him in Queen Square, and besides what he ate, that old Scotch rascal drank nine bottles of port. Port! I might do it on rum, give me a little extra time. But port! Too sticky! Ah, speaking of such matters——"

His eye fixed itself on a bottle upon the mantelpiece; he went to it, uncorked it, smelled it, then smiled upon me beamingly. "I must have overlooked this one last night, Langdon my boy," he said. He filled two glasses and handed one to me. "You can drink this St. James's rum forever and hardly lose any of your intelligence—unless you put a lot of nasty, sticky port on top of it. Look out for port! It's good healthy rum's worst enemy!"

"I still don't understand about Dr. Campbell," I said.

"Yes you do, Langdon. He's agent for Georgia. Ellis is Governor of Georgia; and the agent for the province is Campbell. Whatever Ellis tells Campbell to do, he does. Don't you see? Ellis was Dobbs's friend, and Dobbs got Ellis his place as Governor of Georgia. Then Ellis got Campbell his place as agent for Georgia. Why, it's pretty as one of your own pictures! Campbell's a Scotsman and knows everybody. Charles Townsend, who's the King's favorite, married a Scotswoman, and all Scots stick together like glue. Townsend used to be President of the Lords of Trade and Plantations, and they're the ones that offered £20,000 for the discovery of the Northwest Passage; so Townsend knows how important it is to England to find a quicker way of reaching Japan and the Indies. See how it is? Dobbs sent a letter to Ellis and told him to work for me: Ellis took me to Campbell and told him to work for me. So they're all working for me on Townsend. When my books are published, they'll turn the screws hard, Townsend'll go to the King; and right then, Langdon Towne, you and I, by God, will set off to find the Northwest Passage!"

"You and I, Major?" I cried, and goggled at him. "You and I?"

"You and I, my boy! Wasn't it you provoked my ambition to it? Wasn't it you went with me to St. Francis? You and your notebook? You and I, my boy!"

"How long?" I said breathlessly. "How long will it take us, Major?"

"It might be three years, it might be more, Langdon; but wont it be worth it? Think what we'll see! And think what it'll bring us! We'll be the first white men to go all the way to the Pacific Ocean! We'll lay out a line of forts and trading posts, clear across North America, New York at one end and the Oregon at the other."

Into my mind popped the long hours of figuring I had done on the expense of a canoe journey to the Indian country.

"Where'll you ever get the money for a three-year trip?" I asked. "Why, it'll cost a fortune!"

"Oh no," Rogers said. "Allowing for a detachment of two hundred, the expense wouldn't be unreasonable—not in view of what England would get in return. It wouldn't be more expensive than sending an expedition to Hudson's Bay to discover something that doesn't exist—and England's sent out a dozen of those. Why, it wouldn't be as expensive as fitting out two expeditions for such a gamble as helping your friend Sir William Phips discover a sunken galleon! It's true he found it on a second attempt, but God only knows how he did it! And what was the whole amount of the treasure? A million and a half dollars! Well, there's no gamble about what I want to do! I can find the route to the Pacific. And do you know the value to England of a short route to Japan? A hundred times what Phips found! A thousand times! A million times! No amount's expensive when set against a result like that!"

He was right, of course; I saw that. "What's this Oregon you spoke of, Major?"

"That's the river that runs into the Pacific," he explained. "It's a monstrous big river, the Indians say. We'll build a town on the Oregon, just like New York. The ships from Japan can come in there: we'll load the goods aboard big canoes and transport 'em straight to New York."

"Have you put this information in these two books of yours, Major?"

"My God, no! If I did, some little fiddle-faddle of a King's officer would file a petition for money to make the discovery, and take a regiment of Horse Guards to America to march through the wilderness with powdered wigs, white belts and a drum. You know how far he'd get—just about as far as a dressmaker would have got on that trip to St. Francis! Probably he'd reach Niagara Falls, and then have to be carried back to civilization in a sedan chair! No sir! That's a hard trip and a long one, and there's no one qualified to make it but Rogers!"

I drew a deep breath. Here at last was the answer to my dreams of going to the westward, but it seemed too good to be true; and with a sudden qualm I remembered another great project of this enthusiast.

"Major," I said, "what about that twenty-five-thousand-acre

principality on the shores of Lake George you were planning, and telling the settlers about when we reached Number Four? It sounded stupendous and magnificent at the time. What happened to that idea?"

Rogers drove the cork into the rum bottle and replaced the bottle on the mantelpiece. "Well," he said, "you've put your finger on the one bad spot. I'll tell you what happened about those 25,000 acres, and why. I never got 'em! They were up north of the Mohawk Country, and the Mohawks raised the devil about it! They were bound I shouldn't get 'em. You never saw any people so set against anything as those Mohawks were against my getting those 25,000 acres; so my application was refused. Sir William Johnson was at the bottom of it. He doesn't propose to have any rival principalities or princes in North America. He and General Gage, they aim to control all of North America between 'em, and they balked me."

He looked at me, frowning. "Johnson and Gage, between the two of 'em, they can get anybody hanged for doing what they do themselves! Johnson! Didn't I have to resign my commission on his account, because he wouldn't give me leave to travel to England? I'm a captain on half pay instead of a major right now, because of that! Trying to live in London on five shillings a day!"

He roared with laughter. "Thank God Johnson and Gage don't know what I intend to do about the Northwest Passage! If they did, they'd stop me; but if I can get the King's ear, they wont be able to. The King's ear, my boy: that's what we've got to get. A man with the King's ear can laugh at the General Gages and the Sir William Johnsons; and the King's ear I'm going to have if I've got to cut it off with my own hand! I'll step up to Johnson and Gage and say, 'Look at this, you flibbertigibbets! Whose was it?' I'll ask 'em. 'Do you recognize it? Well by God, it's mine now,' I'll say, 'so step out of my way, children: step out of my way!'"

He reopened the bottle and poured himself another glass. "It's all in the King's ear, Langdon," he said in a confidential whisper, having just been shouting loud enough for the landlord to hear downstairs. "That's what I'm after, and I'm going to get it! He's got two of 'em; and as sure as this is good, healthy, harmless, honest American rum, I'm going to get one of 'em!"

There was a clatter outside the room. The door burst open, and Natty Potter stumbled in, spilling a handful of envelopes and newspapers on the floor. He went down on his knees and pawed them together. "Invitations," he said. "Major Rogers invited everywhere, account the brave Major Rogers' encounter with highwayman." He hiccuped.

"Damn it," Rogers said, "I told you to keep sober till I'd found out what to ask Campbell!"

Potter looked up at him gravely, "Drunk or sober," he mumbled, "drunk or sober, the brave Potter's philosophic mind continues cossantly—I mean constantly—constantly to conceive conceptions. Had one on my way out. This brilliant young artist here, what's he good for, eh? If you do something for him, make him do something for you. Ought to be handsome print hanging in every print-shop—Gallant Major Rogers, future governor Mishla—Mishka—Missika—Oh, God, what a name! Aint possible say it without making a poem for it, and aint possible make a poem on account the damn word don't scan!" He rose to his knees and declaimed,

> "My love is waiting 'neath the silvery moon; but I, alack,
> am on my way to far-off Michilimackinac.

"That's the place!" he said contemptuously. "Michilimackinac! What monstrous and degenerate mentality conjured up such a cacophany—such a travesty on music and onomatopoeia. Ono—ono—that's right: onomatopoeia. It *is* right, is it not? Or is it not? Don't sound quite right. Anyway, that's what this brilliant young artist ought to do."

Rogers was pleased. "That's not a bad idea! Not a bad idea at all! Keep drunk, Natty; keep drunk! Langdon, you could do a picture of me with some little short Indians looking up at me, kind of scared and fawning. Of course you could! A few thousand of those around London wouldn't do any harm."

"Harm!" Potter said. "Be a benefit! Great benefit if it didn't look too much like you, but just enough to familiarize the *haut ton* with something rather like your features! Everybody'd be clamoring to meet the celebrated Major Rogers! Yes, and wouldn't that help to make tradesmen trustful?" This phrase so caught his fancy that he mumbled it over and over—"Trustful tradesmen: trustful tradesmen."

He spoke oratorically. "What, I pause to enquire, would be celestial Heaven's brightest gift to celebrated Rogers and Potter? Trustful tradesmen! Why? Because if they don't trust us, we decline to buy of them—absolutely decline! Why do we so? Because we have our own reasons! What reasons? We decline to name them because they pain us. Why pain ourselves? Forward, then! I have another idea beside that for the universal prints of celebrated Rogers."

"Another idea?" Rogers cried. "Name it, Natty!"

"Name it? I do so with pleasure and pride, Major—pleasure and pride in my own genius. Major, the tale of the untimely end of your gallant father must ring across the land! Must confront every reader in fair England as he opens his favorite journal! What is the taking of St. Francis to any true Briton of this Isle? Little, Major; little! But the passing of your parent, Major—ah, there's where Fame waits on you with tongued strumpets—many-tongued strumpets—I mean trumpets—many tongued trumpets all a-clamoring 'Hola! Hail! Rogers the Great! Hola!'"

The Major triumphantly put on a weskit of yellow watered silk, and thumped his bedizened chest resoundingly.

"By God!" he said, "if I don't get the King's ear, it'll be because he hasn't any to get!"

CHAPTER LIII

THE MAJOR, it sometimes seemed to me, was both the busiest and the idlest man in London; and there were times when he appeared to be the most popular. I made a red-chalk sketch of him in his Ranger's uniform and his tight little infantryman's cap, a musket cradled in one arm and an Indian peering over his shoulder. There was nothing beautiful about the Major's beak-like nose, heavy lips and pouchy eyes; yet, to my amazement and disgust, when a print was made from my drawing, it was instantly pirated by two hack engravers. Not only did their bungling tools remove all character from his face; but the cheap shops were flooded with these execrable prints.

Perhaps because of this, or perhaps because of his unusual height and singular manner of walking with no movement of his upper body, he became as familiar to the crowds in the street as Bute or Garrick or that grumbling, bear-like Dr. Johnson. On the occasions when I walked with him, passersby continually turned to stare; and I could hear them murmuring "Major Rogers"—"Indians"—"the great Major Rogers." He had a habit—not an unpleasant one—of smiling a little sheepishly at those who thus noticed him, and tipping his hat politely. London really liked him, too; there was no doubt of that.

Whenever anything of importance happened in town, the Major seemed always to be among those present. When his highwayman was hanged in chains on Tyburn, Rogers was there, beaming upon the crowd. When there were lists, in the papers, of those who had attended great balls, Rogers' name was on them. He was forever growling at the stupidity of plays he had seen at the Haymarket or Drury Lane. He gambled in the best of company at White's—Heaven knows where he got the money; and he was on easy terms with men at the Cocoa Tree and Brown's. I saw him walking down Piccadilly between Gilly Williams and Sir George Selwyn, his arms linked with theirs; and he was hail-fellow with Lord March, Lord Coventry, Lord Sandwich, Storey and various members of the Hell-Fire Club, men notorious for their debauchery.

Where the funds came from for such dazzling and extravagant association was beyond my guessing. His coats, shirts, hats, shoes and walking sticks were the best that could be bought; he entertained freely and frequently; he went hell-roaring around of nights with loose-living young bucks; and from remarks he dropped in my presence, I perceived that he had made somewhat intimate acquaintance with young ladies in most of the dozens of refined bagnios that were clustered around Covent Garden and Berkeley Square.

A captain's half pay doesn't permit such diversions. I think he must have won most of the wagers he laid; for he was a gambler by nature and a shrewd one. His sheepish smile and his heavy face made him seem an easy prey to schemers, whereas in reality his judgment was swift as lightning, and his courage, as I had reason to know, equal to anything.

Two of his bets came to my ears. He laid a heavy wager with five gentlemen that he would attend a ball of the highest *ton* at Crewe House, wearing no shoes, no stockings, no buckles, no lace; no velvets, silk, satin or brocade; no weskit and no linen or cambric whatever. He went to the ball in a trapper's buckskins, a coonskin cap and moccasins, with a tomahawk and a long knife fastened to his belt; and not only did he win his wager, but he was a tremendous and admired sensation.

Again, when eleven noisy, burgundy-soaked roisterers, Rogers among them, were bickering and wrangling in the banquet room of the Salutation and Cat in Newgate Street, each of the eleven pledged himself to pay ten pounds to the one who told the greatest lie.

When it came Rogers' turn, he said he was not skilled in lying, like London gentlemen; for he had been brought up in a simple home by God-fearing parents. So simple and natural was his father, he said, that the poor man usually dressed in bear-skins; and having a singular face, a trifle hairy, he had one day been mistaken for a bear by his most intimate friend, who was alarmed enough to shoot him through a vital part.

As this incident was not an unusual one in his family, Rogers went on, he would content himself with merely mentioning it as a fact, and would not place it in competition with the superb fictions invented by his companions. He would, however, seize the opportunity to say that America had some natural conveniences unknown in Europe. In western America, for example, there were sections where cold springs, hot springs and boiling springs flowed intermittently from the ground within a few feet of each other. Thus a traveller, arriving at these springs, could remove his clothes and place them, with a small piece of soap, in a warm spring, which would thoroughly lather and rinse the garments, and toss them, neatly folded, on a hot rock to dry. While waiting for this operation, the traveller could catch trout in a cold spring, throw them into a boiling spring without removing them from the hook, and have a well-cooked dinner with but the slightest exertion. Some of the springs, he added, were sensitive: if a stone were dropped into them, they would roar angrily and vomit it twenty feet in the air. Others were phlegmatic, and every eight minutes, year in and year out, would shoot up a column of boiling water a little higher than the roof of Westminster Abbey, but not quite of such volume as would have lifted and floated away the dome of St. Paul's.

At the conclusion of the Major's statement, his companions eyed him doubtfully and began to argue; but the conclusion of their wrangle was that he had earned the hundred pounds. The story that his father had been shot as a bear came into print and achieved a distribution almost as wide as Natty Potter had hoped for it. The conqueror of St. Francis was indeed a "celebrated" personage in England, but not for the taking of St. Francis.

In spite of all his roisterings and play-goings and wagerings and dinings out, I never went to his rooms in the White Bear on a morning visit that I didn't find him at his table, scratching away at his *Journals* and the *Concise Account*.

But after that first morning he never again spoke to me of Elizabeth. I hadn't the courage to ask him what I wanted to—how she looked; what she did; why she wasn't with him; how she stood in the matter of her father's suit against him—ah, and if he still cared for her or she for him!

Going back in my mind to the date of their wedding, I added together the time he'd spent away from her on various expeditions of which he told me, and I computed that of the four years of their married life, they'd spent less than four months together. Yet he wrote her long and affectionate letters. I knew they were affectionate because he often left them lying unfinished on his writing-table; only by being blindfolded could one avoid seeing the scrawled phrases of endearment. My eye caught unwillingly such words as "My Dear Little Angel," "My Dearest Life," "My Dearest Dear Betsy," "Your loving and faithful husband while life remains," "Your affeconot husband."

The word "affectionate" baffled him; as if to torture me, he asked me a score of times how to spell it; and I heard him ask Potter repeatedly: yet when he wrote it down, it was always "affeconot."

Before Rogers came to London, I had a delusion I'd almost forgotten Elizabeth; but seeing him showed me my mistake and cruelly freshened the pictures of her that were in my mind. His noisy talk of bagnios made me shiver and cringe within me. This was a dreadful creature to be the husband of any woman—and yet my admiration for him still lived. Nay, in a fashion it increased, even accompanied as it was at times by a feeling near loathing, and at other times by sheer pity. That old indomitable persistence of his now drove him as he worked at his books and as he grimly pursued his struggle—which often seemed hopeless—to obtain support for his expedition to discover the Northwest Passage. More, I was grateful to him. Not only had he saved my life when we retreated from St. Francis; but here in London he showed himself generous and a good friend. When my inwards sickened of him, I reminded myself that gratitude should outweigh resentment.

Natty Potter was a less puzzling human being, less self-contradictory, and altogether simpler than his employer, the Major—a contrast of which I thought one August morning when he came to my lodgings with a message. "The great and gallant Rogers," he said, "requests the pleasure of your company this afternoon to dine at the home of Dr. John Campbell. How like the Major—the soul of generosity, and vastly hospitable by proxy! You're to bring a portfolio of your masterpieces dealing with that wonderful march to St. Francis—O wonderful, wonderful, and after that out of all whooping. Quotation from the Swan of Avon."

"You're perhaps a little tipsy, aren't you?" I asked.

"Well said!" Potter remarked. "That was laid on with a trowel! This also from the Bard. Why yes, since you ask me direct, I am a little tipsy, but only a little. By no means sufficiently so! A few small gins cours'd one another down my innocent throat in piteous chase—Shakespeare again, if you'll pardon me—but I still retain the famous philosophic Potter mind—the piercing Potter eye."

He repeated "piercing Potter eye" in a thoughtful manner and wandered about the room staring at my sketches, while I went back to work, glad I had hidden the portrait of Elizabeth on the day I learned Rogers was in London.

"Do you still retain your Potter memory?" I asked. "I don't know Dr. Campbell. Are you sure the Major said for dinner?"

"The gallant Major said 'for dinner,'" Potter assured me. He coughed that strange cough of his and added in a faint voice, "I think I'll have to trouble you for a stimulant."

Thinking he was merely up to one of his sponging tricks, I went on with my drawing. "What time does he want me there?" I asked, "and will there be ladies?"

When Potter didn't answer, I looked around. He had slumped into a chair, his thin face the color of dirty snow and perspiration heavy on his forehead and upper lip. I ran for the gin bottle, poured him half a glass and held it to his lips. He took it from me, drained it and shivered weakly.

"Here," I said. "Lie down on my bed. You don't want that gin! You ought to have food! What makes you drink that damned paint-remover on an empty stomach!"

I was enraged with him. "For God's sake, look around you! Walk down to St. Giles's at daybreak any morning, and I'll guarantee you'll see a couple of dead babies in the gutter, thrown there by gin-soaked mothers. Here's an entire nation committing suicide on gin, unless William Hogarth and Sir John Fielding are liars! Haven't you any discretion at all?"

Potter wiped his face on his coat sleeve and with a shaking hand held out his glass to be refilled. Then he took the bottle from me and set it on the floor beside him. "A momentary faintness," he murmured. "It's passing; but if anything'll bring it back, it's a sermon. Had too many of 'em from my family." He sipped at the gin, rolling it over his tongue as though it were fine brandy.

I was sharp with him. "Suit yourself: I have work to do, and I work better when I'm alone. Before you go, let me have the rest of the Major's message."

"If you don't mind," Potter said, "I'll sit here a few minutes. Happens to me sometimes—and I'm usually a little unsteady afterwards. I'll be quiet. Campbell's house is in Queen Square. The dinner's at four; no ladies; and it's important. The doctor's having in someone who can be of assistance to the Major if he takes a fancy to him, so array yourself like Solomon—let your beauty hang upon the cheek of night like a rich jewel in an Ethiop's ear. Once more the Swan."

I meditated on what Potter had said: then took down the sketch I was making and set up a new sheet in its place. Into my mind had come Rogers' description of the sloping meadow at Detroit, of the throng of Indians, of the French garrison marching out to surrender—like seeing flames turned into men, he had said. My sense of color had been growing keener, and I had a sudden feeling I might be able to do such a scene and get something striking out of it. I went to work, and became oblivious to the passage of time and to everything beyond the boundaries of my drawing-paper.

I may have worked three hours when the thought of food occurred to me. I put down my crayons, stretched my cramped muscles, and backed away from the easel to look at what I had done. Then I jumped, startled. Potter, who for me had long since ceased to exist, spoke from just behind me.

"The field of the cloth of flame," he said. He shook his head. "No, no! Too commonplace! Sir, I believe you have talent."

He still sprawled in the same chair, and the gin bottle was empty. When I got a loaf of bread and a wedge of Cheddar cheese from my cupboard, he went at them like a wolf; but when I filled his glass from a pitcher, he stared at me in disgust. "Good God! It's water, isn't it? Don't you know what it does to gun-barrels?" He drank, but with genuine revulsion.

"Hadn't you better be getting back to the White Bear?" I said.

"Oh no!" He jerked his head toward my sketch. "Have you finished the fiery field?" He mumbled the words, "The fiery field; the fiery field," seeming to listen for a harmony that eluded him.

"It's almost done," I said, "except for touching up."

"Touch on," he said. "There's something I want to say—a favor I want to ask."

I went back to the easel and Potter coughed hackingly. "Sir, I seem to perceive a not unkindly quality in you," he said. "May I tell you that it's a singular experience to find yourself something of an outcast; something, perhaps, of a Houyhnhnm. The knowledge that you are is a sort of gnawing, from which you're only free when drunk or sleeping. You wake to a child's peace: then comes the gnawing: the realization. Your family wishes to God you were dead; your efforts are misdirected; whatever you touch is bound to go wrong; you're cursed—lost. But you, sir, can't know the blackness of such a life! You've never had it; you know what you want to do; you're a happy man."

"Well," I said, "if you want the truth, you're sick and gin-soaked. You're no judge of your own condition."

"Ah yes," Potter murmured. "He jests at scars that never felt a wound."

I thought of the countless mornings on which I had awakened to the realization that Elizabeth was lost to me forever: that all my strivings with a pencil seemed doomed to go unrecognized. "Look here," I said. "Get out! How can I do decent work with a drunkard maundering in my ear!"

He ignored this and hitched himself forward to the edge of his chair, looking at me earnestly. "Let me speak. It's been on my mind for years—I think about it in the mornings —conscience crops out; like a dog's dew-claw: useless; but there it is, a remnant of another life. . . . I was on the stage when I married. . . . You have no conception of the temptations. . . . I had it in me; oh, I had it in me; but my family hated me for disgracing them. . . . Birmingham and Bath were mad about me—only a matter of time before Garrick brought me up to London—I knew them all by heart —Shakespeare, Congreve, Fielding—Johnson's *Irene*—all! I could have played any part: any part! I've heard the pit stand up and cheer me: cheer and cheer——"

I interrupted him. "If you want to ask me something, ask it! What is it you think about in the mornings?"

He seemed surprised. "My daughter. When my wife left me, I couldn't keep her! My God, man—not on the stage— not in Birmingham! You have no idea——"

"What became of your wife? Who was she?"

"A beautiful child! A flower blooming in a midden! Her father made pinchbeck jewelry in Birmingham. Rotten rich, he was! That's one thing the whole world must have—imitation wealth: imitation splendor."

"Oh, for God's sake!" I protested, for it seemed to me that really he was acting for my benefit. "What became of your wife and daughter?"

He spoke bitterly. "My wife? Why, after five years her father took her back; had the marriage annulled. Money wipes out everything. It wiped out my romance; wiped me from the mind of the woman I loved—wiped the child from her life and from mine!"

I stared at his thin, flushed face. He looked weak and sick, and was probably, I thought, a little mad; but as he stared up at me, there was a curious calculation, almost shrewd, in his gaze.

"I don't believe a word of it," I said. "The father bought you off, didn't he? It was a Fleet marriage, wasn't it?" Fleet marriages were the scandal of England. They were performed without banns or licenses at the rate of five thousand a year in the unsavory neighborhood of the Fleet prison. I guessed, and guessed truly, that the man had married— as was so often the case in Fleet marriages—for the sole purpose of extorting money from his wife's father.

"Fleet marriage?" Potter said. "It's a lie!" He coughed sepulchrally: looked defiant. "A wicked lie!" Then, with increased defiance, he almost shouted, "What if it was a Fleet marriage—or something like it? What of it, I say!"

"Be done," I told him. "You want something of me. Out with it!"

"Very well," Potter said meekly. "I"—he hesitated, looked at the floor. Then his eyes flicked upward with a furtive plaintiveness. "I—I'm afraid I do want something of you— not money."

"Go on," I said.

"Yes, I will. That pinchbeck father-in-law of mine got his daughter back. Had his eye on a baronet for her—oh yes! Married her to him! Not with a child, though; oh no: that wouldn't do. Wipe out the child! How better do that than leave the little thing to me? So they did. Well, when I left England, I couldn't take her with me—five years old then. Nothing to do but put her under the protection of a nurse."

"A nurse!" I exclaimed. "Protection!" Thanks to the writings of a kind man, Jonas Hanway, I knew a little of the appalling conditions existing among the children of the poor; of the miserable thousands yearly placed by heartless parents in the care of gin-soaked women who went by the names of nurses. Three-quarters of the children, Hanway declared, died before they were five years old.

Potter waved his hand placatively. "I did the best I could. I put her in the hands of a good woman."

"Who told you she was good?"

"Everybody said so: everybody."

"I can imagine it," I said. "I can imagine all England stepping forward to vouch for the lady! How much did you pay the paragon?"

"I don't remember."

"Of course you remember! You were a player without a shilling, and a guinea must have looked as big to you as Westminster Abbey! How much did you pay the woman to keep your daughter?"

"I've forgotten," Potter said sullenly.

"If you want any help from me," I said, "you'll have to freshen up that celebrated Potter memory. When was it you left your daughter with the woman? How long ago was it?"

"She'd be fourteen now." He spoke hurriedly, as if to forestall further questions. "I want to find her—to know about her. If she's alive, I'd like to do something for her. I don't dare to go there myself, for fear the woman might make trouble. You have no idea—whatever I do, I have trouble!"

I worked at my sketch, thinking. Rogers, I remembered, had said Potter was likely to tell you anything; and if I was any judge of human nature, he wasn't one to suffer from qualms of conscience. If he had done nothing for his daughter during the past eight or nine years, he would probably be content to do nothing for another nine. Why, then, should he so suddenly want to find her? On the other hand, he plainly did want to find the child—at least wanted me to find her for him. I turned again to him.

"You're afraid to go yourself, aren't you, Potter? You're afraid in the first place for what you might find; and in the second you're afraid of the woman—the nurse. You think if you went, she'd claim nine years' pay from you that you haven't sent her, and maybe more. You're afraid she might use a debtors' prison as a threat—a threat and maybe a reality. Isn't that it, Potter?"

"Yes, it is." His mouth twitched pitiably. "But I want news of my child, Mr. Towne. Will you find her for me? I can't ask the Major. He isn't——" Potter paused and his eyelids drooped. "He isn't that kind of man. Ann would be fourteen now, and—well, the Major and young females—you'll understand me if I merely repeat he isn't the kind of man I could ask." He looked up appealingly. "I'm in great need of a friend. Will you do this for me, Mr. Towne?"

Here was an errand for which I indeed had no taste, but I couldn't see how to refuse it. "What's the nurse-woman's name," I asked him, "and where'd she live when you left the little girl with her?"

"She lived in Castle Street, between Covent Garden and Broad St. Giles', and her name was Sarah Garvin. If she's moved away, the neighbors could tell you where, I'm sure. You'll do it for me?"

Then, as I nodded grumpily, he got to his feet and shook my hand. "Good man!" he said. "Good Mr. Towne!" His pathos vanished; his air was one of complete relief; and after shaking my hand, he bowed before me like a man of fashion and spoke with airy flourish. "Believe me, my dearest sir; if ever you should need a friend, the gratitude of Nathaniel Potter ensures that you shall not find him laggard in that capacity. Nathaniel Potter, sir, when more effulgent days shall shine upon him—as sometime they surely must —will know how to reward those who extended a Samaritan hand in the period of his adversity."

He went to the door, paused with his fingers upon the latch; and again his manner changed, so that I, remembering he'd been a player upon the boards, could hardly bear to look at him, because I was ashamed for him.

"Remember, she is my daughter," he said, and sniffled as well as he ever did in the theater. "Remember, a father is waiting to hear from you——"

"I will," I said, thinking what kind of father he'd been and to what a life, in all probability, he'd tenderly consigned his child. "What's her name?" I asked him.

"Ann," he said. "Ann for her mother." He sniffled again. "Just Ann Potter."

CHAPTER LIV

DR. JOHN CAMPBELL, with his neat, narrow-fronted house in Queen Square, his own carriage, his bulky *Lives of British Admirals* and his voluminous books on Spanish America and all the rest of the known world, was a credit to English literature—far more so than that dirty-minded old clergyman, Laurence Sterne, who was making a spectacle of himself at fashionable dinners that year, and poor Oliver Goldsmith, who was notorious for sharing a squalid room with a butler and spending most of his time dodging bailiffs.

So great was Dr. Campbell's reputation that when I stood that afternoon before the glittering brasswork on his door, I hesitated to pull the bell for fear I might find myself alone with him and disgrace Rogers by my inability to shine in conversation.

I might have spared myself all worry. The footman, taking my hat and portfolio, caused them to vanish mysteriously, ushered me to an upstairs room where four gentlemen were gathered around a small table on which stood glasses and a decanter of sack. When he announced me, three of the gentlemen neither stirred nor looked in my direction. The fourth, an enormous fat man, surged in his chair, made puffing sounds, waved his hand weakly toward the decanter; then sank back, seemingly exhausted. From this I knew he was my host. Three years earlier I might have thought I had come to the wrong house; but I knew now that the English are not as free with introductions and greetings as are the people of other countries, and often expect guests to solve each other's identity by means of second sight.

Of the other three men, one was the Henry Ellis of whom Rogers had spoken—the Governor of Georgia who had sailed to Hudson's Bay in search of the Northwest Passage. He was dark and thin-faced, his cheeks so deeply scored on either side of his mouth that the grooves had the look of carvings in mahogany. The second, William Fitzherbert, was stooped and weary looking. He had recently been made a Commissioner of Trade and Plantations, and was a man of enormous influence. From bits I had read in the papers, I knew he was a crony of Sir Joshua Reynolds, Garrick and Dr. Johnson. The third, Edmund Burke, was much younger. He had a merry, easy, graceful way with him—an air of polite attention to whatever was being said. Through the influence of Fitzherbert, I gathered after I'd sat down, Burke had within the past few days been given one of the most desirable positions in England: that of secretary to the new Prime Minister, Lord Rockingham.

None of them, I was glad to discover, was what was known as a Wit. I had occasionally overheard, at coffee houses and in the theater, the conversation of Wits, and it almost always struck me that they'd previously prepared their witticisms as soldiers would plant a mine; and that they then laid a fuse under the conversation until, at just the proper moment, the witticism could be exploded. The Wit on his way to club or coffee house, it seemed to me, was like a belle dressing and rouging and placing her patches for a route or assembly; and to my mind a company of people was always pleasanter for the absence of Wits.

These gentlemen now were exercised, it appeared, over some of the shortcomings of the great Dr. Johnson. Seemingly he had taken subscriptions, seven years previous, for a life of Shakespeare, but had ever since been light-heartedly neglecting to write the book.

"After all," Fitzherbert said wearily, "seven years is too long to wait for a book."

"Especially," Burke said, "if one has no other books."

"Aye," Dr. Campbell said. Puffing sounds emerged from his fat lips. "If he'd talk less, and put the talk he saved into books, there'd be no room for my books on the shelf of the British Museum. Johnson's would fill the place to overflowing. Look at the time he wastes answering eediotic questions for that little squirt Boswell!" He made his voice mealy and vapid. " 'Oh, sir; if you could have a third arm, where would you wish it placed?' Good God! Think of the murdered literature that lies at the door of that little drunken ass!" He hitched his stomach into a more comfortable position.

Ellis delivered a weighty opinion. "The doctor's talk has been too much praised. It's like telling a woman she has the most beautiful leg in the world. She'll show it if it kills her."

"Isn't the analogy faulty, sir?" Burke asked. "The lady merely lets you look at the leg: she doesn't kick you speechless with it. Her leg, if admired, isn't a mule's, nor is it a cannonade."

This thought of Mr. Edmund Burke's pleased the others, and they toyed with it in a ribald manner.

The footman announced Lord Bremerton and Sir Joshua

Reynolds, and almost immediately returned to utter sonorously the names of the Earl of Clones and Major Rogers.

Never had I expected such good fortune as to encounter
Sir Joshua here. I hung my mouth open like a fool, so intent
was I on watching him put his arm through Burke's and
hearing him congratulate Burke on his appointment. Kindli-
ness and gentleness shone in his face. He was slightly under
medium height, and wore thick-lensed glasses that gave him
a helpless look. He was pock-marked; and on his upper lip
was a scar that made his mouth pout a little, as a man pouts
when listening sympathetically to an appeal for assistance.

He turned from Burke to Fitzherbert. "My dear dependable
William!" he said in the flat tones of a deaf person, "it's a
pity we can't have a regiment of you to be on the lookout
for the welfare of the nation." From under his arm he drew
an ear-trumpet, which he thrust in his ear and looked expectantly about.

"A regiment!" Clones said irascibly. "You'd need ten regiments of Fitzherberts to get England out of the mess she's
in!"

"What's all this, what's all this?" Bremerton demanded. "I
heard a lady's leg discussed! What leg, eh? Come, come! I
insist! I really insist!" He was a sprightly, erect little man
with a stock so high that if he had relaxed, his head, seemingly, would have vanished in it up to his ears. His friends
in the room called him Bremmy.

Campbell heaved himself about in his chair. "It was a
conundrum, my lord; a conundrum. What's the difference
between the conversation of our friend Dr. Johnson and a
lady's leg?"

Bremerton hopped like an excited sparrow. "Marvelous!
Yes, yes! Don't tell me! Let me see! Lady's leg and Dr. John-
son! Have you all guessed it? Upon my word, I can't wait!
Come, come, Campbell! Out with it!"

Campbell got ponderously to his feet. "One lets itself be
felt, my lord!"

Bremerton struck his forehead with his hand. "By Jove!
Lets itself be felt! Oh, that's vastly diverting! Does the answer go further and say which one?"

Rogers paid his respects to Dr. Campbell and Ellis, bowed
politely to the rest of the company, and came to stand by
me. From the manner in which the others looked him up and

down when they thought themselves unobserved, I could see they all knew who he was, and, too, were curious about him.

That day I was proud of the appearance he made. He wore a suit of shining dark green silk with a weskit of silver cloth. His lace was fine, and this quiet dress became him. I'd feared somehow to see him ill at ease among these distinguished Londoners, but he was as careless and un-self-conscious as he would have been among a group of Rangers. "Did you bring your pictures?" he asked me.

I said I had, and urged him not to forget that Reynolds was here. I didn't, I told him, want to be made a fool of.

"Trust me!" Rogers whispered. He looked exultant. "This is our day, Langdon! Do you see what that old fox Campbell has done? These are all influential men, and nearly all of them know a great deal about America!"

The footman threw open the door and said impressively, "The Honorable Mr. Townsend."

"That's the last of 'em!" Rogers told me hoarsely. "The last and greatest."

This gentleman, Charles Townsend, a holder of so many offices under so many Prime Ministers that he was known as the weathercock of English politics, had a round, smooth, gay, impudent face; a glittering, roving eye; a coat that clung to him and displayed little fripperies that seemed almost feminine. In his walk and in the movements of his hands there was something affected and girlish: yet there was a brilliance in his look that drew the eye and held it. On his way across the room he burst into an explanation of his lateness—an airy, careless recital of his troubles in reaching Queen Square from Whitehall. He gave this account with an air so indescribably comic that the whole company forthwith shouted with laughter. It was a singular sight—this assured, graceful figure with fluttering hands and flexible eyebrows, surrounded by a circle of red-faced men, every last one with his mouth wide open in delighted amusement.

Yet when we had gone down to the dining room and set to work on the dinner, it was fat, puffing Dr. Campbell rather than the brilliant Mr. Townsend who steered the conversation, and did it so unobtrusively that those of us who hoped to benefit most from it were scarcely aware of the steering. The dinner was exactly like every large dinner given at that time—soup at the head and foot of the table: then a saddle of mutton at one end and fish at the other; after that a capon at the head and a platter of pigeons at the foot; and lastly four sorts of ices—grape, raspberry, pineapple and lemon.

It was when we were at the ices that I became conscious of a discussion between Rogers and Dr. Campbell. "Surely, sir," the doctor said, "it is true that a dinner such as this, eaten by a starving man, would result in certain death."

"It may be so, Doctor," Rogers said, "but the starving men I've seen would eat it with no trouble. Sometimes, if they've been starved long enough, they get to be like Indians—or animals." He smiled at me. "You remember the way the men looked when they reached the mouth of the Ammonoosuc and found no food?"

The others at the table had stopped talking and were listening to Rogers, though apparently as yet with slight interest.

"Yes," I said. "It'll be some time before I forget. They looked like sick bears."

"Sick bears is true," Rogers said. "So did you and so did I. Well, if you'd put this dinner before us, Doctor, we'd have eaten it and we'd have taken no harm—except that a few of us might have died of excitement."

"How long had you been without food?" Ellis asked.

"Ah, gentlemen," Rogers said, "I didn't come here to talk about myself and my lean and hungry periods, or I'd have brought a wooden spoon with notches cut in it to remind me of the different mouthfuls I had. For two weeks we had a handful of corn a day—so little that it rattled inside us when we marched. Then there was a week when we didn't have much of anything. Once we divided four red squirrels among fifty men—as clever a bit of carving as you'd find at Vauxhall. Towne shot a partridge once; and I'm sure, gentlemen, you'd have enjoyed seeing four of us gathered around a festal board, measuring that partridge with a pair of home-made calipers to make sure one of us didn't cheat the others out of a sixteenth of an inch of leg-tendon."

The Earl of Clones looked baffled. "Four?" he asked. "I thought you said there were fifty."

"Only four when we carved the partridge, sir," Rogers said. "The others weren't able to go forward. Four of us were going for relief—on a raft."

"On a raft?" Lord Bremerton exclaimed. "Come, come!

Then there was water, and where there's water there's fish. Couldn't you have eaten fish?"

"Yes, my lord, we could have," Rogers admitted. "If we could have afforded to stop and fish, we *could* have eaten them; but to be frank, my lord, we didn't dare stop. If we'd stopped, we might not have been able to start again. And besides, my lord, fish are worthless when you're almost gone from lack of food. They don't give you strength. We were pretty far gone. If you're ever starving, my lord, don't waste time on fish. Try to get hold of a marrow bone. There's more nourishment in a good marrow bone than in a fifty-pound trout."

"How did it feel," Fitzherbert asked, "to be on the verge of starving?"

"Not bad," Rogers said cheerfully. "You've had dreams, haven't you, gentlemen, of being unable to get your hands around objects? You can't grip—you can't lift. If you try to strike a blow, your arm bends: there's no strength to it. You're made of jelly, and can't move."

Everyone at the table nodded.

"That's what starving feels like," Rogers said. "There's some stomach cramps, too, but you can get rid of 'em, generally, by lying down. When you walk, you stoop over to ease your stomach, and your legs buckle. You can't push or strike or lift. Very embarrassing, too, at times." He put his huge hands on the table, eyed them thoughtfully, said, "Yes" in a meditative manner: then grinned sheepishly at me.

The others at the table looked at me expectantly, so I told them how, after travelling three hundred miles through the woods, we had lost our first raft and how the Major, too weak to wield an axe, had burned trees into logs, while Ogden and I hunted food. I thought I saw skepticism in some of the faces, and so, seemingly, did Rogers.

"I have no desire to weary you, gentlemen," he said, "but there's one thing I'd like to say. Unless you've seen America, it's difficult to know what it's like. Even if you have seen it, you've very likely mistaken a slight fragment of it for the whole. It's been my fortune to be associated with many Englishmen who have come to America to lead regiments and armies, and it's surprising how often they found it impossible to understand what lay beyond the hills on either side of 'em. You could tell 'em and tell 'em, but you couldn't make 'em grasp it. Our own people are the same. America, to them, is New York or Boston—nothing more. It just happens that I asked Mr. Towne to bring some drawings here tonight—drawings I wanted to show Dr. Campbell. They're the only ones I've ever seen that give a proper picture of a little corner of our country; and if you gentlemen are so inclined, I hope you'll glance at those drawings before you leave tonight."

There was a perfunctory murmur of assent, and I felt hot and uncomfortable when I caught Charles Townsend glancing slily at Sir Joshua, as if to say, "Good God! Must we see another amateur performance!"

Rogers hitched himself forward in his chair. "It's the size of the country that Englishmen don't understand, and you can hardly blame 'em. Not a hundred people in America know the size of it, and most of those are traders, too ignorant to tell you what they've seen or where they've been. Why, gentlemen, this journey we were speaking about—this trip on which we nearly starved to death—was through country that hasn't had an axe laid to it. There wasn't a road anywhere in the three hundred miles, or a house. We travelled as far as from the tip of Scotland to the South Coast of England—a long way: a long, hard way. Yet that expanse of wilderness, gentlemen, is so small a part of America that by comparison with the whole it's like one little word out of Dr. Johnson's dictionary."

The port was on the table. Dr. Campbell drained a glass as though no liquid had passed his lips for a week. "The Major," he said abruptly, "thinks he knows a route to the Pacific Ocean by way of the northwest."

"You amaze me!" Townsend said. "I thought we buried that corpse when Mr. Ellis returned from Hudson's Bay."

Ellis's dark face flushed even darker. "It's a corpse that'll never be buried—not until Japan and China are buried with it. There's bound to be a shorter way of reaching those countries than any we now know; and the sooner England finds it, the sooner we'll crawl out from under the mountain of debts and taxes that's crushing us."

Mr. Burke held up his glass of port and looked through it at a candle-flame. "And the sooner we'll stop imposing Stamp Taxes on helpless colonies."

"Good for you, Mr. Burke," Rogers said. "You're right. There's something I want to say about that, too. But first I'd like to correct my learned friend, Dr. Campbell. He says I think I know a route to the Pacific. That's been the trouble, gentlemen. Too many have thought they knew a route. Mr. Ellis, no offense meant, thought he knew a route; and so did Mr. Dobbs before him. Look at the time and money wasted by those gentlemen—again no offense meant—and by Capt. Luke Fox, Capt. James, Capt. Scroggs, Capt. Middleton and Capt. Moor, all of them nosing around Hudson's Bay, trying to sail through to the Pacific. Dr. Campbell estimates Englishmen have spent a hundred and fifty thousand pounds in the past thirty years, hunting what they thought was the Northwest Passage. Well, gentlemen, I don't think I know the route: I do know it. Give me an expedition of two hundred men and a free hand, and I'll bring you a map of it in three years' time."

"All I can say, Major," Mr. Ellis said impressively, "is that such a discovery would be the greatest service that could be done to this Nation. I've said before, in print, and I'll say again now, that whoever has it in his power to facilitate such a discovery should consider it an honor to do whatever he can to promote it."

Mr. Townsend made a pretence of looking haughtily at Mr. Ellis. "Are you by any chance addressing that remark to Charles Townsend of the Paymaster's Office, sir?"

In spite of the laugh that went up, Ellis contrived to look innocent. "Dear me!" he said. "I was so carried away by my effort to quote exactly what I wrote seventeen years ago that I even forgot that I spoke in the presence of Charles Townsend."

"Then you'd better repeat it," Burke said, "for the benefit of all of us." He turned to Rogers. "What makes you so sure you know a route to the Pacific, Major?"

Rogers told Burke of his meeting with Pontiac, and of Pontiac's warriors who had come from the shores of the Western Ocean. There was something exciting about his thick, heavy voice. "The existence of that route," he said, "is as certain as this dinner table." He banged the table with an enormous hand. "I could follow it to the Pacific just as surely as I can drink this port." He drained his glass, making one swallow of it.

"How far do you think it is from New York to the Pacific?" Ellis asked.

"I've gone over the maps and over 'em," Rogers said. "Dr. Campbell and I have figured and figured. As near as I can make out, we'd have to travel about six thousand miles."

"Six thousand miles!" the Earl of Clones muttered. "It's unbelievable."

"It's an unbelievable country," Rogers said. "I've travelled over it more than most, to the south and to the west, and I've talked to traders and Indians who've been even farther west and south; and I can't say loud enough or often enough that it'll be a grave oversight—by God, it'll be a crime—if England fails to find out what lies to the westward and secure it for herself."

He leaned forward and spoke directly to Mr. Townsend. "What was England thinking of, sir, not to take Louisiana from the French during the last war, either by conquest or treaty? Why didn't she put an end, once and for all, to the possibility of France playing those dirty little tricks of hers within the American continent? Why doesn't she let me march to the Pacific and open up the real riches of the country, instead of stirring up resentment with Stamp Taxes? You probably wont believe me, because I haven't any way of proving it; but it's God's truth that the country I want to explore is the most valuable territory upon the face of the globe. It's richer than all the rich mines of Mexico and Peru! I'm sure of it! I'm so sure of it that I've made that prediction in my book. I'm willing to stake my whole future on it." He repeated the words, "The most valuable territory upon the face of the globe!"

Burke cast a sly glance at Townsend; then said to Rogers, "I'm surprised, Major, you're not enthusiastic over the Stamp Tax."

"I'm surprised you're surprised," Rogers said. "Most of you gentlemen are friends of Mr. Garrick, according to the newspapers, and you know the terrible time he has when he interferes with the liberty of Englishmen. You remember what happened when he said they must pay three shillings for the seats they've always sat in for two. They tore his theater to pieces! That's the thing that struck me first and hardest about England. If the people get the idea their liberty's being tampered with, they tear something down, right away."

Townsend laughed. "Usually a Prime Minister to begin with."

Rogers gave them a sheepish, disarming grin. "Well, there you are, gentlemen. At bottom, we Americans are pretty much like you. We like our liberty just as well as you do. Put yourselves in our place. His Majesty, I've been given to understand, is of German extraction."

Burke choked on his port.

"Say rather," Townsend suggested, "that he belongs to the princely house of Hanover."

"Yes," Rogers said. "That's what I meant. Well, suppose Hanover, on the strength of having supplied you with your sovereign, should impose a Stamp Tax on all Englishmen. Would you pay it, or would you tear something down?"

Instead of being offended, as one might have expected these Englishmen to be, they stamped on the floor and roared with laughter.

"As a Commissioner of Trade and Plantations," Fitzherbert said, "I think it's my duty to remind you, Major, that any petition you may make for assistance in discovering a Northwest Passage would come before us, and that we are wretchedly poor at the moment. Would it be an expensive undertaking?"

"Not according to my lights," Rogers said. "You reward every victorious general and admiral with more than I'd need. I've figured it out with Dr. Campbell, and we think it could be done for just about what it would cost to send two ships to Hudson's Bay, even including gifts to the Indians and a few hundred traps to let us snare food."

Lord Bremerton raised an outcry. "Gifts!" he complained. "Gifts! All this talk of gifts to Indians, upon my word! Whenever anyone goes to America, he does nothing but run all over the place, hunting Indians to give gifts to! All nonsense, this gift business! Come, come: admit it, sir! Why should those red fellows have gifts?"

Rogers shrugged his shoulders. "Why do you gentlemen always pass port to the left?"

"Eh?" Bremerton asked. "What, what? Two different things entirely!"

"No, my lord; not entirely," Rogers insisted. "If the gentleman to the left of me has the port, and I ask for it, it must pass entirely around the table and come up to me on my right hand. If he merely passed it directly to me, moving it a few inches to the right, he'd be risking ostracism. He wouldn't do it, any more than he'd strike a lady. Now why is it? Why is it almost a criminal offense, in England, to pass port to the right?"

"Dash it!" Bremerton exclaimed testily, "it just is! You can't pass it to the right! Who cares what the reason is? Campbell, Campbell: see here, you know everything, Campbell! What's the reason port passes to the left? Silliest question imaginable!"

Campbell shook his head and emptied another decanter. "Can't say, m'lord. Probably had its rise in self-protection, like so many of our customs."

"You've answered my question, gentlemen," Rogers said. "Making gifts to Indians is like passing port to the left. Nobody knows how it started, but it's something that must be done. I don't mind saying, too, that England hasn't done enough of it. England hasn't been generous with her gifts to the Indians, and France has. There was never such a short-sighted policy. You've saved a few thousand pounds; but in doing it you've made enemies of thousands of Indians, lost battles, and sacrificed territory worth millions."

"What sort of friend is one that can only be held by means of gifts?" the Earl of Clones demanded.

"A nuisance," Rogers said, "but you'd do it if you found yourself in the wilderness and dependent on Indians."

"That's what Sir William Johnson was forever dinning into our ears when I was on the Board of Trade," Townsend said. "More gifts—more gifts to the Indians, or they'd desert us for the French! I found it as tiresome as Italian opera."

"Dreadful red fellows!" Lord Bremerton said. "I never had the misfortune to see one of the wretched creatures. Come, come, Rogers: where are those pictures you spoke of? Let's have them out, where we can see what the horrid chaps look like."

At Campbell's orders, a servant brought my portfolio. Painfully conscious of the amused glances of Townsend and Fitzherbert, I untied it and took out the top one—the sketch I had done that day. Not knowing where to put it on that crowded table, I handed it to Rogers.

"Oh, by God!" he cried. "Detroit!" He looked at me in amazement. "You weren't there! How'd you ever do this?"

"You described it to me."

"By God!" he said again. "I wouldn't have believed it could

be done!" He laughed delightedly, pointing to different part
of the sketch. "See, gentlemen: these are Winnebagoes—thes
are Ottawas—these are Chippeways. These are the Rangers
down here in green, wearing the Scotch caps—the greates
fighters in the world, gentlemen, for our sort of country o
any other. You'll see the day when all war will be waged a
I taught my Rangers to wage it. They're the ones I'd tak
with me to hunt the Northwest Passage."

"May I see that?" Sir Joshua asked.

When Rogers handed it to him, he held it so that all th
table could see. Then he passed it around for inspection an
came to sit by me, his ear-trumpet thrust close to my face
"How long have you worked in pastel?"

"Five years, Sir Joshua."

"Have you been to Italy?" he asked. "Or France?"

I said No: I had taught myself.

"There's a hint of Liotard about that one," he said. "Th
French are far ahead of us in pastel. Have you exhibited ir
London?"

I said I hadn't.

"No, I fancy not," Reynolds said. "Work like that is doubtless a little startling. Yes: a trifle startling. The smoothness o
the Italian school is more desirable. When your stomach's adjusted to pap, you find strong meat offensive. Yes, yes! There's
nothing as unpalatable as the truth to those accustomed to
evade it. Ah—doubtless, however, the dealers have been able
to dispose of a few for you."

"No sir," I said. "They're not interested. Mostly, too, I've
worked on a series. Perhaps some day someone—a collector
or an institution—will prefer a series to scattered pictures."

"Oh, I'm quite sure of it," Reynolds said. "In the meantime,
you have other means of subsistence?"

"I've painted coach-doors and gun-rooms, Sir Joshua. I
did a panel at Vauxhall, too—thanks to Mr. Hogarth's kindness."

"Indeed!" he said. "Yes, yes! That panel of Amherst! Quite
a good composition, too." He sighed. "Hogarth and I weren't
friends, I fear—but I felt it as a personal loss when I read
of his death last October. A great loss to England, too, Mr.
Towne."

"Yes, sir," I said feelingly. "A great loss."

He looked at me, smiled kindly, tapped my shoulder with

his ear-trumpet, then reached into my portfolio for another sketch. It happened to be the one of the canoe overturning on the St. Francis to spill out the dead squaw and her child.

"Yes, yes," Sir Joshua said again. "Very good color in the foliage. Rather brilliant and bold—but not too bold. This would be one of the series, Towne, I take it? Ah, yes! And the number of pictures in this series would be——"

"About forty, Sir Joshua."

"Forty?" he said. "A fine ambition, my young friend! Ah—may we see the rest of them?"

Greatly pleased and flattered, I began removing the sketches from their protectors and handing them to Sir Joshua; while he in turn, after a gracious word upon each, passed them to Lord Bremerton, who sat next to him. And so they went 'round the table—a Master-Canoe Filled with Indians; Whaleboats Entering a Cove in the Mist; Stockbridge Indians in War Paint; and the like.

I heard Rogers shouting enthusiastically across the table, "Look at this, gentlemen! Lake Champlain! There might be a thousand red devils behind any one of those wooded points waiting to jump out at you! See how those headlands float above the water? That's a sign of a storm. A magnificent country, gentlemen!"

The table buzzed gratifyingly over the Major and over my drawings. Sir Joshua turned partly away from me to Lord Bremerton on his right, tapped him upon the arm, and called his attention to something he liked about my Stockbridge Indians in War Paint. "Our young friend designs to produce a series of forty," I heard him saying. "Quite meritorious. You know, it's sometimes profitable for a collector to catch his artist young, Bremerton. It might be quite a handsome thing to possess the whole forty. Even if one paid for them rather lavishly, they might increase in value as time advances, and——"

I heard no more of this conversation; the thick big voice of Rogers, greatly elated, muffled it in my ears.

"You say well, Mr. Townsend," Rogers said. "What eloquence of the tongue can equal that of the pencil? Here in a few moments you've learned more of my country through these pictures than by hearing me talk for years. God bless 'em, I say! God bless the pictures for inclining you to favor the Great Project!"

Dr. Campbell was on his feet. "Gentlemen, the Great Project," he cried, "A toast! Gentlemen, I give you the Northwest Passage! The Northwest Passage and a great leader! Major Robert Rogers!"

At that they all stood, and I with them. Their voices seemed to shake the ceiling as they took up this challenge; and Rogers sat, enormous, flushed with happiness and triumph as they shouted: "The Northwest Passage and a great leader—Major Robert Rogers!"

Then everything seemed in a glow of success and triumph. The Northwest Passage seemed already found—and as for me, I had my own success. Lord Bremerton followed me to the side table where I was wrapping my pictures in their protectors and replacing them in the big portfolio. "Ah, Mr. Towne," he said. "I'll have to see these again! Sir Joshua's opinion has great weight with me: great weight! And I've a particular susceptibility to pastels. Come to Breem some day and see my La Tours. Ah—I'd thought of venturing an offer for purchase—ah——"

"Purchase?" I said, and the blood seemed to rush to my ears so that I wasn't sure he'd said the word. "Purchase? These?"

"That was my possible intention," Lord Bremerton said. "Sir Joshua mentioned a series of forty, and seemed to think that—ah—ah—twenty guineas apiece might not be inappropriate. Ah—eight hundred pounds for the whole series, if you feel inclined to accept."

"I—I do," I stammered. "I—most gratefully accept, Lord Bremerton."

"Gratefully? Tarradiddle!" he said, laughed kindly and gave me a tap on the shoulder.

"When Sir Joshua endorses, I know what I'm getting. Suppose we both go and thank him."

I tried to keep my eyes from blinking as I said, "With all my heart!" but when we looked for Sir Joshua, we found that he'd gone out quietly, after explaining to his host that he must return to his studio and an unfinished portrait.

The gentlemen had withdrawn a little space from the table and, clustered about the towering form of Rogers, were drinking again to the Northwest Passage. With a full heart I drank to it too—and to great Sir Joshua Reynolds and to generous

little Lord Bremerton. When Rogers went to seek the Northwest Passage, I could go with him and paint Indians to my
heart's content at last.

CHAPTER LV

BY WHAT seemed a miracle, I
found Ann Potter in Castle Street, where her father had left
her nine years earlier. From my brief association with Hogarth I had learned that English people of substance and
standing, as well as those associated with them, were singularly reluctant to recognize or admit the depths of misery
and degradation in which so large a part of England's population lived. Why this was so, I cannot say. The gangs of
thieves who slept in attics, cellars and stables; the countless
women of the streets who daily travelled most city thorough-
fares in groups from midafternoon until dawn; the multitude
of dreadful rooms, in each of which six or eight people slept
on one foul bed; the acres of gin-shops that flourished in
the poorer sections, crowded by day as well as by night
with screaming harpies and foul-mouthed brutes—all of
this wretchedness was daily inveighed against by Sir John
Fielding and a few others; and yet upper-class Englishmen
calmly held to the view that in no country were the lower
classes so contented and prosperous as in England.

From the first of my stay in London I knew better; for
in my walks around St. Giles', Houndsditch, Whitechapel and
the Rules of the Fleet, I'd seen misery and horror as an
everyday spectacle. But I confess that until I found Ann
Potter in Castle Street, I'd looked upon all such things in
the capacity of an artist, interested with the eye alone and
unconcerned with what I couldn't remedy. My interest became more personal, however, when I found Ann Potter.

Castle Street is part of the squalid maze north of Covent
Garden. Every fourth house in that enormous rabbit warren
was what was called a tuppenny house—a den where for

tuppence a man could drink a glass of gin and sleep on the floor with a dozen other vagrants in a barren upstairs room. The whole section stank of decayed food, excrement, mold and rottenness. Windows and doorways were black with soot; broken panes were stuffed with rags that might have been there since the days of William the Conqueror. Down the middle of the roadways ran kennels, filled with all manner of slimy refuse: women washed shapeless garments on stools in the street: appeared at house doors to empty pails into the kennels. They wore half-laced leather stays, black with grease and sweat; coarse black stockings, or none: striped linsey-woolsey petticoats able to stand alone with dirt. The sign-boards of the tuppenny houses almost crossed the narrow street, and formed such an upper thicket that only strips of sunlight fell upon the fouled cobbles under foot.

The men in this section were furtive and surly, like ill-mannered dogs. When I stopped to sketch a signboard in my commonplace book—knowing this to be the simplest way to start a conversation—the slinking passersby only muttered obscenities at me and went on. A man in the crooked doorway from which the signboard hung—a sick-looking, lank-haired man in an apron that might months before have been white —stood and eyed me suspiciously.

"Sketching signs," I explained, "for a rich bloke that's making a collection."

He spat with unction. "Making a connection? What's the game, cully?"

To show him I was a man to his heart, I spat too. "Someone said there's a man near here, Garvin, that's got a good signboard. Where's this Garvin live?"

"Ho! Garvin!" the man cried. " 'E owns this 'ouse! 'E's a rich man, Garvin is! 'E owns six tuppenny 'ouses—maybe more! Never a farden for repairs! That's where the money lays! Rot my eyes if 'e don't take in ten or twelve shillings a day."

"Where'll I find him?"

The man spat more affably and gave me the information. "If 'e's drunk," he added graciously, "say 'aye,' master, to everything 'e tells yer; and if 'e wants yer to kiss 'is boots, do it! Might save yer a broken 'ead. Garvin's 'ard!"

The three-story building to which he directed me was no

better than his own. Above the door hung a sign reading "The Jolly Apprentice. Lodging and Refreshment."

A flight of greasy stairs led down to a basement, and in the basement doorway stood a beady-eyed Jew. "Nice port vine," he said in a soft and persuasive voice. "Two nice fat ladies, chust fresh in from der country! All rosy-cheeked!"

A crippled young girl, one arm sadly twisted and one crooked leg shorter than the other, wee-wawed past the Jew, thumbed her nose at him, clumped up the steps of the Jolly Apprentice, one step at a time, and vanished.

"Garvin live here?" I asked the Jew.

"First room you come to," he said; then added eagerly, "Meester Garvin, 'e's gone collecting monnaie. You come in here and vait: take a look at my nice fat country ladies. Don't cost you a penny to look. No? You'll be sorry!"

I followed the crippled girl into the house. There was a horrible, stomach-turning odor to the place, as if rats and men had died and been hidden between the walls: as if all the evil food in the world had been badly cooked somewhere close at hand, then thrown in a corner to decay.

When I knocked on the first door, it was the crippled girl who jerked it open, and beyond her I saw a frowzy bed, a broken-backed chair and a three-legged table. On the bed were three small children. One was an eight-year-old girl who had a black sore on her cheek and a filthy bandage around her head; the others were boys, with the waxy, bloodless pallor of dead children. On a chair beside the bed sat a draggled, sunken-eyed woman with a tumbler in her hand and a bottle of gin on the floor beside her; and she looked round at me between strands of the stringy gray hair that hung down over her face.

"Garvin aint 'ere," she said. She held the tumbler to the lips of one of the pallid children on the bed. He watched me warily, sipped from the tumbler, swallowed with difficulty, and coughed horribly.

"A friend of mine asked me to come here about Ann Potter," I said.

The woman straightened in her chair, hiccuping, and corked the bottle with a fumbling hand. "Wot about Ann Potter?" she asked.

"Where is she?"

"Oo wants ter know?"

"Her father."

"Yus!" she cried. "That sounds like 'im! Leaving me work me fingers to the bone fer 'er fer nine long years: then sendin' around to arsk about 'er wivout so much as a 'thankee, Mrs. Garvin.'" She made a contemptuous sound in her throat that reminded me of a crow, swaying atop a spruce to voice his dissatisfaction at the world.

"He paid you, didn't he?"

"Ho!" Mrs. Garvin cried. "Paid me! 'Course 'e paid me; but 'ow much!"

"Well," I said, "if the little girl's been well treated, and you've been put to unexpected expense for her, I think you'll find her father wont be ungrateful. I'll have to see her, though."

Mrs. Garvin eyed me craftily. "Come back this arternoon an' we'll 'ave 'er 'ere."

"This afternoon? If she's so far away you can't get her here till afternoon, it doesn't look as though you were working your fingers to the bone for her."

Mrs. Garvin looked hurt, solaced herself with a little gin, sniffed, and said, "Sharp, aint you! You go down in the basement and see Dutch Sam. 'E's got a pair of likely new baggages down there. Rattle 'em fer a nower, and I'll 'ave Ann 'ere. Wish a penn'orth to drink first?" She put the bottle on the three-legged table, and, rolling herself out of her chair, lurched to the corner for a glass.

My eye was caught by a movement. The little crippled girl, seated on a box near the door, was looking eagerly into my eyes, pointing to her collar-bone and nodding violently. Then to my horror I realized she was telling me in pantomime that she was what I was seeking: that she was Ann Potter.

When Mrs. Garvin turned back to me, the little girl was still as a mouse on her box, her eyes downcast, her arms and legs at strange, ungraceful angles.

"Thanks," I said. "I can't drink in the morning—weak stomach—I'll sit here while you drink it for me, and I'll make a picture—a picture of you and your children."

I took out my commonplace book. The woman seemed to understand what I would be at. "A pitcher?" she said. "A pitcher of me? Wait!" Then she went to a cupboard, brought forth a soiled lace cap, much torn, put it upon her head, pushed some of the draggled gray hair under it, sat down and smiled glassily. "If it's good I'll give you another drink fer it, an' save it fer Garvin's birfday."

I glanced at the twisted child. "Take this little girl on your lap," I said.

"No, I'd ruther 'ave me pitcher done alone."

"It's not fashionable," I said. "It's the mode just now to have conversation pieces—pictures with two or three figures in them. You can't persuade a duchess to pose unless she has one of her children on her lap and others about her knee, and perhaps her husband across the table."

Mrs. Garvin turned a threatening eye upon Ann. "C'm 'ere!"

Ann limped toward her, but stopped just out of reach.

"You come 'ere!" Mrs. Garvin said dangerously, shot out a claw of a hand, caught the girl's fragile wrist and with one violent jerk landed her insecurely and contortedly upon her lap.

"There!" the woman said. "Make the pitcher!"

I began to sketch, and for the first time had a chance to study the child who had pathetically signalled to me that she was Ann Potter. She was a weazened little thing, and her starved thinness was all too well revealed by her flimsy and torn dress of striped linsey-woolsey—a garment plainly older than the wearer. On her feet, and tied about the ankles to keep them on, were a man's shoes, broken, without heels, and almost toeless. Her poor thin legs were covered with stockings that had once been black, but now were green and full of holes. Her face was streaked with dirt; but under the dirt the pinched cheeks were of a clear, soft brown, and she had fine dark eyes, bright with that terrible precocity nearly always seen in the eyes of the children of poverty. When she was jerked into Mrs. Garvin's lap, I saw her small teeth clench and her lips set in that tight half-smile with which the braver kind of people steel themselves to endure pain.

Something about her confused my thoughts. My plan had been, if I found her, just to report to Potter. Then, after her signal to me, I'd impulsively decided to make a drawing of her for him—a drawing with the background of this witch's hole of a home and the "nurse" to whom he'd consigned her. Such a drawing, I thought, might help to insure better treatment for her from a remorseful father in the future. I knew

I couldn't be sure of that, of course; with a man like Potter, one couldn't be sure of anything. But what the sketch did, as I sat there more and more carefully plying my pencil, was to enrage me with such a father.

I thought of the noble children painted by Sir Joshua, little ladies and lordlets in velvet and lace, about whom his pencil wafted an elfin beauty; and I realized that if the lank hair of Ann Potter could lie in a soft braid around her head, and an exquisite lace kerchief rest upon her piteous shoulders, she might be as lovely as any of those immortalized children who'd been brought in gilded coaches to the great man's studio.

I finished the sketch, and made another hurriedly, shamelessly flattering, of Mrs. Garvin; but before I'd finished this latter, I heard a stamping and thumping in the hall outside. The door burst open, and into the room stumbled a man with a nose all bulbous, like a red sponge. His face was mottled with brown spots, almost as though he were spattered with mud, which he was also; and he brought into all the other smells of that odorous den a combined stench of old, old onions and stale tobacco steeped in rum slops.

He stood swaying in the doorway, peering at me out of eyes nearly hidden by bloated lids.

Mrs. Garvin cackled a scream at him, all in a breath, " 'E c'm 'ere to see Ann Potter, an' I told 'im to come back in a nower, but he's stayed makin' my pitcher."

Garvin looked slowly around the room; then made a sudden threatening gesture toward the three children on the bed. "Garn outa 'ere! Take yer boxes an' git out!"

One by one the three slipped silently to the floor like three travesties of beavers sliding from a bank. They snatched up small boxes from the floor—begging boxes, I realized—scuttled past the drunken Garvin and vanished.

He glowered at Ann. "You too! Git out!"

She moved away from Mrs. Garvin and came warily toward me, staring watchfully at Garvin; and something in that guarded sly movement of hers reminded me of a Ranger slipping from tree to tree when enemies were near.

Garvin made a jump toward her. She dodged away, hopped across the bed like a squirrel, and attempted to scurry behind Garvin and reach the door. Garvin grasped at her, tripped her, tripped himself too. But before he got to his feet, I strode past him, slammed the door and locked it. Then I picked up Ann and stared at her as she stood before me with her bright eyes, like a hungry dog's, fixed on my face.

"This girl isn't crippled," I said to the Garvin woman. "She went over that bed as spry as a cat. Her legs are as straight as mine. What's that mean?"

Garvin got to his feet. "Mind yer own business!" he said thickly.

"This *is* my business, Mr. Garvin," I said. "This girl's Ann Potter, whom I came to find." I patted the child's shoulder and at the touch she flinched down away from my hand, a movement of heart-breaking eloquence; but I took her wrist and pulled up her ragged sleeve to show her thin arm and the old and new bruises—yellow, blue, green and brown—that I knew were there. I opened her meal-sack of a dress and drew it back from her shoulder. There were red weals on the flesh, like claw-marks. I set her on her feet, put her behind me, and went closer to Garvin.

"I was sent here by this girl's father," I said. "I find she's been beaten and mistreated. I find she's been taught to behave like a cripple, so you could send her out on the street to beg. It's a miracle she's lived as long as she has; and if she stays with you, I see a choice of two ends for her. She'll be beaten to death or hanged at Tyburn. Mr. Garvin, if she's beaten to death, maybe you'll be the one that's hanged at Tyburn. It might be better if she went back to her father."

Garvin breathed hard; and his wife, wiping dry eyes with the back of her hand, spoke in a weeping voice. "Drawin' my pitcher fer nuthin'! I wouldn't thought he'd talk as cruel to us that give 'er a mother's care, an' sheltered 'er an' fed 'er when parents cast 'er off an' stopped the pay!" Then suddenly Mrs. Garvin jumped up and became shrewish. " 'Igh an' mighty, are yer, cully? Talk Tyburn to us, do you? 'Ave a care! She aint been worth a damn to us till just now, and the likes of you aint goin' to snatch her away wivout a by-your-leave!"

Garvin laughed hoarsely. "I guess 'e aint! Apprentices can't be took wivout a discharge from the Sessions. Magistrates don't 'old wiv it."

"That's because there isn't an honest magistrate in London except Sir John Fielding," I said, speaking with more assurance than the facts warranted. "Sir John's a friend of mine, and if you want to leave it to a magistrate, we'll go straight before him; but I don't believe you want to. You know what he does to people like you when he gets the chance. Anyway, Ann's not an apprentice. She's a kept child. You were paid to keep her and keep her properly, and look at her!" I turned to Ann. "Can you read and write?"

"Cor!" Ann said, which I knew to be Whitechapel's supreme expression of contempt; and I divined that she meant I might as well have asked her if Mr. and Mrs. Garvin had given her velvet gowns and diamond necklaces.

"I'll 'ave me due!" Garvin said.

"Your due's a week in the Pillory at Charing Cross; but just out of curiosity, I'd like to hear what you think it is."

"By God," Garvin cried, "twenty guineas wouldn't make up for the loss she'd be to me."

"Here," I said, tearing a page from my commonplace book, "write it down. Show me how you're entitled to a penny for losing this girl. Go ahead: write down what she's worth."

When Garvin licked the stub of a pencil and looked uncertainly at his wife, I knew I had him—knew I could take Ann with no fuss and no delay.

"Food for nine years: nine guineas," Mrs. Garvin said promptly.

"Wait," I said. "Potter paid you to take the child. That covered her food."

"It didn't cover her clo'es," Garvin whined, for his tone had changed, "only so long as she stayed the same size as when we got her, an' she growed like a pig! We'd no sooner buy her a pair of good shoes than she'd grow out of 'em!"

"Young man, you just wait yourself," Mrs. Garvin said argumentatively, "you just wait till you have to buy shoes for a brat that aint worth the powder to blow 'er to Chelsea!"

I took another tone with them, seeing that their own had changed. "Very well," I said. "We'll say ten shillings a year for shoes and all other clothing. That's ninety shillings. What else?"

"Wot else!" Mrs. Garvin cried. "There aint a gel in the Parish takes in wot Ann does fer crippled beggin'. One day she come 'ome wiv a shilling, a whole bloody shilling! How you goin' ter make that up to us?"

" 'Ere!" Ann said suddenly in a piping voice. "I told you

that shillin' cove was drunk! 'Ow many times I got to tell you 'e thought it was a penny!"

She turned toward me and put up both thin hands in a strange half-gesture. "You'll buy me, wont you? I aint worth as much as they tell you. They'll let me go easy if you show 'em the money."

I swung around on Garvin. "Thrippence a day for the past two years, and thrippence a day for the next two. Call it eight pounds. Eight pounds you lose by losing her begging. Eight and four and a half is twelve and a half. I'll give you fifteen pounds for the girl. You'll sign a bill of sale for Ann to me for fifteen pounds, or you'll be haled before Sir John Fielding tomorrow."

I took the money from my pocket. Garvin squinted at it horridly and said not a word, but reached for the pencil and the blank sheet from my commonplace book that I offered him, and, still in silence, wrote as I directed.

Mrs. Garvin stretched dirty hands toward the little girl. "Kiss yer mawther!" she mumbled. "Kiss yer dear mawther good-bye."

I felt Ann slide around me, so that I was between her and the woman.

Garvin smiled at me, an exhibition of fangs. "Them fifteen pounds, master!"

I gave him the money. He rubbed the notes with puffy fingers, looked hard at his wife, turned his back to her, went to a corner and fumbled secretly among his clothes. When he turned about, he spoke blandly to Mrs. Garvin. "There, my bird! If I wake up tonight with your paws on me, I'll wring your head off your neck and toss it out a winder! Nobody wont notice it outside. They'll think it's a bad melon." He laughed with gusto. "Good-bye, master! Good-bye and to hell with you!"

That was Ann Potter's farewell from the friends of her youth.

I handed Mrs. Garvin the sketch I'd made of her, and she wept aloud—I couldn't determine whether because of the likeness or her husband's tenderness.

"Come, Ann," I said, unlocked the door, and we went out together.

As we reached the street, she began to hobble along beside

me, crippled again. "No, child," I said. "Not that any more. No more lameness."

She looked at me, astounded.

CHAPTER LVI

THE OWNER of the house in which I lived was Mr. Martin, a Frenchman from Chaumont, who was attached to the King's Kitchen. He was married to a Frenchwoman and had two small children; but the four of them considered themselves as much English as French, and spoke the two languages with equal fluency though not with equal accuracy. It was to Mrs. Martin that I took Ann; and it was she who, in return for one of Lord Bremerton's gold pieces and a promise to paint a portrait of her and her two children, made a place for Ann in her own comfortable rooms. She supervised, too, the washing of Ann's hair, the removal of its population, the first bath the child had received in years, and the purchasing of a brown dress, a wine-colored dress, shoes, stockings, petticoats, and kerchiefs. She even arranged for a teacher to come three hours a day to instruct Ann in reading, writing and how to speak English.

"Give her a meal of real food first of all," I had told Mrs. Martin. "Then do the rest and send her up when you've finished with her. She'll probably be lonely, and I'll paint her picture and talk to her while I'm doing it. I made a black and white sketch of her, but I want to do her in pastels."

When she appeared, however, it was she who did most of the talking; she was amazed at my ignorance.

Crippled children, I learned from her, were of the highest value to parents or other owners of them. The right word for such cripples was "monsters." They were in demand by professional beggars who paid a penny a day for the use of a proper specimen; but the owner of a monster was obliged to have a care about the beggars whom he trusted. Those of the baser sort would inconsiderately remove a monster's clothes, sell the clothes for gin-money, and leave the monster to find its way home naked.

Garvin, she said, was without a peer as a creator of monsters. The three children who had occupied the Garvins' bed at the time of my visit, were, in her opinion, praiseworthy samples of his art. The two pallid boys were kept pale by having tobacco plastered beneath their arms. The black sore on the cheek of the little girl had been raised with hot wax, then colored with soot and varnish.

Ann herself, I found, was disposed to boast a little of the monstership Garvin had taught her, and of her own proficiency in contortion. She was uneasy, too, in her new clothes and new cleanliness; and she was a bad sitter, very restless in anything like a comfortable seat; while the language in which she educated me about monsters made me hope shiveringly that she hadn't talked much to Mrs. Martin.

In the dark brown dress and the snowy kerchief that softened her gaunt little features, and with her hair thick and wavy after its washing, she made me think a little of a younger Kitty Fisher, the actress Sir Joshua had now begun to paint in so many poses. Pitifully foul-mouthed as the child was, marked with starvation, abuse and depravity, and but this moment uprooted from the mud from which she'd drawn what life she had, there was nevertheless something about her that was like a just-hinted glimmer of charm and sweetness. After all, she was the great-niece of the Archbishop of Canterbury; and untended flowers gone to seed in a ruined garden will still be a little different from weeds.

Her voice went on while I sat thinking and desultorily plying my colored pencils. "When 'e got you in a corner, there wan't nuffin to do but yell: then w'en 'e put 'is 'and over your mouf, you bit it. Most generally you'd git away."

"Are you speaking of Garvin, Ann?"

"Yus, but all of 'em was about alike. You could tell by the look in their faces w'en they was goin' to back you into a corner."

"Then you wont miss the Garvins, Ann?"

"Cor! I never missed 'em, not even w'en Garvin was put in Newgate fer debt and the old hell's slut went along."

"For debt?" I said. "Gavin and his wife were in Newgate for debt? How could that be when he had both property and money?"

"I dunno," Ann said. " 'E knows ways of doing anythink, damn his eyes! 'E an' Dutch Sam, they're the best fences in London. 'E found out there'd be a jail delivery on account the King's birfday, so 'e run 'isself into debt and 'ad someone put the damned bailiffs on 'im, damn his eyes! 'E went to Newgate, but 'e got out on the jail delivery, so 'e didn't owe nobody nothink, damn his bloody eyes!"

I sat helplessly listening to her, and knowing that I ought to instruct her in the common decencies of speech; but I felt the task too much for me. I'd leave that to the teacher Mrs. Martin had promised would begin lessons the next day.

"Ann," I said, "you know you have a father, don't you?"

"Who?" she said. "Me? Wot for?"

"Well, you know other children with fathers, don't you?"

"Some of 'em has 'em," she said. "You wouldn't make me, would you?"

For a moment I didn't answer. I thought of Natty Potter; of what sort of a father he'd been to her, and what sort he might be again to her—and I was troubled. Instead of answering her question, I showed her the head I had completed of her: the little portrait I meant to show to Potter before I showed him Ann.

"Do you like it?" I asked.

"Cor!" she said; and this time that singular word seemed to express something like pleasure.

This day passed, and the next, and I hadn't notified Natty Potter that he could see his daughter by applying to Mrs. Martin's. Whenever I thought of letting him know, my gorge so rose against the man that I paced the floor in a sort of furious quandary that ended in inaction. But on the third day after I'd taken the child from the Garvins', a serving boy brought me a note from Potter and waited for an answer. What he'd written was eloquently and perhaps pathetically brief.

"My dear and kindest friend: Am ill in bed. Have you found her? Most anxious. A word in reply, I hope, will suffice to lift the burden from a father's troubled heart. Thine tremblingly, N.P."

His word "tremblingly" seemed well chosen, as the writing staggered almost as much as the writer himself had the night before, I thought; and I didn't doubt he was in bed. I took up a pencil, wrote, "Yes, I've found her," on the back of his note, folded the paper, and gave it to the boy.

The next day he rapped again on my door, and when I admitted him, he handed me another message and said, "I'm to say it's a matter of life and death, sir, and wont you please read it quick and come. I get sixpence extra if I run all the way back to tell him Yes, you're hurrying."

This was the note: "Generous-hearted man: God bless you for saving the reason and perhaps even the life of a friend who erred and it may be even sinned in taking the chance that he might lose track of his own flesh and blood. Your happy message that you have found her lifted half of the burden; and if you will come now in kindly haste, the other half, I am confident, will float away like a zephyr. Pray tell the boy that you will come at once, and I entreat that you will follow on his heels. Complete your noble action, and accept the undying gratitude of, sir, your most obedient and admiring serv't., N. Potter."

"Yes, I'll come," I told the boy, and he was off upon the instant. I put the finished pastel portrait of Ann in my large portfolio and followed, wondering angrily what I should say to this ardent father who seemed to be contenting himself with writing notes about the child he so yearned to see.

At the White Bear I paused outside Rogers' apartment, for I could hear Potter declaiming loudly in his blandest voice. I couldn't distinguish the words; but supposing that he addressed the Major, I knocked on the door, opened it immediately for myself and went in.

Potter was perched carelessly on a corner of Rogers' writing-table; and standing before him was a dry, snuffy-looking little man with snuff-colored hair and a snuff-colored suit whose shoulders were dusted with powder that was probably white but that somehow contrived to look snuff-colored too. He was snuffy in every sense of the word; and I had been long enough in England to know him for what he was—a country solicitor. As I came in, the little man turned toward me sharply, and it seemed to me I had never seen a face so indignant.

"I beg your pardon," I said. "I thought the Major was here —no intention of intruding!" When I would have withdrawn, Potter, without rising from his seat on the writing-table, waved a negligent hand at me. "Come in!" he cried. "Come in!"

"Really!" the snuffy little man protested. "A private conversation, Mr. Potter——"

Potter made an airy gesture. "Oh, not before Towne, Mr. Wheatley! No occasion for privacy before Mr. Towne! You can say anything before Mr. Towne, especially since he's been acting as my agent in the matter."

Snuffy little Mr. Wheatley stared grimly at Potter. "You'll have to allow me to be the judge of that."

"Nonsense, Wheatley! Nonsense!" Potter said. "The little girl is my daughter, you know—the daughter of my dear wife and me! No reason why I shouldn't speak as I wish about my own daughter, even though Lady Venner is her mother."

Wheatley's face was pale. "Be good enough not to bring certain noble names into this matter, Mr. Potter."

"Oh, my dear sir!" Potter cried. "There's no occasion for this attitude! Mr. Towne knows all about it! He knows I placed my daughter in very good hands—with very good people: very good. I've already informed you that it's Towne who's been kind enough to make the investigations." He looked at me twinklingly. "Please assure Mr. Wheatley that you've made the investigations for me, and were successful in them."

"Yes," I said and looked at him hard. "I found the good people with whom you left your daughter, and found her too, if that's what you mean."

"You found her?" Wheatley asked quickly. "She'd been lost?" He looked from me to Potter, who made airy gestures of protest.

"Lost! My dear good Wheatley! This to a father? Ts! Ts! Ts! Pray tell him, Towne!"

I took Ann's portrait from my portfolio. "Not entirely lost," I said. "Here's her picture. I thought her father might like to see it."

Potter seemed to find no sarcasm in my words. "How like her mother!" he said, all at once touchingly sentimental. "Her mother! My own little Ann's mother! How ardently such a mother must yearn to clasp and enfold the little one so unmistakably stamped in her own image!" A triumphant light danced in his eye as he looked at the portrait, and became even brighter as he turned to the solicitor. "You see how precisely like Lady Venner her offspring is, Mr. Wheatley. Must not all the world perceive so profound a resemblance? Eh, Mr. Wheatley?"

Mr. Wheatley's expression, as he stared at the portrait, became bleak. "There seems to be an unfortunate resemblance, I admit," he said.

"Unfortunate?" Potter said. "Unfortunate, Mr. Wheatley? No, no! Not unfortunate! Lady Venner should be happy in the resemblance—happy to have me bring our daughter to see her, as of course I intend. As a Christian gentleman, how could I intend otherwise? Would I deprive Lady Venner, former partner in our sacred union—could I deprive her, I say, of the fruit of our——"

"Enough, sir," Wheatley said with sharpness. "The lady you've mentioned has other children to consider, and also a husband who must be protected from—from learning certain facts. Acting as the lady's private agent, I've already admitted all this! I also admit that since seeing this portrait I am somewhat more amenable to certain arguments of yours. On the other hand, don't believe us helpless, Mr. Potter. There are measures we could take if you drove us too far."

"Yes," Potter agreed suavely. "No doubt! No doubt! But mightn't those measures involve quite a little talk—perhaps even some mention in the public journals? And——"

"Hear me, sir," the solicitor interrupted with visible anxiety. "We prefer, as you do, the more peaceful form of settlement. But in your letters you have mentioned a sum so exorbitant, Mr. Potter——"

"What? Exorbitant?" Potter waved his hand, protesting smilingly. "Is a man exorbitant who merely wishes to pay his honest debts? Word of honor, Mr. Wheatley, the trifling amount I specified would scarcely cover what I owe. Think, Mr. Wheatley, think of me sent to languish in a debtors' prison, and so forced to send the child to its mother to beg for subsistence! Look again at that portrait, Mr. Wheatley, and think carefully of that contingency!"

Mr. Wheatley did look again at the portrait, and seemed to find it ominous; then to Potter he began, "What assurance can we have—what reliance——"

"Word of honor, Mr. Wheatley! The word of honor of a

gentleman that neither I nor my daughter will ever approach the esteemed family you represent, or in any manner ever communicate with them again. Come! I see you're yielding: let's be done with it, Mr. Wheatley."

Mr. Wheatley looked wholly soured by the world; then he seemed to come to some determination. "Damn it," he said, and putting his hand abruptly in an inner pocket, he drew forth a wallet, took out a packet of folded bank notes, and slapped it into Potter's outstretched hand.

I'd been standing, staring stupidly, only half comprehending the scene before me; but this action on the part of the indignant solicitor cleared my mind. I made a motion to amend what was irretrievable, and grasped futilely at Potter's hand as he put the notes in his pocket.

"Give them back to him," I cried, and was fool enough to stamp my foot. "Give them back to him! You've made me a party to a dishonorable transaction, and I'll not have it! I'll not be used for blackmail!"

Mr. Wheatley turned on his heel, took his hat and stick from a chair and stalked stiffly to the door, a snuff-brown study in disdain.

"Wait, Mr. Wheatley," I said. "You needn't have paid that money! I wouldn't have allowed it if I'd known what was going on! I want you to understand——"

Wheatley gave me an icy glance. "I understand, sir, that if you possess the virtue you now seem to claim—after the money is paid—your honesty chooses to assert itself a trifle late!" At the door he uttered a contemptuous snort. "A trifle late, sir!" he repeated, lifted the latch, walked out like an angry, dusty little brown bantam, and slammed the door behind him.

When I turned slowly to face Potter, I found him complacently adjusting his neck-cloth before the mirror, and eyeing my reflection in it with humorous tolerance. "Well, Potter," I said, "you must be proud of your day's work!"

Instead of resenting my tone, he winked at me. "Why shouldn't I be?" he asked. "Why shouldn't I have my due? I didn't ask to be brought into this world, and the world owes me a living. Why should those fat fools in Birmingham have everything and give me nothing?"

"What provision are you planning to make for Ann?" I asked, and I added bitterly, "now that you have money."

He turned from the mirror and beamed upon me. "You've been very kind, Towne," he said, "and I want to show my appreciation. What would you say to a little supper? Just you and the Major and me? We'll make a night of it, eh?"

"Let's speak about your daughter first," I said. "What are your plans for her?"

"Oh, my dear boy," Potter cried jauntily, "what can I do with debts staring me in the face at every turn! Debts, debts, debts! And plans are so unsatisfactory, my dear Towne—so unnecessary! Your experience with Ann proves that! Thanks to you and your jolly portrait, I didn't even have to show her to old Wheatley!" He burst out laughing and slapped his thigh. "Bless my soul! You needn't have looked her up at all! The thing could have been done without that, I vow and believe! I could have told you how to draw a portrait that would have been like enough to the mother."

"Nevertheless, I did go," I said. "I found her and I brought her away. What are you going to do about it?"

"Brought her away? Dear me, dear me!" Potter looked concerned. "Well, since the matter's settled, you'd best take her back, if you'd be so kind. And the sooner the better, no doubt. I'd suggest this afternoon or tomorrow."

Then, as I just stared at him, he shook a waggish finger at me. "My dear fellow," he said, "consider my position—a wanderer on the face of the earth—a man with literary leanings, whose duties require him to be footloose both day and night—how could I burden myself with a child, Towne? When I spoke to you about her, I did have some such thought in mind; but now that I know she's in good hands——"

"Good hands!" I cried. "The Garvins—good hands! Good God!"

But Potter, in his elation, with a pocket full of money, only laughed benevolently. "So? You think she wasn't comfortable? Well, dear friend, I'd trust you with my life, and even with my daughter's. Since you're hard on the Garvins, let's say any other place you choose. She's with you at your lodgings?"

"She's with my landlady."

"Good! Excellent! My friend, I leave it all to you."

"And the money?" I asked him. "You'll make a provision for her?"

"Provision?" Acutest suffering came instantly on his face.

He made despairing gestures; slapped himself upon his chest, where he had put Mr. Wheatley's notes. "Oh, if I only could! But this—this paltry sum—how hard I struggled for it, yet how ignominious the amount! What with the duns hounding me for every penny of it, and the debtors' prison yawning for me, there's not one penny too much to save me! No, my dear Towne! Freely would I give you anything you ask——"

"Me?" I asked. "Give me? Damn you, I'm not asking you for anything for myself!"

"No," he said. "You couldn't in my distress; I know your generous heart. You see my predicament, and you will not press me. A father's heart trusts you, and I can only repeat I leave it all to you."

"You mean you leave Ann all to me?"

"I must; I do!" he said; and, actor though he was, there came the sliest self-congratulation into his eyes. He was afraid that I'd see it there; for he put his hand on my shoulder and bent his head as if to repose his suffering forehead upon that hand. "Best of men, dearest friend, I leave it all to you!"

I couldn't quite hate him; it's hard to hate a natural-born lifelong comedian. I flung his hand from my shoulder. "Stop trying to weep on me," I said, as I went out. "You haven't had gin enough." Then, as I went down the corridor, I heard him singing,

> *"When I was young and in my prime,*
> *I'd neither thought, nor care,*
> *I took delight in mirth and wine,*
> *And rov'd from fair to fair:*
> *I took delight in jovial life,*
> *'Till fate on me did frown:*
> *Until alas! I got a wife,*
> *And the world turn'd upside down."*

I was aware that he didn't care if I heard him. That twisted brain of his amazed me with its cunning. He had known me for a soft-headed fool with a conscience; and having that knowledge, he had used me once and proposed to continue using me. He had known I would take Ann from the Garvins; and he now knew with equal certainty I would never take her back to them. He knew that there was no escape for me: that

I could do nothing but accept the burden he had put upon me: that Ann would be sure of good treatment in my hands, and at no expense to himself.

Well, he was right; and here was I, at twenty-six, saddled with a ward: the grand-niece of an Archbishop of Canterbury—and the daughter of a blackmailer.

CHAPTER LVII

GOOD FORTUNE poured her favors on Major Rogers in a deluge. It was early in October that his two books—the *Journals* and the *Concise Account of North America*—appeared. The kind things said about them in every London publication made stirring reading to me—unexpected reading, too; for I had seen so many intemperate slurs on all Americans in the English papers during the discussion of the Stamp Tax, and heard so many similar scurrilities from the mock-English who dwelt in Portsmouth, that I had come to think no American would ever receive fair treatment from Britons.

They treated the Major handsomely, however. In generous reviews they said he "was a brave, active and judicious officer"—"few of our readers are unacquainted with his name or ignorant of his exploits"—the *Concise Account* was "the most satisfactory description of the immense continent so lately added to the British Empire"—his *Journals* were "authentic, important and necessary to a thorough understanding of the late military operations in North America"—his experiences "would seem almost incredible were they not confirmed by the unquestionable relations of others."

The *Journals* spoke particularly of his statement that the wealth of the Incas and Aztecs was as nothing to that of North America: of his prophecy that the Anglo-Saxon people would find America a home of wonderful scope and resource: of the understanding manner in which he had written of the Indians, and of his prediction that their insatiable fondness for spirituous liquors would clear the continent of them in a century.

Delighted at his success, I went straight to the White Bear to offer my congratulations, and found both the Major and Potter surrounded by journals from which both of them were delightedly cutting the reviews. Potter greeted me gaily, as if no unpleasant word had ever passed between us, while Rogers hailed me boisterously. "By God!" he shouted, "I bet Shakespeare didn't get better opinions of his work. Where've you been keeping yourself? I thought I'd have to walk down to Leicester Fields and dig you out! Have you heard the news?"

"I read the papers at the Turk's Head," I said. "It's wonderful, and you deserve every word of it."

"No, no," he said. "I mean the news about Michilimackinac!"

When I stared at him, he sprang from his chair, slapping his enormous hands together jubilantly. "I got it! They've made me Governor! I'm Governor of Michilimackinac! Governor of the gate to the Northwest! Didn't I tell you I'd get you the chance to paint Indians?"

It seemed too good to be true. "That's wonderful, Major! Have they given you everything you wanted—a Deputy Governor and all that?"

Rogers laughed explosively. "Oh, they haven't given me everything," he admitted, "but I'm Governor, and the rest will come. It'll come! Once I get to Michilimackinac, I'll be where nobody can interfere with me! That's the main thing, Campbell says: to get to Michilimackinac. He and Ellis and Fitzherbert will keep working for me while I'm gone. There's no doubt about it, Campbell said: they'll have Townsend and the King fairly huzzaing for me before I leave."

"When do you think you'll leave?"

"Well," Rogers said carelessly, "I want to write a play, and when that's done——"

"A play!" I almost shouted. "How can you write a play!— I don't mean to be rude—you have to know how to write plays, don't you? Won't it be difficult if you've never written one?"

Rogers' grin was sheepish. "I don't know why it should! You can do almost anything if people let you alone and you go at it hard enough. Lots of people would have said we couldn't go to and from St. Francis the way we did, but we went! I'd never written a book before, but now I've written two."

"But a play!" I said. "What would you write it about?"

Potter handed me a clipping. "I don't believe he's seen this, Governor."

I expected Rogers to look even more sheepish at hearing himself called by this new title; but apparently he was already accustomed to it: he might have been called Governor all his life.

I took the clipping. "The picture drawn by Major Rogers of the Emperor Pontiac," it read, "is novel and interesting, and would appear to vast advantage in the hands of a great dramatic genius."

"Yes," I pointed out, "but it says a great dramatic genius, Major!"

He looked at me sternly. "I know it does! I know it does! How do you find out whether you're a great dramatic genius or not? By writing a play! Aint that what I'm going to do?"

"Yes, but——" I said.

"But me no buts, boy!" The Major laughed vaingloriously. "Natty thinks it'll almost write itself, and Millan says he'll pay fifty pounds on it and publish at once. We could put in two traders to cheat the Indians; a couple of English hunters to kill 'em and browbeat 'em; a pair of braggart British officers, like Gage and Braddock; two or three Colonial governors to steal the presents intended for the Indians—and then a lot of Indians, headed by Pontiac. Campbell says we'll make Indians the fashion in London. Look at what's put on at the Haymarket and Drury Lane—all that 'My-name-is-Norval-on-the-Grampian-Hills' squawking and hollering! Could Rogers, the dramatic genius, do worse? He could not! Tragedy! We'll make it a tragedy! Everybody talks and screams for a few hours, then stab, stab, bang, bang, everybody killed. Huzza for Rogers!"

He gnawed a fingernail. Then he turned seriously to Potter. "Natty, do you think we could get Garrick? Garrick's the man—Garrick as Pontiac! Why, the very name catches the eye!" He extended his arm commandingly, and in a deep voice said: "Come, my red brothers from the West and North; raise up your hatchets and make common cause against these pale-faced plunderers from the East——" He mumbled and muttered; then added, "If honorable peace be your desire," and stared at me vacantly.

Potter looked excited. He strode around the room; stopped to finger a bottle on the chest of drawers; exclaimed sonorously, "The play's the thing, wherewith to catch the notice of the King!"

"Go ahead, Natty!" Rogers said. "Take the bottle along and see if you can't get a start on the first act—two traders, making ready to cheat the Indians—slipping the scales—watering the rum—just a rough outline, so I can go over it and fill it in."

Without another word Potter seized the bottle and vanished into the adjoining room.

When we were alone, Rogers grinned his sheepish grin. "You're wondering about the Northwest Passage, aren't you, Langdon?"

(I wasn't. I was wondering about Potter and his perfectly genuine unconsciousness that he ever had a daughter named Ann.)

"Well," Rogers went on, "I didn't want to mention Northwest Passage before Natty, for fear he'd try to steal the idea. Rum rascal, Natty! Haven't said a word about the Northwest Passage before him, and don't you. He thinks all I want is to be Governor of Michilimackinac. If he knew the core of the idea is the Northwest Passage, ten to one he'd forge papers to prove he'd already discovered it himself. Natty's useful, but you got to be careful with him. Well, I've been working at it."

He unlocked a drawer in his desk, took out a document and tossed it to me.

It was a petition to the King's Ministers, asking that he be empowered to head an expedition to discover the Northwest Passage; and when I ran my eye over it, I recognized all the arguments that Dobbs, Campbell and Ellis had advanced for the need of finding a route to the Northwest.

Even though no Northwest Passage should be found to exist, the petition said, the expedition would be useful in putting an end to repeated, hazardous and expensive attempts to discover it: if, however, Rogers could find the route, the expedition, by establishing a communication with Japan and possibly with hitherto unknown rich countries in the East, would prove of illimitable benefit to England. In this new market, both British and American commodities would fetch large prices, and a new and valuable commerce be opened and secured to His Majesty's subjects.

The Major proposed—if freed from the supervision and interference of Johnson and Gage—to proceed with two hundred men from the Great Lakes toward the head of the Mississippi River, thence to the River Oregon and to the Pacific, there to explore the western margin of the continent.

Attached to the petition was a list of the officers and men he planned to take, and the amounts required to finance a three-year trip. Under Rogers, in addition to the two hundred men, were to be four second captains, four first lieutenants, four second lieutenants, an ensign, an adjutant, a quartermaster, a surgeon, three surgeon's mates, a chaplain, eight sergeants and an armorer to keep muskets in repair, all paid at regular army rates. In addition he asked for eight hundred steel traps to enable the detachment to feed itself as it went along, and for £3000 to spend on presents to be given to the Indian tribes through which the expedition would pass. The total sum which the Major asked to enable him to do all this was a little over £32,000 —a large amount, but nothing compared with the cost of sending Braddock to his doom, or assembling an army for Abercrombie to get destroyed before Ticonderoga. It struck me as being a sound and reasonable proposal—too reasonable, if anything.

"What do you think of it?" Rogers asked.

"It seems all right," I said, "except for the £3000 for presents. If you have two hundred men in your party, you'd be too great a chief, I should think, to give small presents. Is £3000 enough to provide presents for thousands of chiefs, and for three years?"

"No," the Major admitted, "it isn't. I don't believe £3000 is enough for *one* year, let alone three. I told Campbell so, but Campbell wont listen. He has documents from the War Office showing that when Sir William Johnson tried to get £5000 from Amherst, so to give muskets and ammunition to the Indians, everyone, Amherst included, said Johnson was crazy. Campbell says the King's Ministers still feel the same way about giving presents to Indians, and that I can't

ask for more than a quarter of what I need for that purpose."
He winked. "If the petition's granted, we can rob Peter to
pay Paul, though."

"What if it isn't granted?"

Rogers dropped an enormous hand on my shoulder.
"Listen, Langdon! Don't you worry. No matter what happens,
I've been made Governor of Michilimackinac! I'll find some
way of sending my own people to discover a Northwest
Passage, and you'll be among 'em. Does that satisfy you?"

"Thank you, Major. It does indeed."

"Have patience, my boy," he said, "for another month or so;
and after that I promise you that you wont see a white man's
city for years to come." He strode out upon the balcony,
threw back his head, struck his barrel of a chest with both
clenched fists and drew a deep breath of the warm air
of the courtyard—air laden with the odor of horses, saddle-
soap, smoke and ammonia.

"My God!" he said hoarsely, "I'll be glad to get back to
the woods! I'm sick of waking up with a headache and a
mouth that feels like a buffalo-robe—sick of breathing fog
and soot and mud—sick of hearing bawds talk politics—sick
of hearing morphidites talk drivel! The damned place stran-
gles me!" He turned back to me. "Don't you ever feel choked
—smothered?"

"Often," I said. "When I came back from St. Francis, I
couldn't sleep in a bed. I had to roll up in my blanket and
sleep on the floor."

He laughed explosively. "You were lucky! After five years
of sleeping on the ground, there were times when I couldn't
close my eyes if I had a roof over my head. I had to go
outdoors and roll up under a bush! Never, by God, will I
forget how glad I was when Amherst sent for me, a week
after I married Betsy, and gave me a chance to get as far
away as South Carolina!"

This mention of his wife brought up another thought; he
frowned heavily. "Langdon, do you know some scoundrel's
been writing to Betsy in Portsmouth that I've been leading a
hell-roaring life here in London, accusing me of intoxication
and bawdiness, and all manner of light behavior? There's always somebody wants to break up your home as soon as
you show a little high spirits! The Browne family's got
cousins in London, and thinking they're probably like my

father-in-law, I've kept away from 'em; but it looks like they've been listening to scandal and writing these slanderous letters. Listen to this."

He picked up a letter from his desk, opened it and read aloud:

"I have heard on the best of authority that you have been seen with low companions, engaged in wanton and riotous living, and that your debauchery and extravagance is the talk of London. Do you not know that I haven't had a new dress this whole year, except what I have made from old dresses, slaving until late at night in the heat when others are at Assemblies or walking on Buck Street in the cool sea breeze, and using the lace and the ribbon that I have wore already these four years. Is this the way you keep the promises you made to me, and what am I to believe, I would like to know, when you send me nothing but kisses by the thousands and then at once go out to low places with low companions, surrounded no doubt by low women of the town, and there spend the money of which I am so much in need, for Papa does nothing for me, saying it is your duty to provide and have not made one effort to pay the enormous debt you owe him. Papa also says——"

Here Rogers uttered an exclamation of disgust and threw the letter back on the table. "And so on, and so on, and so on! Nag, nag, nag! For God's sake, Langdon, don't ever saddle yourself with a female if you can help it! They certainly raise hell with you if you ever show a little high spirits!"

I turned away from him and looked out of the window. For a minute my face was red. An old rage had come up within me again on Elizabeth's account—and yet there came with it a memory of Hogarth's words when he saw Elizabeth's portrait—"going to be shrewish when she's older." Well, she had indeed a right to be shrewish, I thought; but it disturbed me to think of her being so.

Rogers didn't notice. "Damn all women," he said, and paced the floor; then spoke thoughtfully.

"When you write home, Langdon, you might mention my vast and constant labors, and the exalted character of the noble and important friends I've made. If word got to Betsy

from someone else, it might have weight with her. Damn it,
she ought to realize a man hasn't time to be all debauched
and bawdy, like she charges against me, if he sees two books
through the press in three months; and his companions
aren't so damned low if he's with Dr. Campbell and Ellis and
Fitzherbert a good part of the time, and pushing petitions
before the Royal Ministers and getting the King's ear, and
going to write a deathless tragedy, and doing God knows
what-all! Why, a man like that, she oughtn't to be writing
him he's bawdy! She ought to be proud of him!"

He looked at me ruefully and helplessly, like an overgrown
boy—a person vastly different, as if by sudden magic, from
the confident soldier who a moment since had undertaken
to become a great dramatic genius, to march thousands of
miles through a trackless wilderness, and to fatten the fortunes of England by exploring the western margin of the
North American continent for the first time in history.

This was like Robert Rogers, I thought; he had more than
the two faces of Janus, and all his faces were genuine. It was
as if Garrick played a dozen parts—selfless hero, drunkard,
daring adventurer, debauchee, generous friend, braggart, riot-
er, splendid visionary, whiner, conqueror and whatnot—and
then as if the audience were told that all these roles were the
depiction of but one man. I stood marvelling again, as I so
often did when I was with him.

"Damn it," he said in a peevish voice, "there's times when
I'm almost as fond of her as I was a couple of days before
I married her; but I'm damned if I let anybody nag me! I'm
a peaceful man and I want a peaceful wife!"

Potter came back in the room then, bringing some written sheets of manuscript with him, and I returned to Mrs.
Martin's to find Ann waiting for me in my studio. She was always waiting for me when I'd been out; often enough, too,
her wistful presence prevented me from leaving when I
wished.

When she finished her lessons in Mrs. Martin's chambers,
up she would come to my third floor room with her books,
her sheets of paper stitched neatly together for writing, and
her sewing; and there she would sit, as quiet as a piece of
furniture during the greater part of the time. If I wanted to
run out for coffee, I usually didn't, because of the look that

came into her eyes whenever she saw me rise to fetch my hat. If I thought to go and stretch my legs toward London Bridge and Whitechapel, I was likely to give up that thought because of Ann.

Yet there were compensations to having her always sitting on the far side of the room. It wasn't unpleasant to feel that the somewhat shabby place was no longer lonely, even though it was only a thin child who sat there, sometimes watching me, and sometimes not taking her eyes from her sewing. Nor was she so pitifully thin as she had been, nor looked so undersized now in her decent clothes. Moreover within a week her talk had became respectable, save for a slip now and then, so excellently and energetically was she being taught by Miss Benker, a pinched gentlewoman ferreted out by Mrs. Martin and by her commissioned to make a lady of Ann.

I worked steadily to finish the series for Lord Bremerton; but when that work halted, Ann was a patient model—very different from the first sittings I'd had of her; and I made two portraits of her that I thought better than anything else I'd ever done. To be in the fashion I gave them titles—one "Domesticity"; and the other, smiling at a kitten held between her hands, I confess I called "Puss."

Then one day I was on my way to a picture dealer's with these two in my big portfolio when in the crowd I brushed against Lord Bremerton, and he caught my arm and detained me in his jerky, eager way. Thus Ann brought me luck.

"This Rogers, now," he said with no preface at all, and as if continuing a thought already in his mind, "remarkable personage, my dear sir! Difficult to kill, I fancy! You have great faith in him, Mr. Towne?"

"Yes," I said, "I do. In the woods he's as far above other men as—well, as Pitt is in Parliament. Like all men, he has his faults; but in the woods—well, you can't believe it."

"Quite possible! Oh, quite! Yes! And you think—if he goes—he could march six thousand miles? Good Gad! I mean to say, think of it! Think of such a country! You think he could do it?"

"I think there's no doubt of it. He's a sort of conjurer in the woods. I don't believe there's ever been anyone like him. He knows things by instinct, as a wolverene does."

Bremerton looked petulant. "Wolverene? Tut, tut! What's that?"

"It's an animal like a big badger—a devil about lots of things. In my part of the country they call it 'Injun devil.' You wouldn't believe the things it does. It goes around behind deadfalls and springs 'em. If you set a gun for it, it'll pull the trigger and then take the bait."

"Wolverenes! Astounding country!" Bremerton muttered. "Too fantastic for our statesmen!"

"Well, sir," I said, "Rogers knows things that the rest of us don't. If they give him what he asks for, he'll reach the Pacific or he'll die trying. I believe his name will go down in history with the great explorers—Drake and the Cabots and Columbus."

"Pah!" Bremerton shouted. "They'll give him something, but they wont give him what he wants. They never do! I tell you the country's too big for these dung-beetle statesmen of ours! Look at our Ministers from Walpole on! Yes, yes! I except Pitt! But look at the rest of 'em! Good God! Corrupt, incompetent, feather-brained, debauched, cynical, idiotic! Whenever they find an able man they drop him overboard —try him for high crimes and misdemeanors. Nothing's rewarded but stupidity, treachery and downright knavery! Look at 'em! All of 'em insane over money and position; and they only know two ways of getting either—by marriage or theft! They're like vicious children with toys. Vicious children always break their toys: can't keep 'em: don't deserve to have 'em! That's what our Ministers are doing! They're breaking their toys—throwing America away! They can't keep it! Stamp Tax! Good God! No reasoning with 'em! They'll lose it! Lose what your friend Rogers calls the richest territory on the face of the earth—richer than all the mines of Mexico and Peru!" He glared at me.

"Perhaps they'll change," I suggested.

"Perhaps not!" he cried. "Once a whore, always a whore! Once an incompetent, always an incompetent! Nothing to be done about it, though—no way to stop statesmen who've laid out a course that'll destroy their country. Every nation has to go through it, sooner or later! Ah, well! And you want to go with Rogers, do you?"

"Yes, sir," I said. "I've had my mind set on the Indian country for years."

"Quite right," Bremerton said. "Quite! Magnificent adventure! Pictures of Indians, too!" Suddenly he laid hands upon my portfolio. "What have you here? What have you here?"

I followed him into a shop doorway, where he opened the portfolio and drew one of my portraits of Ann from the protective paper I'd put about it. "Ah," he said. "Hum! Ah yes, there's another." He looked at the other, ha-hummed again, returned both pictures to the portfolio and the portfolio to me. " 'Domesticity,' " he mumbled. " 'Puss.' Very nice, especially 'Puss.' Portraits of the same young lady, aren't they?"

"Young lady?" I said. "No; just a little girl."

"Ah, betwixt and between. Yes. Not neglecting my series, are you? I'm to have it all before you go on the great expedition, am I not?"

"Yes, Lord Bremerton."

"Good! But portraits, now." He seemed to ruminate. "Might do very well if you stayed in London. Pastel portraits will be the same a hundred years from now, with glass over 'em; and paint wont. No, paint wont do it, my lad! With pastel now, the great-great-grandchildren can always see what you really looked like. Ah—you'd have time to do a portrait of Lady Bremerton before you go, eh? Ought to have two—one for my daughter. Ought to have two of my daughter, also. Thirty pounds apiece, eh? Give you some pocket money to help you keep up with that rascal Rogers when he starts for the Northwest!"

This is what I meant by saying Ann brought me luck.

CHAPTER LVIII

I'D FINISHED the series and the four portraits for Lord Bremerton, and had been paid by that kind, odd patron of mine; and it was early in December when Rogers sent me word to pack. "Having completed the last act of my tragedy of Pontiac," he wrote,

"I shall now give a few dinners in return for hospitalities extended to me, and we'll be off."

I had arranged for a thousand quizzing glasses at sixpence each, for a thousand colored prints at a penny each, and for sketching books, large and small, crayon holders, and a thousand cakes of solid color, everything packed in 90-pound bags for canoe transport. As soon as I had collected them, I went to see Rogers. He looked at me warningly when I entered, shouted "Natty"; then, on receiving no answer, he winked at me portentously. "Good news!" he cried. "Good news! I've seen Townsend again!" He was correcting proofs. He counted off the meter on his fingers like a child adding six and seven; then threw the proofs on the table.

"We travel free!" he said exultantly. "The government's sending me over on the next war craft to leave, and you and Natty and the little girl can go as my official family."

"The little girl?" I said. "What little girl?"

"What little girl?" He stared at me. "Why, Natty's daughter, of course. He tells me you've as good as adopted her."

"Oh, he does," I said. "He tells you that, does he?"

"Yes, he does. Isn't it true?"

I laughed helplessly. "It seems so!" I changed the subject. "Have they granted your petition?"

"Oh," Rogers said, "Campbell says there's no doubt it'll go through. Townsend's favorably disposed. You have to nurse those things, he says: nurse 'em and nurse 'em—especially when dealing with Townsend. Townsend's a little absent-minded: apt to forget today what he said yesterday." He slapped his proof sheets. "This'll remind him; and Campbell won't let him miss it!" He laughed delightedly, looking like a big gargoyle. "This'll show 'em how friendly Indians are treated by some of their officers and governors. The first scene shows two Irish traders cheating Indians; the second has two English hunters murdering two Indians for their furs; the third's an English fort, with two English officers cursing the Indians to their faces; but the fourth's the one I'm counting on.

"It's inside the fort. Three English governors, Governor Sharp, Governor Gripe and Governor Catchum, all stealing the presents sent by the King to conciliate Indians. When Pontiac and four other chiefs come in, the Governors talk mealy-mouthed and tell Pontiac how much the King of England loves 'em. So Pontiac tells 'em the truth."

He read to me from his proof sheets, raising his free hand and shaking it threateningly. There was something peculiarly menacing about his huge figure, his round, slate-colored eyes, his thick heavy voice. He seemed, somehow, to be an epitome of the wrongs of all Indians in America, as he declaimed:

> *"Your men make Indians drunk, and then they cheat 'em.*
> *Your officers, your Colonels and your Captains*
> *Are proud, morose, ill-natured, churlish men:*
> *Treat us with Disrespect, Contempt and Scorn.*
> *I tell you plainly this will never do!*
> *We never thus were treated by the French.*
> *Them we thought bad enough, but think you worse."*

He became one of the Governors, speaking in pleading tones:

> *"There's good and bad, you know, in every Nation;*
> *There's some good Indians; some are the reverse . . .*
> *So there's some Englishmen that will be bad . . ."*

As Pontiac, his voice became heavy and threatening:

> *"If you've some good, why don't you send them here?*
> *These every one are Rogues and Knaves and Fools*
> *And think no more of Indians than dogs.*
> *Your King, I hear, 's a good and upright man*
> *True to his word and friendly in his heart;*
> *Not proud and insolent, morose and sour,*
> *Like these his petty Officers and servants.*
> *Let him know, then, his People here are Rogues,*
> *And cheat and wrong and use the Indians ill.*
> *Tell him to send good officers and call*
> *These proud ill-natured fellows from my Country."*

Rogers made a correction in the margin. "These are almost the very words Pontiac used to me," he said. "I ought to get Natty to help me make 'em stronger. By God, it's about time someone made England understand what's happening

out in the Indian country! Look: when the Governors distribute the few presents they haven't stolen, the chiefs give
'em the devil. The first one says:

> "'We think this very small! We heard of more!
> Most of our chiefs and warriors are not here.
> They all expect to share a part with us.'

"The second says:

> "'These wont reach round to more than half our tribes.
> Few of our chiefs will have a single token
> Of your King's bounty, that you speak so much of!'

"The third says:

> "'And those who haven't will be dissatisfied:
> Think themselves slighted: think your King is stingy,
> Or else that you his Governors are rogues
> And keep the Master's bounty for yourselves.'

"Then Governor Sharp speaks up. He ought to be played
by someone like Sir William Johnson—a smug old hypocrite,
able to steal your chronometer while telling you he doesn't
use chronometers. He says:

> "'Indeed you may depend upon our Honors!
> We're faithful servants to the best of Kings!
> We scorn an imposition on your ignorance;
> Abhor the arts of falsehood and deceit!
> These are the presents our great Monarch sent:
> He's of bounteous, noble, princely mind;
> And had he known the numbers of your chiefs,
> Each would have largely shared his royal goodness
> But these are rich and worthy your acceptance:
> Few Kings on earth can such as these bestow
> For goodness, beauty, excellence and worth.'"

Rogers tossed the proofs back on the table. "Aint that like
Johnson?" he said. "Superintendent of the Six Nations and
of all other Northern Indians! Look at Gage, Commander
in Chief of His Majesty's Forces in America! Look at the two

of 'em, thick as two squirrels with the same tail! 'Get me a free hand,' I told Campbell. 'Don't put me under Johnson and Gage!' If I'm going to be Governor of Michilimackinac, I'm going to be Governor!"

We sailed for America a week before Christmas, Rogers, Potter, Ann and I, on His Majesty's frigate *Resolute*, 38 guns, Captain Tolan.

When Ann and I had come on board, she saw Rogers towering over the crowd. "Who's that?" she asked. I told her, and then she frowned as she stared at Potter, who was talking to the Major. "That man with him," she said. "What's his name?"

"His name is the same as yours, Ann," I said, in a voice a little unsteady. "His name's Potter."

She looked up at me. "Did he ever come to that place where I was?" (After her first day at Mrs. Martin's she never mentioned the Garvins by name.) "Did he ever come there, Mr. Towne?"

"I think he did once, Ann—with you."

I took her to the side of the ship, then, away from the noise and jostling of the crowded deck, where good-byes were being said and last stores hustled to the hatchways; and I told her—rather dryly, I'm afraid—that Potter was her father.

She took the information calmly, was merely meditative. "Yes," she said, "the people of that place used to curse him for not paying for me. They said I had a mother, too, but she didn't want me either. You won't want me to call him 'Father' will you?"

"I don't know, Ann. Maybe you'd better, since it's true."

"Then I will, Mr. Towne."

I saw that Potter was looking at us sidelong over his shoulder; and before we turned from the rail, he came up to us, smiling, and put his hand on Ann's shoulder. "Well, Ann?" he said. "Do you know me?"

She spoke without any expression at all. "Yes, Father."

"Bravo," he said. "I'm busy now, my dear, but we'll learn to know each other during this voyage."

I hoped they wouldn't—at least, that Ann wouldn't know him, during the voyage or thereafter, as he was; but I was relieved that the meeting was over and that they met and talked again, when the ship was under way, without embarrassment and, it seemed to me, without much display of interest on either side.

The voyage, on the whole, was a cheerful one; and it was a blithe group that gathered three times a day in the captain's cabin. Not even the biting cold, the mountainous gray seas that racked the vessel until every plank and bulkhead seemed to whine and squeak in agony, or the icy spray that coated guns, bulwarks, ratlines and spars with glistening sheets could lower our high spirits.

Potter, I think, was happy at being freed from shore restraints, especially where drinking was concerned. For no human being on earth did this man have a genuine affection, nor for any place he'd once called home, or for his native land itself; but rum he loved. It was his true love, his heart's dear; and at the sight of it his eye had a lover's sparkle. His laugh rang and his voice grew happy. Deprived of it, he would have pined like banished Romeo; the only true wedlock he ever knew was with the bottle. So he was happy on this ship, where rum was plenty.

Ann, I think, was happy because to be happy was this young creature's nature. The black oppression of her life with the Garvins had passed from her; she was quiet, friendly, eagerly obedient, and had learned to smile contentedly in a way very pleasant to see. After our sailing, she showed almost no interest in Potter, seemed not even to puzzle or speculate about him; and what she seemed to like best was to sit and sew and have me read *Gulliver's Travels* to her. She had a pretty laugh, and I read the passage about Big Enders and Little Enders to her twice in order to hear that laugh of hers twice.

"My dear good Towne," Potter asked one afternoon, as we sat at a table in the great cabin bracing ourselves against the soaring plunges of the ship, "haven't you anything to read but Gulliver?"

"Nothing else so good," I said. "Once you get it in your head and know what it means, you understand people and the world, don't you? You understand the stupidity of war, the folly of trying to build bigger ships than your neighbor, the idiocy of party politics, the ridiculousness of society, the contemptibility of ingratitude——"

"Oh, my innocent young friend," Potter interrupted, pouring himself more rum, "how'll a child understand such things?"

"In the same way all of us understand them—by repetition. Ann, what's the meaning of the man who jumps over the stick?"

Ann didn't even look up from her sewing. "It means a man doing terrible things before people just to please his masters."

"That's right," I said. "Has anybody in England been jumping over a stick?"

"You told me," she said. "All the King's Ministers. Don't other people too, Mr. Towne?"

"They do, my dear," her father said, and seemed to approve of her. Then his fond eye went to the bottle in a rack before him, and he reached for it to refill his glass.

I read the Big Enders and the Little Enders over once again to Ann, and was rewarded by the tinkling little laugh that sounded as if she'd never lived in Castle Street.

Rogers, of course, was in boisterous spirits because his assault upon London had ended in victory; and now he was off upon an adventure that promised widened fame and perhaps a great fortune.

If I'd been of a jealous disposition I could have been jealous of Rogers as easily as of any man in the world. From being a Provincial Major, he had suddenly bounded upward to a height from which he might soon shine as dazzingly as a Clive or a Pitt. He had written two books and a play; he had been made Governor of the most important post in North America; his vision had the breadth of a great explorer and empire-builder; he was strong, audacious, resourceful, gay, brave, fortunate: a leader of forlorn hopes. He had worked hard and untiringly, and certainly if sheer, uncrushable courage ever deserved a rich reward, that quality of his did.

It must be said that on shipboard he celebrated his rosy prospects. Whenever he passed the rum-locker, he poured himself a drink—not because it was such a passion with him as it was with Potter, but because, as he explained, drinking made him like everything and everybody better, especially himself. I think he drank more than Potter, even; night after night the two of them would sit at the cabin table, drinking and carrying on endless arguments. And night after night, late, a lurch of the frigate would pitch Potter from his chair to the cabin floor, where he would lie feebly pawing until Rogers picked him up and thrust him into his little closet of a berth. Then Rogers would come back to the table and keep on drinking as long as the captain or I would sit with him.

On Christmas Eve he put on a beard and a wig of spun yarn, and played Father Christmas—a bellowing, boisterous, rum-scented Father Christmas.

The next morning, roaring with laughter, he climbed the icy ratlines with the crew, thumped the ice from the frozen sails with enormous fists, and helped to furl them as handily as any able seaman. Whatever he did, he did prodigiously. He ate as enormously as he drank, slept instantly whenever he lay down, and remained asleep as long as he liked; he talked with an enthusiasm that wore out the listener.

And I was as happy as any of them—happy because I was going home; because I was about to arrive at the goal toward which all my efforts had been directed for four long and lonely years; because the past few months had given me confidence in my ability to do good work; and because I had now a steadier contentment of mind than I had known since the night the Major had told me he was going to marry Elizabeth.

If pressed to tell why I had this feeling, I probably couldn't have said immediately. Yet I knew well enough that the thought of Elizabeth was no longer a poignant one with me, and that the old sense of loss—of all brightness gone from my life—was no longer a pain: was not even an ache any more. Indeed, when I came aboard ship, I doubt if I'd even thought of Elizabeth at all for a month or so, and I should describe myself as being, throughout that voyage, a young man as light-hearted as any to be found in the world. I liked this sea, that washed the edge of my father's land in Kittery; I liked the stout ship and the high-pitched carrying voices of the sailors. I liked reading to Ann Potter; and one day, when, without letting her see what I was doing, I'd succeeded in keeping her out of the way of her father, who was noisily drunk, I thought I discovered why I'd long ago felt such pain in parting with the

Indian boy Billy, when Rogers took him from me. I thought it was because I'd enjoyed the responsibility I felt in having Billy not only always with me but dependent on me—and so I saw that I'd become better than reconciled to Ann's dependence on me: nay, I'd learned to feel a selfish pleasure in that very dependence of the poor child.

Thanks to northerly gales, our days at sea were an agony of cold and turbulent motion, yet I think the whole ship's company enjoyed them; and in more ways than one they were the shortest days of that year. We sighted the low, bleak shores of Long Island on a gray January afternoon; and four weeks to the minute after leaving London our vessel fired a gun off the Battery in New York Harbor and dropped anchor among a fleet of merchantmen and war craft that would have been a credit to Gravesend.

"Nothing's to be done till I've reported to General Gage," Rogers told us. "We'll go to Fraunces' Tavern, and after I've seen Gage we can make our plans."

We had no sooner set foot ashore than I saw we had been too far from home to know what was going on, and realized why it was that no resident of any foreign country could ever understand America. The crew of a passing pink, outward bound for the fishing grounds, watched us clamber from the frigate's jolly boat to the landing-stage. They must have taken us for Englishmen; for one of the crew bawled out, "You and your goddam Stamp Tax!" At Fraunces' Tavern we were uncomfortable because of the hostility of everyone we encountered, from waiters to guests—until they understood we were not English, as our clothes seemed to indicate. The source of this hostility, too, was the Stamp Tax; and when word went around that one of the newly-arrived travellers was the great Major Rogers, we were astounded at the eagerness with which total strangers came to him to unburden themselves of their bitter hatred of the British Ministry and all its doings.

Even the waiters knew more than I did. They knew the names of those who had favored taxing America; and to my amazement, they held General Amherst to be one of them. Charles Townsend they despised with a venomous loathing. Grenville, the ousted Prime Minister, was more real to them, and infinitely more wicked, than Beelzebub. They knew exactly how the Stamp Act would affect everyone, which was more than Rogers or I knew—they knew how assurance policies now costing two pounds sterling would cost a hundred and ninety pounds under the Stamp Tax; how bail bonds now selling for fifteen shillings would sell for a hundred pounds with the stamps; how the heaviest subscribers to the tax would be the most helpless, such as widows and orphans.

They were in a passion of rage at such injustice, and harped upon it, as outspoken men always do harp upon freshly-smarting wrongs. They were able to spend hours on end discussing the Stamp Tax to the exclusion of all else, and were content to say the same things over and over—their rage at injustice making their repetitions sound new and original in their own ears. Under all the turbulent foam of their profanity and passion flowed a deep and heavy current of determination not to be taxed by idiotic ministers who threw away American money on worthless and unnecessary projects.

When Rogers returned to the tavern from his visit to General Gage, I didn't like the look on his face. He grinned at me, but his slate-colored eyes were hard, as they had been when he was struggling to board the raft in the pool at the foot of Wattoquitchey Falls.

He took me aside, away from Potter and Ann. "You better go home to Kittery," he said. "I'll have to go see Johnson. He's up on the Mohawk. When I've seen him and heard what he wants to do about Indian affairs, I'll come to Portsmouth myself." He coughed. "Don't say anything about the Northwest Passage. I don't want anybody to know about it yet—not anybody!"

"Did you have trouble with General Gage?" I asked.

He ignored the question. "I don't mean for you not to talk about my appointment as Governor of Michilimackinac. The more you tell 'em about that, the better. In fact, tell 'em all you can. Tell the newspapers."

"Then Gage didn't make trouble for you! I'm mighty glad to hear it."

Rogers laughed sourly. "Gage! That fat-faced owl—damned soft-bellied dough-head! He gave me my commission as Governor. He had to! My appointment comes from the King, and Gage isn't important enough to interfere with the

King: not yet he isn't! Oh yes: he gave it to me, but he hated to do it! He told me to report to Johnson, and I could tell from the way he said it that they've cooked up something between 'em!" I saw the muscles stiffen in his arms and shoulders. "By God, I'll bet they'd like to cut my throat! They want all North America for themselves! They want all the credit for everything that happens here! And in their hearts tonight they're damning the King for shoving in somebody who knows how to get along with Indians better than they do —somebody who's already made a reputation for himself!"

"Can't you make friends with them? Can't you work together?"

"Friends with Johnson?" Rogers cried. "My God, man! You'd have a better chance of making friends with a rattlesnake! Didn't I tell you Johnson hated Amherst? When he hates anyone, he never stops hating him. He hates him and he hates all his friends! He knows Amherst's a friend of mine, and that alone's enough for Johnson! That's the Indian in him. He's lived with Indian women for years. He thinks like an Indian, only more so; and you know how an Indian is about those he hates! He never forgets an injury; he'll ruin himself to get even, if he has to. Well, I've fought Indians, by God!" He glared at me; then shrugged his heavy shoulders and muttered, "Well, I only hope to God I can get 'em to let me have a deputy governor at Michilimackinac. Being Governor, I can't leave my post there to find the Northwest Passage unless there's a deputy governor. I've got to get that out of 'em somehow."

Thus when Rogers and Natty Potter set off up the Hudson to visit Johnson, Ann and I took passage for Boston on the midweek packet boat.

In spite of the cakes of ice that floated in Boston Harbor, the snow that lay upon the little islands, and the bitter wind from the east, there was something so spacious about the town on its triple hills, something so fresh and clean about the frigid breeze, that I fairly laughed the cold to scorn. Boisterousness surged within me: I was moved to shout; to exult; to exaggerate. I had a sudden realization that there might be something about this enormous continent of ours that stirred everyone and everything to exaggeration: that made leaves more brilliant in the autumn; the scent of meadows more fragrant in the spring; the cold more piercing and heat more exhausting: that made active men more active, lazy men more lazy, wasteful men more prodigal: that made our people kinder than others—more parsimonious—more generous—more trustful—more suspicious: that made Englishmen more English, magnified the singularities of Irish, Germans, Jews beyond anything known of them in other lands.

Once we were ashore, I lost no time in seeking out my friend Copley. For one thing, I wanted to see him in order to find out how he was and what he was doing; for another, I suspected he'd have information that I might be unable to pick up in Portsmouth without asking embarrassing questions.

His name, I was pleased to learn, had become well-known in Boston; and Ann and I had no difficulty in finding his house—a trig, narrow-chested affair of brick on Beacon Hill, looking across the snowy slopes of the Common and off to the rolling hills of Dorchester and Roxbury.

His appearance was exactly what it had been when I had last seen him in Portsmouth, except that his weskit was of an even livelier taste and his hair more elegantly dressed. His eyes fairly popped from his head when he ran down the stairs and saw me standing in the hall, and from the delicacy of his solicitude, he probably thought I had come back in poverty and distress. I was bundled in a long black London overcoat—fashionable enough in London, but reminiscent of a nightgown elsewhere—while Ann's slender little face, pinched with the cold, peered out over a plaid shawl and two bulky mufflers.

"My dear fellow!" Copley cried. "Where on earth are you from? What—how——" He stared at Ann in frank bewilderment: then recollected himself. "Pray lay off your wraps, ma'am," he urged her. "A glass of sherry, perhaps——"

"Milk," I said. "Milk and doughnuts. This young lady is the daughter of Major Rogers' secretary. Ann, if it hadn't been for Mr. Copley, I'd never have found you, and you'd never have known about doughnuts."

Ann, divested of her mufflers and shawl, curtsied as neatly as if she'd known how to all her life.

We left her before the fire in Copley's front room, nibbling at the first of three doughnuts, while he and I went to the studio on the top floor. "So you saw the Major in London, did you?" Copley asked as we mounted the stair. "I hope he didn't borrow money from you."

"If there'd been any borrowing," I said, "it would have been the other way 'round. He was mighty kind to me. I came back with him."

"Did you, by Gad! You don't mean to say he's going to stay home for a while!"

"Don't be too hard on the Major. Remember, he's a grand soldier and going to be a great man again now. He's been made Governor of Michilimackinac."

Copley pushed open the studio door. "That'll please his wife." But with the opening of the door, I had thoughts of nothing except the portraits that stood on easels in the cold north light of his studio. One was of an elderly gentleman with small, laughing blue eyes and a white wig from which a drift of white powder had fallen on the shoulder of his drab broadcloth coat. He was leaning carelessly on a piece of stone-work, and his hand rested flat against the front of his coat. It was a gnarled and puffy hand—the hand of a man who had spent his days on the seacoast of New England— in Salem, perhaps, or Gloucester or Newburyport. I was ready to swear that if a pin had been thrust into the painted hand, it would have drawn blood.

The other was of an old, old lady in a white cap and a dress of olive brown silk. Black lace covered her white muslin collar: white ruffled armbands half concealed her white silk mitts. She was the perfection of refinement, of quiet, of breeding, of New England kindness and austerity.

On the wall was the most beautiful portrait of all—that of a boy seated at a table on which was a flying squirrel.

I stared at Copley in amazement. "Why, there's nothing better than these in London!" I told him. "You never learned this of Blackburn. What's Blackburn have to say?"

Copley looked solemn. "He said he didn't like 'em! They seemed to make him angry. He's left Boston—gone I don't know where."

"I don't wonder!" I said. "He knew he'd seen a miracle, and that he couldn't make miracles himself, poor man! These portraits are American. These people were born in New England and brought up here. You can see it at a glance. They have New England character—New England feeling, and they're alive with both!"

"Glad you like 'em," Copley said.

"Like 'em!" I cried. "Like 'em! Why, good God! You made me go to London because fame can't be durable in a country where paintings are confined to sitting rooms! Why didn't you go there yourself? If you'd gone to London, you'd be recognized for what you are!"

Copley shrugged his shoulders. "I make as much here as though I were a Raphael or a Correggio. Three hundred guineas a year! That's equal to nine hundred in London. I might go to London and waste a thousand pounds and two years of my time, and then have to return baffled to America."

"Your time wouldn't be wasted," I protested. "You'd see London. How much are you paid for your portraits?"

"Eight guineas. I have got as much as fourteen; but the average is eight."

"Look here," I said, "I'm an unknown in London. Pastel is dead there—dead as a beached whale. It's not fashionable. I made one friend and he paid me thirty guineas apiece for four portraits. And I can't do portraits. I hate 'em, unless the subject's a friend."

Copley's voice was incredulous. "Thirty guineas!"

"Reynolds gets thirty for a head alone," I said. "A hundred and fifty for a full length. He has half a dozen men painting draperies for his portraits. If you want to do portraits and be famous, for God's sake go to London."

He shook his head doubtfully. "I don't know." Then he flirted his hand at the bare and snowy shoulder of Beacon Hill. "I've made a payment on the whole north slope of this hill. In a few years I'll own it. Then I'll make a farm out of it. I want to raise things. I don't want to stand in front of an easel all my life, staring at women's faces. I don't believe I'd be happy in London. Were you happy?"

"No, not till just before I left, and that wasn't like the elation I'm feeling now in coming back to my own country! But we weren't discussing happiness. It wasn't because you wanted me to be happy that you urged me to go to London."

"Well, I'm thinking of going," he admitted. "I've often thought it curious that I got you to go and haven't gone myself. Some day I might send this Boy with the Squirrel to Benjamin West and see what comes of it. He's kind to young painters and——" He broke off abruptly and laughed. "Prating of myself, but of course you want to hear if I've been to Kittery and Portsmouth of late, and what I know of your family and your friends."

"Yes, of course I do."

"At last accounts," he said, "your family are all in good health. My informant, no longer ago than last week, is the great self-styled Captain Huff, who passed through Boston one day ahead of certain minions of justice. He told me Portsmouth was a harder place to live in every year for a man who enjoyed a peccadillo now and then." Copley's eyes twinkled. "I seem to recall that one of Portsmouth's fairest daughters once made a great to-do about your intimacy with him. I suppose you'd still be glad of news of her."

At this I was afraid that I looked self-conscious, and it's true that now I was near Elizabeth again, my heart beat a little faster. "Oh yes," I said, as coolly as I could. "Of course, I always should. She's an old friend."

"Still not quite over it?" he asked compassionately. "Almost but not quite?" Then he went on hurriedly:

"Well—perhaps when you see her——"

I interrupted him: "She's changed a great deal?"

"No, she's just the same; but perhaps some things you didn't see have become more visible. She might even make you a little sorry for her husband."

"Copley! I could never believe——"

"No, no!" he said. "Still the soul of piety and virtue! Still proud of herself for being the wife of the hero. Did you ever think it's possible that's why she threw herself at him—to be the wife of a hero? Painful after your marriage, perhaps, to find that your hero's a peculiar human being; and perhaps the poor Major had to find out a little of the same. For instance, do you suppose that if he'd called on me today with her, he could have left her sitting downstairs alone as you've left that obedient young lady? Why, she'd have been up here fingering her hair, doing all the talking, insisting upon attention, set upon nothing but being the most important person of the trio. My dear Towne, I'm afraid the lovely Elizabeth's really like that."

"Dear me," I said, conscience-stricken. "I'd forgotten I

was leaving that child down there alone so long! We must go."

"Don't think me ungallant to the fair lady of Portsmouth," Copley said as we went downstairs. "I only mean she's proud of being the Major's wife, but not proud of the Major." He laughed in his friendly way. "Don't be offended with me for thinking that in the end you're entitled not to consolation, but to congratulation. You'll forgive this frankness?"

"Yes, yes," I muttered. "I——" But by this time we were at the door of the sitting room, and we heard, from within, a strange voice—the voice, one would have sworn, of a silly and thoughtless woman. "I beg of you," she cried, "really, I beg of you! If you persist—really, a whole bottle of gin—come now, I vow I'll have to send you packing! It's monstrous dangerous—monstrous! Only a tumblerful of it I had at the Coronation, and I assure you I saw three Kings! No, no! You might let Patty fall, and the stairs are so very long —I begged the Earl to make them of something softer than marble—really, you know, if you should fall on her, her poor little head might grow to be like her Papa's the Earl's!"

Copley stared at me, mystified. When he reached for the doorknob, I stopped him. From within the room came another voice, whining, rasping and somewhat slurred. "A insult, that's wot it is! A low, vile insult! Not a day in the past fifty-eight years that I aren't 'ad me two quarts, yes, an' brung up"—the voice hiccuped violently—"brung up eleven fine sons *and* daughters on 'arf an' 'arf—'arf gin an' 'arf slops —an' now 'ere's a bleedin' earl's wife a-tellin' honest Missus Garvin 'ow ter drink 'er gin!"

"Who——" the astounded Copley said, pushed away my detaining hand and threw open the door. In the room there was nobody but Ann Potter. She sat slender and straight in her chair before the glowing fire. But she jumped up as we came in, read in our faces that we'd heard; then, after a moment's confusion, she saw that we were laughing and laughed too.

Copley shook his head ominously. "That's dangerous— dangerous! Two artists in one family! That'll make trouble."

Frightened, Ann looked studiously at the young painter's solemn face, then laughed again.

CHAPTER LIX

I EXPECTED, when I returned to Portsmouth and Kittery, to find everything changed, even as I myself had changed. The outlook of the towns must, I thought, have broadened, just as my own outlook seemed to me to have become a little wider and more tolerant. I had created things that hadn't before existed: I knew more about men, books, politics, art. . . . Kittery, I was sure, would be as glad to see me as I was to return to it.

To my disappointment, nobody but my own family seemed conscious that I had been away.

Silas Mason, who ferried Ann and me across the steel-gray river to the Kittery shore, rowed the same boat he had rowed five years earlier; and the melted pearl that formed the unpleasant pendant to the garnet-cluster he thought of as his nose was apparently the same he'd worn the day I left Portsmouth for England. He eyed the sky in his old familiar way, and greeted me as if he'd last rowed me across the river yesterday. "How do, Langdon," he said inertly. He stowed our boxes amidships, took the oars and added, "Thickenin' sou'west. Might get some more snow." Later, when we were nearly across, he spoke again. "How's things in Boston?" Boston, I suspected, was the utter-most limit of his known world.

"Clear and cold," I told him.

" 'Twas?" he said discontentedly. "Glad I don't have to be there as much as you. Got too many people in Boston nowadays. Can't walk without you get bumped. I want distance around me, I do. Wunt go there no more. Don't see how you stand it."

"Yes, it's a rough life," I said, and he looked better pleased.

The little white houses in Kittery had the well-remembered look, peculiar to river-side houses in winter, of having been temporarily set down in unsuitable locations. There wasn't a

new one among them; all was as of yore—and so did I seem
myself, a futile sort of boy again.

This feeling came on me strongly as I reached my father's
door. I was just young Langdon Towne again, getting home
perhaps after a week's fishing. And after the greetings were
over I think my family had much the same feeling about me
—took it for granted that I was exactly as I had been before
I went away—as penniless, as deluded, as devoid of prospects.
The New England villager may be away from his village a
long time, and may return to it greatly changed; but the
length of his absence and the change in himself will be almost
ignored by the villagers and even by his own family—which
means, probably, that the New England villager loves his village so well that he can't bring himself to countenance a
change in any detail of it.

I think I was feeling embarrassed by this provincial attitude—until my father asked me abruptly about the Stamp
Tax and cried out to know what in Heaven's name the British
Ministry was thinking of to do such a thing to New Englanders? Didn't they know New Englanders wouldn't tolerate
injustices?

I saw that the wrath I had found in New York was a feeble
glow by comparison with this flaming New England resentment of bad government, of short-sightedness, of false reasoning. When Odiorne told in a voice shaking with excitement how a crowd of Portsmouth men, headed by Cap Huff,
had made George Meserve yield up his commission as Stamp
Master and had marched noisily through the town with the
commission impaled upon a swordpoint, I felt within me a
surge of satisfaction that was almost violent. I was proud of
being a New Englander, and I suddenly knew that in all
things fundamental I was less changed than in London I
had thought.

My mother had already taken Ann in charge; and though
I saw that the child found things a little strange at the very
first, and gravely hovered near me when she could, she
adapted herself to New England ways with a really talented
readiness. The mimicry that had made Copley call her an
artist was instinctive with her, as natural as breathing.

We hadn't been in Kittery two days when her voice, her
accent and her manner were almost exactly my mother's;
and on the Sunday morning following our arrival she went

to the kitchen door, looked up at the sky, and said, "Thicken' sou'west. Might get some more snow," so precisely in Silas Mason's intonation that Odiorne laughed till he cried. Ann looked at him without any expression whatever, and I had no doubt she was becoming a New Englander.

When company was in the house, she was as quiet as a shadow; but at other times I'd often hear her chattering to my mother and illustrating her talk with dialogues, speaking in the voices it might be of Miss Benker or Mrs. Martin, or of Major Rogers and the hoarse old Captain of the ship. Her mimicry didn't seem to be conscious imitation: it was always as if she became the person she mimicked.

I think Ann must have spoken privately to my mother about my professional work abroad; and my mother on this instigation must have prompted my father. At all events, on the fourth evening after my homecoming he coughed uncomfortably and asked if I had with me any of the pictures I'd made in London. All the best ones, I told him, had been disposed of, but in my portfolio upstairs were two of Ann that he might think like her. When I brought them to him, he held one in each hand, in the glow of the lamp on the center table. "Hm," he said at length. "It don't seem possible."

My mother came behind him and looked long at the sheets. "What are you planning to do with them, Langdon?"

"Nothing, Mother."

"Nothing?" Odiorne said. "Then what do you make 'em for, if you don't know what to do with 'em?"

"That's a hard question, Odiorne," I told him and I knew I couldn't answer him truly so that he'd understand. "Sometimes I get money for pictures like these."

"How much is one of them worth, Langdon?" my father asked.

"What it'll bring," I said. "Sometimes it wont bring anything. If people don't want a man's pictures, they wont buy 'em at any price."

My father looked at me over the top of his spectacles. "Your mother tells me that Ann says nobody'd buy your pictures for more than barely enough to skimp along on. If you had such bad luck, I'm surprised you kept writing us how well you were making out."

"I made out all right," I said.

"Yes," my father said caustically. "On air a good deal of

the time, wasn't it? Ann tells your mother the landlady told her you pretty often didn't have anything at all to eat."

I looked around crossly at Ann, who sat in the corner of the room, and her hands tightened together in her lap in a frightened way; so I laughed.

"The harder you work, the less food you need," I said airily, and was glad to see those small hands relax their grip upon each other.

"Yes, of course," my father returned with satire. "Always heard these artists were every single one crazy! Another thing—Ann bragged to your mother that not so long ago you sold all your pictures to the nobility. Got to bragging about you so hard that she went on and made ridiculous statements. Claimed you'd got eight hundred guineas for your pictures of Indians, and thirty guineas apiece for portraits— from a Lord or Earl or somebody, whoever it was."

"Yes sir," I said. "That's correct."

My father hitched forward in his chair and stared at me. My brother Nathan whistled unbelievingly. My mother went on knitting; and Ann, in her shadowy corner, looked complacent, I thought.

Odiorne stood up, gaping at me. "Eight hundred guineas for Indians?" he said. "Thirty apiece for pictures of people? Langdon! Wha'd you come home for!" He shouted hilariously. "If it had been me, I'd 'a' stayed there forever!"

My father turned on him. "Yes, Odiorne, I guess you would! You'd have been so busy selling pictures you wouldn't have had time to make any!" He bent over the two pastels of Ann that now lay upon the table.

"Well, Langdon," he said, "I might as well admit it; I thought you wanted to draw pictures because you were too lazy to work the way the rest of us do; but I was wrong. I thought I'd be ashamed of having a son who was an artist." He removed his specatcles and polished them, "As for these pictures, I'd give pretty near anything I've got to be able to say I'd made 'em. It seems to me, Langdon, you know your own business better than we do, and I don't see that any of us is called on to make any suggestions to you."

I stayed away from Elizabeth as long as I could; but in the end I went to borrow Billy from her to use as a model; that was the excuse I made to myself. When I was admitted to the Brownes' front hall by their old Negress, it was Mrs. Browne for whom I asked—though I would rather have talked to the devil than to Mrs. Browne, because there's one thing that can't be denied about the devil by his worst detractors: at least he's interesting.

As luck would have it, Mrs. Browne was in. She came sailing downstairs in a plum-colored dress that gave her a distended look, as though all her dinners for a month were still within her. She saw me, stopped short, turned to go upstairs again hurriedly: then, seeing that this wouldn't do, came down and gave my hand a flustered shake. "Ah, Langdon, I'll——" she said, and bustled away to the rear of the house, where I heard her tapping on her husband's study door. "Mr. Browne!" she called. "Mr. Browne! Langdon Towne is here!" I wondered how many centuries she would have to live with a man in order to call him by his first name. While I fumed uneasily, I heard a stir at the top of the stairs, and saw a face peering at me over the rail. It was Elizabeth.

"Well!" she cried. "I *thought* I heard Mother speak your name." She ran down the stairs with the same graceful gliding movement I so well recalled. It was hard for me to remember she was married. She looked unchanged, and her hand was soft and warm in mine.

"Elizabeth," I whispered. My brain was in a turmoil. I could only repeat her name foolishly: "Elizabeth! Elizabeth!" and cling to her hand until Mrs. Browne sailed back to us like a plum-colored gundelo.

"Now!" Mrs. Browne exclaimed, leading the way to the sitting room. "Now we can learn about the Major! My husband's coming at once. I assure you, all this has been most embarrassing for my daughter—for Mrs. Rogers! Where is the Major?"

"Hasn't he written you?" I asked Elizabeth. "Surely he wrote you from New York?"

Elizabeth sniffled. "I haven't had a word from him in three months! Do you mean to say he's in New York? When did he reach New York? When did he leave England? Why did he leave England? Really! Really! How can he be so inconsiderate of my position!" She pressed her handkerchief to her nose, sniffled again; and with a kind of horror I realized that she was indeed behaving like a married woman: even the sniffle sounded married.

"Now, my dear!" Mrs. Browne exclaimed. "You mustn't excite yourself!" She looked at me, her lips tight. "Perhaps," she said, "perhaps you can explain to us why the Major should have spent all these months roistering and flinging money away in London as if my husband hadn't had to sue him, and not a penny the better for it, and all the time scarcely a word of explanation to my daughter—oh, shameful! Shameful! It's been the talk of Portsmouth! You can imagine our sensations!"

Mr. Browne came in quickly, stared at me out of round, angry eyes, and gave me a moist, limp hand. "What's this about the Major?" he asked. "Like Satan, he goes to and fro in the earth, and walks up and down in it, and we are the last to hear from him, when we should be the first. He gave it out that he was sailing to the West Indies, but instead of that he sailed for London! He has made each one of us to rend our mantles and sprinkle dust upon our heads toward heaven! Have you come as a messenger from him?"

"No, sir," I said. "I came to see if Elizabeth would kindly let me borrow Billy for a few days. I'd like to use him as a model. Ah—the Major's all right. His letters to you must have gone astray. Haven't you heard from him since he was made Governor?"

Mr. Browne started. "Governor!"

"Oh!" Elizabeth cried. "He got it! He got it! He's a Governor!" She ran to her mother. "Why didn't he let me know!" She looked appealingly at me. "You don't know what we've been through, Langdon! Whenever we went out, we could see people whispering, whispering! What's he Governor of?"

"Michilimackinac," I said.

"Great Heavens!" Mr. Browne exclaimed. "That's at the end of the world, isn't it? Let me see—Michilimackinac—well, well! Do you know what—ah—emolument attaches to the governorship?"

"No, sir," I said. "He never mentioned the pay."

Mr. Browne seemed to wince at the word. "That's his careless Irish temperament," he said indulgently. "Well, well! A Governor!"

He went to his daughter and pinched her cheek. "The Governor's Lady! Things will be different now, my dear."

Elizabeth threw an arm around her mother's neck, kissed her; then with a swirl of skirts went to an armchair and disposed herself in it with some stateliness. She was so erect that her chin puffed the flesh beneath it. She fingered her hair, tucking it delicately in place with graceful fingers, and looked at me graciously. "You must tell us of the Governor, now, Langdon. Did you and he speak much of me when you were in London; or were you both so busy squiring the London belles that you had no time to think of the Governor's Lady, poor thing, left moping in Portsmouth without even knowing the position to which she's become entitled?" Then she leaned forward; her expression sharpened and her voice lost its graciousness. "Did you see him with women? What sort of women were they?"

"I saw him with none," I said.

"Yes, but you heard—— Oh, it's too disgusting! George Meserve wrote home that the Major was seen at routs and balls—that every woman in London knew him by sight—that there wasn't a drinking place in the town he hadn't visited."

I laughed. "George Meserve! He doesn't claim to have seen the Major at any of these routs and balls himself, does he? Of course everybody in London knew the Major was there, but I don't believe anybody but George Meserve knew that George Meserve was. In London the Major wrote two books and a play——"

"A play!" she cried. "He wrote a play!"

"Two books!" Mr. Browne exclaimed. "Upon my word— ah, do you happen to know whether they were successful? Were his financial arrangements satisfactory?"

"I don't know," I said. I looked from Mr. Browne to Mrs. Browne, and from them to their daughter; and with a sinking heart I realized that all three looked hungry.

I got up to go. "I thought it just possible I might be allowed to borrow Billy for a week or two if——"

"Ah, yes," Mr. Browne said. "Billy. Ah, yes!" He seemed to wrench his mind from wolfish calculations. "Yes, if Billy were here, of course, you'd be welcome to him: oh, yes indeed! But I sent him to Concord. Yes. Our son-in-law, the Governor, was formerly quite improvident, you know; and I was forced to accept his Concord farm, with Billy and three Negro slaves, in repayment of one of my many loans to him. Now they aren't even mine. Ah—to avoid possible legal complications I transferred the property to my son to hold in trust for my daughter—eventually."

Elizabeth, become the Governor's Lady once more, was stately. "I think I'll have Billy back again to wear a turban and open the door to callers. I think I'll have him and one of the Negroes, too, to attend me on the street. Governors can't live like private persons."

I gulped a little. "Billy's been made a slave?" I asked.

"You speak in a strange tone, Langdon," she said. "You remember he belongs to me, don't you?"

"Yes," I said, and went to the door; but Mr. Browne detained me.

"One moment more, Mr. Towne. What of British opinion when you left? It must have been a painful thing to be an American in London—to try to hold up one's head among British gentlemen while the American scum were questioning the authority of the Crown!"

"I didn't find it painful," I told him. "Most of the English gentlemen that I know were of the opinion that if the King's Ministers indulged themselves in further outrageous follies like the Stamp Tax, England would soon have no American colonies left, and serve her right!"

Mr. Browne, frowning and puffing, stared at me unbelievingly; but Elizabeth, flushed with anger, started up from her chair. "Your friends must have been a low class of Englishmen, Langdon Towne!" she said. "I trust the Governor didn't mingle in the same circles that you evidently did!"

Alas that Hogarth should have been as shrewd a prophet as he was a satirist! I saw then that she looked older and that she also looked—oh youthful dreams! Oh girlhood's glamor —shrewish!

I hadn't become a fine gentleman in London; but I'd learned to make a St. James's bow. In the doorway leading into the Reverend Arthur Browne's hall I now made three: one to Mrs. Browne, one to her husband; and the last—and profoundest—to Elizabeth.

Outdoors I drew a long inward breath and exhaled it whistlingly. The sound was like a marvelling whisper of the name "Elizabeth"; for indeed I was marvelling—marvelling at my former self. Elizabeth! Elizabeth Browne! So that was really Elizabeth Browne! My boyhood seemed to be over!

It was April before the new Governor of Michilimackinac, Major Rogers, came back to the bosom of his family, so to speak. Since I had received no word from him in the meantime, I went at once to the Brownes' as soon as I discovered he was in town, in order to learn his plans.

He had brought Potter with him, and I found the two of them using the Brownes' back parlor as headquarters, and the whole house in a turmoil. In the front parlor was Mr. Browne and a number of his friends, all of them portentously discussing Indian affairs. The Major's past sins, in view of the honor just conferred upon him, had seemingly been forgiven and forgotten, at least for the time being.

In the back parlor the Major was talking magnificently about Michilimackinac. Beneath his hand were maps of the Great Lakes; on one side of him sat Potter: on the other Elizabeth, looking gracious and possessive.

"Look, Betsy," the Major was saying. "Here's Michilimackinac, between Lake Michigan and Lake Huron. It's on the edge of the most beautiful body of water in the world, and we control all the waterways to Detroit, to Montreal, to Lake Superior and the Grand Portage. We're Governor and Governess of a territory to which the petty empire of the Great Cham of Tartary would seem but——"

Here he looked up to see me standing in the doorway, whereupon he pushed the maps from him and slapped the table boisterously. "Langdon!" he shouted. "Just the man I wanted to see! I'm counting on you, Langdon! Betsy's afraid you wont go with me, but I tell her she doesn't know you! How've you been, Langdon, and how's the little girl?"

Potter avoided my eye.

"She's well," I said. Before I could say more, Elizabeth spoke in a hurt voice.

"Why didn't you tell us about Mr. Potter's daughter, Langdon? I have to find out everything from someone else! Why didn't you bring her here to me? I don't see why Mr. Potter didn't arrange to have her come here, anyway. She'd have been such a help in the house. She could have made herself useful in every way, and I particularly needed someone to help me with my sewing!"

The Major cleard his throat. "Let me tell you about what's inside the fort. On the left when you come through the gates——"

But Elizabeth spoke to me sharply. "When will you bring her over to me, Langdon? Since her father's the Governor's secretary, surely you'd be wishing her to stay with us, instead of away over there in Kittery, where he'd so seldom see her."

I smiled uneasily and muttered something to the effect that I hoped she and Mr. Potter and the Major would come over soon, to see how well Ann was doing in her studies. Then I hastily asked the Major whether Michilimackinac resembled Crown Point.

"Crown Point!" the Major cried. "It's as much like Crown Point as St. James's Palace is like a wren-house! Wait till you look out over those straits into Huron on one side and Michigan on the other—two oceans set down amid riches beyond the dreams of man! Why, Crown Point's nothing!—nothing but a guard-house in a narrow lane! Michilimackinac's a fortress between two empires—the white man's empire to the east, and the red man's to the west!"

As a speaker, he had a knack of painting a more radiant picture than other men could draw with twice the number of words. He stirred me when he gripped his desk with his huge hands and crouched over it, telling in that thick voice of his of the endless canoe brigades that moved perpetually east and west past Michilimackinac; of the healthful, cedar-scented air, devoid of mosquitoes and all other stinging insects; of the colorful thousands of Indians who would come with gifts to honor the representative of England's King; of the bluff traders and gay voyageurs; of the new fort, built in the past three years; of the comfortable houses erected for the officers so fortunate as to be sent there.

"Our house," Elizabeth interrupted importantly, "our house —the Governor's house—has a billiard room. I declare! To think I should have to go to Michilimackinac to learn to play billiards!" She seemed to find something irresistibly droll in the very thought of billiards.

"You?" I said unbelievingly. "You! Billiards!"

She shook her head at me archly. "Oh, I shan't let him run away from me again!" she cried. "This time *I'm* going! This time *I'm* going to see what he does with all his idle evenings! Just think! No mosquitoes! No having to wait three months for letters from London! Just think—the Governor's wife and the Governor and all his household receiving tribute from millions of Indians, and drinking tea with the officers, and playing billiards! La! What a future!"

I stared blankly at the Major, who was suddenly so sheepish that he almost looked small. I couldn't believe my ears. Elizabeth, attempting to adapt herself to a post in the wilderness—she, who had been shocked and frightened to hear of my small wanderings in the woods with Hunk Marriner—she, who squeaked and clung to my arm at the sight of a toad in the grass beside the path from her father's door—she was to go to Michilimackinac!

She shook her finger at me. "Langdon Towne, you closemouthed boy! When you were here about Billy, why, instead of talking like a naughty rebel and making us all furious with you—*why* didn't you tell us you'd become a great artist in London and sold your pictures for Heaven knows what prodigious sums, and hand-in-glove with my Lord Bremerton, and not even mentioning him when you must have known we were all dying to hear about London people of *ton!* Thirty guineas for a portrait, indeed! Whatever became of that one you did of me?"

"That one?" I said. "I'm afraid it happened to be destroyed."

She jumped up and patted my hand. "Well, since I never even saw it, you'll have to do another of me in place of it —wont he, Major?" She went to the door, looking back over her shoulder. "Then you'll be court painter, and none of the Michilimackinac ladies will dare to have their portraits done by anyone else."

The atmosphere was easier with her gone.

I thought I had to speak to Potter of Ann. "You'll be delighted when you see her," I told him. "Our Maine food and our Maine air agree with her. You can fairly see her grow; she's beginning to be almost like a young lady."

"Splendid, my dear Towne!" Potter said. "Fatten her all you can, in case we have to go on half rations on the road to Michilimackinac."

I stared at him. "To where?" I asked helplessly. "Not Ann! You can't mean you're thinking of taking that child into the wilderness! She needs schooling! She needs proper companionship!"

Potter seemed shocked. "Proper companionship, my dear

Towne! Don't you consider Mrs. Rogers a proper companion for Ann?"

I felt the Major's slate-colored eyes upon me inscrutably. "I do indeed!" I said hastily, and I added lamely, "I meant companions of her own age."

Potter's smile was faintly mocking. "But my dear good man! You said yourself she's almost gown up. The fact is, I've made a compact of friendship with the Governor's fair lady, and given her my promise—she shall have Ann for her companion and friend."

"Companion and friend," I said bitterly, and it was on the tip of my tongue to say "Companion and lady's maid"; for I'd have been dull indeed if I hadn't seen that Potter had promised to furnish Ann virtually in that capacity in exchange for some favor he wanted for himself.

I put a check upon myself, however, and said stiffly that I thought it better to leave Ann in Kittery, where she was already making progress in her schooling.

"*You* think it better," Potter said, and laughed. "May I remind you that we're speaking of *my* daughter?"

I controlled my temper somehow. "Didn't you turn her over to me?"

"Not at all! I just put her in your charge for a time, but that time's over." Then, as he saw the anger in my face, he confronted me coolly. "Do you wish to go into legalities? Would you have the remotest chance in a court of law to keep me from controlling my own child? Shall we put it to that test?"

I hadn't the shadow of a legal right to the control of Ann; he had me beaten. I knew it, and the knowledge unloosed my temper. "Potter," I said, "I've seen you practise blackmail for banknotes, but even then I didn't suppose you'd be as wily and time-serving a hound as I see you today."

"What!" he cried. "You speak so to me? I'll call you out for this! I'll have you on the field for it; by God I will!"

"You wont!" the Major roared, and his great fist thundered on the table. "I'll have no bickering, by God—not a word more from either of you! Not a damned word, do you hear? I'm Governor of Michilimackinac, and you're both under my orders already, or not a foot do you set on the way to that post! Towne, you're a Tom-o'-Bedlam to think you can tell a man where and where not he can take his own daughter!

I've got to take my own wife, haven't I, damn it? Natty Potter, if I hear any more from you about calling out any of my men, I'll step out on the field with you myself—and stuff every blade of grass that grows on it down your gizzard! I've got too much trouble up on the Mohawk to bear any in my own official family! Where are those letters I told you to write, Potter? Yes, and that list of supplies? Off with you, damn you, off with you!"

The elastic Potter was already appeased. He gave me a whimsical, triumphant glance as he went out, and I knew that poor Ann would go to Michilimackinac.

CHAPTER LX

WHEN ROGERS spoke of the trouble he had "up on the Mohawk," he meant Sir William Johnson, whose magnificent stone residence at Mount Johnson overlooked the heart of the Mohawk Valley.

When Potter had gone out, the Major said to me gruffly, "Sit down! Sit down! I want to talk to you," and told me of the visit he'd made to Johnson after I'd left New York. Johnson had instructed him, the Major said, to wait until June before proceeding to Michilimackinac. In June Pontiac was coming to Oswego with representatives from the Western nations, to make submission to England, and Johnson considered Rogers' presence necessary at the council.

"Was anything said about the Northwest Passage?"

Rogers' explosive laugh was angry. "I wouldn't say anything to Johnson about it unless I had a personal letter from the King in my hand, and all the expenses for that expedition in gold sovereigns in my pocket! Maybe I wouldn't do it even then, unless I had a couple hundred Rangers to keep me from being ambushed by that old viper. Why, do you know what that—that——" He loosened his neckband with a thick finger, spat in the wastebasket beside him, and stared at me from stony eyes. "Do you know what that old wind-belly thinks? He thinks he's going to stop me from giving presents to Indians when I'm Governor of Michilimackinac—not going to let me spend any money at all! Johnson! Johnson, the biggest money-spender and present-giver that ever passed a belt to an Indian!"

"Isn't it possible that you misunderstood him, Major? Surely a man in Johnson's high position wouldn't be so inconsistent!"

"You think not?" Rogers said. "You don't know what men in the highest positions will do when they see rivals coming too close! They'll steal, lie, buy votes, break their promises and go back on their friends! War's a hard business, but politics is worse. According to a politician's lights, Johnson's justified in bottling me up in Michilimackinac without a penny to spend on presents—not one damned penny!"

"But Major, nobody knows better than Johnson that you can't keep Indians friendly without making 'em presents!"

"Know it? Of course he does! Hasn't he written a dozen letters to the Lords Commissioners of Trade to tell 'em that very thing?"

The Major rubbed his big face. "Look, Langdon: the first year Amherst came over here, Johnson's bill for keeping the Six Nations friendly was £17,000. Good Lord, Langdon, I could keep all the Indians of the West friendly and peaceful for half of it! They tell me the Indians didn't get all of it. Somebody else got some. Somebody did, Langdon."

"You mean, Major, that Johnson——"

"Somebody did!" He tapped the table earnestly with a ponderous forefinger. "I only say somebody did. That's all I'll say, and it couldn't have been anybody else but Johnson. I'll be damned if it could! What? No wonder Amherst turned against Johnson and against giving presents to Indians! No wonder he wrote Johnson to punish Indians who didn't behave properly; not to give them presents!"

"What did Johnson have to say to that?"

"Plenty," Rogers said. "He told Amherst it was cheaper to buy up all the Indians than it was to send troops among 'em to keep 'em peaceful. The French first got the friendship of Indians by giving 'em costly presents, he said, and the English couldn't wean 'em from the French without doing the same."

He hitched himself forward in his chair. "Of course, Langdon, he was right, and so was Amherst right. Indians will always be on the side of the government that gives 'em the most presents; but it's also possible to control 'em with troops, and do it fairly cheaply—if you use the right sort of troops. Johnson couldn't do it with Provincial troops. Amherst couldn't do it with the Royal Highlanders, the 61st Foot and a dozen more regiments like that. They'd be ambushed and massacred inside of a month. The only troops that could handle 'em properly would be Rangers, led by—well, by someone who knows how to fight Indians; and that means me!

"Now can't you see, Langdon, what went on in Johnson's mind? He can't control Indians with troops, so he says it can't be done! He says Amherst unjustly criticized him—and he never forgives criticism, Langdon! Never! Didn't I tell you the man's almost turned into an Indian? He hates Amherst for criticizing him, and he hates all Amherst's friends. Well, I'm a friend of Amherst's, so he hates me. And besides that, he's afraid I might get too powerful. Jealousy's an awful common motive in this world, Langdon—commoner than most people know. Don't you see, Langdon, why he hopes I'll be in trouble?"

"I'm afraid I do, Major."

Rogers threw himself back in his chair. "Well," he said, "there's one sure way of getting a governor in trouble with the Indians around his post, and that's to make him follow Amherst's policy. You're a fair-minded man, which is why I'm talking to you. Wouldn't you figure that's what's in Johnson's mind to do to me? I put it to you: wouldn't you think so?"

"I'm afraid I do, Major."

"Yes, sir," Rogers said, and clicked his big teeth. "He'll ruin me if he can; but damme, sir, I'm not afraid of the old fox! I'll lick him and Gage put together with one arm tied behind me! I'm working for something bigger than they ever thought of, and you know what it is."

"Northwest Passage, Major!"

"Yes, sir! The road to Japan, to China—ah, my boy, the road to the diamond- and pearl-strewed Indies! Like a new Columbus, Langdon; and if there's a San Domingo in the way, I wont stop there, like he did! By the Great Jehovah, I'll blow it up!"

"Bravo, Major!"

Flushed and pleased, his chest inflated. "You may well cry 'Bravo!' " he said. "We're working ahead every day on the great plan. I've sent word to Captain Tute and Lieutenant Atherton—good Ranger officers, willing to do anything I tell 'em. They'll come to Michilimackinac. I saw Captain Carver in Boston and he'll make our maps. For two years he's been trying to live on a school-teacher's pay that's only paid half the time. Damned if I don't think he'd undertake to find the Garden of Eden or the Fountain of Youth and make maps of 'em, if doing so would get him out of teaching school. Only trouble with Carver is that he believes everything he hears; then if it turns out to be true he takes all the credit for it, but if it turns out to be wrong he wont take any of the blame. But we got to have maps, Langdon, and he wont try any of his little tricks on me—not more than once! I've even got a man we can hide behind, so the French wont suspect what we're doing: Stanley Goddard. Goddard's the best trader in the Northwest. There's never been a trader who had so much influence with the Indians. So there you are: Tute to act as deputy governor in my place while we're away; Atherton as my second in command; Carver to map our discoveries; Goddard for doing the trading and talking to the Indians; and me to lead the chosen band till the sunset waters of the golden Pacific shine upon our conquering eyes!"

This burst of rhetoric seemed to surprise even himself, and he added thoughtfully, "I ought to remember some of these things for Governorship speeches at Michilimackinac." He looked at me genially. "Well, Langdon, get your sketch books packed! We'll be on our way before you know it."

"Yes, Major."

He got up, stretched himself; then rubbed his mouth with the back of his hand, which seemed to remind him uncomfortably of something. "Look at this house," he said to me solemnly. "All wives and mothers-in-law and Reverend fathers-in-law; a little pee-wee vial of vinegar they call wine on the dinner-table—a damned little vial I could swallow glass and all—and not a damn drop of rum on the place; and if I try to set foot out of doors, don't they all go with me, every step I take—yes, sir; old scripturizing sue-you-for-board-and-vittles Reverend Arthur, too! Whoo!" He threw his arms wide and exploded. "Oh, God! won't I be glad, if I can live that much longer, to be on the road again!"

Thanks to the courtesy due one Royal Governor from an-other, His Majesty's cutter *Curlew*, through the kind offices of Governor Wentworth, was placed at the disposal of Major Rogers to lighten his Western journey by carrying him to New York and up the Hudson to Albany.

Early in June, when the first hot weather of the year was filling the town with the scent of new-cut grass, lobster shells and seaweed, the *Curlew* fell away from the foot of crowded Spring Wharf with the Major, Elizabeth, Natty Potter, Ann and myself on the quarter-deck.

As a Royal Governor, Rogers was no doubt a disap-pointment to those who waved us farewell, for instead of a scarlet coat and polished boots, he wore the uniform of a Ranger officer—leggins of greenish buckskin, a dark green coat circled by a useful belt, and a little black infantryman's cap with its decoration curling up over it like a squirrel's tail. On his advice I, too, wore the Ranger's uniform, Scotch cap and all, that Amherst had given me on my return from St. Francis.

"It may not be the prettiest rig in the world," Rogers had said, "but you'll find it the most comfortable and the most useful, and you'll also find Indians have more respect for it than for a scarlet one."

From the moment we started, it was apparent that Elizabeth wished to fill the position of Governor's Lady as it should be filled. She was all smiles and graciousness, and when we sat at our meals around the table in the diminutive gun-room, she talked so steadily that it was a wonder to me how she found time to eat. If others made an attempt to say a few words, those few words invariably put her in mind of some-thing—as when the cutter's commander, Lieutenant Braisting, had carelessly taken the conversation from her at our first meal, even before we were out of sight of the Isles of Shoals.

"You know," the lieutenant said, "those islands aren't un-like the famous Isles of Greece you hear so much of. Greatly overrated, those Grecian islands. Sailed among 'em as a mid-shipman on the old *Bacchus* a few years ago, and saw a most remarkable——"

Elizabeth darted in on him like a pickerel. "Bacchus?" she said. "Was she named for a prominent Irish family? I've often heard Father speak of the Backuses of Dublin—such charming people! Every single one of the Misses Backus played the harp. If you've ever been in Dublin, Lieutenant, I'm positive you must have met some of the Misses Backus at a rout or assembly."

Even before the lieutenant could say "No," she was off again. "My father says the Backuses all had sweet voices; and when they sang, it was a pleasure to hear them trill the grace notes. You must have enjoyed knowing them, I'm sure."

When Elizabeth had the conversational bit in her teeth, there seemed to be nothing to do but let her run with it. Her questions were rhetorical and called for no answers. If she accidentally received an answer, she ignored it. Yet her hearers, for the most part, seemed to find her loquaciousness pleasing. When she cast sidelong glances at Lieutenant Braisting and stole the talk from him, he only beamed upon her politely.

Ann, habitually a silent girl, was of course all the quieter for Elizabeth's talkativeness, and fell into the position of a tire-woman with a voiceless meekness that was touching and to me enraging too. Airily Elizabeth thought of a thousand frippery errands for her. "Ann, child," she'd say, "I've left my kerchief in my cabin—run fetch it for me, child, will you?" or "Child, I've lost my patch-box! I'm afraid you *never* could find it, could you?"

Handkerchiefs, patch-box, smelling salts, fan, sunshade, powder, eau de Cologne, mirror, scissors, sewing-bag, book— Ann found them all.

In five days we were on our way up the Hudson, a waterway almost as populous as the Thames, and far more exciting. Sturgeons and porpoises leaped beneath the *Curlew's* bowsprit; pigeons passed over us in flocks so enormous that they looked like endless streamers of sooty smoke; scores of little provision boats with leg-of-mutton sails moved downstream in close-packed fleets, looking like children's toys but carrying the vegetables which, on the following day, would fill New Yorkers' stomachs; trading sloops from Albany, loaded with lumber, stone, barrel staves and bales of fur, blundered across our bow, while their crews of fat-faced Dutchmen stared with obvious hatred at the British flag that flapped at our masthead in the soft June breeze. Both shores, except where the massive wall of the Palisades and the rocky slopes of the highlands prevented, were covered with neat farms, houses of brick and stone, flourishing orchards and extensive cornfields; and at night the low lands along the river glimmered like golden gauze from the myriads of fireflies that danced above them.

Rogers warned us against the Dutch, who are despised by New Englanders because of the manner in which Albany Dutchmen not only remained neutral during our wars with the French, but purchased from the French Indians all the plunder captured by the Indians in New England homes. But great as is the New England hatred of the Dutch, it is nothing by comparison with that of the Dutch for England and New Englanders.

"Don't try to buy anything in Albany," Rogers said. "These Dutchmen can skin a sixpence and stretch the skin so you can't tell it from a shilling! A New York Jew hasn't a chance with 'em! They'd ruin him in a week. When they get hold of an Englishman or a New Englander, they charge four times what a thing's worth. There's not more than six good Dutchmen in all Albany. I'm pretty spry at a trade myself, but if I tried to deal with anyone in Albany except John Askin's firm—Scotchmen—I'd be lucky to get away with my leggins!"

That was a side of Albany we were spared. We anchored just off shore, where we could see the brick-ended houses, the scoured white steps to each house, and the benches at the top of the steps on which the householders sat in the early evening; and aboard the *Curlew* we stayed while Rogers went ashore to negotiate for transportation. A little after sunrise the next morning a brigade of bateaux and passenger canoes belonging to Rogers' Scotch friends, the New York merchants Gregg and Cunningham, came out for us, and the bateau-men transferred our bales and boxes from the *Curlew's* hold to the bateaux. When the rest of us were settled in the canoes, the *Curlew* fired a farewell gun and we set off on the second stage of our journey—up the Mohawk River to Lake Oneida, and down the Onondaga River to Oswego on the shore of Lake Ontario.

Oswego was the easternmost of the trading posts as you travelled toward or from the Mississippi, where the French were using every fair and foul method to persuade all the Indian tribes to take their furs down the great river to the French, rather than to Michilimackinac, Detroit, Niagara and Oswego. With the arrival of warm weather every year,

all the Albany traders went to Oswego to cheat Indians, just
as natives of Kittery went fishing in the spring and blue-
berrying in the summer; so Oswego was ordinarily a post of
moderate importance. It was particularly important just now
because of being the nearest post to the Mohawk Valley
and the home of Sir William Johnson. He had summoned
Pontiac and the Indian nations most closely allied with that
great chieftain to meet at Oswego for a Council with the
representatives of the Great Father beyond the seas, and it
was over this Council that Rogers had orders to take control
until the arrival of Sir William Johnson.

Our canoes slid down the Onondaga late on a soft June
afternoon and opened up Oswego with its two forts at the
mouth of the river, the sparkling blue lake beyond, and an
Indian encampment that looked to my unaccustomed eyes as
though it contained all the Indians in the world.

The whole place had the look of an enormous fair. The
fort on the left bank was a handsome one with cannon peering from its embrasures and a British flag flapping idly in a
feeble breeze from the lake. Separating its ramparts from the
river was a broad and grassy parade-ground, dotted with
groups of elms so towering that they must have been a part
of the original forest which looked down upon the Jesuit
missionaries who had founded the post over a hundred years
before.

Across from this fort, on the right bank, was another
fort, unoccupied and dismantled; and it was on the deserted
parade-ground of the abandoned earthwork that the Indians
had pitched their houses of poles covered with skins, bark and
reed mats. Planted in the ground before each tent were lances
from which hung scalps on frames, strips of cloth, medicine
bags, mysterious bundles of feathers. Around these cone-
shaped houses moved the innumerable Indians, decked out
in reds, blues, whites, yellows; up from them rose an unending clamor of barking dogs, screaming children, chattering
squaws, gabbling braves.

Rogers shouted exultantly to me, for he knew how the
sight made my fingers itch for the crayons. "There's four nations, Langdon, ready and waiting for you—Ottawa, Huron,
Potawatomi and Chippeway! They'll keep you busy!"

Beyond the Indian encampment, nearer the shore of the

lake, was a little town of white tents with the fronts rolled up, showing that they belonged to traders.

As our canoes drew in to the landing-stage on the left bank, two drummers ran out from the deep-set gateway, stood smartly to attention and went to beating the long roll. Smoke spurted from one of the embrasures: the bang of the cannon made us blink, and red-coated figures appeared magically upon the parade-ground, hurrying to make us welcome.

Officers of the garrison crowded around the Major and Elizabeth and conducted them toward the fort, and Potter followed; but Ann stayed with me on the landing-stage to wait for the bateau that contained my crayons and drawing books.

The baggage bateaux were still far upstream; and while Ann and I stood waiting, a canoe, driven by an Indian squaw, came diagonally toward us from the far bank. Many canoes from the Indian encampment had taken to the water at the report of the cannon and the rattling of the drums; but this one canoe overshadowed all the others because of its passenger—a man who stood majestically erect in the bow—a grandly sculptured figure such as one might conceive as the monument to some great and victorious general. His arms were folded; one knee was advanced: on his head he wore a magnificent beaver hat, looped up on three sides and edged with gold lace two inches wide: his clothes were pale buckskin, and on the breast of his upper garment was the picture, in indigo, of a blue heron standing on one leg. He was such an imposing spectacle that I thought he might be the king of one of the Indian nations, or perhaps even Pontiac's prime minister. As he approached, he shouted angrily; and I, thinking he wanted the landing-stage to himself, took Ann's hand and swung her down from the stage onto the river bank.

Ann pressed my fingers. "He's speaking to you. He knows you."

To my surprise, this majestic figure was indeed addressing us, and at the same time pointing imperiously at the landing-stage. "Come back here!" he shouted violently. "Hell, can't you see who I am?" He snatched off his superb hat, waving it at me, and this removal released two neatly braided queues of hair so red that it was almost scarlet. Only once before had I seen hair so red, and even as the thought occurred to me,

I realized that this red hair and that other red hair were the same. Moreover, as the canoe drew closer, I perceived something wrong in the anatomy of the man in the bow: he had a wooden leg. This damaged but imperial figure was that of Sergeant McNott, whom I had last seen lying on a knoll at the mouth of Otter River, the torn muscles of his right leg bound with a blood-soaked bandage.

I lifted Ann back on the landing-stage, jumped up myself, and ran to hold the bow of the canoe. McNott caught my shoulder and hopped nimbly to the stage.

"Well if this don't beat all!" he cried. He thumped me again and again on the back, apparently unable to say more.

I got him by the arms and pushed him away. He looked and smelled exactly as on the afternoon when Hunk and I had stumbled into the Flintlock Tavern and first learned about Rogers' Rangers from him.

"Well," I said, "I want you to know I tried to find out about you at Crown Point and at Dunbarton when we came back from St. Francis, but nobody seemed to know where you were."

McNott nodded. "You'd had to find out from a doctor, and you can't find out nothing from an army doctor. He don't know nothing: that's the reason. What became of your friend Hunk?"

"He died the day after I got home," I said. "I guess he was just waiting to say good-bye. He asked after you."

McNott nodded and spat in the river. He felt the sleeve of my Ranger's uniform and looked at my green Scotch cap. "I damn near fell overboard when I saw that hat," he said. "Felt it clear way down in my wooden leg." He looked at Ann. "Who's this?"

When I told him, he nodded again, fingered the material of her dress and absentmindedly ran his hand over her hair. "Figgered it wasn't your wife," he said. "You want 'em a lot solider out in this country. The winters get tough— awful tough." His eyes wandered to the Indian woman who still sat on her feet in the stern of the canoe, holding it from the landing-stage with the paddle. She was staring off into space with the wooden, uninterested expression of a drowsy red hound; and for a squaw, she wasn't bad looking. McNott made just such a gobbling sound as a turkey makes in moments of petulance. The squaw stepped out of the canoe, drew it ashore and sat beside it without so much as a glance at us.

"Did you speak Indian to her?" I asked incredulously.

"Look at her!" McNott bade me angrily. "Would you get anywhere speaking English to her? My God, I had to learn the damned language!"

"Is she—is she—ah——" I asked.

"Is she!" McNott exploded. "I should say she is! I gave two muskets, a horse, half a dozen of the best stroud blankets and a keg of alcohol for her three years ago, and ever since then there's times when it seems as if I was brother-in-law to the whole Chippeway nation on account of her." He looked at me anxiously. "You well acquainted with the Chippeways?"

When I shook my head, he said, "They're good-natured: I'll say that for 'em. They aint sour, like those damned Iroquois; but the trouble with Chippeways is there's too damned many Chippeways, especially if they're all your brothers-in-law. And that aint the worst of it, so far as this lady's concerned. She's only a Chippeway by adoption—though I got to admit she had the best job of adopting done on her that ever was done. Why, hell, there aint hardly a Chippeway alive that don't claim her as a relative! But she aint always been a Chippeway, Langdon; she was born a Sioux. The Chippeways and the Sioux, they've been fighting ever since Noah launched the Ark; and when the Chippeways captured this woman of mine in one of their big woman-stealing battles and didn't have time to kill her, they adopted her. Well, there's more Sioux than there are Chippeways, though it don't hardly seem possible; and if I had to take care of her Sioux brothers-in-law in addition to her Chippeway brothers-in-law, I couldn't make both ends meet. No, sir: I'd just have to hunt up the nearest debtors' prison and move in permanent. Listen, Langdon: if you got it in mind to tie up with an Indian nation, tie up with the littlest one you can find. Try the Mandans or the Blackfeet, and don't have nothing to do with Chippeways or Sioux, or you'll get awful tired of your wife's kin eating with you and using all your things that you aint got right on your person every minute. Thirty to forty thousand brothers-in-law's a trial to any man, I don't care who he is!"

I told him I was here to sketch Indians: not to marry them.

"Good Grief!" he exclaimed. "Aint you got over drawing yet? I should think a man'd go crazy doing so much of 'em."

His eyes wandered to the parade-ground. "You must 'a'
come out with Rogers, didn't you?"

I said I had. "I suppose you know he's been made Governor
of Michilimackinac?"

McNott looked at me oddly. "Know it? Of course I know it!
I bet there aint a Indian this side of the Mississippi that
don't know it. Ah—you run into Lieutenant Roberts yet? Benjamin Roberts?"

"We just got here," I reminded him. "So many officers
came down to meet Rogers that I knew I wouldn't be missed
if I stayed here to wait for our baggage." I turned to look at
the parade-ground. The Major and Elizabeth, surrounded by
officers, were still moving toward the entrance to the fort;
while a crowd of Indians and white onlookers, attracted from
the other side of the river by the new arrivals, kept pace with
them and stared as at something wonderful.

"Come on," McNott said. "I got to see the Major." He
stumped off the landing-stage, swinging his wooden leg in
wide arcs.

"See those two fellers walking behind the others?" he asked.
"One of 'em's got his head tilted over sideways, listening, like
a robin listening to a worm. That's Lieutenant Benjamin Roberts, the dirtiest little pin-tit that ever was!"

"The gentleman with him," I said, "is this young lady's
father—Natty Potter, the Major's secretary."

"Oh," McNott said hastily, "my information comes from
Indians, mostly. Indian talk; Indian talk! Damnedest gossips
in the world! Maybe it aint true, what they say about Roberts." He changed the subject. "See that thin officer walking
on the Major's left? That's Cap'n Peeke Fuller, in command of
this post. On the other side of Rogers is a tall feller with
jaws like a chipmunk carrying acorns. That's Edward Cole,
Commissary at Fort de Chartres, out on the Mississippi. He
used to be a colonel. Great friend of Johnson's. Who's the
woman?"

"Rogers' wife."

McNott stopped to stare at me. "You don't mean to say
he's going to take her to Michilimackinac!"

When I said he was, McNott spat copiously. "There's a feller each side of her," he continued, "one that sort of sham-
bles sideways, and one that's all spotted with freckles. The
shambly one is Jehu Hay, Commissary at Detroit. He's a

colonel, too. The freckled one is Norman McLeod, Commissary at Niagara. He was a major or something like that. They're all friends of Johnson—all of 'em used to go duck shooting together, sleep in the same beds and"—he paused, glanced sidewise at Ann, coughed and continued—"and used to make acquaintance with the same squaws, too. Real close friends." He looked at me intently. "You heard Johnson's new scheme about commissaries, didn't you?"

"No, I haven't heard anything. We just reached here from Portsmouth. What is the scheme?"

"It's a good one," McNott said. "Johnson and Gage rigged up a new way to divide the country. Gage sends out the governors or commandants and don't have nothing to do with trade any more; Johnson takes care of the trading end, and puts his friends out in all the posts as commissaries to regulate the traders, say what they can do, and treat with the Indians."

"I don't believe I understand," I said. "What's left for the commandant or governor?"

"Nothing," McNott said promptly. "Nothing but to take orders from a commissary. How'd you like to do that? How'd you like to be in command of a piece of country, and have to take all your orders from a storekeeper?"

"It sounds tricky," I said. "What's the reason for it?"

"Reason," McNott echoed. "Johnson's a trader himself. Looking at it as a trader, I'd say Johnson had done it to get the control of the whole Indian country into his own hands."

We had almost caught up with the throng of onlookers following the group of officers to the fort. Over us loomed the grassy ramparts, on which stood sentries and soldiers from the garrison.

"Oh," I said, "I'm sure it's not as bad as you make out."

McNott's face grew purple. "You are, are you? Well, let me tell you this——" He shot a quick look at Ann, who still clung to my hand. "Look," he said, "I know what you do to a squaw when she talks too much, and most generally she don't; but I kind of forget how you handle white women. Now what about this young lady here—this Miss Potter? Would she be likely to blab everything she hears, or does she know enough to keep her mouth shut?"

Thinking of the time Ann had told my mother of my foodless days in London, I looked down at her and saw that she, too, remembered. "No, Sergeant," I said. "She wont talk." I felt her fingers tighten on mine.

"That's good," McNott said. "The less our kind of talk gets to the ears of Lieutenant Roberts, the better for the Major. From what I hear, Johnson's working to put Roberts over the Major's head."

"Over him!" I cried. "Put a lieutenant over a Royal Governor! That's fantastic! There'd be the devil to pay in five minutes, and Johnson knows it!"

"Yes," McNott said. "That might be what Johnson wants."

CHAPTER LXI

ROGERS' ATTITUDE toward non-commissioned officers and men was not calculated to endear him to his brother officers; for when men in the ranks weren't marching or fighting, he talked to them and behaved toward them as if they were his equals. Since most officers of all armies are unable to maintain discipline without grinding their subordinates beneath an iron heel at all times, they view with horror any open friendliness between an officer and those beneath him. Thus it was plainly a shock to the scarlet-coated group about the Major, as we were entering the fort, to see him rush shouting upon McNott, seize him by the shoulders and belabor him joyfully as though he were his own lost brother.

The same officers would have been even more pained, an hour later, to see the Major, McNott, Natty Potter and myself sitting together over a bottle of rum in the quarters assigned to Rogers. From the next room came the sound of Elizabeth's voice telling Ann where to put this and where to hang that. "Probably, child," I heard her say, "probably you can't find my garnet pin. It's somewhere in the small hair trunk, but I'm sure you'll never be able to find it." Ann, I knew, would find it.

Rogers smiled fatuously at the sound; then drained his

glass and looked owlishly at McNott. "So you turned trader! Well, there's a fortune in it if you handle it right."

McNott shook his head. "Not for me," he said regretfully. "I married me a Chippeway, and her relatives eat up most of the profits. If I hadn't learned the language so to keep 'em under control, they'd have got my wooden leg away from me before now. As it is, I can keep from starving, and buy me a new hat now and again, and that's all I want—just enough to be comfortable and travel around a little." The sanctimonious mealiness of his voice didn't sound natural.

Rogers eyed him thoughtfully; then looked slowly from me to Potter. Potter was flushed and talkative. "That officer I spoke with, Lieutenant Roberts, seemed to consider an Indian wife as an asset rather than a drawback," he declared. "Very interesting man! I get the idea that Indians worship the very ground he treads on. He told me he'd played Othello to entertain the garrison at Schenectady, and in the invited audience were a large number of Mohawks who went quite mad over him—quite mad! He married an Indian princess—the richest heiress in the Six Nations, and speaks the language like an aboriginal. It's a romance!"

McNott looked at him compassionately. "You ain't seen many of these Indian princesses, maybe, Mr. Potter. They're kind of different from what you expect. This here princess, Mrs. Roberts, for instance——"

"Yes, yes," the Major interrupted. "Natty'll learn all that for himself the first time he goes out among the Indian ladies. What about Roberts himself, Sergeant Mac?"

"Roberts?" McNott said; then glanced thoughtfully at Potter. "Oh, Roberts aint much of nobody—yet. I aint never noticed no Mohawks acting wild mad in love with him, like Roberts has been telling your friend here they was. He give 'em the cape and hat he done that Schenectady acting in, and they liked that; and naturally they hope he'll act some more in more capes and hats. Of course, too, there was that romance your friend was speaking of—Roberts's heiress wife, that's got more wrinkles than there's hairs on a cow's hide, but never gets drunk twice the same day, and can't curse a bit worse than four or five of our own Rangers that was best at it, Major—no offense to your friend here." He gave Potter an only partly veiled sour glance. "Of course, as he says, the romance and all of it, her being considerable under three times the age of her husband——"

"No, no!" the Major said. "What about Roberts himself?"

"Roberts himself?" McNott spoke with elaborate carelessness. "Him? Oh, nothing much. Seems like I did hear old Johnson takes to him a good deal. Yes, seems like somebody told me that this here Roberts and them other commissaries Johnson's been appointing—yes, seems like I did hear they're all about as thick with Johnson as a new litter of pigs is with the sow. I dunno myself, but seems like somebody was telling me something like that, Major." Again he looked sidewise at Potter.

Rogers, frowning, followed that glance. "Natty," he said, "I wish you'd go out now and see that all the baggage is brought into the fort and stowed properly." Then, as Potter rose with alacrity, the Major added, "As a favor, Natty, don't get carried to bed tonight. We want to make a good first impression. Stay just the least bit sober, will you, Natty?"

" 'Pon my honor I will," Potter said. "Just the least bit, Major."

Then, when he'd gone, Rogers looked steadily at the one-legged former sergeant of Rangers. "Stop hinting," he said. "Speak up!"

McNott drew his chair close to the table and spoke in a whisper. "Major, you know how Johnson figures on using these commissaries?"

"I know what I've heard he figures on doing," Rogers said. "I've heard he figures on using 'em to keep traders from wintering with the different nations—to persuade all Indians to come to the trading posts to do their trading; but Johnson must know that at Michilimackinac the traders have got to go out to the Indians, because no man alive can get them to come such great distances to that post to do their trading; so I don't believe it."

"You don't?" McNott said pityingly. "You ain't heard but a little part of it, Major! Listen, if I tell you the rest, will you keep it to yourself and never let nobody on earth know what I've told you? Will you do that, Major?"

The Major looked at him heavily. "Where'd you hear what you're going to tell me?"

"Where'd I hear it? Where do you s'pose? Johnson told Roberts, and Roberts told the Princess Methuselah he'd went and married, and she told every red colored person on earth. Well, I got a princess too; younger and pleasanter than Roberts's, but that same color, and she tells me everything she knows—or else gets maltreated with this here handy wooden leg that's easy to swing when I aint got it on—so she got confidential and told me. You're a gentleman, Major, and wouldn't like to injure no lady, so don't tell anybody I told you, or I'll have to take it out on her for telling me. I'd like your word, Major."

"You have it," Rogers said. "Go ahead."

"Well, 'taint so much after all," McNott said modestly. "This here Roberts, you know he's commissary now right here at Oswego. You're commanding here now, Major, until Johnson comes; so Roberts is under you, aint he?"

"Yes, what of it?"

"Well," McNott said, "all the Indians is kind of looking on and watching to see what happens, you being in command here and Roberts being a commissary that's a friend of Johnson. The Indians is kind of interested to see how you two get along here."

The Major was mystified. "How we get along here? Why are the Indians so interested in that?"

"On account of the future," McNott answered. "I mean, when you're at Michilimackinac. Just suppose—I aint saying when; but suppose some day you'd find this here Lieutenant Roberts promoted from Oswego by Johnson to a real post: made commissary at Michilimackinac, say; and not only that, but put over the Governor at Michilimackinac."

"What!" Rogers cried, and his fist thundered on the table. "Over! Over the commandant?"

"Well," McNott sighed, "I only said *supposin'* it happened. Anyhow, that's why the Indians here at Oswego are watching you and Lieutenant Roberts, and taking kind of an interest in what happens between you."

Rogers looked earnestly at his old sergeant. Then he got up from the table, put on his little black infantry hat and stood to his full height. Once more he looked like the man who'd led the Rangers to St. Francis and brought them back. "I see," he said. "Just now I'm commanding here. I think I'll go out and inspect this post and find out what's wrong with it!"

White men, I have often thought, have one peculiarity in

common. They want their important men to be important in manner; and if the great wear their laurels lightly their greatness is soon doubted. I often forgot, when I was with Rogers, that his equal as an Indian fighter had never been known; that for five long years, winter and summer, he had harried and chastised the Indian enemies of England like some vengeful spirit of the forest; that he had written two books and a play, and been held in the highest esteem by General Amherst and other Englishmen of ability and distinction. The truth was that his ease of manner, his friendly ways and ready smile, his dislike of pomp and ceremony, made him seem a man of ordinary attainments, like all the rest of us.

Indians, however, are not as forgetful as white men. When the Major, McNott and I crossed the river in McNott's canoe and set off on a tour of the Indian encampment, the crowd of copper-colored men, women and children that gathered to see Rogers was so great that our progress became slower and slower, and was at length brought to a halt when five important-looking chiefs in handsomely decorated buckskins stood squarely in our path. They were Ottawas, it appeared, and three of them had been with Pontiac, six years before, when Rogers, on his way to take possession of the French posts, had talked repeatedly with the great chieftain. Two of these very men, with a hundred warriors, had, at Pontiac's orders, escorted Rogers from Presque Isle to Detroit.

At sight of them, Rogers lifted up his big hands delightedly, went to them and clapped each one of them on the shoulder, calling them by name and shouting, "Well, well, well! I never expected to see *you* here!" He was genuinely glad to see them; and the gratification of the chieftains was enormous. Their appearance surprised me; for although their skin was copper colored, their features were as regular as those of the most distinguished white men. One of them, addressed by Rogers as Kab-bes-kunk, might have been Sam Livermore's twin brother.

Rogers fingered their buckskins, beautifully embroidered with dyed porcupine quills, and wagged his head admiringly, while the Indians tried to seem imperturbable. "Look at these," he said to me. "I bet you never saw anything like these before!"

To McNott he said, "Sergeant Mac, tell 'em I'm glad to see 'em: tell 'em I've never forgotten them or their great chief Pontiac, and that I've put all of 'em in a book, so they'll be forever famous. Tell 'em I'm just looking around, and I'll pay a formal call on 'em tomorrow. Tell 'em I want 'em to look out for Langdon Towne, here, who makes colored pictures so the White Father can understand how the great men of the Ottawas and the Chippeways look and dress. Make it strong, Mac. Slather it on."

The Indians turned their attention from Rogers to me, fingered their scalp-locks, straightened their buckskin coats, pulled medicine bags into more conspicuous positions and composed their features in what they doubtless considered more noble lines.

When McNott had finished, Rogers said, "Just ask 'em if everything's all right. I don't want any formal complaints; but if there's anything they don't like locally, I'll listen."

McNott looked uneasy. "Why don't you get an interpreter from the fort, Major?" he asked. "I'm only a trader."

"Go ahead and ask 'em, Sergeant," Rogers said.

McNott spoke briefly to the five chiefs, and Kab-bes-kunk made a prompt and dignified reply. The throng of squaws, children and idle young men swayed and muttered: the smell of bear's grease, medicine bags, paint and hair, blended into that indescribable perfume peculiar to Indians and to the fur of wild animals, was strong around us.

"Well," McNott said, when the Indian stopped, "they got the usual complaint. They say the traders oughtn't to be over here on this side of the river, so close to the Indian encampment. They say it's dangerous, because the traders can't be stopped from selling rum. They say their young men go to the traders every night and get drunk, and there's no telling when they might bust out in a frolic and kill a mess of Chippeways. They say some of the Huron young men might get drunk, too, and come over in the Ottawa camp and take a bundle of scalps. Then there'd be a war."

"I see," Rogers said. "That's a reasonable complaint, and I'll attend to it. Just remind 'em, though, that there's no sure way to keep traders from selling rum, and no way to keep Indians from buying it—not that I know of. I'll move the traders over on the other side of the river, where they can be watched from the fort; but if their young men are bound to get rum, I can't always stop it. They'll have to issue orders to their young men, and enforce 'em, too."

While he waited for McNott to translate, Lieutenant Roberts and Captain Fuller stepped from a canoe onto the nearby river bank and pushed hurriedly through the Indians who surrounded us.

"Major," Captain Fuller said deferentially, "we didn't know you planned to come over here so quick. If you'd let us know, I'd have sent a proper escort with you, so to let the Indians know who you were."

"No need to bother, Captain," Rogers said. "The word got around. I'd met some of these people before, you know—when I took over all these posts for General Amherst some years ago." He grinned disarmingly at Captain Fuller, who looked foolish.

"It appears to me, Captain," Rogers continued, "that you've stationed the traders too far from the fort. Some of the Ottawas have complained, and I think they're right. I'd like those traders moved across the river and close to the fort, where we can keep 'em under proper military surveillance. You'd better move 'em right away, before they have a chance to do anything tricky. Those Albany traders know forty-six ways to skin a cat."

Lieutenant Roberts spoke deferentially. "I'm afraid, Major, I'm responsible for the traders being where they are. I told Captain Fuller to put them there. Before coming here I discussed the matter with Sir William Johnson, and Sir William gave it as his opinion that the traders should be on the east bank, close to the lake shore. Those were Sir William's instructions, Major. I had them from Sir William himself."

Lieutenant Roberts was a young man of medium height, nervous, with a habit of biting his lips and of shifting his bright, quick-tempered eyes from one person to another. Yet he seemed eager to be on good terms with everybody, though I thought there was temper in his shrill and hurrying voice.

When he'd stopped speaking, Rogers shook his head. "We can't risk trouble between the different tribes, Lieutenant, and that's what we'll have if hot-headed young bucks are allowed to buy all the rum they think they can hold. I want those traders moved right now."

Lieutenant Roberts' color heightened quickly. "I protest,

sir! Major, I protest! Captain Fuller, I call you to witness: It's my duty to protest, and I do!"

Rogers stared at him incredulously: stared too, at the silent Indians ranged behind us in a semi-circle. So silent were they, so intent their scrutiny of Rogers, that I heard an Indian's dog, simultaneously scratching his neck and thumping his leg-joint against the turf; and when the animal shook himself, the sound seemed to come from a giant of a dog.

"On what grounds do you protest, Mr. Roberts?" Rogers asked.

"Grounds?" Roberts asked in a shaking voice. "Grounds? Why, I protest because the traders are already placed in accordance with Sir William Johnson's wishes! They're where I instructed Captain Fuller to locate them!"

"Those grounds aren't sufficient, Lieutenant—not under the circumstances," Rogers said sharply. "Captain Fuller, notify those traders to transfer their tents and goods across the river. I'll stake out the spot where I want 'em put."

"Yes, Major," Fuller said. He turned slowly toward his canoe.

"I countermand that order, Captain Fuller!" Roberts called. His voice cracked and his hands shook. "Sir William Johnson has given orders that his commissaries are to be obeyed in all affairs pertaining to the trade. I'm Commissary at this post! I put those traders where they are, and that's where I propose to have 'em stay!"

Rogers' eyes were as gray as slate, and as hard. "I was told to come to this post and take charge of the impending Council of Western Indians," he said. "If there's trouble among the Indians or among the traders, I'm to blame. You can talk all you want about how commissaries must be obeyed in affairs pertaining to the trade; but if I let a commissary exercise his judgment and ignore mine, the impending Council of Western Indians might end in murders and scalpings. Perhaps *you* could explain that to the satisfaction of General Gage, but I couldn't. I was told to take charge of this council; and so far as I'm concerned, the only way to take charge is to take charge. While I'm in charge, Lieutenant, be kind enough not to interfere with me."

He walked past Roberts and swung himself neatly into the bow of McNott's canoe. McNott and I, following, scrambled into the midship section. I looked back at Lieutenant Roberts.

He stood where we had left him. Already the Indians who had surrounded us had broken up and were drifting toward their camp. Captain Fuller, on his way to his own canoe, turned impatiently. "Come on, Lieutenant! I've got a lot to do before sundown!"

Rogers threw a glance over his shoulder and laughed briefly. "That Lieutenant Roberts ought to kept on being an actor," he said. "He ought to keep talking Shakespeare; when he talks Roberts, he's an idiot!"

The traders were transferred; and to outward appearances, all the officers and commissaries at Oswego were thenceforth on the best of terms with Rogers. Roberts appeared to have accepted his defeat; and as for the Indians, they made as much to-do over the Major as though he were the Angel Gabriel preparing to blow the last trump. They came across the river to sit in front of his house and wait for him to come out; and he went daily to their encampments to smoke pipes with them, eat endlessly of strange and unpleasant looking messes, and discuss routes and paths to a thousand different places.

Under McNott's guidance I went myself to the encampment, day after day, to sketch Indians. The first day I took Ann to carry my books and crayons; but when I called to her on the second day, Elizabeth came to the door of the Major's rooms and looked at me archly. It was a look I was coming to dislike as being the forerunner of something I always liked even less.

"Don't you think, Langdon," she said, "that it would be better if Ann stayed here today? Bad boy. Wasn't I a-twitter yesterday thinking of her among all those Indians?"

"I don't see why," I said. "She likes to go. She'll learn a lot, finding out how they live. It's an opportunity."

"Oh, the nasty things!" Elizabeth cried. "The way they dress—some of them have hardly anything on! And a young female——"

"But that's natural," I interrupted. "They wear coverings when they need 'em; but when they don't——"

Elizabeth looked haughty. "That's enough, Langdon. Un-clothedness, even of savages, isn't a subject to be discussed between the sexes. Ann's been placed in my charge by her father, and she's not to go. There are a hundred things for her to do here, where she's needed."

I could only bow to her wishes and go to the encampment with McNott.

Late that afternoon, when I returned to our quarters, Ann ran out of the door to meet me. Had I finished sketching Kab-bes-kunk, she wanted to know. Had he liked the picture? Had I got a good one of him? How many had come to watch me draw? Had they covered their mouths with their hands in astonishment, as they had done yesterday? Had Sergeant McNott said anything funny? What did he say? Had he sent any messages to her? Had Sergeant McNott's wife been along, and had she yet opened her mouth to say a single word?

I gave her the portfolio, and with it a neatly-wrapped bundle of soft buckskin that Kab-bes-kunk's wife had given me to give Ann. She sank to her knees on the grass, put the bundle beside her, and untied the strings of the portfolio. The sketch of Kab-bes-kunk met with her approval; and so intently did she study a drawing of McNott's wife, sitting on her heels in the stern of a canoe with a paddle across the gunnels before her, that her face altered and seemed to become broad and morose, like the pictured face at which she stared. The drawing that pleased her most was one of Kab-bes-kunk's wife.

I liked it myself. She was sitting before a painted wigwam; her hair was cut straight across her forehead; from her ears hung bright blue stones; around her throat were necklaces of black, blue, red and white wampum; her dress was a long jerkin of white buckskin, ornamented at top, bottom and on the sleeves with purple and white porcupine quills arranged in geometric patterns. On her knees rested a cradle of painted bark, and in the cradle was a fat-faced papoose staring out at the world with a supercilious distortion of the mouth. Over the child's head was an arch of wood, from which a dirty string hung to within an inch of its nose.

Enraptured, Ann scrutinized the drawing with clasped hands; then pointed to the string. "What's that?"

"Well," I said, "that's a peculiar thing. It's the child's umbilical cord. The mother ties it to the cradle-arch as soon as the child is born. It protects the child from evil spirits and disease, and such-like things."

Ann looked puzzled for a moment, stared at the picture, then began to turn over the other drawings. Her eager interest in them pleased me, of course; and we'd had a happy hour when Elizabeth's voice from within doors summoned us to supper.

There were but four of us at the supper table that evening; and when the meal was finished, the Major and I were left alone to a bottle of port in the candle-light. Ten minutes later Elizabeth called shrilly from her bedroom for the Major to come to her.

"Damn it," he said, hastily emptied a glass just refilled, and obediently went. Then for a time I heard the piping of her voice and the rumbling of his beyond closed doors. He seemed to be expostulating; and when he came back, he looked seriously dispirited. "Oh me," he said moaningly, as he sat down with me again and reached for the bottle. "Oh me!"

"Anything I can do, Major?" I asked sympathetically.

"Hell, yes, Langdon," he said, "it's all about you!"

"Me, Major?"

"Yes." He shook his head in rueful warning. "If I was you, Langdon, I'd keep away from Elizabeth the next few days. You've got her all in the vapors."

"What?" I had no conception of what he meant. "*I've* got her——"

"She wants me to tell you not to show Ann any more pictures," he said, embarrassed. "She says you're the reason Ann asked her what an umbilical cord is."

"What!"

"That's what she said," the Major went on, reddening. "Says Ann says she wanted to know, because you showed her the picture of one on a basket. Elizabeth says it was damned indelicate of you, and——" He paused, looked at me piercingly and asked, "What *was* it doing there, Langdon? Now I think of it, it does seem peculiar, even in a picture. Elizabeth was making so much noise I didn't stop to think of it; but now I've got my mind clear, I would like to know. What kind of a basket, and whose umbilical——"

I explained; he gave me a strange look, and suddenly burst into a roar of laughter. "Oh, a papoose's! Yes, I see; I see! That's what she had herself all vapored up over, was it? By God, what a life a husband leads! Well, anyhow, you aint her husband, thank your lucky stars; and you can keep away from her, which is something in my fix you couldn't. Of course, she didn't tell Ann what it was. Young females aint supposed to ever had 'em. 'My God,' I told Elizabeth, 'if a young female's going out to Michilimackinac, living among Indians and traders, she's liable to hear what a bateau-man says sometimes when he's swimming ashore after his boat capsizes, aint she? Why, my God, Elizabeth,' I told her, 'pictures of cords and such things wouldn't seem much of a peccadillo.' She wouldn't let me say 'umbilical' again after the first time—put her hands over her ears and squealed when I tried to—anyway, you better stay away from her a while, Langdon."

I agreed, said I'd stay as much away from Elizabeth as I possibly could, and I meant it. It wasn't pleasant to be put in position of not being a proper companion for a young female, especially when that was Ann. It seemed to me that I was beginning not to like Elizabeth a great deal.

The next morning, as I sat on the grass outside the door of our quarters, arranging my crayons and watching for Mc-Nott's red head to appear from the entrance to the fort, Ann burst from the house as if shot from a gun, stopped before me with arms extended, and turned slowly to let me see her. Her hair hung in two thick braids on either side of her face. Around her forehead was tied a red cord, such as Ottawa women use for binding their hair. The saffron-yellow doe-skin jerkin sent to her by Kab-bes-kunk's wife reached to her knees, and beneath it were soft dark brown moccasins and brown fringed leggins. The jerkin was painted, front and back, with small brown likenesses of the beaver, because Kab-bes-kunk belonged to the Beaver clan of the Ottawa nation.

I stared at her. She seemed to have grown overnight—to be taller, softer, rounder. It was the effect, I suppose, of the straight jerkin and the soft colors.

"Do you like it?" she asked anxiously. "Do you think it's pretty?"

"Yes," I said, not wishing to tell her how much it became her. "It's all right. It needs red beads—red wampum—bright red. I'll try to get some for you."

She hopped with excitement: then somehow seemed to shrink within herself. Her face became heavy and stolid: her body took on the appearance of thickness and weight. Her toes turned in: her legs had a stumpy look. Like a squaw, she might have spent half her life sitting on her feet. Even her skin, imagined, darkened and became dusky. She went stodging around me in a circle, grunting and crooning gibberish, her hands folded across her stomach, her body so erect it almost tilted backward. It was beyond me how she did it, but in a moment's time she had made herself into a superb copy of McNott's squaw.

I snorted and jumped up.

She looked at me with dreadful calm and made a sound like the gobbling of a turkey, then turned and walked from me. There is nothing funnier than the rear view of a chunky squaw in motion, and I did what I had never dared to do within sight or hearing of a genuine squaw—laughed immoderately.

When Ann turned, her gaze went beyond me, toward the house, and as I saw the change in her expression, I wheeled. In the doorway stood Elizabeth in a lace cap, a short dressing jacket and a striped skirt. Her nose seemed longer, her face paler, her lips thinner than I had ever seen them.

"Ann!" she called icily. "Come in this moment and put on your clothes!"

Ann looked helpless and hopeless. "I thought," she stammered, "I hoped——" Words seemed to fail her; and worse than that, her vitality seemed to vanish. "Can't I—can't I go with him today?"

"Come in at once," Elizabeth said.

I put myself in the wrong. Like a fool I made an appeal that recognized Elizabeth's complete authority over Ann. "Elizabeth," I said, "there's not the least harm in it! Why not let her go with me? Kab-bes-kunk and his family will be mighty pleased if Ann wears this Ottawa dress when she goes to thank them for it. All the Indians will be pleased. It'll help me, and it might even help the Major."

Elizabeth still stood in the doorway, at some distance from us, but it seemed to me I saw a cold enmity in her eyes. "I need Ann," she said primly. "Even if I didn't, I shouldn't think of letting her go. She must come in and rid herself of this unseemliness instantly."

"Unseemliness?" I said. "What——"

"Those—those garments," Elizabeth explained sharply. "If your mother hasn't brought you up to know that limbs shouldn't be visible, it's time someone told you, Langdon Towne! You're not being a very good influence, I'm afraid. Ann, did you hear me bid you come in this instant?"

Ann bent her head and walked slowly toward the stern figure in the doorway. I picked up my portfolio and case of crayons and went out to the entrance of the fort to meet McNott, whispering to myself things about Elizabeth Browne that I'd have shot a man for a few years earlier.

CHAPTER LXII

W E HAD been in Oswego a week when Pontiac himself arrived, accompanied by his most influential chieftains; and from that moment Rogers almost seemed not to have a home. It was Rogers for whom Pontiac first asked; Rogers to whom he came and for whom he daily sent. Morning after morning Rogers would leave his house before sun-up; and seldom did he return before midnight. I found myself wondering what on earth he and Pontiac could be talking about for as much, sometimes, as fourteen hours a day; and I saw that all the commissaries assembled at the fort were made restless by the intimacy between the two. They seemed to think Pontiac should pay no attention to any white man but Sir William Johnson. It struck me that all of Sir William's friends felt—and I suspected they had caught the feeling from Sir William himself—that all Indians were Sir William's personal property, not to be approached by anyone else.

As for Elizabeth, she expressed her objections with vehemence. I was surreptitiously doing a picture of Ann in her Indian dress early one morning when, through an open window, I heard Elizabeth speaking shrilly: "It was two o'clock this morning when you got back, and here you are going away before six again, without breakfast and never a word to me! I wont see you again until after midnight; and if I should want to reach you, I'd have no idea where you were! I might as well not be married! I sit here all alone, day after day, without a soul to talk to but a young female that never speaks, while you're away doing Heaven knows what, and carrying on with Heaven knows who! All you ever say is Pontiac, Pontiac, Pontiac! I declare, I'm sick and tired of that nasty red Indian, and if you cared two snaps about me, you'd spend some of your time at home instead of across the river in those filthy, smoky places! Why don't you let Captain Fuller tend to the dirty old thing, or Lieutenant Roberts? Why don't you send a messenger to Sir William Johnson and tell him to come here and get his Congress over with? It's his Congress, isn't it? Why doesn't he tend to it himself, instead of making you do it? Why do you let him make you? My Heavens, aren't you a man?"

Rogers burst from the house, coat unbuttoned, belt in his hand and hat on the side of his head. He sighed explosively, wiped his forehead on his sleeve and slowly put himself in order. He beckoned to me. "I'm having an all-day conference with Pontiac and eight chiefs. I'll have McNott to translate, and Pontiac'll throw a guard around the conference, to prevent outsiders from breaking in on it. It'll be the chance of a lifetime to sketch Pontiac, so you'd better come along too."

I took the uncompleted sketch of Ann from the light drawing board I was using. "Ann," I said, "I've got to go. You keep this sketch and we'll finish it in a few days."

She nodded and went down on her knees beside my crayon box. "There's only one crayon holder here," she said, "and only two sticks of yellow. Didn't you say those red buzzards aren't happy unless they cover themselves with yellow?"

I raced into the house and upstairs for more yellow and more crayon holders. When I came down and set off with Rogers, Ann held to my arm and went with us toward the river.

Behind us I heard Elizabeth's voice, a piercing sing-song, making two syllables out of Ann's name—"A-yan! A-yan!"

Ann's hand slipped down my sleeve and clung for a moment to my fingers.

"A-yan!" Elizabeth called. "Breakfast, A-yan!"

Ann turned and went doggedly toward the house; and as

we walked on in the other direction, Rogers glanced back at her over his shoulder. "She's getting to be quite a girl. How old is she?"

I said she must be almost sixteen now.

Rogers whistled, and the pouches under his eyes looked enormous. "Probably takes after her mother. I guess Natty let go of a pretty nice bale of goods when he let her slip."

"What's become of Potter?" I asked. "Seems as if I only saw him about once a week."

"Damn it," Rogers said, "he spends all his time with Lieutenant Roberts. Roberts gives him free rum." He wagged his head. "Langdon, the wisest thing I ever did was to keep my mouth shut to everyone except you about the Northwest Passage! Naturally I told you because it was you told me about Dobbs's book. If Natty knew, he'd tell Roberts when they're drunk together, and Roberts would tell Johnson, and wouldn't that blow us and the whole great plan out of water? It would, my boy; it would!"

That day I saw at least one reason why the Major spent such interminable stretches of time with Pontiac; for when we were all gathered on a small island three miles from Oswego, Pontiac and his eight chiefs seemed only to be interested in sucking at their red stone pipes, staring silently at nothing, and expressionlessly watching me as I sat sketching them. Pontiac, at first, objected to being sketched in everyday apparel. He even doubted the wisdom of being sketched at all, having heard from someone that if his likeness were thus put on paper, it would be possible for the owner of the likeness to do him a mischief by sticking pins into the portrait, or shooting a bullet through it; but he changed his mind when Rogers stood for a small and hasty sketch which he presented to his red friend. "Tell him," Rogers said to McNott, "that he can stick a fish-spear in that, for all I care!"

Pontiac eyed the sketch, front, back and edgewise: then placed it in his medicine bag and offered to send for his headdress of white eagle feathers and his embroidered buckskins. When I smiled and said No, he sat stiffly on his blanket, his eyes fixed and staring. The Major produced a bottle of rum and a rope of tobacco, and made small talk while Pontiac and

his eight attendant chieftains sampled the rum, smoked the
tobacco, but remined haughty and silent.

There was something imposing about Pontiac. He caught
and held the eye. In every way he confirmed what Rogers
had told me and had written in his *Concise Account of North
America,* as well as in his play.

Rogers spoke of him as the greatest Indian that ever lived;
and the Major often insisted that if Pontiac, in addition to
his singular ability to unite Indian nations, had also been
ruthless in punishing infractions of discipline, he would have
been successful in his war on the English, and might have
reigned for years as the red emperor of the West. Certainly
no other red man had ever had the knowledge or the power to
hold together and control such alien and antagonistic peoples
as the Ottawas, Chippeways, Wyandots, Miamis, Potawatomies, Mississaugaus, Shawanese, Saukies, Outagamies and
Winnebagoes; and equally certainly no other Indian had
ever had the brains and foresight to plan such a campaign as
Pontiac planned in 1763—a campaign that in fifteen days'
time took the British posts at Venango, Presque Isle, Le
Boeuf, St. Joseph, Miami, Ouachtanon on the Wabash, San-
dusky and Michilimackinac, and that would probably have
taken Detroit if Rogers himself had not been at that post to
repulse the attack. In addition to planning his campaign, he
organized a commissary department, made and issued bills
of credit which were subsequently faithfully redeemed, and
impressed upon the united nations the urgent necessity of
dispensing with European commodities, and of depending
for clothes, food and livelihood entirely upon their own endeavors. He was a wise Indian—wiser than most white statesmen, and vastly more honest.

Today as I listened and drew, I learned that Rogers had
sought this conference with Pontiac and his chiefs to obtain
information he couldn't have had at an ordinary meeting of
Indians. Ordinary Indian meetings are open to any Indian
who cares to attend them; for an Indian is his own master,
goes where he wishes, and bitterly resents the slightest interference with his liberty. If he wants to enter a stranger's
house, he enters it, and no other Indian thinks of refusing
him. Consequently Rogers, up to now, had held no private
conferences with Pontiac, for there had so far been no such
thing as privacy. This meeting on an island, guarded from

intruders by twenty Indian sentries on the lake shore, was only possible because of the awe and respect with which Pontiac was regarded.

What Rogers wanted was Pontiac's opinion of Sir William Johnson's persistent determination to stop traders from going among the Indian nations to trade; to permit them to do their trading only at British posts; to force all Indians to come in person to British forts in order to exchange furs for guns, powder, shot, knives, beads, kettles and other traders' goods.

"You've got to make it plain to 'em," Rogers told McNott, "that if Sir William Johnson insists on doing things this way, then it's the best way. They can't go contrary to the wishes of Sir William Johnson. If they don't want him to be angry with 'em, they'll have to do what he says, damn it! Tell 'em I want to be their friend, and so I've got to know their thoughts. Tell 'em to tell me the truth; it wont hurt 'em. Pontiac knows I fought against him four years ago; but he knows, too, that men can fight against each other and afterwards be all the better friends. Tell him I've spoken good words for him in England; tell him I wrote good big words about him in a book, telling everybody he's a great man and a friend of mine. He knows I'm going to Michilimackinac, to be the Governor. Tell him I've got to do the best I can for the King and the Indians too, so that's why I want to know what he and his friends are thinking about."

When McNott had translated, Pontiac studied the faces of his eight chiefs, and the chiefs, in turn, rolled dull eyes at him. There was a long silence, and then he began to speak, tapping a knee with a long forefinger to emphasize his words. I had him then as I wanted him, scarlet cloth leggins, silver arm bands, eagle-claw necklace, shaved head and scarlet scalp-lock to which three white feathers were bound with scarlet thread.

"We understand the words our brother has spoken," Pontiac said; and McNott's strained expression showed how hard he strove to translate the Indian's words. "We're here to make friends with the English, and we'll listen gratefully to what Sir William Johnson tells us. We'll accept what he has decided, for we've heard he's unhappy when his decisions are questioned. Therefore we wont question them. Perhaps some'll be benefited by his decision to have Indians come to the forts to trade. Perhaps it'll make goods cheaper. We'll wait and see."

Pontiac looked thoughtfully at Rogers. "Here at Oswego nobody'll be harmed. All the Indians who trade here—Sir William Johnson's friends the Mohawks—live within two days' journey of the fort. So it's an advantage to everyone to have the trading done at Oswego. The same thing's true at Niagara and Detroit, for the Indians who trade there live close to those forts. So if it pleases Sir William Johnson to say that all those Indians must go to forts to trade, no harm will have been done. The Indians I have mentioned will be satisfied, and there will be little difference from the old days."

He hitched himself forward on his blanket and spoke more earnestly. "But Michilimackinac, Brother, is different from all the other posts! We question that the mind of Sir William Johnson is wise when he says he wants Michilimackinac treated like all the rest."

"Yes, I understand," Rogers said to McNott, "but anyhow, ask him why. I want to hear what he says."

McNott put the question; and Pontiac brooded a moment; then picked up three flat rocks, and placed them on the ground with their ends touching a common center. At the center he thrust a twig, tapped his finger against it and said "Michilimackinac." Then he tapped the rocks, calling them by name—"Lake Huron; Lake Michigan; Lake Superior." Scooping up a handful of pebbles, he tossed them one by one beyond the twig; and as each one left his hand, he gave it the name of an Indian tribe or nation—Lake La Pluye, Winnipeek, Killistinoe, Assinipoil, Kamanistiqua, Nipigon, La Pointe, de l'Anie, Au Sault Ste. Marie, Michipicoten, Fon du Lac, Saguenay, Ottawa, Gens des Gros Isles, Millewashee, Folle Avoines of the Lake, Puans of the River Roche, Winnebagoes, Saukies and Outagamies of Ouisconsin.

The pebbles began to fall far, far beyond the twig. "Mandans," Pontiac said. "Pawnees. Shiennes. Konzas. Puncahs. Crows. Blackfeet. Sioux." When he said "Sioux," he scattered the remaining pebbles in a wide semi-circle beyond all the others.

Pontiac's eight chiefs turned triumphant faces toward Rogers and made explosive sounds, as if their stomachs were disordered.

"My brother asks for my thoughts," Pontiac said, "and my

thoughts are these: Michilimackinac has nothing in common with any other British post. In importance it's like the sun compared with the blaze of a pine knot. It's the outermost fort, from which the soldiers of the Great King look out on a vast territory of which they know nothing. In that territory, many days, many weeks, many months travel to the westward, are all the tribes I have named, as well as many others. What'll happen, Brother, if English traders are forbidden to travel to those tribes and live among them?"

Rogers just sat there, waiting for Pontiac to answer his own question.

Pontiac smiled. "My brother could answer if he would. If no traders go beyond Michilimackinac, thousands of the Indians I've named will be unable to come to Michilimackinac to trade. They don't have enough conveyances for bringing their furs to the eastward. Many, if they came East, would have to leave their wives and children for half a year and more. During that time their families might starve: those they left behind would be liable every day and hour to be killed or enslaved by neighboring tribes. It's impossible! The Indians of the West can't come to Michilimackinac to trade."

The other chiefs raised their shoulders, so to have greater freedom in the emission of loud guttural sounds of approval —"Oah! Oah! Oah!"

"They can't come," Pontiac repeated, "they can't come; and at the same time they can't get along without traders' goods. Since they're poor, they can't afford many utensils; so an entire family may, by one accident, lose its winter's hunting unless it can mend the accident. Not much of an accident is necessary. It's fatal to break a gun lock if there's no trader nearby with a stock of gun locks. It's fatal to lose a hatchet, or three knives. If a canoe overturns and one small package of powder is spoiled, that's the end of the year's hunting unless a trader's within reach. One family can't travel for three months, in winter, to reach Michilimackinac and replace a gun lock: to buy another package of powder. Not even Indians could make such a journey in winter. To expect them to do so is foolish. The whole thing, Brother, is foolish. It's worse than foolish. It's thoughtless; it's cruel; it'll cause untold trouble.

"There's only one answer, Brother. If English traders aren't allowed to travel westward from Michilimackinac, then the tribes'll invite French traders and Spanish traders to winter in their towns. My brother knows that the friendship of Indian tribes is given, usually, to the King of that country whose traders live among the tribes. If English traders aren't allowed to pass beyond Michilimackinac, the English King will lose the trade of the Western tribes. He'll lose their furs. The tribes will trade with the French and the Spaniards beyond the Mississippi. As they trade with them, their attachment to the French and the Spaniards will become stronger and stronger, and in the end they'll become dangerous enemies of the Great King in England."

Pontiac took up his red stone pipe and filled it. "What does my brother think?" he asked Rogers. "Does he believe I tell the truth, or does he consider my words foolish? If they're foolish, then all of us"—he waved his pipe-stem toward his chiefs—"are foolish."

"What I believe is of no account," Rogers said. "Pontiac's a great chief, and understands that he's here to talk with Sir William Johnson, and that at the proper time Sir William will come here and explain everything. What I want is information; and here's something else I want to know. If traders or travellers go to the westward this year, will they have trouble? Is there talk of wars or war parties?"

The strain of translating was weighing heavily on McNott. He mopped his face with a red handkerchief and said weakly, "He wants to know what you've heard."

"I've heard the Chippeways and the Sioux are planning a great war," Rogers said, "one that'll put an end to war between 'em."

Pontiac smiled. "My brother heard correctly. They say it's foolish to fight again and again, year after year, without accomplishing anything. The sensible way to fight, they now believe, is to fight until everyone is killed on one side. There's something in what they say; but if the Sioux and the Chippeways fight that sort of war, others'll have to fight to prevent the winner from becoming too strong, and within a short time all the nations will be fighting, because Indians are no different from white men when they make war. They attack traders for no particular reason, and they always have an excuse for stealing anything they happen to want, or for forgetting any promises they may have made to anyone at any time."

At a sign from Rogers, McNott produced a second bottle of rum. Pontiac marked off a portion with his thumbnail, drank his exact portion, and passed the bottle to Rogers. It made an entrancing picture—nine Indians with their eyes glued to the bottle at Rogers' lips.

He passed the bottle to the waiting chiefs and turned again to Pontiac. "My friend, no Sioux have ever come as far east as Michilimackinac, either for a Council or anything else. If messengers and belts were sent to the Sioux this year, asking them to come to Michilimackinac next summer to discuss peace, would they stop their talk of war? Would they come to a Council so far from their homes?"

Pontiac cogitated. His chiefs communed among themselves. In order to think more freely, they lay on their stomachs, or reclined on their backs with legs crossed, or clasped their knees and rested their foreheads against them. They muttered, argued, drew maps with their forefingers, and at length reached an agreement.

"We believe," Pontiac told Rogers, "that the Sioux would come. They'd feel it an honor to come to Michilimackinac and hold a Council with our brother; and there's no doubt that if they did so they'd wait until after the Council before they made war on the Chippeways. We Indians are like white men, Brother. We don't like to take the blame of starting a war; and we always say that we don't want to fight, and wouldn't unless we had to. For that reason we believe that even the Sioux will agree to talk about peace, though they'll probably start fighting as soon as they've stopped talking. The same thing's true of the Chippeways and the other nations. They'll all come a long way to talk about peace, especially if their chiefs know they'll get a few presents from our brother. If our brother can persuade them to be peaceful, it'll be a great thing, for all the tribes can hunt every day and all day, and all the nations will have twice as many furs to exchange. Thus it'll be good for everybody—good for the Indians; good for the traders; good for the Great Father in England."

Rogers looked noncommittal and then suddenly it dawned upon me what he was driving at. If an exploring party went from Michilimackinac to seek the Northwest Passage, and all those far-off tribes of the Sioux, which stood like an enormous semi-circular barricade between the East and the

West, were at war with the Chippeways, not one of us would ever pass the barricade. Our scalps, in all probability, would dangle from poles in the towns of the Sioux, in no way different from those six hundred scalps we had seen moving idly in the dawn breeze before the houses of St. Francis.

CHAPTER LXIII

Not until the 20th day of July, three days before the day set for the Congress, did Sir William Johnson arrive at Oswego. His coming was surrounded with all the pomp and circumstance that might have accompanied the visit of a king. With him were a score of Mohawk chiefs, all tricked out in wampum and feathers, and the braves who paddled them were so bedaubed with colors that they must have spent days painting themselves. As for Johnson, sitting magnificently in the largest canoe, he was a glittering mass of scarlet cloth, gold lace, brass buttons, twinkling buckles, shining leather. Over his shoulders was draped a scarlet ceremonial blanket bordered with gold. When his canoes first came in sight, far upstream, the Indians with him had announced themselves by a continuous firing of muskets, which was immediately answered by a thunderous salute from the fort. Thus the flotilla, majestically approaching the landing-stage, was greeted by every officer, every trader, every Indian in Oswego, all packed together on the river bank.

It may be I was unduly prejudiced against Sir William Johnson, but from the moment I saw him, I disliked him. I disliked his pale, fattish, dimpled face; his fishy blue eye which seemed to me to sparkle only at the mishaps of others; his rasping, unresonant voice; his evident satisfaction with his appearance and position; his vast importance and pomposity. I suspect Tobias Smollett may have been uncomfortably close to the mark when he declared, in his

Adventures of an Atom, that Johnson's high position was owing to nothing more noteworthy than accidentally repulsing a body of the enemy and reducing an old barn which they had fortified.

McNott stood with Ann and me at the edge of the crowd along the river, watching the baronet's gaudy arrival; and the mind of the one-time sergeant of Rangers seemed to be troubled.

"Look at him!" he said, alluding to the great man. "He got a tribe with *his* woman, too; dotes on 'em. Me, if I ever get the chance, damned if I wont up and walk out on that red princess of mine and go back east to Dunbarton, where a feller can marry a woman without having fifty of her relatives come in and use his shaving brush every time they feel like having a mouthful of soap."

"If you want to leave her," I said, "why don't you leave her?"

McNott made a snarling sound. "That's all right for you to say! You aint a trader with a stock of merchandise. Suppose I've trusted two hundred and eight Indians with thirty bales of goods. They go off to their hunting grounds with what they've got from me; and next spring, if I'm lucky, they'll bring back the furs to pay their debt. Well, damn it, you don't think I can sneak away from Princess McNott any time I feel like it, do you? I can't go till I get those furs! By the time I get the furs, I want more money and decide to stay another season. So it goes; so it goes."

"She can't be so very bad," Ann said. "Anyhow, you'd rather have her and the furs than neither?"

"How's that?" he said. "I don't figure that out. Says you, I'd rather have her and the furs than either?"

"Neither," Ann said. "Why couldn't you go away and not wait for the furs, and have her bring them to you?"

"Have her bring 'em to me!" McNott shouted. "Then she'd be there, wouldn't she? You're like everybody else: always telling a man what to do, and if he'd take your advice, he'd be worse off than ever. Besides, look at my wooden leg."

"What's that to do with it, Sergeant?" I asked.

"She steals it!" McNott said angrily. "Every time she thinks I'm going to leave her, she steals it! Does it do any good, me setting on the ground for hours, yelling for her to bring it back? No, it don't! She's got second sight: knows the difference between getting drunk for business and getting drunk for pleasure. I aint got drunk for pleasure twice in the last three years that I aint woke up with my leg gone! Even if I get drunk for pleasure when we're travelling in a canoe, it's always the same—always the same! Wake up and find her setting in the other end with my leg in her lap and a rock tied to it; and if I don't do everything she says, she motions to throw it overboard! By God, I been in more embarrassing situations on account of her and my leg than any man was ever put into by a woman since Potiphar's wife, old Jezebel!" He paused, looked at the brilliant spectacle upon the landing-stage, and concluded bitterly, "Look at him! All puffed up and happy. To look at him, you'd think there wasn't no drawbacks to Indians!"

Johnson had stepped ashore from his canoe, and stood among the officers from the fort, head thrown back, one hand resting on his hip—a proud, imperious figure. Rogers, in his unpretentious Ranger's uniform of green coat and wrinkled greenish buckskin, stood out among the brilliant scarlet jackets like an eagle among a flock of gulls. Sir William hastily shook hands with him; then ostentatiously turned to his favorite commissaries, Colonel Cole and Lieutenant Roberts. I set up my drawing board, and Ann held the crayons ready.

"You aint going to make a picture of that old sulphurbelly, are you?" McNott asked.

"Yes," I said. "I am. That was a pretty cool thing he just did to Rogers. I want to get his face while it's still fresh in my mind."

McNott grunted, and, while I sketched, reverted to his former topic. " 'Course, that woman of mine aint *all* hellion. She aint a bad cook, and she makes maple sugar without dropping hair and leaves in it, which is something the rest of 'em can't do. I guess I got her broke of washing her hands in the drinking water, even. She's got pretty good jaws, too, and if you're in a hurry for some buckskin, she'll chew a hide as much as three days running, so to soften it up. She can split more firewood than any squaw I know, and paddle a canoe mighty well. I figure on winning a real nice mess of furs next spring if I can coax some of those Western squaws into a race with her. And by God, you can say what you want to, but she's got a real smart knack of picking up news. Yes, sir, she's an awful exasperating woman in some ways; but I'll say that much for her: she finds out things; and when she finds out she tells me. Hell, if Pontiac wants to find out why Sulphur-belly aint going to let traders go to the westward to winter with Indians, he'd oughta ask my woman! She knew two months ago!"

He looked over my shoulder at my sketch. "That's it, by God! You're getting him! Rolling his eyes like a fat boy afraid somebody's going to take a piece of pie away from him!"

"You don't really think Johnson made the rule about Michilimackinac just on account of Rogers!" I exclaimed.

" 'Course he did!" McNott growled. " 'Course he did! Don't you s'pose he knows every Indian in North America is more afraid of Rogers than of any man alive? Don't you s'pose he knows he's got to get Rogers out of the way before he can do what he wants to do?"

I turned on him. "Why don't you tell these things to Rogers? Why do you keep them to yourself: then spill them out piecemeal?"

McNott looked contemptuous. "I don't tell Rogers for the same reason you wouldn't be likely to tell him. If I told him everything my woman told me, he'd up and have a fight with Johnson and wouldn't last five minutes. Johnson's mean! If he don't like a feller, he can think up more tricks to get him in trouble than you could think up in your whole life! Yes, and he's got Gage on his side. Do you ever hear of anyone in uniform winning an argument with a Commander in Chief?"

"What do you think Johnson wants?" I asked.

McNott's reply was prompt and violent. "He's after what all these big fellers are after! Land! They're all after land! Funny thing about rich men: the more land they have, the more they want. There aint no satisfying 'em. You'd think Johnson had enough land on the Mohawk to keep him busy all the rest of his life—and so he has, because he aint going to live much longer. He's burnt himself out with his squaws, and he aint healthy. All the land he really needs is a piece six feet long by two wide; but he's like all the rest of 'em: he wants all he can get—all there is—land he'll probably never see—land that'll probably never give him anything but grief."

McNott lowered his voice to a whisper. "You know what

that old rascal figures on doing? He figures on forming a land company with Ben Franklin's son—the one that's Governor of New Jersey—and General Gage and Sir Henry Moore, Governor of New York, and grabbing pretty near all the land between Detroit and the Mississippi River. Yes, sir: all that old feller wants is the whole damned Ohio Valley —about a hundred million acres of land! We used to think Benning Wentworth had some pretty tall ideas when he grabbed a hundred thousand acres; but Benning Wentworth's just a little country boy compared with Sir William Johnson! A hundred million acres he's after; and there aint one soul in North America for him to worry about except Rogers! If he sets out to get a hundred million acres of land, don't you s'pose the Indians'll come running to Rogers to find out what he thinks about it? Don't you s'pose Rogers'll make trouble for Johnson?"

"How'll he make trouble?" I asked.

"How the hell do I know?" McNott cried. "But you can bet he wont stand around with his mouth shut while Johnson hogs half of North America! He'll talk about it, and he'll be listened to in England."

It seemed to me that McNott was vaporizing. His figures were fantastic, and he was speaking great names, assuming that their owners wouldn't scruple to steal an empire. Then, suddenly, I was not so sure. I remembered Clive: the delighted clamor with which the English had commended what they called his moderation when he seized the richest part of India for the East India Company and returned to England with a personal fortune of £300,000. Great adventurers sometimes had great avarice.

"Well," I said, "I hope you're wrong."

"Gosh, Langdon! So do I! If I aint, every one of us that sticks to Rogers will probably get into trouble, one way or another. You and me and his wife—even this little girl here —we'll all have to pay for getting in Johnson's way, most likely. If she was my girl, I'd send her back to Portsmouth tomorrow."

Ann's eyes flashed. "I'm old enough to take care of myself," she told McNott. "If you aren't even able to stop your own wife from stealing your own leg, you aren't competent to tell everybody what ought to be done with everybody else."

McNott eyed her almost respectfully and in a perfunctory

voice said, "Thank God I aint got no half-growed daughters!"
Again he studied my sketch of Johnson. "That's more and
more him," he admitted. "I can almost hear his knees creak
and his insides gurgle. We ought to get a hint, in a day or
two, of how he figures on knocking Rogers' feet out from
under him!"

In this, unfortunately, he was wrong: for Johnson, like a
Mohawk, bided his time so patiently that it was a wonder
any of us escaped the ambush he laid.

With each passing day of the Congress Johnson's jealousy
of Rogers had become more and more apparent. When the
chiefs sought Rogers out, as they often did, Johnson quickly
sent an officer to be near him. Johnson's eye was perpetually
on him. The Major was kept busy, attending to unimportant
details that could have been performed by any enlisted man.

Elizabeth was in a rage. "It's too humiliating!" I heard
her say to Rogers when he returned to the sitting room of our
quarters the second night of the Congress. "He treats you
like a servant! Why don't you stand up for your rights? Why
don't you refuse to do all these nasty little things he makes
you do?"

Rogers looked apprehensive. "For God's sake," he whispered, "speak more quietly! Where's Natty?"

"He's drunk!" she said. "He came in hardly able to stand,
and went reeling out again to join his friend Lieutenant Roberts. He'll go across the river, and wont be back tonight! Oh,
it's disgusting!"

Rogers shook his head at her and nodded warningly toward Ann, who sat quietly beside me, reading her *Gulliver's
Travels.*

"Pah!" Elizabeth said. "You needn't worry about Ann! She
got in his way when he came in, and he slapped her face!"

Rogers grinned at all of us, then explained patiently to
Elizabeth: "Johnson's my superior officer. Whatever a superior officer asks you to do, you do. If you don't you're insubordinate, and that means courtmartial. Don't worry; when
we get off for Michilimackinac, *I'll* be giving the orders."

That was his answer to everything: "We'll be all right as
soon as we start for Michilimackinac."

I almost came to think of Michilimackinac as I had
thought of Heaven in my boyhood—a sunny place, full of

fleecy clouds, with angels in blue nightgowns sitting on
them and strumming five-stringed harps.

The thing that seemed to make the Major most cheerful was
a talk he had with Colonel Cole, the new commissary ap-
pointed by Johnson to Fort Chartres on the Mississippi.

"I asked Cole," he told me exultantly, "how he expected to
make out with the Indians if he couldn't make presents to
'em. Hell, I never expected an honest answer from him; but
he admitted right away it couldn't be done. No use talking
to Johnson about it, though, he said: nothing to do but give
'em presents when the time comes, and hope to God Johnson'll
see the light in the meantime. Oh, we'll be all right as soon as
we start for Michilimackinac!"

For eight days Pontiac and his chiefs puffed at the sacred
pipe of peace and exchanged compliments with Johnson. Then
came the last great day of the conference. On the parade-
ground, before the fort, Sir William had the soldiers build
a long open pavilion roofed with spruce branches to protect it
from the sun and weather. In this pavilion, after a morning
of feasting and drinking, he took his stand, a dominant,
magnificent figure that inconsistently reminded me of Ajax
defying the lightning. Over his shoulders, in spite of the humid
heat waves in which the trees and the lake shore seemed
to vibrate as in a swiftly-flowing current, was draped his
scarlet ceremonial blanket, edged with gold lace. It made
me sweat to look at him.

Around him stood all the officers who had assembled at
the fort, a brilliant company in scarlet and gold. Before
him were the Western chiefs, Pontiac at their head; and
behind the chiefs was all the brilliant great mass of Chippeways, Ottawas, Hurons and Potawatomies. Flat in the grass,
on either side of the pavilion, like things half-snake, half-
human, lay Sir William's Mohawks, who had come with him
for the sole purpose of satisfying themselves that they were
still first in Sir William's affections. The Congress had nothing to do with them; but their jealousy wouldn't let them
stay away. It was a Mohawk trait, McNott said; and since
Johnson had become almost a Mohawk in his private habits
and manner of thought, it helped to account for his own
jealousies.

The speech-making began, Johnson and Pontiac being the

orators. Johnson, wearing an air of noble condescension and seeming about to confer enormous favors on everybody, spoke first. He was verbosely flowery; but put into plain language, what he said was of a simple-enough hypocrisy. The Indians must love the King, their Great Father, who watched over them and gave them rich presents; and, obviously, they must love Sir William Johnson, too, who did the Great Father's watching for him and handed out the presents.

Johnson talked for almost an hour, saying this in fifteen or sixteen different ways. Then Pontiac arose and in a grand, sonorous voice, and in about seven or eight ways, said that he and his people were grateful to the Great Father and Sir William Johnson for the presents, and also—though with less enthusiasm—for being watched over. The Congress had accomplished great good, he added, and he and his people would value the presents highly. He and his people revered the Great Father and Sir William Johnson; and as soon as the presents were handed around, they would begin being grateful forever to Sir William Johnson and also the Great Father.

Then the presents were passed around. All the chiefs received a silver medal inscribed "a pledge of peace and friendship with Great Britain." The medal, McNott whispered to me during the ceremony of distribution, wasn't silver at all, but tin and pewter, with a light coating of silver. The other presents which Johnson gave the chiefs, however, were real enough—ear-bobs, brooches, looking-glasses, strouding, blankets, trousers, muskets, powder, shot, vermilion, fish-hooks and rum.

Half an hour after the presents were distributed, Pontiac and all his warriors had set their canoes in the river, and were streaming out onto the lake and away to the westward, howling Indian songs as harmonious as the scraping of files on metal.

McNott shook his head as we watched them go. "Look at 'em!" he said. "Every canoe so loaded down with gifts that it'll ship water if anyone leans over to spit! Who gave 'em to 'em? Why, open-hearted Big Bill Johnson, because he knows if he didn't, there'd be Indian hell all up and down and round about. Who is it says the Governor of Michilimack-inac must rule thousands of Indians but not make any presents? Why, nobody but this same Big Bill Johnson! I wish him and his Great White Father too had to kiss my wife after she'd been eating ripe whitefish!"

Early next morning we set off by sloop for Michilimackinac. McNott accompanied us, and so did the lady now known to us as the Princess McNott; though to a stranger the princess would have seemed to be wedded to McNott's canoe and its load of goods, rather than to McNott. At night, embracing the goods, she slept beneath the overturned canoe. During the day she sat close beside the goods and the canoe, staring into space.

When Ann worried about her, saying that she looked unhappy, McNott reassured her. "Listen," he said, "you never saw a cheerful-looking horse, did you? All the horses you ever saw had a kind of gloomy look, and I bet you never worried none about 'em. Well, this woman of mine, she's like a horse. She aint unhappy. What would she be unhappy about? She had plenty to eat last night: she'll have plenty to eat tonight: she's got all the clothes she can wear. Hell, she knows when she's well off!"

A sloop carried us over Lake Ontario to the Niagara River, where carts from Fort Niagara hauled our belongings around the falls and to the *Gladwyn* schooner on the upper river. The *Gladwyn* took us the full length of Lake Erie to Detroit, across Lake St. Clair, up the broad St. Clair River into Lake Huron: then sailed northward toward the Straits of Michilimackinac. In the brilliant golden sunlight of an August noon, the approach to those straits was a pleasant one. To our left was the broad opening of the waterway connecting Huron and Michigan: to the right were the high white sides of Mackinac Island, cleanly cut against the sky in the clear air and pure light of the Northern summer; and all around the horizon, beyond the straits and beyond Mackinac Island, was an endless blue rampart behind which, almost within reach at last, lay the winding channels to Lake Superior, to the Indians of the West, to the great River Oregon, to the Northwest Passage.

When we turned into the straits, the fort and the settlement of Michilimackinac unrolled before us on the left bank; and so dwarfed were they by the long, low stretch of dunes among which they nestled that they might have been, as

Ann whispered to me, a fort and settlement on the coast of Lilliput. There was nothing about the place, as we saw it from the sloop—nothing—to bear out the glowing description Rogers had given us two months before in the Brownes' back parlor.

The fort was little more than a stockaded yard, close to the water's edge. Outside the stockade were groups of long barns that I took to be traders' storehouses. At a considerable distance from the stockade a ring of small white dwellings surrounded a patch of farm land. Still farther away were three straggling Indian encampments. Even to me, who expected to see little of it, the place looked depressing. I looked at Elizabeth; she stood rigid, staring unbelievingly at the shore.

The Major, however, seemed as merry as Punchinello; he slapped his hands together and laughed explosively when a jet of smoke gushed from the stockade walls and the thump of a cannon came flatly to us across the water.

The report of the heavy gun seemed to release a spring in that distant toy settlement, for little figures moved like ants within the stockade and at the water's edge. What I had taken for rocks on the shore moved and fell apart. They were canoes and bateaux, and they came slipping out toward us like a shoal of frightened water bugs escaping from a quiet resting place. As they drew closer, we saw they were full of traders, of French voyageurs, of Indians of various tribes. They circled around us, firing muskets and shouting a tumultuous welcome. Then they closed in on the vessel to fasten like leeches against her side. Continuing to ply their oars and paddles, they hustled the sloop to the wharf, which extended outward from the fort's water-gate.

The closer we came to the place, the more populous it appeared. All the canoes in the world seemed concentrated on the shore, overturned and stacked in rows. Two companies of red-coated soldiers marched smartly from the fort, drums thumping, and lined up abreast of the wharf. People appeared in surprising numbers to see us land, but where they came from, unless they had popped up out of the ground, it was hard to see.

When the sloop was fast, Rogers jumped to the wharf to shake hands with the two young officers who commanded the two companies of soldiers. At sight of that careless figure in green coat and buckskins, the whole assemblage burst into cheers and howls of welcome. Rogers smiled and flirted his hand at them, made a hurried inspection of the two companies by walking quickly along the front of the lines, spoke pleasantly to the men, and told the lieutenants to dismiss them. With that the scores of traders, who had been waiting, went for him pell-mell as if intending to mob him. They crowded around him in a circle, all talking and gesticulating, so that they seemed people out of Bedlam.

"Here, here, gentleman!" Rogers said good-naturedly, "give me a chance! You're holding up my wife."

Their shouts and expostulations grew louder. Those in the rear of the circle, in their eagerness to make themselves heard, jostled those in front against Rogers. From the tumult of shouting came such phrases as, "Been here a month!" "Caught by cold weather!" "Damned outrage!" "Have to feed the voyageurs!"

Rogers seized the most importunate of the traders by the front of his coat and used him as a sort of broom to sweep back the others. "You'll give me a chance to get into the fort and settle myself," he roared jovially, "or I'll push you back with bayonets!"

The traders fell away from him, muttering and staring. Rogers pulled at his little hat with both hands, straightened his coat with an angry shrug of his shoulders. "Lieutenant Christie!" he shouted. "Mr. Johnston!"

The two young officers pushed through the ring of traders.

"Who's your commanding officer?" Rogers demanded. "Why isn't he here? Where is he? Why hasn't he put these traders under control?"

"Captain Spiesmaker, sir," the lieutenant said. "He's delayed in Montreal. We expect him any day. We haven't taken any steps because we haven't had any orders. We don't know what steps to take. We've been waiting for you—or for him."

"You've heard, haven't you," Rogers asked, "that no traders are supposed to go beyond this post this year?"

The lieutenant's reply was lost in the storm of groans and objurgations that rose from the traders.

Rogers laughed. "Well, now, gentlemen, you've got to let us go to the fort, settle ourselves and get some food in us. Give me two hours: then I'll meet all of you and hear what you've got to say for yourselves. If you've got a case, you wont find me unreasonable. I hope to conduct affairs at this post in the best interests of His Majesty's Government."

Signalling to the rest of us, he started for the fort's water-gate. Around the gate-post peered a head with pop-eyes and pouting lips: from behind the gate-post came the heavy, ponderous figure of Jonathan Carver.

"Well, by God!" Rogers cried. "I thought you hadn't got here! Where you been keeping yourself?"

Carver showed his teeth in a grin, and his voice was oily. "I didn't want to intrude. I thought you might have forgotten you told me to report here."

CHAPTER LXIV

THE FORT at Michilimackinac was in itself a small walled town, crude, dusty, dreary. The palisading formed an irregular hexagon, its point pressed close against the straits, and at the point was the fort's water-gate, flanked by rough bastions in which 9-inch guns were mounted. On the opposite side of the stockade was a land-gate connected by a narrow road with the French settlement a mile to the eastward and its nearby Indian towns.

Within the fort a score of buildings were grouped around a parade on which grew drooping weeds and sparse grass, baked to a brown mat by the August sun. In the center of the parade was a well, at whose coping stood Indian women, raising buckets of water on a windlass that screamed piercingly.

The fort seemed designed even more for traders than for soldiers; for the far end, near the land-gate, was rimmed with the barn-like warehouses in which traders store merchandise and furs. The near end, handy to the water-gate through which we had entered, belonged to the officers and soldiers; and most imposing of the military buildings, and likewise near to the water-gate, was the one pointed out to the Major as his. To say that this commandant's house was the most imposing of the Michilimackinac buildings wasn't saying much; for though it was built of timbers, its exterior was as cheerless as the Portsmouth jail which Cap Huff held so lightly, and I was sure it was even less solid.

Beyond the commandant's house, close to the palisade, were two log houses for officers; and across the parade were the barracks for the garrison, another group of officers' cabins and a church built of hewn logs.

All the buildings, unpainted and weatherbeaten, seemed scorched by the heat of summer; warped by the winter's cold and driving snow; and their grouping around that barren parade gave them the look of a wilderness travesty of a college.

Drab as was the commandant's house, and outlandish as was the throng that milled about it, kicking up a dust that sifted through all the small hot rooms to muddy the perspiration on our faces, the Major seemed to see everything through that dust as through a golden haze.

He was in high spirits, grinning complacently at his new quarters, at all the dismal buildings, at the Indian squaws and soldiers' wives who peered curiously at us from behind the groups of traders who waited silently for an audience; and he strode up and down the porch, issuing genial and rapid instructions to Natty Potter and Lieutenant Johnston.

"I want a cook and a body-servant, Lieutenant," I heard him say. "I'll have a soldier for a servant, and a French woman to cook. Get me an Indian woman, too, to look after Mrs. Rogers—a young one: not one of those old hags that can't look at a pitcher of milk without souring it. Send for 'em right away, Lieutenant, so they can clean the house and get us some whitefish for supper. Find quarters for Mr. Potter with a trader; but don't bother about Natty's daughter or Mr. Towne. We'll keep Natty's daughter in the house to help Mrs. Rogers; and I guess Mr. Towne can sleep in the billiard room, since he isn't planning to stay here long. I'll inspect the garrison tonight and the town tomorrow. Natty, get your letter-book and write an order for a keg of rum and a keg of wine from the King's stores. See we've got all the glassware and tableware we need, Natty."

His voice exuded contentment.

Within the house, however, Elizabeth was not contented, and seemed struck dumb at the hot little rooms of this musty, creaky house. "Comfortable!" she whispered. "Billiard room!" "A fortress between two oceans!"

Poor Elizabeth! She was repeating the glowing description of Michilimackinac that the Major had given us in Portsmouth. She moved restlessly from one airless room to another over irregular boards that complained beneath her footstep, light as it was: stared unhappily from the dirt-streaked, fly-specked windows: sat silently in one of the rude chairs with which the place was furnished—a forlorn figure of disillusionment. She had a headache, she said, and I didn't blame her.

When the Major came in jubilantly, bearing a platter of whitefish sent him by a soldier's wife, she stared at the floor, her face a tragic mask.

"Come, my love," he shouted, "fill yourself up on one of these and you'll feel better! Best fish in the whole damned world! Come, come; don't be down in the mouth just because this happens to be one hot day!"

He put the platter on the table, picked up a fish by the head and tail, and gnawed it with smacking sounds.

Elizabeth shuddered; but when Ann and I shared one and exclaimed over it, she came to stand beside us. She wasn't hungry, she said, but she consented to try a piece. It would be, she admitted, like shad if it had more bones and more of a fishy flavor.

The Major patted her shoulder. "Go ahead and eat it, my love! You'll like it; and if you don't, you ought to learn to. If you had to stay here all winter, instead of going back to Portsmouth, that's all you'd get to eat." He turned to me. "Langdon, go outside and find Captain Carver. Bring him up to the billiard room. I want to see him before we meet the traders."

When Carver preceded me to the billiard room on the second floor, I was more than ever struck by his cat-like appearance. He put his feet down softly; seemed to prowl around corners; and his unctuous voice was almost a purr.

The Major was knocking a ball around a table whose cover was so ragged that the ball bounced upon it. "I wonder where this table came from!" he said, as we entered the room. "Makes you think the Jesuit Fathers might have played billiards." He put the cue in the rack and beamed at

Carver. "Well, Jonathan, how'd you get here, and where's Captain Tute, and what are the traders saying?"

Carver answered with the elegance of one who reads from a book. "At the invitation of Mr. James Stanley Goddard, Captain Tute and I proceeded to Montreal. Whilst there I encountered Mr. Bruce the trader, and at his solicitation I joined his canoe brigade, leaving Captain Tute to follow later. Mr. Bruce, knowing I was to be associated with you, has urged me to intercede for him. Ah—a most likable and generous gentleman, Major."

"He's pretty anxious to get started, is he?"

"I apprehend," Carver said, "it has been Mr. Bruce's custom to winter among the Naudowessies, so——"

"You mean Sioux, don't you?" Rogers interrupted.

Carver smiled indulgently. "Sioux or Naudowessies. He winters among the Sioux or Naudowessies, and I apprehend he can extend unusual travelling facilities to me if he were to depart soon."

"Hm," Rogers said. "You say he's generous?"

"I think, Major, you'll find him appreciative—highly appreciative."

"Good!" Rogers said. "I'll try to make things easy for him. Any traders that get away to the westward this year ought to be grateful, Captain. Bruce ought to tell 'em so."

"I'll speak to him, Major," Carver said.

Rogers nodded. "Just a hint ought to be enough." He motioned us toward the stairs; and Carver, deferentially waiting for him to go first, seemed almost to rub, cat-like, against the billiard table.

Elizabeth, we found, had eaten two whitefish and, was telling Ann, in a strong voice, how to unpack the ball dresses she had brought to dazzle the socially elect of Michilimackinac.

I was surprised, when my eyes had adjusted themselves to the dim interior of Groesbeck's warehouse, at the motley throng of traders who had assembled to meet the Major.

There must have been two hundred men packed into the shadowy, barn-like room that smelled of rancid pelts, gun-oil, paint and rust. Some wore broadcloth and linen; others were as roughly clothed as any backwoodsman; but the largest number, part French, part Indian and part God knows what, were sallow, slouching, bearded; if they were civilized, they didn't look it.

Before this audience stood a barrel, upended, and on its head, like a grotesque altar-piece, was a keg. When the Major came in, his eyes must have been, like mine, half-blinded; but his nose led him directly to the keg. He stooped to sniff at the spigot. "Brandy!" he said. "My favorite drink—if it's genuine!"

"It's genuine, Major," a pleasant Scottish voice replied. "Remembering your tastes, I picked it out myself, in your honor."

"That's John Askin's voice!" the Major cried. When a red-faced young man with unruly sandy hair stepped forward, the Major clapped an affectionate hand upon his shoulder. "John Askin, the best sutler Rogers' Rangers ever had! John, I'm going to raise a company of Rangers here, just so you can suttle for 'em!"

The Major's eyes, grown used to the dimness of the warehouse, fell upon other old friends among the traders. "Peter Bartie! I heard you'd gone over the falls at Niagara! Gregor McGregor—John Chinn—Aleck Baxter—Forrest Oakes! Not a drop have we had together since we tried to drink the keg of alcohol in New York! This calls for a glass —unless you're saving that brandy for next year!"

The traders crowded around him, shaking his hand. A stocky little man with a hooked beak of a nose had come in from a rear room, with him an Indian woman carrying a basket of glasses. He filled a glass at the spigot of the brandy keg and gave it to the Major.

"No need to save for next year, Major, now we got you! Next year, with your help, we have more and better brandy."

Rogers grinned. "Meaning Stephen Groesbeck sticks to those that stick to him?"

"Stephen Groesbeck and every other one of us!" Groesbeck said earnestly. He raised his glass. "Well, gentlemen, we been waiting and waiting for the Governor, and here he is, a old friend—knows traders, and everything about Indians, and more about North America than anybody in the world: aint never been afraid of nobody, and never wont! Here's to our new Governor, Major Robert Rogers, world-renowned Commander Rogers' Rangers, who puts a end to uncertainty and brings business back to life. Drink hearty, gentlemen!"

The traders cheered and stamped until dust rose from the floor.

A slender little man in clothes too big for him pushed through the crowd to stand before the Major, wringing sad hands. "Major," he said, "I come here from Montreal first thing in the spring, so to go early to trade with Assiniboins——"

"What's the name?" Rogers asked.

"Ezekiel Solomon," the little man said. "Major, when I asked the Lieutenant, he says he can't give me a pass. I say 'If I don't get one, all my voyageurs, they got to be paid; and to pay 'em I must sell my goods at a sacrifice. Then there wont be no furs coming back from the Assiniboins next spring,' I told him, 'and England don't get our furs. You know who gets 'em?' I said. 'France and Spain, they——' "

"You don't have to tell me all this, Mr. Solomon," Rogers interrupted. "What I *would* like to hear is whether Sir Guy Carleton, as Governor of Canada, has ever attempted to discourage you or any other Montreal traders from wintering among the Indians?"

Solomon looked bewildered; but a hundred others answered for him: "No! No! Never! Not a damned attempt! Discourage! Hell, no!"

A sallow gentleman, coatless, caught Rogers' eye. "Sir," he drawled, "being from Montreal myself, I can explain. Bruce is the name: William Bruce: trader to the Naudowessies near St. Anthony's Falls on the Mississippi. Sir Guy Carleton has forwarded petitions from every Western tribe to His Majesty's Ministers, asking that traders be allowed to continue going among them; and Sir Guy himself has said that if traders are prevented from going, England will lose four-fifths of the Indian trade which she now enjoys."

"Aint that what I say?" Mr. Solomon cried. "I told the Lieutenant all that: I aint told him nothing else every day for a week, Major; and all he says is he aint got no discretionary powers!"

The traders muttered and cursed.

"He told the truth, Mr. Solomon," Rogers said. "A lieutenant at this post isn't entitled to issue permits to traders, as you should know! I'm the only one who has the power to issue permits."

The traders were silent, and the twittering of young eave-swallows in their nests against the outer walls seemed to fill the warehouse.

"Now you gentlemen understand," Rogers continued, "there's been some little controversy over whether traders should be allowed to winter with the Indians. Some think the Indians ought to be made to come here to trade; and I don't mind saying there are persons of considerable power and authority who take that side of the question. But as I see it, it's not fair to change the rules in the middle of a game—not fair to say, in mid-season, that traders can't go where for years they've been permitted to go. Therefore, in spite of the differences of opinion on this matter, I'm inclined to issue a general permit to all of you to go wintering."

The traders whispered excitedly among themselves.

"Major," Mr. Bruce said, "if we'd been made to stay here, there isn't one of us who wouldn't have been ruined through no fault of his own, so I don't need to tell you that a permit to go wintering is what we want more than anything else. To be frank, though, we've heard that Sir William Johnson's against it. Now, then, Major: is that true; and if it is——"

"Oh," Rogers said, "I may be stretching my authority a little; but I'm going to let you go, Mr. Bruce. I'm going to let all of you go. You gentlemen know I'm doing the right thing." Seemingly as an afterthought he added, "Of course I know I can count on your support if ever I need it."

While the traders pressed close to Rogers, shouting their assent, McNott nudged me jubilantly. "Aint that the Major to the life?" he asked. "Attack! Attack! Attack! Always attack! Get in the first blow!"

"That sounds dangerous, Sergeant Mac," I said. "Isn't it dangerous for him to run counter to the wishes of Sir William Johnson?"

"Dangerous!" McNott said. "Is a keg of gunpowder dangerous when you build a fire on it? You know it is, Langdon! You know Johnson don't like the idea of the Major being governor here, and wouldn't let him if he could help it. Johnson's bound to attack him sooner or later; and Rogers aint the kind of fighter who stands around waiting for attacks. He attacks himself; and when Rogers attacks, he attacks so hard that those he hits most generally don't never get over it. Maybe it'll be that way now. Anyway, Langdon, I hope so. For all our sakes, I hope so."

Seeing that the Major and the traders were riotously toasting each other, I ventured to ask McNott about another thing that had been bothering me.

"The Major made an odd remark to Captain Carver a short time ago. He said the traders ought to be grateful if he let them go wintering among the Indians. If I understood him correctly, he told Carver to remind 'em to be grateful."

"Well, why not?" McNott asked. "Wouldn't you be grateful to a man who saved you from bankruptcy?"

"Yes, I would," I said, "but it seemed to me the Major was suggesting they show their gratitude in a substantial manner."

McNott's face grew red. "Aint there perquisites to this post, the way there is to all posts? Indians send presents to a governor; and traders do, too. Why shouldn't they? The governor helps 'em make a profit, don't he? And if any governor ever deserved perquisites, the Major does! Do you know what they pay him for being commandant here, tending to all the chores of the place, setting out a bottle for every Tom, Dick and Harry that wants to drop in to see him, hiring a couple of servants, keeping food in the house and doing all the other things a commandant has to do?"

"No, I don't. I never thought to ask."

"Well, you'd ought to," McNott said. "Rogers aint a Major at all, when it comes to being paid. He's a Major by brevet; but on the British army pay-rolls he aint nothing but a half-pay captain, and you know what a half-pay captain gets. He gets five shillings a day! There aint nobody can live on five shillings a day and do the things he's supposed to do; so why in the name of God shouldn't these traders show their gratitude in a substantial way? He can't live here and be commandant unless they do, can he? He can't unless he's found out how to do better'n Adam and Edam did in the Garden!"

"I don't understand it," I said. "How could he accept a governorship if he wasn't given enough to live on?"

"My God!" McNott whispered angrily. "Do you think anybody'd be such a damn fool as to say 'No, sir, thank you, sir: I wouldn't care to accept this governorship I been working a year to get, on account the pay aint high enough?' He would not! And you can bet the Major wouldn't! That aint the way he does things! He's a soldier! He'd grab what they gave him, and argue about it afterwards. My Gosh, Langdon: don't you know all good soldiers are just alike? They do what they're supposed to do, no matter what it costs. They *got* to."

It sounded to me as though the Major might be skating on mighty thin ice, and I said so.

"Yes," McNott said, "it does; but you got to remember, Langdon, that the Major has prob'ly skated over more thin ice than you'll ever see in your whole life."

The Major's voice, loud and thick from emotion or brandy, rang out. "One thing I propose to do as commandant of this post is to make the Western country safe for traders and travellers. You know there's a war brewing between the Chippeways and the Sioux; and you know what'll happen if it comes to a head. Most of you'll lose your hair and your goods; and the Indians'll be so busy fighting they'll have no furs for the rest of us. Now the Sioux and the Chippeways can't be allowed to fight that war! I wont have it! I want every one of you, when you go wintering, to carry messages to the chiefs of all the tribes near your wintering grounds. Tell 'em they're not to fight till I've talked to 'em! Tell 'em they're to come here to Michilimackinac as soon as they can travel in the spring. Make it your business to see they get here—and it is your business! According to my information, the Western tribes have already begun to take their furs down the Mississippi to the French, and you know what that means. It means that if we don't stop 'em, it wont be long before the French have all the trade of the West in their hands; and when that happens, the whole Western country'll be closed to every English trader.

"What's more, England'll never get that trade back without fighting another war and losing thousands of men; so whatever you do, see they get here! Tell 'em there'll be presents for everyone. Those are orders, and I want 'em obeyed!"

"We'll tell 'em!" the traders shouted. "We'll get 'em for you!" "Good for you, Governor!" "A real Governor, by God!"

The Major raised his hand for silence. "Think what it'll mean to you and to England to have peace between the nations! Think! Think of the riches that would pour from that vast treasure-house of Nature! Who so witless as to refuse to give freely to obtain a return so enormous! Who

so shortsighted he cannot see the need of peace? To you I
entrust the task of securing it and of capturing for England
all the fabulous wealth of the West!"

McNott, his face aflame, joined with the traders in shouting furious approval, and thumped with his wooden leg upon
the warehouse floor.

"Mac," I said, "where'll he get those presents he spoke of?
He hasn't any money of his own, and Johnson told him not
to give presents."

McNott eyed me angrily. "Langdon, you're a wet blanket!
What do you care where he gets 'em? Even if he stole 'em,
he could pay for 'em out of that vast treasure-house of
Nature he was talking about, couldn't he?"

I remember that night as a bedlam of roistering, rejoicing
traders, all bent on crowding into the hot front room of
the Major's house to force upon him tokens of their gratitude
and esteem.

They brought kegs of brandy, rum, undiluted alcohol and
wine; rare skins of all sorts—sables, mink, otter; squirrel-
skin blankets; glassware, chinaware, jewelry, rifles, bolts of
cloth, boxes of cigars, bundles of tobacco, fur caps, fur coats,
bear skins and buffalo rugs; saddles; kitchen utensils. One
even brought him a Pawnee slave—a pleasant-looking woman
who, at a movement of her master's hand, crouched beside
a chair or crawled beneath a table, as would a dog, and
remained there until her owner snapped a finger.

A keg of rum was broached to make a punch that the
traders called calibogus; and an hour later the house was
crammed; scores were wandering over the parade, singing,
arguing, fighting; and a dozen, among them Natty Potter,
were stretched unconscious among the weeds beside the house.

I had expected Elizabeth to shrink in loathing from that
howling crew of revellers; but when the drinking was at its
height, she came slowly down the stairs and stopped on
the next to last step, one outstretched hand resting grace-
fully upon the balustrade; the other poised lightly above
the laces at her breast.

Natty Potter himself couldn't have taught her to make a
better entrance; and as the tipsy traders turned toward her
and became silent, she smiled kindly upon them—a living

portrait of a Governor's Lady receiving homage from adoring subjects.

She was a pretty picture, too; her white shoulders gleamed in the candlelight above a dress of pale green taffeta; her billowing skirts, sweeping to the step below the one on which she stood, gave her a fragile and doll-like look. At sight of her I felt within me faint stirrings of my old affection, and hoped she might now become a more fitting helpmate for the strange man she had married.

When Rogers saw her, he lifted his glass. "Gentlemen," he bellowed, " 'low me to present one and all to the sweetest li'l woman in all New England—Governor's Lady, gentlemen —Madame Rogers! Let's all take little drink to Madame Rogers, God bless her!"

They drank to her, and for a time their speech, though thick, was mighty genteel and elegant. The Frenchmen rolled their eyes and whispered compliments so penetratingly that only a stone-deaf woman could have failed to hear—"Mon Dieu, what charm, like a knife in my heart!" "What elegance, what grace!" "Ah, ah! That wrist! Observe its perfection! Ah, heaven!"

The English traders crowded around her, making polite conversation; and to my astonishment, when Captain Carver brought her a glass of calibogus, she accepted it and sipped daintily, looking up archly at the flushed faces before her.

Graciously she held the center of the stage by speaking, in exciting tones, of Portsmouth traders who had come to her attention, though personally unknown to her—how Captain William Whipple had at one time lost his social standing by engaging in the slave trade, but was now esteemed by many of the most respectable citizens of Portsmouth.

As she talked on and on to the circle of swaying, glassy-eyed traders, the hubbub in other parts of the room arose once more, and the slurred hoarse voice of the Major again resumed the guarded speech he had been making to a circle of admirers who hung flatteringly upon his every word. It was a wandering discourse on the oddities of England.

"Most s'prising country in the world," he told them, "only 'bout quarter the size of New England—not a mountain in the place worth mentioning—not a river any bigger'n what a couple hound dogs could make if they turned up on the same tree. Awful restricted, England is, except when it comes to people. Why, people grow there the same as if they was mushrooms—all kinds of people, and more of every kind than you'll find anywhere! More rich, more poor, more soldiers, more beggars, 'n' more drabs—'specially drabs! More drabs to the square inch than there are mosquitoes in South Carolina! Not a King's ship puts into port without being overrun with 'em, or puts to sea without a score hidden below! Not a King's regiment that don't have a hundred riding in the baggage carts. Can't walk on the streets of any city without being mobbed by 'em. Fifty thousand of 'em in London alone! Now a drab's all right in her place; but fifty thousand of 'em's too many for one city, on account drabs have children same's everyone else! Tell you what I think: England's like Indians: Indians'll drink 'emselves to death; England'll drab herself to death!"

The traders expressed befuddled amazement; two, barely able to walk, fumbled their way along the wall toward the door. One, wholly confused, blundered up the staircase, lost his balance and tumbled to the bottom to be seized and ejected by steadier companions.

His partial ascent of the stairs turned my mind toward Ann, lying alone upstairs, deserted by her father, by Elizabeth, by me—a forgotten waif, friendless and helpless in this strange and savage wilderness. Ashamed of my thoughtlessness, I ran up to make sure she was safe; but halfway up I stopped abruptly; for as my head rose above the level of the second floor, I heard my name softly whispered.

In the dim light that reached the dark upper hallway from the crowded room below, I could see Ann's face at the level of my own, behind the columns of the balustrade. Her hands gripped the columns on either side of her face as those of a prisoner might grip the bars of his cell.

"Ann!" I whispered, "you shouldn't be here! Why aren't you in bed, where you belong?"

"It's hot," she murmured. "I wanted to see and hear what they're doing. There's so much to hear!"

"Well," I said, speaking as severely as I could, "you must have heard enough for one night, so go to bed." To soften my words a little, I leaned forward and kissed her. She stayed as she was, her face pressed close between the columns of the balustrade, her eyes closed. Without intending to do so, I kissed her again; then hurriedly said, "Go to your room at once! What would Elizabeth say if she knew you'd been out here like this, talking to me?"

For a moment she didn't move. Then she opened her eyes. "She wont know. I wont tell her. I'll never tell her anything again. I'll say I wasn't out of bed. If I tell her the truth, she says I've done wrong. When I told her what you said about the umbilical cord, she said you were wicked to tell me, and I was wicked to listen. She makes me feel wicked all the time. She——"

There was an increase in the uproar below. I saw Elizabeth run to the foot of the stairs, her billowing green dress held high before her. She wheeled, stamped her foot, angrily cried, "Drunken, clumsy brutes!" then turned again and came quickly up to where I stood.

I glanced apprehensively over my shoulder toward Ann, but she had vanished. When I drew to one side to let Elizabeth pass, she stopped. "You!" she said bitterly. "What are you up to? Creeping up to see Ann?"

"You're upset, Elizabeth," I said. "You're not yourself! What's happened?"

"Happened!" she exclaimed. "Happened! A drunken beast spilled calibogus on my green taffeta! It's ruined! You came up here to see Ann, didn't you? Did you go in her room?"

"No," I said, "but there's no reason why I shouldn't, Elizabeth."

Elizabeth uttered a contemptuous laugh. "No reason, indeed! She may pull the wool over your eyes, but not over mine. She——"

But I waited to hear no more. Closing my ears to the rest of her speech, I ran down the stairs. As I hastened toward the door, Elizabeth's voice came shrilly from the upper hall to stop me in my wrathful flight. "Langdon Towne," she cried, "tell the Major he's to come up immediately! I won't have this house made a pigpen! Tell him to send those disgusting creatures home—if they *have* homes!"

There's something about an angry woman's voice that quells the worst of reprobates; and at Elizabeth's sharp words, comparative quiet fell upon the house that a moment before had been a tumult of drunken shouts and laughter. Traders tiptoed toward the door, stumbling against walls and furniture. When, against my will, I sought the Major, he warned me to silence with an upraised finger.

"I heard what she said, 'n' I aint going to do it, damned if I am! These gentlemen need my assistance, 'n' I find I'll be 'bliged to accomp'ny 'em to town—mere shank of the evening, anyway, my boy! Been a hard day, too, 'n' I guess I'm entitled to relaxation instead of being talked to all night! You tell her I was called away on business—military business."

A trader laughed drunkenly. "Inspection trip. Major's got to inspect number Indian ladies in Michilimackinac available for purposes of military relaxation."

The others frowned at him and made threatening gestures.

The Major looked apprehensively toward the stairway. "Tell her you couldn't find me, Langdon," he said. "Tell her I had to leave suddenly."

"She wont believe me, Major. Wont you speak to her yourself?"

"I will not," he said promptly. " 'F she gets her hands on me, I wont never get to go, 'n' anyway she wouldn't believe me, no more'n she would you. You know she wouldn't believe the Angel Gabriel if he swore he'd been practicing on his trumpet. She'd say he'd been out behind a cloud somewhere, carrying on with a female angel."

From the upper floor came Elizabeth's shrill voice: "Langdon; Langdon! Tell the Major I want him immediately!"

With the stealth and swiftness of a cat, the Major moved to the nearest open window, slid through it feet-foremost, balanced himself on the sill for a moment while he silently signalled his companions to follow; then, with a final meaning glance at me from protuberant eyes, he vanished into the darkness. The traders, scuffling and muttering, clambered after him.

"Langdon!" Elizabeth called again, "why doesn't the Major step up here? How many times must I send word I want him!"

I hurried to the front door. Everyone had fled the house, empty glasses were all about, and the place reeked of rum. On the front steps sat the Major's servant, nodding, and on either side of the steps were two sentries.

I turned back to the stairway. "The Major's not here, Elizabeth. Everybody's gone. Some of the traders are leaving for the West tomorrow morning, and the Major had business with them."

I walked rapidly away toward Groesbeck's warehouse, where McNott had taken lodgings; but I couldn't go fast enough to escape the voice that seemed to slice the night like a knife: "I don't believe it! Our first night here, and he knows I need him, but off he goes to carouse with dirty, common traders! Go after him at once, and tell him to come straight back! Do you hear, Langdon? Why don't you answer?"

In spite of the heat, I shivered—as have most men at one time or another—at what I had escaped in my short life. Only by the slenderest of margins had Robert Rogers saved me from an awful end on our retreat from St. Francis; but the fate from which he had rescued me by marrying Elizabeth I now recognized as even worse.

CHAPTER LXV

THE BREEZE came in from the north on the following morning, fresh from the icy waters of Lake Superior; and it almost seemed to me, when I drew that wine-like air into my lungs and looked out at the opalescent water of the strait and the sculptured white cliffs of the island guarding its eastern end, that the events of the night before had been a fevered dream, brought on by heat, our long journey and our troubled arrival at this fort in the wilderness.

Everything and everybody in Michilimackinac seemed to have been changed by that cool breath from the enormous inland sea just beyond us. The parade was dusty no longer, but almost verdant in the golden rays of the early morning sun. The Major's house had been scoured until it shone by the Major's soldier servant, assisted by a detail of men from Lieutenant Christy's company. The Pawnee slave, installed in the kitchen, chopped wood, peeled potatoes, brought water from the well, and made herself useful to a wrinkled French-woman who had materialized, witchlike, to be the Major's cook.

The Major himself, his eyes pinkly a-swim and the pouches beneath them swollen as if by bee-stings, had poured a pail of water over his head soon after sun-up, gulped down a large part of another pail, and gone striding off to the warehouses, where hundreds of spindle-shanked voyageurs in red woolen caps, gaudy sashes and deerskin leggins were piling bales of goods in heaps, preparatory to loading their canoes.

And early as it was, Elizabeth had already received four invitations to drink tea with the wives of those traders who were so fortunate as not to be married to Indian women. She was pleased with herself, and as gracious as though she had never spoken sharply to me in her life.

"You must tell me, Langdon," she said. "Shall I wear my green striped Cambray or my lavender? The lavender is the very latest, a little extreme perhaps, but wouldn't it be a greater treat for these poor wretches here to see something in the latest mode? Fancy what starved lives they lead! La, it makes me shudder!" She shivered prettily, but when I spoke highly of her lavender, she went upstairs in such high good humor that I boldly called to Ann to take my box of crayons, and set off with her to make sketches at the watergate.

I saw when we reached the shore that the Major's enthusiasm for Michilimackinac had not been wholly exaggerated. The water was clear as the clearest glass, the islands floating in the distance were emeralds rimmed with silver; and on the beach, fishing, shouting and loading canoes, was a gay throng of Indians, voyageurs and traders.

Just off shore canoe brigades were forming. A voyageur stood at the bow and stern of each canoe, holding it fast so that its delicate skin mightn't be split by rubbing on bottom; and other voyageurs, spurred on by their trader employers, piled ninety-pound bales of goods into these craft until I marvelled they didn't sink. They were *canots du maître*—master canoes—bigger than any I had ever seen. They must have been forty-five feet long, with places for crews of fourteen; and on the high prow and stern of each canoe was painted a bright device—a beaver, a flag, a galloping horse, a bear, an Indian's head.

I could have sat sketching voyageurs all day. They were stunted and swarthy, tremendously developed above the waist and shrivelled away to nothing below. In their caps they wore red feathers, a mark of long service in canoe brigades; their leggins were bound below the knee with colored garters; and from their bright sashes hung pouches embroidered with glittering beads. Their manners were gay, too: they smiled continuously, as though they found life an enormous jest; they capered and sang songs; bragged and gesticulated.

I was hard at work, with Ann passing crayons to me as I called for them and keeping inquisitive onlookers from my elbow and easel, when Rogers, Potter and Jonathan Carver hurried from the water-gate and went to where the brigades were forming.

Rogers spoke to Mr. Bruce, and a moment later voyageurs took Carver and Bruce astride their shoulders, waded to the canoes, and deposited them among the bales in the bottom.

I stood up, dropping my crayons. "Why," I said, "I do believe Carver's going already—he's starting! If he's going, why shouldn't I?"

I hurried toward the Major, but he ignored me. Bruce signalled to his steersman, who slapped the water with his paddle and in a quavering voice sang the words, *"Ha, ha, ha, frit à l'huile."*

The crews of Bruce's five canoes broke into the song; and in time with its lilting measure their red paddle-blades darted in and out of the water with the rapidity of tongues of flame; the compact line of canoes moved off to the westward like a gigantic water-insect, paddles swinging with the regularity of machines, sixty strokes to the minute.

From all sides rose the mournful wailing of Indian women —temporary wives left behind by Bruce's voyageurs. To me their discordant howling was an echo of my own disappointment at remaining behind while others set off gaily singing:

> *"C'est un pâté de trois pigeons,*
> *Ha, ha, ha, frit à l'huile,*
> *Assieds-toi et le mangeons,*
> *Fritaine, friton, firtou, poilon,*
> *Ha, ha, ha, frit à l'huile*
> *Frit au beurre et à l'ognon."*

I turned gloomily to the easel. Ann, on her knees beside it, was slowly picking up the dropped crayons. At my approach she rose to her feet.

"Where's Mr. Carver going?" she asked.

"To the westward."

"When's he coming back?"

I shook my head. "I don't know. In two years, perhaps, or three."

"Did you want to go too, Langdon?"

"Of course," I said. "That's why I came here—to go to the westward. Didn't you know that? I thought I'd told you."

When she didn't answer, I looked up to find her smiling a strange, tight-lipped smile that made me think of the first time I'd seen her, when Mrs. Garvin had roughly snatched and held her so that I could sketch her starved body and her grimy face.

She offered me the box of crayons. "You haven't finished the picture."

"I know," I said. "I guess I wont do any more today."

She continued to hold the crayons before me. "It's almost done, Langdon. It only needs red chalk and scarlet for the feathers and paddles. You wont ever see so many brigades starting out at one time: I heard someone say so." She took a piece of red chalk from the box and put it in my fingers. "Look at the canoes, Langdon. Don't they look like arrows?"

I looked at the beach and the strait. There were two hundred canoes loading in the shallows; and already a score of brigades were slanting off to east and west, bound for Superior or Michigan.

As Ann had said, the flashing scarlet paddles gave each canoe the appearance of a vast arrow-head of luminous blue —an arrow-head that would pierce the wilderness for perhaps a thousand miles before it came to rest. Stirred by the thought, I hurriedly finished the first sketch and went eagerly to work on the second; and in the labor of getting my colors on paper, I forgot Rogers, Carver, Ann, and my own disappointment.

Day after day for almost a week the canoe brigades streamed away from Michilimackinac, headed for the traders' wintering places in the West and Northwest; and in all that time Rogers was never out of the company of traders or of Potter. He wrote hundreds of orders, inspecting the contents of canoes, gave verbal instructions to every trader, drank enormously, thought up a hundred things for the two companies of British Regulars to do, and was as busy and as tireless as though ten men were compressed within his huge body.

He was as difficult to corner, too, as ten men, and a week passed before I caught him alone, late at night, figuring diligently in a little black account-book, and scratching his head vigorously.

His oily brown hair had come untied; his green coat, dusty and spotted, lay across a chair; his stock hung loose at his massive throat.

"Come in, Langdon," he said. "Where you been keeping yourself? Painting Indians, I suppose. I told you I'd get you a chance to paint 'em, didn't I? There's no better place for 'em than right here: stay here long enough and you'll see all the kinds there are, pretty near."

"That's not what I want, Major. I want to paint 'em in their natural surroundings—working, playing, hunting. To tell you the truth, Major, I've been pretty worried the last few days. If you've given up your plans about going to the westward——"

"What!" the Major cried. "Given up my plans? What you talking about?" He darted a suspicious look at me. "What put this in your head? Has McNott heard bad news from that damned red Princess of his?"

"No," I said, "but I've waited years to go to the Indian country, and my idea is to get there as soon as I can. When I saw Carver set off with Bruce, and heard nothing from you about when I could go myself, I——"

The Major looked relieved. "You thought I'd forgotten! You thought I'd stopped thinking about the Northwest Passage! Why, Langdon, my boy, the Northwest Passage—that's the apple of my eye—the last thing I'd forget! It's my soul —my life! If I live to be a thousand years old, I'll never forget that! No, sir! That's my great ambition—the thing that's going to make the whole world remember Robert Rogers until the end of time!"

"Well, I'm glad to hear it, Major," I said, "but if Carver's gone, why shouldn't I go?"

"Damn it, Langdon," Rogers said, "you aint any more anxious to get away from this rum-hole than I am, but I can't move an inch till I get instructions from London, and a deputy governor to take my place. When I move, you'll move. Now Carver, he's different. He can make maps, and that's what I want him to do: make maps. The less he knows about what I'm doing, the less he'll be able to talk and the more time he can put on maps. He likes to be important, Carver does, and the people who like to be important always talk too much. You know what would happen if the French learned what we proposed to do: they'd send spies from New Orleans to stir up the Indian nations against us, and where'd we be then? No, Langdon; you'll go West with me and Stanley Goddard and McNott, stopping to talk with all the different nations; not hurrying like Carver. Don't you worry, Langdon: I'll look out for you!"

He rose from the table, ran his thick fingers through his tousled hair, drew a deep breath and expelled it explosively. "No, sir: you aint half as anxious to get away from here as I am! Figures, figures, figures! Not a damned thing to do but peek into canoes and warehouses, and have another drink of rum. I'd rather march a hundred miles through a swamp than spend a day tramping around these warehouses!

"Why, damn it, Langdon, my feet feel as if I had hot frying pans tied to 'em, and I got so much beaver fur in my nose I can't breathe when I go to bed at night! Every afternoon I want to lie down and sleep; but when night comes, I'm so waked up I'd like to go out and tear a tavern to pieces—only there aint any taverns, and even if there were, I couldn't raise the harmlessest kind of hell in 'em without having Elizabeth carry on as if I'd shot her father. Oh, God, when I find out I've got the King's ear, wont I kick up a smoke getting away!"

"Then you think there's no question you'll get it, Major?"

"Just a matter of time, Langdon. Those letters from London are on the way from Montreal right now. I can feel it, just the way I've always been able to feel Indians coming, and northeasters blowing up. They'll get here with the brigades that bring Spiesmaker and Tute, see if they don't, and when they come, my boy, we'll go, Johnson or no Johnson. Why, look at this."

He picked up his little account-book and opened it. "There's the list of goods I've borrowed from Groesbeck so we can have presents for the Indians, and so Elizabeth can be sup-

ported during the three years I'll be away. Three thousand
pounds I owe Groesbeck already, and if that aint being sure,
I don't know what is!"

CHAPTER LXVI

S<small>IX DAYS</small> later, at mid-morning
of an August day whose sharpness foretold a rapidly approaching autumn, the outlook in the northeast bastion
touched off his 9-pounder; and before the white smoke had
blown past the stockade every soldier, every trader's clerk,
every Indian and officer and Frenchman in Michilimackinac
was hurrying toward the shore of the strait; for as all of
us knew, the gun was the signal of a Montreal brigade with
a royal officer aboard.

There were nine canoes; and as they drew closer, I saw
among the passengers the fair hair and the pear-shaped head
of Captain James Tute, whom I had last heard at Crown
Point, bragging to Captain Carver of Indian women whose
admiration for him had led them to follow him about like
dogs. I had disliked him then, but I was glad to see him
now, for with his coming our search for the Northwest Passage was no longer a vague and far-off dream: it was on
the verge of becoming an actuality.

Rogers, grinning happily, shouted a hearty greeting to the
officer who had led the brigade—a pale young man with
flaxen eyebrows and light blue eyes, wearing a powdered
wig, laced hat, scarlet coat, yellow waistcoat, snow-white
breeches and shining black boots. Down one side of his face
ran the long white scar of an old sword-cut. His black
leather stock was so stiff and so high that it pushed his chin
upward and gave him an air of having smelled something
offensive. The Major thrust out a huge hand. "I'm Rogers,"
he shouted, "and you're Captain Spiesmaker, I guess! We
been waiting for you, Captain, and the letters you ought

to have with you. Where are they, Captain? You've got 'em, haven't you?"

The captain made a stiff bow, clicked his heels and drew a packet from the breast of his scarlet jacket. "Compliments of Sir Guy Carleton," he said, and his voice sounded foreign. "I have not separated myself from them once on all this journey. An honor to be of service to a soldier· so distinguished." His little blue eyes stared unwinkingly at the Major, as if to read his thoughts.

The Major beamed. "Captain," he said, "don't think I don't appreciate it! These letters mean more to me than you know! By God, Captain, we'll make this post into something that's never been dreamed of!"

He turned to Captain Tute and gripped him by the arm. "Just in time!" he said. "Just in time!" He held up the packet of letters meaningly, then passed on to Tute's companions, one of whom, James Stanley Goddard, was young but preternaturally grave, as though born old. The other, Phinehas Atherton, had an enormous Adam's apple and huge ears that protruded like miniature snowshoes, so that he looked gangling and immature.

Tute remembered me. "Oh-ho!" he cried. "The painter! How's the painting doing nowadays?"

I told him politely that I still dabbled with colors when I had the chance, whereupon he said I ought to be able to turn a pretty penny re-painting the figures on the prows and sterns of the voyageurs' canoes. I was spared hearing more of his thoughts on Art by Rogers, who took me by the arm and turned me toward the fort. "Now, Langdon," he said exultantly, "it was you who first told me of Arthur Dobbs and the Northwest Passage, so it's only fitting that your eyes should be the ones to see the curtain rise on England's Western Empire that we're to found."

"Bolt the door, Langdon," the Major said, drawing a chair close to the billiard table and hanging his coat over the back of it. "I don't want anyone breaking in on us, not till I've studied these letters and laid my plans. When you marry, my boy, take damned good care to marry a woman who'll keep her mouth shut when you want to think, because if you don't, you wont do a hell of a lot of thinking—not unless you leave home to do it."

He ripped the cover from the packet of letters and ran through them hastily. "Yes, sir, by God," he cried. "Here's one from Fitzherbert—one from Campbell—that's a dun and so's that and that: two duns from that damned tailor—here's Ellis's—and Townsend, by God! Townsend himself! What luck: what luck! Another dun—damn these insolent damned tradesmen—and one from Edmund Burke—your friend Lord Bremerton—ah, my boy, we're made men! Here, damn it: loosen the seal on this letter of Townsend's: my fingers are all thumbs! And don't damage it! These letters alone'll be worth a fortune some day!"

I pried up the wax wafer on the flap, unfolded the heavy sheet, and handed it over. I was excited as he.

"Townsend himself!" he said again. "I knew it!" He ran hastily through the contents: " 'Honorable Robert Rogers, Major and Governor of so on and so on, Captain Commandant of so on and so on and so on; My dear Major; I have this day instructed Dr. John Campbell to recommend to you that, according to our discussions, you proceed at once to explore the interior country and find out the Northwest Passage. His Majesty has been so gracious'—by God, Langdon, we've got the King's ear at last!—'His Majesty has been so gracious as to express great interest in your confidence concerning the existence of a Northwest Passage; and it is my sincere hope that this letter and Dr. Campbell's will reach you in sufficient time to permit you to dispatch suitable and trustworthy officers on this errand without delay. I am sir, your so on and so on and so on, Charles Townsend.' "

Rogers looked up at me blankly, dropped his eyes to study the letter again and slowly re-read it, his thick lips moving. At its end he shook his head and impatiently pushed it aside. He seemed bewildered.

" 'Dispatch suitable officers!' *Dispatch* 'em!" His voice became irritable. "Where's that letter from Campbell? Here it is! Now for God's sake, let's get to the bottom of this!"

Campbell's letter was bulky; and Rogers, scanning the closely-written sheets, grunted with satisfaction. "More like it! That damned letter of Townsend's—busy man, I suppose —gave me a fright, by God! Now here: let's see. Hm! 'Dear Major—Townsend seen the King—King excited over prospect of a short route to Japan——' "

He grinned and wiped his forehead with his sleeve. "Well,

that's clear! We've got the King with us! We needn't worry about Gage and Johnson any more! The King's orders come ahead of theirs—ahead of everyone's. By God, that letter of Townsend's damned near knocked me under the table! Whew! Now let's see:

" 'Short route to Japan.' Yes. 'Desire of His Majesty himself that the Northwest Passage be discovered. Nothing you can do will recommend you more to His Majesty or to his Ministers than to make that discovery.' "

His fist thundered on the billiard table. "They've seen the light at last! The King and all his Ministers want it now! By God, I knew they'd listen, sooner or later! And there's nobody on earth powerful enough to stop me from making that discovery, once I start! Now let's see: what's the rest of it?"

He ran a shaking forefinger down the closely-written page; but before he found the place, Elizabeth's shrill voice, calling from the floor below, interrupted him.

"Governor!" she called. "Governor! Where are you, Governor? Robert! Are you upstairs, Robert?"

Rogers frowned and shook his head at me. "Don't answer!" he whispered. "Let her holler! Damn it, can't I ever have a minute's peace in my own house? Don't answer and maybe she'll think we aint here."

In the silence I heard Elizabeth mounting the stair; the billiard-room latch rose and fell; the door was noisily shaken.

"Robert!" Elizabeth cried. "Robert Rogers! Are you in there?"

The Major stared at me irresolutely.

"Robert Rogers!" Elizabeth repeated. "What are you doing in there? Open the door this instant!"

The Major pushed back his chair helplessly. "My dear," he said, "I've got important letters here—important letters from London. I'm trying to read 'em—got to read 'em, Elizabeth."

"Who's with you?" Elizabeth asked.

"I am," I said.

Elizabeth's voice was dissatisfied. "Why didn't you answer when I first called? You were deliberately rude, both of you. I'm not accustomed to such treatment! Let me in." Again the latch rattled.

"Just let me finish these letters, my dear," Rogers begged. "I must know what's in 'em so I can issue my orders. Let me have another half-hour uninterrupted. What is it you want, my love?"

"I never heard anything so selfish!" Elizabeth cried. "Natty Potter came here and said your friends were coming to dinner —the first I've heard of it! I should think I might be consulted when such plans are made! Who have you asked to dinner, Robert, and how many are there?"

Rogers gazed strickenly toward the closed door. "There'll only be Captain Tute, Lieutenant Atherton and Mr. Goddard, my dear," he said, "—and Langdon, of course. That's all, my love, and you'll be well repaid for giving them a good dinner. You shall have the handsomest piece of brocade among Mr. Goddard's goods."

I heard her murmuring contemptuous words—"nasty traders"—"think of nothing but dirty Indian women"; then she went slowly downstairs and left us in peace.

"I'll tell you this much," Rogers whispered earnestly, "these letters didn't get here a minute too soon! Not one minute! I can stand just so much, and then something's got to give!"

He picked up Campbell's letter. "Now let's see: where were we? 'Nothing you can do will recommend you more to His Majesty or his Ministers'—yes, here we are: 'Strongly advise striking while the iron is hot—waste no time embarking on the discoveries—you should report indications of success at once, as appropriations will then be easy to obtain—wealth of game existing in all parts of North America will make it possible for those you send to live comfortably off the country——' "

He broke off. "What in God's name is he talking about?" Then he went on: " 'When you are certain a route to the Pacific exists, it will be easy to obtain for you an appointment as Governor of the West, and place at Michilimackinac a commandant who will be sympathetic to you and your views——"

As though unable to believe what he had read, his eyes went back to the opening sentence, came down again to where he had left off; raced ahead to the end. He threw the letter on the table; thrust a forefinger inside his stock and dragged at it as if choking; then stared stupidly at the star-shaped scar on the back of his hand.

"Why," he said slowly, "those damned fools! Those damned thick-headed fools! They've given me no money! Those damned he-gossips, spending millions of pounds on their rotten gambles, but not a single damned penny for a sure thing! You can't make 'em understand! You can *not* make 'em understand!" He groaned.

"Think of the months I spent talking to 'em! Months! And now this—'Report any indications of success at once!' 'At once,' for the love of God, when that report'll have to cross five thousand miles of wilderness and three thousand miles of ocean! And they think it's possible 'to live comfortably off the country!' Dear God, how can such dolts stay alive! Damn their shabby short-sighted little brains! Brought up on an island so small you can spit across it, and can't imagine anything bigger than that damned little kitchen garden they live in! Open those other letters! Open that one of Burke's— those from Bremerton and Ellis! I'll see what Fitzherbert has to say. Christ, Langdon, they can't all be mad! They can't be!"

I broke the seals on the other envelopes. They contained letters of congratulation, joyful because the King had been won over to the Great Plan, confident that Rogers would successfully achieve the great adventure and write a brilliant page in the history of British exploration and discovery. "When you are successful, as you surely will be," Burke wrote, "there can be no further misunderstanding between England and her American colonies, for England must see at last the extent of the North American Empire, and misunderstandings will not be tolerated."

The Major's explosive laugh was bitter. "Well, by God, there's no question what the King and Townsend want done! All I'm to do is find the Northwest Passage without money, men, supplies, or going myself! They wont let me have a Deputy Governor, and they've left me just what I was when I left England—a half-pay captain; and on five shillings a day I'm supposed to equip an army to discover an empire!"

"Major," I said, "it can't be true! They couldn't be so shabby! There must be other letters somewhere, giving you higher rank: allowing you a Deputy Governor: granting you money for expenses. They can't hold out hope with one hand and snatch it away with the other! They can't wreck all your plans like this!"

The Major shook his head. "No. There's no other letter. Campbell's the agent for these discoveries. It was his business to get money for me—money and higher rank—and he hasn't done it."

He jumped from his chair. "Well, by God, it'll take more than their mistakes to wreck my plans!" He hitched at his breeches as he had in the old days, when he was leading us on our retreat from St. Francis. "All I needed was the orders. That's all any soldier needs; and I've got 'em! The King wants the Northwest Passage found, and that's enough!"

He strode around the table, a powerful, confident figure. "I'll put Tute in command, and I'll find supplies for the rest of you—yes, and presents for the Indians. I'd rather stay in hell than in this rum-hole of a post, but I'll do it, by God, while the rest of you go out and persuade the Sioux to come in for a Congress next spring—and then I'll join you with enough presents to get us to the Oregon and the Pacific."

"But if they've given you no money, Major," I protested, "how'll you get presents?"

"How?" Rogers asked. "I'll have to do what every soldier's always had to do—I'll have to beg, borrow and steal, and trust to God my country'll pay me back when I've carried out my orders."

He shook his head ruefully. "It's hell's own luck! I've got every inch of the ground in my head, but the rest of you don't know any more about it than you do about Tartary. By God, nothing ever hit me as hard as this—not even when we reached the Ammonoosuc and found no food!"

He was silent, cogitating; and in the silence we once more heard Elizabeth's complaining voice; the sound of her heels clicking on the staircase. Then the door-latch rattled, her knuckles thumped upon the panels, and she shrilly called, "Robert Rogers, open the door! Open the door this instant!"

"Oh hell!" the Major whispered. "Let her in! I guess she means business."

I unbolted the door; Elizabeth, her black eyes snapping, peered suspiciously around the room. "The idea!" she cried, "locking yourself away like this, at such a time of day!" She tapped the toe of her shoe upon the floor. "Robert, what do you expect me to give your guests for dinner? Not a thing to be found but whitefish and a fowl!"

She looked at me kindly and smoothed the white kerchief at her throat. "Have you noticed my new dress, Langdon? Mrs. Bedel made it—Mrs. Bedel of King Street in Portsmouth. The Atkinsons always go to her, and Phoebe Livermore, your friend's sister. Really, her prices are outrageous, three whole pounds for making this, in addition to five pounds for the goods. And I fear she wasn't successful. Such a shame to do badly with such elegant material!"

I tried to speak politely. "It's beautiful, and a perfect fit."

"No," she said discontentedly, "I think it's too old for me." She moved idly to the billiard table. "Oh, letters! Letters from England! Do they say when you're to start, Robert?"

"My love," Rogers said, "I'm sorry to say I've had unpleasant news. I'll be obliged to remain here through the winter. God knows how it happened, but I haven't received the orders I hoped for. His Majesty wishes and expects me to find the Northwest Passage, but my rank hasn't been raised, and no allowance made for expenses. That means my pay remains five shillings a day; and you'll never be able to live on that, my love. Perhaps it'll be best for you to start for Portsmouth when the next trader leaves for Albany."

She stared at him. "Start for Portsmouth? Start for Portsmouth and leave you here alone?" She spoke more rapidly. "Five shillings a day was your pay while you were in London! Five shillings a day is all you've had since last winter, when you came back! You're in debt already, and I guess it wont hurt you to be in debt a little more! You've always found some way to get money when you needed it, and you can still do it! Don't you think I have any pride, Robert Rogers? What do you think my friends would say if I came home while you stayed here? It would be the talk of Portsmouth—yes, the talk of Boston! Heaven knows what they'd say! Start for Portsmouth, indeed! I'll do nothing of the sort!"

"But it'll be cold here, my love," Rogers protested, "and there'll be nothing for you to do all winter——"

Elizabeth spoke sharply. "And what'll *you* do all winter, I'd like to know, if you're left alone to behave as you please? Oh, la! I know what'll happen! You'll take up with one of those nasty Indian women, the way all these terrible traders do! You want to get rid of me, so you can bring one of them into this house! Well, Robert Rogers, never shall it be said I countenanced any such goings on! If you stay, I stay too!"

She swept to the door, gave each of us a final contemptuous glance, and ran down the stairs.

The Major looked at me haggardly. "Damn it, Langdon," he said, "I thought she'd jump at the chance to get back to Portsmouth for Thanksgiving and Christmas! How in hell do you suppose she knew I was figuring on getting a lively young squaw to keep me warm and comfortable?"

CHAPTER LXVII

Two WEEKS later, on the night before we left Michilimackinac to discover the Northwest Passage, the Major had the five of us—Tute, Goddard, Atherton, McNott and me—to supper and gave us final instructions. So fearful was he that his plans might be overheard that our supper was spread on the billiard table, while Elizabeth was left downstairs with Ann to turn visitors from the door.

Natty Potter, who had been pleasantly surprised in the afternoon to receive from the Major a bottle of alcohol flavored with rum, had fallen into a deathlike slumber shortly afterward, and couldn't have joined us even if he had wished to.

On the table were two cold turkeys; and we drank success to the Major from a bowl of flip made of spruce beer laced with rum. "Twenty thousand pounds," he kept reminding us: "twenty thousand pounds you'll receive from the British Government if you find the Northwest Passage; but even if you don't find a water route, and can contrive to cross the Shining Mountains to the great River Oregon and the Pacific, you'll be handsomely rewarded for finding the path. Charles Townsend himself made me that promise, so the twenty thousand pounds is as good as ours!"

When the Major spoke in that thick, heart-quickening voice of his, the task before us seemed almost easy. I knew we could do it, just as years before I had known—with Rogers' voice to spur me on—that even though I was no better than a starved and shrivelled corpse, drained of strength and hope by disappointment and exhaustion, I still could build a raft and somehow fight off death until I had reached the bourne for which the Major aimed.

"You've got your orders," he went on, "and they make provision for everything—for my death—for anything that might happen to keep me from joining you. Follow 'em carefully and you'll be all right. Persuade every Indian nation in the West to send chiefs to my Congress next spring. I'll join you as soon as the Congress is over. If you find yourself in trouble before then, call on your courage and resolution: brave out every difficulty, and you'll be certain of success."

He scooped up another mug of flip, drank it thoughtfully, and added: "When you're west of the Mississippi, you're among Indians that like the French and the Spaniards a damned sight better than they do us. If they think you represent the King of England——"

He circled his scalp suggestively with a rigid forefinger.

"Wherever you go, remember to let it be known you've only one desire: opening trade with Indian nations. Traders: that's all you're to seem to be: traders. And, for God's sake, look out for Indian women! There's no surer way to get wiped out than to help yourself to 'em without the consent of their chiefs."

"Yes there is, Major," McNott said thickly. "Take m'own case. Surest way for me to get wiped out would be to take one without the consent of Princess McNott."

"You're not going to carry your wife on this trip, are you?" Tute asked.

"Why aint I?" McNott demanded. "She's the best wife I got, and I can't do without her until I can get me a better one."

"She'll use up too many supplies," Tute complained.

"That shows how much you know about the Princess," McNott said irritably. "I got her trained. She's trained to do all the work for me, and not to eat nothing till I'm all through eating, and then to be satisfied with just licking her fingers and the inside of the kettle. Anyway, Captain, don't waste time worrying about how many of your supplies my wife'll eat. She's my wife, and I'm going with Langdon Towne, and we'll carry our own supplies."

Rogers drained another mugful and set the mug down with a bang. "Silence! There's twenty thousand pounds reward depending on this trip, and enough honor and advantages to be gained from it to satisfy a thousand men! If I could lead this expedition instead of having to stay here to make things safe for the rest of you and borrow the supplies to keep you going, you know how long any one of you'd last if he started squabbling with the others! He'd last just this long!" He reached forward, seized the second-joint of one of the turkeys, and tore it from the carcass.

"You're to find the Northwest Passage or the great River Oregon!" he shouted. "No squabbling! Keep your damned tempers under control, the way I do, till you've done what you've set out to do! Behave like soldiers: not like tom-cats on a fence!"

He rose to his feet and gestured magnificently with the second-joint. "Remember what's at stake! Gold! Mountains full of it! Rivers—endless rivers carrying the wealth of the West to the King's ships that'll lie in the harbors we find! There'll be cities named for us—mountain peaks, white with everlasting snow, bearing our names and making 'em household words in the mouths of a thousand generations yet unborn—rivers beside which the Thames will be no more than a pint of slops—Rogers River, Tute River, Goddard River—vessels plying on 'em—vessels laden with riches——"

"What's the matter with McNott River?" McNott asked.

The Major waved aside the Sergeant's interruption. "Vessels on 'em," he continued, "crowded with happy travellers, all shouting, 'There's where Major Rogers and his men camped when they discovered this river and the Northwest Passage!' "

"McNott River!" McNott said thickly. "Hooray for Mc-Nott River!"

"Pioneers!" the Major cried. "We'll be the discoverers of the greatest territory the world has ever seen—the pioneers who make possible more fortunes than the world has ever known! The great Columbus sailed to the westward day after day, landed upon a sandy island where there was nothing but seaweed and crabs, and look what happened to him—famous forever, by God—famous, even though he slept in a ship's cabin the whole time, and had cooked food set before him three times a day!

"Will *we* sleep quietly at night? We will not! Will *we* have food set before us three times a day? We will not! We'll

conquer a thousand dangers before which the great Columbus
would have been helpless; and our rewards, my friends, will
be greater! Crowned heads of Europe'll force their attentions
upon us: princesses and duchesses'll shower us with favors:
noblemen and statesmen'll be proud to be seen in the company
of the brave men who out-Columbused Columbus—the daring adventurers who joined with Robert Rogers to discover
the great River Oregon and the Northwest Passage!"

The rest of us rose and raised our glasses. We echoed his
words—"The great River Oregon and the Northwest Passage!" Only McNott was silent, drinking deeply while we
shouted. When we stopped shouting and drained our glasses,
McNott swayed in his chair and said: "Wait till the King
hears about McNott River!"

The Major, fearful that someone might suspect our destination, ordered us off at sunrise the next day, and there were
few on the beach to see us go.

Since daybreak Ann had helped me pack sketching materials in a haversack, and stow away in my cow-hide trunk
in the corner of the billiard room all the fripperies for which
I'd have no use—I hoped—for three years to come.

She laid them in for me—silk stockings, cambric stocks,
tie-wig and bag-wig, hair ribbons, laced hats, shirt- and cuff-
ruffles, London-made clothes and shoes. On top of everything I put the sketch books I had already filled at Oswego
and Michilimackinac.

"We've worked hard at them, haven't we, Ann?" I said,
clumsily trying to ease our parting. "If the house catches fire,
try to save them. They're worth more to me than anything
in the world."

I slammed down the lid, locked it, and hid the key behind
a loose brick in the chimney. "Don't forget, Ann."

She shook her head, a dim ghost in the gray dawn light.

"Well," I said, "they'll be waiting for me. Look around,
Ann, and make sure I've taken everything."

I picked up my haversack, ran downstairs, and hurried to
the water-gate of the fort, where McNott was supervising the
stowing of his mysterious trading supplies and my own compact bundles of sketching materials, quizzing glasses and
colored prints. Tute came to us, as assured as though the
Northwest Passage had already been discovered by his own

efforts. "You'll have extra space in your canoe, Mr. Towne," he said, "for some of our baggage."

"I need that extra space, Captain," I said, "so I can sketch while we're on the move."

"Oh for God's sake!" he said. He turned to Rogers, who stood with Elizabeth, watching us. "I'd like to have it made clear, Major," he said, "just what Towne's status is. Is he under my orders or not?"

Rogers rubbed pouchy eyes with a huge forefinger. "Captain," he said mildly, "you'll find Langdon ready to join with you in anything you propose to do, provided it's reasonable; but he's going on this expedition to paint Indians, according to an agreement I made with him long ago. He bought his supplies out of his own pocket, so I wouldn't feel justified in making him subject to anyone's orders. An artist ought to be free to do things his own way, Captain."

Tute looked dissatisfied.

"I guess, Captain, I'll make that an order," Rogers added. "An artist's got to be free to do things his own way!" He moved nearer to us, close to the water's edge. "For God's sake, don't squabble! Save your troubles till I join you next summer. When I get there, you'll see they don't amount to anything, and never did—just like most troubles." He clapped both of us on the shoulder.

I thanked him for all his kindness to me: then went to say good-bye to Elizabeth, who stood on the high bank looking pale-faced, red-nosed and discontented in the gray light of approaching sunrise.

"Elizabeth," I said, "take good care of Ann, wont you? Her father's worse than useless, and you know I think more of her than anything in the world. You wont——"

Two thoughts struck me simultaneously. Ann was nowhere to be seen; and the words I had just spoken to Elizabeth were almost the selfsame words I had used to Ann about my sketch books—those sheets of worthless paper scrawled with scratchings in colored chalk.

"Why," I said, "where *is* Ann? I thought she followed me here! I haven't said good-bye to her."

"I'll give her the message," Elizabeth said.

"No," I cried. "No! That wont do! I'll have to see her myself! Tell McNott I'll be back at once!" I ran as fast as I

could for the water-gate, disregarding McNott's enraged bellow and Elizabeth's angry cry of "Langdon Towne!"

There was no sign of her on the parade or on the porch of
Rogers' quarters, or in any of the downstairs rooms. I raced
upstairs and into the billiard room, and there she was, kneeling behind my trunk, just as I had left her. In the pale light
that filtered through the dusty window I saw she was smiling
that singular, tight-lipped smile of hers.

I lifted her so that she stood on the trunk, her eyes level
with mine. She was as soft and yielding in my arms as a
kitten.

"Why didn't you come to the water-gate?" I asked, breathless from my run. "What made you stay here instead of
coming with me?"

She didn't answer.

I drew away from her, so to see her face. Her smile
was unchanged; her eyes, fixed on mine, seemed to swirl and
deepen, as do the brown waters of a brook when stared into
overlong; and I, looking into those eyes, almost forgot what
I had meant to say. "The sketch books," I said. "I was joking
about the sketch books. You're not to bother about them;
they're *not* worth more to me than anything in the world."
I kissed her and held her close.

When she still didn't speak, I took her hand, hurried her
down the stairs, out onto the parade and across to the water-
gate. Already the three canoes carrying Tute, Goddard,
Atherton and their voyageurs were on their way toward Lake
Michigan, red paddles flashing and voyageurs gaily singing.
McNott, in a rage, brandished his fist at me from the canoe
alongside the landing-stage and bawled at me to hurry.

Elizabeth caught Ann's shoulder and shook her. "Where
were you, ungrateful child!" she cried. Ann, her eyes on
mine, said nothing.

I patted her shoulder. "Good-bye, Ann. When I come back,
I'll bring you the prettiest presents in the West." I looked at
her helplessly, conscious of words within me, struggling to be
said, but incapable of uttering them.

Again Elizabeth shook her. "Ungrateful child," she cried
once more, "why don't you thank Mr. Towne?"

Without quite knowing how I got there, I found myself in
my narrow nest among the baggage in the bow. "Damn it!"
McNott shouted, "don't you know these Frenchies don't like

to be distanced? They probably wont let us eat till they catch up, and that might be two weeks!"

The steersman chanted, "*Mon Père a fait bâtir maison.*" Like a well-trained chorus the voyageurs swung their paddles and hoarsely continued the song:

> "*Ha, ha, ha, frit à l'huile,*
> *Sont trois charpentiers qui la font,*
> *Fritaine, friton, firtou, poilon,*
> *Ha, ha, ha, frit à l'huile,*
> *Frit au beurre à l'ognon.*"

I looked back at the rapidly receding shore and Fort Michilimackinac's brown palisades, whose pointed tips were golden spears in the bright rays of the newly-risen sun. Already Elizabeth had turned away and was walking rapidly toward the water-gate; and upon the landing-stage stood the Major and Ann, side by side.

I saw the Major go slowly up the sloping shore and into the fort; but for as long as I could see Ann—which was until our canoe turned out of the straits and moved to the northwest into Lake Michigan—her slender little figure never stirred.

What, I wondered, would become of her. Poor Major, I thought—and poor, poor Ann! With a sinking heart I contemplated the cold and empty days that stretched before her, deserted by her miserable father and eternally rebuked by Elizabeth; and I hoped that the Major, softened by his disappointment, would exert himself to show her the kindness that seemed beyond the comprehension of Elizabeth and Potter.

I thought about her and thought about her. Poor, smiling, uncomplaining, understanding, helpful, long-suffering Ann!

CHAPTER LXVIII

Tute, Goddard and Carver! Carver, Goddard and Tute! Those three names have rung in my head for years, like the discords of Indian songs that set the teeth on edge. I have tried hard to forget them, but without success, and I'd be better pleased to leave out all reference to them here. But to do so would be like writing of Julius Caesar and making no mention of Brutus and Pompey: like telling the story of Hannibal and leaving out Scipio Africanus.

Carver had preceded us by a month; and wherever we stopped on our long journey around the northern tip of Lake Michigan, into Green Bay, up the Fox River and down the Ouisconsin to the Mississippi, we had word of him, and it was always the same word—the story of the Menominee and the rattlesnake.

We heard it from solemn-faced Winnebagoes in their harsh tongue; more musically from jolly Sacs, saturnine Foxes and dignified Potawatomies; from gaily-gesturing Frenchmen; from English traders who slapped themselves delightedly in the telling. Everyone, it seemed to us, had heard it; and before we reached the Mississippi I had become so heartily sick of it that every bluejay and squirrel, peering down at us from overhanging trees, seemed to be about to ask: "Have our brothers heard how the white Captain believed the story of the Menominee and the rattlesnake?"

A French trader named Pinnashon had told Carver the story, and Carver wrote it down in a note book as a striking example of the wisdom of the serpent. Pinnashon, it appeared, was crossing the prairie one October day when he met a Menominee carrying a box; and on Pinnashon asking what was in the box, the Indian said it was his pet rattlesnake— his Great Father; that since the hunting season was approaching, he proposed to free the snake until the following spring. Pinnashon asked the Menominee whether he ever expected to see the snake again; and the red man said it would, of course, return whenever it was told to do so.

Pinnashon could not, he admitted, believe such a story: consequently he bet two gallons of rum that the snake wouldn't come back as ordered. The Menominee took the bet, instructed the snake to return on May fifth next; then opened the box and released his Great Father, who glided off through the grass.

On the fifth of May Pinnashon met the Menominee at the same place; but when the Indian placed the open box on the prairie and loudly summoned his Great Father, no snake appeared. Pinnashon therefore collected two gallons of rum.

The Menominee, undiscouraged, offered to bet Pinnashon ten gallons of rum that the snake would certainly be back before sundown on the following day; and Pinnashon, happy to bet on a certainty, agreed.

On the next afternoon, Pinnashon told Carver, the Menominee once more placed the open box upon the prairie and cried aloud to his Great Father, while Pinnashon with difficulty controlled his mirth. Imagine, then, said Pinnashon, his amazement, his consternation, when a snake appeared, entered the box and coiled itself inside with a contented rattle.

"Carver wrote it down in his note book!" said the trader who first told us the story. "Wrote it down and went telling it around to boot, saying he'd heard it from a veracious French gentleman!" He laughed loudly. "Pinnashon's French, no doubt of that; but nobody ever accused him of being a gentleman before, and he'd feel pretty bad if he knew anybody was calling him veracious. Yes, sir; Carver believed that old rascal, and never even thought to ask what made the snake late." He looked at us expectantly.

"Well," McNott said, "I aint no Carver; what *did* make it late?"

The trader snorted. "Hell, that was the point of the story! Damned near broke Pinnashon's heart, him having gone to so much trouble working up to the point, and then not getting asked about it."

McNott stared coldly at the trader. "Brother, what made the snake late?"

"It was a female snake," the trader said. "Aint females always late?"

A month after we had left Michilimackinac, the land on either side of the island-dotted Ouisconsin broadened into smooth plains. Over the plains appeared a far-off drift of smoke: a distant Indian lodge; another and another; then scores which multiplied into battalions, regiments, armies of pointed dwellings of red men.

"Prairie du Chien," the voyageurs shouted, "Prairie du Chien!"

The lodges extended along the plains to the north and to the south in hundreds and thousands, as far as we could see; they stood on the high bank of another river into which the Ouisconsin was bearing us—a river so enormous that it had more the look of a turbulent great lake than of a river. This tremendous stream was the Mississippi, outermost boundary of the America we knew.

When we landed on the right bank, we found the place as populous as Portsmouth, and even busier; and our arrival created no more excitement than the arrival of a gundelo at Spring Wharf.

The noise was something to marvel at. Everywhere among the tents and tepees were drunken Indians, both male and female, howling at the top of their lungs. There were white men, too, drunk and sober: voyageurs; bearded petty traders and traders' clerks; murderous-looking coureurs de bois, whooping and bellowing obscenities; traders' assistants yelling their masters' wares. Sober Indians hopped in circles to the tune of drums, turtle-shell rattles and their own yowlings; sweating Indians played games with all sorts of contrivances —beans, bowls, balls, elongated rackets—and gabbled ceaselessly as they played. As an undertone to this hubbub were the sounds of barking dogs, screaming children, tootling horns.

Goddard, guiding us to the section occupied by English traders, pointed out to us Indians as different from those with whom we were already familiar as trout are different from catfish. He showed us Blackfeet, deep-chested red men in leggins and moccasins the color of soot; Minnetarees from the Missouri River; Peorias, Kickapoos, Ioways, Shiennes; Crow warriors whose hair trailed on the ground: whose profiles from nose-tip to base of skull were one unbroken curve.

It was when we came upon two long rows of lodges made of snowy white skins, painted with suns, stars, buffaloes, antelopes running, that the Princess McNott did a strange thing. She put her fingers in her mouth as does a child who has played disastrously with fire, and hopped as children do when skipping rope. Thus hopping, she approached the white lodges, where Indians were clustered; and among those Indians another woman began to suck her fingers and to hop.

"Oh my God!" McNott groaned. "More brothers-in-law!"

McNott's wife and the other woman put their arms around each other and burst into tears, while all the nearby Indians, men and women too, pressed close around them, the women screaming with excitement; the men looking acutely distressed.

Both the men and the women were dressed in elkskins as soft and white as velvet. The young girls were pretty; the older women lacked the heavy-hipped appearance of Eastern Indians. As for the men, they were tall and regular-featured —the finest-looking specimens I had ever seen, red or white.

"Sioux," Goddard explained. "Naudowessioux."

"Listen, brother," McNott said, "call 'em Sioux and Naudowessioux all you want when there aint none of 'em around; but when there *are*, call 'em Dacotas unless you want trouble."

An Indian as tall as Major Rogers came from behind one of the white lodges, stood smiling down at McNott's wife, and said something that set all the women to hopping once more. The sight of him made my fingers itch for crayons. His face, beautiful to begin with, was softened by a frame of small black-tipped cylinders of ermine-skin which hung from his bonnet of eagle-feathers. Over his forehead the rolls of ermine were short: on the sides they reached his shoulders.

Whatever the names of these Indians—Sioux, Naudowessioux or Dacotas—they, I knew, were the ones I wanted most of all to sketch.

The Indian with the ermine head-dress was Wanotan, chief of the Yanktons, one of the seven great divisions of the Dacotas, whom the French call Naudowessioux or Naudowessies and the English know as Sioux. The very word "Dacota" means "United"; and the Dacotas are a union of tribes who live in amity with each other and unite in war against enemies.

They are great horsemen; daring and courageous warriors; and those whose hunting grounds are far from the traders of the Mississippi River and their rum-kegs are fine people, hospitable, generous, trustworthy toward friends and allies, and accomplished stealers of enemies' horses. But the Mississippi Dacotas known as River Bands, are different. They are lazier and dirtier, their craving for alcohol is something to marvel at; and their leaning toward horse-stealing has broadened into a passion for stealing almost anything from almost anybody.

All this I learned from McNott, whose wife had been a Yankton before she was captured by Chippeways. The woman she had embraced was the daughter of Wanotan and had been captured by the same Chippeway war party that had carried the Princess McNott to the eastward, but had escaped; and the reason the Dacota women hopped with joy was because Wanotan had told the Princess McNott that her parents were dead, but that his lodge was hers and she his daughter.

That was how McNott and his wife and I happened to spend the winter with Wanotan on the hunting grounds of the Yanktons between the St. Peter's and the Missouri rivers, while Jonathan Carver was spending it at the mouth of the St. Peter's with the River Bands; how I was able to accumulate the pastels for the folio edition of *Life Among the Dakotas* which was published by the wealthy Ethnographic Society of London for its members; and how I discovered the true route to the great River Oregon—which Jonathan Carver, like the ingrate he was, later stole without acknowledgement.

CHAPTER LXIX

TUTE AND Goddard seemed glad to be rid of us. "Carver went up the river with Bruce," Tute said, "and Bruce winters near the Falls of St. Anthony, about four miles upstream from where the St. Peter's enters the Mississippi. When you go up the St. Peter's, send a message to Carver and tell him to come back here to Prairie du Chien in the spring with the chiefs he's persuaded to go to the Major's Peace Congress. Do the same yourself, and then we'll all set out together for the great River Oregon and the Northwest Passage."

We discharged our voyageurs, bought two small Chippeway canoes, loaded our supplies into them and set off, McNott and his wife and two Dacota braves in one: Wanotan and

I and two more Dacota braves in the other. Wanotan himself took the steering paddle and guided us through the countless islets of the Mississippi, across the beautiful islandless expansion of its channel at treacherous Lake Pepin, and around the wooded island that conceals the mouth of the St. Peter's from travellers on the greater river. The weather was cold and there was ice in the shallows by the time we reached the blue water of the St. Peter's; so we made no effort to go on to the Falls of St. Anthony to hunt Carver ourselves, but merely sent him Tute's message and pressed on toward the hunting grounds of the Yanktons before ice should stop our progress.

Nowhere is there a prairie more beautiful than that which borders the St. Peter's. I can see it now, dotted with little groves, speckled in low spots by the domes of muskrat houses, undulating off to the distant blue cloud of the Côteau des Prairies—that giant wave of earth which separates the valley of the St. Peter's from the valley of the Missouri, and bears on its crest the red stone from which all Indians carve their pipes.

I can almost hear again the barking cries of Wanotan's mounted warriors, galloping their spotted horses along the bluff at the river's edge to make us welcome.

I need no sketches to remind me of the ever-changing scenes that kept my crayons busy all that winter: Wanotan's braves, with live sparrow-hawks made fast to their heads; papers of pins dangling from their hair; looking glasses suspended from their garments; the white skin tents on the brown prairie in the late autumn; old Dacota women cooking buffalo and dog meat in iron kettles over fires of dried buffalo dung, wiping their fingers on their own hair or on the hair of their dogs, rinsing their hands in the kettle of warm drinking water, from which we were all supposed to drink; bands of buffalo merging into herds so huge that the barren prairie seemed to have sprouted a vast and solid forest of brown scrub; hard-riding young men, their long hair streaming out behind, lashing frantic ponies against the flanks of those herds to leave hundreds of shaggy, mud-caked carcasses on the prairie, bloody gangs of women, children and old men hacking dead buffalo into chunks.

Once more I see the blinding storms of winter that half-buried our village in drifts; the glittering oceans of snow on which we looked out when the storms were over, and black hulks of buffalo wallowing and pawing for food in that vast expanse of white; the swift run of Wanotan's men on snowshoes across the frozen billows to drive lances through those clumsy brutes.

I can feel the interior of the fire-lit tents at night—interiors so reeking with the smoke from buffalo chips, steam from the kettles and the greasy smell of a score of Indians that the lungs and eyes seemed filled with a hot and stinging thickness; feel, too, the pressure of shivering dogs against my back and legs; hear the thumps and yelps as McNott cleared them from him with blows of his wooden leg; smell the soft mustiness of the buffalo robes in which we were wrapped; hear the nightly chattering and gay laughter that went on around me, until I wondered a thousand thousand times how in God's name Indians had ever come to be known as a gloomy, silent race of people.

Sharpest of all my recollections of that winter are those of my incessant and ever-increasing longing for the spring. I was grateful to Wanotan, his wives, his children, his braves, for their unfailing hospitality and their patience in posing for the sketches on which I daily labored; I was touched and flattered, too, by their ever-fresh admiration of my drawings; but the truth of the matter was that my eagerness to start to the westward—to hear the Major's thick voice urging us on and on, always toward the great discovery—made me hate the endlessly unproductive life of the Dacotas and their complete absorption in hunting, eating, fighting, dancing, sleeping and loving. So thoroughly did I dislike it that by the time the ice had begun to rot in March, I was sure that no reward could ever again induce me to seclude myself from civilized society in a wilderness where there were no books or other sources of intellectual enjoyment.

I was doubly anxious to see the Major because of a discovery we had accidentally made.

The discovery came about in this way: when we spoke to Wanotan about the desire of Major Rogers to have peace among all the Western Indians, and asked him to send messengers to other nations asking their chiefs to go to Michilimackinac, he gladly agreed. He would, he said, send messengers south to the Mandans on the Missouri and north to the Assiniboins. "The Assiniboins," he said, "will listen to me, because I permit them to pass unmolested when their war parties travel south to the Missouri to make the journey to the Shining Mountains."

Now in Tute's orders the Major had said that our route in search of the Northwest Passage would be north to the headwaters of the Mississippi, west to Fort La Parrie, and across the Shining Mountains to the great River Oregon. We must, he'd told Tute, be careful not to ascend the Missouri by mistake. Yet here was Wanotan talking of going to the Shining Mountains by way of the Missouri as though it were the only route.

When McNott's wife, at our urging, questioned Wanotan as to why Assiniboins should go south and up the Missouri to reach the Shining Mountains, when they could more easily and quickly go directly west, Wanotan looked pained. Even little children, he seemed to think, should know the reason; he considered it one of those simple things that didn't need explaining.

What Wanotan eventually revealed was that the country of the Assiniboins, in the summer, was flat and watery—too wet for good hunting—so flat and watery that three great rivers rose within the radius of a mile; one the St. Lawrence, another the Mississippi and the third the river that flows north into Hudson's Bay. Because of countless rivers, lakes and marshes, Wanotan said, the mosquitoes were terrible beyond belief, settling on travellers in clouds. Because of the wetness there was little game, and to the westward the country was barren and the Indians poor—so poor they weren't worth fighting.

That, Wanotan assured us, was why the Assiniboins always went elsewhere in the summer, as did the Minnetarees of Fort La Parrie. They came to the place where we now were; then crossed the prairie to the valley of the Missouri, where the land is dry and fertile; where buffaloes, deer, turkeys, geese and beaver are counted in millions; where war parties are rewarded for their efforts because all the Indian nations near the headwaters of the Missouri are rich in horses. Every year, Wanotan said, war parties from the Assiniboins and Minnetarees went into the Shining Mountains to take horses and prisoners from the Shoshonees who live at the source of the Missouri.

McNott looked skeptical. "They do, do they? If they do

it every year, why aint the Assiniboins and the Minnetarees got all the horses by now?"

Wanotan was patient with him. "Because when the Shoshonees lose horses, they go down the river on the other side of the Shining Mountains and catch wild ones. That river runs all the way to the Stinking Lake, in the west, where the land ends."

The Stinking Lake, I knew, was the name given by Indians to the ocean; so the river down which the Shoshonees went to get their horses must be the great River Oregon. "How far," I asked him, "from the headwaters of the Missouri to the beginning of the river on the other side of the Shining Mountains?"

"Minnetarees say two smokes," Wanotan said. Two smokes was the equivalent of thirty minutes.

"Hell," McNott said, "if the Minnetarees can do it in thirty minutes, the Major can do it in less time than it takes Carver to sneeze."

I had a sudden disquieting recollection of how carelessly McNott had once said to me, "And that's going to be the end of St. Francis," and of all the agony we endured in order to achieve that end.

When the ice went out at the end of April, Wanotan and a score of his followers set off with us for Prairie du Chien, true to the promise Wanotan had made to go to the Major's Peace Congress at Michilimackinac; and when we turned from the St. Peter's into the Mississippi we were hailed by an encampment of chiefs from the Dacota River Bands. Among them, as we drew nearer, we saw Jonathan Carver.

"Don't tell him nothing!" McNott warned me. "Let him tell us! That's the only way to handle fellers that don't care what's told 'em!"

When we landed, we found a different Carver than we had known in Michilimackinac. He seemed less obsequious, less feline, more important: in a word, more prosperous. His face was rounder, his eyes less protuberant; he even wore new buckskins, more elegant than our own. Certainly he was a little excited.

"Damned little pop-eye!" McNott said. "What's the matter with him? Looks like he'd gone and bought himself a frisky young squaw, and she's been feeding him beaver-tails and fat white dogs, and making him think he's a skittish young stud-horse! No fool like an old fool!"

Carver gave us a gracious greeting. "Welcome," he called. "Well met! I had your message! How go the labors in the vineyard? Observe my contributions to the Major's Congress!" He waved his hand at the chiefs of the River Bands. "All the great men of the Naudowessies."

"Listen," McNott said sharply, "don't call 'em Naudowessies—not when we're with you! They don't like it."

"My dear Sergeant," Carver said, "you're mistaken. I've been with them all winter, joining them in the pleasures of the chase, sitting by their fires, eating from the same pots in neighborliness and amity, exchanging anecdotes with them in their own language——"

"Oh, you speak their language, do you?" McNott asked. "Speak it well?"

"This morning," Carver said simply, "I addressed them in the Naudowessie tongue."

McNott scratched his chin, opened his mouth as if to call to the Princess McNott; then seemed to think better of it.

"Where'd you winter, Captain?" he asked.

"In the country of the Naudowessies on the St. Peter's," Carver said. "I explored it thoroughly, taking maps and surveys of the land."

"That's good," McNott said heartily. "That'll be a big help when we set out to find the great River Oregon."

Carver stared from McNott to me. "Oregon?" he asked. "The great River Oregon? You mean the great River Bourbon, do you not? The Red River, I believe some call it."

"Gosh!" McNott said, "I forgot you aint seen the orders the Major gave us after you left! Tute's got 'em, Captain, and that's why he sent word for you to be sure to come back to Prairie du Chien. We're all going to start hunting the great River Oregon and the Northwest Passage, and the Major's coming out to lead us. There's a reward of £20,000 if we find 'em."

"The great River Oregon!" Carver said again. "How far is it? My supplies—that is to say, I have no supplies remaining."

"You aint?" McNott cried. "Why, you had a canoe-load when you left Michilimackinac! What you done with 'em, Captain?"

"I gave them as boons to the Naudowessies," Carver said,

"also to the Sacs, Foxes and Winnebagoes, to induce them to attend the Major's Congress."

McNott looked puzzled. "Didn't they give you nothing back? Now me and Langdon, we can't carry all the supplies we got for the few little piddy-widdy things we gave 'em. Every time we gave 'em a piece of sheet iron four inches square, they gave us eight gallons of corn or six bags of pemmican, depending on which we preferred. We still got most of what we brought with us from Michilimackinac. You don't mean you aint got nothing left out of that great big canoe-load of stuff!"

Carver's lips once more were pursed, his protuberant eyes shifty. "The demands on me, I apprehend," he said, "have been more onerous than you would believe. And now, gentlemen, if you will excuse me, I must attend to my friends— my charges." He stared at us blankly, said "Oregon" in a baffled voice, and turned away cautiously, as a cat might turn.

McNott, watching his feline departure, shook his head. "There's something wrong, Langdon! Remember what I told you the day you joined the Rangers?"

"You told me a lot of things."

"Yes," McNott said, "but one of 'em was more important than any of the rest. 'There's an army depending on us for information,' I told you, 'so you got to tell the truth about what you see and what you do. You can lie all you please when you tell other folks about the Rangers,' I told you, 'but don't never lie to a Ranger or an officer,' Remember me telling you that?"

"I never forgot what you told me that day, Sergeant."

"No, I guess you didn't," McNott said. "I guess you wouldn't 'a' come out of that St. Francis expedition as well as you did if you hadn't remembered everything you was told, and behaved according. Well, Langdon, Carver aint telling us the truth. I'll go farther than that and say he's just a plumb liar. I'll bet you a white buffalo robe he never went more than twenty miles up the St. Peter's, even; and he didn't make no oration to them Indians in their own tongue, because if he did, he wouldn't be calling 'em Naudowessies. I say he never explored nothing; and what's more, he's telling us some kind of a lie when he says he never got nothing in return for giving away his presents and supplies. Well, Langdon, what's the reason for it? He aint lying just to hear himself lie, is he? Of course he aint! He's lying so we wont know what he's been up to, just the way every liar does; and what I want to know is, what's he been up to?"

Carver got away for Prairie du Chien before we did; but not a thing could we learn about his activities from the chiefs of the River Bands. The Princess McNott heard someone refer to him by a Dacota name meaning "Moon-buyer," but when the chiefs were asked about it, they only looked puzzled and shook their heads.

"Damn it," McNott said, "nobody wouldn't 'a' called him that name right out of a clear sky. They might 'a' called him 'Pop-eye' out of a clear sky, or 'Man-who-walks-on-egg-shells,' but not 'Moon-buyer.' He had to buy something to get called 'Moon-buyer.' What do you s'pose he bought, Langdon? Whatever it was, he aint got it with him, that's certain!"

We had to give it up; but on the way to Prairie du Chien I thought often of Carver's odd behavior when McNott had mentioned that we were to go in search of the great River Oregon and the Northwest Passage. His whole appearance had abruptly changed. From being confident and gracious he had suddenly become apprehensive and furtive. The more I thought of it, the more it seemed to me that Carver had been afraid of something; and yet I knew that whatever else Carver might be, he certainly wasn't a coward. It was all beyond my comprehension.

I was no better satisfied when McNott and I reached Prairie du Chien and hurried to Tute's tent in that crowded and tumultuous Indian metropolis; for not only did we find Tute, Goddard and Carver with their heads together, but Carver had again resumed his air of condescension and importance. As for Tute and Goddard, they greeted us pleasantly, which in itself was unusual, since Tute had never before taken the trouble to conceal his dislike for me.

My first question, of course, was for the Major, but Tute knew nothing, so I told him what we had learned from Wanotan—that the way to reach the great River Oregon was by way of the St. Peter's River and the Missouri, and not by the route laid down in the Major's orders. The three men heard me in silence. At McNott's insistence I had reserved for the Major's own ear some of the most important information that Wanotan had given us; but neither Tute, Goddard nor Carver asked for further details.

"That's very interesting," Tute said. "Very interesting. I'll inform the Major. Got to write him soon, anyway." He cleared his throat and looked inquiringly at Carver, so that I knew he had no particular desire to hear more from me.

"When are you figuring on starting, Captain?" I asked.

"Just as soon as we get the Indians safely away to Michilimackinac," he said. "The French and Spaniards are fighting tooth and nail to keep 'em from going. They're offering 'em all sorts of inducements to come to New Orleans. Only today they stole ten of Captain Carver's Naudowessies: persuaded 'em to keep on down river instead of going to the Major's Congress as they'd promised; so we got to keep talking to 'em."

"We want to get started as soon as we can, Captain," I reminded him. "If we don't get as far as we ought to get this summer, the trip'll probably take us an extra year, even with the Major leading us."

"Don't worry, Mr. Towne," Tute said heartily. "You tend to your painting and we'll tend to the worrying." He smiled; and so did Carver and Goddard. Unless I was greatly mistaken, there was something behind those smiles besides amiability, and that something looked to me like veiled amusement. My doubt and bewilderment increased; but not even the best guesser in the world could have guessed the fantastic secret shared by Goddard, Tute and Carver—the secret we were soon to learn.

I had hoped against hope to find a letter from Ann at Prairie du Chien, and my disappointment when I didn't was greater than I would have thought possible. I had long intended to write her a letter to send by Wanotan with my winter's sketches; but now that I was in Prairie du Chien I put off writing from day to day in the hope that traders might soon come through to the Mississippi from Michilimackinac, and that one of them would have letters for me—perhaps a letter from the Major and certainly one from Ann.

Indeed, I hardly had time to write, so frequently did I visit the landing-place on the Ouisconsin where brigades al-

ways landed. Each night I told myself hopefully that a brigade might arrive at sun-up the next day with letters; and
when sun-up passed, I'd stand there an hour or more, straining my eyes up river, hoping to see a brigade come in sight
from behind the little islands. Late in the morning was a
good hour for brigades to arrive, so I was always there then,
and also from sundown until dark. Never before had I felt
such restlessness and irritation as that which drove me on
my daily journeys to the landing-stage; and not until dawn
on the morning that Wanotan was to leave did I give up
hope, get out paper and pen and sit down to write Ann.

The muted sounds of daybreak gave way to the pandemo-
nium of an Indian encampment: I heard McNott cleaning his
teeth with ashes and complaining that the Princess McNott
must have put a pole-cat and an old undershirt in the fire before retiring on the preceding evening: I heard Tute pre-
senting pewter medals to a party of Indian chiefs; and still I
wrote on and on. I found nothing remarkable in the fact
that my pen raced over the paper at three times the rate I
had ever known it to move before, or that the labor of
writing filled me with a lightness of spirit such as I hadn't
felt for months; or that again and again I sprinkled upon
the pages, as freely as punctuation marks, the words "Ann
dearest."

It was only when I found myself writing, with a feeling of
tightness in my breast, how long the days had seemed after
our canoe had left Michilimackinac; how sharply the picture
of her upon the landing-stage of the fort was etched within
my brain; with what poignancy that picture swam before my
eyes whenever our voyageurs, on the long journey down the
Ouisconsin, sang (as they were forever doing), "*Fritaine,
friton, firtou, poilon; Ha, ha, ha, frit à l'huile*"—it was only
then that I put down my pen, picked up the sheets, and
hastily read them over with a rapidly-growing realization of
what I had done, and at the end a complete understanding of
the reason for my restlessness during the past winter.

What I had written, I saw, was a love letter. If I had
thought at all, when I began to write it, I would have thought
that I felt for Ann only the fondness which a brother feels
for an affectionate younger sister; but I knew better now. My
feeling for her was so deep that no child as young and inexperienced as Ann could ever understand it.

I sat there, staring at the pages—at the "dearest Anns" swimming upon them as thick as islands on the Mississippi. I shouldn't, I told myself, send her such a letter; but within me I continued to argue. Ann was more than a child, wasn't she? Surely, too, she wasn't inexperienced! And wasn't she both tolerant and wise? Hadn't she seen and understood the bestiality of London slums? Didn't her understanding of everything she saw and heard verge at times on the miraculous?

I thought so; and yet—into my mind came the memory of her eyes looking at me from between the balustrades of the dim upper hall at Michilimackinac; of how she had continued to kneel there without moving, when I kissed her. Would anyone but a child have acted so? Would anyone but a child have hidden herself without a word on the morning of our departure? Would I, going in search of her, have found her crouching in a dark corner, dry-eyed and smiling, unless she had been a child? And if she weren't a child, would she have stood motionless and unresponsive while I held her in my arms and pressed my lips to hers?

That kiss, I now admitted, had been no brother's kiss.

Of course, I told myself—of *course* she was a child—a mere child still. I took a fresh sheet of paper and began again—"Ann." Her name, alone like that, looked forlorn. I added a word—"darling"; then crumpled the sheet and thrust it in my pocket.

Why had Elizabeth been so fearful of my influence on Ann—so insistent in her wish to know whether I had gone to Ann's room—so observant of Ann's habit of looking at me—so resentful of her appearance in the Ottawa costume presented to her by Kab-bes-kunk's wife—so determined that Ann's limbs, as Elizabeth so delicately put it, should not be displayed? Why had she felt obliged to speak of all these things unless she considered Ann no longer a child? And how was it that she had seen Ann looking at me? Not as a child, certainly, or Elizabeth would never have spoken of it.

I didn't know what to think, and so groaned unhappily; then laughed at myself for groaning. If Ann was a child, she wouldn't always be one. Perhaps by the time she got my letter——

Confused and troubled, I took a fresh sheet of paper, wrote the word "My" upon it, scratched it out and wrote

"Dearest," scratched that out and wrote "Dear Ann," threw down the pen, tore the paper in a dozen pieces—and heard McNott's voice shout, "Well, for God's sake!"

He was standing at the door of the tent, looking at me; and as I stared blankly at him, he came in and looked over my shoulder. "What the hell you writing that takes so much tearing up?" he demanded.

When I hastily placed my hand over the pages, he scratched his jaw and looked contemptuous.

"Listen, Langdon," he said, "Wanotan's waiting to get away. You been five hours writing that letter; and five hours, by God, is enough time to tell anybody anything! Why, I'll bet a dollar you've wrote ten times as much as there is in the Bible about the creation of the world! You finish that up quick, or the French'll get Wanotan away from us just the way they did those ten Dacota chiefs of Carver's."

He looked at me moodily. "By God, it wa'n't natural for them ten Dacotas to go off that way, when all their friends went to Michilimackinac to get presents from the Major. I bet they were scairt of something. Now I wonder——" He rumbled and bumbled to himself.

Once again I ran through the letter to Ann, took out the pages on which I'd told her how long the days had seemed without her, tore them to bits, and added another page— "I'm sending my pastels in your care, because you understand better than anyone how much they mean to me. They have protectors between each sketch, and since they're sewn in a double thickness of buffalo hide, the package is waterproof. Don't let it be opened, and when I come back, Ann dear, we'll open it together."

Utterly dissatisfied, I sat and stared at the last words. There was more, much more, that I wanted to say; but my thoughts churned uselessly within me.

"Listen," McNott said violently, "if you got anything more to say in that letter, say it. If you aint, sign your name, for God's sake! If you can't sign your name, draw a picture of yourself; but do *something!*"

"Yes," I said uncertainly, "I guess that's best—a picture of the writer and his best friends, Sergeant McNott and the Princess."

Mollified, McNott watched me sketch a canoe broadside to the beholder. In the stern sat McNott's wife grimly clutching a detached wooden leg; amidship sat McNott, gaily waving his cap; and in the bow was I, holding aloft a paddle whose blade bore the words, "Love to Ann."

CHAPTER LXX

No PERSON is so persistently vindictive as is a small-minded, short-sighted man toward those who have openly accused him of wrongdoing. That was the chief reason why I said so little to Carver, Tute and Goddard when our suspicion of them became practically a certainty. We were sure they were lying to us, but we couldn't prove it; and there was, of course, just the bare chance that they were telling the truth. Even if we had known at the time what we later discovered, I would have hesitated to make any open accusations for fear their vindictiveness would have led them to lie to the Major about our newly-acquired knowledge, or to conceal it from him.

We would start up river for the great discovery, Tute had told us, at sunrise on the twenty-first of May; and dawn of that day found me packing the last of my sketching materials. McNott and his wife had risen earlier and gone to load our canoe, together with the two Dacota braves, Tokacou and Moukaushka, left by Wanotan to attend us on our travels up the St. Peter's, across to the Missouri and up that river as far as we wished.

When I hurried to the landing-stage, I found Tute, Carver, Goddard, Atherton and their interpreter, all smiles and cheerfulness, standing by their heavily-loaded canoes; while McNott, already settled amidships in our own, stared stonily before him with that same white look around his mouth that I had seen on that far-off unhappy morning when he had furiously attempted to kick discipline into the raging Rangers at Otter River.

Thinking he was in a bad humor because I was late, and hoping to get his mind on other things, I said, "It's like a dream, Sergeant Mac, setting off at last to find the Northwest Passage. It's——"

McNott interrupted me brusquely. "I guess you aint seen who's paddling 'em."

For the first time I looked at their canoemen. Every last one of them was a Chippeway.

At a loss what to do or what to say, I swung my pack into the canoe, then went to Captain Tute, who beamed upon me. "We're heavily loaded, Mr. Towne," he said, "but I think you'll find you'll have all you can do to keep up with us."

"Captain," I said, "we're following the Major's orders, aren't we? We're going to try to find the great River Oregon, aren't we?"

"Why, yes," Tute said. "Yes. Of course we are!" Probably his hearty laugh was intended to be reassuring.

"But you've got Chippeways, Captain," I protested. "Chippeway paddlers and a Chippeway chief as well."

"I have indeed," Tute said, "and as I say, you'll find it hard to keep up with us. Best paddlers in the West, Chippeways are. And this chief, Ongawe—why, everybody says there's no better guide anywhere!"

"But they're *Chippeways*, Captain," I said again. "They're not familiar with the Western country we've got to go through. And we're going through Dacota territory. You know the Dacotas don't think much of Chippeways. And didn't the Major's orders say to take Dacota guides—Sioux guides?"

Tute's smile vanished. "Yes. I believe they did say something like that." He just stood there, looking at me. When I turned to Carver, Goddard and Atherton, in the vague hope that they might uphold me, they only stared intently at the ground.

There was nothing to do. I went back to our own canoe, picked up my paddle, slid into one of the amidship seats, and waited for Tute to lead the way up river.

Hoping against hope that our fears were groundless, we stayed as cheerful as we could, kept our mouths shut, and our eyes and ears open. The Chippeways, as Tute had said, were great paddlers, able to outdistance us; so perhaps, I told McNott, I had misjudged Tute and Carver. McNott only snorted; and at the southern end of Lake Pepin, where the Chippeway River enters the Mississippi, the blow fell.

Tute's and Carver's canoes had gained on us all that afternoon, and toward evening we saw them drawn up in the shelter of the bluff at the junction of the two rivers. When we drove our canoe out of the dusky water of the Mississippi and into the clear current of the Chippeway, Tute walked to the water's edge to watch us come in. He looked serious.

"We've had bad news, gentlemen," he said. "We're going to have to alter our course a little."

I looked at McNott. His face was scarlet. "Sergeant," I said, "don't come ashore till you've cooled off." I climbed from the canoe and walked up the beach with Tute to where Carver, Goddard and Atherton sat beside a fire, gazing absently at their shoes, as seemed to have become their habit when near McNott or myself.

"Our canoemen," Tute went on, "refuse to continue on up the Mississippi, and our guide also considers it unwise. That leaves only one alternative. We'll be obliged to leave the Mississippi here. We'll follow the Chippeway to its source: then cut over to the end of Lake Superior and wait there for supplies."

I stared from him to the others, and in the heavy silence the distant laughter of their Chippeway canoemen, angling for catfish, seemed derisive.

"You're going to give up your hunt for the River Oregon and the Northwest Passage?" I said heavily. "Give it up before you've started?"

"Certainly not," Tute said. "I don't know what put that idea into your head. We're just going to the Grand Portage on Lake Superior. There's no better spot as a starting-place for Fort La Parrie and the Northwest, as you know."

"But it's off the track, Captain! We want to go up the St. Peter's River. Fort La Parrie's too far north for our purposes. And if you spend any length of time on Lake Superior, you'll never get within striking distance of the Shining Mountains this summer! You'll have to come all the way back to the Falls of St. Anthony and the St. Peter's. Don't leave the Mississippi, Captain, just when we're almost at the St. Peter's."

"My dear Towne," Tute said kindly, "it's out of the question. Our canoemen absolutely refuse to pass through the Sioux country."

"If that's the only reason," I said, "let 'em go. McNott and

I'll go forward to the Falls of St. Anthony and get Dacotas—Sioux—for you."

Tute shook his head. "Unfortunately, Mr. Towne, we're much in need of supplies, and the place to get them, of course—provided the Major sends them—is at the Grand Portage."

I looked helplessly at the heap of 90-pound bales that had been unloaded from his two canoes. There must have been thirty of them—almost two full loads. "But you've *got* supplies," I said. Behind me I heard the sound of McNott's wooden leg in the gravel, and of his heavy breathing.

"Supplies of a sort," Tute admitted. "Captain Carver has none at all, and these of mine are only calculated to get us to Lake Superior. They're not suitable for use among the Sioux."

"Why aint they?" McNott asked. "Sioux wear papers of pins in their hair. They're glad to get anything. Even if you didn't have nothing but diapers and stays and false teeth, they'd be suitable. Hell, Captain, I'll guarantee to make diapers all the rage with the Sioux. You can't——" He stopped when I took him by the arm.

To Tute I said: "Captain, if these supplies aren't suitable, you can exchange 'em for suitable ones at the Falls of St. Anthony when the traders come down from Michilimackinac —and they'll soon be down. Captain Carver can draw against the Major for supplies, too—the way you must have done."

"My dear Towne," Tute said, "what makes you think we haven't considered these possibilities? There's a very good reason why Captain Carver can't draw supplies against the Major. The traders wont supply him."

"Why not? They supplied you, and the Major's orders were that supplies could be drawn against him as needed."

"Yes," Tute said patiently, "but I got my supplies before the traders saw how many Indians were going to Michilimackinac for the Major's Congress. There'll be seven thousand at least—seven thousand Indians looking to the Major for presents. If the Major gives presents to seven thousand Indians, he'll be obliged to buy the presents from traders, and the only way he can pay the traders is with drafts on the Indian Department—isn't it?"

"I don't know," I said. "Yes, I suppose so."

"Yes," Goddard said, "it is."

"Well," Tute said. "Sir William Johnson *is* the Indian Department; and if Johnson should refuse to honor the drafts, none of the traders would ever be paid. What's more, the Major would be thousands of pounds in debt. So you see, Mr. Towne, the traders are afraid to let Captain Carver have more supplies. That's why we must go to Lake Superior and wait for supplies to come directly from the Major."

I made a final desperate attempt. "But, Captain: you've got enough gifts with you to carry us wherever we want to go, and if we go by way of the Missouri, we can live off the country, all of us—something you can't do around Lake Superior. It's alive with buffalo; swarming with muskrats as easy to catch as chickens. Probably the Major *will* be thousands of pounds in debt, as the traders say, but he'll never get out of debt unless we help him discover the Northwest Passage. That's all we've got to do, Captain: get the proof that the Major's right: show that he was justified in his search for the great River Oregon. If we can do that, Captain, no man in America would dare to refuse to honor the Major's drafts. Any expenditure he might have made would be upheld. If Sir William Johnson dared to refuse to honor his drafts, he'd be removed from office, and rightly so. Once we've made that discovery for the Major, nobody can touch him—nobody! He'll be the greatest man in North America."

Tute slowly shook his head. "What you say may be true, Mr. Towne, but we'll do the Major no good if we go to the westward, make this discovery, and have insufficient supplies and gifts to get us back home. Further argument's useless: we've made up our minds. I'm in command of this party, and responsible for it. I can't afford to gamble there'll be buffalo and muskrats where we'll need to go. You've been in the Rangers, and you know that's one of the things the Major always insisted on: Don't take chances. I must know I've got enough supplies to ensure our safety; and the place to get those supplies is at the Grand Portage on Lake Superior; so that's where we're going. Have your canoe loaded and ready to start at sunrise tomorrow."

"Captain," I said, "I hope you'll reconsider. I know the Major used to tell his men not to take chances when they weren't necessary; but he made exceptions when there was something to be accomplished, as when he led us against St. Francis. You weren't there, Captain, but you can take my word he took more chances than we'll ever be called on to take."

"There was nothing else he could do, was there?" Tute said. "We'll start for Lake Superior at sunrise."

God knows how McNott restrained himself from trying to throttle at least one of our leaders. As for myself, I could have shot Tute, Carver and Goddard without a qualm; but I didn't even dare show my resentment.

"In that case," I said, "McNott and I—we'll go on to the St. Peter's so to have things ready for the Major when he comes out. We'll leave word with the Dacotas, and they'll tell him where to find us. After being with the Major at St. Francis, and knowing how he feels about finding a route to the Pacific, I take it he'd want us to go forward if we could— so I guess we will."

CHAPTER LXXI

HOPEFUL UNTIL the last that Carver, Tute and Goddard might change their minds, Mc-Nott and I stood on the sheltered beach where the Chippeway runs into the Mississippi and watched the two heavily-laden canoes slide off into a rosy mist. All five of our erstwhile companions saluted us politely enough as they drew away; and it seemed to me they looked complacent, like men inwardly rejoicing over large winnings at the gaming table, but trying not to show it.

Sick at heart, I told McNott to stop his cursing and get the canoe loaded. "We'll go on to the Falls of St. Anthony, just above the mouth of the St. Peter's," I told him. "The Major's orders said for Tute to winter there; and even though Tute didn't, that's where the Major'll send word by the first trader to leave Michilimackinac."

McNott slapped his wife noisily on the rump to speed her in the loading. "Langdon," he said, "those fellers know what they're doing. They're thick as thieves that just robbed a hen-

roost, and there's something they all know about together—
something that makes 'em want to go up into the Chippeway
country."

He thoughtfully fingered the slit in his damaged ear. "Now
for God's sake, Langdon, why should they want to go into
Chippeway country? What's the real reason they turned off
from the Mississippi? It certainly aint because they lack supplies, and it certainly aint because they're afraid of Sioux.
Hell, Langdon, Carver may not have gone far up the St.
Peter's, but he was thick enough with those Sioux we found
him with, and he knows they're friendly to travellers, just as
well as we do. He was safe with 'em, wasn't he? Safe as a flea
on a porcupine's back!"

He shook his head. "By God, I can't figger it out! Carver
gave those Sioux plenty of presents, too, because we saw the
looking glasses hanging on 'em, and the brass curtain rods
in their hair, and those pretty checkered calico shirts; but
they hadn't given him a damned thing, so far as I could make
out! 'Taint natural, Langdon; but I'll be damned if I can see
any reason for it—and if there aint a reason, I'm a Win-
nebago!"

We not only discovered the reason at the Falls of St. Anthony, but with the help of little Ezekiel Solomon and the letters he brought us, we got back our confidence, which Tute
and Carver and Goddard had almost destroyed.

Indian women assemble in great numbers at the Falls of
St. Anthony in the spring of the year, partly to enjoy the
majestic beauty of the thirty-foot-high curtain of snowy water
that hangs straight across the Mississippi, partly to take fish
by the thousand from the pool below the falls, but chiefly
because of their eagerness to greet the first spring traders
who come out from Michilimackinac with the latest thing in
calico bed-gowns, colored paint, blue glass beads and red
broadcloth for trousers.

From these women the Princess McNott heard what it was
that even Wanotan had concealed from us—probably because
he was ashamed to reveal it—and what it was that the
chiefs of the River Bands had, doubtless because they feared
the consequences, also denied knowing. It explained why
Carver was called "Moon-buyer," why he had suddenly be-

come so important and gracious, and why he and Tute and Goddard had gone up the Chippeway River.

Carver had met the chiefs of the River Bands just before McNott and I had found him at the mouth of the St. Peter's in May, and had distributed gifts among them. After the distribution there remained to him several bales of interesting presents. Later he addressed the chiefs through an interpreter, telling them the desire of the White Father at Michili-mackinac for peace between the Chippeways and Sioux. If, he had told them, they didn't stop fighting the Chippeways, traders would never again be allowed to come among them.

Now on the eastern side of the Mississippi there was an enormous stretch of territory claimed as hunting grounds by both the Chippeways, who had towns all through it, and by the River Bands who lived only along its water-front. This piece of territory extended from the Falls of St. Anthony to the Chippeway River, along the Mississippi, and also extended an equal distance inland from the river. Roughly, it was one hundred miles square. Since it was claimed by both Chippeways and Sioux, no Sioux could hunt on it without being regarded by the Chippeways as trespassers, whereas the Chippeways who already lived on it were held by the Sioux to be intruders. Thus the Sioux and the Chippeways were perpetually going to war over this square of land, and persuading their allies to go to war over it as well.

When Carver told the River Band chiefs that there must be no more fighting between Chippeways and Sioux, two of the younger chiefs, already famous for their skill at horse-stealing, had an idea. Their idea was to sell all the debatable land to Carver in return for his undistributed presents, but to retain all hunting and fishing rights in the property. Carver thought highly of the idea, wrote it all out in English, and the two chiefs signed it.

"That, by God," McNott told me, "is why they call Carver 'Moon-buyer.' That pop-eyed idiot has a deed to land that never belonged to the Sioux anyway, and they have as many rights in it as they ever had."

"You say they signed it?" I asked.

McNott put the question to his wife, then said, "Yes, but they didn't sign their own names. They signed names that never existed." He sighed. "Look at her, Langdon! Look at her! Not a damned hell's inkling of right and wrong! She thinks it's funny! It's that misguided sense of humor she picked up from living with Chippeways! Look at her, roaring with laughter!"

I looked at her, but her face was expressionless. "She's not laughing," I said.

"Not laughing!" McNott cried. "She's damned near bursting! Put your hand on her stomach and you'll feel her!"

I took his word for it. "Mac," I said, "Carver wouldn't be such a fool as to believe he could buy a piece of land a hundred miles square—an area greater than all New Hampshire—for a few blankets and mirrors and papers of pins."

"Why wouldn't he?" McNott asked. "Didn't he swaller Pinnashon's story about the rattlesnake? Why do you s'pose ten of those chiefs went down river to New Orleans instead of going to Michilimackinac like they'd promised Carver they would? Because they figured Carver'd find out what they'd done! Hell, they needn't 'a' worried! Carver wouldn't never found out nothing by himself, and if anybody else tried to tell him that deed of land wasn't good for nothing, he wouldn't 'a' believed it, would he? You know damned well, Langdon, that a feller like Carver wouldn't never believe nothing that made him look like what he is—a plumb damned fool!

"And another thing: that pop-eyed idiot went and told Tute and Goddard and Atherton, and they've quit thinking about the Northwest Passage and the great River Oregon! They've gone up the Chippeway River to look at Carver's land, by God! That's why they had Chippeways with 'em! They'd made up their minds before they left Prairie du Chien that they was going up the Chippeway to look at Carver's land, and I betcher they figger on making £100,000 apiece. Yes, sir: figger it out for yourself—10,000 square miles they think they got, and that's 6,400,000 acres, and they ought to be able to sell it to New Englanders for two shillings an acre anyway, because Carver came from New England and the place is full of damned fools just like him!"

McNott looked at me darkly. "You know what they're figgerin' on doing, Langdon? I'll bet they're figgerin' the Major's scheme is just a waste of time and not worth bothering with, seeing that they got this great big parcel of land right in their hands. Yes, sir, I'll bet they don't intend to go another mile to the westward. If I'm right, the Major's having a knife stuck into him on one side by Tute and Carver and Goddard, and on the other side by Sir William Johnson and General Gage and that little rat of a Lieutenant Roberts! I don't like it, Langdon! I don't like it a damned bit!"

It hardly seemed possible that Carver could have been such a credulous nincompoop; yet he had repeatedly shown himself to be gullible; and he would, Rogers had said, do almost anything to escape the grinding poverty of a schoolmaster's life. As for Tute, I was willing to believe anything of him. Was the world, I wondered bitterly, wholly made up of Tutes and Carvers—people so shortsighted that they considered it more important to amass a heap of tarnished shillings than to explore a new world?

"Well," I said to McNott, "there's one man who'll never forget the Northwest Passage and the great River Oregon. Thank God we can depend on the Major. We'll wait till we hear from him, and then we'll go on!"

The first trader to reach the Falls of St. Anthony was Ezekiel Solomon, a little Jewish trader who had wintered on Lake Superior close to Michilimackinac, had returned to the fort at the earliest possible moment, and with the business energy of his race had set off at once for the Mississippi. With him, to my inexpressible relief, he had two letters for me, one from the Major and one from Ann.

The one from the Major, he said, was a duplicate, and a copy would be sent to Lake Superior in case I had moved north. I hardly heard him, so intent was I on the thin little letter from Ann, wondering what was in it, wishing that Solomon would turn his back long enough to let me snatch a glance at its contents.

I heard him clearly enough, however, when he said, "She's a nice young lady. I never seen one like her."

"Yes," I said, "she is. She is indeed." I felt I was probably speaking too enthusiastically, so I added in what I hoped was a paternal tone, "A very well-behaved little girl. When did you see her, and was she looking well?"

"Yes," Solomon said, "she looked good. If I had a daughter, that's the kind I'd like." His beady little eyes looked me up and down. "She'd be useful in trading business, on account her persistence."

"Persistence?" I asked. "That doesn't seem quite the word to apply to Ann. She's really a quiet little girl, Mr. Solomon."

"Maybe you aint paid enough attention to her," Solomon said. "She aint so little, and she don't never stop eskin when she wants something pretty bad—like having a letter carried to you."

"I don't think she realized she was bothering you," I said.

"Oh, no bother!" Solomon said quickly. "But good for me you aint gone nowhere yet, odderwise I spend weeks writing letters to Miss Potter, telling what I heard about you, who seen you, what you been doing, where you gone, when you coming beck, how many paintings you got done. How much time that leave me for trading and Indian society, eh? Not none!"

I drew a deep breath and laughed, and I know I laughed unsteadily. "Well," I said, "thank you for bringing this letter. I—I——"

"Thenks!" Solomon cried satirically. "No thenks to me! What if I said I don't take it, ha? Then she look at me! Something come out of her, some feeling, some——"

He made groping gestures before his face with a half-clenched hand. "I never see nothing like it. She makes feelings in you without saying nothing. S'pose I tell her—I wouldn't do it, but s'pose I did—s'pose I tell her No, I wont take no letter, on account having lots business! She don't do nothing, just move the eyes!"

He clenched both fists before his face and forcefully thrust them straight toward me. "Right away something come out and go into me—here; here; here!" Successively he gripped his throat, clasped a hand over his eyes, smote his breast with a clenched fist, then added, "Without no trouble I cry like little baby!"

He seemed puzzled, then fumblingly said, "I think she maybe got something in her—something different, like us Jewish fellers have feelings in the fingers so we know good cloth when we touch it."

By some singular alchemy, Solomon's words, inept though they were, brought Ann's face and her proud, tight-lipped smile so clearly before me that my throat contracted and I couldn't speak. Nor could I wait longer before opening her letter. Regardless of Solomon, I had to have a glimpse, no matter how fleeting, of the words she had sent me.

With clumsy fingers I broke the seal and unfolded the sheets. Solomon shifted uncertainly from one foot to the other, then turned from me. The opening words were, "My dearest Langdon."

The restlessness and uncertainty that had so long oppressed me were gone as though they had never existed; never had I seen a day more beautiful: a scene more ravishing than the Falls of St. Anthony, with its thundering curtain of snowy water hung between the fresh green covering that spring had spread upon the banks of the Mississippi. The whole world was so brilliant that I laughed in sheer joy. "Wait!" I shouted to Solomon. "Come back!" I folded the letter and buttoned it in the pocket of my buckskin shirt, where it seemed to press against me as if there were life and warmth within it.

"You haven't told me a word about the Major!" I protested. "How's he getting along at Michilimackinac, and what did you hear about the Congress?"

"Didn't hear nothing else," Solomon said. "Lake Michigan so full of Indians going to it, it's dangerous. In the Straits you can't hardly turn around without bumping canoes. Nothing ever seen like it before—not nowhere."

"And what do the Indians think of the Major?" I asked.

"Mister," Solomon said, "they think he's the greatest man in the world!"

"Splendid!" I said. "Splendid! He *is* a great man, Solomon—a born leader with the vision of a statesman."

Solomon nodded, twitched at his baggy buckskin shirt, examined the sky dubiously and muttered something about unloading.

"There's nothing wrong at Michilimackinac, is there?" I asked quickly. "The Major's not having trouble, is he?"

"I should be one to say anything against the Major!" Solomon protested. "Aint he fixed it so I go wintering instead of bankrupt, the way Sir William Johnson fixed it for me to be?"

"There *is* something wrong!" I said. "What is it?"

Solomon's big head settled back, bird-like. "I don't know nothing," he said, "only what I heard once from my granfadder. A rabbi he was—a big rabbi." He cupped his hands

at the level of his waist as if he held within them an enormous invisible ball. Evidently his grandfather was heavily
bearded. "My granfadder said a statesman or a soldier what
takes strong steps independent of everyone, wont never gain
nothing by it so long as he lives, only hatred."

"Perhaps," I admitted, "but unusual circumstances make
exceptions to every rule, and the Major's an unusual man."

Solomon turned his hands palm upward. "My granfadder,
he said that was a rule there wasn't no exception to."

He tramped off to unload his canoes, his scrawny neck
protruding from his voluminous shirt like that of a plucked
chicken.

Vaguely uneasy at his words, I lightly touched Ann's message through the buckskin above my heart, but picked up
the Major's letter and opened it.

"Esteemed friend [it read], you will be glad to hear
your work last winter is now bearing fruit, and Indians are
poaring into Michilimackinac from north, south, east, and
best of all, from the west. Peace anamates every bosom:
also the desire that traders be aloud to come amongst
them hereafter and allways. It is a magnifasent spectacoll,
and my bosom swels with pryde to think by my efforts peace
will rane amongst our red brothers. I have recd bad news.
That little 2-faced snake Lt. Roberts has been aptd Com-
massary at this post and is expected daily but by God he or
no other Lt., no matter by whom aptd. cannot lord it over
me and issue me his orders which have no more wit behind 'em than a sneeze, and you may be sure I will beat
him in the end. I have wrote to Capt. Tute. I have not
recd the goods which he must have obtaned in return for
all his gifts, which is causing me grate concern. Pleas make
sertain these goods are dispatched immediently if not al-
reddy done. Also Capt. Carvers. If I can obtane the goods
from Capt. Tute and Capt. Carver, I can make ready to
go myself to the westward, but untill then I shall be much
hampered for lack of money, which I have done everything
to get. Be assured that when successful I will loose no time
in setting off, and we will reach our destanation if we have
to go there on our hands and knees. Meanwhile continue
to the westward for your discovery as if I was with you.
Let nothing stand in your way and do not let your courage

and resulution faile you in the attempt. Appart from this everything is quiet hear, and Mrs. Rogers sends affeconot good wishes. I am sir with Esteem your most Obdt. humble Servt,

"Rob¹ Rogers."

I gazed at the Major's familiar handwriting with something of the veneration with which, on our journey to St. Francis, I had so often looked at the man himself. He was still the same indomitable and resourceful magician who had dragged me from the rushing water at White River Falls, miraculously hauled himself—a bullet-scarred, knife-slashed skeleton—upon the sooty raft from the foam-streaked pool at the foot of Wattoquitchey Falls, and shouted at Bellows at Number Four, "Those men of mine are going to be fed, or by God I'll raid every house in the settlement!"

He'd never change, I thought: never; and I laughed aloud as I once more scanned the evidences of his lack of change: "Peace anamates every bosom"—"a magnifasent specatacoll" —"that little 2-faced snake"—"do not let your courage and resulution faile you"—"affeconot."

I seemed to hear his thick voice, back in the White Bear Tavern, asking me how to spell "affectionate." No: he wouldn't change: he was the same great leader he had been at St. Francis. He would, as he said, take us to our destination even though he had to lead us on his hands and knees. That indomitable spirit of his would spur even a Tute or a Carver to high endeavor!

I laid aside the Major's message and felt free at last to draw Ann's letter from my pocket. "She makes feeling in you without saying nothing," Solomon had said; and I knew from the unsteadiness of my hands, as I opened the pages, that he had been far short of the whole truth.

"My dearest Langdon [it read], I am sorry this letter is not a long one. When you went away I thought I would write in a diary what happened every day so you would know what has been happening and how cold it was and what Indians came to the fort and whether they were good to paint, also that I thought about you every day, both at morning and night and while writing in the diary and at other times too. At first when you went away I thought perhaps I would die, and I told in the diary every time I felt like dying, as I thought you would be glad to hear. You would have been surprised how often it was. Now it is not so often, of course.

"The reason I did not send the diary is I lost it. I kept it under the mattress on my bed and that is where it was lost. I felt very sorry when I went to get it and found it was lost. I thought I would die, because I wanted you to read it. It is hard to lose things here because there is nobody to talk to about it.

"The Indians who have come have been very poor and have all needed anything they could get, especially rum, which they don't have any of and need very much. They have not been good to paint as they have all been dirtier than any you ever painted when I was with you. Oh Langdon dear I have missed seeing you do pastels and make people come to life on paper and get colors all over yourself. When I see an Indian that you would like to sketch I almost die because you are not here. I hope you are finding lots of Indians to draw. I suppose there are lots and lots of them where you are, but if you can't find enough there are plenty here.

"I was sorry about my diary because I told in it about learning how to do the Pawnee woman, also the French woman who cooks, I can do her very well and talk the way she does when Mrs. R. has been in the kitchen and spoken about the soup having too much water in it, also Mrs. Cardin a French Woman a friend of Major R's who has been to talk to the Indians at Arbre Croche for him and take rum to them. Sometimes she takes some herself and then eats cloves and I can do her very well, I think you would like to see me do Mrs. Cardin because she is soft and rolls her eyes and moves her eyelids very fast and leans against people as well as speaking quite affected, especially when saying Mrs. R's dresses are the most beautiful she has ever seen, and worn with such an air. Mrs. R. goes to her house to take tea and likes her very much and is never cross about her the way she is about all the other ladies.

"You will be sorry to hear Mrs. R. doesn't feel well. Sometimes her back hurts her, and sometimes she has very bad migraine, and sometimes she feels faint. As soon as she gets over one thing, she catches something else, so she is not very good company. She does not like it here and does not like to have the soldiers and their wives come to call, she says they are common, but the Major likes it because the soldiers' wives are gay and are fond of drinking rum and dancing and singing, and they are not angry when the Major slaps them, but just laugh and swear and slap him too.

"There is not much to do here in the winter and the Major gets very tired doing nothing, sometimes he falls asleep in the afternoon and doesn't wake up till the next day, and sometimes he goes to the village and cannot get back because of snow and so sleeps there. I wish he could go away and do something, because I think he would like to, and he is different from the traders and other men in the place. When he is standing with others, you don't notice the others, but only see the Major, so I think he must be a great man perhaps. Sometimes he makes me think of a kettle on the stove, quiet but all boiling inside. He walks around and around all the time when he is in the house, and sometimes you can't hear him at all, and then there he is, staring at you. He talks very loud, sometimes, and says he will be all right, so I think perhaps he is worried for fear something wont be all right.

"He sent my father to Lake Superior to talk to the Indians because my father wouldn't keep sober and would fall down on the ground outdoors and sleep there, and cough a great deal. There wasn't anybody to take care of him, and after all I am his daughter, so I nursed him as well as I could and he was a little better and then the Major sent him to Lake Superior. Perhaps when he comes back he will get well if I can keep him from getting rum and can nurse him again. I am sure I wont catch what he's got, because I don't have colds and never cough at all.

"The Major has been very nice to me and speaks very kindly, sometimes I wish he wouldn't be so kind but I don't think he means anything, just thinks he will be playful because I would like somebody to play with.

"Oh Langdon dear I miss you, and I am so sorry about my diary because you would have known how much I missed you if you had read it and now you will never know.

"Please send me a letter. I would like a little picture of you. After you had gone I knew that if I had asked you you would probably have made a little picture of yourself for me before you went, and when I thought about it I thought I would die because I hadn't spoken about it before you went away. If you have time will you please make me a little picture that will go in a letter and send it to me so I can have it? I will keep it where it can't be lost like the diary. I miss you. I hope you are well and having a good time and that you are having good weather and painting some beautiful pictures. Oh how I wish I could see them and you.

                                                              "Ann."

I read the letter over and over, alternately elated and enraged at the revelations Ann had made: elated—and half-choked too—by her confession of complete desolation when I left, her concern for my painting, health and happiness, her desire for a sketch of me; but hot with anger at what she gently called the loss of her diary. And why shouldn't she be able to talk to anyone about her losses? Why in the name of God couldn't Elizabeth give Ann, that lonely little girl, the sympathy and love that every girl should have?

In my imagination I saw her, alone in her dark and narrow room, without friends and without companionship, practising the soft and kittenish ways of the clove-eating Mrs. Cardin: sitting for hours in the steamy kitchen and for lack of other occupation absorbing every petulant movement, every indignant syllable, of that outraged French cook.

Her astounding power of reproducing the words, manner and appearance of others had also given her the ability to draw clear pictures with her pen; but clear as were the outlines of those pictures, there were tones within them that baffled and troubled me.

The neglected Elizabeth, seeking sympathy with her imaginary ailments, I could see and understand; I understood how Mrs. Cardin, by her flattery, had lulled Elizabeth to a false security. But what of the pictures of the Major? What of his restless and silent stalking through the house? Of his sending the drunken, stricken Potter to the icy shores of Lake Superior? Of his drinking with the wives of common soldiers? Was it possible, I wondered, that his disappointment at being forced to stay in Michilimackinac through the winter had been too much for him to bear? That, I was sure, wasn't the answer. Nothing, I told myself, was too much for Robert Rogers to bear. No labor, no disappointment, could crush the hero whose dauntless courage had brought us safely through the perils and the heartbreaks of the St. Francis expedition.

The sentence over which I puzzled longest, and to which I most frequently returned, was the one in which Ann had said, "Sometimes I wish he wouldn't be so kind, but I don't think he means anything." How had he been kind to Ann? She needed kindness; so why should she be reluctant to accept it? What was it that his kindness might have meant if Ann hadn't decided—as she evidently had—that it meant nothing?

Trying to laugh at the morbid fancies that a harmless word brings to a man's brain when he's in love, I folded the letter, fastened it securely in the pocket of my shirt, got crayons and a mirror from my haversack and went to work on the small portrait for which Ann had asked. As I worked, my mind grew calmer.

Why shouldn't the Major be kind to Ann? He's been kind to me, always—as kind as a father could have been—kind and sympathetic. Of course his kindness in Ann's case meant no more than it had meant in mine. It was paternal. He was sorry for her because Elizabeth ignored her, and he wanted to make amends—perhaps out of friendship for me.

That was it: friendship! Men stand by their friends, always.

I felt an overwhelming relief, touched the little letter curved like a shield against my breast, and was happy in the thought that it had come in time to buoy me up on the long, long journey on which we were to embark next day.

CHAPTER LXXII

WITHIN A month of the day we left the Mississippi and started up the St. Peter's, we were sure that the Major's great plan was feasible. The Shining Mountains could be reached and crossed; the great River

Oregon could be descended to the Western Ocean. We found two women—Snake Indians—who had been captured by Minnetarees where the Missouri River rises in the Shining Mountains. They had been brought down the Missouri and sold by their captors to an Ahnaway chief.

"If Minnetarees can do it, the Major can," McNott said. "There aint nothing an Indian can do that a white man can't do better, and that Rogers can't do best of all."

As for food, three hunters could have kept an expedition of fifty men bountifully supplied with food. The prairies between the St. Peter's and the Missouri were alive with game. Buffalo herds were so enormous that the thought of counting them would have been ridiculous, like attempting to count the stars in the sky or herring when they run in the spring. Rabbits, prairie dogs, antelope, muskrats were everywhere. Plover, ducks, geese, grouse rose up by the millions.

When we had crossed the prairie and come into the valley of the twisting, rushing, sand-filled Missouri, the banks of that turbulent river seemed at times almost to crawl with turkey, bear, elk, beaver; the wooded runs that gave the nearby prairie the look of being fenced off into farms were rich with Osage plums and grapes; the creeks full of pike, bass, trout, fish resembling salmon, catfish, crawfish and fat mussels.

The eagerness of all the red men we met, Dacotas for the most part, to have traders come among them with guns, powder, shot, knives, kettles, hatchets and cloth for clothing was pitiful—a constant refutation of Sir William Johnson's insistence that Western Indians come to the Eastern forts to trade. They killed their fattest dogs in honor of our coming; danced and howled around our tents all night; made us speeches that droned on for hours.

They were poor, they said; only a few among them had made the long journey down the Missouri to trade with the French and Spanish; and those few, too often, had traded their furs for knives that broke, powder that wouldn't burn, guns that exploded, kettles that cracked, cloth that rotted. If traders could come among them, they would soon be rich, for furs were plentiful; so they would do anything, promise anything, if the White Father would send traders.

When I replied that we were only seeking locations for

trading posts, and that the White Father himself was following in our footsteps, they set the prairie afire as a signal to
him. That, too, was how each settlement gave notice to the
next Indian town that friends were approaching—by lighting
the mat of dry grass that lay under the summer's growth,
so that a sheet of flame ran before the wind, casting a
crimson glare on the billowing smoke that rolled above it.

With the tireless Major to give us increased speed, Mc-
Nott declared, we'd slip through all the Indian nations and
over the Shining Mountains like a clam sliding through a sea-
gull. This remark he made so often that I grew sick of
hearing it; and he made it, I knew, because he thought I
was dubious about our chances of going safely through the
Blackfeet and the other nations farther up river. He complained with increasing frequency, too, of my lack of spright-
liness when we camped at night.

"You're getting to be about as cheery as a mustard-pot,
Langdon," he told me. "If I wasn't naturally a sunshiny
feller, I don't believe I could stand it, night-times, sittin'
in front of a smoky fire and fighting mosquitoes with you
and the Princess McNott! Damned if I wouldn't cry myself
to sleep!"

The sergeant was right in one way, but wrong in another.
I was indeed increasingly serious, but not because I doubted
our ability to go forward. I couldn't understand why the
Major neither joined us nor sent a messenger to tell us
when we might expect him; and I was bothered, too, by
haunting phrases from Ann's letter. Whenever I had a moment to myself, I took it from its wrappings to look again
at the words I had long since learned by heart.

It was a limp little letter now, from the countless times it
had been folded and unfolded by hands always grimy from
groping for meat in the kettle, cleaning a rifle, tugging buffalo
or deer skins from still-warm carcasses, poking at fires and
struggling to protect our clumsy wooden pirogues from the
shifting sandbars and the treacherous buffetings of the Missouri.

To guard it from the perspiration that drenched me when
the waters of the Missouri didn't, I carried it in a mink-skin
medicine bag that I had bought from a Dacota; and no
Dacota medicine man ever treasured the "medicine" that
saved him from enemy arrows, the scalping knives of Paw-

nees and the displeasure of the Great Spirit more zealously than I treasured Ann's letter in its little mink-skin case.

Although Ann had said she was sure she would come to no harm from nursing her father, my mind darted like a frightened salmon from one dreadful possibility to another; and as is so often the case in a lover's broodings, I could only imagine the worst: only see Ann lying wasted and helpless, racked by coughs: sacrificed to a worthless parent who contributed less to the world than the shaggiest buffalo on the plains through which we travelled.

And with increasing frequency I brooded confusedly on the sentence that had come to loom more darkly in my mind's eye than all the others—"sometimes I wish he wouldn't be so kind." It had grown to be a sort of torment.

But in spite of McNott's fears and hints and upbraidings, it was he, poor man, who brought our slow but steady progress to a sudden halt.

The channel of the Missouri twists so violently in places that we sometimes paddled our heavy pirogues for miles in order to get forward a few hundred yards; and at such times I went ashore to shoot for the pot, while McNott remained in one pirogue and his wife in the other. So fiercely, too, does the stream hurl itself around curves, and so angrily does it bite at overhanging banks, that in places it seems like something malevolently alive, snarling and snapping at those who venture near it. As if by magic it rolls up sandbars in midstream where five minutes before there was nothing but rushing water, and in even less time it pounces upon and gobbles sandy islands large enough to hold a hundred men. The appearance and disappearance of these sand-spits must be closely watched; for the rage of the current as it spews them out and gulps them down becomes terrible.

McNott had just put me ashore, and I was scrambling up the bank, when I heard a strangled shout. The pirogue, returning to midstream, had been caught by one of the river's sudden frenzies, and tossed broadside on a sandbar which was melting away to nothing. The rushing current threw the pirogue half-over; Tokacou fell from the stern and went whirling downstream; but before the boat could be completely overturned and our load of supplies scattered and ruined, McNott swung himself onto the sandbar, seized the gunwale and by main strength held it from going under.

I leaped from the bank and splashed through the shallows to his aid. Tokacou came floundering upstream, wet feathers dangling from his hair, his mouth wide open, like an enormous draggled bird. By the time we reached McNott, the sandbar had been eaten away, the hungry roar of the current at that spot had subsided to a growling discontent, and the pirogue floated free, no harder to hold than any boat in swift water.

"My God, Mac," I said, "I never thought you'd save it!" He just stood there looking at me.

"Get in," I told him. "I'll go back where I left my musket." He didn't move; and I saw, then, that he couldn't get in— that he couldn't even take a step without assistance.

With a horrible cold feeling in the pit of my stomach, I took him beneath the arms and dragged him to the beach. When Tokacou had brought the pirogue ashore, we lifted McNott over the bank and laid him on the prairie. He hadn't said a word; but when he felt dry ground beneath his feet, he rolled over on his face, got to his hands and knees, and bright blood gushed from his mouth just as it pours from a deer when his throat is first cut. There was nearly a quart of it—so much that it lay in a glittering pool between his hands, forcing us to pick him up and move him again.

He seemed to feel better with all that blood out of him. "I must 'a' busted something, Langdon," he whispered. "I'll just lay here the rest of the day, and let the Princess make me some of her Chippeway tea. I'll be all right tomorrow."

He wasn't all right. Tokacou ran forward and signalled his wife to come back; and when she had joined us and examined McNott, she unbuckled his leg, peeled off his wet buckskins and wiped away the Missouri River sand that covered him from head to foot. Then, without a word, she left him and went to grubbing up weeds and pulling leaves from shrubs. When she had boiled them in a kettle for an hour, she poured off a quart of brownish-green fluid and brought it to McNott, who accepted it with an expression of acute repugnance.

He drank it slowly, shuddering after each swallow; lay back and closed his eyes; then turned on his side and threw it up. His wife said nothing, but I saw her go to the kettle and sample the brew herself. Since she retained it and took no further steps, I gathered she was satisfied with it.

The next morning he was no better. We made buffalo broth for him, but he refused to drink it, saying it was all right to get down, but not worth the trouble of bringing up. When he tried to stand, he couldn't. Even to crawl was beyond him; his hips and legs wabbled and gave way like those of an animal with a bullet between front- and hind-quarters.

That day we made our camp permanent, packed the supplies beneath the overturned pirogues, and sent Tokacou to the nearest band of Dacotas to tell them they could have half the meat we killed if they'd help us drag it in.

The frequency with which McNott demanded water was harrowing, and his wife sat beside him all day and all night, giving him water and hourly searching him from head to foot to keep him free of the ticks that infest the banks of the Missouri.

When the Dacotas came and pitched their white lodges nearby, we hunted buffalo, deer and bear which the women dried and pounded into pemmican; and a wrinkled medicine man, after consulting Mrs. McNott, spent an afternoon dancing around the patient, blowing on a magic whistle, banging on a magic drum, and singing magic songs in a voice as raucous as the squeal of a rusty hinge; but his only effect was to make the sergeant irritable.

Half of the water he drank stayed down; but he not only couldn't eat: he didn't seem to want to. Buffalo hump, buffalo tongue, beaver tail, grouse's breast—none of these delicacies interested him. He just lay quietly on his buffalo robe, staring up at the top of the tent; and with each passing hour he seemed to grow thinner and weaker.

If only the Major could come up with us, he would, I knew, have medicines with him, and possibly some of them might help McNott—though I didn't see how any medicine could be of benefit if he had broken something inside him.

Eight days after he was hurt, a little after sundown, his wife came to me and jerked her head toward the tent. I went in to see what McNott wanted, and found him looking almost dead.

"Langdon," he whispered, "I'd like to have you write a paper so I can sign it. I'd like to have you write down that I got four hundred and sixty-two pounds, seventeen shillings and ninepence in Montreal, and that——"

"Now listen, Mac," I said, "don't talk that way."

"Why not?" he asked. "If this damned stomach don't starve me to death, the damned ticks'll eat me up, or the damned cold'll freeze me solid. Hell, I aint got nothing in me but water, so I ought to be as easy to freeze as a puddle; and those Northern Lights, they been tuning up. Last night I thought somebody'd lit a yeller fire outside, and it wa'n't nothing only those Northern Lights, getting themselves polished up for winter."

"Nonsense!" I said. "We'll have you eating in a week or two, and then we'll go on."

"It aint so," McNott said quietly, "and you know it. There aint nothing I want to eat, and I guess that's a sign. What's more, I can't walk, so shut up and listen. I got that money in Montreal, held by Gregg Cunningham's agents. You write out a paper. I want you should have four hundred pounds of it, on account you're educated and can spend it better'n most people—and because you're about the only feller I know that wouldn't care whether or not I gave it to him.

"The rest of it—the sixty-two pounds, seventeen shillings and ninepence—I want to go to the Princess McNott, damn her! She's kept me from having a lot of fun since I got acquainted with her, but she aint never interfered with my business, nor dropped sand and twigs into pemmican when making it, like most of 'em do, nor fretted me with a lot of useless talk when I wanted to do some quiet thinking—and that's more'n you can say of most women, Langdon.

"I aint never had to hunt for her when I needed her; and by and large I've prob'ly been better off with her than I'd 'a' been with one o' these mammerous young minks that's like to be missing for an hour or two whenever there's a dance or a drinking party; so I guess she better have the sixty-two pounds, seventeen shillings and ninepence.

"And don't give it to her in a lump, Langdon, or relatives'll get it off of her, the way they do off of all females. Fix it so she gets about two pounds a year for life: then she'll be rich enough so everybody'll be polite to her, but not so rich that she wont have to hustle a little to make both ends meet. If there's anything I hate, it's a woman so well fixed she don't have nothing to do but sleep and eat and find fault with what everybody else is doing."

I shook my head. "I wont do it, Mac. You've got no business to lose hope. You're forgetting you've been a sergeant of Rangers, and learned your lessons under Rogers. You know better than most what he tried to teach all of us: that there's always a way to escape, even when you're tied hand and foot; and you're never finished till you're dead."

"You do as I say!" McNott insisted, his voice a travesty of his old-time violence. "Hell, Langdon, you might as well do it. Here we are, twelve hundred miles from the outskirts of nowhere, and me too weak to blow my own nose. There's only one end to that. I suppose maybe if we had that young Pelletier doctor here, the one that cured 'Zekiel Solomon of the spotted fever there aint supposed to be no cure for, he might be able to do something."

"Pelletier?" I asked. "Where's he live? Montreal?"

"Montreal hell!" McNott said. "He's the Michilimackinac feller that gets a bale of beaver if he cures you, and nothing if he don't. He's smart, Pelletier is. Yes sir; I certainly wisht we had him here."

"Mac," I said, "if you think Pelletier can cure you, there's no question what we'll do. We'll go back. We'll start for Michilimackinac right now. We can go down this river six times faster than we came up; and if we can cross over to the St. Peter's before it freezes, we ought to be able to make it—if you can stand the trip."

McNott half sat up. "Stand it! I can stand anything better'n lying here and being eaten alive by ticks!" Then he sank back. "No. We'd never make it, Langdon. We better wait for the Major, like you planned."

I looked at him hard. There had been eagerness in his voice, but now there was only resignation, and I thought I knew why.

"Mac," I said, "I don't mind turning back. Anybody'd think, to hear you talk, that it's a disgrace to turn back, once you've started forward; but it's not so. I never yet made a decent picture without going back and doing it over a dozen times. Do you figure I'd be satisfied with a painting if I was too proud to re-do it when there was something wrong with it? Or feel I'd got anywhere if I went forward and you died, and I knew I could have saved you by going back?"

The look of eagerness came back into his eyes.

Disregarding his faint protests, I ran from the tent and called McNott's wife. "Back!" I shouted at her. "We're going back!"

To show her what I meant, I turned a pirogue right-side up, dumped a bundle into it, and made motions of sweeping the entire camp down river.

As realization dawned upon her, her face quivered. For a fleeting moment I thought I saw her lips curve with the beginning of a smile; and her waddle, as she went to draw the tent-pegs, was almost a run.

Not even Rogers himself could have broken camp more quickly than we did. The relief of moving after a week of inaction and suspense was like wine; and the knowledge that at the end of our journey I would find Ann was like a whip scourging me on.

Twenty minutes later we were on our way down river, while along the bank galloped our friends the Dacotas, plaintively howling for us to return, and lashing their ponies in a vain attempt to stay abreast of us.

We found Wanotan and the entire population of his town —chiefs, braves, women, horses, children and dogs—at the landing-place on the Missouri where the Dacotas leave the river to travel across the prairie to the St. Peter's; and they made as much of an outcry over us as though we ourselves were royal governors. McNott was treated as ambassadors are treated: placed on a buffalo robe, picked up by six young men and carried to Wanotan's lodge, which Wanotan vacated for him so that he might have the best of shelter and care.

While the women knocked a dog on the head and prepared him for the pot, all the men gathered outside Wanotan's dwelling to howl strickenly over McNott's plight. What was more, their concern was genuine. They wept genuine tears, threw ashes on their heads; and some slashed themselves with knives. I thought at first they were thus solicitous only because we were their friends and had spent the preceding winter with them, but I soon found out it was due to the fact that we were the representatives of Major Rogers.

Whatever I wished them to do for McNott, Wanotan said, they would do. Ponies, dog-teams, travoises, a skin lodge, snowshoes, braves and women to help transport him as far as the Mississippi—all these I could have, and anything else I wanted, because we were ambassadors from the great man at Michilimackinac.

Never before, Wanotan declared, had the White Father in England sent such a great warrior to advise and govern his red children. When the Yanktons had gone from Prairie du Chien to Michilimackinac, he admitted, they had expected to find a governor like all other governors: one who talked much and said little—who took no notice of the needs of Indians but spoke often of the white man's needs—who gave little and demanded much—who was friendly to Indians until he got what he wanted, and then spoke harshly to them, as men speak to dogs.

Instead of that, said Wanotan, they found a governor who was kind, wise, generous; one who had gone to the trouble of bringing chiefs from all the nations to the greatest gathering of Indians ever seen. From them he had asked nothing except that his red brothers would build a Chain of Peace that would extend through all the nations from the rising to the setting sun, so that traders could travel safely to every nation and put an end to poverty, famine and misery among them. The wisdom of his words and the generosity of his presents, Wanotan said, averted a great Indian war, nor would the chiefs who had been at Michilimackinac allow a war to take place so long as they could be sure that their differences would be heard and decided by such a great chief as Major Rogers.

To hear Wanotan's extravagant enthusiasm for the Major was more than pleasing; for it was as good as an assurance that although hunger, cold and endless labor might hamper my effort to get McNott to Michilimackinac, I would not—thanks to the Major's foresight—be in perpetual danger of having my head split open by tomahawks.

What, I asked Wanotan, had he heard about the Major's journey to the West? Had he started yet? Was it known where he proposed to winter? Wanotan, however, knew nothing of the Major's plans.

Before we sat down to the dog-feast that night, McNott, who had eaten no solid food since we had turned back, but had somehow contrived to keep life in his attenuated body by reluctantly sipping a cup of broth and then waiting grimly for the waves of nausea to subside, told me weakly that he thought he wouldn't mind having a little piece of loin of boiled dog.

When I went with it to his lodge, I found his wife waiting

outside. She took the piece of dog-meat, ate it herself, shook her head warningly at me; then picked up a cup and preceded me into the tent. When she held the cup to McNott's lips, he sniffed at it suspiciously.

"Where's that piece of dog?" he asked.

"All gone," I said. "It wasn't a very big dog."

He nodded and pushed the cup away. "I s'pose that's goose soup; but it smells to me like someone washed his leggins in it. I might as well wait till they kill another dog. Right now I don't want nothing but some water that aint been washed in."

Thanks to the urging of Wanotan, who accompanied us, and to the eight young Dacotas who took turn about carrying McNott in a buffalo robe, and the panting dogs that dragged our baggage on travoises across the Côteau des Prairies, we reached the St. Peter's and got down it before it froze, travelling comfortably in our own bark canoe that we'd buried when we came up from Prairie du Chien the preceding June. What was more, we got down just in time; for snow was falling when we reached the point where the St. Peter's enters the Mississippi, and in the morning there was a foot of it on the ground. The greater river was so full of freezing snow and jagged ice-cakes that we camped where we were and waited for the weather to moderate.

It was while we waited that three things occurred to raise my hopes for McNott. For the first time since his accident he had a craving for solid food; he got to his one foot unaided and stood firmly upon it; and he flew into one of his old-time violent rages at the Princess McNott.

There was a settlement of River Band Sioux at the mouth of the St. Peter's; and when Wanotan told them who we were, they too gave us a cabin to ourselves. Since chiefs from these people had been among those who had cleverly got Carver's goods away from him by giving him a deed to a large part of North America, we thought it best to move our few remaining bundles of merchandise into the cabin with McNott, and for his wife to guard them until we could cross the Mississippi.

That was how I happened to bring Mrs. McNott, for her supper, a meat-covered marrow-bone from a buffalo, and how she happened to be eating it in McNott's presence. He watched her turning the bone in her hands and gnawing as she turned, as though eating corn on the cob.

"That don't look so bad," he said to me in a sepulchral faint voice. "When she gets through playing with it, damned if I don't believe I'll get her to split it, so I can eat the marrow."

He gobbled an order to his wife, who continued her gnawing as though she hadn't heard.

"Funny," McNott went on, speaking to me, "funny I aint thought of marrow-bones all the time I been laid up. Maybe if I'd thought of 'em sooner, I might 'a' started eating sooner."

His voice seemed to strengthen, and he again gobbled sharply to the Princess, who rose, wiped her greasy face with the back of her hand, wiped her hand on the back of her trouser leg, and stolidly carried the marrow-bone from the cabin.

Licking his lips, McNott continued his discourse. "I dunno nothing better for a delicate stomach than marrow, whether it's boiled or roasted. It's sweet and it melts in your mouth, so you don't have to chew it. A feller that's suffering from too much rum, so he can't touch no ordinary vittles without wishing he was dead, he can eat marrow. It just kind of trickles all through him, and soothes him where he needs it most. Yes, sir; I wish I'd thought of marrow-bones sooner!"

When his wife returned, she carried a cup and silently gave it to him.

"What's this?" McNott demanded. "Where's that marrow-bone?"

I think he thought she'd hid it behind her back, because he drank from the cup, muttered "dishwater," and continued to look expectantly at her; but when he returned the empty cup she gobbled briefly and returned to her seat beside our bundles of merchandise.

"What!" McNott shouted. "What!" In the firelight his face looked as dark as his wife's, and I knew that emotion, as in the old days, had made it as scarlet as his hair.

"Damn her!" he said to me, his voice shaking, "she says I can't have nothing to eat till we're across the river! She says I got to keep on drinking dishwater. Here! I'll see about that, by God!" He rolled over on his knees, caught the wall of the cabin and rose to his foot. "Gimme my leg, Langdon! I'll show her my word's still law." Holding to the wall, he hopped a step toward his wife.

She reached behind her, picked up McNott's leg and held it over the fire.

McNott, a furious skeleton, bared his teeth at me in a horrible grin. "Yes," he said savagely, "and she'd do it, too, just to keep me from having a nice, healthy marrow-bone! I take back every damned word I said about that sixty-two pounds, seventeen shillings and ninepence! She can't have 'em! She's out of my will entire, Langdon! You take it all and give her nothing, and let her find out what it means to oppose the wishes of somebody that's twice as unreasonable and got twice as many legs as me!"

Three days later the river was free of ice-cakes; and Wanotan, to make sure we crossed safely, went with us to the mouth of the St. Croix River, while four of his men, in another canoe, paddled abreast of us, carrying the travoises and the two dogs which Wanotan had given us to drag McNott and our baggage on that last long stretch of frozen river, snow-covered highland and countless lakes that we must cross to reach Michilimackinac.

It was at the mouth of the St. Croix that McNott had his first marrow-bone. His wife had brought a dozen of them with her, and when with sepulchral sucking sounds he had extracted the soft interior from the one she allowed him, and had covered his face and hands with grease, he shouted irascibly for more—a demand which his wife ignored.

Each day, after that, he ate meat—at first only the marrow-bones, and small bits such as the livers of porcupines or deer, or the raw breasts of grouse, scraped to a jelly.

From a Chippeway town on the St. Croix, McNott's wife demanded guides, hunters and a sled as though it were our natural right; and when she distributed to the chiefs a handful of quizzing glasses, she got not only two young braves and their squaws to help us on our way, but five gallons of corn and five bags of pemmican.

By the time we reached the headwaters of the St. Croix McNott was eating a portion of everything we shot, and climbing from the sled when we struck bare ground, to hobble along beside the dogs.

On the day when we saw to the south of us, in the distance,

the cold blue waters of Lake Michigan, he asked for pemmican and cursed as loudly and foully as he ever did when his wife refused to let him have it.

Three days later, with the Straits of Michilimackinac just beyond a low range of hills to the east of us, a blinding snowstorm came out of the northwest. We made ourselves a burrow behind a ledge of rock and built a snow dome above us, and in that fetid little hole we lived three days—the seven of us and the two dogs. During those days McNott boasted to the four Chippeways of his exploits, kept tight hold of his wooden leg, ate freely of pemmican, and heartily damned the squaw who had made it.

He lectured the Chippeway women on the advisability of keeping their hair out of their cooking, saying that no man would put up forever with a careless cook; but he nullified his words by continuing to dip into the food which he reviled. It wouldn't be long, I saw, till Caesar was himself again.

CHAPTER LXXIII

WHEN THE storm stopped, we went on to the northern bank of the Straits of Michilimackinac, straining our eyes for a glimpse of the fort on the far shore. We could barely see it: only the roofs of the buildings within the stockade were visible above the ice-cakes that the north wind had piled high against the southern side of the straits in a barrier that glittered like scoured bayonets in the frosty morning sunlight. Among those roofs I picked out the snowy tip of the Major's, beneath which I knew I'd find Ann—and I hoped I'd find her as warm and yielding as the ice beneath us was cold and hard.

Spurred on by the thought, I pulled harder at the sled than did the dogs; and when we had crossed the Straits to the foot of the slabs of ice, I pulled off my snowshoes and pushed McNott back on the sled. "Keep off that rough ice," I told him. "Don't take chances at this late date. Wait here with the baggage, and I'll see the Major and have some men sent back to help you. If he's still here, he'll probably turn out both companies to bring you in."

"Wait hell!" McNott said. "Aint I been away from civilization just as long as you have? There aint nothing, now, that could stop me getting over that ice—not nothing! You could put a bullet through my heart, Langdon, and I'd keep right on travelling long enough to get where I'm headed."

"Maybe so," I said, "but you stay with the baggage. Otherwise I'll hold you down while your wife takes off your leg."

I clambered up the face of the ice-reef and set off toward the fort. As I drew closer, I saw the water-gate was open, and that a sentry, bulky in bearskins, stood in the gateway, watching my painful progress. I almost shouted to him to run and tell the Major; but on second thought I decided to save my breath. I remembered the Major's surprise and pleasure when I had unexpectedly walked in on him at the White Bear in London; and if the Major was still in Michilimackinac, I longed to savor that friendly pleasure again.

I crawled down from the ice-barrier, stamped the snow from my moccasins and marched up to the gate. Over the sentry's shoulder I saw the parade that I had last seen on a smoky, golden September day, over a year ago, and had then thought desolate. It was the same, yet not the same. On the right were the King's storehouse, the guardhouse, the little church; and far beyond them all, at the end of the parade, were the barn-like warehouses of the traders, among which moved a few ant-like figures, swathed in furs; close at hand, on the left, was the Major's house. Long icicles, hanging from its eaves, somehow made it look as if it had been untenanted for many a dreary day. But ah! It wasn't untenanted, I knew. In that house was Ann!

No doubt the sentry thought me mad, for in my elation I laughed in his face. "Towne," I said, "Ensign of Rangers, acting on commission for the commandant."

The sentry looked puzzled, but lowered his musket and stood to attention.

I walked through the gateway and started for the Major's house. "He's here, isn't he?" I asked the sentry over my shoulder.

"Who? Captain Spiesmaker? He went to the Settlement. Lieutenant Christy's officer of the day."

I stopped. "No, no! I mean the Governor, Major Rogers."
The man looked queer. "Yes," he said, "he's here. He's
under arrest and in irons."

He swung his musket. The bayonet, describing an arc, glittered with a light that stabbed at my eyes. It came to rest,
pointing at the guardhouse. "He's in there," the sentry said.

I thought I hadn't heard correctly. "He's in there? That's
the guardhouse!"

The sentry nodded.

"He's in the guardhouse?" I said. "Major Rogers? In irons?
In the guardhouse? For God's sake, what for!"

The sentry shook his head. "We don't know. Nobody ever
told us. Maybe because he treated soldiers like human
beings."

I still couldn't believe I'd heard what I thought I'd heard
the sentry say. "But the commandant—the Governor!" I protested. "They can't do a thing like that to the commanding
officer at a post!"

"That's what they did do, though."

I set off at a run for the guardhouse; then my brain cleared
a little; I stopped again and went back.

"You've got nothing against the Major or his friends, have
you?" I asked the sentry.

He laughed. "Not me! He invited me and me wife to his
house for a rout last month, and we went. He's been treated
bad, the Major has, and I'll say so to anybody." As an afterthought he added, "Except Captain Spiesmaker and Lieutenant Christy."

I wondered whether my long journey from beyond the
Mississippi had affected my brain—whether I had been overcome by the storm through which we had just passed, and
was only dreaming that I was within the fort at Michilimackinac, listening to the fantastic utterances of a sentry out
of a nightmare—a private soldier who claimed to have accepted an invitation to a ball at the home of his commanding
officer.

I rubbed my eyes and stared hard at him. No: he was no
phantom. He was still there, and he was real enough, for his
breath had made his mustache both wet and icy, and the little
hairs within his nostrils were frosted white.

"Well," I said uncertainly, "I've got to talk with him, but I
want to send word to someone that my party's out yonder

on the edge of the ice-cakes with all our belongings—Sergeant McNott and his wife and some Chippeways. The sergeant's a friend of the Major, and he's been sick. Will you get word at once to Stephen Groesbeck for me?"

"I'll tend to it," the sentry said. "I hope you can do something for the Major. There aint been more than one damned officer come to see him a single time—not even while they were letting him starve to death!"

I looked at him hard.

He said, "Yes, by God," and then I set out for the guard-house at a run. This time I didn't stop.

There was no sentry at the door of the small squat building, so I tried the latch. It was locked. I shook the door; but it was heavy and immovable, made of hewn planks. When I listened I heard, beyond the door, a faint clanking sound—such a sound as comes up from a brig's fore hatch when a chain cable is being stowed.

I ran around to the side of the building. There was a window in it, high up: a window in which thick iron bars were set, but in which there was no glass or skin or oiled paper as protection against the outer cold. I screened my eyes from the pallid glare of the December sky and peered between the bars. On the far side of the barren room was a wooden bed-place and on it lay a bulky figure.

"Who is it?" a familiar thick voice asked. My heart sank at the sound of clanking chains as his legs moved and he lifted himself on his elbow. He uttered a straining grunt, half groan, as he made these movements.

"It's Langdon Towne, Major," I said. "In the name of God, what happened?"

"Langdon!" the Major cried hoarsely. "Did you find it? Did you find the Northwest Passage?"

"No, Major," I said. "McNott was sick and I had to bring him back; but you can do it, Major! You can do it with fifty men including some boat builders! It's just about the way you said it was, only you have to go up the St. Peter's and across to the Missouri. The Missouri goes all the way to the Shining Mountains, and the Oregon's on the other side, only thirty minutes away. It can be done! We'd have done it easily if you'd been with us."

"St. Peter's!" the Major exclaimed. "Don't tell Carver! Don't tell anyone! By God, I'll beat 'em all and find it yet."

The chain rattled, and again the Major groaned and cursed. "These shackles!" he said, and from the way he spoke I knew he was sweating with agony. "These damned shackles wont let me get up, Langdon! They're too damned tight! They're so damned tight my legs feel as if they'd burst!"

The sounds from that cold, dark room, and the miserable odor that came out from it through the barred window, made me sick. "Major," I said again, "what's happened? How'd they ever get you in here?"

"Oh, orders," he said bitterly. "Orders from Gage! Orders from that damned fat spider of a Gage! That's all I know. Spiesmaker had an order from Gage removing me from office and putting Spiesmaker in my place, and telling Spiesmaker to put me in close confinement till I could be carried to Detroit or Montreal for trial. Well, he did, Langdon! That damned toy soldier threw me in here five minutes after he got the order, and not a word did he say to me or to anyone else as to why it was done. And the hell of it is, they won't be able to take me to Detroit or Montreal till the ice breaks up in the spring! That means three more months of this!"

His voice grew shrill, and I saw his big hand thump against the side of his bunk. "By God, I don't care how long they keep me here, or how hard they try to kill me, Langdon! They can't kill me! They've done their best; but by God, I wont die! They can starve me and break my bones with their damned irons, but I'll crawl out of here on the stumps of my legs in the spring, by God, and find out the lying whelp that's responsible for this!" He panted like a dying dog.

"But they can't do things like that, Major!" I protested. "They have to let you know why you're put under arrest!"

The Major's voice was calmer. "No they don't, Langdon. I thought they did, too; but they don't. I don't know what I'm charged with! When I asked Spiesmaker what he was doing it for, he just turned his back and walked off, damn him! I haven't seen him since. I've sent word to him and tried to find out, but he never even answers!"

My eyes, by now, were more accustomed to the dark interior of the guardhouse, and I made out that the irons on the Major's legs were horse-shackles, fastened with bolts and joined by a heavy chain. I saw him push himself upright with his huge arms, and draw his knees slowly up, as though to swing them over the side of the bunk. Then the chain clanked; the Major expelled a breath that was part hiss, part groan, and fell back limply on the hard boards.

My muscles quaked as I watched him, even as they had shaken at Wattoquitchey Falls, when Ogden and I stood helpless while he struggled, in the pool, to capture the raft that meant life to all of us if he could board it, and certain death if he failed.

"My God, Major," I said, "I'll go see Spiesmaker. I'll——"

"It wont do any good," Rogers said. "Elizabeth went to him, but she got no satisfaction. Satisfaction!" He laughed drearily. "You know what they did to her when they found she'd come into the fort and was talking to me, the way you are? They kicked her away from the window. Booted her."

"They booted her!" I whispered. "Booted Elizabeth!" My mind, wholly confused by what I had seen and what he had told me, fumbled slowly for the truth. "Wait, Major: you say they booted her when she came into the fort? Isn't she living in—where's she living, Major? Where's Elizabeth living? Major—where's Ann?"

"Elizabeth's living in the town, of course," Rogers said. "They threw her out of our house. You wouldn't expect them to show her any courtesies, would you—not with me rotting here and every last one of 'em afraid to say a decent word for me or show me any sign of kindness. Not even Carver! Not any of 'em! I——"

"Major," I interrupted, "is Ann with Elizabeth?"

For a moment he was silent, and I thought he hadn't heard. Then he said, "With Elizabeth? Why, last I heard Elizabeth was with Mrs. Cardin—very talented French lady —sent her to Arbre Croche to talk to the Indians last spring. She——"

"And Ann," I persisted. "Is she——"

The Major's voice became hurried, apologetic. "Very hard on Elizabeth, Langdon—I wouldn't take what she says too seriously—upset, of course—likely to say anything that comes into her head. You'll——"

It dawned upon me suddenly that the Major wasn't answering me about Ann.

"Major," I said, "this that's happened—seeing you like this—it's as though the earth had fallen out from under my feet! I must see someone I can trust—try to find out the reasons for the way they're treating you—try to find out what's to be done. I'll have to find Ann, Major; and then, if I can, I'll come back at once."

There was, it seemed to me, a sort of timidity in the Major's voice when he called after me, "Wait, Langdon; I didn't tell you——"

What it was he had to tell me, I now knew, must wait; more important than that or anything else, to me, was Ann: where she was, and why the Major had failed to answer my questions about her. I was frightened.

On the way from the fort to the town, I overtook a feckle-faced young man swathed in a blanket coat, blanket trousers, two mufflers and a fur hat. When I asked where Mrs. Cardin lived, he moved his head gingerly among his mufflers and eyed me with a shrewd blue eye. "The Widow Cardin, aye!" he said. "The hoose wi' the blue door and blue blinds. You can't miss it!"

I thanked him and hurried on, but he quickened his pace and kept abreast of me. "From the looks of your clothes," he said, "you've come a long journey."

"Middling," I said, "middling."

"And have you heard about the Major's misfortune?"

"Yes," I said. "I have." I didn't want to talk to him or to anybody until I'd seen Ann and freed my mind from the dark depression and the darker forebodings that weighed upon me. Ann must be with Elizabeth, I thought. She must be.

The young Scotsman was not to be denied. He hurried along beside me, his head withdrawn, turtle-like, into the turned-up collar of his blanket coat. "Maybe," he said, "maybe you'll be knowing what's the reason for it. Maybe you've heard why they chained him up like a mad dog?"

I shook my head. "How should I know? I've been to the westward for a year. Don't *you* know?"

"My Cod!" he cried, "there's forty-fifty traders here that want to find out, but never a thing can they learn except that Sir William Johnson wouldn't honor his bills! Why wont he? That's what we want to know! Five thousand pounds' worth of goods the Major bought from us, but 'twas only what he had to have to save us from a war—and everything that he bought, what's more, he gave to the Indians. It looks to us as if the wrong man had been thrown into them irons. It looks to us as if Sir William Johnson ought to be wearing 'em—not Rogers."

His clack set my teeth on edge, and I wondered how Scotsmen had ever achieved a reputation for taciturnity. "Well," I said, "I can't help you out; but those of you who've been in Michilimackinac during the past year must have made some pretty shrewd guesses as to why this has been done to him."

"Aye," he said. "That's all they do: guess. That's all they talk about—why the Major's in irons. 'It might 'a' been this,' they say, or 'it might 'a' been that.' And all of 'em together don't know nothing! Just a lot of he-housewives, tittle-tattlin'! Cod, how I hate tittle-tattlin'!"

He raised a long, thin neck from the collar of his blanket coat, glanced over his shoulder with the look of a freckled sheep, then withdrew his head even deeper into the shelter of his mufflers. "There's a story going around that he was figuring on deserting to the French, him and his wife, this winter: that he was going out to Lewis Constant on the Mississippi and then down the river to New Orleans, and that's why he was put in irons: so he couldn't go."

I stood stock-still, staring at the be-muffled Scotsman. If the Major had joined us to lead us in search of the Northwest Passage, he would have come to Prairie du Chien, of course, and the French name for Prairie du Chien was l'Ouisconsin—or Lewis Constant. I thought I saw how the rumor might have started. If the Major had ever let slip that he planned to go to Lewis Constant, nobody could have imagined that he contemplated anything so fantastic as striking off into the Northwest from there in an attempt to reach the Pacific. Any other conjecture would have been more reasonable; and if an enemy had hinted that it was the Major's intention to go down the Mississippi into French territory, the explanation would have been believed.

"By God," I said, "I think that's it!"

The Scotsman looked at me pityingly. "Hoots!" he cried. "It's plain you know nothing about travel to the westward! Who'd go with you? Not Indians! They're too busy hunting! Not voyageurs: they're lost without their canoes. You'd starve or you'd freeze! And what do you think would happen to you if you had a woman along? A white woman?" He snuffled and again contemptuously ejaculated "Hoots!"

But I'd already started off once more at a sharp stride. It wasn't sharp enough to distance the Scotsman, though; he still kept at my elbow. "Na!" he said. "Na! 'Tis a silly tale. To my way of thinkin', you'll have to look for a smaller, cosier reason. 'Twas maybe not his trouble with Lieutenant Roberts, as some say—though that Roberts was as mean a rat as ever lived, aye; and the Major put him under arrest and sent him down country with good reason; but there's a story going round that as soon as Roberts got down country he——"

We had come to the neat whitewashed houses of the French settlement. "Oh, for God's sake!" I said desperately. "I'm not interested in rumors. The Major's a friend of mine."

"Aye," he said cheerfully. "I knew you'd no be going to Mrs. Cardin's unless 'twas so. 'Tis as you say: rumors aint interestin' to any sensible man. I'm not interested in 'em myself. If you ask me, 'twas the Major's fight with Potter that was the start of all the trouble; for they're all saying that Potter's the favorite son of a Duke, or maybe of a Pairsonage." At the look on my face he added hurriedly, "Now that's no rumor, for 'twas in Bostwick's house that Potter lived; and I'm clerk to Bostwick, so I know what I'm talking about. Aye!"

"He quarrelled with Potter?" I asked. "When was this, and what did they quarrel over?"

"Quarrel, man! 'Twas a battle! They just rolled on the ground like wildcats!"

"A fight! The Major and Potter? What about?"

" 'Twas two months after the Indian Congress," the Scotsman said, "and a terrible thing it was! They come tumbling out of Rogers' house, storming and swearing and rolling in the dirt, and the whole place in a turmoil about it for weeks."

I stopped again and faced him. "What was it they fought over?"

"Ah," he said, "it must have been something dreadful, for nobody ever found out, not even when Potter up and boarded the schooner and sailed off down the lake, without——"

I seized his arm and shook him. "Potter's gone? Potter's left him too?"

"Aye! Took his daughter with him and set off in the schooner for God knows where. 'Twas the last sailing in August."

"What!" I shook the man again. "He took her with him?"

He pulled away from me. "Certainly he took her with him! Where else would a man's daughter be, except with her father?"

I stared at him, mumbling, "She went with him?"

The Scotsman must have thought me either insane or wicked, for his blue eyes were suddenly suspicious. "There's the Widow Cardin's house," he said, pointing. He wiped his red nose on the back of a woolen mitten; then turned and hurried away, casting furtive glances at me over his shoulder as he went.

Mrs. Cardin, who admitted me to her warm little blue-shuttered house, chirped like a bird when I asked for Elizabeth; and, thinking of Ann's description of her, I wondered whether she would lean against me. She was as fluffy and softly rounded as a sparrow; but her round black eyes were sharp and hard, more like those of a watchful sparrow hawk; and her little hand, when she placed it in mine, seemed to fit my palm bonelessly. I thought I knew, when I felt the soft suggestion in that hand, how the Major had happened to make her an ambassadress to Arbre Croche; and I could even guess why Elizabeth had come to live with her. Poor Elizabeth, always suspicious of the wrong things!

She glanced appraisingly at my buckskins, black and shiny from grease and hard wear. "Ah, you are new in this place —a friend of that poor Major, yes. You come from Detroit, perhaps, to tell Madame Major why that poor husband has been so treated, and that it is all a mistake?"

"No," I said. "I come from the other direction. I think if you'll tell Mrs. Rogers——"

She made big eyes at me. "But that is wonderful!" she whispered. "You are brave, to travel this country when she is frozen!" She tilted her head, bird-like, and smiled invitingly.

"Mrs. Cardin," I said, "I've got to see Mrs. Rogers: now: alone."

"But of course!" she exclaimed. "We see each other later, eh, and talk together?" She pressed my arm reassuringly,

and went lightly from the room. Mrs. Cardin, I suspected,
had made short work of the Major.

The heat from the cylindrical iron stove almost suffocated
me, and the smells of civilization—of perfume, dust, paint,
stale cooking, upholstery, dry wood—seemed horrible after
my year on the prairies and in the lodges of the Sioux. I
marvelled at the accumulation of trash that filled her crowded
sitting room—French chairs, pictures in frames, a spinet,
heavy brocaded curtains, china figures of shepherdesses in
billowing lace petticoats: marvelled at the thousands of miles
they had come by canoe and at the things men do for
trade that's worth little when they get it, and to please
women who are worth even less.

Then I heard Elizabeth's step on the stair and she came
quickly through the doorway, swung the door shut behind
her and stood there with her hand upon the knob. Her eyes,
perhaps, seemed a little larger; her nose a little sharper, her
lips a little thinner than I had remembered them; but I
couldn't be sure. Her lips, I recalled, had always been a little
thin: her nose always a little sharp.

She swept me from head to foot with that sidelong glare
of hers; and my greasy buckskins must have offended her.
She looked at me in silence for a moment; I didn't speak.
Then she slipped past me and settled herself on a French
chair with a deal of skirt fluffing.

"Well, Langdon," she said, "you're the last person I ever
expected to see! Not that I expected to see anyone! I might
as well not exist since the Major's troubles began."

"Elizabeth," I said, "if there's anything I can do, I'll do it.
I saw the Major—saw him through the window. He said he
didn't know why he'd been put in irons. Surely that's not
true, is it, Elizabeth?"

"Why shouldn't it be?" she asked. "He's done nothing—
nothing! Of course, it's all due to that Sir William Johnson;
but we can't imagine on what grounds the dreadful creature
has dared to do this to us! It's not because the Major had
to give presents to the Indians. That was six months ago;
and if there'd been anything wrong about that, he'd have
been put in irons long since."

She pressed her handkerchief to her nose. "Oh, Langdon,
the humiliation of it! I don't know how I can ever, ever,
ever hold up my head in Portsmouth again!"

"But if he's done nothing, Elizabeth," I said; "there'll be nothing humiliating about it. He'll have a chance to be heard, and then—if he's innocent—he'll clear himself."

"A chance to be heard!" she cried. "How'll he have a chance to be heard if they starve him and freeze him and crush his legs with fetters! And if he dies, there'll be a stigma on our name forever! What, oh, what mortification for my poor father!" She began to sniffle. "And oh, to think of that awful creature doing such a thing, without warning, to a Governor! A Governor! It was a title I was so proud of!"

"Elizabeth," I said abruptly, "where is Ann?"

Elizabeth's bowed head lifted, and her tear-filled eyes grew hard. "Please!" she said. "Please! I've endured enough without hearing that name again. I don't permit it to be uttered in my presence."

I was merely bewildered. "I mean Ann Potter," I said. "Ann Potter."

"I wont speak of her."

"You wont speak of Ann! Why not?"

Her eyes flashed angrily. "I don't choose to."

"What!" I said. "You don't mean to say you're angry with her—angry with a child who——"

"Child!" Elizabeth cried, suddenly fierce. "Child, is she? Does a child try to rob a woman of her husband?" She sprang to her feet, pale and shaking. "Child!" Her voice was almost a scream. "Trying to take my own husband away from me—beneath my own roof—eating my food—wearing the clothes I gave her—and then before my very eyes——"

I caught Elizabeth's wrist and sat her down in her chair. I was cold all over, as if the last drop of blood in me had drained away. "You're insane!" I said. "You don't know what you're saying!" I shook her.

She wrenched her wrist from my grasp and stared up at me, her eyes soot-black in her chalk-white face, on which lines and blemishes stood out with dreadful clarity.

"Insane?" she whispered. "No, Langdon! Oh, indeed, no. I tell you she threw herself in his way! She invited it! When I'd leave the room purposely, Langdon, they'd be close together when I came back—close together, and she looking up at him like a sick sheep. Once I found them over your trunk, she hiding behind the lifted lid, pretending to be hunting for something among your things!"

She clutched the arms of her chair and again her voice rose. "Don't know what I'm saying, indeed! That minx pulled the wool over your eyes, but she couldn't pull it over mine! I watched her and I caught her! You're all alike, you men—any woman can make you think black's white! You know nothing about what I tell you, and yet you dare—you dare to question what I saw! You and her father too! The idea of that sot, that Potter, who never drew a sober breath, thinking he had to defend her! He, that drunken thing—that miserable creature! What greater accusation than to be defended by Potter! I know what I know, Langdon Towne! She's a baggage; she's a drab; she's a——"

I gripped her shoulders. "Elizabeth! You've said enough! You've said too much! Now you'll be still!"

She sank back in her chair, watching me with frightened eyes, while I stumbled to a chair myself and tried to think. Truth to tell, I was deadly sick—sick in body as well as in mind—at what Elizabeth had said.

I knew now why Rogers and Potter had fought; why it was that both of them had concealed the reason for their fight from everyone in the garrison and in the town; why Rogers had warned me that I mustn't take Elizabeth's words too seriously.

I remembered how Rogers, at Oswego, had looked at Ann, over his shoulder, and asked her age: how he had commented on the probable beauty of her mother. Up from the dim recesses of my memory, too, came the words Potter had spoken when he asked me to search the slums of London for Ann. "The Major and young females," he had said, and stopped.

And that poor creature Potter! Something that had been in him when he'd once been a gentleman—some old spiritual spark—must have glowed again, and he remembered after all he was a defenseless girl's father. That last spark of manhood had sent him—drunken sot and miserable creature though he was and would be to the end of his days—flying at the throat of his colossus of an employer.

I understood everything now: understood that here was the end of a part of my life that for years had seemed to be its greatest and most fascinating part. Yes, I knew, then, that all of me that had centered so long upon Robert Rogers was at an end, and that my own part in his life was at an end, too, forever. How could it be otherwise when Ann, my Ann, had suffered a sickening persecution, a hideous love-pursuit, at the hands of this man?

I looked hard at Elizabeth. Her eyes wavered and sank before mine; and I understood something else: understood that she, poor thing, knew that what she had so shrilly told me had been cruelly distorted in the telling, distorted thus for her own wrecked pride's sake.

"Elizabeth," I said heavily, "I think I know what happened. It's probable that Major Rogers will expect to see me again; but he wont, and I think he'll understand why he doesn't."

I stood up. "Now, Elizabeth," I said, "I'm going after Ann. Where's her father taken her?"

She shook her head. Her fingers, locked together in her lap, writhed and twisted.

"Didn't she leave any message for me, Elizabeth? Any letter? It wasn't like Ann to go away without a word to me. She sent me a letter to the Falls of St. Anthony—yes, Elizabeth: another thing: she spoke of a diary——"

Elizabeth sprang from her chair. "No!" she cried, and stamped her foot. "No, no, no! I don't know! I wont listen! Don't say her name again!"

Her face reddened, twisted horribly, and the features seemed to dissolve and run together. "I can't stand it! I can't stand it! I want to go away! I want my mother! I want my sisters! It's horrible here—horrible! The cold and the ice! The snow whispering against the windows—whispering, whispering—and the wind—the wind!"

Her voice broke into a sort of wailing moan. "And the awful people! The awful, awful people! Indians everywhere, dirty and greasy, staring and staring! I can't bear it! Nasty little Frenchmen, leering and grinning! And that Captain Spiesmaker! Captain Beast! Captain Brute! Trying to kill my husband—trying to kill us both—I'd rather die than stay here. Oh, God, I wish I was dead!" She groped blindly for her chair, sank into it and sat there sobbing and hiccuping.

"Well, Elizabeth——" I said.

Her sobs, dreadful to hear, went on and on.

"Well, Elizabeth——" I said again. Then, as her weeping grew only louder, I opened the door and left her.

CHAPTER LXXIV

I STOOD IN the icy street below that blue-shuttered house, trying to stand straight and think clearly—to overcome the cold sickness that gripped my stomach and made me bend and shiver.

I was sure of one thing: Ann hadn't gone away from Michilimackinac without a word to me. Somewhere, or with someone, she had left a message, but with whom? Not, in all likelihood, with a servant if she had written something she didn't want seen. In fact, there wouldn't have been anyone she could have trusted if she had lost the friendship of the Governor. Friendship! My gorge rose at the thought of her, kneeling behind the opened lid of my trunk, shrinking from the stare of those hawk-eyes above her and——

"The trunk!" I shouted. "She was behind the open trunk!" A drunken, bandy-legged voyageur, with a scarlet ribbon fluttering from the tasseled end of his stocking cap, shied away from me at my shout and bawled protestingly as I went pelting off toward the fort and Captain Spiesmaker's quarters.

At the land-gate of the fort, I found the sentry peering interestedly toward Stephen Groesbeck's warehouse. He spared me a hasty glance.

"It's that McNott," he said. "That trader who used to be in the Major's Rangers. He just came back from the Mississippi. They say he's sick, but when he found out what had happened to the Major, he tried to break down the guardhouse with his wooden leg! They had to drive him off with bayonets and put him under guard!"

I saw a cluster of men, some of them in uniform, outside one of Groesbeck's windows, and heard a faint violent bellowing that I knew came from McNott; but I couldn't stop then. I hurried on toward the church, behind which stood the captain's house.

The captain's orderly let me in; and when the captain himself came to the door of his sitting room and looked coldly at me, his chin held high by a black leather stock that reached almost to his ears, I didn't blame the garrison's enlisted men for hating him. The sword-cut across his cheek and chin was a solid white against his waxy skin; his close-cropped hair seemed to bristle; his pale, close-set eyes stared coldly at me. "Yes?" he said. His voice, peculiarly accented, was sharp and abrupt; the voice of a martinet.

"Captain," I said, "I met you here a year ago, just before I went to the Mississippi."

He put his hands behind his back and looked me up and down. "Ah! What you want?"

"When I went away," I said, "I left a trunk—a box—in Major Rogers' care."

"Ah," Spiesmaker said. "Another friend of the fine Major!" His little gray eyes looked hard as bullets. "Please, you come in and I say one word."

He turned on his heel and went with quick steps into his sitting room, a hot little box of a room with a sheet-iron stove in the corner, buffalo skins on the floor and bearskins hung around the lower walls to keep out drafts. On a table were a few German books: on the mantel were specimens of ore—copper, lead, iron, silver—all neatly labelled in German. A liver-colored dog with a pointed snout and an abbreviated tail rose from behind the stove and sniffed searchingly at my buckskins. Upon them must have been an elusive fragrance from our two Sioux dogs; but when Spiesmaker shouted at his animal, it went back to the stove and sat behind it, looking at me sadly, as if he echoed back at me my own despair.

"Now," Spiesmaker said, turning to me. "Here is that one word I wish to say. You can do nothing! Not nothing! When the time comes, this fine friend of yours goes for a court-martial, where he belongs; and I warn you! You were not here when the trouble happened, and I recommend it to you strongly, you don't have nothing to do with that courtmartial. Not nothing!"

I hardly heard him, so busy was I with my own heavy thoughts.

"That McNott—he was with you, yes?" Spiesmaker went on. "He has made a fool of himself thinking he could alone fight this garrison, and look where he is! Under arrest! I am in command! Nothing can be done—nothing—except what I say!"

"Captain," I said, "I want my box: my trunk. That's all I want. Will you help me get it?"

Spiesmaker looked incredulous. "Don't you help that Mc-Nott make trouble! You have been one of those who wasted away the King's stores, trading on the Mississippi for the account of your fine friend, the Major. You are one of them, and McNott too: also Goddard and Tute and Atherton. I tell you, if you try to make trouble, it will not be permitted to you, ever again, to trade on this continent."

"Captain," I said, "I'm not a trader: I'm a painter. I didn't go West to trade: I went there to paint Indians—to persuade them to come here for the Peace Congress—and I had orders to go. It's not my fault my trunk's where it is, or that the house is now closed against me. Will you give me an order for the trunk, Captain?"

Spiesmaker nodded and smiled. "Peace! A Peace that does good only to a few traders! Bah! And you go West to paint, eh? Where's your paintings?"

"I don't have them here," I said.

The captain shook with silent mirth. "Of course!" he said. "What you painted you haven't got. The Peace you went to make wasn't worth making. The Nordwest Passage your friends hunt for isn't nowhere; so nobody does nothing he goes to do! You know what I think? I think you prepare a passage so Major Rogers passes safely through the Indians to join the French at New Orleans and be maybe a colonel." He eyed me craftily.

"Oh," I said, "that's nonsense, Captain! Will you send your orderly with me so I can get my trunk?"

"Nonsense?" he asked sharply. "No, no! he had a great scheme for betraying this post, killing us all, and deserting to the French!"

"Just a moment, Captain," I said. "That's twice you've accused me of having a hand in a traitorous plot. Didn't you seize the Major's papers and search them? I've been given to understand you did."

Spiesmaker shrugged his shoulders and pursed his lips.

"If you did," I went on, "you know why we went to the westward. You saw our orders——"

"Orders!" He laughed. "Anybody can write any orders that come into his head."

"True," I said, "but you also saw letters from Charles Townsend, from Dr. John Campbell, from Henry Ellis, from Edmund Burke, from Edward Fitzherbert, telling him to issue those orders. I hope you don't think anybody would be so foolish as to forge those gentlemen's names to letters!"

"There were no such letters," he said.

I looked at him hard, and he returned my stare. His eyes were steady; not a muscle of his face moved.

"There were no such letters?" I repeated stupidly. "You seized his papers and went through them, and there was no letter from Charles Townsend among them?"

His eyes never left mine. "Is it likely that a great gentleman like Charles Townsend, Secretary of War, Chancellor of the Exchequer, would write familiarly to a person so unreliable, so full of wild and dangerous schemes, as your fine Major?"

I had an impulse to answer him, but overcame it. "Captain," I said, "I don't want to argue with you. I only want my trunk, so I can get some drawing materials from it, and use what's left to raise a little money. I must leave here at dawn tomorrow, if I can."

"You must leave here!" Spiesmaker cried. His face brightened. "You want to leave now? You go to the eastward, perhaps?"

"Yes," I said, "I must catch up with Potter, if it's possible. You don't know, do you, Captain, where Potter was going when he left here?"

Spiesmaker behaved like another man. He stepped to the door, called his orderly, and from a drawer in his table took a key. "No, no!" he said. "I'm sorry: I do not know. It was long ago in August, and after his fight with the Major he shut his lips tight. He had been badly treated by the Major, and I think he wished to go to England, but whether from New York or elsewhere, I cannot say."

When the orderly came in, Captain Spiesmaker handed him the key, gave him instructions to get my trunk and carry it wherever I wished; then bade me a punctilious and almost cordial farewell. I never saw him again, nor did I wish to.

The orderly, huddled in his bearskin coat, waited in the

tomb-like hall while I raced upstairs. Every room in the house, except the little cubicle in which Ann had slept, bore mute witness to the sudden departure of its unhappy occupants. That room alone was clean, and bare as a cell.

The large corner room, in which the Major and Elizabeth had slept, was a hoorah's nest of soiled bedding, rumpled garments, old letters and ancient Portsmouth newspapers. A striped petticoat trailed from a chair; an empty bottle lay on the bed.

I ran to the billiard room, where my box, spread with a buffalo robe, had been placed in the corner as a seat. The buffalo robe lay in a heap in the middle of the billiard table; but my box was still there, and the key where I had hidden it behind a loose brick in the chimney.

I went to the trunk and rubbed my fingers over the white letters I had painted on the cover a year and a half before. Their rough surfaces reminded me how black flies, blown by a soft northwest breeze, had flown against the wet paint: how Ann, kneeling beside me, had patiently attempted to free them with a pinpoint. I tried to remember only that, and not to think of how she must have looked, kneeling behind the raised lid when Elizabeth had walked in and seen her cowering there.

I got the lid open at last, and stood staring down at the neatly-folded brown coat that lay on the top. There was a strip of red flannel across it, and I knew Ann must have put it there as a sop to the moths. On either side were pieces of camphor—more of Ann's thoughtfulness, of course; but nowhere was there a letter. I felt carefully around the edges of the trunk; looked beneath the six sketch books—two of them filled and four unfilled—that I had left tied together; then, in a panic, tossed the garments every which-way and hunted through their pockets, but found nothing.

My mouth was dry with disappointment. Never in my life had I wanted anything so much as I wanted the word I knew Ann must have left for me. I knelt before the trunk, my eyes closed, trying to think what she would have said if she had been kneeling there beside me. "Of course, Langdon," she'd have said, "I wouldn't have gone away without leaving a message for you, and of course I'd have left it where you'd have been sure to look—where you'd have had to look, sooner or later."

I opened my eyes and stared at the jumbled belongings on the floor. There was nothing among them that I had to have —nothing except the sketch books.

"Oh my God!" I shouted. "The sketch books!"

The voice of Spiesmaker's orderly echoed through the empty house. "Anything wrong, sir?"

"No," I called, breaking the string that held the books together. "No: everything's all right. Just a few minutes more!"

I carried the books to the single window, looking out on the darkening parade—the books between whose sheets Ann had so carefully placed protective-papers—the books that were more valuable to me than any of my earthly possessions. With shaking fingers I turned the leaves—and there it was— there was the message, written in that pretty slanting hand taught her by the stern Miss Benker.

"Langdon dear," it began. I drew a deep breath, and crouched beside the window, holding the book close to me, perhaps in the vague hope of catching some of Ann's warmth and sweetness.

"We are going away [it read]. I hoped there would be another letter from you saying where you are, and perhaps I could send a letter there to tell you. Every trader who has come back I have asked about you, but none of them have seen you since you left Prairie du Chien, and they know nothing. They had seen Mr. Carver and Mr. Tute and Mr. Goddard, but they said you were not with them, and they said it would be useless to send any more letters to you, as you would never get them. What they said is not true, because you said you would come back. I know you will come back, dearest Langdon, because you need me to make your crayons and put the papers between your pictures, and because if you don't come back I don't want to live, and wont, so you *must* come back.

"We are going to Montreal because my father says we cannot stay here any longer. He had a terrible, terrible quarrel with the Major, dearest Langdon, and I am afraid I was the cause of it. I am very sorry. It is terrible that the Major has to stay here all the time, drinking with the traders and forever being bothered by Mr. Roberts so there isn't anywhere for him to go and nothing for him to do but get drunk. I hoped he would go away and join you and Mr. Carver and

Mr. Tute, and when he couldn't it must have been very bad for him. He just drinks and drinks, and after he has been drinking, it has been hard to keep out of his way. Sometimes I was very much frightened. Of course he can't help being the kind of man he is.

"I have prayed and prayed that you would come back, and whenever the sentry fired a gun for a brigade, I ran all the way to the gate because it might be you.

"My father is still sick. I do not think he will live much longer. He says he can get some money in Montreal, though I do not know how he can do it. Perhaps Lieutenant Roberts is going to help him get it, because I have seen them whispering together. My father has talked a great deal about England and several times each day he recites what Shakespeare said about it—'this seat of Mars, this other Eden, demi-paradise' —so I think that if he *can* get money in Montreal, he will go back to England.

"We are going in the *Gladwyn* schooner tomorrow early. I must tell you that at last my father has been very kind to me, and I hope that if I can nurse him into a little better health I can show my gratitude to him. I hadn't expected he would help me in a trouble, but he did, and you will respect him for that, won't you, Langdon?

"I feel very far away from you, and yet must go with him farther still. Maybe when you have found this you will come to Montreal, where I shall be watching for you every day. Ah, how I will watch.

                                                            "Ann."

From the window, in the gathering dusk, I could see the guardhouse on the far side of the parade, its window a black patch upon its cheerless wall. The bitter wind, rustling its icy fingers at the eaves of the building in which I was, must be darting through that black window like frosted knife-blades to slash at the flesh of the sick, miserable, stricken man who lay in the darkness, shackled to a wooden bunk.

He couldn't, Ann had said, help being the man he was; and neither, alas, could I. If, in spite of what had happened, I had wished to help free him from the army's brainless and inflexible grasp, there was nothing I could have done. At this moment I despised him, and yet I felt like a traitor to leave him there, helpless, chained, tormented. If by wishing, or by any act of my will, I could have freed him from his dreadful situation, I might have done so; but I wasn't sure, even, about that. I could only think of Ann; and I didn't know: I didn't know.

CHAPTER LXXV

STEPHEN GROESBECK'S snug home lay against the side of his warehouse as though the warehouse, having given birth to a miniature of itself, were suckling its young; and to me the warm interior of that small white building seemed a haven in which I could have slept forever—if there had been nothing on my mind.

Dutchmen, I have often heard it said, are pig-headed and avaricious; but Groesbeck, though a Dutchman, was both generous and understanding. When I pounded on his door that evening and dragged my trunk into his hallway, he quacked at me like an excited duck, pushed me into his neat parlor and sat me down in a cushioned barrel-chair: then waddled to the dining room for the rum bottle.

While I drank he stood staring at me and shifting uneasily from one foot to the other, extremely duck-like.

"Gott!" he said, when I put down the glass, "what a devil-nest—and now comes this McNott—this sick man—tearing off his leg and trying to smash down houses! Gott sei dank he aint healthy and got two whole legs or we all be in jail with bayonets around!"

"Mr. Groesbeck," I said, "I've got a brown suit in my trunk and some other odds and ends. The suit's London-made and not much worn, and the trunk's a strong one. Will you take all my things in trade for enough equipment to get me to Montreal?"

"I guess we have no trouble making arrangements," Groesbeck said comfortably. "We got plenty time for trading: you wont have no travel till April-May. *Gladwyn* schooner, she can't get in here before May, I don't think. Here, take another little glass rum and lay back easy! You aint got nowheres to go, so don't sit on the chair-edge. Tomorrow we talk trade."

"No," I said. "Tomorrow's too late. I'm starting for Montreal at daybreak."

Groesbeck made sounds like a mallard champing its beak on water-plants. He shouted a sentence at me in German: then grew calmer. "Everybody's crazy, except me!" he said. "What you talking about, going to Montreal? How far you think you get? No, no, no! You stay here, get yourself nice young Indian girl like everybody else: then when the ice goes out, you start for Montreal and cost you nothing—not one damned penny."

"I'm going the first thing in the morning," I said. "My mind's made up."

Groesbeck seemed to flap abbreviated wings. "Um Gottes willen!" he cried. "Daybreak! Daybreak! For why! Aint you had enough—from beyond the Mississippi to here through snow and ice; and now off again, never stopping, like Flying Dutchman! You freeze your fingers: freeze your toes: freeze everything off you! For why, du—du——" Breath failed him.

"Private reasons," I said. "Private reasons, Mr. Groesbeck."

"So," he said. "I tell you now, you can't do nothing for the Major in Montreal! You aint heard all the story, my young friend, and——"

"I don't believe I want to hear it, Mr. Groesbeck. I—to tell you the truth, I'm very much disturbed. Potter——"

"Pah!" Groesbeck shouted. "Potter! Dreck! Rauber! Nobody believe what he say! He is bad! Schrechlich! Waste not your life for that verdammte!"

"You don't understand," I said. "What you say is unfortunately true. He has a daughter, Mr. Groesbeck——"

"Ah!" Groesbeck said.

"She was in my care for a time, when she was younger," I went on. "I know Potter; I know him too well; so—yes, Mr. Groesbeck, I'm starting for Montreal at daybreak."

"You see the Major before you go?" he asked.

"No."

He waddled up and down the small room, casting sharp glances at me and making muted sounds such as ducks make on good feeding grounds.

At length he went to the window, pushed aside the heavy

hangings, and peered out. Then he turned and called sharply in an Indian language. An Ottawa squaw in a knee-length green velvet jerkin and bright red trousers came silently from the dining room. In her ears she wore imitation diamonds the size of a teal's egg. She stared at me while Groesbeck addressed her, and, when he had finished, walked majestically from the room, toeing in.

"My wife," Groesbeck said absently, and added, "too bad you aint staying. I got two more diamond earrings, and I give you both." He paced the floor, muttering; then cogitated aloud: "You never do it alone—never; but maybe you do it if you go with the right people. There's chust a chance: chust a bare chance. Well, we see: we see!"

The door opened and McNott came in, propelled by the squaw. He stood there, a murderous expression on his face, while the squaw, after admiring her diamonds in a gold-framed mirror, retired silently to the dining room.

"Sit down, my friend," Groesbeck said. "Do not speak loud. If they find out you come through that liddle trap-door, they close it up and you don't get out again till they let you out. They keep you there all winter."

"Where's my wife?" McNott asked.

"In the kitchen," Groesbeck said. "She's eating yet. Already she's eaten three dinners."

McNott limped to a chair and sank into it. His wooden leg was dented, and from the end a splinter six inches long had been broken. He accepted a glass of rum from Groesbeck, downed it and shivered.

"Langdon," he said huskily, "did you see him? Did you see where they put him? Did you see what they did to him?" Forgetting his shattered peg he rose suddenly to his full height; wavered; caught the back of his chair. "My God, Langdon," he shouted, "they can't—they can't——"

Groesbeck sat him down again. "Don't shout," he said. "It don't do you no good."

McNott pounded his knee. "Langdon," he said, "you got educated brains. You can figure out some way to help the Major. You got to! These damned rats around here—every one of 'em's dodged into his rat-hole! The Major saved their bacon for 'em; but now he's in trouble, by God, they're hiding and squeaking! These people aint flesh and blood! They're sawdust and ice-water!"

"Mac," I said, "there's nothing I can do. I can't even stay here. I've got to go to Montreal. I'm starting at daybreak."

McNott stared, openmouthed. "Montreal! You can't get nobody to go to Montreal with you—not at this time of year—without you give 'em a slop-jar full of gold! Montreal, for God's sake! You *can't*, not when the Major's in trouble. And you saw him! He told me you did! He said you'd be back! By God, Langdon Towne——" He began to struggle with the buckle of his leg strap.

"Now wait, Mac," I said. "Something's happened you don't know about. Potter started for Montreal four months ago and took his daughter with him. You know what sort of man he was. Well—I've got to get to them."

"Oh, God!" McNott cried. "A damned little spindle-shanked snub-nosed waxwork, and you'll go skating and hollering all over hell's pig-pen after her when the greatest fighter in the world is lying over there, chained to the ground and freezing!"

Groesbeck sharply slapped McNott's shoulder. "Listen! You don't know nothing you're talking about! You speak about rats full of ice-water! Phoo! You let me tell you something."

He levelled a finger at the sergeant's face and spoke slowly: "Not you and not nobody else in this part of the country can do one thing for the Major! They got him. They waited and they waited; and when it got too late for anyone to help him, they sprung the trap, so!" He snapped his fingers.

"Now see," he went on. "You know how much I gave to the Major, so he could send supplies to Tute and Carver and the rest, and let them discover the Nordwest Passage? Three thousand, two hundred and seven pounds! I am willing, because it will be a great thing for me, for England, for trade, for the Major, for everybody. All the others, they gave something also, to keep peace between the Sioux and the Chippeways. They gave not so much as me, no, but more than they can afford to lose. And all of us gave more and more, thinking we would get it back because we were doing good. And then——"

He smacked his palms together. "Crack! The trap snapped! The Major's in jail, two months' journey from New York, so it aint no use appealing to General Gage. Our goods are gone and we wont never get our money. But still we have something left, and all of it—all—is in our trading business. If we also lose our trading business, we starve or die in debtors' prison."

He sat down heavily. "Do you know, my friend, who gives the permits for traders to travel in Nord America? In Canada it is Daniel Claus, superintendent of Indian Affairs, and he is son-in-law to Sir William Johnson. In New York it is Sir William Johnson himself. The Major did what Sir William told him not to do: therefore he has been insubordinate. You see, my friend, what will happen to any trader who takes sides with the Major against Sir William Johnson. You see, also, why none of those he helped can now help him. The Major is finished, and those who help him will also be finished."

McNott stared at him and said nothing.

"There's one thing you're overlooking," I told Groesbeck. "Spiesmaker admitted searching Rogers' belongings and seizing his papers, but he denied finding a letter from Charles Townsend among them. Now that's a lie, because Townsend wrote him and told him to go ahead with his plans to discover the Northwest Passage—told him the King wanted him to do it. You can't be insubordinate if you follow the King's orders, because the King comes ahead of everybody. Townsend may be a slippery customer, but he'll never deny he wrote that letter. If Johnson and Claus try to make trouble for you, they'll be in worse trouble themselves when Townsend swears—as he must—that he wrote that letter to Rogers."

"There, by God!" McNott cried. "Didn't I tell you that Langdon Towne had educated brains?"

Groesbeck shook his head. "Townsend wont never swear to writing that letter. Then everybody knows it wasn't written."

"Damn it, Mr. Groesbeck," I said, "he *did* write it, so he'll have to swear to it. No matter what they say about Townsend and his Stamp Tax, he's a courageous gentleman."

"Yes," Groesbeck said, "he was. But not any longer, my friend. He's dead."

"Charles Townsend," I repeated unbelievingly. "Charles Townsend dead? When did he die?"

"Didn't you hear me," Groesbeck asked, "when I said the trap wasn't sprung till all was ready? Charles Townsend died in September, and the news reached New York in October.

Crick! The trap is set! So General Gage wrote an order for the Major to be put in prison and his papers seized, and sent it to Michilimackinac by the last boat to arrive here before the Straits were frozen. Crack! The trap was sprung: the Major was put into chains so tight he can't walk—chains so tight nobody can't get 'em off, only a blacksmith. And then—they seize his papers! And would you believe it, my friends, that letter from Charles Townsend—it wasn't there! So he never got it, and he was insubordinate after all!"

Groesbeck poured himself a glass of rum. McNott reached for the bottle, filled a tumbler with a shaking hand, swallowed the dose at a gulp and sighed shiveringly.

"By God, Langdon," he whispered, "Johnson beat him. Nobody ever beat the Major before, but Johnson's done it; and oh God, didn't he do it! The Major talked and he talked—yes, he can still talk; but he aint the same feller. I guess maybe it's because he aint able to attack. He couldn't attack if he wanted to; and even if he could, I don't believe he'd know what to attack! By God, Langdon, when I saw him there—that feller that all the French and all the Indians in Canada couldn't hurt for five long years—that feller that saved us all, a hundred times—when I saw him trying to get up and not having the power to do it; trying to talk and not being able to finish on account of his legs hurting him so, I —well, the Major's gone, and so's the Northwest Passage."

McNott made a strange, half-choked sound. His lips, nose and eyes were pursed together in a singular contortion; tears were trickling down his chin and falling on his clenched, chapped hands.

Then I stood up. "Mr. Groesbeck," I said, "will you look at the things in my trunk and make me as large an allowance as you can? If I get to Montreal, I think I can repay you some day."

"Yes, yes, yes!" he said impatiently. "I give you everything you need—coat, toque, blankets, moccasins, rifle, snowshoes —all! What I cannot give is men to go with you. That is what worries me."

"Don't let it," McNott said. "Me and the Princess, we'll go with him." He unbuckled his wooden leg and thrust it into Groesbeck's hands. "Here, tell one of your men to put a new peg in this limb of mine, and have him make me a special snowshoe-leg with a steel peg and a fry-pan riveted onto the end of it with angle irons."

"But you haven't seen the doctor," I protested. "You can't——"

"Doctor be damned!" McNott shouted. "The only time you need a doctor is when you're scairt of getting sicker. Well, I aint going to get sicker—not unless I have to watch these skunk-water soldiers raise hell with the Major. I'd go crazy if I couldn't do something about it, and I guess I can't —not here. I might be able to do something, though, on the road to Montreal."

CHAPTER LXXVI

WE DIDN'T get far on the way to Montreal, and in spite of the sadness of the circumstances that stopped us, the delay, like most delays, did no harm in the end, though when it happened I was sure it would prove the ruin of us all. And I, at least, was able to turn it to account; for I was enabled to do pictures of the Chippeway divinities who dwell within the hollow earth-ball and emerge to protect and plague mankind—Kitchi-Manito, the Great Spirit; Manabozo, the giant ancestor of everyone; Mitchi-Manito, the evil spirit; and the scores of lesser godlets who haunt the streams and forests of the Chippeways. From these sketches grew the frescoes in the central hall of the Ethnographic Society in London.

When we left Michilimackinac in the bitter gray dawn, McNott was as silent as his wife, and his grief and rage not only seemed to give him added strength but to fill him with a savage restlessness. Growling inarticulate nothings, he'd let us put him on the sled with our meager baggage; but before the dogs had gone a mile, out he'd get and swing along at his wife's heels, muttering furiously to himself. I knew how he felt; my own fear that something might happen to Ann— that she might have been left penniless in Montreal—filled me with such a consuming desire to reach her that I didn't want to stop for anything—not even for food or rest or storms. When we did stop for food and rest, we did so because McNott's wife made us; and it was she who saw to it that we stopped always close to a deep drift in the lee of a thicket or against the bank of a stream, where we could burrow for shelter in case of a storm.

It seemed unfair, in view of her foresight, that she should have been the one to suffer; but that seems to be the rule in this world—for the thoughtless to outlive those by whose labors they are preserved.

The snow caught us on the sixth night after we left Michilimackinac, and penned us at the foot of a ledge for what were to prove the longest days of my life. Only one day's supply of fresh meat remained to us when we made camp; and to have ventured into that howling smother of whirling snowflakes to hunt would have been certain death. So there we stayed, the three of us and the two dogs, huddled together beneath our buffalo robes for warmth, dipping into our precious store of pemmican, like a ball of beavers beneath their icy roof, until the sun came out to turn that rolling countryside into a mass of fleecy, glittering billows.

When we crawled from our shelter, we were eager for fresh meat, and the dogs were ravenous; so McNott went to cutting firewood while Mrs. McNott and I strapped on our snowshoes, took the muskets and struck off in opposite directions, each of us breaking trail for a dog that lunged so eagerly after us that the tips of our snowshoes rapped their snouts.

"Shoot any damned thing except yourselves!" McNott told us. "Owls—crows—wildcat—fox. There aint nothing I couldn't eat, barring you; but prob'ly the dogs aint so p'tickler!" I sent my dog Jennie into hardwood thickets, hoping she might find deer scraping in the snow for moss or feeding on tangled vines, or perhaps surprise a fox stalking a buried partridge, but the whole world seemed to be as empty of life as it was full of snow. I heard a giant woodpecker whacking tentatively at a tree, as though making ready to deliver the one final blow that would burst it in pieces; saw a red squirrel, high in an oak, hopping precariously from one branch-tip to another, but that was all.

When, therefore, I heard a far-off shot, I was relieved.

Hoping the Princess had found a larger target than a rabbit, I scanned each distant thicket in the direction she had taken, thinking she might come out and signal to me; but nothing moved upon that glaring white expanse, except a slowly-undulating layer of the blue smoke from McNott's fire.

Then I saw McNott hobble out from the ledge against which the fire burned, and from far beyond him there came to me clearly, in that still, cold air, a frantic barking.

Jennie looked up into my face and whined, so that I kicked at her with my snowshoe to keep her quiet.

The barks abruptly altered to a shrill yelp that was almost a scream, and as abruptly became barks again. Jennie growled and lunged back along our tracks, her hackles up.

McNott, I saw, was waving to me, but I had already turned and was running as fast as I could toward the far-off barking. When I passed the clumsily-laboring Jennie, she fell in behind me, whimpering and growling. The barking, I thought, had stopped, but as I ran on I heard the sound a dog makes when he has hold of something, worrying it—a sort of spasmodic strangled cough.

The sounds came from beyond a thicket of spruce and birch, and when I skirted it I came on a circular pit or amphitheater in the deep snow such as deer make for themselves when drifts prevent them from travelling. Half a dozen staring, trembling does were crowded against the high bank at the far side, and in the center, pitching, shaking its head, striking with its forelegs, was a buck trying to free himself from our other dog whose jaws were locked on his throat.

On the trampled, yellow snow at the bottom of the pit lay McNott's wife, face down, her musket six feet away. There were gouts and blobs of blood all around her, and her blue jerkin was smeared with it.

Blood streamed from a hole in the deer's ribs, and the dog at his throat—whose spasmodic worrying growls never ceased—was horribly slashed along the back and belly, so that blood spattered from him as the deer plunged and threw its head from side to side. It was easy to see what had happened. McNott's wife had shot the deer, knocked it down and gone into the pit to cut its throat and drag it out. As deer will, it must have come to life, lashed out at its enemies with its hoofs—and to be struck by a deer's hoofs is as bad as being hit with a tomahawk.

When I stopped and took a deep breath, so to shoot straight after my long run, Jennie flung herself past me and into the pit, leaped for the deer, got him by the hind-quarter; and that horrible small amphitheater seemed to be filled with a blurred revolving wheel of deer and dogs. Fearful of wasting a shot, I floundered over the edge, snowshoes and all, landed on my hands and knees, crawled to McNott's wife and pushed her closer to the wall. Behind me the growling and worrying of the dogs, the thrashing and strained bleating of the buck, were horrible.

When I turned, the plunging beasts towered above me, a tangled mass of flying hoofs and bloody fur, so close that I pushed the muzzle of my musket against a tawny side and pulled the trigger. The flint flashed in the pan; the musket, unfired, was almost wrenched from me by the furious movements of the struggling bodies. I felt the crunching impact of the deer's hoofs against my shoulder, my side, my thigh: felt the bloody body of the wounded dog strike hot and wet across my face; and somehow, amid all the snarling and striking and whimpering and hoarse breathing, I got to my feet and swung the musket barrel against the deer's back with all my strength. He coughed hard and stood still, so I swung again. This time he went down on his knees, and from the way his hind-quarters slewed around as the dogs tugged and hauled at him, I knew his backbone was broken.

I stood looking at him. My legs were shaking, and the stock of the musket had broken off in my hand. My brain seemed to move slowly. Something must have happened to McNott—the deer ought to be killed, of course—I primed my musket, then saw that the barrel was badly bent. I took out a knife, caught the deer by the nose and pulled back his head to cut his throat; but I couldn't because of the wounded dog, whose teeth were still fastened where I wanted to cut. His eyes were shut, and at intervals he made a bubbly wheezing sound and feebly wrenched at the draggled crimson hair between his jaws.

I couldn't seem to figure what to do about it. The deer saved me the trouble by groaning and going slack in my hands.

I went over to McNott's wife. She lay where I had pushed her, and I saw that the deer's hoofs had cut her jerkin just above her waist. When I took her by her shoulder and rolled her over on her back, her eyes were open and she looked calmly at me, but made no effort to sit up. There were more hoof slashes down the front of her jerkin. I saw her eyes move to my shoulder and travel down to my knee, and when I followed her glance, I saw that I, too, had cuts in my clothes. I understood then why my brain had moved slowly. My shirt and leggins were warm and wet against my side; and I knew I'd have to get away soon if I wanted to get away at all. What, I wondered dully, had happened to McNott?

I leaned against the side of the pit and must have slept a little, for when I heard McNott's voice, I was lying on the blood-spattered snow and my leg burned as though a hot poker rested against it. McNott was above me, at the top of the bank. "Langdon!" he was shouting. "I got the sled, Langdon! Can you get up, or shall I unhitch Jennie for you?"

I contrived to sit up, and was conscious that the movement started my side to bleeding again. "Unhitch her," I said. "We got to drag out that deer. We'll need it."

McNott's eyes were wild. "I had to dig out that damned sled!" he said. "It was froze to the ground, and I knew damned well we'd have to use it!"

He vanished; and when he came back with the carrying-string, I got it around the deer's horns somehow. McNott had to tie us on the sled, and when he and Jennie dragged us back to camp, there was little to choose between his wife, the deer and me.

I could hear McNott dimly through the feverish fog in which I seemed to swim, and his voice appeared to me to come from gargantuan figures that struggled for possession of my brain and held me back from some vast task that groaned aloud to be accomplished. Most terrifying of all these suffocating specters was Rogers, whose large face and staring eyes, painfully distorted, would swell within my aching eyes until every corner of the world was crowded with him; while I, a little naked mannikin, strove and strained to get away, but, like a quivering jelly, couldn't move. McNott's voice, issuing from these nightmare faces, incensed me until I wasn't sure what I heard.

"Damn her," I thought he said—and I thought, too, he said it whimperingly, "damn her, aint that just like her—just does what she damn pleases and don't care whether you like it or not. Here, Langdon, you'll be all right—roll over and let Jennie lick them cuts—I'll stay here—that's all right, Langdon, I aint goin' away—hell, I can't—here, for God's sake keep on licking them cuts, you damned hyena—I'll stay here, Langdon, and not a damned thing I can do except keep them damned wolves away—by God, if I ever get my fingers on one of those damned hell-critters, I'll pull out his toe-nails with my teeth—here, Langdon, eat this———"

That awful voice of his went on and on for an eternity, scourging my brain with nettles and filling my heart with inexpressible woe, and when unexpectedly it stopped I found that the gargantuan faces were gone too; that the sun was warm on my face and that a whole deer—a sleek doe, with clean, unbloodied coat—lay handy to the front of our shelter. When McNott saw me looking at the deer, he gave me a cup of water and a tender slice of raw meat. "Here's a nice little piece," he said in the mealy voice some people use to invalids, "tenderer than that other old thing!"

I turned my head to look for his wife, but couldn't find her. "How's your wife, Mac?" I asked, and was surprised to find my voice thin and reedy.

"Who? The Princess?" McNott asked. "She died." He spoke carelessly. "Served her right! She'd oughta knew better than go down in with a lot of snow-bound deer and make all that trouble for everybody."

I rubbed my forehead, then looked at my hand. Under the dirt on it, it had a waxy look. "When did she die, Mac?" I asked. "I—I———"

"Hell!" McNott said cheerfully. "She's just as well off. When you think of all the Indians in this world, what's one more or less?" He went to the entrance of our shelter and looked up at the sky.

"Mac," I said, "I couldn't feel worse if she'd been my own wife. I can't hardly believe it! She was a good woman, Mac—a mighty good woman."

McNott's voice was defiant. "I gave her hell, but she never said a word. She was cut pretty bad and there wasn't no way of finding out where she was hurt worst." He spoke more rapidly. "The hell of it was, Langdon, there wasn't one damned thing I could do! She never said a word, damn her, but I knew damned well that if I could find a camp of Chippeways, they'd be able to do somep'n for her, and maybe, by God, even fix her up! She——"

He stopped, coughed loudly and drew a deep breath.

"A good woman," I said again. "Quiet and good—a lady if ever I saw one."

"It was those terrible damned wolves," McNott said. "They came around and howled, and I couldn't leave. I—I didn't dare to go for help."

Sergeants, I saw, have feelings like everyone else, no matter what they say or what people say of them.

A week passed before a band of Chippeway hunters came across McNott's tracks, followed them to one of the drawings on birch bark I'd made for him to leave in conspicuous places, and so came to help us. I was struck by their reverence for the dead; before they loaded us on the sled and started for their winter camp on the Mattawa River, they built a platform high up between four trees, wrapped the frozen body of our poor companion in her buffalo robe and placed her on the platform; then deposited beside her things they could ill afford—tobacco, powder, paint. Each one gave a part of his most valued possessions. I don't wish to argue with the churchmen who hold all Indians to be savages, but it has seemed to me that Indians who haven't been wrecked by rum and white men's tricks have a better grasp of the ten commandments, and practise them with greater regularity, then any churchmen I know.

Of our life with the Chippeways, there is little to tell. In the beginning I insisted on being taken at once to Montreal, raged at my own weakness and damned the stringy-haired old Indian women who puttered around our tent, sniffing at my cuts with dirty noses, and applying dirty-looking remedies with dirtier hands.

At first I blamed the old women because the slashes on my thigh wouldn't close, though later I knew they weren't to blame, since the cuts on my shoulder and side healed neatly beneath their treatment. For a long time, of course, I thought they were in league with McNott to prevent me from going in search of Ann.

Eventually I came to be grateful to them; for not only did they heal my cuts, but it was they, too, who squalled to me about the huge, deformed and ugly Mitchi-Manito, who puts

evil thoughts into the minds of men, until in desperation I
took crayons from beside my bed and made a sketch of
Mitchi-Manito; a hump-backed monster with pouchy eyes,
blackened teeth and a pendulous lower lip, stooping to whisper in the ear of an Indian. When I turned it around and
showed it to the old hags, they screamed horribly and dashed
from the tent. Their terrified howls brought a dozen scowl-
ing Chippeways to the tent; and to appease them I hastily
drew a sketch of good-natured Manabozo, the giant demi-
god at whose antics the Chippeways laugh immoderately.

That was the beginning of my slavery to Manabozo. At
first it was only the Chippeways from our own town who
came daily to beg for pictures of him; but soon word went
up and down the lakes and rivers concerning the white man
on the Mattawa who made likenesses of Manabozo, and whole
towns of Chippeways came and waited silently outside our
lodge to be shown his portraits—Manabozo sending the
muskrat to the bottom of the sea for soil with which to create
the earth; Manabozo building the bridge across the Straits of
Michilimackinac and dropping the rocks; Manabozo creating
good weather with his smile, and his sour-faced brother
Peepuckwis raising storms with his frowns. So busy did they
keep me that almost before I knew it, winter had drawn the
warm green mantle of spring over her white shoulders.

Not until late in May would the cackling old women agree
that I was sufficiently recovered to take the long canoe journey to Montreal, with its bumpy rapids and its tedious carries; and it was June when we drew up to one of the landing-
stages of the big canoe wharf at Montreal, and McNott and
I climbed ashore to hunt for Natty Potter and Ann.

Both McNott and I had hoped, for different reasons, that
we could find out about Potter without going to the office
of the Indian Commissioner for the Northern Department—
Daniel Claus; but I soon realized we might search and ask
questions forever in that huge city of warehouses, merchants
and Frenchmen without finding anyone to tell us what we
wanted to learn.

"There's no getting away from it, Mac," I said. "I'll have
to see Claus. Potter couldn't have come here without Claus
knowing about it, but I don't believe anybody else has ever
heard of him."

McNott looked uneasy. "Yes," he said, "I guess one of us'll have to see him, and I guess it better be me."

"You!" I said. "You earn your living by trading. He's bound to ask you things that'll make you lose your temper, and first thing you know, he'll revoke your trading license."

"Oh," McNott said, "I don't lose my temper as often as you think I do, and two places where I make it a rule never to lose it is when I'm in a trade or a fight. Now your trouble, Langdon, is that you aint a trader, and you got an awful bad habit. You tell the truth when it aint noways necessary. This Claus is Sir William Johnson's son-in-law, and Johnson wouldn't 'a' sent him up here to warm his tail in this job if he wasn't just the same kind of yeller-bellied throat-cutter that Johnson is. If you go to see him, you may not lose your temper, but you're pretty apt to tell him the truth about a lot of things; and if you do that, you won't find out nothin' you want to know. No, Langdon, you're a good artist, but you're a terrible bad trader, so I'll be the one to see Claus."

McNott, when he returned from his visit to Claus, was more cheerful than I had seen him in some time; he beamed upon me as he told me what I most wanted to know.

"They sailed from here in September," he said. "Him and Ann. They was only here one day, and then there was a barkentine sailing for Liverpool, so they boarded it and went."

I got up at once. "I'll have to find out when the next vessel sails for England, Mac, and try to ship aboard her."

McNott smiled paternally. "The next one is a Indiaman chartered special by Gregg Cunningham & Co. to carry furs, fast. Name of *Admiral Vernon*. She sails day after tomorrow. I thought you might like to go on her, so I got this." He tossed a sealed letter to me. "You take that down to the captain of the *Admiral Vernon*, and he'll give you passage to London and three meals a day, all without it costing you a shilling."

I turned the letter over and over. "Who's it from?"

"Who do you s'pose it's from?" McNott asked, tolerantly. "It's from Claus, of course!"

"Well," I said, "why should Claus do anything for me? I can't accept anything from——"

"Oh my God!" McNott shouted, his complacency gone. "You don't want to testify at the Major's trial, do you?"

When I didn't answer, he reasoned with me. "Listen, Lang-

don, you needn't be afraid I'll start a argument with you over
the Major. I like him and you don't. You aint never said
much, but I've done some figgerin' about him and Ann, and
we don't have to go no farther with it than that. But with
Claus it's different. I got kind of mixed up when I talked to
him, and I guess Claus got to thinking that it's me that don't
like the Major and you that do. That's just one of those
fundamental trading mistakes that anyone's bound to make
sometime or other.

"So there ain't nothing underhand or mysterious about
this letter. Claus knows you're here in Montreal, because I
told him so, and I guess I let slip that you used to be a
good friend of the Major's; and on top of that Claus picked
up the idea you might not be able to testify at the Major's
courtmartial. In fact, I guaranteed you wouldn't if only
Claus would fix it so I could get you aboard the *Admiral
Vernon;* and it's so, aint it? You couldn't testify at the Major's trial if you went to England on this *Admiral Vernon.*

"Seeing that Claus expects the Major to be brought in
from Michilimackinac almost any day, he's pretty anxious to
get rid of everybody that might have a good word to say for
him. So if you sail on the *Admiral Vernon,* Claus'll be satisfied, and you wont owe him nothing and wont be indebted
to him for nothing. And besides, the way I figure it, Johnson
and Claus are skinning everybody they can, and if you can
get anything away from 'em, it's your duty to do so."

I was silent, thinking of Ann, hurried away from Montreal
by that ailing, miserable father of hers, in spite of having
told me in her letter that she would be waiting and watching
for me. And Potter, penniless Potter—how had he obtained
sufficient money to embark for Liverpool within twenty-four
hours of his arrival? In view of the letter McNott had brought
me, I felt certain that Potter had obtained help from the same
source, but I couldn't imagine on what grounds.

"Listen, Langdon," McNott went on, "what's happened
between you and the Major aint none of my business; I aint
tried to pry into it or talk you out of it; and now, by God,
you got to give me equal consideration! You can stop being a
friend to the Major, but you can't stop being a friend to me
—not without a fight, you can't! Traders tell me that Johnson and Gage and Claus between 'em have got it all fixed so
the Major wont have a damned friend in Montreal when he

gets here—at least, not one that'll be in a position to testify for him. They're either going to buy 'em up or drive 'em out. Well, I aint scared of those three pot-bellied hornpouts, and I want to help the Major; but damn it, I can't do it unless they think I hate him! That's why I done all that trading with Claus today, Langdon, and got you that letter so I could say 'Look what I done, Claus! I got Langdon Towne out of the way for you!' Now for God's sake don't let that damned New England conscience of yours spoil everything just out of cussedness! I swear to God, Langdon, I'd rather have the smallpox than one of these New England consciences they talk about! Conscience hell! It aint nothing but not daring to enjoy yourself, and not wanting nobody else to! Now then: what's it going to be?"

"I'll use the letter," I said.

McNott looked relieved. "That's the first time I ever had to argue anybody into taking something for nothing, Langdon, but of course I don't know any other artists." He hesitated. "Maybe you'd like to hear what I heard Johnson and Claus and Gage are figuring to——"

"I don't believe I want to hear it, Mac," I said. "I'll use the letter, and that'll have to be enough."

I heard it, willy nilly, though not from McNott—heard it, together with a lot I wished I'd never heard; and I saw more, too, than I like to remember even now.

Since I had no clothes to my name but the Chippeway buckskins in which I had entered Montreal, I borrowed money from McNott for two complete suits. The tailor worked all night to have them ready, and early on the morning the *Admiral Vernon* was to sail, I went with McNott to pay for them; then together we walked silently down a side street toward the dock at which the *Admiral Vernon* lay. My few belongings were aboard; and I should have been in the best of spirits to be setting off for England; but true friends are few and not easy to relinquish.

It was a relief when our minds were taken from the discomfort of our sudden speechlessness by the sight of two men running toward the wharves, and then another. McNott swung his wooden leg a little faster. Behind us we heard hoofs rattling on the roadway, and two horsemen pelted past us at a gallop.

"Oh, my God!" McNott said. He broke into that hobbling run of his.

"Who was it?" I asked.

"Claus," he said. "Old turkey-neck Claus himself."

We came out of the side street onto the town's slovenly-looking water-front with its muddy roadway and sagging warehouses against a background of ships' spars cocked every which-way. Fifty yards from us a crowd had formed at the end of an open dock, and newcomers were pelting from all sides. One man ran out from the crowd, perhaps to carry the news of what he'd seen; and as he passed us he shouted up to spectators at open windows: "It's Major Rogers! He's the one that don't walk good." Those at the windows slammed them down, and I could hear running on the stairs.

I felt a sudden surge of hot excitement within me at that unexpected shouted mention of Rogers' name; but the warmth gave way at once to icy bitterness. I stopped short and turned away.

McNott caught me by the arm, and at his imploring look I went on again with him.

Over the heads of the crowd I saw a group of soldiers and canoemen, newly landed from a brigade. Towering above all of them stood Rogers, supported on either side by a soldier. He wore no hat; his hair was long and matted; his beard was an inch long; and the pouches under his eyes were brown, as if smudged by a finger dipped in burnt umber. His green uniform coat was streaked with dirt, and one of his legs was bent at an unnatural angle.

As I stood staring at him with a feeling that might have been horror or pity or disgust, or a little of all three, one of the soldiers stooped, picked up a dusty three-cornered hat, put it, a trifle askew, on Rogers' head, and gave it a slap with the flat of his hand. Rogers looked at him in rueful amusement; then lifted his big hands and jerked the hat firmly into place. At that old familiar gesture, which I remembered as the inevitable prelude to all our cruel marches and all our bitter labors on the St. Francis expedition, my eyes smarted in spite of myself, and I didn't dare look at McNott.

Claus, who had been standing near Rogers but saying nothing to him, shouted something, made an impatient gesture, and stepped to one side.

Preceded by four soldiers, followed by four more, and supported by two others who had him beneath the arms, Rogers moved forward at a gait that was half a stumble and half a hop. I saw him turn his head and speak to Claus, but Claus never so much as looked at him.

As that shabby, half-crippled giant hobbled toward the rough and muddy road, the crowd fell away; from it came a spattering of applause and shouts that swelled to a cheer. Claus, once more on horseback and staring angrily from side to side, rode slowly after Rogers. The cheering died and those who cheered stood silently staring after that battered, stumbling man in the dirty green coat.

"Well," I said. "Well——"

"No!" McNott cried, and seized my wrist. "Don't go yet! I got to find out, and you got to wait while I do. There aint nobody else I can talk to, only you, and I'll prob'ly have to talk to somebody after I find out. Prob'ly I'll say things I wouldn't want Claus to hear—damn his little half-pint soul to hell—and if I say 'em to anybody but you, Langdon, they're bound to get back to him. You're the only friend I got, Langdon. You got to wait!"

I waited, of course, and went with McNott toward the soldiers and canoemen who had come to Montreal with Rogers. They had lifted the canoes to the wharf and were stacking the baggage, while a discontented-looking sergeant of the 60th Regiment, gloomily aloof, silently watched their activities.

McNott halted beside this morose figure, drew a carrot of tobacco from his pocket, dusted it on the front of his buckskin shirt and bit off a full inch. Then he held it toward the sergeant. "Chew?"

The sergeant only grunted coldly.

"Just come down from Michilimackinac with the Major?" McNott persisted.

The Sergeant gave him a basilisk stare.

"Used to be a sergeant myself," McNott said. "Used to give 'em hell, too, before they took this leg away from me."

The sergeant looked more human. "Provincial?" he asked.

McNott's face grew scarlet. "Provincial!" he whispered hoarsely. "Do I look like a Provincial, you pork-eater? Aint you Royal Americans had any training, for God's sake? You must be a hell of a sergeant, you must! Here, take a bite of this tobacco before I push it down your throat!"

The sergeant seemed faintly surprised, took the tobacco and bit hugely at it. When he would have returned it, McNott waved it aside. "Keep it," he said. "You aint left enough of it for me to bother with. That's prob'ly the reason the Major looked half-starved. Prob'ly you Royal Americans got first bite at his rations, and didn't leave none for him."

The sergeant spat enormously.

"I guess things aint what they was when I was in the army," McNott went on. "Some prisoners we didn't bother to keep, but those we did keep, we kept. On the march they et what we et, and we never abused 'em the way you fellers abused the Major."

"Abused him!" the sergeant cried. "You don't know what you're talking about!"

"Oh, don't I?" McNott asked. "I fought with Rogers, I did, and one of the things I learned was to keep my eyes open. I guess I can tell when a man's been abused—hell, aint I seen enough of 'em lashed half to death by those damned Regular officers of yours?—and the Major's been abused! Hell, his leg's damned near broken off! I don't need but half an eye to see that!"

"Well, by God," the sergeant said, "*we* didn't do it! We aint no murderers!"

"Brother," McNott said, "maybe you aint murderers, but you're associating with 'em, the way I see it; and you can tell an awful lot about a feller from his friends. Now me, I'm McNott. Being a trader's my business, just the way being a sergeant of Rangers used to be. Them that's friends of mine, I'm a friend of. I see to it they don't get into trouble on account of me, and if I get a chance to help 'em out, I do so. Both of us being sergeants, I don't mind telling you that I'd kind of like to help the Major."

The sergeant laughed bitterly. "A hell of a chance you or anybody else'll have to help him! They're going to settle his hash for him, they are, and there aint nobody going to be allowed to interfere! Why, when——"

"Who's going to settle his hash? Who's they?"

"Why, Gage and Johnson and the Captain and that little weasel Lieutenant Roberts and anybody else that works for Johnson and Gage! Why, when——"

"The Captain?" McNott asked. "You mean Captain Spies-maker?"

"Certainly I mean Captain Spiesmaker!" the sergeant said. "Why, when they set out to put the Major aboard the *Gladwyn* schooner, the whole damned Chippeway nation lined up along the Straits and tried to get Spiesmaker to stop. Told him it meant the end of their peace with the Sioux, because there wasn't nobody else that understood Indians. Thousands of 'em there were, all painted up, and all howling as if every last one of 'em was losing his best friend."

"And I guess they were," McNott said. "I s'pose Spies-maker was real sharp with 'em."

"He argued with 'em," the sergeant said, "but they wouldn't listen to him. They told him white men always punish their wisest counsellors and reward their fools, and that he was doing it too. So the Captain put the garrison under arms, turned the guns on the Chippeways, moved the *Gladwyn* off shore so the Chippeways couldn't rush her, and then he threw the Major into a whaleboat, irons and all, and had him rowed out and hauled aboard the schooner like he was a sack of corn. By God, that was something I wont forget in a hurry—all them Chippeways dressed up in feathers and red flannel and buffalo horns, and all yowling till it made your hair crawl, and the Major coming up over the rail at the end of a rope, and his wife standing there on deck and staring into that sweating white face of his—never stopped grinning, the Major didn't, and I bet the irons damned near broke his legs off—and Carver standing beside Mrs. Rogers, looking as if he was thinking of something else, the little misbegotten piece of dead fish!"

"Carver!" McNott groaned. "Carver!"

The sergeant spat. "I dunno what would have happened if the Major hadn't been shackled, or if they hadn't pushed him down onto the ballast right away, because those Chippe-ways followed along the shore, throwing all their English belts and medals into the lake. We could hear 'em yelling. Wouldn't wear belts, they said, given to 'em by a Great Father who treated his son the way the Major'd been treated. We thought, even after we got out into Lake Huron, that they might get canoes and come out and take the Major."

McNott drew a deep breath. "Oh my God!" he said.

"Why wasn't I there! If I'd only been there, we would 'a' come out and taken him!"

I wanted to ask about Elizabeth, but I couldn't make my tongue utter a word about either of those two tragic figures. The picture of Elizabeth, pale and open-mouthed, staring into that suspended, slowly-revolving face on which stood damp beads of agony, seemed to burn within my brain.

The sergeant looked pityingly at McNott. "It wouldn't 'a' done the Major no good if you'd come out. Then they'd had a excuse for killing him. They aint had a excuse yet; but they done their best, I'll say that for 'em! They tried hard at Michilimackinac, and they tried a damned sight harder on the Gladwyn. They threw him down on the rock ballast, irons and all, and it was cold—real cold. They wouldn't let nobody go down to see him—his wife nor nobody. Once a day they'd throw him some food and let down some water in a bucket. We could hear him, through the bulkheads, groaning. That's what's the matter with his leg. My God, I don't know how he stood it! He aint human!"

McNott moistened his lips. "What happened to his leg?"

"The irons were too tight," the sergeant said, "and the cold weather made his legs swell up pretty near as big as your thigh. When the Gladwyn got to Niagara, they took off the hatch and hoisted him out, and he was a sight! The bone in his leg had split open on account of the irons, and the marrow had squeezed out through the skin—enough to fill a teacup."

"Jesus!" McNott whispered. "What did his wife and Carver do about it?"

The sergeant seemed surprised. "Do? Why, there wasn't nothing anybody could do. Nobody wasn't allowed to do anything. His wife's going to have a baby—four months along, she is—so they sent her home quick; and Carver, he started for New York in a sweat because they told him that if he hurried, maybe Gage would give him the back pay that the Major owed him and Johnson had stopped him from getting."

McNott just stood there, opening and closing his big hands.

I had heard all I could stand. Sick at heart, I turned and walked away, but even so I couldn't help hearing the sergeant's angry voice.

"Even a half-wit could see," he said, "they'd figured he'd be dead by the time he reached Niagara. The story we heard is that Johnson and Gage want to get all the Western Indians to bring their furs to Fort de Chartres, so that settlers'll go out and buy land in that section from Johnson and Gage's land company; but damn it, Johnson and Gage don't know how to persuade the Indians to go to Fort de Chartres. They just wont do it. Either they go down and trade with the French and Spanish, or they go to Michilimackinac, so Johnson and Gage figure the only way to get 'em to Fort de Chartres is to get rid of Rogers. That's what we hear; and when those rats make up their minds to get rid of anyone, they do it. We hear the Major's going to be kept in prison till he rots; and if he wont rot, and he makes 'em give him a hearing before a courtmartial, we hear they're going to fix it so he can't get any witnesses, and we hear Lieutenant Roberts'll produce witnesses who'll swear he planned to turn Michilimackinac over to the French."

My gorge rose. I shouted to McNott, quickened my pace, and set off for the *Admiral Vernon*. I wanted no more of the land: no more of the stench of politics, of trading, of baseness, of disloyalty, of perfidy, that seemed to meet me everywhere I turned. Into my mind came the scenes that Rogers, ages ago in London, had read me from his play—scenes in which Governors Sharp, Gripe and Catchum revealed their knavery; and I knew that Sharp, Gripe and Catchum had been the merest faint shadows of Johnson, Gage and Spiesmaker. More than that, I knew that no villain upon the stage can equal, in brutal and malignant rascality, many of those honored gentlemen who, by ruthlessness and sharp practice, have achieved the highest offices and are bent on holding them.

When McNott caught up with me, his face was white and his eyes seemed almost to crackle; but he walked silently beside me until we reached the wharf and stood in the shadow of the tall yellow masts of the *Admiral Vernon*.

"Come aboard, Mac," I said. "We'll have a drop of rum before she sails."

He drew a deep breath and shook his head. "No," he said. "No. I got so much to think about, I wouldn't be good company, Langdon." He spoke almost gently. "If I'd 'a' been there, Langdon, I'd 'a' got him, so I'm going to stay right in Montreal till he's courtmartialled, if I have to stay forever. I'll find some way to testify for him, and there aint nothing on earth I wont swear to! Not nothing! If you're fighting Indians, you got to fight 'em the Indian way—you learned that in the Rangers, Langdon; so if I get a chance to fight Captain Spiesmaker or Lieutenant Roberts, I'll fight 'em the Spiesmaker way and the Roberts way—and maybe, by God, maybe I'll get a crack at Carver and Tute!"

He patted me on the shoulder. "We had some pretty good times together, didn't we, Langdon? Well, you run down in the cabin and see if you got everything, and then come up and let me know in case you need something more."

I ran down the gangplank, dodged the shouting sailors who labored frenziedly at the hatches, saluted the captain on the quarterdeck, and dodged into the spacious cabin. My pack of Chippeway sketches was in my small bed-place off the cabin, and so were the clothes from the tailor, packed in the carpet-bag I had bought with the money borrowed from McNott.

There was also a letter sealed with an enormous red wafer bearing the stamp of Gregg, Cunningham & Co. Since I had no friends in Montreal, I racked my brains, as I pried off the wax, as to who could have sent it. When it opened, a slip of paper fell out—a bill of exchange from Gregg, Cunningham's Montreal office on Allen MacPar & Co. of London for £100.

The letter read: "Dear Langdon: We had some good times together. I have tore up your note for the clothes. To hell with it. You will need this £100 a grate deal more than I will, and I don't propose to have any argument about it. If you need any more, draw it off of Allen MacPar & Co. When I come to London and get me a uptodate leg, I will let you paint my picture and that will make us sq., which we allready are anyway, only your damned New England conshiunce probally wont think so. You know what I think of New England conshiunces. Respctfly yr. humble and obdt. servt. to command.

                    "Rob't McNott (Sergt. of Rangers.)"

I ran from the cabin to the deck, jumped on the bulwarks, swung myself into the mizzen ratlines and scrambled up them until I could see the entire wharf. Nowhere upon it was there a sign of McNott.

"Mac!" I shouted. "Mac!"

I climbed higher up the ratlines and shouted again, but never an answer did I get.

CHAPTER LXXVII

To THE traveller who has once seen London, the city thereafter seems to him a second home—one to which, even under ordinary circumstances, he returns with pleasure. Why this is so I cannot say. Perhaps it forever summons up the past, as does a familiar face, by something ever-reminiscent among its multitude of scents and sounds and scenes—its tumultuousness and silences; its darkness and brilliance; its throbbing church bells and blaring bands; its spacious green parks and crowded houses; its scents of horses, perfumes, cookery, leather; its all-pervading soft fragrance of coal-smoke tinged with a hint of the sea.

I would have been happy just to see again that city in which I'd been so lonely and so poor; but since I came back to it in search of Ann, who had filled my heart for aching month on month, the place was a fever in my veins.

If Potter, after landing in Bristol, had gone to London, I knew that Ann would surely have visited her one friend there; so when the *Admiral Vernon* came to anchor at last on a July evening, I hurried ashore with a breathless eagerness, gave a boy a penny to carry my carpet-bag and bundle of sketches, and set off as fast as I could go through the narrow, crowded, fishy-smelling streets of Whitechapel; up the curving ascent of Fleet Street, with its well-remembered print-shops; along the Strand to Covent Gardens, where light ladies from neighboring bagnios strolled gaily in the twilight and called shrill pleasantries as I hastened past; and through the little streets to Leicester Fields and the green door of Mrs. Martin's house. How many happy days I'd spent behind it, and how often I'd opened it to go hungry and disappointed up to bed! I hoped hunger and disappointment didn't await me now.

The pounding of my heart sounded to me as loud as the thump of the knocker—and suddenly there was Mrs. Martin before me, her eyes round as crown-pieces. She stared at me and stared at me: than called wonderingly upon her Maker in syllables that pattered swift as summer rain. Seizing my shoulders, she pressed her cheek to mine.

"You!" she cried. "You, you! Langdong! Enter! My God, how I have a blow here upon the bosom to see you thus unexpect! Quick, quick! Enter, enter!"

She tugged me into the hall; seized my bag and bundle from the boy; pushed me into her parlor with its gilt furniture, its scent of cinnamon and dried rose-leaves, its green, red and yellow carpet that had always hurt my eyes.

On the wall above the fireplace hung the pastel I had done of Mrs. Martin and her two children to repay her for her kindness to Ann when I had brought her there, dirty, half-starved and clad in filthy rags. The sketch had been framed in blue plush, so I knew the Martins valued it highly.

"Mrs. Martin," I said, "I've come to find out whether I can have my old rooms back—and whether you've seen Ann: whether you know anything about her."

Mrs. Martin, sitting on the front edge of her chair, bounced upward twice, as though springs beneath her had been rapidly released. "Yes!" she cried. "Yes, yes, yes, yes! Ah, what a mélange! I am excite! No, no, no, Langdong! No, no! No! You cannot have it! You cannot have those room! They are occupy! Oh, my God, what experience!" She clutched her knees with both plump hands, rocked herself backward and forward; and from her burst peal on peal of laughter.

I took her arm and shook her. "You say you know where she is? Where is she?"

"It is *she!*" Mrs. Martin screamed. "You don't understand? That poor little one has those room herself! She is here, in this house! Mon Dieu, mon Dieu, who could have expect that this long day, this day of mutton for dinner and cold ham for supper, would bring such an affair at the end!"

I got to my feet. "If she's here," I said, trying to speak calmly, "I'll go up to see her. Is her father here too?"

Mrs. Martin caught my hand. "No, no, Langdong! How you are misunderstand! She is not here! One half-hour before you arrive, she go out. Ah, the poor one! When she come here, she have nothing—not one penny! Her father, he die on the ship coming to England, and she walk all the way from Bristol to London, poor little one!"

My heart seemed to turn over. "She's gone out!" I whispered. "Out at this time of night! What do you mean? Where's she gone? How's she living?"

Mrs. Martin shook her finger at me. "Ha, ha! No, no, no, Langdong! She live good—yes, good! Only last month she commence, and before that time she has never one penny: never one! But now I think she will have many—as many as she want! Ah, how I am glad for her, that she no longer must save each farthing, and walk, walk, walk so not to spend nothing! It is not too late, Langdong: why you don't go see her now?"

"My God!" I said, "that's the one thing in the world I want to do! Where is she, and what's she doing?"

"She is give lecture on sauvages," Mrs. Martin said. "Sauvages of North America."

"A lecture—on savages—on Indians!" I said incredulously. I couldn't imagine Ann—Ann of all people—standing solemnly before solemn people, and lecturing them.

"Ha!" Mrs. Martin cried. "A lecture, yes, but such a lecture as never before was given in London. Those who attend scream with laughter, and rouge falls from the faces of old ladies who have not smiled in years. Look, I tell you where is this hall—not five minutes walk—where she lectures on the sauvages."

I was running when I got to the two square lamps that flanked the entrance of Half Moon Hall, but the sight that met my eyes within that entrance stopped me in my tracks. On each side of the foyer was a long, narrow sign reading, "Entertainment by a Young Lady of Family who has Dwelt among the Savages of North America," and supporting those signs were framed pastels—my own pastels—of Wanotan in his head-dress of ermine skins; of Dacota hunters on snowshoes lancing a struggling buffalo in the snow; of a Dacota woman stripping the white skins from the poles of her lodge; of a Dacota medicine man in all his panoply of buffalo horns and otterskin bags, tootling his magic whistle, like a savage Pan, in the ear of a sick Dacota girl. What stopped me, however, wasn't the pastels, but the sign beneath them:

Pastels of Indians of North America
Executed by Langdon Towne in the American Wilderness
Loaned to the Lecturer
By the Ethnographic Society of London

The Ethnographic Society of London! Every lover of the Arts in London knew that richly endowed Society, not only because of the generous sums it spent on sending artists to far corners of the world and on publishing their resulting paintings, but also for its beautiful building, designed by Robert Adam, which had been under construction when I was last in London. The Ethnographic Society! I couldn't believe my eyes. This long sea trip; this hurried walk through London; this strange exciting talk with Mrs. Martin; this foyer with its advertisements of a Young Lady of Family and its pastels of Yanktons from the St. Peter's River—all these things could be nothing but the jumbled phantasmagoria of a dream.

I went closer to the sketch of Wanotan and raised it from the wall—and from behind me an outraged voice shouted "Here!"

I turned and saw, behind a window marked "Tickets," a fat little man in a white wig that had a blueish cast from lack of powder, and a black silk suit that, for the opposite reason, had a grayish tinge about the shoulders.

"Not to be touched!" he said severely. "What in God's name is there about those pictures that makes individdles want to touch 'em? Don't you know works of Art aint made to be handled? Look at 'em all you wish, but let 'em alone!" As an afterthought he added, "Sir."

They were real after all!

I begged the fat man's pardon. "I forgot myself," I said. "My interest was aroused—A Young Lady of Family— most interesting. Could I have a ticket?"

"Performance half over," he said, mollified. "Take it at half-price, sir. One shilling sixpence."

As I drew the money from my pocket, he added, "May I ask, sir, whether your interest was aroused by the hint of mystery in the lady's announcement, or by the subject-matter of the lecture?"

"Both," I said.

He nodded complacently. "Ah, I thought so. I told her she'd got to be mysterious. Look at my last attraction, I told her— Sig. Paolo Battisto and his Acrobats of the Highest Italian Nobility! That's what draws 'em, I told her, and she soon found I was right!"

He came out from his cubicle, opened the door between the foyer and the hall, and silently waved me in.

A curtain hung between the door and the auditorium; beyond the curtain I heard Ann's voice—and at the sound of it a hand seemed to close tight around my heart and hold it from beating.

When I pushed the curtain aside, I saw her sitting in the center of the stage in just such a yellow halo of light as might strike through the mist of a forest clearing at sunrise; but whether the mist came from the lights of the stage or from my own eyes, I couldn't tell. There was a roaring in my ears that prevented me from hearing what she was saying, and a weakness in my knees that made me cling to the curtain for support.

I saw Ann smile and walk off the stage, a slender little figure, as straight as a lance; the shadowy audience burst into sudden loud applause; I found a seat for myself in the back row, got into it somehow, and sat there with my heart pounding at such a rate that I was sure the sound was audible five rows away; but when I glanced furtively at those near me, I saw they were doing too much sniffling and nose-blowing to pay attention to me.

The setting was simple. In the center of the stage was a log, backed by a semi-circle of spruces; protruding from the trees at one end of the semi-circle was the bow of a *canot du maître* daubed with an Indian's head; at the other end was something that seemed to be the base of an Indian lodge, and beside it a black pot suspended over a fire from a birch tripod.

When Ann came back, she wore a gray shirt and a pair of deerskin leggins, carried a small bundle of odds and ends, and went straight to the log, sat down upon it, put the bundle on the floor at her feet, and began to talk as she might have talked to my mother in Kittery, and as she had spoken to me innumerable times of things that interested her.

While she talked, she took first one thing and then another from the bundle and donned it—garters for her leggins, a gaudy sash, a beaded tobacco-pouch, a red woolen cap, and last of all, a scarlet feather in the cap—and amazingly it was no longer Ann who sat there, talking to us, but a voyageur speaking broken English, swaggering and bragging and throwing us a burst of song or a snatch of French profanity that made my ears tingle: wagging his pipe at us to emphasize his importance and magnificence, the speed of his dogs, the crushing weight of the burdens he had carried across portages, the beauty and lines of his canoe, his superhuman bravery and quickness at shooting rapids. He was the greatest man who had ever entered the Northwest; there was never a night that he couldn't eat three suppers; he had saved the lives of forty-seven men; he had had fourteen wives and sixty-two children; he had earned thousands upon thousands of pounds, and every shilling of it he had spent on pleasure —on tobacco and finery; on love and wine; no man in the world had been so happy as he, and if he were young again he would do exactly the same things—for he was a voyageur, and voyageurs never see small wolves: they never, never see small wolves!

He roared with laughter, and the audience roared with him, and off he went, swaggering still and bellowing that song I had heard so often at Michilimackinac:

> *"Fritaine, friton, firtou, poilon,*
> *Ha, ha, ha, frit à l'huile,*
> *Frit au beurre à l'ognon."*

Out of our sight, he sang a second verse. His voice faded and changed: changed to Ann's voice—and she was there before us again, a woman deserted, but still bravely singing, in a gay farewell, the song the voyageur had sung. *"Ha, ha, ha, frit à l'huile"*—upon her face was that determined little smile she had worn when my own voyageurs paddled me away to the westward to the tune of that same song on that far-off August morning.

Then her smile became forlorn, her figure drooped; her hands came up in a queer half-gesture of despair; and she sang another verse—a verse whose airy, meaningless words made horrible the singer's loneliness and longing for the lover who had left her:

> "*C'est un pâté de trois pigeons,*
> *Ha, ha, ha, frit à l'huile,*
> *Assieds-toi et le mangeons,*
> *Fritaine, friton, firtou, poilon,*
> *Ha, ha, ha——*"

Her voice seemed to twist my heart, to choke me, to blind me. I couldn't sit quietly and endure another syllable of that song—not without making a spectacle of myself.

Scarcely knowing how I did it, I got myself from the hall and back to Mrs. Martin's, where Mrs. Martin admitted me with glistening eyes. Seeing a flood of questions hovering on the tip of her tongue, I brusquely told her I'd wait for Ann in my old rooms, and that nothing was to be said to Ann of my presence.

"I want to tell her myself," I said. "You understand."

I sat down and got up again perhaps a thousand times: I walked the floor of that small room in which for four long years I had stood before my easel, working and re-working on the sketches no one wanted; and all four of the years together, as I now looked back upon them, seemed shorter than this endless waiting for Ann.

Yet when I heard a key rattle and the street door open, my mouth was dry; my palms were moist; I wasn't ready; I hadn't thought what to say to her; or if I'd thought, I couldn't remember.

The door closed softly; there was a silence, as though someone stood at the foot of the stairs, listening; and I held my breath, trying to hear above the thudding of my heart.

Then there were quick footsteps on the stair; and outside the door Ann's breathless voice said, "Langdon." I wet my lips and tried to speak, but couldn't; nor could I even move.

The door swung open, and in the opening Ann stood framed.

With both hands she clung to the latch, her eyes reaching out to me. And then her knees gave under her. At

that I came to life and caught her in my arms before she
fell.

"I knew it," she panted. "When you went out, I knew it.
I knew it was you. I knew it *had* to be you. Terrible people
came and talked at the end—talked and talked—and I knew
it was you, Langdon! I couldn't make them stop talking!
They brought me a chair, but it was too slow: too slow!
Feel my heart, Langdon darling!"

When I stumblingly tried to tell her all the thoughts and
longings that had so long burdened me, she whispered again
and again, "Yes, Langdon: I know! Yes, dearest Langdon;
I always knew."

If it hadn't been for Mrs. Martin, God knows how long I
might have stood there, telling her over and over again the
doubts and aching fears that had preyed upon me during all
my travels—feeling against my cheek the soft movement of
her lips as she murmured, "Yes, Langdon, I know! I know,
Langdon dearest!"

Then I heard Mrs. Martin's door open, and cursed a little
at the sound of her footsteps on the stair; but when, through
the open doorway, I saw the eagerness of her face and the
brightness of her eyes, I remembered she had been good to
Ann when Ann had no money—and with that recollection
there came a flood of other things about which I wanted Ann
to tell me: her father: the Ethnographic Society: her acting;
for anyone with half an eye could see that she was a great
actress.

"Ah!" Mrs. Martin cried, "how I am happy!" She came in
and stood beside us; sighed blissfully. "I told Meestair Martin
this night it is what I planned, years ago, for you two; for it
was plain to me even then that this little one here, she was the
one for you! I am Arlesienne, Langdong—and from les
Arlesiennes, love has no secrets!" Her voice became practical.
"What you do now, Langdong?"

"Why," I said uncertainly, "perhaps I could—let me see,
the White Bear—no, not the White Bear—another tavern."

"Pah!" Mrs. Martin cried. "What a race, these Americans
—no thought for the future, no thought for the monnaie, always waste—why don't you get married?"

Ann still clung to me, her cheek against mine.

"Yes," I said, "of course. Of course we will." I held Ann

closer. "As soon as Ann's willing—as soon as we can make arrangements."

"Willing!" Mrs. Martin screamed. "Arrangements! Mon Dieu! What a race of people! What a race! Cold, like ice! This girl is sick, I tell you! She is sick from love! I, I, Jeannette Gregoire Martin—I have talked and talked with her! Have I not seen how she waits and waits for you? How she hopes and hopes? You think I am blind, Langdong? Her heart was burst, almost, because she heard nothing from you—because she has not the monnaie to return to America to hunt for you! And you—you say you will marry when she is willing: when you can make arrangements!"

She struck her forehead with her clenched fist. "Bon Dieu! Should she appear to you to be eager when you make no appearance of eagerness—when you, in the moment of finding her, speak of leaving her for the White Bear? Ha! Yes! The White Bear! Mon Dieu! How it is well named, that tavern for American white bears! Have you no élan, no esprit, that you must wait for arrangements? Look what you save if you marry now, this night, this very moment!"

Ann sighed and her lips moved against my cheek.

"At this time of night?" I protested. "And without banns? Without a license?" But in the moment of my protesting I saw what Mrs. Martin had in mind—a Fleet marriage—a wedding before one of those soiled and dubious divines who plied their strange calling in the shadow of England's most famous and most miserable debtors' prison.

It was a Fleet parson who had married Natty Potter to Ann's mother. All the Fleet parsons were awake, tippling and hoping for trade, throughout the small hours of every night. To Fleet parsons, banns and licenses were idle vanities, no more necessary than honor in a bridegroom or virtue in a bride.

"A Fleet marriage!" I said. "That's what you're thinking of, isn't it? I wouldn't want Ann to have a Fleet marriage."

"And why not?" Mrs. Martin demanded. "Why do you not ask *her* what she wants? Look at her, Langdong! Look! What you see in those eyes? You see fear of a Fleet parson? No, no, no! You see hate for a Fleet marriage? Jamais de la vie!"

She shook her finger at Ann. "Pourquoi t'attardes, tu, Ann?

Si j'ai passé par là moi! Vas-y, Chérie, sans plus attendre!
Lance-toi vers le seul ciel qui compte!"

Ann laughed unsteadily. "I'll put on another bonnet, Langdon dear, and then I'll be ready."

CHAPTER LXXVIII

For an artist, there is no
earthly condition nearer heaven than to be alone with his
work and the lady of his choice; and thanks to Ann, I had
everything my heart desired.

For a year we stayed on at Mrs. Martin's. When Ann's engagement at Half Moon Hall was finished, she refused to continue with her lectures in spite of my arguments.

"Remember what Copley said," she told me. Her voice
shifted and took on the quiet gaiety peculiar to Copley.
"'Dangerous—dangerous! Two artists in one family! That'll
make trouble.'"

So I remained the only active artist of the family, and I was
active indeed; for even after we moved, for convenience, to
the small house in Cavendish Square, I was busy completing
and arranging for publication the series on the Dacotas which
the Ethnographic Society had ordered. It was Ann whom I
had to thank for this immediate employment, for it was to
the Society she had gone with my pastels in their wrappings
of buffalo skin on her arrival in London. Out of this work
grew the idea for the huge ceiling in the Society's building—
the circular fresco which shows the cycle of the Chippeway year against the background of Chippeway divinities—
a fresco that took so long to plan and paint that there were
times when I thought Ann and I would be old before it was
done. So it was Ann who brought me everything.

It was from Ann's own lips, at the end of long days'
work, that I learned the story of her ghastly voyage with her
father, learned also that which made me think back to Rogers
with more of pity than I had thought to feel when I bitterly

set off from Michilimackinac on that cold December dawn. How darkly blind a man can be when caught by violent emotion, if he is unable or unwilling to seek out all the facts.

"You know, Langdon," Ann said, "gunpowder can be useful when it's properly directed; but when it's exploded out of time, or not given the right sort of outlet, it does terrible things—as it did to Sergeant McNott and your friend Hunk Marriner. And Major Rogers was a sort of human gunpowder. You mustn't blame him for his treatment of me. He was suffering. He was cramped; hedged in; stultified. He wanted to do what was right, and you and I both know that he was well able to; but foolish men battered him and blocked him—let him stand idle when he should have been put to doing something great. That was his undoing, my dear. Being the sort of man he is, he had to explode—and of course he exploded in the wrong direction."

I knew she was right. She was always right; but the most I could say was a grudging "Perhaps."

"When we came to Montreal," she said, "my father had only the few shillings his friend Lieutenant Roberts had given him. Between us we had nothing—nothing, except your pictures, and those I tied to me at night for fear my father would take them and sell them. He hated the Major, Langdon—oh, how he hated him!—and he had a letter from Lieutenant Roberts to Colonel Claus in Montreal. Do you know Colonel Claus, Langdon?"

I nodded.

"He's not a nice man," Ann said simply. "My father was sick—very sick. On the way to Montreal he coughed and coughed until his clothes were drenched at night, and there'd be blood on his handkerchief in the morning. So in Montreal he went to Colonel Claus, and told him that in return for passage to England he'd write a letter proving that the Major was a thief and a traitor; swearing that Robert Rogers planned to desert the British and join the French, and that this desertion would cause an Indian war and dreadful misfortune to the interests of Great Britain."

"I see," I said, "I see. I knew your father must have done something for Claus, but I couldn't guess what. And did he write the letter?"

"Yes," Ann said sadly. "He wrote it and read it to me. None of it was true, though there was a little shadow of

truth in everything—just enough to deceive those who knew
no better. One sentence spoke of how the Major had urged
my father to join him in deserting to the French, and of how
indignant my father was at this insult to his honor. You remember, of course, how sensitive my father's conscience
was, and how he scorned, always, any suggestion of double
dealing."

I laughed, and took Ann's hand and kissed it.

Her fingers twined themselves around mine. "When I asked
him not to give the letter to Colonel Claus," she went on,
"he paced the floor, gesticulating, playing a part. 'I am a man
more sinned against than sinning,' he said. 'Put in this honest
hand a whip to lash the rascal naked through the world!' And
then, Langdon, he laughed and coughed and coughed, and
there was blood on his handkerchief!"

She was silent and so was I, uncomfortable at this picture
she drew of her miserable father, dying with perjury on his
soul. If I felt so, how, oh how must she feel?

Often, in the slack moments of the hard-working life we
led, our talk took us back to the days of hardship and heart-
break through which the two of us had lived; and I had
ceased to be surprised at finding Rogers' name upon my lips.
With Ann in my heart and my home, my bitterness against
him had faded more and more, dulled by the patine with
which time smooths the unhappiest experiences. He had come
to seem unreal to both of us: never again, we knew, would we
see that strange, strange man. He was a memory only. . . .

And then I picked up my morning paper to learn that
Rogers himself was back in England! In a shaking voice I read
the news to Ann, and we stared into each other's eyes with
amazement and perhaps even a certain apprehension.

"What will he do next?" Ann whispered.

Next? Who could tell, indeed! Hadn't he said, when a battered hulk, chained to a wooden bench in the guardhouse at
Michilimackinac, "By God, I wont die! I'll beat 'em all!"

He was so far from dead that the coffee houses buzzed
with the tale of how he had been tried by courtmartial late
in 1768, had been acquitted of the charges brought against
him, and now, here in London, had actually taken a house
in Charing Cross, as fashionable a spot as there was in the
city.

How the man did it, when he was in debt to the tune of thousands of pounds, God alone knew. Even more wonderful than his house in Charing Cross, the King himself received him at Court, and was so taken with him that he was publicly seen to place his arm around the Major's shoulders! Rogers, trapped, beaten and kicked by Johnson and Gage, had escaped from the trap to be embraced by His Majesty King George III!

We heard rumors that Johnson and Gage's great scheme to become the owners of an empire in the Ohio Valley had been frustrated by Rogers, because of his influence with the King; heard, too, that Jonathan Carver and Phinehas Atherton had come to London to fawn upon the man they had betrayed; that Rogers was again petitioning to be allowed to find the Northwest Passage and the great River Oregon—this time with fifty men, and by way of the St. Peter's and Missouri rivers. And again and again I heard he was trying to obtain reimbursement for the vast sums he had spent to keep the Western Indians peaceful and to hold their trade for England.

Then one June morning, on the back page of the *Morning Advertiser*, in the very spot where, seven years before, I'd seen the account of the Major's encounter with the highwayman on Hounslow Heath, was one of those biting little paragraphs in which coffee-house patrons took such delight:

"Among recent arrivals at the Fleet Prison was Major Robert Rogers, late Commander of His Majesty's Rangers in North America, late Captain Commandant of the garrison at Michilimackinac."

That was all. He had been jailed for debt; and if his debt was anywhere near as large as I had reason to think it was, the Major's days of freedom were over.

All through these quiet years of work and home life, I had seen time and again that Ann had completely forgiven the man. I had never asked myself whether I too had forgiven him, perhaps because if ever and whenever I thought back to the specific treachery he did to Ann and me, I despised him. At other times my hatred seemed not to exist. And so, when Ann came to me and said, "You must go to the Fleet, Langdon; we can't leave him there to rot," I was sure, without taking thought, that I hated him still.

I shook my head. "See the Major? It's impossible!"

Ann looked at me. I saw her face as I had seen it in the

Major's dim hall at Michilimackinac, held from me like a prisoner's by the bars of the balustrade. How right that little Jew had been, at the Falls of St. Anthony, when he clutched his throat, smote his breast and said, "She don't do nothing, just move the eyes, and right away something come out and go into me—here; here; here!"

She put her hand upon my arm, still looking into my eyes. "Langdon," she said, "those were little men who kicked him when he was down before. Prisoners in the Fleet don't have many friends to help them."

Hadn't Ezekiel Solomon added: "Without no trouble I cry like little baby?" Yes, Ezekiel Solomon had been right!

The feeling of humility was new upon me.

CHAPTER LXXIX

I HAD THOUGHT of the Fleet Prison as I had thought of all jails—as a stone building filled with straw-strewn cubicles, from whose iron-barred doors peered wan prisoners in chains, and before which paced morose guards in uniform, jingling huge keys on iron rings; but it wasn't like that.

When I reached Ludgate Hill and walked down Farringdon Street, I found a grated window in a blank wall. Above the window were cut the words "Pray Remember Poor Debtors Having No Allowance," and behind the grating stood a man hopefully rattling pennies in a tin cup. The cup came out of the bars appealingly toward me as I passed, and I dropped a shilling in.

A few paces beyond the window was an arched doorway— as busy a doorway as ever I saw. Messengers raced in and out; waiters with trays and hampers hurried anxiously through. Ladies whose profession was dubious made small-talk with cadaverous-looking doorkeepers who stared fixedly at those who came and went.

When I stated my business to one of them, he looked help-

lessly baffled until I drew a shilling from my pocket. Then he
became alert and loudly bellowed, "Cryer!" In response a fat
man with black teeth and a nose like three ripe strawberries
reluctantly and with the assistance of an eight-foot stave
hoisted himself to his feet from his seat on the outer pavement and eyed me appraisingly.

"The celebrated Major Rogers," the keeper told him. "Upper side, Number 12, but 'e'll be in Bartholomew Fair if they
aint shut off 'is credit."

The Cryer's eyes never left my weskit pocket, so I gave
him a shilling too, and was led along an arched tunnel and
out into the bright sunlight of a high-walled prison yard that
was more like Southwark Fair than a prison.

The main building, beneath which the tunnel had brought
me, was four stories high; and at each one of the scores of
open windows in this huge structure was a man or woman or
both, laughing, drinking, screaming, making love, holloing to
people in the court below.

Above the doors and windows of the basement hung
painted signs—Alderman's Coffee House; Jos. Starkey, Bil-
liards; Bartholomew Fair Wine Room; J. Cartwright, Tapster;
A. Keith, Latin & French Taught; Bull & Garter Tap Room;
John Figg, Barber; B. Lands, Racket Master; Bambridge,
Haberdasher.

The court itself was a tumultuous throng of men, women
and children of every condition—some in rags and some
dressed in the height of fashion. Crouching against the front
of the prison were men huddled in foul and tattered great-
coats in spite of the warmth of the day, so that I suspected
they wore next to nothing beneath. Others, stripped to shirt
and small-clothes, ran furiously and with rackets drove ivory
balls against the towering wall that shut the courtyard from
the outer world. Still others played at skittles, Mississippi,
fives, cribbage, backgammon, whist and games unknown to
me. Around a tent which did duty as an ale-house, roisterers fought and sang; bedizened women strolled among the
players, their shrill laughter rising penetratingly above the
unending tumult of the place.

As I stood at the mouth of the tunnel, staring at the motley
crew in the courtyard, I was aware of faces turned toward me.
"Garnish!" I heard someone shout. "Pay or strip!" In an instant the cry was taken up on all sides, and every man in the

courtyard, seemingly, stopped what he was doing to press close up to me. Those who were closest clutched at my arms and coat as if to tear off my clothes.

" 'Ere, 'ere!" the Cryer bawled, making play with his stave, "can't you see 'e aint no Collegian? 'E's a wisitor! Garn out of 'ere!"

The prisoners slowly dispersed, grumbling, except a few who remained to whisper urgent pleas for money, and a plump young woman in a striped skirt and a low-cut bodice, who seized the opportunity to smile kindly upon me and adjust her stocking-top before my unfascinated gaze.

The Cryer lifted bushy eyebrows at me. When I shook my head, he slapped her smartly on the buttocks with his stave, ignored her outcries and addressed me briskly. "Lucky thing for you, Master, you 'ad me along of you, or you'd be garnished proper."

"I wont forget it," I assured him. "What's the meaning of garnish? What did they mean by 'Pay or strip!' "

"Ho!" the Cryer said. "You aint never even been in the College before, Master! Anybody wot comes in, the first thing 'e 'as to pay is Garnish, so all them old Collegians can get drunk; and if 'e aint got no money, Master, they take 'is clo'es and sell 'em. They got to 'ave their Garnish, aint they?"

"Do the women pay Garnish too?"

"Women!" he exclaimed. "There aint no women in 'ere!"

Since there were at least a hundred women in sight, I could only wave my hand helplessly at them.

"Oh, them!" the Cryer said. "They didn't get put in 'ere! Nobody gets put in 'ere, only men. The women just come 'ere. Some of 'em's wives, and some of 'em's just friends of the debtors. Some of 'em's laundry-ladies, and some of 'em run errands on account there's some errands that aint delicate for a man to go on. The rest of 'em's just 'ere on business or pleasure. Glad of a chance to do pretty near anything, Master."

He became confidential. "That little gel out there in the yeller bonnet—they speak 'igh of 'er. Begins with a farden for just a mere kiss, and so on. If you 'ave a fancy to a little innocent trifling——"

"That's very kind of you," I said, "but I'm here to see Major Rogers."

"Heach man to 'is taste," the Cryer said. "I'll cry the Major

in the court, an' then I'll cry 'im in Bartholomew Fair; and if
'e aint in neither place, Master, I'll 'ave to 'ave a penn'orth o'
Bob to cry 'im on the Master's Side an' the Common Side.
'Ard work, Master, cryin' out a man from among the two hun-
dred an' forty-three debtors in this place. A penn'orth, eh,
Master?"

"Yes, yes," I said. "That's agreed." His words meant next
to nothing to me; but the heat of the courtyard and the stench
of latrines were almost overpowering.

He stepped forward to a more commanding position in the
court and in a gin-hoarsened voice bellowed "Major Rogers."

Nobody paid the slightest attention. Not even by the turn
of an eye did that idle crowd of debtors and drabs acknowl-
edge the name that had once been the bane of the whole
French army; the name that had commanded the respect of
every Indian nation in North America, had put new hope
into all the disconsolate traders of Canada, earned the
high regard and support of the King's Generals, of the King's
Ministers and of the King himself.

The Cryer turned to me, and his strawberry nose seemed
to steam with annoyance. "You come along of me. Saves
time, in case 'e's sleepin' in a corner an' 'as to be waked up."

I followed him into the basement of the huge building—
the section evidently known to the inmates as Bartholomew
Fair; and on each door the Cryer rapped with his stave and
shouted "Major Rogers!" Sometimes there was no reply; sometimes a volley of oaths and hoarse laughter answered him;
sometimes he nimbly dodged a shower of dirty water or beer-
dregs.

"'Ard work, Master," he assured me again. "That's the
'ell of this place—the macaronis and the beaux! A mechanic
or a squire, 'e's all right; but damn these 'igh-born Mohocks
that ain't never done a lick of work in their lives! They aint
got no respect for nobody! Seems like the 'arder you work,
the more they 'ate you."

All the rooms in Bartholomew Fair were used as tap
rooms, kitchens, coffee houses, tobacconists', barber shops,
card rooms, club rooms, eating houses, each one as dirty as it
was dark; and though we looked into every room, we found
no sign of Major Rogers.

The Cryer groaned. "Mebbe it'd be best for our 'ealth's

sake to 'ave a dram afore we climb to Upper Side, Master," he
said hopefully. "Cruel 'ard climbin', them stairs is."

When I refused, he led me to a stairway so foul that dirt
had caked on it in knobs and knots, and we stumbled up
flight after flight, through an assortment of odors by comparison with which an Indian village was as fragrant as newly-cut
sweet-grass.

In the dark gallery of the topmost floor the cries of the
racket-players, the shrill laughter of the women, the hoarse
shouts of roisterers in the courtyard below, came to us dimly,
as though choked and stifled by the stench of the place. The
Cryer went confidently to a closed door, rapped upon it with
his stave and bawled, "Wisitor for Major Rogers!"

He placed his ear against the panel and nodded to me with
a sly and knowing grin. " 'E's there," he whispered. From
within came creakings and hurried movements; then a heavy
silence.

The Cryer thumped again upon the panels, and this time a
familiar voice sluggishly shouted, "Yes, yes, damn it! Nobody
deaf here!"

The key turned in the lock, and the door was flung open.
In the doorway stood Rogers, a little unsteady on his feet,
long brown hair hanging lankly on either side of his broad
face, dirty white cambric stock askew, and shirt stained
with streaks and splotches.

Behind him I saw a truckle bed with a tousled gray blanket
on it, a battered pine table and two stools. Peering with
feigned interest from the open window, which looked on the
rear of the prison, was a young woman in a pink and white
striped skirt, a bright blue blouse and shoes whose heels were
so worn on the inner edges that she seemed almost to be
standing on her ankle-bones. She wore no stockings.

Rogers stared at the Cryer, head hanging and underlip
slack. The pouches under his eyes were enormous, and glittered as if wet or newly greased. "Well, who is it?" he said
thickly. "Don't wish to be disturbed when resting."

His eyes moved slowly from the Cryer's face and heavily
met mine. "Oh," he said, swaying a little. "Didn't see you.
Who is it? Bad light here." He caught at the door-jamb
and peered hard at me.

"Why, Langdon!" he said uncertainly. "Langdon Towne!"
He shot a furtive glance at my escort; at the young

woman leaning from the window; at the dishevelled bed; then passed his hand clumsily over his thick lips and spoke to the Cryer. "Well, what you waiting for?"

The Cryer turned to me, showing blackened teeth. "We mentioned a dram—a penn'orth of gin, Master." His face was like that of something seen in a dreadful dream. Everything around me—Rogers, uncertain of speech and with wavering, bloodshot eyes; the wretched cell of a room and the sour stench of it; the lump of a woman, staring from the window with the same witless instinct that leads an ostrich to thrust its head beneath the sand—all of this had the quality of nightmare; and my understanding of it was as foggy as a troubled dreamer's.

I fumbled for a penny and dropped it in the Cryer's palm.

"Servant, Master," he said. "Servant, Major. Pleasure to oblige a gentleman."

He stooped and looked under the Major's arm at the woman in the window. "Glad to see you in good company for once, Sadie," he added, and left us.

"Damned whelp!" the Major said. "If Fitzherbert hadn't died, I'd put an end to all this insolence! Come in, Langdon: come in! Ah—that's my nurse at the window: my nurse. Had a bad time with my leg, Langdon, my boy. Prob'ly you heard."

"Yes," I said.

"By God!" Rogers said. "I've got some scores to pay that no debtors' prison can ever take notice of! Forced the marrow right out through the bone and the flesh! Have to have a nurse look out for it—bandages and all that."

He went to the girl, who continued to stare bovinely from the window, and placed a huge hand on the small of her back, which was broad as a cow's. "You needn't wait any longer today," he said, "but if you're here tomorrow, you can look in to see how I am." He coughed in earnest of delicate health.

She withdrew herself from the window and turned a fat, expressionless, dead-white face toward the Major. "Needn't wait any longer? I come up here for them two shillings, and here I waits till I gets 'em!"

"Shillings?" Rogers repeated vacantly. "Two shillings?" He slapped his breeches pockets, and seemed suddenly to recall something half-forgotten. "Damn it!" he mumbled.

"That remittance was late again! Langdon, my boy, could you spare me a few shillings for a matter of a week?"

I hurriedly gave him all the silver I had. He counted it carefully, moving his thick lips—"eight, ten-and-six, eleven-and-six. Eleven-and-six, Langdon. I'll make a note of it."

He flung one of the coins to the fat girl, who picked it up with an air she tried to make disdainful, and deftly concealed it somewhere about her voluminous bodice.

"Now you got your two shillings," Rogers said heavily, "suppose you get out and stay out."

"Stay out?" she asked in a strange hoarse whisper. "Don't you want me to look in tomorrow, like you said?"

"I do not!" Rogers said. "One thing I insist on's sissiplin —displin; and you, you damned fat dough-faced slut, you started getting insubordinate! Here you'll wait, you says! Well, my beauty, jus' try it! Jus' try somep'n like that on Major Robert Rogers of Rogers' Rangers! You come in here again and I'll drop you out the window, 'n' then I guess you'll think twice before you start telling a commanding officer of Rangers what you'll do an' what you wont do!"

She fled past him, and I could hear her scuffling down the gallery on her worn-out heels.

Rogers, muttering to himself, went to the bed, fumbled fruitlessly beneath the blankets, looked between the bedstead and the wall, lost his balance and sat heavily upon the travesty of a mattress.

"Damn it," he said, passing huge fingers through his disordered hair, "these women aint got one damned grain of reticence or anything. Show 'em a bottle of gin 'n' they aint sassfied to drink only half it! They drink it all, unless you watch 'em; then take the bottle home to put vinegar in. You don't happen to have a drop of gin about you, do you, Langdon?"

I shook my head.

Rogers struggled to his feet. "Sit down, sit down!" he said. "Don't stand there as if you were waiting for orders! No question of rank now, my boy! Be free and easy with me—like an equal."

Then he rubbed his hand across his forehead and frowned, as if trying to remember something. "You've always— you've always——" He rubbed his brow again. "Damn it, what was it I just thought of? What is it I'm trying to say?

Oh yes!" He seemed to brighten a little. "You've always looked up to me too much—that's the trouble: you've always looked up to me too much." He looked at me sternly. "Not that you oughtn't to. Of course you ought! I'm Rogers! Major Rogers! Rogers of Rogers' Rangers!"

He laughed. "But you know that, of course, because you're Langdon Towne, so what's the use of my telling you? Here, Langdon, sit yourself down on this stool while I clean up a bit; then we'll go down to Bambridge's Whistling Shop 'n' have a drop or two to old friends 'n' the Northwest Passage."

"I wont stay," I said. "I dropped in to see whether there was anything I could do———"

"Wont stay!" Rogers cried. "Never heard such nonsense! You'll stay 'n' have supper! Mos' interestin' society you'd want to meet, right here in this damned College. Good's an education—linen drapers, naval officers, prize fighters, architects, sculptors, cap'n from the Royal Hussars, poets—all of 'em up to their ears in debt, so they put 'em in prison, Langdon; the last place in the world where they'll ever have a chance to get out of debt! I tell you, Langdon, you're in good company when you're in the Fleet! No, Langdon: I aint goin' let you go—no sir! Not till I've done the honors —'n' had a chance to think whether there's anything you can do for me, like you said. Guess I can find somep'n."

He lurched to a chest of drawers, took a tie-wig and a green coat from the bottom drawer, opened a bag of flour, and with an old piece of flannel clumsily powdered the wig as well as his soiled cambric stock. He re-tied his hose, which were wrinkled around his ankles, tightened his knee-bands, examined the shoulder of his coat and shook his head angrily at sight of an open seam through which a corner of padding protruded. Muttering to himself, he pushed the padding out of sight with a clumsy forefinger. There was a singular stale smell to him, of perspiration and wine-dregs, gin and bad tobacco.

"There," he said, clapping a laced hat on his head and taking a final look at himself in a mirror that reflected him both dimly and contortedly: "that's better!"

He ushered me out, carefully locked the door of his miserable chamber, and on his way downstairs continued his discourse, but with a tongue that seemed stiff and unmanageable. "When I think what I been through in the last five years,

Langdon, I'm s'prised every time I look in the mirror. Aint
changed at all. Have to have a little more gin than I used to,
on account of my leg 'n' malaria, 'n' helps you sleep, too.
Makes it hard when—ah—remittance don't come, 'n' can't get
credit for gin, even if it's to be used as medicine, the way
I use it. Very fortunate, you coming 'long like this, Langdon,
making possible have gin again tonight. Ah—le's see, what
was it, now—what was it I was jus' talking about?"

"You were saying how little you'd changed, Major."

"Yes, so I was! To tell you God's honest truth, I'd feel
just about as good as I ever did if only I could get away
from the damned prison an' get started on somep'n again
—somep'n big. Ah, my boy, I got some real good plans, if
only I could get what's owed me!"

He hurried me into the courtyard, where the throng of
strollers and racket-players had dwindled at the approach of
the supper hour, and went limpingly down the basement
stairs into the long gallery of Bartholomew Fair.

At the doorway over which hung the sign reading "College
Haberdasher," he fumbled for the latch, and in his eagerness
to enter almost sprawled on the floor when the door gave
way. The shop was a strange one, for the owner stood behind a counter on which was nothing save two cravats, badly
wrinkled, a fly-specked stock and a half brick.

"Two Bobs," Rogers said thickly.

"You aint got credit, Major," the man said.

Rogers' eyes rolled wildly. "Damn you, Bambridge, they're
for this gentleman—my good friend Langdon Towne. One
of my Rangers, Bambridge, you damned little worm—not only
a Ranger but a great artist, too. So let's have a little ordinary
courtesy, Bambridge! For the love of God, Langdon, give this
snake three shillings!"

I gave the man a gold sovereign, and when he had bitten
it and rung it on the half brick, he brought out two pint
bottles of gin from under the counter. Rogers snatched one
of them, wrenched out the cork and poured half the contents
down his throat. "Ah!" he sighed. "Ah! That's terrible stuff,
Langdon, but it's better'n nothing. Bambridge, you damned
weasel, why don't you keep something fit for gentlemen to
drink?"

"Maybe for the same reason you don't never have nothing
to pay me with, Major," Bambridge said.

"Impudence! Always impudence!" Rogers said sadly, then grunted and finished the remainder of his bottle in three long, lingering swallows. "Hah!" he said. "Now my young friend Langdon, come with me!"

I followed him out to the corridor and he laid a wavering course toward the end of it, whence came a clatter of china-ware, a babel of shouting, and bursts of maudlin song. The two end rooms bore the imposing name of Alderman's Coffee House; and the Major, bawling jovial greetings, piloted me between tables at which sat men and women who were chiefly remarkable for the dishevelment of their wigs and their garments—all of which seemed strangely askew.

In a corner of that noisy, smoky, rancid place we took possession of two stools and a greasy, rickety table. The Major planted his elbows on the table and at once went to talking rapidly, as if he feared I might have something to say that he might not care to hear. When a waiter brought us ale, boiled potatoes and mutton swimming in a transparent gravy that tasted of hair, he chewed enormously and stared at me out of eyes watery above those glistening pouches that were the color of a russet apple.

"Le's see," he said. "Does memory play me one of its tricks—it does sometimes, my boy—or didn't I purchase two bottles of gin from Bambridge? Two, I think. Two, I swear! My dear old friend, what became of the other?"

I brought it forth. The Major said "Hah!", drew the cork, laced his ale with gin, and gulped down the contents of the mug as if he burned inside. Then upon the instant he ate voraciously again, but somehow contrived, even with his mouth packed with food, to keep on talking.

"Yes, Langdon," he said, his speech becoming thicker and thicker, "it's damn aggravating to be kept away from food 'n' drink 'n' decent lodgings jus' because you can't get what's owed to you. You know how much this damned government owes me, Langdon? Ten thousand pounds, by God! Yes, sir! A thousand pounds was all they allowed me, 'n' I'd spent ten thousand more on King's business, keeping the Indian trade for England, 'n' look at what I've got out of it! A courtmartial 'n' sickness 'n' a two-shilling room on the Upper Side of the Fleet, 'n' not a penny to spend! If you value your peace of mind, Langdon, keep out of public life and don't ever try to do anything for your country!"

I could hardly bring myself to look at this miserable man —this grimy, gin-soaked giant who had been the flashing spear-head of the British attack against the French troops that had hoped to keep all of North America for the King of France—this garrulous, red-eyed, wheezy derelict whom I had known as Wobi Madaondo: the White Devil whom the Indians had feared as they feared no other English leader.

He hitched himself forward to the edge of his chair and rubbed his greasy thick lips with the back of his hand. "Now listen, Langdon; all I got to do is show 'em I'm going to get ten thousand pounds and——"

Heavy-hearted as I was, I couldn't help laughing. "Ten thousand pounds! Talk sense!"

"No, listen," he insisted. " 'Taint as hard as you think! I got some mighty fine schemes, Langdon; mighty fine. I been working on 'em—yes, 'n' I got 'em prac'lly worked out! Now you take this Northwest Passage: it's there, 'n' you know it's there, 'n' I'd 'a' got there if it hadn't been for that skunk Johnson. Why, damn him—d'you know what that rat did, right while he was having me tried for giving presents to Indians? He 'n' Claus was having a Congress 'n' giving 'em twenty bateau-loads of presents so't they'd bring their trade to Fort de Chartres! Twenty bateau-loads, by God—twice as much as I had to give 'em—'n' the Indians wouldn't pay a damned bit of attention to him!" He laughed bitterly. "God, Langdon, when I think what that old skunk did to me jus' because he wanted to hog all the credit for everything, it makes me puke!"

He groaned, drank deeply and looked bewildered. "Well, as I was saying—jus' what was it we was discussing—had it right on the tip m' tongue——"

"You were speaking of the Northwest Passage, Major, and of——"

He slapped the table. "I cer'nly was! Johnson stopped me once, but he wont do it again. No sir! This time there wont be nobody stop me! This time I'll get there, because this time I'm going to take Englishmen with me. No sir: there aint one damned bit o' use trying to get anything out of Englishmen if you're an American, because Englishmen know Americans aint civilized and don't have to be treated like civilized people. Englishmen think it's an honor for Americans to be 'lowed to associate with Englishmen, 'n' honor ought to be 'nough for 'em.

"Yessir, you got to take that into account when you deal with Englishmen! Well, you know who's going with me next time? Pickersgill, by God! Yes, sir! Captain James Cook's lieutenant! Cook's been nosing around for the Northwest Passage, but he can't find it 'n' he never will; but Pickersgill's going with *me,* 'n' I'll find it for him, 'n' he'll collect the money for all of us. 'N' D'Arcy's going—you remember D'Arcy, don't you—Amherst's aide! Yes, sir! Pickersgill 'n' D'Arcy; 'n' this time with Pickersgill to navigate for us, 'n' Captain Cook himself to meet us when we get to the mouth of the Oregon, we're going all the way across the Pacific, 'n' come home by way of Japan and Siberia! Why, we'll be the greatest discoverers in the world! We'll bring gold 'n' ivory 'n' precious stones from Russia, 'n' all the perfumes of Araby that Lady Macbeth herself talks about, 'n' myrrh 'n' frankincense, 'n' all the spices of the gloried East—I mean the storied East. Why, hell, Langdon, those damned Tartars out there, they're just the same kind of people as Chippeways 'n' Winnebagoes. They look like 'em and act like 'em; 'n' I'll handle 'em just the same as I handled the Chippeways! I'll have an army of 'em lugging sables all the way to England for me, see if I don't!"

He laughed loudly and contemptuously. "Ten thousand pounds! Why, ten thousand pounds aint a drop in the bocket —bucket. I'll come home with diamonds like rocs' eggs 'n' pearls that would 'a' strangled Cleopatra, 'n' enough money to buy every stick 'n' stone 'n' Lord in London. You wont never hear 'nother word about Stamp Taxes or any other kind of taxes on Americans—not by a damned sight, Langdon! Why, not even such a bloody idiot as this minny-headed Lord North would run the risk of losing a country full of diamonds 'n' pearls 'n' splices 'n' franklcense 'n' everything. Make a hell of a difference to America, 'f they let me show 'em the Northwest Passage, 'n' don't you forget it!"

He pushed himself erect in his chair and bent a stern gaze upon me. "What you lookin' so glum for, Langdon? Don't be downcast! I'll take you, too! I'll make your fortune, jus' like I used to. I'll find a place for you in this expedition, never fear! You've heard me promise, so why don't you

look happier?" He stared. "You want to go, don't you?"
"No, Major."

"Why not?" he asked, frowning heavily. "Why don't you?
You know it'll make you rich, don't you? Look, Carver's in
London, damn pop-eyed mealy-mouthed pussycat! You know
what that weasel-footed snake's been telling people? Been
telling 'em I never had authority send him hunting Northwest Passage—saying he was the one invented idea of discovering Northwest Passage! Planning to write a book about
his travels, they tell me, 'n' 'splain how he thought up everything all by himself, for God's sake! When he heard I was
figgerin' on tryin' it again, he began to crawl around on his
belly, wanting to go with me, 'n' I wont take him! Not one
damned inch! Carver 'n' Atherton—they both want to go,
but to hell with 'em! I'm a great feller, now they've found
I've got some Englishmen going with me——"

"Have they been here to see you?" I asked.

Rogers stared at me gravely. "See me? 'Course not! They
aint got any money, not any more than I have. Money's
the only thing that'll help me, 'n' I need more'n any of them'll
ever have!"

He signalled carelessly to a waiter for more ale, and in
so doing nearly fell from his stool. Righting himself, he
hiccuped. "Now here's somep'n I need awful bad. You know
my brother James?"

I said I hadn't that honor.

"Well," Rogers said, "he's a real good boy, James is: real
good. He aint as good a officer as me, because he's one of
those fellers that stays in one place till he sends down
suckers 'n' gets himself all attached to the land, kind of. He
ain't good company like you 'n' me, either, but he'll work
harder clearing stumps off a piece of land than I would trying
to get the King's ear—damned near. He aint got 'magination,
that's James' trouble. No 'magination. Well now listen——"

He blinked, focussed wavering eyes on his cracked and
blackened fingernails, and rubbed a clumsy forefinger across
a star-shaped scar on the back of his hand. Into my mind
flashed the picture of Ogden and me—starved, shivering,
fainting, half-dead skeletons—standing in the drenching rain
at the mouth of the Ammonoosuc while Rogers rubbed rolls
of dirt from that same star-shaped scar and told us he was
starting down the Connecticut after food to keep us alive.

"Le's see," he said thickly. "What were we all talking about?"

"You were speaking of your brother James, Major."

"That's it," he said. "James. Somebody's got to write James —somebody he'll believe. Not me. He don't believe me. Don't believe his own brother! By God, he even thought there was something in that story Potter told about me—the one that pigeon-breasted Mohawk-marrying Roberts got him to tell —the one about me joining the French! My own brother! Me, the father of his only nephew! Didn't know I was a father, did you? Father of a li'l baby boy—li'l Arthur—born just after that damned trial, while I was in Montreal. Jus' imagine that! Innocent li'l child, 'n' 'bliged to be born under a cloud on account of Roberts 'n' the rest of those damned lying, murdering swine, Johnson 'n' Gage 'n' Claus 'n'——"

He must have been about to utter Potter's name, for he broke off, looked startled, shook his head; then said, "Poor li'l Arthur," drew a long, quivering breath, and moisture stood in his bloodshot eyes.

I tried not to think, even, of Elizabeth, the girl who, in her long-dead youth, had been horrified by uncouthness, becoming the mother of Robert Rogers' child.

The waiter set a gallon tankard of ale before us, and stood looking down at Rogers.

The Major, waving him grandly to me, said, "Don't bother us, boy. There's something I wanted to tell you, Langdon."

I paid.

"Something you'd like to say to me, Major?" I asked.

"There cer'nly is, 'n' you'd never believe it, not hardly! He's here! He's in the Fleet!"

"In the Fleet!" I exclaimed. "Your brother James in the Fleet?"

"Who?" Rogers asked. "James? Hell, no, Langdon! Roberts! I'm talking about that damned screech-owl of a Roberts! It's him that's in the Fleet, and not only in the Fleet, but over on the Common Side to boot. Serves him right, the dirty Mohawk-marrying screech-owl! Tell you what I'll do, Langdon: I'll have him paraded for you—give you idea how low a man can fall!"

He pounded heavily on the table with his pewter ale-mug, and his shout for the waiter rang out above the tumult of bellowing and singing all around us almost as it had rung out at White River Falls when he told us to jump for our lives.

"Le's see," Rogers said, when the waiter answered his call. "I need a penny, 'n' I don't b'lieve I got one." He fumbled with thick fingers in his pockets. "Could you let me have a penny, Langdon?"

He took it from me, examined it closely, and held it up before the waiter. "My friend," he said, "listen to your orders! You're to go over on the Common Side 'n' find Benjamin Roberts."

"The gentleman you poured the beer over?" the waiter asked.

"The same," Rogers said. "Go get him. Tell him I got a mutual acquaintance here. Tell him he'll get some ale—not on his head, this time, but down his throat—'n' maybe some meat. He might get sixpence, even."

The waiter took the penny and went away. Rogers passed his tongue over his thick lips. "Yes sir," he said triumphantly, "that dirty Roberts is right here in the Fleet, 'n' wha's more, he's over on the Common Side! Lives in a cell with a dozen others, 'n' don't eat unless somebody drops money at the Beggars' Grate! He'll run fifty miles for sixpence! But the bes' joke of all is who put him in the Fleet! You jus' simply wouldn't believe it if you saw it painted in one of your own pictures!" He laughed so uproariously that a disheveled fop at a nearby table rose and stared coldly at us, only to sit down quietly when he saw Rogers.

"Major," I said, "if you want to tell me something about your brother, you'll have to tell me quickly. They close the gates soon, I'm told."

He steadied himself by clutching the table-edge with his huge hands. "Stay over night—pleasure to have you share my room," he said vaguely. Then, with an effort, he fastened his eyes on mine. "You write my brother, Langdon. He's rich! Got thousans 'n' thousans of acres in New York, 'n' aint never let go none of 'em. You tell him you saw me—health greatly impared by coffinement. Being kep' from great projects. Northwest Passage, Langdon, 'n' that aint all, not by a damn sight! I aint told you about the others. Listen:

"That feller Gage, he never had one damn thing to court-martial me for. He jus' tried to murder me, tha's all! He 'n' Johnson 'n' Spiesmaker, they figured anybody'd die if he got thrown onto the ballast the way I was, and took to Niagara in cold weather; but Gage was the one to blame, because he ordered the courtmartial, thinking I'd be dead before I ever had to testify. Well, I'm alive, 'n' I've got a case against him, by God! I'm going to sue him!

"Ten thousand pounds? Why, hell, I'll get *fifty* thousand pounds out of that dough-faced pot-belly before I'm through with him! You tell my brother that! Tell him all he's got to do is assume my obbaglations—olligations—obligations, 'n' I'll get out of here and pay him back ten times over—a hundred times! Why, it aint possible for him to lose, Langdon!

" 'N' listen: I met the Ambassador from the Dey of Algiers before they threw me in here—feller the shape of a haystack, Langdon, 'n' mustaches like a pair of sickles, 'n' wears trousers cut like a couple balloon jibs. You know anything about Algiers?"

I shook my head, sick of his talk, sick of the Fleet, sick of everything.

"Listen," he went on, and his great red face worked, as if he prevented it by main strength from becoming slack and muscleless. "This Dey of Algiers, he needs fighters, 'n' he aint afraid to pay for 'em. Needs good officers on his ships, 'n' good officers ashore. Got all the sholdiers he wants, but aint got no officers that know how to show sholdiers the right way to fight. Why aint he? Because there aint none, only me!

"Well, this Dey of Algiers, he's got good sense. He knows about me, 'n' he knows my way of fighting is the only right way there is. His Ambassador—old sickle-whiskers— he come to see me, 'n' he says 'You come on down to Algiers, Major,' he says, ' 'n' we'll make you a general, 'n' half of what you capture is yours,' he says. 'You'll get your general's pay,' he says, ' 'n' if you capture a ship with a cargo worth ten thousand pounds, five thousand of it's yours,' he says.

" 'Give you a house to live in,' he says, 'all blue tiles 'n' palm trees in the garden 'n' a nice view out to sea, 'n' any number of wives up to six—young ones—pick 'em out yourself—have more'n six if you want 'em,' he says, 'but the Dey wont pay for only six. Any others you'll have to buy with your own money,' he says. What you think of that! Six wives, all perfumed 'n' wearing gauze pantaloons!"

He regarded me triumphantly, then looked concerned. "Don't tell my brother James about the six wives. Don't say nothing 'bout wives at all. Jus' tell him I can go down 'n' render valuable assistance to the Dey of Algiers, any time I get out of here, 'n' if I don't get out of here pretty damned quick, I'll most likely die of one thing or another. You know what to tell him. Jus' put in some of that Harvard College language of yours. I *got* to get out!"

Swaying on his stool, he raised his ale-mug and drank sonorously; and the ale, trickling from the corners of his mouth, dripped on his soiled cambric stock. He set down the mug with a bang, pawed clumsily at the damp spots, and made sounds of exasperation. It was a relief when someone stood at my elbow, and a hesitant voice said, "I believe I've already had the pleasure."

I looked up and saw Lieutenant Benjamin Roberts, but a pitiably different Roberts from that scarlet-coated favorite of Sir William Johnson, who had attempted to assert authority over Rogers at Oswego. His coat and small-clothes were caked with dirt; his stockings were pulled under at the heels to conceal holes; a soiled kerchief was tied around his neck in place of a stock; and the hair that curled around his ears was dusty and full of bits of straw. Everything upon him, as seemed to be the case with all the others in that wastrels' abode, was somehow crooked—somehow improperly adjusted. His haggard face was thin and dirty; his lips dry; only his eyes were the same—cat's eyes, in which, when the drooping lids were lifted, lurked wariness, resentment, jealousy.

Rogers frowned at him, rubbed a huge hand across wavering eyes, and laughed foolishly. "Didn't know you, Lieutenant," he said. "What you doing in here? Somebody give you some money?"

He swayed forward, then pushed himself upright.

"The waiter told me you asked for me," Roberts said.

"Who, me?" Rogers cried. "Think I'd ask for you, you malfeaslin', Mohawk-marryin' rattlesnake in the grass?"

"Look here, Major," I said, "you remember telling the waiter to ask Lieutenant Roberts to join us, don't you? Sit down, Lieutenant, and have a mug of ale. Have you had supper?"

Roberts snatched at a stool and sat close to me. "Supper?" he asked almost whimperingly. "Supper?"

I called the waiter; ordered another plate of mutton and potatoes; another tankard of ale.

"Supper!" Rogers repeated. "Him! He aint had a supper since Sir William Johnson refused to honor his draft for a hundred pounds—one hundred penny-weeny pounds, the yeller-bellied old Mohawk! Wouldn't spare him a hundred pounds to keep spying on me 'n' spreading his dirty damned lies about me! Roberts, you're a dirty, chicken-breasted Mohawk-marrier—nothing but a cheap hundred-pound debtor! Look at me! Ten thousand pounder; 'n' you, you li'l pint of snow-water, you aint got 'nough resoffleness— 'sourcefulness—to scratch up a hundred pounds. Jus' a pint of snow-water, half poured out!"

"I can't have this, Major," I said. "You asked Lieutenant Roberts to come here, and the least you can do is treat him decently."

"Nothing of the sort!" Rogers said thickly. "I asked him to come over so's you could see how far a dirty, chicken-breasted, Mohawk-marryin' polecat would run for a quart of ale, 'n' how much he'd swallow from a offser he did his damnedest to murder. Tha's what you did, you damned tippy-toed tin sholdier! You paid Potter to swear I was going to join the French—dunno how much—not a hell of a lot— brains like yours 'n' Potter's can't think bigger'n a hundred pounds! Yes, 'n' if it hadn't been for your testimony, you damned Mohawk-marryin' skunk, the Board o' Trade would 'a' granted me sixty square miles on Lake Champlain, 'n' I'd be fixed for life 'n' wouldn't 'a' had a debt in the world!"

Roberts said never a word; and when the waiter brought the ale and put the platter of greasy mutton and gray potatoes before him, he went at them voraciously, making wet champing sounds and casting wary glances at Rogers from the corners of his eyes.

Rogers laughed drunkenly, poured himself a mug of ale with a hand so unsteady that he deluged his weskit in the pouring. He drained the mug without stopping for breath; then swayed on his seat, breathing stertorously, huge hands clutching the table, big head sagging, and focussed protuber-ant eyes on Roberts.

"Go ahead 'n' eat, Mohawk-marrier," he said. "You think

you stopped me; but you aint! You're the one that's stopped!
You 'n' Johnson 'n' Gage 'n' Claus—there aint none of you
can stop me, only for jus' a few days, as days go in this
part of the world! You can't see what I see—off, off, beyond
the mountains—you li'l foxes under your own li'l stone
walls—I'll show you, by God—show every damned one of
you blind li'l foxes—all tail 'n' no brains! Oh, God! Aint
there nobody in this whole God-damned world but li'l blind
foxes! I wish—I wish——"

He paused, half-rose from his stool, and his staring, bloodshot eyes swept in a dazed half-circle above our heads. Then
he tottered, grasped blindly at the table, sprawled to the
floor with a crash and lay motionless in ale-moistened grime.

Roberts, busy with his mutton and potatoes, didn't look
up. Those at the next table disapprovingly eyed the huge
body beside their stools, but made no complaint.

Roberts pushed back his plate, wiped his mouth on a shiny
sleeve, filled his ale-mug and leaned toward me confidentially.
"I hope, sir," he said elegantly, "that you will place no cred-
ence in the Major's words. It's true I've been shabbily treated
by Sir William; but the canard about the bribe extended to
Mr. Potter, sir—and on the word of an officer and a gentleman, sir, it *is* a canard that——"

"I know all about Potter," I interrupted.

Roberts buried his nose in his ale-mug and watched me
over the brim.

I rapped on the table to get the waiter's attention; and
when he came and stood looking down at Rogers, his expression was one of admiration. "Strike me!" he exclaimed.
"It aint often the Major's able to get like this!"

"Will you help him to his room?" I asked.

"Pleasure, Master," he said. "Leave 'im lay till the crowd
thins out; then me an' Sadie'll look out for 'im. Sadie always comes huntin' for 'im along towards midnight; an'
till then, Master, 'e's as well off 'ere as a baby'd be in 'is
cradle."

I felt in my pocket: then saw Roberts' eyes fixed eagerly
on my hand. "Here's a shilling," I told the waiter. "Look
out for him; and when Sadie comes, tell her to tell him I'll
send something to the gate for him tomorrow—and that
I'll write the letter he spoke of."

The waiter nodded. When I turned away, Lieutenant Roberts followed me toward the door; but when I ignored him, he left me alone and I went out from the stench and turmoil of Bartholomew Fair, across the dim and echoing courtyard of the Fleet, and beneath the arched passage into the freedom of Farringdon Street and Ludgate Hill.

Rogers, I knew, had reached the height of his career—had come to a real grandeur of soul—on that terrible day when, at the end of our retreat from St. Francis, the woodcutters had dragged our raft ashore and helped the three of us to stagger to the stockade at Number Four. I saw him as I had seen him in the flickering firelight of the fort: gaunt, barefooted, covered with bruises, hung with tattered strips of strouding. I remembered the shredded leggins hanging on his emaciated flanks; the ribs and bony chest that showed through his torn rags; the chunk of bread in his scarred, sooty, pitch-stained hands; and as if it had been yesterday I heard his thick voice saying: "Get me some beef—fat beef. I'm going back—back to my men—back to the Ammonoosuc!"

And now I had seen him so low that a man could go no lower this side of the grave. But far as he had fallen, yet something—some imperishable last glimmer of that old spirit—still survived. There was an inner force that had been warped and twisted by narrow men and a narrow woman, but that had never been wholly crushed and never could be.

More than that, I suspected that even still the man who lay in the mud of the Fleet was better than the mere sodden husk of Robert Rogers. But for Fate and Ann Potter, I suspected, there in that same grime might lie Langdon Towne. There, too, but for the grace of God, might lie any of us, our talents quenched and our best dreams beaten.

CHAPTER LXXX

I THOUGHT this time that Robert Rogers was surely finished: that he was a stranded wreck, doomed, if ever freed from the rocks, to sink like a

stone; but he was far from finished. I wrote to his brother
James, as I had promised; there was nothing more that any
man could do. Then, absorbed by the two-year task of de-
signing and executing the Great Spirit painting for the ceiling of the central hall of the Ethnographic Society, I tried
to forget not only Rogers but everything that might distract
me from my work.

I pretty well succeeded, for although my father's letters,
with their open bitterness against the English, made me increasingly uneasy, I almost convinced myself that he was
placing too great an emphasis on affairs that were less grave
than he implied. I believed what I read in the London newspapers and held, with most of the few Englishmen I saw,
that the fighting in America was merely the rioting of turbulent, greedy ragamuffins against men of property. It seemed
a little odd to me that the King's Ministers should feel called
on, early in 1776, to despatch Lord Howe and his brother,
with a fleet of Britain's strongest men-of-war, to make over-
tures of peace to mere rioters; but British Ministers, I told
myself, did unaccountable and idiotic things.

It was Copley who brought me face to face with what I'd
so sedulously avoided. He had come to London, had been
given a royal welcome by Benjamin West, Sir Joshua and
everyone else who knew his work, and immediately became so popular that I'd seen him half a dozen times before
I could get a moment alone with him. He seemed to me to
be a changed Copley, inclined to be more artificial in his
manner—more the courtier.

"I heard of an old friend of yours recently," he told me.
"While dining at Lord Mansfield's, I had a chat with Admiral Sir Charles Leighton—striking figure: marvelous color-
ing—and he asked whether I'd ever heard the name
Rogers in America. Of course I mentioned your old commander the Major, and he at once said 'By Jove, I fancy
that's the chap.' It appeared the Admiral had just come
from the Mediterranean, where he'd run across a seafaring
person who told him the Dey of Algiers had a new general
from the Americas—fellow named Rogers, the seafaring
person thought. Said he'd fought two battles for the Dey
and won both of them—roaring drunk both times. Would
that be the Major, do you suppose? What ever became of
him?"

There was little doubt in my mind. Thereafter I'd have another picture to add to those so indelibly graven on my memory—to those of him grubbing in the Ammonoosuc meadows for the tawho to keep us alive; threatening to raid the settlement at Number Four if food weren't sent to his starving men; gesticulating grandly and declaiming lines from his great tragedy, *Pontiac*; sprawled in the filth of the Fleet Prison; and now, sitting cross-legged on an Algerian divan, roistering with gauze-pantalooned wives, yelling with hoarse mirth and slapping them, fond and drunken.

"Strange," Copley continued. "Strange he wasn't sent to America to teach that riffraff a lesson. They'd have got short shrift at Lexington and Bunker Hill if they'd had to face Rangers under Rogers."

Short shrift! Riffraff! This from Copley! How many Americans were talking this way? Was my father in the category of riffraff? "Rangers against Americans!" I said. "Rangers wouldn't fight Americans! What are you talking about?"

Copley looked at me shrewdly. "You're not thinking of going back to America, are you, by any chance?"

"To tell you the truth," I said, "I've not thought of it. I've been too busy with my ceiling." Inconsequentially I added, "Anyway, it'll soon be over, with Lord Howe offering reconciliation."

"Yes?" Copley said doubtfully. "Well, take my advice and don't go back. Stay where you are! It's no longer possible for an artist to make money in America; and what's worse, it's impossible for him to have a mind of his own or say what he thinks."

I may have looked skeptical, for he became emphatic. "It's the simple truth! If you're even suspected of wanting to say a good word for anything English, you're fortunate if you're not tarred and feathered—if your property's not seized—if your family's not left penniless and starving. Why, by God, Langdon, do you know what that scum—that rabble—did to me? The news got around that Colonel Watson of Plymouth was my guest, and just because he'd never been afraid to say he preferred to be governed by Parliament rather than by riffraff, those damned yokels undertook to break in my door and ransack my house. I had to argue with 'em for two hours. If they'd ever got in, they'd have destroyed every painting I owned."

How could I possibly believe him? Was the world coming to an end?

Copley went on: "You can't even imagine what it's like unless you've gone through it! There's no culture left in America: no refinement. A good two-thirds of the people are being terrorized and browbeaten by the other third—abominable malicious louts! Those who had the property and good taste to order portraits are being driven out by the clowns. No! It's no place for an artist. Nothing but noise, irritation, confusion, persecution! I'll never go back. Benjamin West'll never go back. And if you're a wise man, Langdon, you wont think of going back!"

I began then to think of going back, however; for my own family certainly sympathized with those louts of whom Copley had spoken, and I couldn't help picturing with increasing frequency my own early days in Portsmouth, when Elizabeth Browne and her father had withdrawn the light of their countenances from me because of my persistence in consorting with louts—with those coarse and profane swearers, Cap Huff and Hunk Marriner. They were the scum and the rabble of whom Copley had spoken. McNott and Jesse Beacham; my father and my brothers; John Langdon, my father's friend, for whom I'd been named: they were the riffraff. The cultured ones—the ones who were being browbeaten and terrorized by those abominable malicious yokels —were people like Wyseman Clagett, Sheriff Packer, Benning Wentworth, Sir William Johnson, Daniel Claus, the Reverend Arthur Browne, his sour-faced lady and poor Elizabeth!

Yes, I thought more and more of going back, but I said nothing of it to Ann; her happiness was an unfailing delight to me, and not for worlds would I have done anything to mar it. She made our little house in Cavendish Square a haven of rest after the long hours I spent lying on my back and plying my brushes on that endless ceiling; and each morning I went encouraged to the task that had seemed impossible of achievement the night before.

It was in the summer of '76 that we learned of the astounding thing those louts had done. Not only had they refused to consider the reconciliation which Lord Howe had so graciously proposed; they had even declared America a free and independent nation, and defied England's army and navy. When I read this news, I felt a singular impulse to laugh—not in amusement at their insane presumption, or in contempt at their impotence, but in almost tearful admiration of their magnificent bravado. I didn't laugh, for I felt Ann's eyes upon me; but since she said nothing, I was silent as well.

Not long thereafter something happened that made us talk of it. On one of those evenings in late autumn, when the moon, struggling to pierce a silvery blanket of fog, gives a silent, ghostly quality to the half-seen shapes that float along London's streets and squares, Sam Livermore, my old friend from Portsmouth, walked in on us so suddenly and unexpectedly that for a moment I thought he was a ghost himself.

As he sat before the coal fire in our little sitting room, fair-haired and smiling, he seemed not a day older than on that fateful evening when he had piloted me from the home of the Reverend Arthur Browne to Stoodley's tap-room, and written the letters that started Hunk and me for Crown Point and Rogers' Rangers. He only differed from the Sam I'd known by being slower and more guarded in answering questions—which I thought only natural for one who had risen to the post of King's Attorney for the Province of New Hampshire.

When he'd made his compliments to Ann, I showered questions on him. How had he learned our address? When had he last been in Portsmouth? What had brought him to London?

He replied by producing an unsealed letter addressed to me in my father's handwriting. When I opened it, I found it contained only the words, "My dear son: We are all well and send you our love by Mr. Livermore, seeing that he once did you a service long ago, though you may have forgotten it."

"Well," I said, handing the page to Ann, "that's the most peculiar letter I ever received from any member of my family!"

"These are peculiar times," Sam said.

"But he speaks as though I might have forgotten what you did for me!" I said. "Why on earth should I have forgotten?"

Sam shrugged his shoulders. "Oh, just a precaution, no doubt."

A suspicion of the truth dawned upon me. "Precaution! I think I see! Well, I haven't forgotten. You're safe here, Sam, and welcome."

"I was sure of it," he said, "but it's always well to be careful. Ah——have you by any chance heard anything from Major Rogers recently?"

"He was in the Fleet Prison for debt," I said, "and I saw him there——"

"Yes," Sam said, "we know about that."

"You know about it! How——"

Ann spoke quickly. "Langdon went to see the Major at my request, Mr. Livermore."

"I thought perhaps you'd have more recent news of him," Sam said.

I shook my head. "I haven't—though Copley told me he'd heard a rumor Rogers had fought and won two battles for the Dey of Algiers."

"So I understand," Sam said, "but that was some time ago —if ever. There's been nothing, for example, in the past week or two?"

"Certainly not. What makes you think *I* might have word of him?"

"You went to St. Francis with him," Sam said. "An old friend and all that. I thought he might have come to you for help in—well, in raising officers."

"Officers for what?"

"For a new corps of Rangers to replace those he raised in Connecticut and lost at Mamaroneck last month."

"He lost Rangers! And at Mamaroneck," I said slowly. "Who was he fighting for at Mamaroneck?"

"Lord Howe," Sam said. "Rogers and his Rangers acted as advance scouts for Howe when he moved out of New York to attack Washington at White Plains." He smiled kindly and added, "Your brother Odiorne helped to turn back Howe at White Plains. He's in the Massachusetts Line."

"Rogers in Connecticut," I said, trying to comprehend what Sam had told me. "Leading New England Rangers against New England troops! Against my brother Odiorne!" I sat silent, imagining men in greenish buckskins, slipping silently from tree to tree, drawing closer and closer to a group of sleeping New Englanders, all of whom had faces like Odiorne.

I looked helplessly at Ann, who sat staring at her folded hands.

"Yes," Sam went on, "we've had a lot of trouble with the Major, Langdon: a lot of trouble! I don't believe we'd have stopped him before White Plains if his Rangers hadn't been new and raw and if we hadn't sent trained troops against him—twice as many as he had."

Bitterly he added, "If we'd sent militia, they'd be running yet! My God, you wouldn't believe human beings could be such cowardly rats as our militia regiments! God knows what's going to become of us if that's the sort of vermin we're breeding! You're mighty lucky to be over here, Langdon, where you're not forever in a rage at the stupidity of mankind: where you're—where you're safe!"

We sat silently for a time. Then I said heavily, "Now you're out in the open, let's have the rest of it. How else did Rogers give you trouble?"

Sam's voice was exasperated. "Oh, with his reputation, and his damned endurance! Say 'Rogers' to militia anywhere between Providence and New York, and they throw away their muskets and start running; but fast as they run, by God, they can't move as fast as the Major! When they first set me to work on him, with Captain Peters, there were times when we thought he wasn't a real man, but some sort of he-witch, riding all over hell on a broomstick!"

He glanced over his shoulder. "No danger of your servants hearing me, is there?"

When Ann said they slept in the basement, he looked apologetic. "I have to be a little careful."

"You don't need to be careful, Sam: not in this house."

"Well," Sam said, "Rogers came to America over a year ago, and right away he began to nose around our lines. One day he'd be in Baltimore; then he'd be in New York; and a few minutes later, seemingly, he'd be in Portsmouth."

He shot a quick glance at Ann. "Called on Elizabeth while he was there, but I fancy he'd been"—he coughed—"somewhat free with the ladies. His health didn't seem of the best, and she had rather a bad time with him. Yes, rather bad. Well, he left Portsmouth and headed for the Connecticut River, and by that time General Washington had put Peters and me to following him. It was like trying to follow a black squall on a dark night. It occurred to us he might be taking a jaunt, just for the fun of it, over the route he covered when he went to St. Francis. He went through Number Four, up past Wattoquitchey and White River Falls, stopped at Hanover to see Dr. Wheelock, and then went on, past the Cohase Intervales, and we lost him.

"Later we got word of him in Albany, traced him into New York, out of New York and back up the Hudson. We lost him in Vermont, found him again in Concord, followed him to his brother James', tracked him to New Jersey, back to New York, over to Philadelphia—and that was all the General could stand! Rogers was up to something—God knows what—well, we arrested him at last in Philadelphia and threw him in prison just before Congress signed the Declaration of Independence; and a few days later, right under our noses, he slid out from behind those bolts and bars and past the sentries as easily as your friend Cap Huff gets out of the Portsmouth jail! He stole a boat, disappeared down the river, landed at Staten Island, and joined Howe just before the British took New York. Then he went over to Connecticut and raised his Rangers."

Sam shook his head. "Tires me out, just thinking of how he raced around. Peters and I got so we made silver bullets for our pistols, in case we had to take a shot at him." He looked thoughtful. "I'm not so sure a silver bullet, even, would do the trick."

I pondered his amazing story, and then, for lack of something better to say, stammered, "So Cap Huff's still getting in trouble, is he?"

"He's doing better than that," Sam said. "He joined the army and went to Quebec with Arnold, and when he came home he bought a farm in Kittery—one of the nicest farms on the river; then went right back to Quebec. Said he had to go back to get enough money to fix up his farm. God knows how he expected to get it. He said something about wishing you were in Kittery, so he could get you to paint the inside of his house just the way you did the Warners'." Sam laughed. "Good thing you're not going home, or he'd probably persuade you to do it."

I looked again at Ann. Why was she still staring at her interlaced fingers?

I turned back to Sam. "What I don't understand is why you're in London."

"Damn it," Sam said wearily, "we've got to know about Rogers! What's he going to do? He's like a cloud—a damned black cloud—hanging over us: full of lightning: apt to strike anywhere. He's got Washington worried to death. When he was beaten at Mamaroneck, he vanished. We heard he'd gone to Halifax, intending to recruit another corps of Rangers in northern New Hampshire and Vermont; then raid the coast—Falmouth, Kittery, Portsmouth. So I turned myself into a downtrodden Loyalist and went to Halifax, cursing the cruel New Englanders who'd driven me out; but it was a waste of time, because Rogers wasn't there. He'd gone to England, the Halifaxers said, to get some of the Ranger officers who'd fought with him in the old French war. So I came to England too, but I can't find him, Langdon! He's worse than the Wandering Jew—worse than the Flying Dutchman! Damn him, swooping around like something out of a fairy tale—like a warlock. Well"—he threw out his arms in a despairing gesture, rose to his feet and took a couple of turns up and down the room. "Well, that's how it is, and I'm going back by the first boat. My work's there. I've got to find out whether there's anything in the story that he's going to raise more Rangers in New Hampshire and Vermont. Do you want me to take a message to your family?" He looked at me oddly. "I suppose you're planning to stay here for some time, like Copley and West."

"Yes," I said, "I guess I am, Sam—quite some time. I'm doing a ceiling for the Ethnographic Society, and it's not finished yet. Then, too, Ann likes it here." As I said it, I turned to her. She was not staring at her hands any more. Her eyes were on mine, and there was a look in them that brought me to my feet. "Ann!" I went over to her. "You *do* like it here, don't you?"

For two breaths she made no answer. Then she said, "Isn't the ceiling almost finished, Langdon?"

"Almost," I said, wondering. "There's a herd of buffalo to be done, and some small figures on horseback."

"I'm glad of that," she said, "glad of that, because now I can say what I've often wanted to say." She turned to Sam. "An artist needs encouragement, Mr. Livermore. If he's a good artist, he's never satisfied with what he does. He's forever doing over and doing over, and feeling uncertain about what he's done; so he oughtn't to have worries over

and above his work. What he most needs is peace of mind—
and I've done all I could to see that Langdon had it."

I caught her hand. "You have, Ann!"

Sam nodded understandingly.

Ann turned back to me. "Now I'll answer you, my dear.
I've been happy here, but I'm not any more. I don't like
it for myself, and I like it even less for you. You're known
as a painter now; and the better you're known, the more
elaborately we'll have to live if you want to continue to be
well known in London—more servants, more dinner-parties:
more of everything: always more and more. You can't escape!
It's happening to every artist you know—Copley, West, Reynolds—all! Well, my dear, there's only one end for an artist
who's caught in such a circle—only one end, and that's dis-
integration and disaster. It's not so in America, Langdon.
You can live simply, and still be a great artist; but you can't
do it in this land of flunkeys and fawning—this land where
nobody gets anything except by the accident of birth or
favoritism!"

She spoke again to Sam. "Langdon's forgotten the only
London I knew before he took me out of it—a London of
dirt and despair—of men and women not half as decent as
brutes—of men and women soaked in gin—of children
kicked, beaten, starved, educated in nothing but crime and
vice. I never knew a day that wasn't misery and horror! I
never knew a man or woman who didn't grovel before someone—whose lives didn't depend on somebody who had the
mastery over them!"

"That's a small part of England, Ann," I said; "one you'll
never have to see again."

"No!" she said, and seemed to fling the word from her.
"No! It's a large part of England, and not the only part I
don't like! I don't like the rich young rakes who made nights
hideous for me at Half Moon Hall—so hideous I couldn't
have gone on, even if you hadn't come back! I don't like the
bagnios that all the gentlemen—gentlemen!—visit so frequently, nor any of the other things that go with bagnios
and rakes."

She rose to her feet, her hands clenched. "Do you think I
can ever forget the day we sailed into Boston Harbor, or
the freshness and cleanness of the wind that came down
from those three blue hills to blow the last of Castle Street

from me? I wanted to cry and to shout, Langdon! And the people! Those strange, strange, free people, who walked with a swing such as never was seen in England—who thought for themselves, grovelled before no one, knew no awe of any man: who'd never known what it was to be kicked and cursed by gin-soaked devils—never had to beg or steal or hide in cellars like starved cats—never been afraid of being insulted if they were seen speaking to those above them, or contaminated if they said a kind word to those beneath them! And until I forget those things, how can I be happy in a land where half-grown children are sentenced to death for stealing a loaf of bread, where noblemen think less of the poor than they do of dogs?"

She stopped abruptly, and in the silence that struck against my ears like a blow, I heard Sam swallow twice.

I found her hand and held it tight; and what we had to say together, our eyes said for us.

"Well, Sam," I said; but my voice broke on his name, so that I had to cough to ease the choking fulness within me. "Well, Sam, we won't be in England as long as I thought. Wouldn't you like company when you start for home?"

I never regretted going back, not even when things looked darkest; and I often wished that when disappointments and disaster at last overtook Copley and West, they might have been heartened by the sights and sounds and scenes that lay close to my hand but couldn't be found in London—the glitter and gleam of fields, trees, rocks and sea beneath our burnished Maine sky; the soft wind from over the river with its odors of ships and wet sand; the trembling haze above the marshes, the scent of heather and sun-baked mud, and the far-off calling of feeding curlew; the gentle roaring of the breeze in tall pines; the slap-slapping of pollock-schools, whacking the surface with their tails as they moved upstream in the stillness of dawn; the secret pipings of mallard drakes exploring the tinkling waterways of a marsh, and the distant throbbing of partridges, boastfully beating their breasts; those vast armies of small white clouds, planed off at the bottom by industrious celestial carpenters, and ranged around the horizon as if to shield New England's rolling meadows from attack; the recurring broken harmony of song-sparrows and robins, pouring out full-hearted hymns of gratitude at the beauty and richness of this land of ours.

We built our house, when New England was safe at last, on a point above my father's, far enough away to provide the solitude without which, Ann insisted, no worthy piece of art has ever come into being, but not so far as to be beyond the reach of old friends, without whose sympathy, I know, an artist cannot work.

It was on a gusty autumn evening that I heard an old friend's voice bawling hoarsely to me from the river; and when I threw open the door to let him know I was at home, I saw approaching, in the light that flooded the path, three figures instead of the one I had expected.

"Found him in Stoodley's," Cap Huff bellowed, "asking where you lived, so Sam and I brought him over personal, stopping at my house to let him see the kind of pictures you can paint when you do it for love."

This oft-repeated remark of Cap's never failed to embarrass me; for the paintings of Cap's marvelous marches and triumphs, which he had modestly commissioned me to place upon the walls of his sitting room, had brought me a richer reward than any I had ever done—the string of pearls that now were Ann's. We often wondered where he got them, but Cap, though he seemed to rack his brains, couldn't tell us. He had, he said, picked them up, but he disremembered when or where.

"You stopped at your house for rum and nothing else," I said, and looked hard at the figure walking between Cap and Sam Livermore. There was something familiar about his head, cocked a little to one side as if listening—and even before the light shone full on his face I remembered following that same figure, that slightly tilted head, through swamps and rivers, storms and forests, for an eternity packed into two short months.

"Captain Ogden!" I cried.

"*Colonel* Ogden," Sam corrected me, "just back from England and even farther east, for all we know."

Ogden smiled and said nothing; but when, in the sitting room, he bowed over Ann's hand, he brought his heels together and bent low, as had been the custom of some of the foreign officers who fought in our army.

"I saw your paintings in London," Ogden said, while Ann mixed flip for us, "and when my ship put in at Portland, I thought I'd stop to tell you so—and give you this." He drew a small book from his coat pocket, opened it at a certain page and handed it to me. The title-page read: "Travels through the Interior Parts of North America in the Years 1766, 1767 and 1768, By J. Carver, Esq."

"Well I'll be damned!" I said. "Jonathan Carver!"

I looked at the page Ogden had indicated. There it was: the story of Pinnashon and the rattlesnake: the account of his meeting with the Sioux at the mouth of the St. Peter's River. But where was the rest of it? Where was the account of the commission Rogers had given him to draw maps? Where were Tute's orders from Rogers to take Carver under his command and go in search of the Northwest Passage? Where was the mention of the vast tract of territory that the Sioux had sold him? Where was the explanation of the indignities inflicted on Rogers by Gage, Johnson and Spiesmaker? Nowhere! I glanced up at Ogden with bewilderment and indignation.

"Why," I said, "the man's not only a liar, an ingrate, a traitor: he's a thief and a fool! He's falsified every date in his book! He's twisted every fact he's told, and left out most of the things he should have told! Look here: he 'named Goddards River after a gentleman who desired to accompany him!' Desired to accompany him, for God's sake! Goddard was his superior officer! And he says the idea of finding the Northwest Passage was his own idea; never even mentions Rogers! He says the St. Peter's River and the great River Oregon rise within a few miles of each other, when their sources are God knows how many hundreds of miles apart! He's even stolen most of his book from the Major's *Concise Account of North America!*" Disgusted, I threw the book on the table.

"I thought as much," Ogden said, "but the fact remains that it's the most talked-of book in Europe today. It's been translated into three or four languages, and it wouldn't surprise me at all if the world remembered Carver long after Rogers had been forgotten."

"Damn it!" Cap shouted. "Aint that always the way? Look at all the things I done in the war, and some damned general or colonel—no offense, Colonel Ogden—always got the credit!"

"That's not quite true, is it?" Ann asked. "Aren't you always given credit for the times you broke out of jail?"

Cap eyed her uneasily.

Ann turned to Sam. "Has there been any news of the Major recently?"

"None that I've heard," Sam said. He laughed. "But wherever he is, I'll warrant he's raising the devil with someone! What a chase he led us, and what a trail he left! I think I told you Elizabeth divorced him and married that hard-drinking privateer captain, Roche, who commanded Paul Jones's old ship *Ranger* for a time."

"Wasn't his brother James proscribed?" Ogden asked.

"Proscribed!" Sam said. "Everything he had was confiscated because he had the misfortune to be the Major's brother. He barely escaped to Canada, leaving his wife and children penniless here."

"My God!" Cap burst out, "I don't know a damned thing about Brother James, but the Major sounds plumb dishonest to me! I bet he'd steal from his own soldiers!"

Ogden looked at me and we both laughed. "My God, man!" Ogden said, "that's the one thing he never would have done!"

"Well," Sam said, "I thought he'd steal the whole of New England from us before he was through; and maybe he would have, if he'd ever drawn a sober breath. There wasn't an officer in Quebec or Halifax he hadn't borrowed money from, and not one he'd repaid. We're well rid of him! He seemed to ruin almost everything he touched. The last thing he did before he finally sailed for England and left his brother to face his creditors was to collect a bounty for raising seven hundred men, when he'd only raised forty."

Cap was shocked. "And they paid him? Aint that just like the English? Wasting money on kings that aint no good to 'em, starting wars they don't know how to finish, and paying all outdoors for things they don't know nothing about! They hadn't ought to be trusted with money—not with ours, anyway!"

"The Major went back to England?" I asked. Ogden was just back from England. I caught his eye. "Didn't you hear anything of him there?"

Ogden hesitated. "Why—ah—no," he said. "No. Not a word. I think he must be dead."

I knew Ogden wasn't telling the truth. He *had* heard of the

Major: probably he had seen him, and perhaps even preferred to think of him as dead.

And then Ann surprised us all. "Dead?" she said softly. "Rid of him? He'll never die, and you'll never want to be rid of him and what he stood for!"

She rose, crossed the room and slid aside the shutter. The wind of late October rattled the windows, and we heard the scurry of dry leaves whirling against the door with the sound of moccasined feet running across frosty grass. A bellowing squall plucked at the corner of the house.

"That sounds like his voice," Ann whispered; "his voice and his footsteps, searching, hurrying, hunting! Ah, no! You can't kill what was in that man!"

THE END

Kenneth Roberts Novels

NOW AVAILABLE IN FAWCETT CREST EDITIONS

ARUNDEL has had 33 printings in the original Doubleday edition, and was a selection of the Family Reading Club, the Doubleday Dollar Book Club, and the International Collectors Library. It has been published in England, Germany, Sweden, Denmark, Italy, France, Spain and Czechoslovakia.

CAPTAIN CAUTION has had 20 printings in the original Doubleday edition, and was a selection of the Peoples Book Club, the Family Reading Club, the Doubleday Dollar Book Club, and Talking Books, American Foundation for the Blind. It has been published in Spain, Sweden, Hungary, Italy, Iran, Norway, West Pakistan and Czechoslovakia.

THE LIVELY LADY has had 21 printings in the original Doubleday edition, and was a selection of the Peoples Book Club and the Family Reading Club. It has been published in England, Germany, Spain, Sweden, Finland, Romania, Italy, France and Czechoslovakia.

LYDIA BAILEY has had five printings in the original Doubleday edition, and was a selection of the Literary Guild, the Book-of-the-Month Club, and the International Collectors Library. It has been published in Argentina, Brazil, Norway, Finland, England, Australia, Sweden, Switzerland, Denmark, Holland, France, Hungary, Spain, Italy and Yugoslavia.

OLIVER WISWELL has had eleven printings in the original Doubleday edition, and has been published in Australia, Sweden, Switzerland, Brazil, England, France, Czechoslovakia, Spain and Italy.

RABBLE IN ARMS has had 22 printings in the original Doubleday edition, and was a selection of the Family Reading Club, the Doubleday Dollar Book Club, the International Collectors Library, and Talking Books, Library of Congress. It has been published in Australia, Germany, England, Italy, Sweden, Spain and Czechoslovakia.

MORE FASCINATING HISTORICAL NOVELS
by
KENNETH ROBERTS

ARUNDEL   M650   95¢
The story of Benedict Arnold's expedition into Canada

BOON ISLAND   T1057   75¢
The story of the struggle for existence by the men of the *Nottingham
Galley* after it went to pieces off the Maine coast in 1710

CAPTAIN CAUTION   T1157   75¢
The adventures of privateers, slave traders, adventurers and heroines
during the War of 1812

THE LIVELY LADY   M432   95¢
The adventures of a Maine privateer captain at sea and in Dartmoor
prison

LYDIA BAILEY   M1041   95¢
Americans involved in Toussaint L'Ouverture's revolt in Haiti and
in the war with the Tripoli pirates

OLIVER WISWELL   M648   95¢
The story of the American Revolution as seen by a Loyalist willing
to give his life for his convictions

RABBLE IN ARMS   M730   95¢
A sequel to *Arundel*, chronicling the two-year struggle of the American Northern Army to halt the British invasion

FAWCETT WORLD LIBRARY
Wherever Quality Paperbacks Are Sold

If your dealer is sold out, send only cover price plus 10¢ each for postage
and handling to Book Department, Fawcett Publications, Inc., Greenwich,
Connecticut 06830. Please order by number and title. If five or more books
are ordered, there is no postage or handling charge.

**A COMPLETE CATALOG OF FAWCETT PAPERBACKS AVAILABLE FREE,
ON REQUEST.**

Those who enjoyed *Northwest Passage*
will also want to read:

LITTLE BIG MAN

by Thomas Berger   Crest M1271   95¢

A brilliant comic novel that presents the cowboy as human rather than heroic. "This is an epic such as Mark Twain might have given us . . . it's a delicious, crazy, panoramic enlargement."
—Henry Miller

MY LIFE AS AN INDIAN

by J. W. Schultz   Premier T386   75¢

An intimate and absorbing portrait of the Blackfoot Indians, their habits and personalities, by an Easterner who became a member of their tribe.

TO BE A MAN

by William Decker   Crest T1222   75¢

A novel portraying American cowboy life from the turn of the century through World War II. "What gives the book its distinction is the ring of authenticity in its people, its events, even its animals . . ."
—Wallace Stegner, *Life*

A WOMAN OF THE PEOPLE

by Benjamin Capps   Crest T1172   75¢

The bestselling novel about a white girl who is captured by Comanches and grows to womanhood among them. "A tremendous, profoundly moving, authentic novel of the West."
—*Christian Herald*

FAWCETT WORLD LIBRARY
Wherever Paperbacks Are Sold